Sub Martis: STARSHIP

SANDI CAYLESS

www.sunskerrypress.com

www.sunskerrypress.com

CONTENTS

1: BOOTCAMP

The sleek, red twin-finned craft rose to the apex of its flight and tilted like a predatory bird, to descend in a lazy double spiral that left a trail of azure haze through the thin Martian atmosphere. The trail had traced a figure eight across the rose-hued sky.

"Two points off for being a smartarse," Lieutenant Copper Milkstone commented to her friend Lieutenant Linen Lyrican as they watched the display from the vantage of the observation deck of the Flight Dome of Beagle One Basecamp, one of Mars Fleet Academy's training stations. "I hope we're not expected to do *that* after another month's training."

Linen turned to look at her friend. "You mean you haven't done the figure eight manoeuvre in flight training simulations?" she asked, her gold-flecked eyes glowing in mock surprise.

"No. And neither have you, so cut it. I've seen your results and you've only had one perfect landing out of three in sims and *that* was in a standard military shuttle."

Copper leaned back in her chair to look up again through the overhead dome. "See that, he's sending out a green trail now," she noted. "Flight instructors! We should be up there practising, not sat here watching him show off his paces in a fancy fighter."

"He's the one in the classy uniform with the gold wings and insignia that says he's the boss," Linen shrugged. "Besides, as an instructor he needs to keep his flight hours up, doesn't he?"

"He gets plenty chance taking rookies like us up. And talking of classy uniforms, who the hell did they get to design these fizzing jackets?" Copper complained, running a finger around the inside of her collar. "Gray Woodelms it certainly wasn't."

"Itch Factor Incorporated," redheaded Linen grinned. "They should have got my Ma: she'd have built in a comfort factor and more pockets. Never mind, we'll be in flight suits later for yet more flight training. They wouldn't let any of us loose solo in a fighter unless we can show we can handle one upside down, backwards and falling out of the sky with no engines."

"That'll be the sol: on two months basic training that seems to be stretching to four, none of us will get near that standard. Here we are, Class Alpha Zero One out of the new and exciting Beagle One Basecamp and the pride of Mars Fleet Explorer and Space Corps and what have we got: at least another month of endless flight sims, classwork, physical jerks, memorising rules and regs even God's never heard of, washing our socks, spit-polishing our billets, saluting our seniors and whatever else they throw at us! Weren't we promised only six sevensols basic in boot and then on-the-job training with whatever base or ship we're assigned to? In our case the almighty *MSS Drake II*, with the scary Colonel Elle Chryse Moritz in the command chair."

"We signed up, though I admit we *were* actually pushed into it by the aforementioned scary Colonel Moritz and promised six sevensols of officer training in bootcamp and we've done that already and then some. But they reckon we've *all* at least another six as the new squadron's not near ready to launch yet – though you can bet that most of our team-mates will not be assigned to any of them. But let's face it, although these uniforms aren't a cut above the rest, once we get the *Drake's* insignia attached to our jackets, we'll stand out in any crowd."

Although most were not destined to become pilots, all new recruits to Mars Fleet's fast-track officer training scheme were given basic flight instruction and those with aptitude or previous training were expected to continue. As both Copper and Linen had completed their basic flight tickets and were qualified to fly short-range mid-atmospheric civilian craft, they had little option but to spend part of almost every sol in flight simulations or in actual flight with an instructor either aboard with them or watching every manoeuvre they made from a station on base, with the facility to take over control should he or she so wish.

Aboard their assigned starship the duo knew that they would be classified as science specialists, both being part of the way through their PhDs under the auspices of Lowell College of the University of Mars, but in common with their newly-recruited peers they were doing the groundwork that would bring them up to the standard required for junior officer ranks aboard any ship of Mars Fleet. Unlike their fellows, they knew the identity of the ship in which they were to serve, but this they had agreed between them to keep under wraps. Bound for the flagship of a new squadron of top range vessels that would be heading out on a shakedown cruise, they suspected that a degree of envy might result that could make life a tad uncomfortable if it were widely known. Holding the ranks of lieutenant whilst in training as a result of their first degrees plus their tertiary education, they had already fielded sufficient flak from those of their cohort that had been assigned the training rank of ensign.

"Here's Instructor Captain Meltdown on the way in, so we'd best look sharp," Linen announced as she stretched lazily.

"One sol you'll accidentally call him that to his face and it's you that'll be for meltdown," Copper warned. "Where the hell are Blazells and Dingle? Aren't they supposed to be watching every move with us and profiting from the experience?"

"Grabbing a last caff in the mess, I'll bet. They've seen all this before, just like us. Talk of the devil… you guys have just missed the magnificent Meltdown showing his wings."

"One sol he'll land on his nose and it's his underwear he'll be showing," Copper prophesied.

"Hope I'm there to see it," Linen shot back. "You two ready for a trip in the four-man trainer?" she asked the newcomers.

"Depends who's at the helm for lift-off," Gadget Blazells responded. "If it's you, Lyrican, I want a back seat."

"You don't need to pack your sick-bag just yet, Blazells, Lieutenant Milkstone's in the hot seat for this jaunt," Linen told him, her face creasing in a smile. "But let's go meet Captain M, he's obliged to brief us before we take off and then watch every manoeuvre from his control seat. We could always reprogram his flight-schedule pad with the Leisure Dome as our endpoint this trip and stop off for an hour?"

"Then we'd be grounded and it would be your fault," Copper told her. "This is Mars Fleet's Basecamp Beagle, not Pillinger Junior School's Detention Centre for unruly students. Besides, as the Leisure Dome doesn't have its own spaceport, we'd have to land at the main spaceport and take a land shuttle. You try sweet-talking Beagle Port Control into letting us land without a permit."

"Sometimes I wonder how you two made it in here," the earnest Dingle put in. "You don't strike me as Service material."

"We got drafted, more or less," Copper informed him sourly as the foursome strolled off the observation deck and across the hall in the direction of one of several briefing rooms.

"How come?"

"Relatives in the Service that thought they knew better than we did," Linen lied smoothly. "And promised us no more than a month and a half in boot. They fibbed. How come you ended up here, Dingle? You're not exactly Service material either."

"Couldn't find a job after my degree that paid any better and I'd gone through cadet training in school and quite liked it. The recruitment office said it was similar here, only more advanced *and* I was virtually guaranteed the training rank of lieutenant."

"And you believed them? You mad fool."

"Tell me about it: cadet school was a holiday camp compared to this, and I'm only an ensign and will be when I'm assigned," Dingle said mournfully as he led the way into the briefing room. "After the breeze they call the Service Entrance Test, this comes as a shocker."

The four spun out the time in casual chitchat until Instructor Captain Max Meldyn stalked in. His uniform was standard issue for his rank, but he wore it as if it *had* been designed by the celebrated Gray Woodelms for the hero in a high-budget tri-dee holo-flic. His teeth shone at his four trainees.

"Right, let's get to it, people. Sit," he commanded. "We'll go over your route and then we'll see if you know the inside of the Ares-Class Mark IV four-man shuttle as well as you know your own backsides..."

Forty five minutes later the four trainees had escaped to the hangar, suited up and were slotting themselves into their allotted positions. As Flight Captain, Copper soon had them organised.

"Lyrican, you're navigator and comms on the outward leg. You'll take over on the way back Blazells, but for now you're weapons: we've a logged short stopover at the mil base out to the north of Mendel Dome but meanwhile keep your hands on the trigger in case our instructor lets loose unscheduled target drones. Dingle, you're survey and mapping and make sure you keep your eyes peeled: you can bet Ground Ops have moved a few mobile work domes around since the navi-comm self-updated. Web in people, we haven't got all sol."

"You don't need to sound so efficient, our talk's not being monitored," Linen told her friend.

"Want to put credit on that? I bet this thing's got more bugs than a flea-infested sewer," Copper responded as she called in to their local flight control to confirm their status.

Having carried out the obligatory pre-flight safety checks and obtained the relevant permissions, she set for taxi to the take-off pad. As she had several hours of sims and actual flight under her belt and was well able to handle a civilian version of the craft, she lost no time in further chat. Once airborne, she set the small shuttle on course for their first scheduled destination of a newly established military station beyond Beagle's most northerly sub-dome, Mendel.

Beagle One Basecamp was a recently-established facility for training fast-track recruits to the Fleet branch of the Service, the body on Mars charged with planetary defence and similar vital concerns. After a widely-publicised increase in fleet recruitment, owing to a surge in outer system exploration for new resources and the building of new starships to carry out the work, several such new training centres had been established planet-wide. Beagle One was located to the west of and beyond the ancillary systems dome that served Beagle's central dome, Pillinger; it had once been a drilling site for water ice extraction. The Basecamp comprised a main base dome, a flight training dome with attached launch site and a dormitory dome where both trainees and instructors lodged. Despite its designation as Beagle One Basecamp, there was no Beagle Two.

The small training shuttle cleared the basecamp and followed a north-easterly course in order to avoid overflying populated centres. The planned course took the craft between Mendel, the most northerly habitation dome of Beagle Complex, and the Astrobiology Field Dome, a prestigious science centre under the auspices of Mars Deep Mining Consortium that Copper and Linen knew very well, it being the field base for their PhDs.

Linen pointed this out to their fellows as the glittering plas-crystal of the AF Dome's upper sections slid by on their left.

"Aren't you cutting by a tad close, Milkstone?" Dingle asked anxiously from his rear seat.

"Check your chart, Dingle: we're flying over the north end of the new sub-tunnel route that will eventually link the spaceport and the AF Dome. And as I've set a straight line for Beagle One Military Station, that takes us this close – as long as nothing's thrown at us to cause us to divert."

"Confirmed," Linen put in from the navigator's position at Copper's side. "Doesn't seem to be much action going on as far as the tunnel goes," she went on. "You charting it, Mr Dingle?"

"I'm charting," he replied automatically. "But I guess most of it is underground, so we won't see much surface works."

"We have another craft in our sights," Copper noted a short time later. "Let's check it out. This is Flight Six-Five-One-Three out of Beagle One Basecamp on a training mission east of you. Do you read us, over?"

"Loud and clear Six-Five-One-Three! This is Flight Alpha Two-One-Niner out of the Astro-Field Dome en route to the north, over," a well-known voice replied.

"It's Kezza and the Amber-Scamper!" Linen exclaimed.

Intensely conscious that they were possibly being monitored, Copper tabbed her link and replied formally. "Well met, Captain Brownpelt! Copper Milkstone, Flight Captain. I take it you're heading to the Warren site station, over?"

"We are, in atmospheric flight; is Linen with you, over?"

"I certainly am, Kezza. Great to hear from you," the redhead cut in without as much as a by-your-leave. "Flying high, I see. How many have you aboard and who are they?"

Before she could add anything further Copper's voice cut in with a warning of incoming and a curt directive to Blazells to man his station and target the blips she could see on her screen.

"Six-Five-One-Three diverting eastwards. Have a good trip, Alpha Two-One-Niner, out. Get those damn drones, Blazells!"

As Copper activated the crew protection gear and felt the webbing tighten round her, she hauled back to pull the shuttle's nose up in an effort to avoid one light-drone that had ducked the virtual fire of her craft's weapons. Acutely aware that this was not a simulated flight and that she had three other bodies to safeguard, she increased acceleration to reach a clear area of sky. It was Linen, manning the secondary weapons station, who took out the remaining drone.

"Well done, Flight Six-Five-One-Three: confirm destruction of all your targets," the voice of Instructor Captain Max Meldyn came in over the comm. "Continue your mission and return to base as directed."

"I wouldn't put it past him to try that again," Blazells snarled angrily from the back. "He was listening in! You shouldn't have started that chat with your buddy on the other flight," he added irritably to Linen. "Bet that's what triggered it."

"If your fingers and eyes had been where they *should* have been, I wouldn't have had to take out that last drone for you," Linen returned equably.

"Cut the chat people and attend to your business," Copper ordered. "We dissect this flight back at base. Lyrican, plot us the most effective direct line to Beagle One Military Station."

"Aye, ma'am," Linen responded with a twinkle in her eye as she complied speedily.

The shuttle reached its endpoint without further trouble and after a rapid about-turn and a reordering of positions they were on the return leg. The sage Captain Meldyn thought it prudent to retest their reactions by sending up another clutch of light-drones but no other trials were aimed at them and they touched down at Beagle One Basecamp on time.

Blazells' recriminations against Linen continued as the four made their way from the re-pressurised hangar to their assigned briefing room, despite Copper's sharp instruction to button it. Their instructor, a sardonic grin on his face, was waiting to greet them but the anticipated ear-bashing did not materialise. The flight was gone over meticulously and no blame apportioned, although Meldyn requested to be apprised of their connection with the captain of the passing flight.

Captain Kezza Brownpelt was in fact the pilot of the second dual-operational land-hover shuttle belonging to the Amberline research group, to which Copper and Linen officially belonged. It had been heading out to the Amberline research site at which they had both worked before being assigned to the Fleet as trainees. The captain was also the niece of Linen's ex-landlord back at Lowell Dome Complex and hence the redhead knew her well. The details were retailed to Meldyn as briefly as possible: that Copper and Linen were PhD students was known but the extent of their work and the prestigious group of which they were still effectively a part was not common knowledge and for various reasons they preferred it that way.

Linen wiped imaginary sweat from her brow as the four, now released from duty, were allowed to depart and make their way across to Main Base Dome for well-earned mugs of caff.

"That went well," the redhead said, selecting her drink.

"No thanks to you," Blazells retorted.

"We weren't penalised," Copper pointed out. "You're lucky he didn't drop a point off you for missing that light-drone."

"I think we did okay," Dingle put in. "As a team, we're quite good. Maybe they'll match us up next time as well?"

Copper's glance at her friend clearly spelt out that she hoped not: she had seen enough of the other two to last her until the end of their training. All she said, however, was that she hoped their furlough would be announced soon as it was high time. As they were heading into what normally would be rest-sols for a large proportion of Mars' citizens and were more or less half way through their extended stint, it would be a logical time.

"You could sweet-talk Captain Meltdown and find out about our leave," Copper said to Linen once their two colleagues were safely out of earshot. "He likes the cut of your jib."

"He likes the cut of anything female and stylish that's half a decade younger than he is," Linen countered. "*And* that he thinks worships his every word," she added impishly. "But I'll give it a go after our next class if I see him: navigation isn't it?"

"It is," Copper said briefly. "We'd best down the rest of this and go fish our learn-pads from out our lockers."

"At least we must be *close* to our first and only furlough," the redhead went on. "We were told it was about half way through our training, weren't we? And we don't have far to go, as we have our own place in Beagle."

"Your Grammy's place, you mean," Copper corrected her.

"Thanks to Grammy, but she told us in no uncertain terms that it was ours for the duration. Unit Five, Court Nine, Road Five off Memory Avenue. Make the rest of them jealous..."

"I wouldn't go broadcasting it, half of them are jealous of us as it is," warned her friend. "And everybody will want to come along for a party and free billets, and given some of the rum recruits we have in our class, you don't want them abusing your Grammy Magenta's stuff. *And* they will."

"You have a point. But from what I hear, most of them are hatching plans of their own, after a party somewhere in Pillinger Dome, once we know about the timing."

"Why don't we suggest Dirty Deneb's for any party? If they did damage there, you'd never notice."

"Another good point," Linen agreed, nodding. "And we could hobble as far as my Ma's place if we didn't want to face the longer walk home," she added.

"Talking of fam-units, I had a link from Majorelle," Copper mentioned as they marched along to the line of lockers.

Majorelle Moritz was a friend of the two who had once lived next door to Copper in the Kellyn family unit on Road Eleven in Lowell Dome Complex and had paired with their old friend Lofty, the owner of a somewhat downmarket diner that they, as impecunious students, had patronised regularly. She was also the niece of Colonel Elle Chryse Moritz, whose introduction into their lives had since seemed to lead to nothing but trouble.

"*I* didn't," Linen declared. "Why didn't she copy to me?"

"Because it was a tip-off about Ma Kellyn; Ma's still peeved that I flitted from her place when we started training here, but – wait for it – according to Malachite's landlord Pa Larimar, Ma has apparently expanded her little property empire again and has landed a block of ex-rental apartments in Beagle Central, of all places. How Pa Larimar found out Malachite doesn't know, but with Malachite working at Lofty's and knowing Majorelle once had an apartment at Ma Kellyn's, he passed it on. If it's true and knowing Ma, she must have snapped them up for a song. But as she's no doubt looking to rent them all out speedily, Majorelle warned me in case Ma calls to try to rent me one. They're on some backstreet called Skady Lane, wherever the blazes that is."

Linen began to laugh. "Better known to the locals as Shady Lane. It's at the end of a private road that starts at Blur Street, passes the back gate of Beagle Law Enforcement HQ and links with the far end of Skyring Street. It's the teeny bit of road that begins at the end of Skyring and cuts through to Zaranj Street, not that far from Styllaflax in fact, but over the back," she went on, naming a small fashion store that was run by art students from Beagle College and to which she had dragged a reluctant Copper some time before.

"But so close to Central, apartments can't come cheap," her friend objected. "How could Ma afford a whole block?"

"If apartments you call them," the redhead grinned. "It used to be Law Enforcement's accommodation block for rookie cops and junior officers that were assigned to Beagle Central. Most of them didn't stay long, by all accounts. But it's surrounded by what looks like cut-price warehousing, or was once. It's maybe so underused it's being sold off. I expect the newbies have to find their own lodgings these sols. Your ex-landlady *will* have picked it up for a song, though: you know Ma Kellyn and all this way away from Lowell it would have had to be a bargain price, even given Ma's legacy from her late Uncle Whatsit at Phoenix."

"Uncle Singeol Kellyn," Copper reminded her. "She always hinted that she and her brother Pinker inherited little but given what she's done so far, with her fancy apartment at Lowell Leisure Dome as well, *that* was probably a blind. Maybe Pinker was coerced into chipping in for the purchase – Ma can be very persuasive when she wants to be, just like someone else I could mention in fact, and Pinker's a walkover."

"Could be," Linen agreed. "And I expect your sly reference was to my distant relationship to Ma. But didn't Ma sue that swindler calling himself Dusty Kellyn that tried to cheat her out of part of Uncle Singeol's estate? She maybe got a packet out of that. So we must check out this Skady Lane place and see what it's all about when we're on this leave we've been promised."

"I rather hoped we'd check out the Leisure Dome for a sol or two and then have a couple of nights on the town eating real food and not stuff that tastes like it's Earflaps' reject stock. But what's this private road off Blur Street out back of the Lock-Block called?" her friend asked curiously.

"Private Road," Linen informed her.

"That figures."

"But better known to the locals as Rookie Road, as that's the way the rookie cops had to walk to report in."

"Only in Beagle..."

"We Beagle-ites are known for our ready wit as well as our charm," Linen said roguishly.

"And a few other things best not mentioned," Copper returned. "But enough already, let's collect our stuff and head in for the next lecture. It's just like our undergrad sols, except you don't get any time off for bad behaviour."

* * *

Some time later and back in the twin quarters they shared, Linen set the privacy lock and turned to her friend.

"I sweet-talked Captain Meltdown at break and he says we're all due furlough, but it's not within his remit to say when: we get leave when our contract says we do. And that's two sols from now, I found out from the office. But I won't be sweet-talking him again. He's rather put out."

"Why, what did you do to him?"

"He tried to sweet-talk *me* into spending part of my leave in his company…"

"Surely consorting with your own trainees is strictly against regs," Copper interrupted.

"Sure is, kiddo. So I told him I'd planned to spend part of it with an aunt who's in Mars Fleet as I know she's due planet-side sometime soon."

Copper's eyes widened. "Lor' I bet he backtracked once you let slip who it was. I assume you *did* tell him that Colonel Moritz was your Auntie Elle?"

"Of course I did: that fib's been going the rounds so long it's almost true. And Colonel Moritz was all right about it when she found out I'd used it to get the persistent Wolff Waterbone off my tail when he was trying to make his way into my confidence – and elsewhere – after I'd persuaded him to persuade the almighty Mars Deep Mining Consortium to fund my PhD. So there's no problem. Meltdown will never check it out as he knows questions would be asked."

"As I've told you before, you're the dizzy limit. You *will* have to behave once we're well and truly graduated as fleet officers, you realise."

"Like hell! I signed up for a stint in the Service with Auntie Elle breathing down my neck but I don't recall agreeing to bend my knee to any old authority."

"Check your contract," Copper advised. "It'll be there in the small print at the bottom of the holo."

"Whatever; how's Spook by the way? You haven't mentioned him much recently?"

"Because we're mostly in company is why. He comes and he goes. He's here now. I think he's getting all excited because he knows what's going on and hopes to get back into space soon."

Spook, an alien entity that had awoken when the deep tunnel system in which its ship had been buried for millennia had been disturbed, had latched onto the unconscious Copper when she had been injured in a rockfall. She and Linen had been working within the ancient tunnel system known to their research group as the Warren, deep under the surface of Mars, as part of their PhD projects. It had been the various remarkable finds at their site and elsewhere on Mars and their conjectures in relation to them that had brought them to the attention of Colonel Moritz and in part had led to their present situation. As far as Copper was concerned, Spook was intangible but definitely *there*. They were connected on some subliminal level that she could not fathom but she had grown so used to him that she was almost comfortable: almost, but not quite. Linen believed that she had likewise developed some sensitivity to the entity, but was far less receptive to it than her friend.

"You'll have to tell Auntie Elle about Spook once we're on board the *Drake*, you know. You did let out to her that you had the impression that several times an alien mind had reached out and touched yours for a fleeting second, when first we figured there *was* an alien ship buried out beneath the Glory Hole."

"I guess, though I don't think she quite believed me. She thought it was the after-effects of that bang on the head I got in the rockfall. We *did* get the impression that her team had found evidence that there was an active life-support system in Spook's ship, though they were never able to breach it," Copper replied.

"But we'll have to get used to calling her Colonel Moritz even when we're not in her company, you realise? I suspect we'll see little of her anyhow; we'll be stuck in our lab getting on with our PhD stuff until something really exciting happens. I hope I don't get space-sick. I've never been in a *moving* starship before."

"You'll never notice. It's equipped with gravity generators, so it'll be just like our lab back at Lowell except the scenery outside will shift. Even Trisk will be there to keep us company, and we'll be well away from people like Lomax Gratikule and Wolff Waterbone and other Mars Deep Mining Consortium lackeys at the Extra-Martis Missions Survey Office up at Viking One that are endlessly demanding reports and project updates," Linen pacified her. "Not to mention out of the immediate orbit of our ex-College colleague the Divine Thulia, as she's based at Vee One as well and likes to wag her tongue in our direction too often for comfort. Although as MDMC's still paying our PhD disburses, I suppose they'll *have* to get reports via the EMMS Office from us now and again."

"But you can't get *off* a starship," Copper lamented. "There will be rec areas and so on, but we'll be trapped."

"Lor' we're all trapped under the domes here, so where's the difference? You're just getting nervous the closer we get to take-off, saying goodbye to all that's familiar and saying hello to a strange environment."

"Stop psychoanalysing me, it's annoying."

"There, there, little Cop."

"That as well. And you can stop too, you're as bad as she is."

"Are you grumping at Spook?" Linen demanded.

"Yup. And I get the feeling that he agrees with you."

"So you're outnumbered. But we're on leave in a couple of sols!" Linen crowed, picking up a pillow and throwing it at her. "You'll feel better after a soak in a decent tub and a good meal."

* * *

By the time the signal sounded to announce dinnertime, the whole training wing had heard of their forthcoming six sols of furlough and plans for a get-together were in the air. Someone had found out that the Service would provide a shuttle-bus to take them as far as the Orbital Route that circled Pillinger Dome and a list of inexpensive local lodgings was doing the rounds. As inset trays clattered and rations were selected from the options available at the servery in the mess hall, the lines of uniform-clad trainees were swopping ideas of where to head to and what to do once they got there. It was as the pushy Lieutenant Gadget Blazells had decided that in his opinion something classier than the dingy Deneb's Diner was called for and was listing a number of much more upmarket watering holes of his acquaintance that an electrifying idea occurred to Copper.

"Giordano's!" she exclaimed to the line at large.

None of their fellow diners had heard of the place and were agog to know where and what it was. As the two from Lowell explained its position in the Mars Deep Mining Consortium-run Astrobiology Field Dome, curiosity was sparked. None of their mates had visited the AF Dome but all had heard of it and of MDMC. That Giordano's was the largest leisure bar and diner in the place and possibly on the planet and was space-themed to boot went down very well. When Linen announced that it was known to customers as The Black Hole, as once inside, it was challenging to find the way out, almost everyone decided that it was the ideal place to mark the beginning of their leave.

"Well done, Cop," Linen whispered to her friend as the two made their way to a small booth. "He only wanted his ideas to be given top billing and Dirty Deneb's doesn't suit the taste he thinks he's got. And I've had another great idea – tell you later."

Later turned into much later as the ideas for furlough and a good time at the AF Dome were debated. Several of the trainees had called up specifics on the diner and were impressed by what they saw. The reservation was made and confirmed and credit extracted from those who had decided to attend. Both Copper and Linen were plied with questions and were hard put to keep under wraps much of their background with respect to the AF Dome and the reasons for their extensive knowledge of it.

Once back in the familiar setting of their quarters, Copper turned to her friend. "Okay, out with it – your idea."

Linen's eyes lit up and she grinned. "I'll check in with Thars – he *did* say keep in touch after all, as he's our senior mentor – and see if we can get overnight billets at the Psi Complex! That would save us having to come back to Pillinger and then having to find transport back to ours. We're still Lowell PhD students with the Amberlines, so we should have access."

"For work," Copper said shortly. "Thars won't sanction it for a pleasure trip to the Astro Field Dome with a bunch of Service rookies out for a night of drinking and dissipation."

"Hardly pleasure, given many of the company, but let's have a think: we have a couple of sols before we set off."

Linen's idea of a think was a rapid finger-tapping session and then a short link to Thars Amberline, the head of the Amberline Geology-Astrobiology Research Group at Lowell College, and technically in authority over the two students and their work. The redhead prudently waited until Copper was in the shower before contacting the professor, as she suspected that her idea would not appeal much to her friend.

"We have a billet for our fun at Giordano's," she announced when a damp Copper surfaced from the hygiene cubicle.

"You what?"

"I called Thars…"

"At this time! It's nearly midnight!"

"*Here* it is; it's not at Lowell, it's different time-wise than we are, but Thars is about anyhow, and so's Avrom, as he's making up time to go buggy racing later in the sevensol. And we have a billet," she repeated.

"So what have you mortgaged our souls for that you swung that?" Copper demanded dangerously as she towelled her hair.

"Well, we *will* have quite an early start on the Satsol after the party," the redhead warned. "We'll be off in the Scamper to visit the guys out at the Amber Warren…"

"What! You've promised we'll do some work, haven't you?"

"Just collecting a few extra samples is all, so that we have more than plenty for our trip away with the *Drake*…"

"We have plenty already! They're all in storage at Lowell and we have to get them shipped up to the *Drake* before we leave so we'll have something to keep us occupied while we're headed to wherever it is we're going! *That* was made quite plain when all this shenanigans began. And what about our enviro-suits, our sample tubes, our instruments…"

"Thars was heading out to the AF Dome in a couple of sols anyhow, so he's agreed to come out early; he'll get our enviro-suits shipped out pronto and get Avrom working on the details. We have our MEDICs here in any case – all our data is stored in them – and the bits of kit Auntie Elle gave us: we didn't dare leave *them* behind. Thars knows our schedule, so it'll be a quick turnaround as he'll organise the Scamper's schedule. And we'll get to see our friends out at the Amber-Warren…"

"Damn, hell and blast!" Copper exploded, her face creasing as if she was thinking rapidly. "Oh Lor', not Spook as well! He wants to be closer to his ship!"

"Handy having a disembodied alien as a familiar, isn't it?" grinned Linen.

"Who for, you or him? It certainly isn't me! I wanted a trip to the Leisure Dome."

"Look, we'll still have time," Linen pointed out. "We head out Frisol for the party, our first leave sol is technically Satsol, and we're not due back here until the next Frisol…"

"You mean back here Thursol eve if we're due on duty early, and I bet we will be. And what about our plans to stay out at our own place? What about the visit to that apartment block in Skady Lane that's now Ma Kellyn's, supposedly?"

"We'll have time for that! We only need to hop over to the Warren, one sol out in the field, back the next to the AF Dome and then Beagle Central – plenty of time. And don't forget that we'll have at least a couple or three sols after we finish training before we have to join our ship," Linen reminded her.

"Which we'll be spending at Lowell sorting our stuff: Auntie Elle's not going to sanction a sol off to have a good time when there's a ship to launch that's already well behind time," Copper snapped rebelliously.

"How d'you know she's *well* behind time?" Linen retaliated.

"Trisk told us when he linked in the other sol with the list of quarters still free aboard that he'd charmed out of the officer in charge and his suggestions of the best ones, based on what he's seen, remember? I figure she's late because they're still trying to retrofit her hull with the self-repair organo-metallic material that was developed based on the alien material that makes up most of the alien hulls and other artefacts that have been found on Mars to date. They hadn't quite got there the last we heard and if I recall, the colonel was a bit cagey about how much of the stuff was in production, given it was clandestine and under military jurisdiction."

"Trisk said six sevensols or so to the launch," Linen smiled. "That's hardly well behind time. Good to have a friend aboard the *Drake* that's looking out for us isn't it?" she went on blithely.

"Stop changing the subject in the hopes I won't notice," said Copper. "At this rate we won't have much furlough for the next frocking half-year!"

"Look, it'll be good to see the guys out at the Warren again if nothing else and make sure they keep their eyes on our site for us. And Spook sure as shells wants to check his ship, as he won't be seeing that again if he decides he's in the Service for the duration as well."

"He can check it anytime he wants: I figure he must be able to move close to light speed. It's just that he doesn't like leaving me alone for any length of time. But have it your own way, both of you. I wish I'd never mentioned Giordano's."

"It *will* be much better than Dirty Deneb's and we can easily sneak away if the company gets too annoying. I guess we'll have to check on the shuttle we need to get us over there and book places. The other guys can sort themselves out," Linen decided. "They're the cream of the crop of recruits after all."

"You can damn well book it."

"Done. Wonder if Lieutenant Korin Karst will be on table duty for the eve?"

"Once he sees your face he'll change his shift," Copper warned her.

* * *

The following two sols were spent in eager anticipation of the leave that all the trainees now knew was in the offing. The major highlight of the penultimate sol in harness from their point of view was that Copper and Linen were given the chance to take out a two-man low-atmosphere craft that seemed to be a cross between a shuttle and a fighter. It gave them some sort of idea of what it might be like to fly a combat vessel and both had been exhilarated by the ride, despite the vexing interference of Captain Max Meldyn. *He* had enlivened their sortie by sending a small fleet of virtual combat drones in after them. As their route had taken them through Hebes Chasma, a deep and sheltered channel north of Valles Marineris that was tough to navigate, they had been severely tested and had little time to enjoy either the experience or the view. Copper had piloted the small ship around the central plateau to avoid the many rocky trenches and highly scored cliff faces whilst Linen had taken out the drones, swearing softly and continuously.

"He did it deliberately," the redhead complained testily to her friend after a rigorous debriefing that had itemised their every error. "Now I've given him a serious brush-off and he's realised that I don't hang onto his every word in breathless adoration, he's trying to make things difficult."

"The advantage is that it *does* test us almost to our limits," Copper soothed. "Though I suspect he'll regret it if he breaches the upper threshold of *your* temper."

"Don't have one. You're the grouch in our team," Linen told her, chuckling. "I must drop Auntie Elle into the conversation when next I see him, just to keep him in line. We'll have enough to put up with when Blazells finds out we've been allowed up in the MV2 flyer: he's trying to be the hotshot of our cohort and takes everything personally."

"You realise now that you've told Captain Meltdown about Colonel Moritz, he'll think she's pulled strings to get us aboard the *Drake?*"

"Hardly; we're the best of the best after all and try as he might, Max the Melt can't ignore that fact. We're just lucky we had the opportunity to get our provisional pilots' tickets before we were dragooned into the damn Service, although we owe a lot of that to the use of Rustin's flight simulator. We must give it him back one sol, if ever we get out to Wells. Whoops! Here are Blazells and Dingle and the Gadget's not a happy trooper."

One half of the approaching duo was undoubtedly in a foul temper and expressed it by a snappily-worded salute and a curt nod in passing. Ensign Dingle was more affable and voiced his congratulations as he mentioned that he and his team-mate were set for test flights in the simulation suite.

"Good luck, Foxy; you too, Blazells," Linen said impishly as they passed.

"You're taking a risk, lady. Did you see Dingle's eyes light up when you called him Foxy?" Copper demanded. "He'll think you're taken with him and he'll be asking you for a date."

"Only being polite. But Foxin Dingle's too shy to be asking anyone for a date without a lot more encouragement that that."

"You were deliberately winding up Gadget Blazells' prop," her friend accused.

"Naturally: he asks for it by his attitude. And besides, he's sweet on me and trying to hide it," Linen announced blithely.

"No he isn't, you annoy the hell out of him. In fact you annoy the hell out of most everyone, including me at times."

"Why thank you, I do my best. But let's cut the chat and find a caff well away from prying ears and eyes. I'll fetch Gerald out of my locker and we can use him to organise our schedule. We have a whole hour to work out the best way of spending our furlough to advantage and it's only half a sol away."

"Good idea; I'll bring Gemima, as we have a link from Trisk to check out. I hope he's managed to put the word in for our new billets aboard the *Drake*, though I would have thought it would be first come, first pick."

Their erstwhile Amberline Group colleague and now one of the senior science officers aboard the *MSS Drake II*, Lieutenant Trisk Addystone had had the advantage of a very short spell in basic training and an established position aboard ship. As an outgoing and friendly individual, he was also adept at persuading others to see his viewpoint and the two trainees were in high hopes that he would have engineered some comforts for them aboard their soon-to-be assigned ride. Stopping only long enough to abstract their Mobile Encyclopaedic Detection and Information Consoles, or MEDICs, from their lockers, the two made their way to the trainees' mess.

Once they had commandeered a small table in the mess well away from everyone else, they eagerly called up their link. Trisk was as cheerful as ever and his smiling face lit up as the image projecting from Copper's MEDIC, Gemima's, holo-generator port expanded outwards. Their friend's message was short and to the effect that he had suggested to the harassed individual tasked with organising the *Drake's* accommodations that it might be as well if the scientific research personnel aboard the starship had billets near one another, for the sake of efficiency if nothing else. The officer had not been taken in but had marked two comfortable berths close to Trisk's as assigned to incoming crew and ticked another job off her busy schedule. The diligent Dr Addystone had also tacked their names alongside his on the door panel of what would be a sizeable office near his main lab: it had not yet been allocated and he hoped they would be able to commandeer it when it was operable. The whole science section had been removed from deck ten to deck five owing to some structural constraints, the deck ten area labs being given over to the engineering department. Trisk was happy enough with the upset and the move: although further from the crew quarters on deck nine, they would be closer to their local mess.

"The joys of housekeeping on board Mars Fleet's finest," Copper laughed quietly. "We'll have to pay him back once we're actually up there. Best send him a thank you. But it sounds like the *Drake's* nowhere near ready for launch yet. She was pretty near finished when we saw her last, I thought."

"We only saw the bits that we were shown by that Lieutenant Commander Khilph and then by Colonel Moritz," reminded Linen. "And that wasn't much. We didn't see any of the crew berths or even the engineering decks. We should call up the specs of every big ship we can and try to get a feel for what we might have to navigate around once we're aboard."

"Let us see what we might be in for, you mean," Copper said. "But I agree. Now we're officially Fleet, we should be able to get access to that sort of information. Or at least, Gerald and Gemima should, as they were given access to military and other databases way back, when Colonel Moritz jumped into our lives and started to take over."

"We were told we'd be given a sol away to be shown around a ship and it hasn't happened," Linen remembered. "Normally it would be part of training to be assigned short trips on training ships, but because of the recruitment upsurge, we've missed out. Lor' knows how many more recruits are out there in all the other basecamps that seem to have sprouted up over half the planet. I'm amazed nobody's twigged that it's not just because of the expansion of the Fleet's exploration budget that there are all these new ships building that need crews to man them."

"Well I'm not going to enlighten our lot if the question comes up," Copper said decidedly. "Least said and all that; and they'd freak and want to know how I knew. But we'd better get on and organise our schedule. There had better be time for a couple of sols of nothing but R and R or you're in trouble."

"Then let's move it. I've had a number of our buddies asking for details of cheap lodgings so I'll check out one or two in Beagle Central that I suspect are passable and see if they have spaces available. There's only morrow-sol left for booking up. Gerald," Linen instructed her MEDIC, "Check if there are rooms available in the following locations in Pillinger Dome: Asaph Hotel, Helix Hotel, Pallas Hotel and Mary House."

"You know all those places?" Copper demanded.

"Yes, they're all this side of Beagle Central and close enough to the Land-Hover Station to get over to the Astro Field Dome reasonably easily; and they're the least expensive. Saying that, they're not cheap, but I'm not going to suggest any of our lot try out the two rooms that are let out in the basement of Beer Belly Pete's Bar in Bee Street, or the Blue Gene that's on Shergotty Street, further away. I wouldn't let either of those out as a dog kennel, not even for Osterley. The Shuttle Shed at the far end of Barnes Street has a few letting rooms, I think, but I wouldn't swear to it. You can often pick up an economy billet near Beagle College out of semester time and there you're close to decent drinkeries like Susie's Cider Factory and Fiddlers *and* the student med centre if you go overboard on the drinks or get caught up in a brawl. Some of our lot wanted to know the best upmarket bars to take a date, but they can find that out for themselves, I'm not a frocking directory of Beagle Central. But maybe I should tell them what places to avoid?"

"Lor' they're all big boys and girls, they'll work it out one way or another," Copper told her. "But they'd best pocket a supply of Oxypep if they're visiting any dens you recommend or they'll never make it back to their billets. Do you *know* all the dubious drinking dens in Beagle, by the way?" she added suspiciously.

"Most of them – though only by reputation, of course," Linen responded.

"I'll bet. Anything else I should know if we're augmenting the education of our fellow rookies?"

"Don't book a room at Mary House if it's the last one to be had in Central Dome," the redhead advised. "It's known as Scary House and the owner's called Scary Mary. So I've heard. But if he asks, tell Blazells it's the best one on offer."

2: FURLOUGH ONE

Beagle One Basecamp was buzzing as the exuberant bunch of freed trainees hefted travelling carryalls onto shoulders or skids and made for the military hover destined to ferry them along the link road from their base to a military dock at the crossing point of Evolution Avenue and the Orbital Route, outside which they could board public transport to Pillinger, the central dome of Beagle Complex. Most of the rookies had their billets arranged and were anxiously conning confirmation messages on their wrist-comm units and planning the quickest routes there. It was Frisol afternoon and the majority intended to scout out the local territory before setting off to Mars Deep Mining Consortium's Astrobiology Field Dome and their assignation at Giordano's.

Copper and Linen settled into handy seats, having dumped their larger and more innocuous pieces of luggage in the hover's aft cargo bay. They had decided to make for their earmarked quarters in MDMC's Psi Complex in the AF Dome rather than stop off at Linen's mother's apartment or at their own place, a unit within an enclave named Court Nine that was a short way down Road Five, one of the side roads that led off Memory Avenue. The avenue itself was one of the four major routes out of Beagle Central; it terminated at Bruno, one of Beagle's sub-domes, and had the major advantage of a convenient link road known as Route N1 about half way down that led directly to Beagle's Leisure Dome.

"Be good to see the guys again," Linen mentioned as she wriggled into a more comfortable position. "Wonder how many students are out in the field?"

"And who they are," Copper added. "If Noa and Syriana are in residence, this maybe wasn't such a good idea."

"We've only got one sol!" Linen admonished. "Besides, we're out this eve to Giordano's, so unless they're at the AF Dome and with time in hand, we'd not meet them. Syriana was severely put out that we were fast-tracked into the Service though," she went on with a snicker. "Despite her always saying it's a poor career move in anybody's books."

"She just figures that once again we've got something over on her and it rankles," Copper told her friend. "But enough of her and her temper already. Why aren't we moving? We have a land-hover to catch."

"You're too anxious by far. Here we are, she's powering up. We'll catch a hop-on, hop-off at the edge of Hirst Street and then north on Zarnecki Avenue and we'll be there in no time."

With a boisterous roar from the trainees, the hover set off and as Linen had prophesied, the trip to Dome edge took only long enough for them to check itineraries and decide that they would have sufficient time for a quick sortie around the labs and the Amberline Common Room at the Psi Complex before they would have to prepare for their evening of debauchery.

Having collected their excess luggage from the cargo bay, the two bade goodbye to their fellows and made for their ongoing transport stop. To their joint irritation, Gadget Blazells, with Dingle in tow, hopped up beside them. That pair were heading for the Plaza Hotel, an upmarket place that was very close to Beagle Central Station and within a walk of the Land-Hover Station that would provide their ride to the AF Dome later in the sol.

"Not an inexpensive choice of lodging, Foxy," remarked the redhead to her colleague. "Comfortable but pricy, but you won't have too much trouble finding your way home from the Astro Field Dome at any rate. Are you there for the duration or is it just the one night?" she enquired playfully, smiling up at him.

Copper was hard put to hide her amusement as the stuttering Dingle replied that he and Blazells would be resident there for a couple of sols, after which they planned to venture out to Beagle Leisure Dome and find some stopover nearby.

"We may see you there later in the sevensol: we're planning a short trip out that way. But the Leisure Dome – the Sirius Hotel is the best accomm there, but if you can afford the Plaza, I expect you can afford the Sirius. Try Dominion Holo-Suites if you need a thrill, they're the best on the planet."

"Is the Sirius the place *you* stay when you're out that way?" the steely voice of Blazells cut in sarcastically.

"No, Cop and I have a place we can use out on Road Five off Memory; we tend to berth there when we're in this neck of the planet," Linen responded, as Copper's eyes widened at this breach of the agreement to tell no-one of their apartment.

"So why are you headed for the hover to this precious Astro-Field Dome you're so keen on, then?" he demanded.

"Because we have free billets and free subsistence courtesy of our research group in the AF Dome is why. *And* we'll be able to walk there from Giordano's after the party. It's a no-brainer, really. And we have things to do, people to see, places to go out that way. Are you sure you can afford the prices of the Plaza Hotel?" she went on to Foxy Dingle, who appeared to be drinking in every word.

"I checked the tariff, it looked okay," stuttered the young ensign as he eyed her anxiously.

"Please yourself. We need to swop buses here for the trip up Zarnecki, this one goes straight through to Memory, but there's one waiting. Let's to it, people."

* * *

At Beagle Land-Hover Station, the two outbound travellers made straight in, having helpfully pointed out the way to the Plaza Hotel to their two messmates. Copper was bursting for a private word with her redheaded friend and began as soon as the other two were out of sight.

"Right, lady: what possessed you to mention our place on Road Five? You promised…"

"I didn't say our place, I said a place we could use," Linen pointed out righteously. "If anybody asks, which they didn't, it's my Grammy's, as you're always alleging anyway."

"You're splitting quarks," Copper accused. "Anyway, why were you winding poor Dingle up? Poor sap is now probably convinced you're keen on him and have his interest at heart and is screwing up his courage to ask you out on a date."

"He'd wet himself if I said yes."

"Probably. But you're making him nervous, you bad girl."

25

"He can cope, he's an officer in the Fleet – or he will be once he's assigned. He'd better get used to it. Besides, truth be told, I was only annoying Gadget Blazells. He can't see why anybody'd be interested in Foxy Dingle over himself."

"Leave the lad be. Is the Plaza so expensive, anyway?"

"Yup! It's next to Central Station and links to the spaceport so of course it's not cheap. Where's our hover departure dock?"

"Five: it's up on the board," Copper said, hauling her carryall over one shoulder. "And it's in."

She led the way over to the relevant dock and boarded the shuttle bus, flashing her travel pass at the ident port in passing as she scanned ahead for an empty booth.

"This one'll do," she puffed as she slung her baggage under the double seat and slid over to the window.

Linen disposed of her own gear and slid in opposite, casting enquiring eyes over her surroundings as she settled her smaller carryall on her knee. "Not too busy; I don't recognise anyone in range but there must be a few of ours coming or going. We could start up the Amberline space ditty and set things off?"

"No we couldn't. When are you going to learn not to draw attention to yourself?"

"When I'm too old to care," Linen told her. "Ten minutes yet before we leave. How's Spook, by the by? Getting excited?"

"Yes, as a matter of fact. How could you tell?"

"Your face. Feels he's closer to home then? If he considers that ship of his home, that is. Did you ever work out where he actually goes when he's not around your neck? D'you think he *can* link to his ship anytime from wherever he is on the planet? He seemed to know what was going on with it, didn't he? He knew that those military drones of Colonel Moritz were trying to breach it but that was when we were down the Glory Hole."

"How the hell would I know? And keep your voice down or people will think we're weird. You'd better not mention Colonel Moritz or our work in a public place either – Lor' knows we've had enough trouble over it already and just 'cos we've now been drafted doesn't mean it'll get any easier."

"You have a point," Linen conceded. "Auntie Elle will have our ears if she thinks we're spilling beans. But you know, I'll be glad in a way to get back to our Dragon's Nest and our Glory

Hole, if only to see that nobody's fingered anything since last we were there."

"So will I; Thars promised our sites would be left untouched, but with the military all over the place, who knows what might go on behind his back? I know the techs keep a tight rein, but given Auntie Elle's now up there commanding a new starship, who's in command of her late clutch of underlings? And can they be trusted?"

"That's a can of worms and no mistake," Linen agreed. "But we can do nothing until we get there, so hand over the crispy chips and let's talk about something else. What our friends and ex-neighbours back at Lowell are up to would be a good start."

The journey to the Land-Hover Station at the Astrobiology Field Dome was over before they had covered that ground and by the time the two had disembarked and found their way to the hop on, hop off travelator that took them to the MDMC Psi Complex, they were more than ready for some new excitement.

Once at the impressively colourful plas-glazed portals of the Complex, Copper raised her wrist to the external reader plate and the panels parted to allow them both entry.

"It seems an age since we've been here," she sighed, looking around to get her bearings before striding over to the reception point to have her implanted Amberline Group student ident upgraded to allow her access to the facilities at the Complex.

Her friend followed suit and the pair were told to choose their favoured quarters from a list presented.

"Our lot must be thin on the ground," Copper noted as she perused the list and chose S3-42 as being handy for the elevator.

The receptionist concurred. "There are only two students in at the moment apart from you, though there are a few of yours out in the field, at your Amber-Warren and Nuryaninov sites," he said. "Your Prof's out at the Warren station; shipped out a couple of sols ago."

"What students are in?" Linen asked.

"Dol Rosso and Ahmet," she was told. "But they're off back to Lowell soon."

"Kurt and Decius," Copper nodded. "Friendly enough," she added in a low voice as the two sailed off and into their ride down to sub-floor three.

The emblem S3-42 glowed gaudily green as they approached the appropriate portal, the door panel having recognised their implants and permissions.

"Let's ditch our stuff and head up to the Ref Snug and see if Silver's about," Linen suggested. "He can give us the lowdown on what's what. We have a few hours to kill before we have to prettify ourselves and head on across to Giordano's."

"We'd best check our gear has arrived and if it's ready for our trip out morrow-sol, given Thars is out on site already and he said he'd arrange to have it shipped here. According to our schedule, we'll be off in the Scamper at oh eight hundred, so we'll have to have everything set," Copper warned. "We have our MEDICs and our scanners and the bits and pieces that your Grammy and Auntie Elle gave us ages ago, but nothing else in the way of kit, unless Thars had some other stuff sent out. And we'd best check in with Maize as well and let her know how Majorelle and Lofty are doing – she'll expect it."

"Lor' at this rate we'll not have time for a jar with Silver!"

"Tough. This was your bright idea in the first place, so it's your fault. Sort your bunk and get us a couple of mugs of caff while I check the comm logs to see if we have any messages."

"Yes ma'am! At once, ma'am! The Service is the right place for you, ordering me about like this. Just as well I like it," Linen smirked, complying.

Copper seized a cushion and threw it at her friend's head on her way over to the comm. A quick run-through confirmed that there were no updated messages for them. She therefore put a quick call in to Maize Mallis, Thars Amberline's Exec at the AF Dome and a cousin of Majorelle's mother. Maize was free and looking forward to seeing the two.

* * *

Half an hour later and Copper and Linen could at last make their way over to their group's stores and main lab. They wanted to ensure that their enviro-suits were not only there, but packed up for transfer to the Scamper, one of the two craft used by the Amberlines for cargo and people transport. Maize had told them that the Scamper was in the main AF Dome hangar and was loading for the early start on the morrow. Captain Kezza

Brownpelt and her second, Commander Chrysa Pennyplate, were supervising operations.

The two found lab coveralls and hauled them on, scanning around for familiar faces. Apart from two techs belonging to their group in the stores, the place was deserted.

"It's like a Ghost Dome," Copper said, shivering. "Where the hell's everyone?"

"Break time," Linen informed her as she collared Jho Jaros, the senior of the two techs, and asked after the enviro-suits.

"Still in the packaging sent over from Lowell," she was told, as he indicated the relevant case. "But we're short-handed so you'll have to wait awhile before I can spare a tech to get them and the rest of the gear out to the Scamper. There's nothing else here for you two: Prof Amberline told us you'd be in but you'd have your own kit and you'd be using the standard samplers and corers that are out on site."

"Fair enough, Jho," Linen twinkled at him. "How about we take the lot over to the hangar for you if you'll lend us a trolley, help us stack them and let us use the runner-hover – we'll bring the trolley and runner back, promise."

"You're all heart," Jho told her, grinning.

"That and cheek," muttered Copper *sotto voce*.

"Come on, Cop, let's sign these suits out, get the rest of the stuff loaded and let these boys get to their caff-break," Linen said, ignoring her.

"Furlough starts here," was the groaning reply as Copper grabbed an end of one of the boxes and began to haul.

* * *

It was some time later that the two found themselves back at the Psi Complex and in the Ref Snug, a small bar and diner for the use of residents outside the main refectory on sub-floor one, discussing the sol's doings with their old friend Silver Yarrow, the barkeep. They had been inveigled into helping load the gear they had brought over to the hanger and had then spent a relaxed quarter hour in chat with the two pilots. They had come away with the knowledge that both would be allowed to sit up front for the morrow's ride out to the Amber-Warren, and if circumstances were favourable, the craft would be set to atmospheric rather than land-shuttle mode and the two trainees could take a turn at the controls.

"You now realise that these will be our last ales of the sol and we'll have to remain virtuously sober for the whole eve out at Giordano's," Copper reminded her friend sternly, raising her small glass. "Weather's set fair, so there should be no problem with our hands on the helm, given we *are* qualified – well nearly – to fly military as well as civilian craft."

"So we'll be able to keep an eye on what's going on without disgracing ourselves, and we'll be able to remember everyone else's indiscretions, which means we'll have ammo to mortify them later. Must make sure we have our wrist-comms so we can capture the data for posterity," Linen giggled.

"Bet you're glad she's your friend rather than your enemy," Silver remarked conversationally. "But how's life in the Fleet, and why the blazes did you sign up in the first place?"

The two provided an edited version of the pressures exerted by others and the inducements offered in the shape of good pay, fancy uniforms and the training ranks of lieutenant, as well as being able to continue their PhDs aboard a starship, hopefully equipped with the latest that technology had on offer. The fact that their immediate superior would be their old friend and colleague, Dr Trisk Addystone was an added advantage.

"You know," Copper remarked as they made their farewells and set off back to their quarters, "I wonder why Colonel Moritz *did* push to get us aboard the *Drake*? I suspect she had Grammy Magenta Firewall giving a shove at the back as well. Was it so that she and her Intelligence cronies could keep an eye on what our research – and Trisk's come to that – was pulling out? And have all our relevant samples in a place where no-one else, including our sponsors, the almighty MDMC, could get their paws on them, in case the brighter of their tame lackeys could work out exactly what it was we actually found? And then make massive profit of it…"

"It's not profit they would make, I suspect, it's more likely to be leverage," Linen responded in a low voice as they turned into room S3-42. "We were *not* chosen by accident to carry out the testing of those miniaturised stealth surface science bots all those months ago, Auntie Elle admitted that much. And as a result of it and what we found, our lab stores were broken into, we were hounded – by your ex-pal Mizzle Chert for one and that damned reporter Stellaria Firedrake for another – and we were chased and shot at by some nasty people. Not to mention being on the receiving end of aggravation from those two MI minions of Colonel Moritz. A lot of people seem to want their hands on the evidence we've dug up and figured out. And unfortunately for us, you are one of the very few known to be responsive to the materials the powers-that-be think are alien artefacts. I suspect if *that* was widely known, you'd be very sought after by a number of highly unscrupulous people."

Copper stopped in her tracks to look at her friend. "Frock! I hadn't thought of that! You think we were drafted into the Fleet for our own protection?" she asked.

"There's only one other person we know that's been able to cause a response in the alien organo-tech that's been found."

"Trisk!"

"Exactly. And where's he right now? Senior science officer on board the *MSS Drake II*."

"Maybe that's why your Grammy was keen on us to have a look-see aboard the *Drake* and why your Ma didn't completely flip when she found out we were going to sign up – they knew in advance that we would be better off there than out at Lowell or even at our site," Copper surmised. "Given our joint talents, the work we're involved in, the mission that we think the new Fleet starships are set for and the commercial ships that are prepping for *their* missions. MDMC's new supra-light boat is set to launch before the *Drake*, according to Stardust Flashnews."

"She is," Linen agreed. "And Alecta Lattim will be wearing the gown my Ma designed for her when she launches it. I must check in with Ma: she's probably a better bet than the media for the launch schedule, as she'll be able to get the lowdown now that Ms Lattim is one of her famous clients."

"Your family would be top class as spies, if ever you thought to set up in the espionage business," Copper told her. "Your Grammy Magenta has the expertise in gadgetry that could bring down a government and your Ma has the ears of high-profile thespians that gossip to all and sundry."

"Too many out there already," the redhead responded dryly. "MDMC has its moles, Military Intelligence has its moles, every big consortium, industrial or otherwise has its own snoops and spies looking into everyone else's business so they can scratch their way to the top or scratch someone else's eyes out. But let's grab a caff and then get organised for the eve."

"And get set for our early start morrow-sol. I'm exhausted already and we haven't even started to be sociable yet."

* * *

The expanse of Giordano's gleaming façade lit the walkway in myriad scintillating hues as the two stepped off the travelator, across the short walkway and onto a welcome mat limned in luminous pink.

"Bet this has impressed most of our cohort that have made it thus far," said Linen, looking up at the external display. "We're booked into the Officers' Mess. Whoever took the booking seemed to think it was funny given who we were and they said we would all fit into the table space available."

"They might not find it so amusing, once they see the actual mess our lot make. We should maybe have suggested they set us up in the Cadet Recreation Zone. At least there they should be prepared for pee and puke."

"Please, Lieutenant! We are about to dine!" Linen exclaimed as she stepped through the door, more in order to impress the silver-clad attendant approaching from the expanse beyond than as an attempt to rebuke Copper.

"Good evening, officers; I'm Lieutenant Korin Karst and I'm at your service, welcome to Giordano's…"

His voice trailed off as he took in Linen's red hair, tastefully tied up in a spangled net, and the stat bars that both had decided to wear openly on their jackets. The pins had been given them by Colonel Moritz some time before to ease their admission to some Service sites and as a means of alerting ranking personnel to their status as civilian auxiliaries. As the insignia represented a newly commissioned branch of the Fleet, it was unlikely that any non-military person would understand their significance. Karst looked keenly at the metallic blue bars with reddish edges and a diamond shape within a square that denoted status. He clutched his menu-pad tightly to his chest, tongue-tied. Copper raised an eyebrow.

"We have reservations," Linen explained. "We're with the crew out of Beagle One Basecamp. Here's our confirmation."

As the holo expanded from her wrist-comm, the attendant's eyes widened in unease.

"Yes, ma'am. This way."

His back and his blue hair registered acute alarm as he turned to lead them to their assigned area. They followed at his heels along winding, metallic-walled passageways until they reached the familiar holo-portal of the Officers' Mess, its low-key grey and red walls looking stark after the riot of colour outside.

"Any starship with those systematics would never make it out of space dock," Linen remarked in the passing, pointing out part of the wall decoration that purported to be an engineering spec suggesting that deck three systems were operational.

"We have rearranged some of the seating to accommodate your party by retracting the enclosing partitions and setting extra chairs. Ensign Kerillan Greyspoke and I are your assists for the eve," their escort announced formally, in a tone that suggested he now regretted agreeing to do the shift. "Weren't you post-graduate students previously?" he added, unable to comprehend quite what was going on.

"We were," Linen informed him archly. "We're now assigned to the Fleet. Which means we're legitimate lieutenants."

He clutched his menu-pad even closer "Please place your orders at the console of your choice and specify your credit-ident number to assist accounts calculation later," he told them and then excused himself, turning on his heels at a speed that impressed them. He still looked dazed.

"Wants to make sure we don't run off without paying the rest of our bills," Copper chortled as she waved over at a couple of their peers who had made it in. "The place looks bigger with the partitions down – shame, the changeable wall colours would have had them all playing find the most clashing combinations. But I guess they can do it with the tables, they're all chameleon plasformic. Our lot are quite thin on the ground so far, I see, but as we had to cough up a sizeable deposit, I'm sure most of them will haul in eventually. What say we sit with Ferret, Zills and Inkle at that table over by? That way, if Blazells and Dingle turn up and want to join in, we'll be placed for a quick getaway."

"Have it your way," Linen agreed. "But I suspect we'll all be playing musical tables before long, in view of the usual off duty high jinks in the mess back at basecamp."

"These three are fairly harmless, normally," muttered her friend in an undertone. "And remember, no booze."

Their fellow trainees had already sampled copious amounts of some brew or other by the look of them and the boisterous welcome the new arrivals received. Upon enquiry, the three let out that they had spent half the afternoon in dissipation in some den in Beagle Central and were definitely up for more action. Linen immediately sized up their comrades nearby and informed Bass Ferret in a low but penetrating voice that Ensign Bonny Skate was sweet on him and he should start there.

"She'll eat him for dinner," was Copper's opinion as Ferret decided that ordering an exotic cocktail as an opening advance to the comely ensign was his best way forward.

"Shall we dance, Lieutenant Milkstone?" Ensign Dex Inkle demanded with a hiccup, standing up and extending a bent arm.

"No we shan't," Copper told him. "Firstly, there's no music, secondly there's no space, and thirdly, I've paid for half my dinner already and I want to collect before it gets too busy in here. I've changed my mind," she added to Linen. "I want to sit in a quiet booth over there."

"Oh no you don't. Just have a squint at the menu and order something. I've put in for a couple of custom-made Sparkle Specials on my tab, so they should be turning up soon."

Grumbling, Copper turned to the console and began to skim through a lengthy list. The quick Zills had stepped in to capture the disappointed Inkle and drag him off into a fumbling waltz around the other tables, to the consternation of their assigned assist, Ensign Greyspoke, who was attempting to deliver drinks.

"Hope you're getting overtime pay," Linen told her as the attendant parked two tall fizzing glasses by her elbow. "You'll deserve it by the time this lot are finished."

"They're all Fleet trainees?" Greyspoke asked, eyeing a bunch of four who had just arrived.

"Yup," Linen informed her.

"Lor' help the planet," she responded as she hurried away.

As the place filled up and the atmosphere became thick with argument, innuendo and the soft thumping of some background music that someone had set off, Copper and Linen ate their way through their rations and sipped at innocuous concoctions that were becoming more lurid as the evening passed, Linen having decided to see what she could invent drink-wise that looked lethal but did no more than cause tickles up the nose.

"Blazells keeps looking this way," Copper noted as she swept up the last of her crockery and slung it into a handy waste slot.

"Probably looking at Zills and Inkle canoodling. You'd think they'd go somewhere private, some of us are digesting dinner."

"*I'm* digesting dinner; you're capturing evidence to use later, aren't you?"

"I might be. Where's Ferret got to? Bon-Bon Skate chewed him up and spat him out, has she?"

"They've both gone AWOL," Copper told her, swabbing her hands industriously with a cleansing wipe. "Blazells is en route here with Dingle at the back of him. Evidently unable to capture dates. Or something else… He's eyeing up our jackets! I bet he's spotted our stat bars and curiosity's killing him."

"Oh good! This could be fun."

"No it couldn't. Behave yourself or I'll report you to Colonel Moritz."

The redhead gave an expressive shrug and looked up at the approaching duo. "Do sit down," she invited. "Haven't had the chance to talk to you all evening. Enjoyed your meals?"

The two complied and slid into vacant chairs. It was obvious to Copper at least that although both had been drinking neither was the worse for wear. It was also apparent that Lieutenant Blazells was intensely interested in the jackets that both she and Linen had removed and draped over the backs of their chairs. She took her own measures as her friend engaged the two in light-hearted banter. It was Blazells who brought the chat to a close, indicating that he wanted to go and have a word with some friend in the corner.

"Before you go, Blazells," Copper said, a glint in her eye as she held out her hand palm upward. "I'd like my stat bar back. The one you removed from my lapel a couple of minutes ago."

"I don't know what the hell you're on about!" he said angrily.

"Oh no?" Copper twisted the elegantly-jewelled bracelet that Linen knew was a cleverly crafted wrist-comm unit around her wrist and ordered a holo playback.

"Naughty, naughty," Linen's eyes crinkled up in merriment at the discomfited lieutenant as the holo showed his hand sliding across his body to detach the small pin, surreptitiously slipping it into his pocket.

"You will return my stat bar now, *Lieutenant.*" Copper's eyes bored furiously into his and her lips curled in anger as Dingle's jaw dropped. "Or I *will* have you up on report. It *is* trackable, by the way and if I have to scan for it publicly, believe me, I will."

The stat bar was replaced on the table and the young man swallowed nervously.

"You're dismissed," Copper told him sharply. "You will of course *not* mention this to anyone, either of you. You got that?"

"Yes, ma'am," the pair responded.

"Get the hell out of here!"

"Yes, ma'am."

"Nice impression of Colonel Moritz," Linen congratulated as the two slunk off with anxious looks at one another. "Is it okay to laugh now, ma'am?"

"You got a copy of his antics I take it?" Copper said in reply.

"Course I did, it was obvious he was trying for a closer look. He took a risk trying to filch the thing, though; I thought he was smarter than that. *Is* it trackable by the way?"

"No idea, but it sounded good. I've had enough; I want out of here and so does Spook. When I get upset, he gets upset."

"Aw! He worries about you! That's cute!"

"No it frocking isn't, it's unnerving. Pack your traps and go make our excuses to those of the gang that are still awake. I'm going to close out my tab and then head to the comfort station to get rid of that last triple cocktail."

"Yes ma'am!"

When Copper returned, her friend was rounding up her property and checking the table for anything inadvertently left behind. She announced that she had paid her bill and was ready to leave: everyone who should have been informed had been.

As they moved off, the thumbs up and cheery waves alerted Copper to something or other. "What did you tell them about our early retreat?" she demanded suspiciously.

"I told them we were heading off to get tattoos," Linen told her, grinning toothily. "Most of them believed me."

"Damn you, Lieutenant! I'll have your ears for that!"

That rejoinder caused the much-chastened Blazells to cast a startled look at the pair as they passed the table next to the exit where he and his crony had taken refuge, hoping to hide in the dark and finish their drinks. Linen had noted their reactions.

"What are you going to do? Report me to the colonel?" she demanded loudly and tartly.

"You're asking for trouble, lady!"

"Don't have to ask; I generally get trouble without asking."

"Will you behave?"

"Did you see those two hiding behind the jugs of ale trying to look invisible?" Linen asked. "You've seriously scared Gadget Blazells and poor Dingle will be afraid to speak to us again. How the hell he's ever going to learn to give orders as an officer is beyond me."

"So it seems is controlling your tongue. Tattoos! Mind you, I've always secretly fancied a tattoo…" Copper admitted.

"Funny, so have I. Maybe we should look into it when we're back in Beagle after our stint out at the Warren. But we'd best make tracks and hit the sack, we've an early start."

"If we ever find the way out of this place… Ah, green floor lights say we go this way…" Copper announced, pointing.

* * *

Back in the safe harbourage of their quarters at the Complex, Linen set about dredging up gear for the next sol whilst Copper organised mugs of Chocó-crème. They had met Silver and one of the techs on the way in and had perforce been obliged to spend a cheerful ten minutes explaining their fancy clothing and their outing and trying to avoid being invited into the Snug for a nightcap.

"Peace at last! At least there's only the two of us here," the redhead announced as she kicked her field carryall into a corner and dropped into a squashy chair, raising her feet onto the small table alongside.

"Don't be too sure," Copper told her, setting the mugs on the table and sitting down likewise. "I feel as if my personality's beginning to split and with Spook here as well, that's four of us at least."

"You know, you *will* have to let Colonel Moritz in on Spook once we're aboard the *Drake*. She's going to figure that there's something up, if the chief medic doesn't twig beforehand."

"Stop giving me things to worry about and drink your drink. I want to grab some sack time before Gemima starts telling me it's Satsol and it's time to get up. Lor' am I glad we got most of our stuff aboard the Scamper, it means one less job. Are we the only travellers? I can't remember anyone else being mentioned?"

"We are. Just as well, if we're going to be up front. There's enough gossip doing the rounds about us as it is… You first for the shower and don't take all night over it."

* * *

The two were up early the following sol but by the time they had cadged a lift to the main hangar on the small runner-hover kept in the vehicle bay of the Psi Complex and had given a hand with final loading, it was too late for breakfast. Captain Kezza Brownpelt had a tight turnaround and the Scamper would spend only a short time at the Warren station, they knew. Accordingly, the duo stepped aboard when requested and made their way forr'ad to the flight deck to take their allotted places. Copper sat beside Kezza in the co-pilot's chair whilst her friend slid in at her back alongside Commander Pennyplate; they would switch when told to do so by the Captain.

"I'm taking her out in flight mode," Brownpelt told the two visitors. "I've cleared it with Thars that you two can take the helm out over Isidis for a short time, but that's it. Clear?"

"Aye, Captain," the two responded in unison.

The captain kept up a running commentary as she held the Scamper in a low flight north-east over Isidis. Once out of local Beagle airspace she increased her altitude and prepared to hand control to Copper, having ascertained her readiness.

"Pilot Two, you have control."

"Roger that, I have control," was the automatic response as Copper, feeling the thrill of total command, smoothly took the helm with hardly a bump in flight to show for it. She kept her heading, deviating only once to skirt a raised area of patchy terrain lest some erratic gust of wind caused undue turbulence. She explained her actions as she went, earning a murmur of approval from Brownpelt.

"I have another craft on my screen," Copper noted a little later. "She'll cross our flightpath if she maintains her current bearing. Best check it out. This is Flight Alpha Two-Two-Six out of the Astro-Field Dome en route north; we have you in our sights. Do you read us, over?" she relayed.

"I read you, Flight Alpha Two-Two-Six and have you on my board," a male, slightly puzzled, voice replied. "This is Flight Six-Five-Two-Four on a training flight out of Basecamp Beagle One to your north east; heading directly back to base, over."

"Alpha Two-Two-Six to Six-Five-Two-Four: on your current course you will come within four hundred metres of our flight line; request you deviate to give us airspace, over."

"Negative on deviation, Alpha Two-Two-Six; I'm on a tight schedule and straight beam, over."

Copper hissed through her teeth and snapped the link on. "Six-Five-Two-Four, you read as a two-man training fighter, please confirm, over."

"Confirmed, over."

"We are a civilian personnel and cargo carrier, four aboard; we thus have priority over a training flight unless you have an emergency situation. Request you state your emergency or alter course as per flight priorities defined in MAT Procedures, part 1, chapter 4, section 9, over."

"I have no emergency, will comply, Flight Alpha Two-Two-Six, over."

"He's cooking it," Linen noted conversationally from behind.

"Alpha Two-Two-Six to Six-Five-Two-Four, roger that. I appreciate your compliance, Flight Captain; out."

"We don't usually do stand-offs here, Lieutenant Milkstone," Captain Brownpelt remarked as Copper cut the external link.

"The Manual of Atmospheric Transport Procedures table of flight priorities provides a very comprehensive record of who's got priority and one thing I do remember is that training flights are at the very bottom of a very long list. He was in the wrong."

"Bet he'll eventually realise it was you: he sounded as if he recognised your voice," Linen advised her gleefully. "He'll have your ears for it back at Basecamp. Best let me take the hot seat for a while until you get your temper back under control."

"I take it you knew that pilot?" Pennyplate surmised.

"Instructor Captain Max Meltdown," said Linen. "Our senior flight trainer, no less. Bet he's got someone up with him he's trying to impress, hence the testosterone show. But he *is* a damn good pilot, I'll give him that."

"But not much else," Copper added.

"Who's at the top of the priority list for giving way in general airspace anyway?" Linen asked. "Frocked if I can remember."

"The President of Mars. And even *she* would have to give way in an emergency. Preparing to return control to you on your mark, Captain Brownpelt."

* * *

The remainder of the flight, with Linen at the helm until the site station hove into view, was uneventful. As Kezza had taken over at that point the two students had leisure to look out at the familiar terrain around the Amber-Warren. Both noted that the military presence in terms of exploratory pits, service facilities and land craft was still evident. Some ground crew were visible around the temporary structures but it was rather quieter than it had been when last the two had seen it. As the Scamper was brought into the hangar and safely docked, the pair looked at one another and sighed in unison.

"Back!" Copper breathed. "Let's help with the unloading and rout out Thars: he said he wanted a word when we got in."

Linen agreed and the two set to work with a will, the hangar techs assisting to free the pilots for their about-turn pre-flight checks. They were still hard at it when Thars Amberline strolled up, hands in pockets.

"Chilly," he greeted them. "Enjoy your party last night?"

"Mostly," Copper told him. "We'll have time for a sortie to the Dragon's Nest this afternoon. What have the military bods been up to since last we were out this way?"

"Pulling back, as far as I can tell," Thars replied with a quick lift of his eyebrows at her tone, which had lost some of the deference she was wont to display in his company. "Let's talk in the mess, it's noisy here. The techs will finish up. I'll be along in a bit. I want a word with Kezza."

"You all right, Cop? You were pretty sharp with Thars back there," Linen asked as they made their way down one of the two tunnels that led to the hub, the central area of the site station that housed meteorological and other essential services and from which the other habitable station areas radiated.

"Was I? It must have been Spook. I get the impression he's doing mental somersaults now he's close to his home territory. Go find your ship," she added.

"You'd best not start speaking to him out loud or people will think you've gone space-loopy," her friend warned.

"Can't help it. I'd swear my link to him is becoming stronger. It's really beginning to freak me."

"Freak *you*? It scares the panties off me. But here's Mik Mack on the lookout for a chat," noted Linen as they turned into the mess and one of their favourite techs waddled up. "The whole place evidently knows we're back."

"We're back and didn't have breakfast," Copper corrected. "Let's find the eats first and then talk."

Having explained their state of starvation to the tech, he was all understanding and helped load their trays and fuel their mugs with hot caff. They found a table over in a corner, waving to those of the technical and ancillary personnel that they knew, and sat down to listen to Mik expound all the latest gossip from his neck of the planet. Thars Amberline joined them minutes later and the pair soon found that, as they had suspected, their colleagues Noa Dunelm and his partner and field-mate Syriana Steefens were also in residence, although presently out on site.

"Those two charm chickens haven't changed, even if they're now legally paired," Mik Mack informed the two students in a low voice. "But Ms Steefens definitely wears the britches in that partnership," he chuckled in an undertone.

"You don't have dual quarters out here at the station for students," Linen said matter-of-factly. "Do they rate permanent crew quarters while they're here, given their paired state?"

"Certainly not, they're in temporary residents' quarters, same as everybody else, including me," Thars told them. "How they arrange their own domestic concerns is up to them."

"Too much information!" Copper wailed. "Have a chipper, Thars, they're good."

The Prof was quick to remove a chipper from her plate with a grunt of thanks. "Military training seems to have given you an edge of steel, Copper," he remarked. "Enjoying it?"

Copper considered, eyeing her red-haired friend quizzically. "I'd rather be at Lowell," she admitted. "At least there you could take time out, within reason. But I expect it'll be better when we're assigned."

"Why *did* you opt for the Service?" Mik asked curiously.

"Everyone wants to know that," Linen told him, nodding her agreement to Copper. "We'd rather let the rumours fly about and leave you all in the dark."

"Please yourselves, duckies," Mik laughed, his face creasing. "Out to your site now, are you?"

"Once we've stowed our kit," Copper told him, pointing to the stack of kitbags by the table. "I expect most of the dorm quarters are free."

"Had them left especially for you two," the tech said.

"I'll bet. But we'd like to get out on site sooner rather than later, if our enviro-suits are unpacked and if there's a handy bus heading that way."

"I might be persuaded to get your gear and the bus ready for you, if you tell me why you're going Service."

"Tell you this eve over a beer," said Linen persuasively. "But only if you tell no-one else, not even Ambrose."

"Deal," Mik agreed, rising. "I'll leave you to finish your late breakfasts in peace and make sure your stuff's set. What will you both need in the way of scanners, scrapers, corers and the like?"

"We don't need scanners, but sample sleeves and scrapers – and the auto-sampler for loose floor goop," Copper stated. "I don't expect we'll be excising, but I suppose we'd best have one Obsidian corer."

"You got 'em, Lieutenant Copper, ma'am."

"Just hop to it, Mr Mack," she replied. "And you don't need to salute, I'm not in uniform."

"You might have to field a bit of similar flak," Thars warned. "It's pretty common knowledge that you've joined up and will be carrying on your PhDs as science officers on some ship of the Fleet. No-one's quite sure why."

"Bet you are," Linen laughed up at him.

"I may have an inkle or three, but I won't push it. What sampling are you hoping to do and what are you planning to do with your specimens and your data? You'll have a lot to ship up to wherever you're going, I understand."

His eyes twinkled as he regarded the pair. He evidently was party to a great deal that he was not telling but neither of his students was sure just how much.

"We'll have time to pack our Lowell gear before we ship out," Linen told him. "As Trisk did," she added mischievously. "Pity we won't have a super tri-dee sim aboard the... whatever ship we're assigned to. That would help matters along."

"I wouldn't be too certain of that," the Prof chuckled with a teasing wink. "I understand that off duty facilities aboard the latest of Mars' finest Fleet ships are pretty extensive, especially the larger, long-haul examples, so you never know. Ask Trisk, when next you hear from him. I'm sure he's worked all that out by now. But back to my former question: your schedule while you're here..."

* * *

"Thars is one savvy article," Linen declared to her friend as they strode down the temporary residents' corridor to choose their cubicles. "He knows damn well what's going on."

"He's worked on Mars Gov and military contracts for years so he's bound to have picked up a lot," was Copper's opinion. "And with his rep and with Trisk as one of his star students, he'll be someone they can all trust with secrets."

"You reckon?"

"I reckon. But here are our usual billets, eight and ten. Let's lock our idents in, dump our gear and change into the necessary for our enviro-suits. Then we'd best get our butts to the suiting room: Mik Mack's no slouch when it comes to organisation."

They found both Thars and Mik Mack in the suiting room when they reached it a few minutes later. Their suits were hung on the rail and they swiftly stripped off their warm coveralls and eased themselves into the almost skin-tight protective garments that had been designed to their physical specifications.

"Never gets any easier," Copper grimaced as she fastened the tight neck catch and checked the breather attached to her belt.

She carefully hung up her discarded coverall, abstracting her MEDIC and a couple of small items from one of its pockets and securing them within a leg pouch of her protective outfit. "Got Gerald?" she added in a low voice to Linen.

"Sure have. Let's off. Thanks for organising our stuff, Mik; appreciate it."

"I know *you* do, Treasure; some don't," he rumbled at her. "Ironstone's taking the bus out. Ambrose is on site so you'll see him once you get there. I'm staying out with Thars to upgrade a couple of systems. You'll have about three hours. Suit you?"

"Just fine," she replied as she and Copper followed the other two out of the door.

The hangar was as cold as usual and not busy. The Scamper was nowhere in evidence, having evidently made her departure in short order. The small hover-bus that would be their ride was already prepping, with tech Skella Ironstone at the controls.

"Hop aboard, Dragonets!" Mik ordered cheerily. "We don't have all sol."

With a short greeting to Ironstone in the passing, the two scrambled in after him and strapped themselves into their seats, closely followed by their senior mentor. All four fixed on their breathers for the short trip to the field site.

In a very few minutes the small craft was skimming across the open rocky terrain towards the enviro-bubble that shielded the site externally. As the bus pulled up at a projecting outcrop that designated the site entry, Copper and Linen peered out at a couple of temporary work domes that were almost close enough to walk to. All but Ironstone scrambled out and made for the airlock, kitbags containing their smaller pieces of equipment in hand. When the outer door had sealed and the inner space pressurised, they stepped past the inner airlock and down to the sand-coloured floor.

"Sign yourselves in, you two!" greeted Ambrose Grock, the tech in residence. "Good to have you back for a sol or so! Your buddies are out at their site but they'll be in for a break shortly."

"Shame," muttered Copper as she removed her breather. "I was hoping for a bit of peace."

"Just link into the site holo and stop the moaning," Linen instructed. "We'd best stop for a bit and be sociable."

"Why? Where does it say on my frigging contract I have to be sociable?" Copper demanded as she linked in, watching as the small image tagged 'Milkstone' materialised on the site map alongside the 'Lyrican' that denoted her field-partner.

"Small print at the bottom," she was told. "Hop in and sort us a choc. How are you, Ambrose?"

As the tech led the way into the small site office, he answered in his usual jocular fashion, motioning the latest arrivals to the bench space. Mik Mack had disappeared off to help with the unloading but he and Skella Ironstone soon reappeared with the kit. Copper had organised the drinks and soon the party were joined by the two students who had been out at their site.

Noachis Dunelm and Syriana Steefens had done sufficient work for one sol, Noa informed the group as he jettisoned his pack and saluted his fellow-students with a flick of the hand.

"You two got here, I see," he said. "Well, we're off as soon as we've sorted these sample sleeves. Get us a drink, will you, Syr, and I'll get our stuff out to the bus."

"We're fine, how are you?" Copper retorted in an undertone as Ms Steefens walked past them without a word and turned to the drinks dispenser.

"Had a good session in the field, Syriana?" Linen called out.

"Good enough," was the sour reply as she turned with two mugs in her hands. "*Some* of us have had to work our socks off for sevensols on end, out here and back at College." Her eyes were challenging as she regarded the pair critically.

"Tough luck," Copper told her shortly with a mocking grin, shrugging. "It must get wearing, same old, same old."

"Have this seat if you're tired," Linen put in as she stood. "Come on, Cop, we'd best get out to our site. We need to get as many samples as we can under our belts for taking back with us before we return to our exciting pursuits over at Beagle. And of course, we have several sols of furlough to fit in first."

"We'll maybe see you at the station later," Copper grinned maliciously at Syriana, whose lips had pouted at the suspected put-down.

"Yes, you two had better get on," Thars Amberline advised. "You're not here to waste time. Your site's waiting for you."

"Sir, yes sir!" Copper responded smartly as she turned swiftly to gather up her gear, causing her mentor to raise an eyebrow and Syriana to straighten up, baffled.

"Got Syr on the run, then," Linen laughed up at her friend as the two, Ambrose's safety briefing echoing in their ears, set off down the trail that would lead them to their Dragon's Nest site. "You're certainly creating an impression among our lot here with your new and masterful ways. What gives?"

"Spook. We have to get down to our site pronto, there are one or two things we need to see to," was the ominous reply.

"Like what?"

"Wait and see," Copper replied curtly. "Tunnel walls have ears. And I bet not all of them are friendly."

"You're scaring me – I feel I need to pee."

"So pee; you've got an enviro-suit on after all."

"Thanks," Linen grunted.

"You're welcome."

3: UNDER THE GROUND

Copper kept up a stealthy check of their way using Gemima as a scanner, to the perplexity of her friend. Linen could see nothing amiss as they tramped the main route, known as the High Road to those who used it, that ran the length of the upper part of the tunnel system. Sundry signs at several side passages that warned of hidden dangers and decreed that only authorised personnel had access were still *in situ*, the result of the incursions at their site and its environs to assist military digging some while back, but nothing new was obvious. As the two reached the blue floor beacon that marked the turning that eventually led to their site, they detached their breathers and automatically clamped them over their heads preparatory to stooping down to make their way through the narrowing passage that led to a wider level path and thus the Dragon's Nest.

Copper, in the lead, halted, straightened up and checked her suit's alarm before removing her breather, motioning her friend to do likewise. She looked around the small cavern, its greenish-grey roughly-textured walls spattered by encrustations of yellow and brown mineral deposits and broken by hollows, niches and extrusions. The faceted surfaces, jutting stalactites, rock piles, lava balls and other formations emphasized the volcanic nature of the system of which it was a part.

"Lights!" Copper called out as she stepped over onto a set of ramped steps that led down into their lower site, which they had termed the Glory Hole on account of the precious crystals that encrusted the majority of its wall surfaces.

At her back, Linen watched puzzled as her friend, MEDIC in hand, carried out a thorough scan of the smaller cavern.

"We'll set up the light grid here first and see what's changed since last we were down. I'll use Gemima as she has all the data in her matrix. Once the grid's in place, then we'll see…"

"We'll see what?" Linen demanded.

"What's changed, if anything," Copper said in reply, holding up a cautionary hand. "But first…"

In one swift movement she removed a small thick cylinder of polished metal from her leg pocket and set it down on its three flat round feet atop a handy boulder. She activated the device and as they waited, a blue ring slowly began to radiate from it. Linen's eyes widened, watching intently as the privacy bug carried out its three dimensional scan around them.

"There's no active scan in operation, then," Copper noted in grim satisfaction. "I'll leave it running, just in case."

"You think we've been breached?"

"Spook thinks we've been breached. At least, that's the impression I got when we started off from the office. Let's set your privacy bug up top, and then find our floor marker in here and get the grid up."

They worked quickly, cursing a sharp fluctuation in remanent magnetisation that was interfering with their readings, until a grid-map of light, projected over the rocky walls around them in a fine tracery of blue-white, shone out softly. Each pentagon of the display was subdivided into smaller gridded sections, each of which was saturated with colour and would expand outwards in response to the touch of a glove. The display would also react to verbal requests for additional data. Copper swiftly requested a visual readout of changes since last the two had mapped the site.

A quiet susurration told them that Gemima was calculating and in moments the answer appeared. There were two breaches: one took the form of a fine channel that pierced the wall which separated their lower cavern from the tunnels beyond that were part of the military excavations around the Warren; the second was a minute conduit that began on the ground in the far corner of the space – in that corner beneath and beyond which they knew was buried a small alien ship. Both apertures were open to air at their exits. Tiny piles of fine, powdery rock close to the sources of the breaches in the Glory Hole suggested that the coring had been done from the far side, where a pressurised air system was obviously operational.

"Shit!" Linen gazed at her friend in something akin to fear. "Looks like some person or some people have cored through to the Glory Hole from the military side of things – from the wall section nearest our site and from the place we know Spook's ship is half-buried in the rock. What the hell does it mean?"

"It looks suspiciously like somebody's figured that we, or our group, are somehow connected to the find of that ship and want more data that they think we might have or be able to dig up. As we've been drafted into the Fleet, it doesn't take much to realise that we must be the link…"

"But whoever it is would have to know that one, we found what we did, and two, we are now in the Service… that points to someone with military knowledge at a high level."

"I know; that's what's scaring me," Copper admitted. "We've always suspected that there must be security leaks in the Service, in fact so has Colonel Moritz, and this smacks of it big time. Let's get as much as we can on the breaches while we set the auto-sampler to gather floor litter. We *will* have to come back with loads of stuff or Thars will wonder what the blazes we've been at down here. But we'll have to contact the colonel on the QT and let her know."

"I know. She'll be livid. We'd best use the multi-scanners she gave us, or maybe not: they're linked to several classified military sources and databases – and their use will be noted."

"Good point. I brought along our usual scanner as a blind, so it'll have to be that, until we speak to Colonel Moritz. We can take samples near and a little beyond the breach points; that may give us a clue as to how they were made. They're so tiny it must have been with miniature corers or the like. We'd best also make sure that nothing's been sent through the breaches – though if nano-probes were deployed and then retrieved, how the hell we'd be able to tell I don't know."

"I'm beginning to be really glad we're assigned to the *Drake*. She seems a whole lot safer than a big cavity a long way under the surface of Mars with an alien ship not a rock's throw away from it that's sending a signal to who knows what and where, and a whole lot of nasty people more interested in it than they should be," Linen sighed. "I'll get Gerald onto setting up the grid up top and checking to see if we have any changes up there. You start the scanning down here."

Copper agreed and the two settled to their work, but they felt that they had achieved very little when Ambrose called in some time later that there was half an hour left and they should start to pack up. It appeared that Thars and Mik were almost done.

"Damn!" Linen cursed. "This frocking increase in remanent mag is making data acquisition a lot more trouble that it should be. Why the hell *does* it fluctuate so much?"

Copper had begun to shrug, but her face suddenly creased in a smile, and some relief.

"What?" her friend demanded.

"Spook: we know that some of the remanent magnetism in areas like the Warren was deliberately engineered by his people to hide their tech. I don't know how he did it, but he's the one responsible for this latest increase. Whatever's been going on, he figures it could be dangerous for us and he's protecting us."

"So now we've got your disembodied alien friend looking out for us down here? Just dandy. What will he do as an encore? Find the baddies and give them a telling off?"

"Don't be a flooshy and start packing, or we'll be the ones given a telling off. Did Gerald's scans show any differences in the Dragon's Nest?"

"Not that I could see right off and as my privacy bug's still showing clear, we're currently not under surveillance – at least surveillance that we can detect. Let's get the hell out of here, it's been one helluva sol and I want my dinner. And we've got Mik Mack's ears to tickle with why we joined the Service. We'll just have to embroider the tale of pressure from relatives that made out it would be a good thing and offers we couldn't refuse."

* * *

Once back at the site station and having securely stashed their precious samples and kit, the two lost no time in de-suiting and heading to the dormitory showers to refresh themselves for the social evening they suspected was ahead of them. Mik Mack was quick to claim their company the second they turned into the mess. He had commandeered a small table that would make it difficult for others to join them and once they had settled with their trays, he quickly brought up the subject of their recent decamping to the Service, folding his arms expectantly.

"That's certainly a very good story," the tech agreed as he sat back at the end of the recital, chiefly recounted by Linen. "And I'm sure most would be taken in by it. What's the real reason? You're not telling me that the offer of extra pocket money, fancy kit and lots of good times out beyond the orbit of our little ball of rock here are sufficient to make the likes of you pair of savvy solbeams toe a line like that?"

Copper shrugged as Linen oiled her tongue for a further attempt to baffle their inquisitor. Something in Mik's face made her change her mind.

"Look, Mik," she said in a very low and urgent voice. "This goes absolutely no further, not even to Thars. We *were* subject to persuasion from on high by people with our best interests at heart because our researches are showing results, a lot of which are of great interest to some very nasty people that are not above making life very difficult, if not dangerous, for us around our usual haunts. And we *have* been threatened and our stuff broken into. And we're scared."

Copper turned in silent disbelief to her friend, a questioning look on her face, her upraised hands requesting an explanation.

"He'd only have gone digging," Linen explained. "And then gotten into more trouble than he – or we – could handle."

Copper looked closely at the tech. "This hasn't come as a surprise to you," she observed acutely.

"No," Mik admitted. "I figured you'd found out something big-time that was getting a few big cheeses rattled, given the incursions back at Lowell; we hear how things are out here. And not many students have a friend like that colonel that asked to see your site *and* let you and Trisk see over those diggings of theirs out yonder. And young Trisk has joined the Service as well. Though he did finish his PhD and was in the market for employment. This won't go any further. But just you look after yourselves. And if you find yourselves in a tight spot anywhere in this neck of the woods, you give me a call. You hear?"

"We hear," Linen smiled. "Now where's this beer that was promised?"

"On its way. Sit tight."

"Don't fret it," the redhead advised her friend as Mik strolled off to the dispensers. "He won't talk. I *did* guess he knew more than he was letting on: he knows the troubles that have followed our published, and unpublished, work. And he's nothing if not persistent – he would have worked out it must be something to do with our findings, as the military was taking an interest, and his meddling might just alert whoever violated our site that they were about to be exposed."

"And the consequences could be very bad. We need to talk to Auntie Elle sooner rather than later," Copper pronounced.

"Not from here, it's not secure, so close to those damn military digs. I don't think I would even take the chance of using our wrist-comms, despite them being to my Grammy's spec and better than the best military ones available as far as security is concerned – *and* they were authorised by the colonel. It'll have to wait 'til we get back to Beagle. And I'd like to go over the scans we did this sol to see what we have," declared Linen.

"But not now. Just look who've come in: our two favourite colleagues. Thanks, Mik," Copper added as the tech rolled up and placed a large and frothing mug in front of her.

"So how are the Service hotshots?" Noa enquired jovially. "Earning your pay there and still getting a student disburse?"

"Pull up a chair if you can find one big enough for your personality," Linen invited. "You too, Syriana, haven't seen you for hours. How's life treating you? You both look very well."

The ever-outgoing Noa quickly complied and began the tale of his and his partner's doings, whilst the latter sat down sulkily and narrowly eyed the two, trying to figure out exactly what the gains were and what she was missing out on.

"So how did you manage to get such comfortable billets as officer training and then get time out to drop in here?" Noa demanded at last.

"Friends in high places, I expect," his mate put in with a lift of her lip.

"Naturally," Copper responded, not rising to the bait. "We have friends in high, low and various other places too numerous to mention. We thought we'd come on over and visit a few of them while we grabbed a few more samples to keep us busy while we're up there." She pointed skyward with a finger.

"Not where I'd like to be; you could get killed up there," said Syriana.

"You could get killed down here," Linen told her. "At least up there you get to see the sights and you get paid regardless of the down time."

"Sights! The inside of whatever rust-bucket you're assigned to! It'll be yes sir, no sir, three bags full, sir. Let me tidy away your plate for you, sir."

"That would be ma'am, yes ma'am," Copper grinned. "And aboard ship, you tidy away your own plates; the non-comms have better things to do that run after the likes of us."

"And how would you know? You've never been aboard a starship in your life," Syriana sneered.

"Oh but we have," Linen contradicted. "We were granted the privilege of a tour around the *MSS Drake II* some time ago — friends in high places," she added.

"Were you now?" Mik put in. "What's she like? I've seen some of the stuff on the media channels about her. Something special, I gather."

"She is that," Linen agreed. "But we can't disclose military information to non-mil personnel, Mik, sorry. And we *do* have to advise our security ops if we're pushed on such matters."

"Understood," the tech smiled.

Syriana had evidently had enough, and deciding that she had rather eat her dinner anywhere but in the present company, she hauled her partner to his feet and both set off in quest of food and a quiet place in which to discuss an impending report that they were in process of producing for their sponsors.

Copper waved mockingly at the retreating backs. "See you later, guys! Not," she added to her two friends at the table. "I suppose we should upload the data we got while we were out," she went on to Linen. "Save us the trouble morrow-sol. And weren't you going to link to your Ma?"

"If you're trying to get rid of me, duckies, just say so," Mik laughed, tilting his head at them. "I won't be offended. I know you'll have heap of beans to get done. But I meant what I said earlier," he went on in a quiet and serious tone. "You have any problems out here, you give me the nod. You hear?"

"Aye, sir," Copper rejoined facetiously. "And thanks for the beer. It takes away the taste of Syriana."

"Don't I just know it," he responded, rising.

"Blast!" Linen said softly. "Here's Thars, and I bet he wants the lowdown on what we found at our site."

"As far as we know, nothing's changed," Copper hissed in an urgent undertone. "We need to take this carefully in case we *are* being monitored."

"Got you. How do, Thars! How's tricks?" demanded the redhead as the professor ambled up to them and sat down.

* * *

It was two hours later that the two students managed to prise themselves away from their friends among the personnel at the Warren. Using a link to Corona Lyrican as an excuse, they made for the common room, captured a comm booth and set privacy to prevent interruption. Linen's mother was home and pleased to hear from them, but they made the connection short with the promise of more gossip later when the two returned to Beagle.

"Now to the field lab," Copper declared. "It's so perishing cold in there we're unlikely to be disturbed. You can upload all our scanning data and prelim runs on the floor samples to the Amberline Databank while I do some analysis of the nitty gritty that Gemima got on the breaches in the Glory Hole."

"Deal. Let's move it before someone else decides they want a chat and pins us down again."

The duo set up one of their privacy bugs in a secluded space in the deserted lab lest any unfriendly ears were listening. Their task took some while, but the results from Copper's MEDIC indicated that both breaches *had* originated from the military side of the intricate system of tunnels of which the Warren was a part, and not in that operated by the Amberlines. The channels also appeared to be recent and had been made by some device akin to a miniature Obsidian corer.

"Whoever did it must have retrieved their lode drill as soon as it was done," Copper reckoned. "The bore through the wall is low down but there isn't that much rock to core through. It's the one from Spook's ship up and back here that bothers me, though. It would have had to be pretty directional and whoever did it knew the direction, knew our site was here and had entry to the location of the ship… That points to someone working in the military diggings out yonder that has high priority access."

Linen pondered for a moment. "Remember that MDMC and their lackeys were first in here before ever the Amberlines were let loose, so there would have been maps made. *We* have the site holo, after all, so even with the new tunnels that our techs opened after Thars got contracts in place, MDMC and anyone connected to the project would have had those. It's their site after all; they laid claim to it and decided that students were the cheapest way to explore and analyse it, after their exploratory pits didn't show up anything valuable enough to waste their own time and effort on."

"Allegedly," Copper put in.

"Granted; but MDMC Acquisitions would have been on the lookout for new sources of costly minerals such as diamonds at first and that came up dry, so we were put in. And then our results caused a few head scratchings; and what with the other things that were happening on other sites around Mars, the finds that suggested higher life, the supposedly alien artefacts, the stuff that our chums Fudge and Chocolate amongst others brought in aboard the *Lithium Star*…"

"Not to mention Auntie Elle's original finds when she was out on the edge, aboard the *Wayfinder* on that collision-reduction mapping mission way back," Copper added. "That's what really started it all, the *Wayfinder's* chance finds of what they thought were traces of alien tech and then the *Lithium Star* found similar, but attached to what they thought were the remains of the *MSS Griffon* and a clutch of rockery. And Trisk and his original PhD research projects turned up pollen that he worked out had been altered by organo-tech in ages past when Mars was supposed to be a deserted, almost barren world, apart from a few vestiges of primitive life. But that doesn't explain why now there have been a couple of holes bored through to our site. Why us? Again…"

"As Mik Mack pointed out, not many students have a friend like Colonel Moritz; and when we were having trouble with the Press in the person of Stellaria Firedrake and others not so long ago, even Wolff Waterbone and our former College mate, the ever-ditsy Thulia Numbridge, were roped in to try and make us cough up the story of what we thought we'd found."

"Desperate for the lowdown," Copper agreed, nodding. "But this is recent coring, just as we happen to come back to our site for a few last-minute sampling ops? That smacks of intentional infiltration by the bad guys and a big time security leak in the bunch that are digging out there."

"They won't be out to erase us," said Linen soothingly. "But they might be out to pick up bits of information that we may let slip as we carry out our final sortie at the Dragon's Nest and the Glory Hole. But as people knew we were heading out this way, there *has* to be a leak here or in MDMC. Thars would have let Lomax Gratikule or the Waterbone at the Extra-Martis Missions Survey Office know: our projects come under the EMMSO's Planetary Survey Missions Project banner after all *and* they're still paying our fees. I haven't heard much from the Waterbone lately, I have to say. Maybe Auntie Elle scared him off."

"Maybe Thulia's got him cornered," Copper suggested tartly. "She was certainly oiling his ego for her own ends last time we saw them. But enough already. *We've* been compromised; how many of the other Warren sites have been?"

"I shouldn't think any: ours is closest to the military diggings and we're the ones causing the stir, so where would be the point of risking further incursions? And our site is also the one closest to Spook's ship. Where in hell is Spook anyway? I can't sense him, and I often can when he's around."

"Only when he lets you, but he's not here. He tipped me off about the problem, so I expect he's around his ship. He maybe goes there to recharge or maybe just to keep an eye, or whatever he uses for an eye, on things. But let's finish up for the eve. And morrow-sol, we keep to mundane chat and we do *not* mention the colonel or the *Drake* or our training or anything, even if our privacy bugs show clear."

* * *

Early the following sol found Copper and Linen up and in the suiting room in preparation for their new round of sampling out at their sites. Thars Amberline was already suited and made his way out, with the admonition to them to be quick. He was busy stacking supplies aboard the waiting hover-bus when the two strode into the hangar, kitbags slung over shoulders and various items of non-standard ware stashed about their persons.

"No Dunelm or Steefens?" Mik Mack demanded truculently as they approached. "Well, we're not waiting. We have yet more systems upgrades and a new tech to break in. This is Flinn Jecks. He's starting with Thars on site as soon as we're in. Get on with loading those sample sleeves, man, and don't be all sol about it," he ordered as the new tech eyed the students up and down.

As the loading proceeded Linen took a quiet opportunity to enquire of Mik about Mr Jecks' credentials, causing the tech to look curiously at her. "You think he might be trouble?"

"No idea. But a new appointment just as we heave-to sends a shiver where it shouldn't. And he keeps staring at us."

"Got you. I'll find out and keep you posted," Mik promised.

"Last sol out, is it?" Ambrose greeted the two students as he popped out of the bus, where he had been checking the craft.

"It is," Copper told him. "So we'll have to make it a good one and get plenty to keep us busy."

"So move it, we're almost done. Breathers on, you included Mr Jecks. Where are your two colleagues?"

"Weren't suiting up," Linen said briefly. "They'll have to catch the next ride, *if* they're coming out this sol that is. Syriana was mouthing off about the amount of stuff they had to do and a due report that was hardly started yet just as we left the mess."

With the bus loaded and prepped, the team set off for the short hop to the field site. Once there and disembarked, routine unloading began and it was fifteen minutes before Copper and Linen could set off to their site. It was Jecks' polite request that he would like to see the Dragon's Nest that caused Mik to look up, and not benignly.

"You're here to assist with the updates and to learn the ropes in the office here," the tech told the rookie. "Students' sites are sacrosanct: no tech breaks that rule unless in dire emergency or unless given authority by a senior and that means the Prof here, the site manager Mr Orrus or a senior tech. You got that?"

"Yes sir," was the startled response.

"Good. Now for the most important job of site tech at the start of the shift: the safety briefing. You two ready?"

"We're all ears," Copper told Mik and the tech launched into the usual list of cautions to be observed whilst on site.

The pair then sent off down their customary route, Copper raising a cautionary finger to her lips and giving a slight shake of the head that signified that any chat be limited to trivial matters that could safely be overheard, at least until they could check their surroundings.

Once safely within the Dragon's Nest, the two removed their breathers and looked quizzically at one another. Copper smiled grimly, removed her privacy bug from her pocket and began to set it up. Linen meanwhile had hauled out a small scanner and diligently began a top to toe sweep of her friend whilst listing aloud the samples they should take. She handed the device to Copper, motioning her to carry out the same procedure.

"You're clean," Copper announced finally, the privacy bug indicating that the upper cavern was not being bugged at that particular point. "What was this in aid of?"

"Just in case someone had planted a bug on our persons or our suits," Linen told her. "As our suits are generally hung up on the rail after decon by one of the duty techs, we'd have no way of knowing if they'd been tampered with behind our backs. That Jecks was eyeballing us both pretty closely, I noticed, back at the station; not usual in a newbie in a new job, I thought. So I asked Mik to check him out on the QT. He'll get back to us."

"Just as well our suits haven't been, or this Jecks would know by now we're onto him. I saw his eyes following us as well and it creeped me out a bit. His eyes are an odd shade of pale grey and he doesn't look like the usual run of new techs: he looks like he's been around a few blocks in his time. It's starting to feel like we're back at Lowell and being hounded by those misfits that were trying to hack into our sample stores at College and bug our talk at Mitty's place, remember?"

"I do. And the mess they made of it," Linen chuckled. "But these sorts of coincidence are not just chance. We really need to assume that our every move out here is being monitored. Let's talk shop. No more mentions of bugs, spies, spooks or anything else from here on in if we can possibly help it."

"You got it; let's unload our MEDICs and start them off. I trust them against any Amberline scanner. We'd best get the Obsidian corer warmed up for action as well. We can collect a few deeper block samples from areas we haven't done before.

And I want some near-floor and on-floor particle samples from our site below, especially near wall edges; it's more difficult for the auto-sampler to get in there after all," Copper said, giving an enigmatic wink.

"Ma'am, yes ma'am, Lieutenant Milkstone, ma'am."

"Just hop to it, smartarse."

They speedily unloaded their kit and then directed Gerald to generate and project the illuminated grid-map of the upper site. The light-web was soon superimposed over walls and floor. As the grids filled with data they were relieved to see that nothing had apparently changed from the previous sol. They decided therefore on auto floor sampling of the Dragon's Nest whilst they checked the Glory Hole below.

Once down the ramped steps the two began their usual sweeps, keeping up a stream of petty chat until Linen's privacy bug indicated that they were not being monitored. Gemima was then unpacked and positioned at the pre-set locus in order to establish the lower grid-map. Some soft swearing ensued at the shifting levels of interference from the inherent magnetic anomalies of the surrounding strata, but soon the small crystal-studded space was encompassed by a fragile web of light infilled with various muted colours.

Copper eased her aching shoulders, sighing softly. "What we got?" she demanded, carefully scanning the two locations that had been penetrated. "Anything new I wonder… Damn!"

"What is it?" queried Linen.

The answer was a sharp intake of breath as Copper examined the floor space critically. "This channel leading to Spook's ship is marginally wider that it was yestersol and here's some of the substrate that's been scraped out. Someone's sent a micro-mole of some sort through and it's pushed the scrapings ahead of itself and hasn't collected them all up. Whoever it was probably thought we wouldn't notice, as the floor of this place is deep in the dust of ages anyway."

"Poor judgement on their part. But what's it mean?" Linen demanded. "Someone very small is planning a visit?"

"Or someone may very well be preparing to send something through. The question is what, and when?"

"Are they such dimglows that they figured we'd not notice?" Linen replied. "But it looks like the coring certainly originated on the far side. That points to a perp with military credentials or at least with access to systems on the other side at this moment in time. And we're not supposed to be discussing this sort of thing down here."

Copper shrugged. "It's freaking me. But if it *is* us they want to be listening to or whatever, they'll have to be quick. We only have the rest of this sol and then we're off."

"They maybe want access through here after we're gone as well. You could ask Spook. He's not come back yet, has he?"

"No, but he's close. Funny, I'm beginning to miss him when he's not around my neck like an invisible scarf."

"Careful or I'll start to get jealous. But seriously: you *can* link to him when you try and you *do* get the impression of where he's at – remember the first time you tried to link to him back at Lowell and you saw in your mind's eye the cavity his ship was buried in? Or at least that's what you thought it was."

"It was," Copper said, sighing. "It was more than a feeling, it was almost certainty. I'll give it a go. You go topside and check that we're still not being bugged and that Gerald's still working."

"He'd better be," Linen sniffed, setting off up the steps. "I'll start block-sampling as well; the corer should be ready by now."

Copper set herself down on the gritty floor and closed her eyes, trying to recreate the sensation that told her Spook was with her. Seconds later, she knew that she had contact. She had no need to articulate even in thought the concerns that pressed round her, for immediately she was aware of a subtle wave of concern and an image that was almost clear of a subsurface cavern, subtly and eerily lit by angled bulkhead lanterns. There was a substantial protrusion of an iridescent red-green material from the bedrock of one wall. It was, she knew, part of Spook's ship, which had been buried there eons before and in which the alien entity had hibernated until the activity of humans in the tunnel system around it, allied to incoming signals from off-planet, had activated his suspension system and awoken him. His physical body had not survived the shock of awakening, but his life-essence he had been able to separate off. It was that which had latched onto Copper all those months before.

The cavern itself was empty of the scientists that had been tasked with finding out all they could about the alien ship and trying to gain entry to it. They had not, as Copper knew, been able to penetrate the craft, nor could they scan anything more than the ship itself would let them: it was organo-technology of the highest order and as such was programmed to defend itself. As Copper, eyes still closed, saw the scene unfold in her mind, she was aware of a shift at the entrance to the area: a suited and gloved individual with some small instrument in hand had slid in and set something off. Copper knew instinctively that it was some sort of jamming device: the recording devices that were in place to monitor the chamber and its secret were evidently being overridden. Whoever it was would not have much time.

The person moved into the open, assiduously scanning the space. He or she knew what they were looking for, for as soon as the crucial location was reached, a small auto drill-mole was abstracted from a pocket and set to work. Manipulations of some hand-held guiding device were made and the operator quickly made for the exit, deactivating the jammer.

Copper came to with Linen shaking her gently. "Dozing off, are we, Cop?" the redhead enquired lightly, a cautionary look in her eyes and a tightening grip on her arm warning of trouble. "What you need is a strong caff. Pity we can't bring any down here, but that's the way the planet spins. Never mind, we can take a break in an hour or so and see what Mik's been up to back above. Meanwhile, sampling."

As Copper came back to full awakening, she realised what had alerted her friend: the privacy bug was no longer giving out its blue glow that signified they were safe to talk. A subtle pink emanation from the tubular device suggested that some sort of monitoring operation was in progress.

"We had a long haul yestersol here and in the lab and were up early," she responded in what she hoped was a casual voice. "Besides, I've already sorted out all these sleeves for what the auto's collecting."

"Then let's get 'em filled, sleepyhead! And then you can give me a hand with the block samples. We may as well pack as we excise. We can take a couple back to the office with us and leave them and the filled sleeves there until we finish up. It'll mean less to cart back up at the end of our stint. We'll need to spend this eve getting everything sorted for shipping out."

"Whatever," Copper responded as she mechanically began to pack the closest sample sleeve with the material that the auto-sampler had collected. "This place doesn't get less dusty, does it? You reckon Noa and Syr made it out here yet or are they still in the mess?"

"We'll find out. That sampler's sounding a bit scratchy, you think it needs an overhaul?"

Copper caught the unspoken hint and pulled out the scanner that Colonel Moritz had given her, despite her friend's warning glance. Ostensibly examining the busy sampler, she directed the device towards the widened aperture that led down and along to the cavern she had so lately seen in her head, shielding the holo-output of the device with her gloved hand.

"I'll get the techs to give it a service when we're done," she said, nodding fractionally. "But it should do for now. I don't think it's about to fail on us just yet. It had better not, we've still got a heap of stuff to do."

"Maybe I should call Mik and get him to sort us out another one, just in case?" Linen suggested. "The one up top is working its little socks off as well and we need them both operational if we're to get all the material we want."

"Good call. You do that while I finish loading these sleeves. Where are the rest of them? We'll need a couple more."

With Copper grumbling inconsequential nothings about their workload to herself, her friend called into the site tech back at the office to explain their concerns.

"It may be nothing but it very well *might* be something," she heard Linen say pointedly. "Thars back from his systems testing or whatever he was doing yet?" she added.

"No, still out," was the reply in a slightly puzzled tone. "You two coming in for a break soon? Your buddies Mr Dunelm and Ms Steefens have just gone out to their site; they've only just got here and have a lot to do, so they said."

"In which case, we'll come on in. We can bring the sampler with us and you can give it the once over. Get the caff on!"

"Will do. See you soon."

"Let's get on it," the redhead said to her friend. "We go *now* and we won't have to put up with Noa and Syr whining about the work they have to do when they come in. You know what they're like."

"Don't I just," Copper replied. "Let me get this sleeve filled and I'll deactivate the sampler. The mag's pretty high this sol, so I may as well switch the grid-map off. We'll no doubt have to recalibrate the whole damn thing when we come back, we always do. You never get the same readings twice in this place."

The two quickly gathered up their tackle, Copper carefully lifting Gemima from the floor and looking round to see that nothing was left behind. She had no intention of leaving any of their precious kit to the mercies of whatever had caused the privacy bug to issue its warning.

"Lights off!" Linen bawled as the two ascended the ramped stairway up the Dragon's Nest. "No point wasting power," she added as she covertly pointed to the privacy bug in the upper site that was operational and still showing blue.

"We take everything of value with us," Copper said quietly. "The sample sleeves and packs we can leave. Let's hit the trail."

Before they did so, the two repeated the scans of each other that they had carried out prior to their beginning their sol's work and, those showing clear, set off down the trail, monitoring every step of the way. By silent but tacit agreement, they had decided that no exchange of information would be made until they knew they were very safe from eavesdropping.

Mik, waiting in the site office, uttered nothing bar a quick greeting and the information that the caff was on tap. He made a point of stepping over to the dispenser array to produce their drinks as the two began a rapid assessment of the office itself.

"We're clean and so are you," Copper announced to the tech as she swept the immediate area with her eyes.

"What in blazes is going on?" Mik demanded. "I figured from your call that something was up."

"Our lower site's being bugged," Linen said shortly. "Can't tell you how we knew but it is. Don't know if they have visual or just audio." She looked interrogatively at her field-partner.

"Both," Copper confirmed. "At least that's what my ops data shows. But as we've switched off the lights and we're here, there won't be much to see or hear for now. We brought all our gear back so it wouldn't be tampered with. But I've had an idea how we can put a temporary stop to the snooping at any rate, as long as the source hasn't moved away from where it was."

"How?" Linen demanded.

"We move the rocks about. And I suggest we also send out a spy-cam ourselves, through that fissure connecting the Dragon's Nest with the Glory Hole – the one that opened up after the marsquake that led us to discover the Glory Hole in the first place, when we were here on our first sampling tour way back."

"Why through the fissure?" Linen asked. "Why not just set it up in the Glory Hole?"

"Because we do it on the QT and that means *not* down there. Can you get us the necessary right now, Mik? We can leave it running; the opening in the Glory Hole is high up, so it's not a place we would normally reach to sample without scaffolding in place. We can link another scanner to the cam and capture any data. That would show if our site's being infiltrated when we're not there. Because we won't be in a very short time."

"Give me a sec," Mik Mack replied grimly as he made a quick connection of his own. "You get that caff down you while I sort one or two things."

A short time later, Mik looked up. "Ambrose is on his way with a bunch of kit including a replacement auto-sampler. He's bringing what you need on the quiet and in the same case. He won't ask questions and I'll sure as hell make sure we're not under surveillance when we discuss things. You're positive you can do the needful at your site? After the earful I gave Jecks, I can't come with you." He paused to scrutinise the pair. "You reckon Jecks may have a hand in it? I haven't been able to dig up anything on him, which is a mystery in itself. Usually a tech's background info is available to those with relevant clearance. Which includes me, as far as juniors are concerned," he added.

Linen shrugged. "I'm not sure. Back at the station he struck me as too watchful of us, odd in someone who'd never seen us before; and for a new tech he was too much on the inquisitive side. Cop caught it too. So we checked our site very carefully."

"What *can* you tell me?" Mik asked.

"Nary a thing," Copper told him regretfully. "But it looks like our research is still causing disturbances in some places. We can't pin anything on Jecks, though; he might just be naturally nosey. And as the bugging started *after* we'd been down a while, it wouldn't have been him – he' still out with Thars and on the site holo, right?"

"Still showing loud and clear," Mik verified as he indicated his station, where two of the images were labelled 'Amberline' and 'Jecks'. "But they've not been in for a caff and cake break. You'd better have something to eat to keep you going. I'll post you on who's in and when, if you like. You'll need another respite if you're going to be out all sol. But this bugging worries me: at your site only or a few other places as well?"

"Can't help you there, Mik; but our site and the outer tunnels close by are the ones that link to the mil digs on the other side. Although those digs go down further, beneath the lowest levels of the Warren, *that* we do know," Copper told him.

"And how do you know that?"

"Saw some of their site maps when we visited the Base Camp ages ago," she replied smoothly. "But let's eat. We'll need all our energy just to keep our eyes and ears open."

"You do that and I'll stack the samples you've brought in. Keep an eye on the holo and my comm while you're at it."

The two complied as they chose their victuals and set to, but nothing came in apart from a notice that the hover-bus had left the station and was on its way. Minutes later, a cheerful halloo at the inner hatch told them that Ambrose had arrived. His arms were full and he deposited the kit he had brought in, telling the three that there was more to come. The unloading took another ten minutes and by that time Copper and Linen were ready and eager to return to their site. They gathered up their kitbags, now supplemented by the spare auto-sampler that Ambrose had brought, with many a significant nod at its bulging case.

* * *

Once back at the Dragon's Nest and by now highly-attuned to interference, the two students lost no time in carrying out thorough scans of themselves and their two sites. As before, the upper chamber was clear of surveillance devices as far as their privacy bug and scanners could tell. Gerald was set up to project the grid-map over the rock fascia, and once that was in place the new floor sampler was removed from its casing, checked and set to collect floor grit. The pair then carefully extracted the extra gear that Ambrose had included. Familiar with similar devices, Linen quickly inspected the small hover-cam, set it to wide-field and readied it for launch. Copper in the interim had crouched down to reach the crystal-studded aperture, well-hidden beneath a low ledge, which led down to their lower cavity. It was large enough to insert a gloved hand and its spec was in Gemima's memory matrix. Once she was satisfied with its operation, Linen passed the cam to her friend; Copper carefully cupped it in her hand and slid her arm into the fissure, obeying Linen's low-voiced commands as to positioning.

"Think that's it. Can't tell as no light below, but it's in hover-mode so we can tweak it later. We'd best get on: if we *are* being currently monitored, the watcher is bound to know we're back here," Copper said quietly as she removed her arm and shook it.

The two gathered up their remaining tackle and made the descent into the Glory Hole, calling for light as they did so.

"Let's get our grid set up down here," Linen began. "We can leave scanning ops and sampling to run up top. That new auto-sampler seems to be running okay, but the mag is still high."

As Copper fired up her MEDIC for projection of the light-grid, she looked over at her field-mate, who had begun to pull the second auto-sampler from its case.

"We need to make sure we get uniform coverage of the floor sections," Linen said. "Let's check what the grid says once it's operational. I'll haul out our big bio-geo-chem-scanner and set it up; and we'll need the vac static sampler as well. Gemima, veil the floor sections by intensity of sampling once you have a clear grid," she ordered the MEDIC.

"Complying," was the terse reply.

"Damn this mag!" Copper meanwhile was grumping. "It's still not settling. Ah, there we have it… hmm we've done a lot centrally as far as sampling the floor goop is concerned but a lot less near the walls. As the damn auto-sampler's programmed for uniform coverage, it should be more constant than that."

"Look at the material on the floor," the redhead responded. "The sampler skirts around some of the larger pieces as it can't swallow them. We'll just have to move them even if it means a site reconfigure. Give me a hand to lug this fizzing great boulder over to the wall and out of the way for a start. And we should clear those lumps away as well – they're from that time the floor above caved in. But carefully, we don't want to move or damage something that might be important; this site has to remain as pristine and undamaged as possible, *that* was the deal. Gemima, scan and catalogue changes to current site layout and update your grid-map."

As the two worked, removing the smaller pieces as a start, Copper made shrewdly sure that she checked the grid for places of sufficient screening that could safely be used to store the slack from the under-sampled floor spaces. She issued her orders competently but calmly and in under fifteen minutes both the exits of the two known breaches had been blocked to some degree. A quick scan after that had indicated that no other infiltrations had been made, but the privacy bug, then set in operation, still showed that monitoring was operative.

"We've still the block excisions to make up top," Copper reminded her field-mate. "We've sampled grids Alpha 001 through Delta 020, but we're short on substrate from the mid to upper levels. Though I suppose we'd best vac-sample here, since we are *not* going to be coring. These damn things can be noisy and they stir up a bit, but let's get to it. Help me shove this boulder over a bit: I may as well use it as a seat."

Grinning, Linen obeyed; the larger of the two breaches was thus effectively blocked by a very hefty lump of rock, upon which Copper sat in triumph. The privacy bug was still showing pink, however, suggesting that the leak in the other wall had not been plugged entirely. Linen made a cut-throat sign with her hand and pointed to the second opening, but her friend nodded negatively, tapping the side of her head; any view from a micro-cam would be obscured, but it would be useful if the two could plant misinformation in any listening ears. A thumbs up showed that Linen had got the message.

"If you start here, I'll head on up and see that our ops up there are still running smoothly," the redhead suggested. "There may be one or two things that need a tweak."

"Done," Copper replied starting up her vac.

She cannily left it running as she swept the entire area afresh with her military-issue scanner. As far as she could tell, there was nothing amiss and no additional devices had been planted.

* * *

A couple of hours later and Mik called them up to ask if they were ever coming in for their break. Noa and Syriana had been and gone and the Prof and Jecks had finished their work and had left for the site station. This was invitation enough and the two closed operations down in the Glory Hole, removing all of their own equipment and ordering lights out. They repeated the manoeuvre in the Dragon's Nest and were soon on the road to the office.

"Thought you'd have swapped shifts by this time, Mik," Linen greeted the tech as she stepped through the door.

"Ironstone was feeling a bit off-colour," he winked up at her from the desk. "So I volunteered to cover for her. I told Thars so when he and Jecks came in."

"When did you tell *her*?" Linen chuckled as Copper, feeling a frisson of anxiety, pulled out a scanner and began a sweep of the environs.

"Clear in here," she announced. "Just what systems were Thars and Jecks upgrading?" she enquired.

Her tone caused Mik to look intently at her. "The enviro-systems just off the High Road, close to the areas that were less damaged in the last 'quake and that the techs hadn't got around to; they weren't priorities as none of you lot are working them," he replied. "You reckon I should get another tech to check the work out?"

"Might be worth it," Copper told him, raising an eyebrow. "Thanks to you and Ambrose for the kit, by the way. Seems to be working okay," she added.

"No problem, cupcake. Grab a bite, both. You won't have much time left at your site, and that will be you for the duration now, won't it?"

"Yup. Be grateful if you could keep an eye – both eyes – on our site for us," Copper added, looking enquiringly at her friend, who nodded.

"Will do," he agreed warily. "Make sure you two Dragonets keep me updated on your link info. It'll be chill to have a couple of buddies aboard a starship. But for the moment, I think I'll get Ambrose to come on out with some stuff. He can have one of the other techs bring him out in the bus and can stay over for a bit. There's always plenty to do out here."

"Good idea," Linen nodded. "But now we eat: as you say, we don't have a lot of time. And no doubt Noa and Syr will want to get back to base sooner rather than later – they always do."

"Tough," the tech said robustly. "In my book, you two have priority."

"Just don't tell them that or we'll never hear the end of it," Copper warned as she picked up her mug.

* * *

Several hours later and the two Amberlines were gazing with a mixture of sadness and elation at their lower site. Mik Mack had called in some time ago to say that their two colleagues had quit for the sol and gone off with Ambrose and the bus, but that he would remain on site until they had finished as much as they wanted. Having completed their work above, they agreed to vac-sample another section of the Glory Hole, but leave the smaller of the breaches untouched: they had noticed upon their return that the debris against the aperture had shifted slightly, which implied that a current watch was being kept on them. Both were wise enough to realise that mock ignorance was likely to be their best course and had made some play at filling any listening ears with a fictitious account of where they planned to spend the remainder of their leave.

Once back topside, a thorough scan of the Dragon's Nest revealed that the situation there was *status quo*: the recorder cam in the fissure leading downwards was operational and no further incursions had been observed. They locked the cam in place and abstracted its linkage. They planned to pass that to Mik later.

"Let's collect our blocks and scrapes and head out," Copper said quietly but wearily, shrugging her shoulders to relieve the tension.

"I'm going to miss our dragon and her nest," sighed Linen as she scanned the misshapen lumps of stone that had suggested their site's name. "But onwards and upwards, I guess. In our case quite far upwards; and we have a lot to get through at the station if we're catching the first transport out Moonsol. Isn't

Captain Jeffers due in at some point? If so, it'll be the Scuttle, joy of joys. *He'd* never let us have a turn at piloting her, even if Opal was agreeable."

"Wouldn't want to, with Jeffers breathing down my neck. Pass the bio-geo-chem scanner over and I'll pack it in with this," Copper ordered. "That's about it – all except our little bug here. From now on in, no chat that isn't idle."

"Got you. One of our first stops in civilisation is going to be a spa. I need a long, hot, fizzy soak in scented waters and a long, cool cocktail."

"This was your idea in the first place, so don't moan at me about your aches and pains; they're your own fault."

As they packed and collected their belongings and made their way by the various passages that would take them to the office and the exit to the Warren, they continued in amicable banter. Suddenly Copper stopped dead, grabbing Linen's arm in a vice-like grip. She pulled her sideways and into one of the numerous tunnels that led off the main path.

"What is it?" her friend hissed urgently.

"Don't know, but Spook just screamed in my head to get off the High Road," Copper whispered back. "Down here, quietly; it's darker."

The two could hear a scuffling and dragging sound from the main highway and moments later a couple of suited individuals passed their refuge, dragging what looked like a third.

"Haven't got a lot of time," one panted hoarsely. "Just dump him down here somewhere, he'll not realise what hit him when he wakes up. At back of this warning sign will do. You'll have to get back to the office to keep an eye on the comms and stuff."

The two Amberlines crept further backwards when they realised that the two were about to haul their burden to within a couple of metres of them, at a small tunnel they had just passed. They flattened themselves against the wall and waited, hardly daring to breathe.

"That'll do," a second voice puffed. "I'll give you a hand with the mole-drill and then get back up here in case those two dimglows come on in."

The two moved off further down.

"Dimglows? That would be us?" Linen whispered.

Copper was divesting herself of her kit. "You got a weapon of any sort? Your stun?" she muttered.

"Nope – wasn't expecting to have to use it."

"Then warm up the Obsidian corer."

"You're kidding!"

"I'm not. Drop everything else. We're heading on in."

4: FURLOUGH TWO

Copper crept to the end of the passage and peered round the corner; she could see no sign of the two heavies and pulled her field-partner forward. As Linen gestured down the way to where the unconscious individual had been dumped, her friend shook her head grimly.

"Can't help him at the moment and we need to get to the office before one of them does," she whispered. "We're on the site-holo: one look and they'll know exactly where we are."

"Shit!"

"Exactly. Move it."

"It'll be Mik, won't it?" Linen puffed as they made the office.

"Guess so. In here, shut the frocking door and hand over the corer. You call in a mayday to the station, but be quiet and make sure you speak to Thars. I only hope those two are working on their own or we could be in real trouble."

"I figure we're already in real trouble," Linen muttered as she tabbed the relevant connections.

"Now what the hell else is there round here that we could use as a weapon? Lor' knows what they stunned Mik with, but I bet both those thugs are armed. Make that quick and then get over here," her friend ordered, checking the site-holo.

Neither of the two strangers was showing up on the holo, leading Copper to conclude that they were not linked into the system. That was bad, as she would not know when they were approaching. One lone figure, tagged Mack, was unmoving in the sector that he had been dumped.

"Damn!" Copper muttered to herself as she cast around for something heavy.

She dropped the corer to drag a low crate over, positioning it just inside the entry portal. Panting heavily, she retrieved the coring tool and scanned the space for suitable weaponry. A large rock-core extractor had been left against the far wall near the dispensers and she grabbed that, hefting it in her free hand. It would have to do.

"Security detail on the way; they sort of know the score. Got the site paramedic as well," Linen told her.

"Get behind me and hang onto that. Hit anything that isn't me," Copper directed.

"No way! I'm at your side!"

"Like hell. I'm taller than you and if I go down, you'll still be standing. When the hell will you ever learn to take orders?"

The minutes trickled by. Suddenly Copper's head reared up. "Something's on the way!" she hissed, activating her corer and bracing herself.

The door of the office slid over and there was a muted curse as the individual stepping in caught a foot on the crate. It was enough to warn him that he had company and he spun, the weapon in his hands locked in position. He was too late: Copper lunged, the corer held up for action. She sliced down diagonally: the beam swept across him, catching his arms, the weapon and one leg. The firearm fell useless as the man let out an unearthly scream, staggering backwards.

Her training kicking in, Linen jumped out, the core extractor wielded like a club. She scanned the cowering form. The man had huddled into himself and was shaking, the blood beginning to flow. The girl kicked the broken gun away from him and cast a quick look up at her friend.

A movement on the floor alerted Copper and she brought a boot down quickly on one of the injured man's hands: the other was reaching for something inside his pocket. "You try it, you're toast!" she warned as noises at the entry alerted the two students to new arrivals.

Copper had the Obsidian corer ready to slash at anything that came through the opening, but she pulled up as a suited and helmeted form brandishing a weapon stepped in, closely followed by a second. There were more outside.

"I take it you're the cavalry?" she remarked calmly. "One down and there's at least one other that we know about on the loose somewhere out there."

The leading figure pulled off its helmet to reveal the face of a woman that neither of the students recognised. "Mirrin Birks, station security team," she stated as she cast her eyes around to take in the situation. "He's a mess. Your work?"

"Yup," Copper said shortly. "Didn't know the station *had* a security team."

"I double as a site mechanic," was the wry reply as another person stepped over the threshold. "What's the deal?"

"You two all right?" the voice of Thars Amberline cut in.

"We're fine. Where's the medic? Mik's out there and hurt; I'm not sure how bad. Linen, you go with them to show the way and pick up as much of our kit as you're able to bring in. They'll need back-up," Copper told Birks. "His accomplice is not on the site-holo so we don't know where he is, but he was going to be using a mole-drill so you may be able to track the drilling. He'll be armed and dangerous: don't take chances."

"We've got trackers, we'll find him. What about *him*?"

"Mr Jecks will live, I expect. The corer will have cauterised most of his lacerations after the initial bleed. But check him over, he's got concealed weaponry."

Leaving one of her number and a shocked Thars Amberline behind, the security officer made off to issue orders and search as much of the site as possible.

The professor was eyeing his student in perplexity. "Are you sure you're all right, Copper?"

"Fine, Thars. But why did Jecks and whoever is out there not show up on the site-holo?" she demanded as she deactivated her Obsidian corer and set it down. "He must have logged in when he came onto site, it's mandatory, and Mik was here."

"Jecks was a new start – he doesn't have an implanted ident yet, so I guess he must have removed his temporary wrist-ident or cut the link. But who's the other one? And what the hell's going on? Why is the Warren being targeted by them?"

"Search me," Copper shrugged, although a few ideas were percolating in her brain. "But the military are still digging in our backyard, so it may have something to do with them."

The security officer examining the white-faced rogue tech on the ground straightened up. "He was packing a bit of an arsenal. You're lucky he didn't get to use that phase rifle on you, you'd have been a puddle on the floor. Or this stun blaster: *that* would have given you a headache."

"I know," Copper said harshly. "I recognised the rifle and I know the sting it has. Why d'you think I hit first and didn't stop to ask questions?"

"You recognised the rifle?"

"I've used one – in practice sessions on an authorised range," she added as the man's eyebrows shot into his hair. "Check his boots," she went on. "You can hide one or two surprises in a bit of shoe leather."

Jecks looked up at her in bafflement, his eyes red. Whatever his brief, her credentials had not been part of it, Copper figured, and he had no idea of her training or her abilities. She surveyed him in return and in her mind's eye she suddenly saw what she thought may have been one of the answers to why the Warren had been infiltrated. She strode over to the desk and examined the site-holo critically, tabbing up a few enquiries. Suddenly she slapped her comm link and issued a staccato request to Linen.

"Tell Ms Birks and her team to head on down to the keyhole tunnel section near the Dragon's Nest, but take the right hand branch just before the low passage into our site. An unexplored bit beyond the red delineator has just recently been logged as a query up here under an unidentified ident; and as Mr Jecks has just tried to jump up, I guess he's a tad anxious that I think it might have been his."

"Copy; will comply," Linen responded formally. "Mik will be okay, by the by, severe stunning and grazes and lacerations due to rough treatment, but he'll do. Paramedic's on it."

"Copy that, Milkstone out."

"What the blazes are they teaching you in that basecamp of yours?" Thars demanded in a low voice as he walked over to examine the site-holo.

"How to deal with the likes of him and his nasty friends," Copper responded with heavy irony, nodding at Jecks. "But I'll let your security deal with it: I don't think he'd appreciate what I'd do to him."

"I'd say you'd done plenty," interrupted the security man on the floor, who had been listening. "He needs a medic."

"His victim has priority," Copper retorted pointedly as she began to rummage in a nearby locker. "But I have my GHQ so I *am* qualified to render emergency aid. The primary assist kit is in here. Get him down flat on his back if you can do it without causing him too much pain. I'll need it for full body scan."

"Don't you touch me," the injured man groaned as he tried to back off.

"Button it," he was told by the security officer, who carefully prised his tightly folded limbs apart and helped him lie prone.

Copper had meanwhile tugged out a large carryall and begun to set out its contents. She quickly unpacked a medi-scanner and set it up adroitly to assess the damage, pulling out its extensible scaffold, which she set over Jecks to include as much of his body as possible.

"Hold it steady," she instructed Thars, who had knelt down to lend a pair of hands.

As the scanner moved along the scaffold, its readings were captured and converted into advice as to treatment, displayed on a holo-readout that expanded over the device. Copper was more than relieved to note that there was no damage to Jecks' major organs, but a couple of tendons in one hand had been sliced, the weapon he had sported having taken the brunt of the hit on his torso. As the scanner sent out its holo-projection of the most appropriate places to position various dressings, she unpacked the relevant materials.

"The right hand first," she murmured gently. "But I'll give you a hypo shot to dull the pain before I start."

She had almost completed her ministrations when Linen breezed in with the information that Mik was on his way back to the station, another hover was on its way in and more medical assistance had been summoned from the AF Dome.

"But the military base on the doorstep must have a medic on hand," the redhead continued, looking down at Jecks as she dumped the kit she had carried in. "Want me to give them a buzz? They sure as hell must realise something's going on here, with all the hullabaloo outside."

"Not my call," Copper said warily, looking at the professor.

"Do it," he responded. "Just say accident, don't give details."

By the time that Linen had found someone willing to take her link and agree to her request, Birks had called in with the information that she and her team had apprehended the second suspect. They were escorting him to the site station, where he would be held securely until enquiries were made.

"Where?" Linen demanded. "I don't recall noting a cell on the premises."

"Shut up and fetch me the gurney," her friend ordered. "We'll have to strap this guy in, he won't be walking anywhere."

The Amberline party had collected its gear, secured the field site and made it as far as the site station when a Ground Ops medical doctor, a Captain Bardin Deck, finally turned up. Both Mik and Jecks had been installed in the small treatment room off the end of the decon suite, where Copper thankfully released the care of her patient to the medic and his assist.

"Not bad, young woman," the doctor congratulated her as he looked over the arrangements. "But he'll need way more than I can do for him here. What exactly happened?"

"It's Lieutenant," she informed him acidly, eying him closely. "Lacerations from an Obsidian corer. It uses thermo-energy and micro-beams to cut through rock, usually. By the way, you may find inclusions from a Mark Three military issue phase rifle in his wounds. And you keep both your eyes on him," she told the security guard who had been posted to watch Jecks. "I'm off to decon, shower and eat," she added to Mik, who was now awake. "I'll come back and see you later. Keep smiling, it makes the rest of the universe wonder why."

"Aye, aye ma'am," he grinned up at her. "And thanks, to you and little Lieutenant Linen out yonder."

"Any time, Mik," she replied with a half-salute.

She found Linen in the decon suite; the redhead had divested herself of her enviro-suit and visited the sonic shower. Cleaned up, she was sliding into a warm coverall.

"Stowed all our own kit and our samples in a secure locker, but they'll need sorting," she greeted Copper. "It's going to be a long night if we're off with the Scamper or the Scuttle in the bright and early."

"I'm going to need a long beer to get through it. But now we have our two perps under wraps and maybe scared off the one or more on the other side of the tunnel wall, I'm inclined to give Auntie Elle a call. Just let me get out of this and into something more seemly. The techs can do all our suit-stashing and stuff for once. Our samples and our own kit are all we'll be dealing with."

Copper completed her decontamination speedily and both made for the showers and a thorough scrub, having decided that a call to Colonel Moritz would be wise before a sortie into the mess. Thars relinquished his small site office to them without question and they were soon ensconced, every privacy device they could think of being brought in to provide security.

"She'll wonder what the hell's up," Linen surmised as she set her privacy bug operational. "How are you going to explain that you were suspicious of bugging at our site in the first place? *And* that you knew that someone on the other side of the wall had cored through from the site of Spook's ship?"

"I had a feeling. And we tend to set up our privacy bugs as a matter of course anyway; we've done that since we got them, given all the troubles we had back at Lowell. As for the coring from the site of the ship... that was the direction in which the breaches led, we worked it out," her friend replied. "And as the scrapings were our side of the breaches, it was obvious they had cored through to us. As for what was happening on the other side... The problem is, I don't know if I was seeing the actual, or something that had happened before we got down there," Copper reflected. "It looked like the perp only had a few minutes to work. If the site of the ship isn't manned, I reckon it's under constant surveillance and interference that causes loss of visual would result in checks being made pretty quickly. The mag anomalies everywhere down there probably cause signal loss quite frequently, so they'd be used to it and maybe blasé. But it *would* be checked out."

"You'd best put that to the colonel as speculation after you tell her we noted that the site had changed and then we realised there were very narrow channels where there hadn't been before – she's used to quirky notions as far as we're concerned. But here's the link coming through now," Linen warned.

The colonel *was* very surprised to get their call. She had been off duty aboard the *Drake* and in her own quarters when it came in, but knew them sufficiently well to know that they had not called to ask after her health.

"Lieutenant Milkstone, Lieutenant Lyrican," she greeted the two. "What's your problem?"

"To the point as ever, ma'am," Copper answered. "And we have a problem that concerns you and your people out on our site here at the Warren…"

"You're spending your furlough working?"

"Long story for another time, ma'am," replied Copper, looking fractionally at her friend. "But for now…"

As briefly as possible, she outlined what had happened, their reasons for their actions, the information that they had garnered to date and their conjectures regarding the same, the obvious conclusion being that there were infiltrators within the Service teams working on the diggings in the local area – and possibly more than two among the Amberlines.

"I think Jecks and his sidekick were trying to cut through the substratum to reach the ship from our part of the tunnel system, judging by where the second guy had started his drilling," Copper said. "The ship's half-buried in bedrock, so the military team on your side can only access the part they can see. But they must have known that the ship *was* there *and* the best place to get to it from our side, so that suggests a lot of planning and serious infiltration. Though what would happen if they *did* try to break into the ship I don't know," she added. "I doubt they'd be able; I don't expect your people have yet, have they?" she added ingenuously.

"I figure you know damn well they haven't," Colonel Moritz replied curtly. "And they're not *my* people any more. You two are, amongst others. And I'm sure there's a lot more to this than you're telling me. I don't recall ever telling you that the ship was half-buried in the surrounding substrate for a start. But even on a secure channel, the matter is not up for further discussion. I'll take it from here. You two get on with your leave: you may not get more for a very long time."

"Yes, ma'am," they replied in unison.

"Was that a threat or a promise?" Linen demanded as the link was cut.

"I'm too tired to care; but relieved in a way. We know the colonel will get on the case right away and she'll get the troops out here dealt with. She'll get her people to sort the site cam and stuff we left as well, I expect. What Thars will do with Jecks and his partner in crime, I don't know. Get onto whoever at Lowell has the job of assigning techs to projects, I guess, and roast them for allocating him a criminal – and a damn dangerous one at that, given the hardware he was packing."

"You're telling me: that phase rifle at the max setting could have killed you," Linen stated.

Copper shrugged. "It could have done at that. All I can say is that thanks to Sarn't Biskott and Sarn't Senior Fitness Instructor Chi I was up for it; not to mention the weapons instruction and practice that Sarn't Kevloki has been shoving down our throats for the last however long it's been. But let's eat and then we'll have to start our packing and storing and loading and whatever else there is to be ready to ship out morrow-sol. Do we know what ride we're on? Or if there *is* one early?"

"Nope to what shuttle, but I heard that there's a shipment due in late this eve, so there will be one heading out. We can get the techs to lend a hand with the some of the sample stuff if we need it done in a hurry, they won't know what it is – hell, *we* don't know what most of it is."

"Good luck with organising the techs," Copper told her.

"Aw, I'll sort something out. Dinner here we come."

After a substantial meal, interrupted by several site personnel burning to know what had happened out in the field and a very snappy Thars defending them from the most persistent of the gossipmongers, the two thought that they had better drop in and see how Mik was faring. He was still in the treatment room but had been promised a berth in quarters more salubrious than his own for a few sols to get over the worst of his bumps and bruises. Jecks had been moved under tight guard directly to the superior facilities of Beagle Hospital's secure wing, where a crew of law enforcement officers from Beagle Central was to meet up with the escort and take over its duties. What had happened to Jecks' accomplice and any others apprehended at the military site they did not know.

The injured tech was in much better shape than he had been a few hours previously, sitting up and reasonably chirpy. Much happier than Thars, Copper was quick to point out as she and Linen sat either side of their friend and proffered the small mug of ale they had brought in on the sly.

Mik looked around at the room, empty bar themselves and the military med assist in the far corner, who was checking up on something or other. He set the mug on the side locker with a word of thanks, bit his lip and twisted his mouth up as if he knew something.

"Come on, Mik, out with it: what's eating at you?" Linen demanded.

"Thars had Birks go over the office out by to make sure nothing was disturbed until the law had had time to examine the scene of the crime – or one of the crimes," he uttered hesitantly.

"And?" the redhead urged.

"Wasn't a lot of life left in that phase rifle after you'd carved it up," he said, looking at Copper. "But it had been set to kill."

"Oh shit!" Linen breathed, both her hands creeping over her mouth as Copper compressed her lips tightly.

The redhead stood up and hurried round to the other side of the bed. "Oh Cop!" she groaned, wrapping her arms around her taller friend. Suddenly she dropped her head onto Copper's shoulders and burst into tears.

"Hey, can it, honey, I'm still here," Copper muttered gruffly, trying to extricate herself and keep hold of Linen at the same time.

The med assist turned round to see what the noise was about and made as if to come over. Mik shook his head violently and gestured him away. "I shouldn't have mentioned it, maybe," the tech said in a low voice. "But I don't suppose anyone else would have, until the whole thing came out. Thars is livid, so Birks told me, and very conscious of what the outcome might have been."

Copper had by this time made it to her feet and was trying to manoeuvre Linen into the empty chair. Mik held out a wipe and she took it gratefully.

"It's okay: I didn't know it at the time, so it's okay," she said, wiping the wet face.

Linen looked up, lips still trembling, straight into her friend's eyes. She hesitated for a second before she burst out, "You're a damn liar, Copper Milkstone, you knew damn well."

"I'm a damn liar," Copper agreed. "But I'd have got there first anyway. I had mental back-up."

Linen stared at her for an instant and then sagged tearfully. "Thanks be for disembodied aliens," she said inarticulately.

"You what?" demanded Mik, concerned and curious.

"Nothing," Copper said very quietly. "You did *not* hear that. You didn't hear anything and you don't know anything except that we asked you to check out Jecks. Drink your ale and tell us how you're feeling."

Mik did and after a short bout of questions and answers, the two left him to sleep. Linen had recovered sufficiently to smile and suggest that the next stop should be the hangar, where she had slung all their belongings and samples into an empty locker.

A scant half hour later and the two were seated in a booth in the common room, meant to be linking to friends outside but in reality sipping ale and talking. They had pocketed their MEDICs and their various other clandestine bits and pieces, but Linen had cajoled the on-duty techs not only to pack up their other kit and samples but to arrange for its loading on board the Amber-Scamper, which had come in for them at Thars' summons, and for onward shipment to Lowell College for safe storage.

"You'd get a cookie by knocking on anyone's front entry and asking, you would," Copper grumbled to her friend, but she said it with a smile. "And don't for frock's sake tell Syriana that you engineered it or she'll make a point of coming over to whine at us. You know, if it wasn't so late I'd be tempted to try and ship out tonight – the billets at the Psi Complex are far more comfortable than the ones here."

"I could try and sweet-talk Kezza," Linen suggested.

"No – she and Chrysa have done enough and they're entitled to their rest as well. We'll be off soon enough and back to your Ma's place to see her and start our furlough."

"But don't let out what's happened, though," Linen warned. "Ma would freak."

"I know. Colonel Moritz wouldn't want it spread around in any case. Neither would Thars, come to that. I expect he'll want a word or six before we leave."

"Starting about now," her friend replied. "Here he comes… Do we mention the unlawful ingress at the Glory Hole and the cam we left to monitor the place?"

"No we don't," Copper cautioned as their senior mentor hove to and requested their attention.

Professor Amberline was as curious as almost everyone else to know how the two had realised that the Warren site had been the target of subversive activity, and more importantly, the gritty details of the quick reactions that had resulted in the capture of the two known moles. He was almost pacified by Linen's story that her unease at the overly nosey Jecks had led to their more than usual caution in their sortie to their site and her request that Mik check out his ticket. It was too bad that Mik had been attacked, but as Copper pointed out, if Jecks and his accomplice had not acted as they did *when* they did, both she and Linen would have been on their way back from the Dragon's Nest and clearly visible on the site holo to anyone who happened to look.

One thing about which Copper was adamant: the two would depart as planned the following morning. Any follow-up of the incidents at the Warren would have to be made via their senior officers at Beagle One Basecamp. Looking at the inflexible face, Thars agreed. After delicate enquiries into his students' states of health both physically and mentally, he left them to the rest of their evening.

"You know, you've got Thars well and truly floxed," Linen told her friend. "He just can't get over the change in you. Neither can I, at times. Spook here now?"

"Yes. *You're* sometimes aware of him, don't you feel him?"

"To be honest, Cop, I haven't tried. There's been so much going on. We were supposed to be on furlough but I feel as if I have the weight of the planet on my shoulders. This was to be a one sol stopover and what's happened? Our work site's been invaded, we've been spied on and damn near shot and now that the Military and Beagle Law Enforcement have been brought in, we're part of a criminal investigation."

"Don't you worry about that, Colonel Moritz will sort it out. It's about Spook's ship: someone or some people other than the ones legitimately involved now suspect or know what it is, and possibly that it's been sending out a signal; and also maybe that it did start to let the colonel's people get readings from it they couldn't get before. So the ante's been upped, the whole case will be taken over by Military Intelligence and everyone else will be capped."

"We are going to get utterly fried once Colonel Moritz finds out about Spook, you realise that? She'll work out why we knew a lot more than we told her and she'll be pissed."

"We worry about that when she finds out. What in hell was I supposed to do? The Intelligence Service has been breached, it has to have been, so *had* I told her, someone would have found out and even if they didn't believe it, you think I'd still be here?"

Linen shot a look at her. "Did Spook tell you that Jecks' rifle was set to kill?" she asked.

"He doesn't *tell* me anything – I just get a feeling or intuition about things that I know isn't me. So I knew someone was heading in and that they were really nasty and I knew I had to hit out first. So I did, almost without thinking. Okay, months of drill honed my reactions and I caught the full lock on the phase rifle, but without Spook, I may well have hesitated."

"So he gives you an edge."

"That's about it. I'm beginning to think that he must have been in some sort of military service or fleet when his kind were on Mars. His ship is small, tiny in fact, and *possibly* a scout of some sort, but..." she trailed off.

"He's getting to be too much again, isn't he? You need a break from him. *I* think you're getting too dependent on each other and you're absorbing some of his experiences."

"Don't be ridiculous, how could I? He's an alien entity, able to operate in non-corporeal form and as far removed from me on a mental plane as I am from a cat..."

"Depends on the cat. Look at Ma Kellyn's Altair: he could read you like a book and knew what side his dinner bowl was buttered as far as *you* were concerned," Linen pointed out.

"Thanks for that. I'm now an alien's pet, am I?"

"Oh stow it! You're tired is what you are, and grumpy. Let's go capture another ale and then hit the sack. That at least should keep the busybodies here off our backs. Or maybe I should let you shout at them; you'll scare them into silence."

"Thanks for that."

"And Cop?"

"Yup?"

Her friend's face crumpled. "Don't go getting shot at again. I don't think I could take it."

Copper put soothing arms around her. "Oh Linen, honey! It wasn't a big deal and we're both still here. I *knew* it was going to be okay, really I did."

"No you damn well didn't! You've always been a lousy liar and I've always been able to tell! And if you *had* been hurt, or worse, it would have been my fault! I was the one that arranged all this, just so that we could get a free billet at the AF Dome for a measly eve out!"

So that was it, Copper realised: Linen was blaming herself for all that might have been. But if the two had not been precisely where they were, the Warren and all their work there may have been seriously compromised, as would operations at the military site; and Spook's ship and everything in relation to it would have been open to the intrigues of whatever unfriendly forces were out there. And there were many, as they both knew only too well. As she gently and clearly pointed all this out to her friend, she had the satisfaction of seeing Linen's smile return.

"Maybe you're not such a lousy liar after all," the redhead told her. "I almost believe you. But not quite."

"Nightcaps for us both," Copper announced. "Chocó-crème with a good shot of scotch in it: I'm sure I can persuade Ambrose to pony some up from somewhere. And I promise I'll bark at Noa and Syr if they get too close."

* * *

Early Moonsol brought a cheerful Captain Kezza Brownpelt into the mess and over to the table where Copper and Linen were having breakfast.

"We're all set to go when you are, your stuff has all been loaded and checked through," she told them. "Thars brought me up to date on what's been going on, mostly. I'm not going to pester you for details. I guess you're both pretty sick of it all."

"Thanks for that, Kezza: we've really had enough," Copper told her with feeling.

"I guess you won't want to take the helm on the way back into the AF Dome either; we *are* going high for the ride."

Both shook their heads and she smiled at the expressions.

"You did good," she said. "I'll make sure all your stuff gets sent in the right direction for Lowell Central and I'll ice anyone who tries to make waves. You two enjoy the rest of your leave."

"We intend to," Linen twinkled. "Once we've picked up the stuff we left at the Psi Complex, we'll catch the next Land-Hover over to Beagle and then we'll see."

"Spa at Nollixa's," Copper decided as the captain departed to her craft. "If we can offload at your Ma's fam-unit, we can head out. You Ma will be at work, won't she?"

"I expect she will, it's Moonsol after all. But she knows we're on furlough and this will be the only one we get before we head out to our ship, so she may have a plan or two in place."

"As long as they don't involve Magenta," threatened her friend. "That would be the cream that broke the cupcake."

"No comment at this time," Linen grinned enigmatically. "So swallow your caff and let's fetch our carryalls and wave bye-bye to all our mates. Most of them are here and eyeing us up anyway. Though not Noa and Syr, I see, but no loss there."

The two collected their kitbags and made their way from the dormitory wing to the central hub of the station. Mik was there and first in line to bid them farewell. Despite his injuries he had hobbled over early to make sure he would not miss them and each was given a warm hug. Various others proffered hands and slaps on the back, and waving cheerfully, the pair set off for the hangar. They found several more well-wishers there and had perforce to exchange a few words. Thars had prudently boarded the Scamper and was waiting for them.

"Off now?" he demanded gruffly. "Don't forget to link. I'll be expecting regular updates on your PhD work and I'll see you both back at Lowell before you set off into the blue yonder. I have to hang on here. Take care."

He smiled, shook their hands warmly and was gone, but both students realised that their professor was sincerely affected by what had happened in the short time that they had been around.

"Stow your stuff and web in," Kezza Brownpelt directed as she peeped around the Flight Deck entry. "We're set to go."

"Aye, aye, Captain," Linen called chirpily, slapping her pack into a locker and plumping herself down.

Copper had done likewise and with a mock salute at their pilot, she signalled her readiness for departure. Sinking into the cushioned seat, she turned to her friend.

"It's been one helluva furlough so far. Wonder what could make it any worse?"

"Oops," Linen grinned back, a finger at her lips.

"What the blazes have you done now?"

"Had a link from Ma before we went for breakfast…"

"And?"

"Grammy's headed for Beagle. She'll arrive morrow-sol. She called Ma, and it's as much a surprise to Ma as it is to me," Linen went on. "I half-wondered if Colonel Moritz had been in touch with her, but I wouldn't have thought so."

Copper shook her head. "That's all I need! You might have let on when you found out, dammit! But no, the colonel would *not* have called Magenta, I'm sure. Your Grammy has her own contacts, though, and I bet she's found out that something went down at the Warren. Has she been called back to the *Drake* about the systems she helped to install there, do you know?"

"No. But she wouldn't tell me if she had. Drafted we might be, but we're still trainees and she's savvy enough to know that other eyes and ears are on us at Beagle Basecamp, whatever."

Copper turned to the viewing port at her elbow to watch the sunrise over the plain of Isidis and her mood lightened. Even with the ebullient Magenta Firewall on the horizon, it was good to be away from the turmoil of the preceding sol and to be looking forward to some peace – however long that would last. They had completed a sizable amount of work that would see them through their stint aboard the *Drake*, she fervently hoped, and had had the chance to bid goodbye to some very good friends. She settled back comfortably and closed her eyes.

Some time later, a familiar vibrating told the Amberlines that the shuttle was powering down and that they were coming in to dock at the Astrobiology Field Dome's main hangar.

"Here we are back again," Copper sighed over at her friend.

"Sure are, kiddo," was the response. "I expect we should offer to help unload."

The two were quick to tender their services but were politely told to get lost. They shrugged and set off to the Psi Complex to find their billet and wrap up there. That took in a few squabbles over what was to go where and who would carry what. An hour later, and with a quick trip to sub-floor two to take their leave of the Amberline lab techs, followed by hops up to bid goodbye to the Prof's exec Maize Mallis and to their friend Silver Yarrow in the Ref Snug, they set off for the travelator ride to the Land-Hover Station.

"It's like treading old ground," Copper sniffed as she looked around, dumping her baggage at her feet.

"It *is* treading old ground," Linen told her, her gold-flecked eyes scanning the vista likewise. "We've been this road so many times we could do it in the dark and with plugs in our ears. But we won't see it for quite a long time, I should imagine. No more Giordano's, no more Bern's Buttery, no more trips down to the rec area for quiet walks in the Psi Gardens at the Complex... Just look at the solbeams gleaming through Dome roof and sparkling off the edging struts. We'll have to carry all that in our memories to come back to when we're feeling homesick out in the great yonder, a great expanse of nothing as the only view on our starlit horizon..."

"Bottle it; you'd bring tears to a prosthetic eye, you would," Copper admonished her severely. "You're yanking my chain anyway."

"Course I am. Best way to cure melancholy and you've got it bad, I could tell by the temper and the cushion-throwing earlier. Where's Spook, by the by? I get the feeling he's not around."

"In a holo-jar in a glass-candy store looking for sweetness and light, how would I know?" retorted her friend, a tad crossly. "Sorry, you're right, I *am* snappy. Reaction, I guess. Whoops! He's just turned up. He's so tuned to me now he seems to be able to pop up at my merest whimper. I wonder how the hell he can do it so fast. It's disconcerting at times."

"Sounds like it could be downright awkward. What if you were in a tight clinch with some good looker at a romantic nightclub and he wanted a piece of the action?"

Copper looked at her, waving a finger. "Will you behave? We're in a public place."

"Aw, nobody's around to listen. And even if they were, they wouldn't understand the discussion and they'd be showing their bad manners. But here's the station, we'd best go find our ride. Want to sing the Amberline space ditty for old times' sake?"

"Nope. And *you'd* better not start it or you'll be sitting on your own."

"There, there, temper, temper. It's Docking Bay Two and we have a few minutes to spare. I expect we'd better sort our tickets to ride or we'll not get on. I'll put them on my wrist-comm, but I'll need to pay for them separately: our service providers won't let us charge non-comm expenses to them."

"Very wise," Copper snickered.

The wrist-comms had been a gift from the ever-generous Magenta Firewall, but as with most of Magenta's hardware, they were more than average and had several quirks, one of which was that comms were not chargeable. They were also practically indestructible, had been specifically made for the two and were genetically bonded to them, thus no-one else could use or abuse the devices. They were also chameleon, which meant that their colours and facets could be changed to suit the wearer's apparel or taste. Linen's mother, Corona Lyrican, had been responsible for their design, but the pair had long suspected that Colonel Moritz had had a hand in their acquisition, Grammy having mentioned that they had been "okayed by the woman Moritz" when she handed them over. The two friends were also highly suspicious that the gadgets were trackable.

Copper and Linen quickly found their appointed vehicle and sat back in their chosen seats to watch the reddish vista that was lightening as the sol advanced towards noon. As the hover slid into its dock at Beagle's Land-Hover Station, the two decided simultaneously that a travel-cab would be the best means of onward travel to the Lyrican family unit and hang the expense.

They quickly hailed a vehicle and as it made its way along wide Zarnecki Avenue and past the classy BC Hotel, Copper snuffed up a lungful of air and looked around at the by-now familiar highlights, the shops, stores and businesses, colourful and well-lit, that gave Beagle Dome Complex its popularity and charm.

"It's beginning to feel more like home than Lowell," she told her companion.

"We have our own place here, don't forget," Linen smilingly responded. "But we'll trespass at Ma's for this sol at least; it'll save us having to organise the housekeeping out at Road Five."

The cab shot out of the end of Blur Street and so out of Central Dome into Memory Avenue, turning quickly right into Road One. Court Six was a short way along the road and as they rolled up outside Unit Five and came to a halt, the cab door slid open and the two passengers tumbled out, hauling their hand luggage. Copper paid whilst Linen retrieved their larger carryalls. Soon the redhead was proffering her personal ident at the front entry, which opened into the welcome warmth and soft colours of the small lobby.

The two stepped down to the internal door and over the threshold to the inner space. Like most dome dwellings, the unit had no windows to the outside, but the gentle ambient lighting made up for it. The airy hallway in shades of blue was broken up by doors in various colours. One such in pink had been labelled *Copper.*

"I see Corona's as well-organised as usual. As you look so much like her, I'm always amazed you're not even a quarter as tidy as she is," Copper remarked.

"Are you a clone of either of your folks?" demanded Linen.

"Point taken," Copper admitted, halting precipitately as an alarming thought suddenly occurred. "Where's Magenta going to camp when she turns up morrow-sol? Here or at ours?"

"We'll have to ask her. She may decide to hang on at Ma's to give us time to ourselves. She does have *some* tact, you know."

"But not much. And I bet she'll want a lowdown on all that Thars said and did and how he looked out at the station to keep her cockles warm for a month or two. I bet she keeps a secret pic of him under her pillow," Copper laughed.

"I dare you to ask!"

"No way, she'd brain me. But I think I'll change before we hop off and find Nollixa's for that spa. And sink my face in a mug of Chocó-crème, if you could dredge such a thing up."

"Ma's always got stuff in store. You may even find some in the hospitality station in your room."

"Can't be frocked starting it up. Besides, I'm sure the fam-kitchen's handier."

"I'll dump my bags and organise it. You go change and then head to the fam-hub," Linen ordered.

"Yes ma'am."

The cosy Lyrican family hub was a warm and attractive space that Corona had furnished stylishly but simply. Copper, snugly attired in a comfortable two piece suit, wandered in and tucked herself up in the corner of one of the pair of comfy red sofas.

"Here we are!" Linen declared, appearing from the kitchen with a brace of large mugs. "Your Chocó-crème, milady. Ma left a link for me: she won't be back until six or so, so we've to make ourselves comfortable and she's taking us out to dinner at the Carnelian Crucible. She figured we wouldn't be up for the BC after a spell in the field."

"She so right: the BC Hotel is far too swish at the end of a hard sol's travelling. And the Crucible's just a nice stroll down Memory," Copper said as she sipped the warm, hot drink.

* * *

An hour and a healthy long walk later found the two friends in the compact Nollixa's Therapy Salon, a spa and beautification bureau on Wells Street, a road that led off Artisan Square. They had been shepherded into the basement of the place and put in possession of a suite, where they lazed in a warm, bubbling vat of scented water, sipping citron fizz and gossiping.

One aspect of Beagle Central visible in sol-light that had not changed from their last visit, they agreed, was the number of individuals in uniform adorning various street corners. Trainees were not encouraged to disport themselves in military attire off-camp, the inference being that these people were the authentic article. As many of the insignia were Fleet, it implied that a few ships were orbiting at a distance sufficiently convenient that the crews could shuttle down for shore leave.

"From here on we wear those stat pins Auntie Elle gave us," Copper informed her friend. "We're on leave and I refuse to be hounded by off duty grunts out for a good time at someone else's expense."

"You reckon we'll be hounded?" Linen enquired.

"Of course we will; your hair's a magnet for every trooper that has a line in sweet-talk that he or she thinks will have you falling at their feet."

"We can look after ourselves, as I think we just proved out at the Warren. And with you at my back, I don't need any other protection."

"With me at your back *and* the tongue in your head, you mean. But I'm seriously not up for idle banter with a bunch of dimglows, however attractive they appear on the outside."

"Ma'am, yes ma'am," Linen responded with a mock salute. "Let's hit Jinx for a creamy caff when we're done here, it's not far. And then we can have a look-see around the stores on Artisan. I haven't bought any new kit for ages and I'm itching for a rummage for some tasteful traps. The last thing was that leisure suit for cold nights out at the station I got at Midnight's."

"Midnight's place is at Lowell. That's one helluva long way to go for a look in a seedy clothes emporium that smells like a pile of used socks."

Linen looked at her friend, startled, for a long moment. "And Midnight's is one heck of a lot more than a seedy clothes store," she said slowly, her brow creasing. "Even Colonel Moritz told us to treat *that* place and its owner with respect and Midnight is more enigmatic than a four-dimensional block puzzle. But no: you've just twanged a string at the back of my mind. You won't believe this but…"

"I'll believe it, believe me…" Copper groaned.

"Shut up and listen! There's a store not a million metres from here that I've heard of but never been in. Ma used to say that it was more trash than dash and more tacky than a bucket of glue. It was so dark you couldn't see what you were buying and it *smelt like old socks*… Remind you of anywhere?"

"That's got to be coincidence," Copper argued.

"Maybe. It was one or two years ago, it might not be there still. But I wonder… You won't believe the name of it either," Linen said impishly.

"Try me."

"Nightfall."

"You're right, I don't believe it," Copper told her crossly. "You're winding me up like a string-powered propeller."

"I'm not, Cop, trust me. I'll look it up on my wrist-comm…"

"I wouldn't if I were you: if you *are* right, and I still doubt it, somebody will pick up on the enquiry. Our wrist-comms are mil issue, we've suspected that for ages. You think they're not going to set off an alarm somewhere if that kind of query is input?"

"You have a point. Let's get out of this and get topside for our face-makes. Time's nearly up anyway. Then Jinx: we'll use a public info-station and ask for directions to cheap clothes stores near here. I'm sure Ma said the place was way out at Dome edge and in this quarter, at the back of Skady Lane somewhere. You think the guy running it will be called Nightfall?"

"Like hell! And at back of Skady Lane? I've got that horrible feeling of here we go again. Why do our lives always seem like a tangled ball of plas-wool that some giant kitten is playing with?"

"So that someone like Auntie Elle can come along, straighten out the strands and then have them woven into an even more complex pattern," she was told.

In reply, Copper splashed her in the face with a handful of scented spa water. "Bottle it," she ordered.

The two made for the prettification station aloft to complete their personal enhancement and soon found themselves on the road again and heading into Jinx, a small café on the corner of Wells Street and Artisan Square. The place was busy but a free table by the window caught their eyes and they sat down.

"Two creamy caffs," Linen said, tabbing the order into the table-top menu-pad. "I'll pay, since you're in such a temper. And it's probably my turn anyway."

"Given I paid at Nollixa's, it's your turn. Does this table have an info-point?"

"Course it does, this is a classy joint and one of Beagle's best cafés, I'll have you know."

"It's warm and clean and the seats are soft, so I believe you," Copper retorted, glowering at a military threesome leaning on the counter, who were eyeing the pair openly. "Never fails," she went on, as one of the trio detached himself from the group.

"Hello there, ladies," the man leered.

Linen raised an eyebrow, looking at Copper, whose eyes had narrowed as she took in the interloper. "Please go away," the redhead said politely. "This is a private conversation."

That and Linen's predictably captivating smile was invitation enough and the trooper pulled out the free chair at their table. "Can I sit down?"

"That's between you and your personal medic," Copper told him shortly. "We're busy, soldier; back off."

"You're not being very polite to an officer that's in the trade of defending you and yours from all that's out there," he went on with half a glance at his frankly observing colleagues. "Let me buy you both a drink."

His free hand rested on Copper's shoulder for a fraction of a second in an obviously oft-practised move of seduction and he turned a soft smile on her.

"I said back off, *sergeant*: you try that again and I'll have you up on charges," she grunted at him, straightening up, her lips curling into a tight snarl and her eyes sparking fire.

At his hesitation, she pushed her chair back and stood up to eyeball him squarely. "And believe me, I *have* the authority," she snapped. "From here on in, we wear our ranking pins," she added shortly in an aside to Linen.

"Aye, ma'am," was the smart reply.

"Move it!" she ordered.

The shaken serviceman, yet unsure as he glanced at the still-smiling redhead, swallowed nervously. Alarm was beginning to crease his face and he slowly backed off with an attempt at an apology. Copper sat down and scraped her chair noisily over the floor. "You got a note of his insignia?" she loudly demanded of Linen.

"Yes, ma'am," she replied, scanning all three with her wrist-comm. "Grunts!" she added, looking skywards.

The waiter brought their order over himself to catch a closer look at the duo: the interchange had caused a few heads to turn and his had been one of them. Copper, still furious, motioned only to the table with her head and stared him out. He placed the cups carefully and told them that they could tally up at the counter whenever they were ready.

"I like this new, masterful you," Linen whispered over. "And it seems to have an effect on everyone you meet. Although I wouldn't try it on Colonel Moritz if I were you: I bet *she* doesn't think imitation is the sincerest form of flattery."

"Just drink your caff and interrogate the info-point about this place you're so keen we check out."

"Aye, ma'am!"

As Copper slowly savoured the warm drink, she kept a wary eye on her surroundings. She was beginning to wonder if she *had* unconsciously been imitating their formidable ally and soon-to-be commanding officer. If so, she had better nip that little habit in the bud.

"What's the vex?" Linen enquired suddenly. "You look as if you expect something unpleasant to happen."

"Just a vague unease, as if something's out of kilter," she replied. "As if there's a kink in the universe or something. Don't know if it's me or Spook. I only hope you're packing your stun. I must get hold of one: a legal one, not like the one Magenta gave you. What's the deal on this Nightfall place?"

"It's half way down Dowson Street, in the direction of Dome edge. Not too far from here in fact. We go out onto the square, head east to where it meets Zaranj Street – at Styllaflax in fact – and hop along a nameless street in the same direction that leads to a five way intersection: Skyring Street, Skady Lane, Private Road and Dowson Street."

"That's only four: what's the fifth?"

"The nameless road you've just come down," Linen pointed out. "Look at the holo."

"By the time we've done all this walking I won't have any feet left," Copper complained in a low tone. "And time's getting on if we've to meet Corona at six. And we'll have to lose those grunts at the bar; they're still casting eyes at us when they think we're not looking and throwing back cups of caff that they've added additional refreshment to. I'm heading for the comfort – you keep an eye on them."

"Yes ma'am."

By the time that Copper returned, her friend had paid the bill and was ready to leave. The two made for the exit, well-wrapped against the cool air, and set off along their chosen route, pausing now and then to look at inviting store displays and to take a quick peek back the way they had come. Copper sighed. It had taken twenty minutes to reach the nameless road that joined the top of Dowson Street and by that time the two were more than grateful for the hours of drill they had had to put in back at Beagle One Basecamp. Copper was also beginning to regret that she had worn less than comfortable bootwear.

"Right, here's where we see what's been following us all the way from Jinx," Copper at last muttered. "Got your stun?"

"In my pocket," Linen replied. "Turn right here and we're in Skady Lane."

The two sauntered around the corner and then began to run, skipping through the first opening they came to and flattening themselves against the interior wall. They seemed to be in some sort of entrance tunnel, beyond which a hazy light suggested somewhere open to Dome roof.

"That block further down must be the ex-rental apartment complex that Ma Kellyn's taken on," Linen whispered, puffing. "But where this leads I don't know."

"Get back and give me the stun," was the only reply.

They could already hear the heavy footfalls drawing closer to their concealed space and with a quick glance at Linen, Copper drew the mini-stun blaster up towards her face. The footsteps stopped just out of their view and she could almost see the hand gestures of the leader of the pack pointing to where they were. He turned in to find the business end of the gun in his face.

"One more step and you are toast, mister."

The man stepped backwards and into the arms of the buddy behind him. Both fell to the ground, the third member of the trio prudently retreating to a safe distance. Copper lowered the weapon toward the crumpled heaps on the walkway.

"Names, ranks and numbers, boys," she demanded. "You have *way* overstepped your marks this time."

"Our authority," Linen added, tabbing her wrist-comm.

The holo that emanated from the jewelled device was the insignia on the stat bars that the colonel had given them. Linen gave the bleared eyes only seconds to take in the badge before she snapped it off. She then took a careful image of the two on the ground, both of whom were attempting to stand up, and the third who had been trying to sneak off around the corner.

The sergeant dully stated his name, rank and serial number as requested; the other two were a sergeant and a corporal.

"You're lucky we're too busy to bust your asses to hell and back," Copper told the three. "Get the hell out of here. But I *will* be making a report and you *will* hear more of this."

As the three slunk off, Linen faced her friend. "You sound more like Colonel Moritz than Colonel Moritz," she said. "Let's find Nightfall's before anything else happens."

"You realise this is all your fault for wanting to check this place out?" Copper pointed out, handing back the stun. "And believe me, you'll be hearing more about it later. But as we've come this far, we'd better get on. And I'm still creeped out. This sol hasn't ended yet."

The small clothing emporium that was labelled *Nightfall* and sported an obscured window in numerous shades of murky grey bore a remarkable resemblance to their erstwhile clothing haunt of Midnight's on Coblentz Street, not far from Lofty's in Lowell Central. The two turned in. The place was even set up the same, with dark décor, a limited range of goods on view, a musty smell and a suspensor net of lights hovering at ceiling height. As they had expected, one of the set detached itself and drifted over companionably. The two looked at one another: they had long suspected Midnight's devices to be monitors and not simply handy illumination for the benefit of customers.

"You've not been here before," the slim dark-haired woman who had separated herself from a console behind a counter that was close to the door observed with an inscrutable smile as she came to look them over. "I'm Nix Nightfall and this is my place. How can I help?"

Copper stared sternly at the light that had buzzed her left ear and folded her arms. Linen oiled her jaws for work and smiled back at the proprietrix.

"Good quality military issue stuff, by the look of it," she said cocking her head at a nearby rail. "And some of it is chameleon fabric. What do you have that's not on display? I might be interested in an outfit for a festive event."

"Might be or are?" was the swift comeback.

"That depends on the goods," the redhead responded.

Ms Nightfall consulted her console and tabbed a couple of buttons. She raised an eyebrow. "Are you aware that you're being followed?" she asked with what seemed like quiet interest.

"They're *still* following us?" Copper questioned. "Then they must be dimmer that I thought. They're three half-drunk grunts that have been on our tails for an hour. Is there a back way out of this place, or is that a stupid question?"

"There are no stupid questions – only stupid questioners," Nightfall said. "And I guess you're not one of those. But you'd better have a look at your tails. They don't look like half-drunk grunts to me. And there are only two of them."

5: NIGHTFALL

Copper and Linen traded quick glances as Ms Nightfall spun her console in order that they could see. Her external spy-cam had picked out two lean individuals in very smart but non-descript clothing. They seemed to be studying the holos emanating from a store along the way. One was positioned in order that he had a good view of Nightfall's entryway.

"I wouldn't have thought that a show of the best in internal sanitation systems engineering would be riveting viewing for a couple that look like that pair," Ms Nightfall remarked. "You two in some sort of trouble?"

"Are we ever in anything else?" Copper muttered. "I don't recognise them. Do you?" she asked her friend.

"Nope. But I always think the best form of defence is attack. We could go and ask."

"On what basis? We know you're following us, tell us why or we beat the living crap out of you? They look as if they might just be trained to deal with that and we might get more than we bargained for. Do they know where we're berthed, I wonder?"

"Ah. You have a point. That could be quite awkward," Linen said, nodding.

"Or out-and-out dangerous, and for more than us. Magenta's marines might be a place to start. At least from there we can put things into operation."

Copper meant the planet-wide security service with which Magenta Firewall had registered the two months before. A quick call summoned a protected and well-armed travel-cab, manned by a skilful pilot, which was capable of much more than ground-based locomotion. The two, with Magenta and Corona, had first used one to escape the machinations of some nasty individuals in Beagle Central that were linked to several intrigues including theft of organo-technology. The friends had also called the link up later back at Lowell, to rescue them from the clutches of the very tenacious Ms Stellaria Firedrake of the Interplanetary News Network, who had been trying to prise information about their research out of them.

"Grammy's paying them a retainer for us, so we may as well make use of it," Linen grinned. "I'll give them a buzz."

"We'll order transport out of here," Copper enlightened Ms Nightfall. "It shouldn't take long, I hope. Meanwhile, I'd like a copy of that visual and then we can browse."

Nightfall looked at her customers, tilting her head to the side. "You're cool, I'll give you that," she said.

"So are you," Copper shot back as she recorded the holo of the strangers that the woman had helpfully called up, copying it to Linen. "Keep an eye on those two, if you don't mind," she added, turning away.

"Maybe we should just stay here for an hour or so," Linen remarked as she moved off in the direction of a nearby clothing rail. "Bore them into leaving the place."

"Don't be a flooshy: we're going out for dinner tonight and Corona would scour the streets if we didn't show. And Magenta would send in her idea of reinforcements, once she found out. Beagle would never get over it."

"Who do we call when we're safely aboard?"

"Who else?" Copper demanded.

"Auntie Elle's going to be utterly sick of the sight and sound of us before this spell of furlough is over," Linen prophesied.

"Furlough? Oh yes, that was what we were meant to be on," Copper retorted irritably. "Having a good time on Service pay. *That's* happened so far, hasn't it?"

"But you're not overly worried, I can tell. They're not out to wipe us off the planet? And Ms Nightfall is okay?"

Copper swiped fruitlessly at the over-friendly hover-light as it manoeuvred sociably closer. "Push off!" she ordered it testily.

"Have a look at this jacket," her friend interrupted. "It's plasleather, a nice shade of deep red and it would make you look more than cool, especially if it had insignia of some description attached. It's based on a military design and I bet I can find one in my size as well. Try it on."

"If you insist."

"I insist. This *is* a clothes store after all. And I'll pay, so no arguments."

By the time Copper had tried on the jacket and found it to be a perfect fit and more than flattering, Ms Nightfall called over to say that a hover had pulled up and its operator had stepped out. The entry chime sounded and a tall individual, clearly armed and dressed in a dark uniform that both recognised, stepped in.

"Someone called a cab," she announced.

"I did," Linen acknowledged, snatching the jacket from her friend's hands and approaching the woman. "We'll take this," she added to Ms Nightfall. "Can you source another in my size? We can call for it morrow-sol."

"I can and this'll be thirty credits," the proprietrix said.

"It will not; I'll give you twelve," was the instant response.

"Will you come *on*, lady?" Copper burst out as the redhead began to haggle.

They settled on twenty and Linen paid up promptly. "We'd best hit the flightpath. Where are our two shadows?" she asked as she collected her goods.

"Still out there and eyeballing that cab," Nightfall said. "Have a good eve and don't take a straight way back to your base: they may have their own ride round back. I'll see you morrow-sol."

The duo followed their cab pilot outdoors to the larger-than-typical sleek, dark travel-cab with obscured windows that stood at the side of the walkway.

"Hop in," their driver instructed as she sized up the twosome outside the systems store and deployed a key that released the vehicle's door panel.

Once inside, the duo settled comfortably into the rear seats and waited. Their escort slid into the front position, released the screen that provided privacy and enquired their orders.

"We need a secure visual link, long-distance," Linen told her.

"You have it. Activating," the woman said, and a console slid out from the side of the cab nearest the redhead.

"Meanwhile, let's go for a ride," Copper said. "Where to?"

"The BC Hotel," Linen suggested. "We can nip in for caff."

"Dressed like this? They'll throw us into the street!"

"Then a tour around Dome Central. These toughs may have friends we haven't seen yet," Linen warned. "And we have a *very* private link to make."

"The comms console is self-scrambling and this vehicle has jammers," their pilot told them. "You'll also find route and info holos in the door consoles. Take your time."

She closed and sealed the privacy screen and the vehicle let out a low hum as it picked up power.

Linen began to make the link. "Wonder what time the ship keeps?" she muttered "If the colonel's in her bunk, she may not thank me for waking her up."

"AMT standard, I should think. But too bad: this has got to do with the deal out at the Warren and with our researches — and other things best left unsaid. So it *is* her business. And more unfortunately, ours. Get on while I unroll this info-sheet and see what gives with the outside planet."

Without further ado, Copper unfurled a tri-dee sheet she had pulled from the cab door. As she had expected, the route they were taking was clearly visible, their cab depicted as a holo-image in red. She figured that they were heading into the heart of Dome Central as they had just turned into Blur Street and were moving westwards. Copper was also aware than another holo was keeping pace at their back.

"I've made contact," Linen informed her. "The colonel will take our link in her office; I think she's on the bridge."

Leaving her friend to update the officer and pass on relevant information, Copper kept her watch on their cab's progress. "We've turned into Zarnecki and are heading north. They're still on our tail. I can't see any others that might be shadowing us, but I guess the pilot will keep us informed," she reported.

"You two lead interesting lives," Copper heard the colonel remark as she continued to trace their route and to work out how to activate what seemed to be some sort of scanning gear that could probe the local environs outside the cab.

"That damn hover's armed!" Copper announced indignantly when she finally managed to obtain readings. "Whoops! We've just turned off at Ng Avenue! I guess we'll be doing a tour of the backstreets! Web yourself in, we've been here before!"

Their driver called in to advise the same as the vehicle picked up speed and began some rapid manoeuvring and Copper was hard put to maintain her position without losing sense of the info-sheet. For the benefit of Linen and Colonel Moritz, she tried to keep up a running commentary.

"Cutting into Spry Street! That's us on Thomas – Delbrück now – back onto Ng Avenue! And our tail is trying to keep up. Lor' it must be obvious to those nanobit-brains that we know they're following! We're heading down to Kelvin – we're turning into Kel... no, we've cut north-west onto Shoemaker," she corrected herself. "What in blazes the travelling public is making of this..."

She had no intention of having a look out of the window to make sure, as her geography of Beagle was less than perfect. "Right onto Bridges Street," she called out as her finger traced the track on the info-sheet. "Left at Spry, heading for Mädler-Beer... now heading south-west... that's Grey's Gym. We're turning off onto Nelms Crescent – we've definitely been here before! She's heading for the Public Gardens and across..."

"First IDC Mars," Linen laughed over. "I'll cut now, ma'am, and update you later," she added, killing the link on the comm.

A sharp turn had the pair holding onto their seats and each other as the travel-cab spun. The green spaces of the Public Gardens outside whirled around.

"Just as well this is a hover, that manoeuvre would have churned up a few turves!" Linen gasped. "She's trying to outface that hover on our tail – but at least it hasn't attempted to disable our systems, I've not noticed a power drop. What are we going to do, gun it, ram it, run around it in circles?"

"Not in sol-light in a public space and for sure with a frigging audience!" Copper gulped as a sudden uprush told them what to expect.

As had happened on their previous ride in the same area, they felt the abrupt upthrust as their craft launched skyward and spun, to descend rather forcefully on the vehicle beneath with a crunching and grinding of grating metalwork.

"Reinforcements!" Copper warned, tapping her info-sheet.

"Ours of theirs?" Linen demanded.

Their pilot provided the answer. "I've called in back-up," her voice advised over the cab's audio system. "My colleague will deal with our pursuers and no questions asked."

"This is some service!" Linen crowed. "We'll have to tell Grammy they're worth every credit."

"I suspect Magenta already knows," Copper said ruefully. "You can update me on what the colonel said back at base."

"What's your final destination, ladies?" the pilot requested from the front.

"Road One off Memory, Court Six, Unit Five," Linen called. "And if there's a link to leave positive feedback on this little adventure, let us know. You deserve a bonus."

"All part of the service, ma'am," was the chuckling response. "Besides, you'll be charged for the additional assistance."

"Just as well we're not the ones paying," Copper observed wryly. "What time is it? I've lost track?"

"Just after five; we'll have time for a quick soak in a hot tub before Ma gets in. And I'll shove your new jacket in the thermo-clean, I bet it needs it."

"Another topic for discussion," Copper told her. "Mars has got more covert ops and secret services than the worst spy holo-flic I've ever seen."

"That's what makes our little planet such a great place to live," Linen assured her with a smile as their travel-cab turned and settled gently into its normal operating level before moving off sedately.

"Heading on down Antoniadi Street now," Copper informed her friend. "We'll pick up Arago and then direct on Blur and out to Memory, I guess."

"Quickest way," Linen agreed. "This dinner had better be good – I expect you'll need it."

"You're telling me! There's a great bunch of gadgetry in this side pocket, by the way," she added. "This cab is a marvel. Wish I had a Spirit Hover like it. Wonder if we have weapons here *we* could use?"

"Dream on! But I'll be glad to be back home. And we don't mention a word of this to Ma, remember? *And* we must head into Nightfall morrow-sol to pick up my jacket. Hope she'll have it laundered before she hands it over."

"You'll have to pay for it first," Copper warned. "Our chum Midnight would never let us off with anything… well, I suppose we got good deals, being who we were and who he was."

"We never found out exactly who and what he was," Linen reminded her. "Wonder if every frocking Dome Complex on this entire planet has its own version of Midnight and Nightfall? And what they're called?"

"Wonder after dinner: this cab has a turn of speed, we're on Blur already and I need a good hot soak."

* * *

Copper had little time for a soak, for her friend routed her out quickly as a link from Colonel Moritz had come in. The two sat in Linen's room to see and hear the message, which was to the effect that the two suspects that had followed them had now been apprehended. They were allegedly part of one of several concerns that were trying to poke sticky fingers into the reasons behind the military activities currently underway over half the planet. The now widespread suspicions that alien artefacts *had* been dug up on Mars, particularly around Beagle, and that the Fleet, amongst others, were gearing up to set out on outer-Sol system exploration in relation to that had only whetted their appetites for more information and a piece of any action going.

The research that the Amberline Group was involved in was obviously closely linked to the situation, in view of the diggings adjacent to the Warren site and the problems that had occurred both at the site and back at Lowell College over the past several months or more. That both their facility and the two researchers had been targeted was not surprising: as the formidable Stellaria Firedrake of INN had noted previously, Copper and Linen not only packed a great deal of prize hardware for lowly students, but they also had high level and very interesting friends that took a good deal of interest in their work.

"So yet again, be on the alert because we seem to be the target of some very nasty people," Copper concluded. "Just dandy! And didn't Colonel Moritz say way back that her people knew most of the bad guys involved and that her lot had them under surveillance? Though she *did* mention that there were other villains out there that they were trying to keep track of, as far as possible. At this rate, I'll be glad to get aboard the *Drake*.

At least aboard her we should be almost safe from prying eyes, snooping noses, searching fingers and fizzing guns!"

"Chill it, Cop: it's only a walk in the park," Linen counselled. "We can deal with it – all three of us."

"You knew Spook was with us all the way, didn't you?"

"Yo; I think it's up to him whether he lets me know he's close. That's why sometimes I can't tell if he's hanging round your neck, or wherever. You're the one he linked to, after all."

"Hmm. I've got a lot to thank the Amberlines for then," Copper responded dryly.

"Well naturally: a place as a PhD student in a major research group, a reasonable disburse that comes in regularly, hard work, fun times, the chance to dig into the deeps of our little planet; and now the opportunity to get into the great beyond," Linen told her.

"Not to mention getting followed, threatened, shook about in an armoured vehicle, the company of very strange people and an alien that thinks I'm its surrogate mother," the redhead was informed severely. "But I hear noises in the passage; that must be your Ma back from work."

Corona Lyrican called out to let them know of her return and both stepped out to say that they were catching up on research work, which was almost true. The usual round of welcome was followed by the information that Ms Lyrican senior was off to freshen up and change and would see them for a quick chinwag before their dinner date at the Carnelian Crucible.

Indeed it was scarcely a quarter of an hour later that Corona reappeared and settled into one of the comfortable sofas in the family hub with a cup of hot caff and a smile. She had much to tell them in little time, she announced, the main item being that Magenta would turn up on the doorstep at about noon morrow-sol, being already on her way: she had had to stop over at a station called Ember for some reason connected with her work and would come in from there.

The two trainees looked at one another. Station Ember was a military outpost close to Moreux Crater in the Ismeniae Fossae region and a No Fly Zone existed around it on all their current flight charts. As a civilian, Ms Firewall was privileged indeed if she had been allowed to land there. Her mode of transport was also piquing the two friends: no civilian craft would be allowed within fifty kilometres of the place.

"Wonder what her business was?" Linen asked nonchalantly.

"As if you two didn't know!" Corona said irritably, watching the pair. "But I won't ask as I suspect you won't tell me."

"Sorry, Ma: we signed up for the Service and it goes with the territory, even if we're only guessing. But what's with *you* these sols? Any more lucrative commissions amongst the rich and famous that we should know about? I guess Alecta Lattim has picked up all the gear you designed for her?"

"She has, but so far I haven't seen her wear any of it for any big occasion; although the event she ordered the gown and extras for can't be far off," Corona replied.

"The launch of MDMC's big boat, we figured," Linen said. "It must be close. I reckon MDMC was trying to beat the *Drake* out of dock, but its launch was delayed for some reason as well – probably lack of parts. The *Drake's* in Phobos Station II Space Dock and the MDMC boat's in its own dock in Mars orbit. I must check in with Quartz to see if she knows more."

Quartz Craterhouse was an old friend of Linen's who once was a production worker in the MDMC shuttle sheds on Chryse Planitia. She was now a steward with Linking-Shuttle and having kept in touch with her old friends at the shuttle sheds, she was a useful source of information on the latest rumours circulating in that quarter.

"More likely that MDMC wants to know where the *Drake's* to be heading and its lackeys are hanging fire 'til they find out," Copper interjected. "We still don't know its name."

"Who cares," Linen said, shrugging. "But Ma, do you have more commissions in the offing?"

"Two or three," Corona acknowledged. "I have a selection of my pieces in an exhibition in the Twilight Gallery on Zarnecki. I got the space on the back of the Galaxia Sandbar commission – Ms Sandbar was good enough to publicise the accessories I did for her pairing and they've brought me in a few new customers. But my clients have as much right to privacy as you two, so that's all I'm saying about that. However, on another note: what do you think to this?"

As she spoke, Corona called up an image on her wrist-comm which hovered in the air above the device, shimmering into holo-clarity. It was a diadem of blue and white gems in a delicate tracery of platinum.

"That's a beauty, Ma!" Linen exclaimed. "Looks like it's for a pairing. Anyone we know?"

"Phoebe Orphistene," was the response.

"You what? Auntie Phoebe? You're joking!"

"Don't be rude!" Copper butted in. "Are you saying that Ms Orphistene isn't likely to get paired?"

"That's not what I mean and you know it. But after her sad little affair with the big and nasty Wolff Waterbone, I thought she'd given up trusting anyone who made promises. I hope she knows what she's doing."

"No comment," Corona said. "I've seen the man: he's well-spoken, presentable and seems to be fond of her. *And* he works in one of our labs, so we'll all be keeping an eye on her – and him."

"I hope he knows what he's taken on, with you lot policing the situation," Linen chortled. "Any other surprises while we're at it?"

"I rather thought you'd have things to tell me," was the reply.

"Can't, Ma, you should know that by now. But we had a little bit of fun on the way out to the Amber-Warren – or at least Copper did. And it's bound to have repercussions back at base."

Linen went on to give an amplified account of their run-in with Captain Max Meldyn over priorities when Copper had the helm of the Scamper. That kept them busy until it was time to change for dinner and thus safely deflected other searching questions.

* * *

The Carnelian Crucible was a large restaurant down Memory Avenue and facing Road Five, off which was located the family unit owned by Magenta Firewall and in the long-term custody of Linen and Copper. Their six next-unit neighbours, agro-students at Beagle College whom they had met when they, Magenta and Corona had been upgrading the unit after Magenta had acquired it, had endorsed the Crucible as a place where the goods were both economical and edible. One of the students moonlighted as a waiter at the restaurant to earn extra credits, supplying his employers with cut-rate luxury foodstuffs that he and his mates grew in a pink plas-glass greenhouse outside their own door.

The night air along Memory was cool and all three were well wrapped up to combat the chill. As they turned into the warm and inviting place, they looked around. Their acquaintance Flyx Ztarmish was nowhere in sight, but Copper noted one face that she knew. She nudged Linen surreptitiously and nodded in the direction of a tall man in the company of a couple of others.

Lieutenant Commander Grayn Bilkitt was an officer in the Intelligence Branch of the Service and part of a group known as Outer Mars Operations. The two had met him and his superior, a Lieutenant Colonel Toxi Karben, through Colonel Moritz, and had taken an instant dislike to the acid-tongued Karben.

"What's he doing here?" Linen whispered. "I thought we'd seen the last of him months ago – when we met him and Karben in here in fact. You remember?"

Copper did, very well. "Military's still all over the place," she reminded her friend in an undertone. "Though he's in mufti and so are his buddies. They might not be part of his division."

"Like hell, look at the three of them: they all came out of the same mould," Linen hissed back.

"What are you two muttering about?" Corona demanded after she had agreed their reserved table with one of the serving staff and they were heading over.

"Not now, Ma; let's sit."

"Okay," Corona insisted as the three took their seats. "What are you so het up about?"

"Recognise one of the people at that table behind you; he's senior level Service, but I can't tell you more. Don't turn and look. What are they doing, Cop?" Linen questioned softly.

"Eating," her friend replied. "He hasn't spotted us yet. No you don't!" she added as Linen's eyes lit up. "Leave them be, I'm sure he won't want to renew our acquaintance. At least his boss isn't with him."

"Spoke too soon, Cop. Guess who's just come out of the comfort?"

"You've got to be kidding me!" was the furiously whispered rejoinder as Copper turned to look.

"I'm not: Lieutenant Colonel Karben. And *she's* in civilian rags. Maybe they were expecting a quiet eve out on the Dome," Linen grinned mischievously.

"This furlough's getting madder by the minute," her friend declared as the aforementioned Colonel Karben caught her eye and froze fractionally.

Copper smiled, nodding apparently politely but with a steely expression on her face. Linen civilly acknowledged her likewise as a very puzzled Corona took stock of the woman.

The colonel strode over to their table, unable to ignore them. "Ms Milkstone and Ms Lyrican, I believe. May I ask what you are both doing here?"

"We're having dinner," Copper replied sardonically. "And it's Lieutenant Milkstone and Lieutenant Lyrican," she added with a lift to her eyebrow.

That was met with a look of frank disbelief. "Since when?"

"Private information. We won't pry into *your* business here, naturally. I expect you're also having dinner. Enjoy your eve. And please give our… salutations… to Commander Bilkitt."

"Salutations?" Linen repeated as Karben, with a sharp look at Corona, bid them a curt farewell and turned on her heel.

"Well I wasn't going to say respects or compliments, was I? We're not exactly the best of friends," Copper reminded her.

"Bet she's off to check up on our records," Linen sniffed. "But what are she and Bilkitt and their chums doing here? Mind your tongues, I bet now she's spotted us she'll be keeping an eye and an ear. Hey, we could wind up their props for them!"

"Could we hell; she'd know. I bet the two of them remember the last time we did that and they obviously got an ear bashing over it from Auntie Elle," Copper responded.

"Will the two of you just look over the menu and choose your food," an irate Corona butted in. "I have no idea what in hell is going on and I suspect I don't want to know, but we are here to eat. Let's do that."

"Yes, Ma. Sorry, she's the kind that brings out the worst in us. They were neither of them particularly courteous to us the times we met before. But at least we've put the cat among their shuttle ducks…Wonder who their two associates are?"

"Who cares, let's eat," Copper told her. "But keep an eye out: Bilkitt's giving us the once over."

"Smile at him; it'll drive him doozie."

Copper did, raising a flirtatious shoulder that caused him to frown in annoyance, as Ms Lyrican senior ordered the pair of them to behave or she'd have them out by the ears.

"You'd think you were a couple of teenies! How you'll get on when you have to obey orders aboard a ship, I don't know!"

"Truth be told, Ma, neither do we," Linen confessed. "But hey ho! Let's keep the conversation to levels you don't mind others hearing about. I know this table has noise suppression that's supposed to block sound both ways, but there are a dozen easy ways round that. Tell us about Phoebe's partner for a start, and when the legal pairing ceremony's to be. And tell *her* to give us a call if she has any trouble: we'll soon sort him out."

The meal passed in amicable and innocuous banter, but both trainees kept a close watch on the table at which the officers sat, smiling whenever one of them caught their glance. Linen did suggest calling in at their apartment off Road Five on the way home but the idea was firmly vetoed by Copper. With the four personnel opposite no doubt all trained to ferret out secrets, she had no intention of mentioning its location or giving any snoops a lead on where it was. In any case, she was a tad concerned that their walk back to the Lyrican place might be the subject of unwanted interest but was wise enough not to mention anything to her companions.

* * *

As far as the two Fleet trainees knew, they were not followed from the restaurant. The four at the nearby table had left half an hour before they did with barely a glance in their direction, but Copper caught the impression of irritation at their interrupted evening. The whole smacked of unlikely coincidence however, and she and Linen, dissecting the incident later in Linen's room, came to the conclusion that either there was more going on in Beagle than they realised and Military Intelligence had been called in, or the events in which they *had* been involved were stirring up a lot more than expected. In any event, Karben had seemed genuinely surprised that both now bore the rank of lieutenant, which implied that her and Bilkitt's presence there was nothing to do with them.

"Or nobody told them," Linen suggested. "Colonel Moritz is now in command of the *Drake*, so she should be out of their hair, but that doesn't mean that she can't call on MI if there's a problem. And there seems to be one with the ship out by the Warren, which brings in Outer Mars Ops, as that's their sphere of activity. Not to mention us, as we probably know a bit more than most about the situation. There must have been a serious breach in the system out on Isidis if that's the case. And we've long suspected a leak in Intelligence as well. Auntie Elle didn't deny it when we hinted way back, at any rate."

"Whatever's going on, we're in it up to our butts yet again," Copper snorted in annoyance. "I suggest you set your privacy bug tonight and keep your stun handy – if not that little number you pulled on Auntie Elle's troopers when they picked us up for that meet with her way back. I take it you still have it?"

"Yup, but as it's not legal I tend not to carry it about. Some store security system would surely pick it up and sound an alarm Might be troublesome explaining it. But you'll have Spook as back-up; he'll be able to wake you up if there's trouble."

"There had better not be, is all I can say," Copper muttered darkly as she prepared to head off next door to her own room and a warm soak in the tub. "See you in the solshine."

"Sure will. We have to head off to the shady Ms Nightfall to pick up my jacket, don't forget. And it's just the right shade of red to go with our stat pins."

"Don't think I hadn't noticed," her friend told her. "See you on the flipside."

* * *

The morning dawned at the usual time for their latitude in the northern hemisphere's summer and the two were reasonably early about, as they wished to see Corona before she set off for work. Corona had decided to finish at her employ earlier than usual in honour of her mother's visit and to keep an eye on her two guests as far as possible. She was less than satisfied with the explanations that she had received the night before, but as the two were fully adult and had been for a number of Mars years, she realised that there was little that she could do but attempt to keep them under control.

There had been no alarms overnight and the duo was in hopes of a quieter sol than the one before. They set off on foot to Ms Nightfall's emporium just after Corona left and spent the walk in quiet speculation as to the real nature of Nightfall's operation and why a downmarket clothing emporium seemed to be the chosen undercover option for both her and the enigmatic Mr Midnight of Coblentz Street in Lowell Central Dome.

"If they're part of Military Intelligence they're savvier than Karben's bunch, or they appear to be at any rate," Copper said softly. "I'd put them on a par with Magenta's marines: they're hardly official but they're an operation you can count on. Maybe they're similar, only spies."

"If you need a spy, you call them?" asked Linen doubtfully. "That hardly seems… you're yanking my chain!"

"Course I am. Now you know what it feels like; you've made a career of yanking mine," Copper told her as they turned into Private Road, there being no signs to bar their way and it being the speediest way to their destination.

"It'll give us a look-see at Beagle's main Law Enforcement premises as well," Linen had argued. "I've actually never been there before."

"I'm glad to hear it, if surprised," Copper told her. "I'd have thought you'd know it inside out. You seem to know most places around your mother-hub rather well."

"I'm a Beagle-ite: we all do," Linen informed her as the two marched along.

They were unmolested the entire length of the road and reached their turn-off to Dowson Street with no trouble.

"All these years and we thought it was off-limits," Linen marvelled. "It was probably only a ruse by Law Enforcement to keep nosey dustbaggers out. We haven't even seen one officer of the Law."

"It's maybe caff-break for the early shift," Copper suggested. "Wonder how Ms Nightfall manages to source things at such short notice?" she went on.

"In view of what she seems, it's hardly surprising," returned Linen. "But our jackets will look chill with our ranking pins on them, especially when no-one's quite sure what they represent."

"What's bothering me is why we didn't notice those other two on our tail yestersol," her friend admitted. "And why Spook didn't give me a clue," she added, somewhat put out.

"He did; you just didn't listen aright. You *said* you were edgy, as if you felt something wasn't right and the universe was out of synch. You knew we were being followed but not who by."

"By whom," Copper corrected tetchily. "I *can* sometimes see what I think he sees, or would see if he had eyes."

"How do you know he doesn't?"

"We are not going to get into the realms of speculation on the sensual capacities of an ethereal alien," Copper said firmly.

"I think you mean sensory," the redhead corrected. "Sensual smacks of something else, and if his capacities are sensual, I'd be worried."

"Believe me, I'm already worried," Copper retorted dryly as they reached their destination.

Ms Nightfall was expecting them and had the dark red jacket for Linen on her countertop. It seemed either new or freshly laundered, as it was shining.

"Thirty credits," she greeted them with a smile.

"You're a businesswoman and no mistake," Linen informed her. "I'd like to inspect it first. And I'll give you fifteen, since you took the trouble to source it."

"No you won't. Twenty five."

As before, they settled on twenty and Linen examined and then tried on her new acquisition gleefully, twirling in front of a handy mirror. "Very nice and it suits me. We'll make quite a pair," she went on to her friend. "We'll have to wear them when we meet Grammy later. Wonder what her plans for the sol are as regards us? I bet we head out to some nice eatery or other. We haven't seen her for an age. I'll take it wrapped for now, if you don't mind," she added to Ms Nightfall.

Copper was scrutinising her surroundings closely. There were some differences to Midnight's store on Coblentz Street, but the suspensor set of lights was practically identical she noted, as was the positioning of the counter and the back area that held all manner of interesting things.

"If this is a standard set-up for this type of business, it would be better if there was more variation," was her summation in an ironic tone. "Else somebody's going to notice and put two and two together to get a whole heap."

"Just ignore her," Linen advised Ms Nightfall as the two shouldered their carryalls and made for the exit. "She gets these notions."

"Another thing I've noticed is that we haven't seen many of our cohort about. Weren't most of them supposed to be staying local and seeing the sights?" Copper said when they were clear.

"We haven't been here that long and I'm sure most of them are sightseeing around the local bars or out at the Leisure Dome having what they think is a good time," Linen told her. "But enough of this already. Where to now? We have time before Grammy shows."

"Skady Lane," Copper replied. "We *were* going to see what Ma Kellyn had got herself into, after all. Though I haven't heard from her, as Majorelle thought I might."

"We'd best call up Majorelle and Lofty later, to see how they are and what Osterley's been up to, and all the folks back at Lowell," her friend agreed, linking arms. "Just back up the way we came and then turn left into Skady. It's a bit of a junkyard, as we noted from our very short stop off yestersol."

"Let's hope we don't have the same problems," Copper said with a surreptitious look around.

"Nobody's in sight; this doesn't seem to be a very popular neighbourhood," Linen noted.

"At least for law-abiding citizens."

A short time later found them strolling along the insalubrious Skady Lane, a narrow and overbuilt street where the buildings tended to loom. The apartment block further on that they had noted from their refuge the sol before soon reared up, its grim façade pierced by a number of small windows. They agreed that it looked like some sort of rental apartment complex that Ma Kellyn would have bought for a reasonable sum. The structures either side looked like industrial units but were anonymous. The main entry to the block, which was called Skady Apartments if the lettering on the tiled flooring under a small covered portico was accurate, was a semi-opaque plas-glazed panel that had seen better sols. Unable to peer through, the two examined the ident-reader carefully.

"As this place was once for the use of rookie law enforcers, it's probably triple encrypted; but if this is Ma's latest venture on the property market, she'll have it changed as soon as," was Copper's opinion. "Whoops! Somebody's in there, I can see a shadow and the lights have just come on."

"Maybe it's one of the existing tenants," Linen guessed. "We should hang about and ask."

Copper could sense no imminent threat and agreed. Seconds later, they realised their mistake. The two had stepped out of the entry to make way for the departing individual whose outline they could see through the misty glazing. If the outraged intake of breath was insufficient, the pursed mouth and widening eyes made it abundantly clear that Ms Drusy Kellyn was less than enraptured to see them on her doorstep.

"Well! And what may I ask are you two doing here?" she queried truculently. "This is private property!"

"The street isn't, Ms Kellyn," Linen calmly asserted. "And we were passing."

"This is a bit off the beaten track to be *passing*," Ma disputed in freezing tones.

Copper took a hand. "We were passing this way, Ms Kellyn, because Linen and I were attacked just up the street yestersol," she said quietly. "And we are here to scout out the area and see if we can get a clue as to who and why."

Ma drew herself up and looked her ex-tenant in the eye. "I take it Law Enforcement has been informed?"

"No," Copper said shortly. "Our own people have and they are dealing with it. But we want more information."

Ms Kellyn scrutinised the pair of them shrewdly. "You didn't take much hurt," she observed.

"We can look after ourselves. We're military-trained after all. But I must say it *is* a surprise to see you here."

"My being here is none of your concern," was the sour reply.

"Naturally not," Copper said evenly. "And we won't pry. But you didn't happen to have been here yestersol and seen two characters sneaking about where they shouldn't, about sixteen hundred hours?"

Ms Kellyn was still watching the duo narrowly. "What did they look like?" she demanded.

"Like this," Copper responded, calling up the holo that Ms Nightfall had passed on of the two well-dressed and muscular individuals that had trailed them.

Ma shook her head. "I've seen nothing like those two. This *is* a respectable neighbourhood, after all."

That was a fabrication if ever there was one, the two realised, but Ma would never admit to it. As further delicate probing on the characters likely to be found in the environs of Skady Lane yielded no results, Linen suggested that as they were headed into Artisan Square, perhaps Ms Kellyn would like to accompany them to Jinx Café for some light refreshment.

Copper's eyes blazed but she held her tongue, realising that her friend had an agenda of her own. That being the case, Ma carefully locked the premises and acquiesced. In rare harmony the three made their stately progress back to the unnamed road and then on along one side of the square, where a cut across to Wells Street brought them to the café. They had kept to safe topics such as the doings of common acquaintance on the way, but once comfortably seated and in possession of a creamy caff apiece, Ms Kellyn had to hear about the trials and tribulations of being Fleet officers in training. The two were only grateful that none of the other customers appeared to be members of said Fleet and dismissed the subject as soon as they could.

Ms Kellyn was marginally impressed that the two had spent a short part of their leave in actual work rather than in dissipation and were now awaiting the arrival of Linen's relative from out Viking way. She was still intently watching the pair and chewing something over in her mind. Linen skilfully brought their friend Majorelle Moritz into the talk: she was a favourite of Ma, having been an exceptionally tidy and quiet tenant whilst living in the Kellyn family unit and having been legally paired from there, to Ma's credit.

"Not a pairing I would have predicted, Majorelle and that Mr Amaloft, but they seem to be well-suited," Ma rumbled. "And *he's* well set up, owning the diner *and* the family unit; though that dog of his must be a sore trial to such a clean and tidy person as Majorelle; it's never away from the vats down cellar. They have a Spirit Hover," she added. "*You* have family here," she went on to Linen. "They live close?"

"My Ma's place is on Road One off Memory."

Ma nodded. "A big place is it?"

"Yes, as fam-units go," Linen told her. "The usual fam-hub and kitchen, three fairly large sleeping quarters, a small office, a decent storeroom and space outside for a hover, though she doesn't have one of those. Close to work too – she works in a lab in the Science Park off Mohs Road, so she's just a step away, really," Linen, clearly seeing where the conversation was headed, explained artlessly.

"I expect her Landlady or Landlord is reasonable as far as rent is concerned?" Ma hazarded, slightly put out.

"Oh she doesn't have one – she owns her place."

This was big news to Ms Kellyn and her eyes bulged as she pondered. "Our family, however distant, has always been careful with its resources," was the result of the cogitation. "Mostly," she added, evidently considering Linen as one of the exceptions that proved the rule to be nothing more than minewash.

"The woman Firewall," Ma continued. "I expect *she* owns her own place?"

"Oh, Grammy does, out at Deep Two, south of Viking One. And she also owns her business, as you know."

Ma Kellyn was more than aware of that, having discovered some time before that not only was she distantly related to Linen through Ms Firewall's late partner, but that Magenta's late mother was Curiosity Lyrican Lear-Grange, one of the most prominent mathematicians that Mars had ever produced, and a very competent mineralogist to boot.

"I expect you stay at your Ma's when you're here?"

"Yes, that's where we are at the moment," Linen's eyes crinkled up in amusement.

"But perhaps you'd prefer your own place, you and Ms Milkstone here. Independence is usually the better option, rather than battening on family."

"Talking of family, how is your brother Pinker?" Copper put in dryly, knowing that Ma found her sibling trying at best and intrusive at worst.

"Same as usual: trying to scrounge a billet for his bi-annual leave from work," Ma snapped. "He's not lodging at mine, Altair doesn't like him. But back to accommodation: you'll both need somewhere when you're not out in whatever ship you'll be given once you finish your training. A nice small place that's handy for home and easy on the pocket."

"Not many of those to be found," said Copper.

"I just happen to know of one or two that will soon be on the market and not a stone's throw from here that would suit."

Both feigned innocence and with the application of a little more flattery and the supply of another cup of creamy caff, Ma was finally induced to let slip that she had recently come into possession of the block known as Skady Apartments. Linen had regretfully to acknowledge that she and Copper had access to a sizeable family unit owned by her Grammy Magenta Firewall, and close enough to be very useful. But as they had numerous colleagues who were all destined to be officers in the Fleet and thus reasonably good bets as tenants who were paid regularly and were frequently away from home, they could pass on the details of said apartments to them, if Ma so desired.

Ms Kellyn ruminated, scenting possible profit but unsure of letting out details to the two. Linen pressed the matter in her inimitable style, suggesting subtly that if they could see what was on offer themselves, there were one or two instructors, recently assigned to Beagle One Basecamp, who were also probably in the market for comfortable local accommodation to which they could retire during their periods of leave, when their cramped base billets became too restrictive for their social lives.

Copper was hard put to refrain from smiling as the suave features of Instructor Captain Max Meltdown flitted into her mind. She nodded however and hinted that Captain Meldyn might be a prime candidate as she was sure he preferred a more private space than that offered by Beagle's usual run-of-the-mill hotels for his spells of furlough.

Ms Kellyn's eyes had lighted at the information: she evidently had not considered the lately-instituted basecamp as a profitable source of tenantry. The upshot was that she would provide the two trainees with a limited tour of one or two of the apartments within her less-than-complete premises the following sol, if they would meet her there at thirteen hundred hours precisely. They agreed with alacrity and she bid them a speedy farewell.

"Off to tart up a couple of the billets and their surrounds to make a good impression on us," grinned Linen as she settled the bill. "If they're cheap enough and bigger than your average boot box, they might be right up Max Meltdown's avenue as a cosy place to bring his conquests, well away from the prying eyes of his colleagues."

"It would be funnier still if we could inveigle a couple of his colleagues to sign on with Ma as well," Copper smiled in return. "This furlough's turning into more fun that I was beginning to expect. But we'd best get back to your Ma's place if we're to be there when Magenta turns up. And I'm getting antsy."

"Best watch our backs on the way then," Linen responded. "Follow me. We'll stay on Artisan and head down to Blur. It's a busy area, so we should be safe enough in broad sol-light. And there're a couple of stores and galleries to look in on the way."

"Just keep your stun handy. But now we're technically Fleet, does that mean we *can* legally pack a little heat? Or would that be only when we're in uniform?" Copper asked in a low voice as they walked onward at a swift pace.

"Not even then unless we were on duty, I suspect. You don't see uniformed troopers parading the streets with guns up their sleeves, do you? Our escort from Grammy's marines was armed – but then she *was* on duty. And it's just occurred to me that *her* weapon didn't set off any security systems at Ms Nightfall's."

"I bet it damn well did, but she knew exactly what was going on and turned a blind eye – or at least a very sharp eye. But let's keep moving. Something's sending a frizz up the old spine and I don't know what it is."

"I do," Linen replied as she grabbed her friend's sleeve to point out something in a store window. "Just hold here. I spy a couple of people not ten steps behind us that stop when we do and they don't seem very intent on window shopping. Move a bit to the right… It looks a lot like our old buddy Lieutenant Colonel Toxi Karben of Military Intelligence, in mufti. And she has a friend in tow that doesn't look like her sidekick Bilkitt. What do we do?"

"We keep walking and if they *are* on our tail, we outface them. For people working in MI that think that's covert, they're dimmer than a pair of dirty brass doorknobs."

"Don't think so – she's figured I've spotted her and she and her pal are headed this way."

6: MAGENTA

Copper and Linen turned, waiting for their pursuers to catch up. They then saw that Karben's buddy was one of the unknowns with whom she had been dining at the Carnelian Crucible. The colonel was quick to acknowledge them.

"*Trainee* Lieutenants Milkstone and Lyrican," she said.

"Colonel Karben," Copper responded formally. "And you are?" she asked of the stranger, as the colonel made no attempt to introduce him.

"Not your concern!" Karben snapped.

"How rude," opined Linen in an aside to her friend. "I'm Lyrican; this is Milkstone," she added to the man.

"What are you two doing here?" Karben demanded acidly.

"We are on furlough, Colonel, as I'm sure you know. We are based at Beagle One Basecamp, as I'm sure you also know. Our base is thataway," Copper added, pointing west.

"I'm aware of that!"

"And as we have less than a sevensol of leave, we don't have time to get very far. May I ask why you're tailing us?"

"You got as far as your research site up near Nili Fossae," the woman rapped curtly.

"May I ask why you're tailing us?" Copper repeated coolly.

"I want a word. Why did you decide to head out to your site, having only a few sols of leave? How did you manage to work out that your site had been targeted by undesirables? And then deal with them? And then there was that little fracas the other sol that ended in a vehicle chase through the Dome. And who was that woman you were talking to in the café just now?"

"That's a lot of information to demand on a public street in the middle of the sol. And it's none of your business, ma'am. If it was, I'm sure you'd be able to get your hands on the answers without our help. *You* have resources we don't."

Linen was watching her friend in some concern. Karben was not a friendly individual and never had been, to them. And she was a high-ranking officer in the service of Mars Intelligence. She was not someone to annoy, however satisfactory the sense of besting her might be.

"Answer the questions."

Some of Linen's anxiety had percolated through and Copper smiled, giving a slight nod. "We made for the Warren to collect additional samples as part of our research; we *are* continuing our PhDs once we're assigned aboard a ship. We examined our site minutely, as routine, and found it had been breached – from the military site close by us, in fact. Thus we suspected infiltration and took steps to find and stop it, as far as our *own* site was concerned. As for yestersol, we realised we were being followed for reasons unknown to us but we suspected in relation to the intrusions at our site and elsewhere, and took steps to curtail that, as I'm sure you've been informed. As for the old friend with whom we were enjoying a quiet caff, that is private. But if you'd really like to know more, we are meeting her morrow-sol at thirteen hundred hours. I can supply you with our rendezvous and we can *all* have a chat."

"Belay that, Ms Milkstone! You *are* technically part of the Service and so am I – and your superior by a long way."

"Which, ma'am, if I may make so bold, gives you no right to detain and question us. We are Fleet trainees under the direct authority of our superior officers at Beagle Basecamp. If you need additional information, I suggest you go through those channels to get it. But as we have an urgent appointment for which we are already late, you will have to excuse us…"

"Not so fast!" the man with the colonel put in.

"Yes?" Copper asked with a direct and questioning gaze.

"We haven't finished with you," he told her.

"Then I'd be obliged if you'd cut to the point. How can I help you further?"

She had called his bluff and he knew it. Before he could fill the awkward pause, however, Linen cut in with a quiet chuckle.

"Our urgent appointment has come to find us."

The redhead waved her hand energetically in the direction of a smartly-attired individual who was marching towards them like a small battle-tank. "Well met, ma'am!" she called out.

The two MI officers had turned as one to see who was on approach vector. There was a quick flicker of semi-recognition in Karben's eyes, followed by a glance at her obviously-puzzled colleague. From that exchange, Copper realised that he at least had not seen Magenta Firewall before.

"Good to see you again, ma'am," she stated formally. "You must have made good time."

Magenta looked the two strangers up and down. Karben she nodded at. They had never been formally introduced as far as Copper was aware, but Magenta had seen the lieutenant colonel at least twice before and knew that Linen and she had some sort of connection to her through Colonel Moritz.

"I made good time from Station Ember," was the response, causing a tightening of Karben's lips that did not go unnoticed. "Am I interrupting something?" Ms Firewall went on, aware of the atmosphere.

"Shall I make the introductions?" Linen broke in brightly. "I'm afraid I don't know *your* name," she said to Karben's crony. "But Ms Firewall, this is Lieutenant Colonel…"

"That's enough!" Karben grunted. "We have to go. I will no doubt see you two later. Dismissed."

"I didn't realise we had been summoned," Copper said to the retreating backs. "We'll take a cab back," she added, unhooking her small scanner from its chain.

She quickly ran the device over Linen and then handed it to her friend, who repeated the scan.

"Clean," Linen announced. "They didn't plant a bug on us."

"A cab?" Magenta asked.

"If they *had* bugged us, I wasn't going to let on we could walk home," Copper explained. "But you must have made very good time, ma'am. How come you came looking for us? And how come you *could* track us down?"

"None of your business. And enough of the ma'am. But we'll take a cab and head to Road Five for a chinwag, as Corona's still at work. I've been hearing all about your latest exploits and it's better your mother doesn't know," she told Linen. "I'll link to her later and tell her I came in early and I'm with you two."

The travel-cab Magenta summoned was one of the fleet of secure vehicles that had provided escort to the two girls the sol before. Neither said anything, but boarded as requested. Once security had been invoked at Ms Firewall's request, she turned to the two, who were sat side by side.

"Okay, who were those two? The woman I recognised from the BC Hotel when we had a run of trouble there, and then later we saw her at the Carnelian Crucible, but that was some while ago. If I recall aright, you said then that she was one of Colonel Moritz' team. I reckon she's not now."

"We think not," Linen agreed, "Now that Colonel Moritz is in command of the *Drake II*. Lieutenant Colonel Karben used to have to answer to her, and didn't like it. She's MI, and we first met her when the colonel called her in to hear what we had to say about our research. She was pretty dismissive at the time, but some of our ideas were closer to the bone than she liked and she rode us a bit over them. We met her by chance at the Crucible yestersol eve and let slip that we were lieutenants. That seemed to wind her prop a little," Linen laughed.

"By chance?" Magenta queried.

"I wondered about that," Copper put in. "After the leaks at the Warren site that *we* twigged and almost certainly leaks at the mil dig next door that may or may not have slipped past MI, a few knuckles would have been rapped. Karben was possibly one of those in charge and hence on the receiving end of said mass knuckle-rapping. When she realised that we had been the ones involved at the Warren, she probably figured that we knew more than we were telling. She wouldn't be as far as she is up the MI tree if she hadn't. They're not altogether dimwits in that branch of the Service."

"I'll bet," Linen agreed. "She must have realised that we had headed out and figured that this is where we'd be. I think it was probably coincidence that she and her playmates were in the Crucible last night when we hailed her. But as she had seen us there before, it was maybe a good call on her part. But I bet she knows about your place on Road Five, Grammy – she'll have made enquiries last time, you can be sure."

"But she didn't know that we were Fleet trainees: *that* seemed to surprise her," Copper stated. "I guess she would have found out pretty quickly, but then she spotted us in the Crucible last eve and probably had eyes kept on us. And as she needed heads on poles, she thought ours would fit nicely. She was wrong."

"I'll say," Magenta beamed. "You're a right pair of hotshots, as I've said before. The woman Moritz had her head screwed on when she decided you'd make a good bet for the *Drake*. But once we're at your place we'll get settled in and I'll order some eats. And then you can tell me all about the shenanigans at your field site."

* * *

Court Nine on Road Five, when at length they reached it via the vast Memory Avenue, was almost the same as usual. It was certainly tidier than the wrecker's yard with which Copper had compared it when first she saw it, but it would win no prizes for style or structure, being no more than a haphazard semi-circle of quasi-spherical plas-crete bulges huddled close to one another. All sported two windows at ground level.

Unit Five was rather more in keeping with the average family unit, with its fresh coat of pale pink wash that made it stand out from its ochre-tinted fellows, its holo-plants flanking the neat doorstep and the trim recessed bay for transport access. The pale pink plas-glass edifice was still in evidence in front of their student neighbours' place at Unit Four, its greenery sprouting in all directions. The nosy ex-miner inhabiting Unit One was also still there, judging by the partially-complete Spirit Hover on its frame outside and the roving door-cam that swept over the party the second they disembarked. The other units looked as usual, grubby and unloved, but the court itself was clean.

Copper and Linen had not seen the abode for some months but had been kept informed of the upgrades it had received by Magenta, who had been at pains to consult them at every step.

"You'll see some changes to the place since the last holo I sent you," Ms Firewall apprised them. "I know I told you that this is *your* place, but I've kept an eye – you never know who's up to what behind your back," she added darkly as she flashed what was evidently an implanted ident at the door reader plate. "We'll set it up to your Fleet implants," she announced. "That way you don't have to carry your solid ident. More secure that way. Lights!" she bellowed as she led them within.

The front entry panel opened into the well-lit main hallway, the walls either side of which were interrupted by several doors. The family hub and the kitchen were the first of these, on either side of the entry. A small comfort closet came next with a door opposite that which led down to the cellar via a set of stairs. The three doors to the sleeping quarters were further on and two of them had been labelled *Copper* and *Linen*; the third was branded *Guest*. There were a couple of other panels that led into a closet that had been organised as an office for Magenta and a further store. The door panel at the far end led out onto a flight of steps that gave on to a sunken yard at the back of the property.

The two younger women looked around the main hall. They had seen the holo of the fresh pale green wall colouring, but it somehow looked brighter in actuality. The doors were all in a soft tawny shade and the hexagonally-tiled floor matched that.

"Check out your rooms," Magenta ordered. "I'll call up the rations. Everything we'll need for that's in the fam-kitchen."

Copper's room had been decorated to her taste in warm shades of russet and ochre and the comfort closet was snug and bright in deep cream and golden yellow. The flooring was thick and soft. There was a large bed, a wall-hung entertainment unit and two sets of inset storage drawers. The task-desk fitted unobtrusively into one corner and a sizeable hospitality station occupied another. Magenta had clearly been busy for the latter was furnished with a drinks dispenser and an array of drinks tabs, as well as a small range of utensils; a handy cupboard was filled with some of her favourite provisions. A holo-pic limned in green light beside the entry bore an image that she recognised as Scalenyx, the holo-dragon she had met on a trip to Beagle's Leisure Dome with Linen and Corona several months before. Copper sniffed, and unaccountably, tears began to prick her eyes. More than curious now, she slid the neat panel doors of the wall closet aside to disclose shelves, a lockable cupboard and rails. Hung there was a sleep suit and a house-robe in her size, with a pair of house-shoes on the floor. One corner was taken up by a flight simulator, lent to her and Linen months ago by their ex-College friend Rustin, who was now a met officer out at Wells Dome Complex. She removed her wrap and set off to find Linen.

"Rustin's sim made it over from Lowell with my stuff from Ma Kellyn's: we should send it on to Wells before we finish our training. And your Grammy's fitted one or two surprises," she greeted her friend, who appeared to be rummaging in a drawer.

"You're telling me. This drawer's got some of the stuff I left at Ma's place in it so I have lots of changes of clothes. And she didn't mention the spanking new comms linkage at the desk, or the pic of Blueberyl by the door. Wonder what else she's done that she didn't tell us about?"

"You've got a holo of Blueberyl!" Copper exclaimed. "I got one of Scalenyx. Your Grammy's had words with your Ma over them, I bet. I didn't expect all the stuff at the hospitality either. Maybe there's a tri-dee holo-suite in the cellar?" she suggested.

"Don't count on it," her friend advised. "Grammy's well-off but she's not made of credit. I wonder what she's done to the fam-hub: if I recall, we suggested green and cream shades for that with toffee-coloured seating, but you know Grammy."

"Only too well," Copper returned as they set off down the hall to the kitchen. "But…"

"But? You're still uncomfortable about accepting all this, aren't you?" Linen guessed.

"Well, yes. She's *your* Grammy after all…"

"I keep telling you we can go shares. Did you ever tell your folks you were going Service?" Linen asked curiously.

Copper bit her lip. "No. Didn't seem to be any point; they didn't appear much interested when I said I'd started at Lowell on my PhD and I rarely hear from them, so…"

"You tell them, and let it go," her friend advised, linking an arm through hers. "Let's see what's going on."

Magenta was hunting in a high cupboard and turned with a set of plates in her hands. "It'll be here soon. Park your butts at the table, there's plenty of room."

There was: the central table in plasformic would seat six in comfort and the well-appointed space seemed to have all else necessary for ease of use. Copper did not remember choosing pink and red as the colour scheme but it sat well with the rosy light that suffused the room from the window. The view outside was evidently so uninspiring that semi-opacity had been set as the preferred view.

The summons at the outside entry that denoted the arrival of lunch was answered by the formidable Ms Firewall and a cheery server strode in with a selection of boxes, which he unpacked, setting their contents out dexterously around the table.

"We'll not be fit for dinner this eve if we eat all this now," Copper muttered.

"You don't need to clear your plate," Linen reminded her, a knowing grin creasing her face. "Grammy wanted a few words about our work, remember?"

She remembered, and once their attendant had departed the three began. Copper had been right: Magenta was impatient to hear of their trip out to the Warren in minute detail, especially the actions of Professor Thars Amberline, for whom she had a poorly-hidden soft spot. The repercussions of the incidents out there as far as the recent alarms that the two Amberlines had had in Beagle were also discussed: Ms Firewall was aware of the trip in the travel-cab and the back-up that had been deployed and had been suitably annoyed. On the back of that, she was particularly glad of a few arrangements that she had put in place, she informed the two mysteriously.

The gist of these arrangements had to wait until the three, the remains of their repast in the recyc and their implements in the wash-box, had made themselves comfortable in the family hub. That space was exactly as the two had specified as far as décor in green and cream, washed-tan sofas and chairs and units in pale plas-oak was concerned; an arrangement of what looked like spangled netting strung with lights that made up the ceiling caused Copper to look round, as did the superfine silver lines running down every wall. It was perhaps Spook that caused the momentary frisson of electricity that ran down her back and she turned almost accusatory eyes on Magenta.

"This place is sewn up tighter than a high-level meeting of Mars Gov's war committee!"

"You figure?"

"I figure. Why?"

"You're good," Magenta congratulated. "Almost too good. And you're right. There *are* secure systems in every room, but this is the nerve centre. Not that I expect you'll have to use it, but I believe in covering every base, even the ones you can't see.

And *I* may need it. While that holo-pic of darklight over Isidis is outlined in green light, this place is secure. If ever you see that green change to red, you have problems of a breach somewhere. Every room has a similar holo-pic and the same applies."

"Ah, that would be the pics of Scalenyx and Blueberyl in our rooms," Copper nodded to her friend. "But who's in the holo-pic in the room labelled *Guest?*" she asked, compressing her lips tightly as a vision of Thars Amberline jumped into her mind so vividly that she almost voiced it aloud.

Linen caught it in the fragile telepathy that existed between them and smirked. "Ma's dragon, Perlossica?" she put in hastily.

"Sunset over Olympus Mons," Magenta said shortly, scenting the covert exchange. "But I have these for you," she went on, opening a carryall that she had maintained a clutch on since lunch. "That one's for you, Copper, as is this. And this is for you," she added to her grand-daughter, handing over the small but solid packages.

Copper undid the larger of her gifts quickly. From the neat, finely crafted plas-leather casing she slid out a small handgun, turning it over in her hands carefully. She had practiced with hand weapons during training at Basecamp, but the one she held was smaller, neater and lighter and slid into her palm as if it was made for her. She looked in silent amazement at her friend.

Linen held an almost identical firearm, but in a deep red to Copper's blue. She was also fingering it almost lovingly. "It's so tactile," was her assessment. "And it's a work of art. Grammy, these are beautiful. Legal?" she asked.

"If you have the relevant licence tags. Which you do: I've arranged it. There were no problems as you're Fleet trainees and thus deemed capable of handling firearms," Magenta informed them. "You'll wear the tags at all times in case you're asked to produce them. You'll find them in the holster cases; the cases have secure clips by the way, so you can attach them to a belt or secure them in a pocket or carryall. And the firearms will bond to you by the same means I used on your wrist-comms. Do that now," she instructed. "See where the catch is flipped on and off? Flip it off and take tight hold of the handgrip… keep a hold… that's it. That blue glow means it's recognised your imprint and can't be imprinted a second time."

"How lethal are these?" Copper asked as she flipped the safety catch on again and examined the handgrip of the piece in interest.

"Lethal enough," Magenta told her. "Slide the baseplate open – they'll take standard charge-caps for the smaller military issue Personal Protection Firearms, A01 to A03, which makes them useful; and they're both loaded, so watch it. You'll know more than I do about PPFs, but these can be used to deadly effect if you hit the right mark. If ever you find yourself having to use them on an assailant, aim for the limbs, not the head or the main body. That way you'll disable but not kill."

"Grammy, this is good of you, very good, but why? It's freaking me a bit and I can sense Cop's getting restless. Are we liable to be in such trouble that we'll need weapons like these?"

"What do you think?" growled Ms Firewall.

Copper spoke grimly. "I think you're right. We're running into some mighty peculiar people. The phase rifle that frocking maniac Jecks was toting out at the Warren was set to kill and he was aiming it at me *and* aiming to use it, only I got him first. Thanks a million, Magenta. I wouldn't want to use it in anger, but if I had to, I reckon I could."

"I reckon you could too," Linen told her with a twist to her mouth. "I reckon we'd both have been toast if you hadn't been so quick off the mark."

Magenta looked at them both in consternation. "You didn't mention the part about the rifle set to kill when you were giving me the lowdown earlier," she accused.

"Slipped our minds," Linen told her, with a deep sigh, biting her lip. "What's in the other parcel, Cop?"

Copper had almost forgotten her second present, but put her PPF to one side to undo the smaller package. She let out a quiet laugh. "This was your idea, wasn't it?" she said to her friend as she held up a mini-stun blaster almost identical to the one that Linen owned and which had been supplied by her Grand Dam.

"Well, I might have mentioned to Grammy that you were hankering after one," she admitted. "But *these* are a surprise."

"Just don't tell your mother about the handguns," Magenta warned. "She worries enough as it is. But I'd better show you around the rest of this place and point out the bits and pieces of tech I've put in place which you'll have to set up each time you leave. You'll be staying here until you head back to your base I expect? I thought we'd dine at the BC Hotel tonight, by the by. Corona knows. I hope you brought some suitable traps? If not, we'd better get you kitted out. And you'd best tell me what plans you have for the rest of your leave. I don't want to be treading on your toes if you've something arranged."

* * *

Back at the Lyrican family unit later, Copper and Linen were in the latter's room unpacking the quality apparel that Magenta had insisted on supplying and that had been the result of a short shopping trip around Beagle Central.

"Grammy's seriously rattled, that's for sure," Linen said in a quiet voice, trying in vain to find a clear space in which to hang her new outfit. "Surveillance light-arcs along the hallway that are to be switched on as we leave? Every room with bugs in place? Don't go down into the cellar on pain of loss of privileges? That makes me suspect that people know that she or we or both are likely to be in residence."

"Magenta's rattled? The socks are being scared off me," said Copper as she swept a chair clear of detritus. "But *we* know that others know of our involvement in all this. We know the area around the Warren, and all round Beagle in fact, has more alien artefacts than the whole rest of Mars. Beagle *is* the epicentre of all things alien and hence the focus of most of the activity. And the work on the sub-tunnel from the spaceport to the AF Dome has been slowed because more alien artefacts are being turned up along that route as a result of the digging. Although I haven't heard the latest on that for a while, it's being kept under wraps."

"Still going, I expect, as a complete halt would raise awkward questions among the union employ reps for a start. But enough of that: these overlay pants suits are more than classy enough for the BC and they'll match our new jackets."

"And if we have to vault a gate or two, we'll be able to do it without showing the planet our panties," Copper put in dryly as she held the lower part of her suit aloft, allowing the gauzy overlay to billow. "We could wear them without the glitzy bits for our assignation with Ma Kellyn morrow-sol as well: Ma likes a bit of style. There's a thermo-unit at our place, isn't there?"

"Yup, it's in the kitchen," Linen confirmed. "We'll have to organise more stuff to take over there if it's our base from here on in but we don't have time just now. I think we should stay over here tonight and then head out first thing. Otherwise it's a heap of hassle and you never know who you might meet along Memory Avenue at night."

"Agreed. It'll take you an hour just to bag this stuff up. And I've no intention of being the target of groups of feral youth prowling the highways and byways of Beagle, or even a horde of Mars Fleet's finest out to spend their back pay on whatever they consider a good time – and there seems to be plenty of them about, not counting our lot. Wherever the blazes *they* are: I've seen nary a one. You first for the tub or me?"

"You. You can have ten minutes, so you'd better make it a shower. And don't use up all my Blue Diamond soap-sub. And set the tub to clean when you're done."

"You just clear up the mess in here," she was told. "Sharing with you is like sharing with a crazy puppy with six legs that likes to empty closets and then jump about in the contents."

"Aw! You love me really!" Linen called, throwing a towel at her friend.

"Just as well we've only a few sols left of furlough, cupcake: a month of this and I'd cream you," Copper growled, snatching the towel as she headed in the direction of the hygiene cubicle.

* * *

The wide Zarnecki Avenue blazed with smart galleries, stores and restaurants, but the glittering BC Hotel outshone them all. Their travel cab shirred to a halt at the entry portico and Copper slid out, stopping to view the spectacular illumination. Sighing, she made her way after Magenta and Corona through the fluid holo of rippling colours that fell like a waterfall of light from on high and into the opulent interior. Linen brought up the rear, looking to left and right to see if she could spot anything or anyone of note as the group followed an attentive escort to the Smoky Pearl Lounge, where they were to have a cocktail before dinner in the main restaurant.

"A couple of bits of brass," Linen noted as she cocked her head in the relevant direction. "Don't know them."

"How about semi-brass you *are* acquainted with?" Copper murmured. "Ensign Foxy Dingle and he seems to have a date."

"No way! You're right, it is and he has. Ensign Zakarina Zills no less. Wasn't she locked in facial combat with Ensign Dex Inkle over at Giordano's last we saw her?"

"She evidently won, or figured he wasn't worth the effort; which he wasn't, let's face it. I bet Zak Zills made the move on Dingle. If she'd heard that he was holed up at the Plaza Hotel, she'd be in there, scenting credit," Copper whispered as she inclined her head at the pair, who had evidently spotted them.

"They're not exactly dressed for dinner at the BC," observed Linen, waving over as she and Copper ostentatiously removed their red plas-leather jackets to display their finery and settled into comfortable chairs at a small table.

"What are you two jabbering about?" Magenta demanded as a courteous waiter sloped up with their pre-dinner cocktails.

"Two of our cohort," Linen told her. "On a hot date, maybe and stopped in for a cocktail. But where Dingle got the trouser credit for drinks in this place I don't know."

"We know nothing much of his background," Copper said to her. "Maybe his folks are well off."

"Maybe they are, he *did* do a degree and he's still wet behind the ears. Still, I wish him joy of Zak Zills. She's the champion wrestler of our squad," she informed the two older women. "She can even beat Copper on a good sol."

"Belay that, Lieutenant," her friend said snappily. "Hand to hand isn't wrestling, though Zills makes it look that way. And she has a height and weight advantage over the rest of us. She'd make a fearsome security officer."

"As long as it's not on the *Drake*," was Linen's response. "What are they staring at?"

"Us. They're probably looking for those tattoos you told the guys we were going to get. They'll be wondering where they are, since these suit-blouses are a tad revealing about the shoulders and almost everywhere else as well."

"I'd forgotten about that! We'll have to get it organised."

"I'm having a blue dragon on *my* butt," Copper announced. "Where do we go?"

"Will you two behave?" Corona ordered sharply. "But there's a place on Artisan Square by the name of Ivyleaf Designs that'll do you a tattoo if you're set on it. Though I suggest an arm or a leg: laser burn on your butt hurts."

The two looked at Ms Lyrican senior in surprise and then at each other.

"Do you have a tattoo, Ma?"

"Mind your own business, lady," Corona responded with a twinkle in her eye. "And try your cocktail: it's a Sunspot Surprise and a house special. We have a few minutes before dinner."

Those few minutes were spent in an assessment of the other occupants of the bar, but no-one else appeared of any interest. Linen was forbidden by her friend to approach their two fellow-trainees, but both could tell that Dingle was gratified that he had been seen in company.

"Bet he hopes we'll tell everyone back at base that he was out on the Dome with a date," Linen giggled. "It'll up his charm score no end."

"As he and Zills will no doubt bleat about meeting us here, he can do it himself," Copper told her. "Though I suspect we're going to be on the receiving end of a heap of lip about all this."

"We can handle it. But here's our summons to table, so let's go see who else is about that we know. Hang onto your jacket: we don't want our stat bars going AWOL."

"You two aiming to turn heads with those are you?" Magenta demanded, having caught the exchange.

"Pays to give out that you have clout, Grammy, you should know that," Linen answered. "But if you see anyone in here that you know and think we should know, tell us."

"Get on in and mind your manners. I'll give you the nod," Ms Firewall added more quietly. "I don't see anyone so far."

"Except Karben and Bilkitt," Copper interjected. "Maybe *they're* on a hot date. They didn't expect to see us in here, that's for sure. Look at the outraged faces over the plates. And here we are at a table in direct line of sight. Isn't that handy?"

"They have to eat somewhere and Beagle's not a big place. And they'll be billeted here, they're upper top brass," her friend surmised. "Wonder how long they're around?"

"I wonder *why*," was the mordant response.

The first part of the dinner passed peacefully enough despite the flashing smiles that Linen felt bound to bestow to annoy the two from Outer Mars Ops every time one of them looked over. It was towards the end of the main course that Magenta figured why the officers had prolonged their dinner way past dessert: a small metallic cone with two fine blue crystalline rings around it that she had set on the table, with a finger to her lips to caution the other three, had begun to glow and to send out a discrete holo-note. Ms Firewall slid the gadget to Copper, who instantly grasped what was happening. Discretely, she tapped her ear and pointed to the nearby table.

"Nice try, Colonel Karben, Commander Bilkitt," she said in a cold voice. "But I suggest you turn your listening device off and retreat while you can or I *will* make a very public scene about your bugging our table. And I will of course be reporting this incident. Have a very nice evening."

As the cone's holo died, Copper and Linen turned their eyes on the two officers. The former began a rapid verbal note into her wrist-comm as Colonel Karben rose and approached.

"What in hell was all that about?" she challenged them furiously.

"So you were listening!" Magenta spat, eyes flashing and just as livid as the colonel. "Whatever badge you wear that you think gives you the right to bug private conversations cuts no ice with me and I suggest you back off now. I've met your kind before and believe me I know how to deal with it."

"Out," Copper ended her link, flicking off the button of her wrist-comm, steepling her fingers and looking up at the colonel.

"Did it never occur to you two that we're keeping you under surveillance for your own protection?" Karben demanded in a low voice.

"No, it never did," Copper told her blandly. "Are you?"

Karben compressed her lips. "I'll be taking this up with your senior officers!" she snapped. "And as for you, Ms Firewall, you are treading on dangerous toes. I suggest you watch your step." She turned and strode off.

"Who were you calling?" Linen asked her friend curiously.

"No-one, I was just making a note. I don't really think we can annoy Auntie Elle with this, she's had enough of us to last a lifetime."

"*I'll* be making waves," Magenta said to the duo. "You heard nothing, Corona. Finish your dinner and we'll have a look at the dessert menu. Those two are off to sulk somewhere, no doubt."

"That's a chill piece of kit," Copper marvelled. "It gives you the source of the scanning beam very accurately."

"You have it to add to your collection. I have another one somewhere," she was told. "I developed it as a prototype for something else I had in the pipeline ages ago. It has its uses."

The remainder of the meal passed with no further incident and all four decided that an early run back to the home unit was preferable to more adventures.

"Wonder where Dingle and Zills have sloped off to?" Linen speculated, looking into the Smoky Pearl Lounge as they passed.

"Dingle's quarters," was the laconic reply.

* * *

Wedsol found the two up betimes in order to arrange the transfer of their various belongings to their place off Road Five. Corona had left for work and Magenta was away on some spree of her own. Linen looked around at the mound on the floor of the sleeping quarters she shared with her friend and scratched her head, deciding that a travel-cab would be the best option.

"It'll charge you excess baggage if you load all that onto it," Copper remarked. "Wouldn't you be better calling a removals transport?"

"Very funny. Where's your stuff?"

"In the hall, all packed up. What do you need a hand with and what can you leave 'til next time?"

With a great deal of argument and an exchange of thrown cushions, Linen's packing was finally completed and a travel-cab ordered to take the two and all their goods and chattels to their own place, a few blocks east from their current location. As the cab progressed along Memory Avenue, Linen looked around.

"I feel like I did when I left home for my job of rock-sorting out at that geo lab at Argyre, years ago," she said. "Except I was going in the opposite direction and Ma was with me to wave me off at the spaceport."

"*Our* next job will be a lot further out than Argyre," Copper stated. "Wonder who'll be seeing us off then?"

"All our mates at Lowell, I should think. We'll have to leave from there as we'll need to collect the samples we're taking and have them transported to our store aboard the *Drake*. I expect we'll get our orders, shuttle up to the ship and then report to somebody. But here we are. At least we can get straight in using our implants now – saves hunting out idents."

With more wrangling and a cheeky wave at Unit One's door-cam, which was swiftly set in motion the second they arrived, the two paid the cab and tumbled through their own front entry, hauling kitbags, carryalls and boxes behind them.

"These light-arcs make the place look like some upmarket penitentiary," Copper complained. "Can't we change them to pink cross-hatching or something?"

"Later. Stow you kit in your room and then we'll check the place out. Then we'd best head for this Ivyleaf Designs place Ma mentioned. You still want a tattoo?"

"It seemed a better idea last night, but I'll still go for it if you will."

Linen's eyes creased gleefully. "Deal done. I'll have my gold dragon, if they can get the colour right. I have a copy on my wrist-comm that I made of the hard-holo Ma gave me."

"We'd best look smart for Ma Kellyn, but I don't think she'll appreciate the glad rags we wore to the BC. She'll think the tops are indecent," Copper declared. "But comfortable kit if we've to show flesh for the tattoo. I still think my butt's the best option."

"Ha! You just don't want people to see it. And you might not be able to sit down after it's done."

"Don't be a flooshy, your Ma was just yanking our chains. It doesn't hurt," Copper told her as she kicked her larger carryall into her private room. "I hope," she added to herself.

Half an hour later and shipshape, the two were enjoying a small mug of caff in the fam-kitchen. They had decided that a cab ride to Artisan Square would save effort and leave time for a walk to Skady Apartments and their rendezvous with Ms Kellyn.

"Bet she's been working like a green-arsed gnat since we saw her last to get the place half-decent for the holos she expects us to take," Linen smiled across the table. "But I hope we can coax a couple of our instructors into taking her up on a place: most of them must have had to ship in from outside as Beagle One's a new base and if their quarters are anything like ours, there's no place to hang your hat, much less to swing a mouser."

"We'll find out soon enough. Finish your caff, our ride will be here in a dot," warned Copper. "But we'd best start getting used to shifting under our own power again or our muscles will think we're torturing them once we're back to Sarn't Biskott's phys drills every frocking sol."

"We could practice our hand to hand later if you like? The fam-hub here's large enough," Linen offered.

"Just get your stuff."

"Yes ma'am."

* * *

Their travel-cab had indeed turned up at the door and in a very short time the two were within the tasteful interior of the body art salon at Ivyleaf Designs, a small operation that would artistically adorn almost anything within reason, for an agreed price. Linen had opted for a small illustration of a holo-dragon named Blueberyl that she had once ridden in the Fantasy Realm of the Dominion Holo-Suites facility at Beagle's Leisure Dome. Copper's choice was her own ride on the same occasion, a hard-holo blue dragon that had rejoiced in the name of Scalenyx and to which she had become inexplicably emotionally attached.

"That's chill!" the enthusiastic redhead breathed as, work complete, she could see in the mirror the tasteful artwork that now decorated the back of her upper left shoulder. She twisted and turned to view the design from various angles as she waited for her friend.

Copper was equally enchanted with her own tattoo, in a similar place on her own frame. A quick shrug of her shoulder and the blue creature seemed to move, its scales shimmering.

"I see you didn't aim for your butt in the end," remarked Linen as she admired.

"Oh didn't I?" Copper pulled a section of her lower clothing down to reveal another tattoo on the upper left quadrant of her left buttock.

"What in blazes is that?"

"Absolutely no idea," was the reply. "It flew into my head and was so clear that I drew it on the board; the therapist copied it into the auto-laser, and here it is. That's what took so long."

It was a symbol that neither could link to anything they had seen before. It was roughly rhomboidal but consisted of curls and flows within and without the main shape. It was a dark blue with pinkish infilling.

"The colours aren't exactly as I imagined," Copper told her friend. "But it was hard to pick out what I think I was seeing in their colour charts."

Linen looked closely at the design and then at her friend. "Think you had help?" she asked quietly.

"Maybe. Let's pay our bills and head on out. We have plenty of time, so we don't need to rush."

"We can keep going out of Artisan and onto Zaranj," Linen decided as the two regained the walkway. "That way we come into Skady Lane from the south side and see what's down there. We didn't get beyond Ma's apartment block the other sol."

"I'm still wondering how Ma could afford to buy an entire apartment block. Even with financial aid, it wouldn't have come *that* cheap."

"Maybe she *did* persuade brother Pinker to cough up some credit; he inherited half-shares from Uncle Whatsit Kellyn when he passed on up at Phoenix. *And* they had the apartment to sell, if I recall," Linen said.

"That was up in Phoenix," argued Copper. "That's hardly a place you'd get top price for anything, seeing it's in the northern polar region."

"You'd be surprised: salt mining, water abstraction, minerals, metals... lots to be dug up, up there. And as Ms Kellyn *was* a target for those crooks trying to dun her out of some of the estate, it must have been substantial."

"She'll not tell us, so let's start walking. My butt's nipping," Copper went on after a moment. "Yours?"

"Not my butt, no. Other places, yes. But now we're out in the open and I see no prying eyes, what's with the tattoo on your butt? Spook?"

"That's what I figured. The symbol was so clear that I had to draw it; and the therapist asked what it was, so I had to say it was a tribal design I'd been toying with for a while as a tattoo. So naturally he suggested that he would do it at a reduced rate, since I'd got one already…"

"And to allay suspicion, you said yes," Linen guessed.

"That's about it. If anyone asks, it's just a fancy motif that I picked out of an auto-designer random sampler tablet."

"So nobody can ask for the same design… good thought," Linen agreed. "Still, it beggars the questions what is it and why does Spook want you to know about it."

"No doubt I'll find out some sol. Meanwhile, I'll keep it under wraps as far as possible."

"Not difficult, given where it is," Linen laughed. "Just be careful in the communal shower block back at base."

As the two strolled along Zaranj Street they speculated on what Ms Kellyn had been doing to the apartments within the block since last they saw her. They had called up the spec of the property on Linen's wrist-comm but learnt little: having been in the hands of Law Enforcement previous to the recent purchase, information had been restricted and sales particulars had only been available on application to the relevant body.

"Trust Ma!" Copper sniffed. "But it's not a massive block. It seems to have two levels above the ground floor and only one below and it's long and narrow at the front. But there's no clue as to apartment size. You mentioned they were tiny?"

"By all accounts but I've never been closer to it than we were yestersol," admitted Linen. "We'll soon find out: here's where we turn. And cut-price warehousing about sums up *that* piece of dereliction," she added, pointing ahead. "I wouldn't want to be walking down here on a dark night. It's fenced off and there are warning signs but it doesn't say what about, just keep out."

"Don't even think about scanning," Copper warned. "There will be hover-cams sweeping the place even if we can't see them. But it can't be very underhand surely, given it's so close to ex-Law Enforcement accommodations?"

"Best place for any dark dealings: who would try anything or look too closely?"

The two continued and found that they were a few minutes early. They used the time to attempt to scout out the rear of the property but found the way barred on both sides by high gates.

"Just the edges of the block and the buildings on each side," Linen noted. "And everything's the same shade of dull. But this pathway looks cleaner than yestersol. The tiling of the entry's been spruced up, the plas-glazing of the porch is cleaner and the missing bits have been replaced. Ma wants the front to make an impact, then. I suppose I should start gathering visuals."

The semi-opaque plas-glazed panel that made the front door had also been scrubbed and the legend 'Skady Apartments' set in, lest any visitors missed the name on the ground beneath their feet. The ident-reader that permitted entrance was new, as was the series of buzzers, and several less than discreet door-cams were angled to catch the whole area of access.

"Twelve apartments," Copper noted from the buzzer array. "Three on each level. Don't think I'd want a basement place."

They were interrupted by the opening of the front entry and the solid form and dour countenance of Ms Kellyn, who greeted them shortly with the observation that they were on time, which was unusual in a dome where many, particularly tradespeople, seemed unable to read a chronometer, or to keep to prearranged schedules. She gruffly invited them to step over the threshold.

"I expect you won't stop long, having a lot to do," she went on, eyeing the pair.

Copper was having trouble keeping a straight face: a holo-pic of Ma's cat, Altair, was set above a row of mailboxes on the wall opposite the entrance. Apart from those and some secure-cams in strategic locations, the small hall was empty of everything but pots of holo-plants in two of the corners: Ma was evidently not inclined to encourage loitering by providing seating.

"Elevators *and* stairs," Ms Kellyn pointed out. "But as I have still a lot to do up there, I thought I'd give you a tour of two of the roomy apartments on this level. The lower level is accessed that way."

As the levels above and below seemed to be only partially lit and strange scouring and bumping noises could be heard issuing from nearby, the two assumed that an army of cleaning bots was in operation. Ma was by this time extolling the cleanliness of the main lobby and the fresh wash of pure colour she had used for the walls: the previous blue and silver check smacked too much of the erstwhile occupants, she told them severely. And the lighting had had to be increased – all manner of muck had been hiding in the corners when first she viewed the place.

There were four entries on the ground level, three of which were labelled four, five and six; the last bore the legend *Private*. Ms Kellyn had chosen number four for their first visit, and the privacy light, the external memo board and the high level of security were pointed out in a tone that demanded appreciation. Copper knew Ma of old and trod the ground carefully.

The main apartment room with its pink colour-washed walls was hardly larger than Copper's small home had been at the Kellyn residence on Road Eleven off Flagstaff Avenue back at Lowell, but it sported the usual Linking-Laundry facility; it was also equipped with a heat box, a luxury that Copper's place had lacked. The two visitors were wise enough not to draw attention to its deficiencies in terms of lack of generous closet space as doors to catering, hygiene and sleeping units were spotlighted by the landlady.

"A *separate* sleeping unit, as you can see," Ms Kellyn pointed out, scenting the lack of enthusiasm as she flung the door as wide as it would go into a diminutive chamber that contained a short bed and sliding closet space that had been left open to make the room look larger. "With a *real* window to the front!"

Copper nodded, not trusting her tongue. The more fluent Linen let loose a few choice phrases and swept the area with her wrist-comm, informing her friend that it would certainly impress one or two of their instructors back at base. Probably, Copper thought, only not those that Ms Kellyn would want as tenants.

"And what rent are you asking for this size of apartment, Ms Kellyn?" she enquired politely.

Ma drew herself up in annoyance. "Rates are on application," she announced. "Tenant's contracts are sacrosanct, you should know that. And as you have an apartment you can call on and won't need one of mine, I'll thank you to remember that."

"Of course, ma'am. But we *will* be asked."

"I'll give you my details for these apartments and prospective tenants can link to me. There's no call for you to hand out my facts and figures willy-nilly. This way to the very handy kitchen."

The very handy kitchen was tiny, but larger than the catering units in Ma's apartments back at Lowell, Copper admitted. The freshly furbished hygiene cubicle was also spacious and sported a sizeable tub. In view of the dimensions of many of Beagle's Law Enforcement officers and their resultant appetites when off duty, that was not surprising, Linen informed her in a low voice. Ma had evidently changed the décor, but the appliances were the original.

"I *will* be replacing those in here," Ms Kellyn added as she pointed to a sagging sofa and two chairs in the main apartment. "The shelving and entertainment unit will be left, as will the task-station, dining fixtures and that low table; though *that* will have to be resurfaced. Whoever had it last was as bad as Young Bronze Jerryd: *he* has no consideration for my property at all."

"Is Bronze still with you at Road Eleven, ma'am?" Copper enquired of a rather unruly ex-neighbour.

"He's on his final warning! A spoilt carpet was the last straw, but he's paid for the cleaning of it. Though I now have a very polite young lady, a friend of young Maressan's intended, Jenika, in *your* old place," Ma smirked. "And she likes cats!"

"That's handy," Linen remarked. "As Altair knows your old place like the back of his paw and where you kept his bowl and his Kittychew Crumblies. You left them there, I expect?"

"Of course I did; you can't have pets at basecamp and I'd no use for them. How are Maressan and Jenika, anyway, ma'am? Both still with you at Road Eleven and well, I hope?"

"Naturally. They're ideal tenants; well, apart from that home-brew, but Jenika will soon have *that* pastime under control once they're legally paired and sharing an apartment. But *this* place is very spacious and is more than sufficient for a singleton, or even a couple," Ma went on, eyeing the two. "Though I don't expect you get much of *that* at your training camp."

Copper was tempted to ask what *that* meant, but agreed that quarters for those in legal partnerships were not an option at Beagle One Basecamp.

"Time is marching on," Ms Kellyn announced. "You'd better see the second apartment. It's number six, down the hall."

She led the way regally and the two followed, grinning at one another, through the next but one door panel. As the place lit up, they could see that it was almost identical to the previous place, with only the wash covering the various walls changed to soft green and the one real window in the main room rather than in the sleeping unit. As Ma enumerated the virtues of the place, Linen enquired if these were examples of the larger of the apartments available. The response was a frosty stare and the statement that prospective tenants would be invited to view if they needed more information, and would she like an interactive plas-film describing the superior amenities on offer and the convenience of the block to anyone working in or near Central.

Copper's mind had slipped elsewhere and with a quirky smile asked Ma if any of the homes were currently occupied. The icy eyes narrowed suspiciously as the landlady took in the question and chewed over the veiled insinuation behind the enquiry.

"That's none of your concern."

"It is if they're up to no good," she replied.

"Cop?" Linen demanded.

In answer, Copper walked over to the door viewer and called up the area just outside the apartment. There was a face looking up. The attached body held some sort of scanner and the hands were manipulating the device. Copper tabbed the door open.

"Can I help?" she demanded as Ma Kellyn spluttered in fury behind her.

The man had pulled something from a pocket but both girls were faster and he found himself staring at the business ends of a pair of small weapons.

"I keep mine set to kill," Copper announced calmly by way of explanation.

The man held both hands up but his face was hard and impassive, evaluating her, wondering if she were bluffing.

"I don't," said Linen and fired.

7: A TASTE OF COMMAND

Linen considered the prone form on the floor, prodding it with her foot. "I thought he'd be better out of action," she said to the other two, not looking up. "I didn't like the look on his face or the gun in his hand."

"You and me both," her friend told her. "We'd best get Law Enforcement I expect; they're only down the road after all. Just as well it was your mini-stun you pulled. Your PPF would have blown his face off. But it must be set to heavy stun, otherwise he'd still be standing."

Ms Kellyn was visibly shocked and Copper left Linen to sort out the link whilst she assisted the woman to the sofa and made her sit down.

"Is the drinks dispenser operational?" she asked, pocketing her own firearm.

"I have supplies down the hall in the Private store," Ma said, handing her a security ident with shaking hands.

"You sit tight, ma'am, we're dealing with it," Copper advised as she set off. "I'll get some caff organised," she added to Linen in the passing.

Five minutes later, with Ms Kellyn recovering from her fright and sipping well-sugared caff, a chime at the entry signalled the arrival of a brace of officers of the Law. Linen headed off to let them in. Unspoken exchanges between the trainees had resulted in a swift examination of the insensible man and the abstraction of two weapons and another scanner, which were now sitting on the low table. As far as they could tell, the intruder carried no identification but they had no way of rapidly assessing implanted IDs. The two had also tacitly agreed that they knew nothing about the situation and were in no way inclined to speculate about motive. Copper took it upon herself to suggest to Ma that she took advice from a local crime prevention officer and upped her security: a property in process of upgrading was likely to have new and potentially expensive equipment around and thus might be a target for light-fingered reprobates.

The two officers had set off their hover-cam as soon as they entered. One knelt to examine the body, which was by this time recovering its senses, and to make sure it was suitably secured. The other introduced himself and his colleague as Officers Jay Sleet and Dirk Pellin and enquired what had occurred. Linen began to give her account of the situation, admitting that she had rendered the man in his current state, as he had pulled a gun and had looked as if he was quite capable of using it. She considerately informed them of her rank and handed over the stun that she had used on him. Copper raised an eyebrow and pulled out the licence tag for her more deadly handgun, which she wore around her neck. She was still on the sofa solicitously assisting Ms Kellyn, who by this time had regained most of her composure and all of her temper and was raging over the attempt on her property by a weapon-toting person unknown.

"I have one tenant in possession," she announced. "He came with the building, but that isn't him. I've never seen that piece of trash in my life. But how did you know he was at the door?" she demanded of Copper.

"I heard something outside; that's why I activated the viewer. I expect you don't have full soundproofing set yet, ma'am."

Ma knew her ex-tenant sufficiently well to know that she was not being totally candid but said no more than that it was lucky that she and her friend were armed, or who knew what would have happened.

The two younger women were required to explain why they were viewing the property as a medi-bus was summoned for the alleged felon. They were still talking when two paramedics with a gurney strode in to collect him. Officer Pellin set off with the group while his partner scooped the weapons and scanners into an evidence sleeve for removal to a secure place. Officer Sleet's view that a team of experts would have to inspect the building for means of entry and any other clues as to the motive for the attempted crime was met with outrage by its owner. Ms Kellyn gave vent to her displeasure in no uncertain terms and Copper and Linen were only glad that they were not to be faced with a trip to the local police HQ down the road for fuller statements, at least at the present time.

"How did he get in?" Ms Kellyn demanded.

"He wasn't carrying anything other than the weapons and the scanners that I could find," Copper said. "No credit, no ident, no key. So that's a mystery. It could be that he dumped his gear after he got in, or he has a host of very sophisticated implanted hardware that he used. Or someone let him in, the question then being, *where* is that someone now? Or is there another way in that you don't know about, or has he been here for some time and his goods are stashed elsewhere?"

"Maybe a window was left open?" Linen suggested.

"They're non-operable," Ma put in. "The emergency exits are clearly marked but they're for exit not entry. This place is very secure: I made sure of that as soon as I got it."

"In that case, ma'am, he must have had help," the LE officer announced. "Where is your current tenant based now?"

"Apartment two down below," Ma retorted with a dangerous glint in her eye. "And if he's had a hand in this, he's out; I won't have criminals on my property. Though I haven't seen him for at least a month; in fact I've only met him the once, when first I viewed the premises. He travels a lot, he told me, and only uses the apartment as a base when he's in Dome. But if he's sublet it or handed the ident to strangers then he's out. Let's check it."

She would brook no argument, despite the officer's plea that they call for back-up and she set off like a guided missile, the other three trailing.

Apartment two was empty, according to Officer Sleet's hand-held probe. Ma therefore let them in using her pass ident, scrutinising in some suspicion the hover-cam that had followed them. Copper and Linen looked around. They had no intention of using any of their own equipment to scan the place, but it was uncommonly tidy for such a downmarket block. That was one reason that Ma had probably accepted the place with a tenant *in situ*: tidiness and absence were greater virtues in her book than credentials.

Ma had no qualms about searching in closets and personal space. There was very little there. The only clues they had that the place was in use was a collection of expensive unguents in the hygiene unit, some edible greenery in the catering unit's frig box and a smart jacket over a chair in the sleeping unit. The laundry hopper held a couple of used towels but nothing else.

"We'll have to go over every micron of this place and we'll need the details of this tenant, ma'am," Officer Sleet declared. "His name – you said it was a male, didn't you – his business, his length of tenancy, his references as far as you know."

Ma drew herself up. "I have all I received from the previous owners – your *own* accommodation branch, by the way – on my info-pad," she announced, sliding the device out of her carryall. "As far as I'm aware, Mr Jecks moved into the place only…"

"Jecks!" Copper and Linen had uttered the name at the same time and in a tone that immediately alerted the other two to something amiss.

"You've heard of him?" Ms Kellyn demanded.

"Flinn Jecks?" Copper demanded. "Let me see the ident pic!"

"Shit! That bastard!" Linen exploded.

"I take it you both know him?" Officer Sleet asked as Ma drew in a scandalized breath at the expletives.

"The last *we* heard of him he was heading out under security escort to Beagle Hospital for treatment; he was supposed to be handed over to Beagle Law Enforcement to be dealt with once he got there," Copper told the officer with a grim mouth.

"Why?"

"Because three sols ago, Sunsol to be exact, that bastard tried to kill me. Fortunately, I got him first. Your people should have all the information: the incident in question happened out at the Amber-Warren field station of the Amberline Group of Lowell College. I have no idea if Ms Kellyn's current situation is linked to Jecks, but at the moment it's not our immediate concern. We have to go."

"You are material witnesses," the officer maintained.

"I doubt it. I advise you to check Ms Kellyn's internal secure cams as well as your own. Those and your examination of the scene should give you all the material you need to proceed with your case against the person you have in your hands now. Ms Kellyn, if you'd give me the contact details for your apartments,

I can pass them onto the appropriate parties when we're back at our base."

Ma was eyeing Copper in unrestrained amazement: this was not the well-behaved and unassuming ex-tenant she thought she knew so well. She promised to link the information across once it had been updated and supplied Copper with her current link information. With barely a murmur she led the two upstairs to the front entry, the ineffectual Sleet bringing up the rear.

Once safely in the cooler air of Skady Lane, Linen turned to her friend. "You've scared the underwear off Ma, you know: she's not sure what to make of this new you. But what do we do now? Auntie Elle?"

"I don't see an alternative. But we're not going to request a private link, we'll just leave an advisory on what's happened and she can take it from there. She'd no doubt be updated at some point anyway. But not in the open, we'll do it back at our place. And the hell with it, we take a cab, I'm seriously strained. Let's head to Artisan Square and pick one up there. And the rest of this sol had better be quiet or else."

* * *

"It's Grammy," Linen said some time later in the comfort of their own family hub. "She's taking us and Ma to the Carnelian Crucible for dinner tonight. And she's got something arranged for us morrow-sol at oh eight hundred hours someplace special, so she says we won't stay out too late tonight. And morrow-sol she'll take us to lunch after whatever it is she's planned and get us back to our place in time to collect our kit and get out to the dock at the crossover at Orbital and Evolution to catch one of the mil transports back to basecamp."

"I thought this was our furlough, not hers," Copper huffed. "I bet she's heard more of what's going on and wants us in her sights for as long as possible before we head on back to base. I suppose we'd best check the time our transport leaves: I for one don't want to be hanging about a transfer station for an hour. Oops! Here's a message... just an acknowledgement from the colonel that she received our link. Nothing else."

"Good. I hope that means we won't have to stand up before a Justice and say what happened," Linen stated. "It'll be taken over by the Service, as it all seems to be part of the same thing, including the leak on their side. Ma Kellyn will be pleased: the last thing she needs when she's trying to rent out apartments is a criminal investigation on the go and a whole pile of heavy boots all over her place. She left anything about the apartments at all?"

"Not a thing," Copper told her, rechecking her wrist-comm. "But I've had a link from Mik Mack reminding us to keep in touch once we're back at base."

"I got that too. Spook still around? I guess it was him tipped you off about the face at the entry, was it?"

"It was," Copper sighed. "He's always around more when we're out this way – closer to his home base, I suppose."

"Cheer up! Without him, I suspect we'd have been toasted once or twice."

"Without him, we wouldn't be so deep in all this intrigue over alien life on Mars in the dim and distant past," Copper said sternly. "Nor trainees about to be shot into the great beyond on a starship of the Fleet, just to keep us in line and out of the way of the machinations of very nasty people with thumbs in a lot of very strange pies," she added.

"But think of all the fun we'd have missed!" Linen grinned.

Copper threw a cushion at her.

* * *

The evening meal at the Carnelian Crucible was enlivened by the tale, well-watered down, that the two were induced to tell Magenta and Corona over their afternoon adventures in Skady Lane. Linen, to turn the conversation as she fiddled with their table's entertainment controls, demanded a hint on the pleasures planned for the morrow. Magenta would not be drawn, apart from the fact that the treat would take up two or three hours.

"Just be ready at oh eight hundred hours sharp, when I'll be there to collect you," her grandmother warned. "And dress comfortably for walking, no skimpy blouses or strappy sandals. And bring decent carryalls."

This was enough to set the two off, but no amount of cajolery would provide a clue. Resorting to a series of ingenious suppositions, a fractional uplift of the brows at the notion that the outing was away from rather than towards Dome Central suggested to Copper that the Leisure Dome was the most likely objective; she was gratified when her articulation of the idea elicited an annoyed snort from Ms Firewall.

"Any more harassment and neither of you will be going!" she announced at last. "Colonel Moritz is welcome to the pair of you, is all I can say. I hope she knows what she's taken on!"

"So do we," Linen laughed. "But we'll leave it at that and say thanks a million in advance."

In Copper's view, a million thanks were liable to be several hundred thousand over the odds: she knew Magenta and knew that thanks might not be what they felt at the conclusion of whatever was in store.

* * *

Magenta had arranged a travel-cab on Thursol to take them to their appointed destination and she and it appeared promptly on the doorstep of Court Nine, Unit Five. The two were already kitted out for the sol ahead. A lengthy debate the previous eve on their return to their place had led Linen to infer from the proposed walkabout and the need for carryalls that they were in for an epic shopping spree, but Copper was not sure. It was a blind, she decided: Magenta was as accomplished a deceiver as Linen when it suited.

As the cab bowled along the majestic Memory Avenue and turned left down Route N1 for the Leisure Dome, the two had time enough to dissect the previous sol's exploits and enlighten Ms Firewall on the more alarming aspects that both had thought prudent to conceal from Corona. Enough was said by Magenta to let the two younger women realise that their enlistment to the Service and their coming posting to the *Drake* had been in some way engineered as a safety manoeuvre to protect them from the increasing dangers posed by organised groups trying to gain a toehold in the race to make the first physical alien contact by any human, as far as was known.

"Apart from the *Griffon*," Copper pointed out. "That appears to have been contact and no mistake."

"Wasn't that logged as a collision rather than a shake of the hand or the tentacle?" Linen argued, winking at her friend.

"Colonel Moritz will know more, no doubt," Magenta broke in. "And you'll find out more once you're aboard. But even with a privacy shield in place in here, that's not a topic for discussion and don't you two *ever* get to talking about it, even in fun," they were warned. "But here we are," she twinkled as she released the opacity controls to let the two peer out at their destination. "It's time you got some experience under your belts if you're to make a career out in the space-lanes."

"Dominion Holo-Suites!" both exclaimed.

"That's about it. I have business in Dome here, but you two are booked into something that *may* help your education a bit."

"Not another ride on our dragons across the fantasy world of Ultima Azuria Beta then?" Copper surmised.

"That won't help you aboard a ship of the Fleet, especially like the *Drake II*, on an exploratory," Ms Firewall admonished.

"I bet I know! It's the Adventure Suite isn't it?" exclaimed Linen, eyes shining. "Are we going on a sim trip to the outer planets?"

"I'd rather the one that gives you command of an explorer ship on an interplanetary survey," Copper said hopefully, trying not to dance up and down. "That would be the chillest ever."

"That's the one I figured would be most helpful, not that I've been on it. But it's quite a popular sim, so I had to book well in advance," Magenta notified them.

"It's also the priciest, if I recall," Linen put in quietly to her friend as Magenta paid off the cab. "Grammy, you are the best."

"I don't quite know what to say," Copper added, almost overwhelmed. "I…"

"Oh stow it, girl, and get on in. I know what I'm at. Just don't send your ship into too much trouble that you break an arm or something, because I won't be held responsible."

Once through the entrance of Dominion Holo-Suites the three made straight for reception, intimating to the hovering attendant that their suite had been pre-booked. Their first duty was to agree to the insurance proviso that any injuries as a result of individual indiscretion would not be covered. As the related safety briefing covered practically every activity they were likely to be involved in, it was almost certain that they would have no chance of winning a claim for anything whatsoever, however they behaved. That being the case, the older woman looked to the ceiling, bid them a speedy farewell and told them that she would see them topside later.

The guide assigned to the duo led them to their suite entry and tabbed their selected programme sequence. Having chosen to experience the simulation as a pair, she told them, one would have command of the Starship *Explorer* and the other would be the first officer. She handed over two large idents bearing the relevant logos and left them to it, suggesting that they follow the corridor they would find on the other side of the entry.

"Wonder how many arguments there are for block bookings of four or five?" Linen asked as she generously decided that her friend would make a better captain than she would and handed over the badge that bore the legend *SS Explorer* and three stars.

"Whatever fleet this *Explorer* belongs to, it isn't Mars Fleet," Copper said, accepting the emblem and slapping it on her jacket. "This isn't a captain's ranking insignia for sure."

"You're probably an admiral or something," Linen told her. "But after you, Captain, ma'am!"

The officer they found behind the door greeted them with a salute, eyeing their badges before addressing them respectively as Captain and Commander. He informed them that he was Lieutenant Blue and he was there to escort them to the bridge. A pale grey corridor, the schematics of which suggested it was level one, led to an elevator at the far end.

"You're not a holo," Copper noted astutely as they walked along. "Here to keep an eye on proceedings?"

"In this particular simulation, the management are required to maintain a watching brief."

"In case customers get rowdy?"

"Not exactly," he replied. "Some people can get carried away, especially those assigned as weapons officers, but in case there are visitors unsure of proceedings or shipboard protocol."

"Who don't know how to give or to obey orders, you mean," said Copper.

"More or less," Blue responded. "This way."

"Looks nothing like the *Drake*," Linen muttered to her friend in an aside meant to be heard. "Where are all the servo-outlets, the info-points, the bots, the busy personnel stuffing bits of kit down hatches in the deck?"

The brightly-lit lift seemed to be rising, if the whizzing lines of arrows on the info plate were anything to go by. Their escort advised them that were headed directly to the bridge above level four, where the duty crew was in readiness. The *Explorer* had received orders to depart upon their arrival.

"Not before I've checked my boards, it won't," announced Copper as some unseen voice informed them that they were passing level three.

"Bridge!" the voice called crisply and the elevator panel slid aside to reveal a curved, pale grey space of moderate dimensions with ops stations set about it at various angles to left and right.

"Captain on the bridge!" Blue announced and all the visible officers snapped smartly to attention.

"At ease!" Copper called out almost automatically and with a small frisson of pleasure: she was used to being on the receiving end of that response when having to salute senior officers during training sims back at basecamp.

"Your station, Captain; yours, Commander," Blue said with a slightly curious glance as he indicated a trio of chairs, which were set slightly higher than those around about, in the hub of the space and with a good view of the large holo-grid set up opposite the elevator.

Copper assumed the centre seat and Linen slid in at her right.

"Who gets the other one?" Linen wanted to know as she pulled an operations board across her knees and looked at the holos that were beginning to form.

"The duty officer of the sol, Commander," the efficient Blue replied. "At this time, I have that post."

"Then you'd better sit down," was the reply as Linen looked around.

Copper was doing likewise. Each of the bridge stations was clearly labelled with navigation, helm, comms, weapons, science and engineering being the most obvious. At each one, colourful arrays that were presumably instrument panels lit the spaces up.

"How much that the designers of Giordano's had a hand in the colour scheme?" Linen enquired facetiously at her elbow.

"I have planetside Central Docking Control on the comm, Captain," the comms officer announced from her station. "They are assigning us helm control: we can leave at our discretion."

"Course plotted and laid in, Captain," the navigator sang out.

"Best get this show on the road, then," Copper winked, looking at her sidekick.

"Heading four two three one mark two," Linen responded as she pointed to her ops board. "That's galactic grid delta four by six and the Fairway star system's our scheduled port of call. Our listed mission is to survey the third planet to assess the potential for exploitation or habitation. It's charted as uninhabited by sentient life, based on long-distance scans."

Copper had pulled her own ops panel over to examine the output and was amused to find that the map thereon showed the ship, its heading, and the instructions she should be giving her holo crew. Despite Blue's presence, an irresistible urge to see how far the system programmers had allowed for wayward clients seized her and she called out:

"Give me helm control: I'm taking her out."

She could hear Linen's quiet chuckle as a fleeting ripple of sound spread around the bridge before the voice of the officer at the helm announced transfer to the captain's station and the pattern on her board changed to show the docking web and the route that would have to be followed to allow the *Explorer* to make her way out and onto their designated course.

"We'll have to engage the light drive to get anywhere fast, I expect," Linen remarked as Copper grasped guiding toggles that had popped up and began to manoeuvre the vessel through the imaged tunnel of light that seemed to be the way into free space. "And those are nothing like the controls of the standard Ares-Class Mark IV four-man shuttle."

Their path lit up on the main holo-grid viewer against a star-spangled backdrop and the light-well that was supposed to allow them to travel at speeds in excess of light speed grew centrally.

"Take over, helm!" Copper called and was gratified to hear a response of "Aye, Captain," from the helmsman.

A swirling vortex of light filled the viewer, pulling the eyes into it as the officers, human and holo, were pushed down into their seats. The vortex flattened out to form a streamlined tube of bluish white and a voice could be heard across the bridge. "Speed increasing to LS 3... 4... 5... maximum LS achieved!"

With a jolt, the pressure eased and everyone straightened up, the helmsman calling out that they were now travelling at full safe velocity, their ETA at the Fairway star system being forty three minutes. The officer at the science station confirmed that no other ships were detectable close by and the one known star system that they would pass close to was Vernal Six.

Several minutes elapsed and the central viewer, now showing their course through what appeared to be a normal starfield, was moving swiftly. A gentle thrumming vibrating through the space indicated that all systems ops were running normally, the only interruptions being updates relayed by the officers of the various bridge stations. Linen had called up the spec of the *Explorer* and found that she was a small vessel as starships went, with a crew complement of only forty three.

"Comfort station's over there," she nodded to her friend. "In case you get space sick or worse. And the crew includes two catering personnel, a therapist, three medics and an exec officer. Doesn't explain what they all do, though."

"Vessel approaching on intercept course!" Blue interrupted. "Reading as hostile! She's targeting us!"

"Show me!" Copper demanded. "Red alert! All hands to battlestations! Get all the tactical info on her you can. Evasive!" she yelled as the main viewer expanded to show stars rushing apart and a dark grey ship lit in red approaching, clearly directly. Her size could not be judged, but the weapons officer had announced that she was big and requested targeting orders.

"What's her weapons' status?" Copper barked.

"Warming them up," Linen announced at her side. "Looks like we're in her sights…"

"Target her weapons and her engines!" Copper ordered. "Helm, keep us out of her targeting eyes!"

"Aye, Captain," echoed around the bridge and the crew was flung sideways as the *Explorer* shot out of the line of fire of the oncoming vessel.

"Suggest you lock in safety webbing, Captain," Linen said, attaching her own. "Looks like we're in for a rough ride."

She repeated the orders to the rest of the bridge crew and kept up a running commentary on the status of the ship as they were thrown this way and that and spears of light shot across the starfield.

Copper kept her own eyes on the main bridge holo-grid and found herself issuing orders to all the main stations on course, targeting and outcomes. She had used space hazard simulations before in entertainment and training situations, but this one was something else and as she conned over the bridge stations' data that was relayed to her own ops board, a small fizz at the back of her neck spread down her spine and around her ribs that she hardly recognised. As the pace of the battle seemed to slacken and the whirl of the starfield slowed to display a much-damaged enemy vessel that was out of firepower, Copper released her safety webbing and got to her feet.

"All stations, damage reports!" she demanded. "Get them to my ops station! How are our engines, Chief?" she demanded of the engineer. "I could hear them complaining."

There was a slight pause, as if the programme was reacting to the situation but thinking about it first. Linen raised an eyebrow, watching her friend intensely.

"Medical station, report in: I want our casualty list," was the next order. "And theirs," she added. "Where's that tactical on them, Lieutenant?"

This last was to the science station; the officer immediately sent the relevant data to the captain's console, calling out that the enemy ship was dead in space and suing for surrender.

"Comms, find out who they are and what the hell they were at," Copper ordered. "Get me a visual of their bridge."

"Negative on visual, Captain, their systems are shot," was the immediate response. "They're asking to leave in peace."

"Like hell! They'll only come back with reinforcements. I want their full spec and then we'll tow them to our nearest base in this sector and hand them over to the authorities. Relay that to their ship and get me their commanding officer right now…"

"Aye, Captain…"

There was a bloom of flame as the enemy ship exploded in an intensifying ball of fire, dazzling the watchers. As the *Explorer* rocked in the shock wave, Copper was flung to the deck.

"Evidently towing them out of the combat zone isn't in the programme," Linen noted impishly as she hauled her friend to her feet. "You all right, Cop? That was some display."

"Me or the holo?" Copper demanded.

"You. Holos like this I've seen before. Not as fancy to be sure, but more or less predictable. *You* on the other hand… You were really in the mental state. Why?"

"Been there before," was the short answer. "Cancel red alert! All hands stand down! All stations report!"

The ship had not been too badly damaged, the engineering officer confirmed, and was able to continue her pre-set course. Copper ordered the science station to scour for survivors and salvageable remains but the search came up negative on both counts. The fly-by of star system Vernal Six was next on the schedule and that was accomplished with little more than an exchange of comms with the locals and a look over their night-time southern ocean, which was alive with a multi-coloured phosphorescent bloom that could be seen from space.

The Fairway solar system was reached without incident and Copper gave the order for low planetary orbital insertion of the third planet as a prelude to the scheduled survey, clarifying her initial height as one thousand five hundred kilometres above mean surface level. According to her available instruments, that should be sufficient to evaluate any life on or under the planet and its levels of complexity. The star itself was a red giant and loomed like a great eye in the holo-viewer.

"It'll look big from down there," Linen informed her. "But we're not ordered to go down, are we?"

"At my discretion," Copper smiled. "Which means we go down if it's safe to do so; but I wouldn't risk taking the ship down, though I see she *is* cleared for emergency surface landing. So we go down in a shuttle, *once* probes have suggested it's safe to do so. You up for that? You can pilot the shuttle."

"Yo. You with us there, Lieutenant Blue?"

"Yes, Commander," was the reply. "Probes?" he went on to Copper.

"You don't think I'd risk taking personnel down there if I hadn't checked out potential biohazards? There *are* such things as biosafety protocols you know."

"I'm not a science specialist, Captain," Blue replied warily. "You know how to fly a shuttle, Commander?" he added to Linen, obviously a little out of his depth.

"Of course I do," Linen told him. "Wouldn't be in this chair if I couldn't, would I?"

"I expect not, ma'am. But may I remind you, Captain, that it is unadvisable for both ship's senior officers to be absent at the same time."

"Noted," Copper responded dryly. "But let's see what the scans are showing and then let's release sampling probes."

As the various stations reported their findings after several decreasing orbits in various inclinations of the planet below to produce a practical coverage, it was obvious that the world Fairway Three was essentially untenanted by sentient beings, or possibly any lifeforms above the level of mice that they could read, even in low orbit. Surface scans disclosed a dry, cratered place but there were several caches of what read as underground water that existed beneath large rocky outcrops scattered across vistas of gritty pinkish sand.

"It's like a large pink Mars with lumps of glassy red rock all over the place," Linen summarised, her brow crinkling as she scanned the composite readout. "It's as if much of the silica in the upthrust of crustal matter was fired. Systems of canyons and gullies on the surface of the main mass, deeper areas that could be impactive in origin and it looks like we have subterranean voids, like the Warren maybe, but bigger, below them. There are even polar ice-caps but they're small at this time; the ice reads high in nitrogen and phosphorus. Atmosphere higher in oxygen than Mars, lower in carbon dioxide; surface temperature range is slightly higher than home and there are indications of biomatter, particularly in these greyish areas but the planet won't support human life unaided."

"Neither does Mars. But if we have water ice and there are underground voids, we have habitation potential. But we need more data on any biological matter that's down there that might cause us trouble before we go anywhere, so we send probes in first. Science station, ready biosampling probes for drop – I want as much info as we can get on potential biosignatures. Let's target a section of the middle latitudes for a start."

Again, a perceptible pause was apparent before the science station duty officer reported that the probes were set to go on the captain's mark. Copper gave the signal and watched as a fleet of tiny blips was discharged from the *Explorer* and began to spread out in a wide field over the targeted surface below.

Quite suddenly a judder shook the ship and the wail of the red alert began to fill the air.

"Cut the noise!" Copper bawled. "What in blazes is going on?"

"Something's launching from the planet!" Blue called out.

"How can it, if it's not inhabited?" Linen demanded. "That's what initial distance scans showed, wasn't it? And ours haven't pointed to anything different."

"Increase orbit to three thousand kilometres; plot an evasive course," Copper ordered. "Can we outrun them? They seem to be some sort of missile. There's no organic content."

"So much for non-sentience," Linen shrugged, webbing herself in. "Here we go again…"

"They're moving with us, Captain!" the weapons officer bellowed.

"Then take them out! Helm, maintain evasive action but keep us close enough to target those missiles."

As the *Explorer* slewed and the expanding spread of her own firepower lit up their simulation sky, the crew clung tight to its seats. One particularly sharp jolt threw the weapons officer out of his chair and he tumbled across the deck.

"Commander Lyrican, take over weapons station! Medic to the bridge!" Copper ordered as she unhooked her webbing and stepped down to assist the officer, who was attempting to regain his footing.

Linen was quick to comply and tied herself in securely when she made it to the appropriate station. Copper, with Blue's assistance, helped the injured officer to Linen's empty chair and webbed him in. Blue looked hunted.

"All missiles accounted for, Captain!" Linen confirmed after a prolonged chase. "Tracking back to source… they seem to have emanated from beneath a rocky outcrop at nine one point two east by four three north on the grid. But we have no associated biosigns in that zone at all. Science, what have we got on that area?"

"Deep fissuring, kilometres below surface; numerous void spaces detected. But I agree, no biosigns. Perhaps they're old protective measures, set to launch when something big gets too close?" the officer hazarded.

"Which means there would be detection systems operable. So where are they and why didn't we detect them?" Copper questioned.

"They started when we dropped our probes," Linen told her. "Programmed to activate when they're being scanned?"

"Possibly; but I'm not dropping more probes just to find out, in case the system learns and sends up bigger ammo next time. Stand down red alert, all hands. How's the weapons officer?" Copper enquired of the medic who had appeared on deck and was ministering to the injured officer.

"Fine, Captain," was the bright reply. "Superficial only; he can return to duty."

"Then hop to it, Lieutenant. And you'd better get back to your station, Commander," she went on to her friend.

As Linen was doing so, the comms officer called out that they had received an urgent summons to return to base without delay for new orders.

"Time's running out," the redhead deduced with a grin as she slid into her seat. "That was fun. Think Colonel Moritz would let me loose at the weapons station aboard her ship?"

"Like hell. Acknowledge orders, comms; navigation, plot us the quickest course home and then let's cook it, full safe speed."

"Aye, Captain," echoed around the bridge as Copper again called for status updates, scanning her ops board carefully.

The return to their point of origin seemed to be rapid and was accomplished with no further alarms. Linen had been right: their allotted timespan was running out.

"Central Docking on the comm, Captain," announced the helmsman once the *Explorer* had come in safe to their allotted bay. "Requesting transfer of helm control to maintain station-keeping."

"Transfer at your discretion, Lieutenant."

"Aye, ma'am. Transfer complete and now at station-keeping. Safe to disembark."

"Captain and first officer required for immediate debriefing in port, on the outcome of the mission to Fairway Three," the comms officer announced.

Blue leapt to his feet. "This way, Captain, Commander," he said smartly, leading the way off the bridge and into the elevator that would lead them to the pale grey corridor of level one.

Once in the lift, he eyed the two in some puzzlement. "If you don't mind me asking – are you *actual* officers? You seemed to know what you were at."

Linen inclined her head in the affirmative. "Well spotted," she said genially. "Lieutenant Lyrican, Lieutenant Milkstone."

"Which ship do you belong to, if I might ask?"

"That we can't tell you," Copper put in. "But thanks for your assist. It was an enjoyable experience."

Linen concurred and as they made their way along the deck to the exit, she kept Blue occupied by small talk. He seemed reluctant to let them go, but bid them farewell and disappeared behind his door.

"Off for a caff before the next lot," Linen surmised. "Looks a bit harassed. Bet he's not had many like us before. But we need to talk, Captain, ma'am."

"Not here. We'd best see if Magenta's turned up. I guess she knew our likely timescale," her friend said.

"I'll bet. I also bet you need a caff."

"I do; and a visit to the comfort station. Not to mention a quick shower. I suspect I've got one or two bruises from the overactive gyros that were causing the sim movement."

"You and me both. But there's Grammy. Lor' it's only just past noon! It seemed a lot longer!"

"I think that's the idea," Copper smiled as they walked over to Ms Firewall, who had commandeered comfortable seating by the exit and was sipping a beverage of some description.

"Take the weight off and tell me all about it!" she bellowed over. "Want the souvenir holo-vid?"

"No thanks, Grammy. But it was fun. Though I think we gave them a headache or two."

"That's what I like to hear!"

After a quick rundown on the details of their adventures on their virtual interplanetary survey mission, Magenta hauled the two off for a late lunch. She decided to make for Dome Central and asked if they had any particular choice of venue. Copper looked to Linen as the fount of knowledge in that area and the redhead was quick to suggest the Shuttle Shed on Barnes Street as a place she had often wished to visit but never had.

"It's an eating and drinking den with a hardnosed pilot theme, so I've heard," Linen said with a wink.

"I've heard that and a lot more besides," Magenta growled as she waved to the travel-cab she had ordered. "You two want to go there, I suggest you get more hand-to-hand combat training under your belts. We'll try the Engine Room on McClintock Road: it's similar but less rowdy and close to your Ma's work, so she'll be able to join us for a bite and get a look at the pair of you before you sail off back to your basecamp. I'll link her now. You two get in and behave while I do that."

"How did you know Blue wasn't a hard-holo?" Linen asked quietly as the two settled down. "It's difficult to tell sometimes that they *are* holos, I grant you, but…"

"He was wearing scent and it wasn't parfum de holo-system lube," was the flippant reply. "And he kept eyeing you up like a lovesick flooshy while we were on the bridge."

"More fool him, he wasn't my cup of creamy caff. And what was with all the action? Weren't we on an interplanetary survey? That suggests more than one planet," Linen continued.

"When you've only got three hours real time, surveying a bucketload of alien landscapes probably isn't a viable option."

"Especially when you decide you want to launch probes to look for biosigns before you'll risk sending a shuttle down. I expect the artificial intelligence of the system had a lot of quick thinking to do over that," the redhead laughed quietly. "But you figured out what was going on as if it wasn't new to you; *and* you said you'd been there before – Spook?"

"Spook. He was with me, I felt it."

"But I thought he was in a small scout, a one-man or one-alien craft," puzzled Linen in a whisper.

"He was when we found him – or rather when he found me. And he'd been there for millennia," was the equally soft reply. "But he must have had some sort of life before he ended up in that ship – and I'm beginning to think his ship's more than just a scout. But that's what I reckon the déjà-vu was. I felt I knew what the situation was like."

"What's keeping Grammy? Can't track down Ma at the lab? Oh, here she is," the redhead added as Magenta climbed in. "Made the link to Ma?"

"Yes, she'll join us," was the brief reply. "Let's go."

"You realise we'll have to leave a lot out when we retail our exploits to our colleagues back at base?" Linen informed her friend as the travel-cab set off.

"I can't imagine many of them will be very much interested," was the reply. "They'll be too busy trying to get back into shape and keeping their heads down; we're way more than halfway through now, so that's us on the final stretch."

"We should have been finished by now and would have been if there hadn't been delays to the *Drake*. What caused them anyway, do you know, Grammy?" demanded Linen.

"No. Even if I did I wouldn't be discussing them here, and neither should you," Magenta apprised her abruptly. "You never know who can listen in to a travel-cab, for all they're said to be private and sound-proof. You two got your packing done for heading out later?"

"Mostly," Linen admitted. "You, Cop?"

"All done," Copper told her.

Magenta kept the topics to mundane until they reached their destination. The Engine Room was a small feeding and watering hole on McClintock Road and a short way from the main artery of Blur Avenue. It was run on lines neat enough to qualify as vaguely upmarket and the three soon found themselves seated and awaiting Corona Lyrican, whose employment at a laboratory in the nearby Science Park would allow her to join them quite quickly. Ms Lyrican was timely and once settled and the privacy shield around their table invoked, the exploits of the sol had to be discussed again. It soon became obvious, however, that the two older women had more on their minds than light banter.

Copper had received the first warning as a vague anxiety that grew as she listened to the general chit-chat with which Magenta was attempting to lighten their ears. Ms Firewall was evidently restless, which was an unusual event as it was.

"What's happened?" Copper eventually demanded bluntly. "Something's been going on that we don't know about and you're both disturbed by it."

Linen nodded. "I was beginning to get the impression that all this jawing was a cover for something. Come on, out with it. What is it, Grammy, Ma?"

"Your friend Jecks and his playmate – the one you damaged at your landlady's new place – have been sprung from the tight clutches of Beagle Law Enforcement," was the answer. "I had a link from Colonel Moritz to warn me as I was trying to link to your Ma," Magenta told them. "The Law evidently had been told that the Service was going to be relieving them of their charges. Only it wasn't the Service that got there first. Two medics at Beagle Hospital have been hurt as well as a couple of law enforcement officers. There's an all-points bulletin out for the villains but they've evidently got friends in high places and they'll be well away by now. But basically, watch your backs: there's no saying if this will track back to you, but be careful. It's probably the goings on out at your site that's at back of it – some people want their hands on what they think is down there and they want it fast. That's what led to your trouble in the first place. And they are very nasty people, as you're well aware."

"Damn!" Copper hissed softly, realising what had triggered her anxiety: Spook was getting worried about his ship.

"Once we're done here, we're all going back to yours," said Magenta. "You get packed up and I'll get you out as planned, as there's a transport heading over to your base from the military dock at the Evolution and Orbital Route crossover that'll have your name on it. So eat up."

Copper sighed. "Damn!" she said again. "When will we *ever* get any peace? If you're not finishing those chippers, pass them over," she ordered her friend. "I need sustenance."

"The sol something dulls Cop's appetite we're *all* in trouble," Linen said affectionately. "We can take care of ourselves. You shouldn't worry about us, Grammy."

"It comes with the family contract," Magenta informed her roughly. "You should read the small print."

"I love you too, Grammy. And Ma. Just you two look after yourselves and stop scratching your heads over us. We'll be fine," Linen went on, winking over at Copper. "We've got all the back-up we need."

"I'm not even going to ask," Corona put in. "I'll order some ale. I think we all need it."

* * *

The next couple of hours followed Magenta's outline, more or less. There was a link to Copper from Ma Kellyn relating that the info-sheet Ma was preparing on her apartments was delayed as *certain people* were ferreting about her property like precious ore prospectors down a mine and Ma was not about to let them out of her sights just to organise plas-paperwork. She hinted heavily that her ex-tenant and the redhead probably knew more about the goings on than most people should, but Ma was not about to poke *her* nose into *their* concerns. On another note, had Copper heard anything from Majorelle recently? Ma always liked to keep in touch.

"Colonel Moritz," Linen nodded when she heard. "Wonder if Ma spotted her around Dome somewhere and this is her way of trying to find out why?"

"Isn't she supposed to be on board the *Drake*? I thought the commanding officer always had to be on hand, though I expect she has a first officer and a second officer, come to that. Why is she still concerned in all this? I thought it was the property of Outer Mars Ops or whatever Colonel Karben's bunch is called."

"And look how smart they are," Linen said ironically. "But we're her contacts and about to be part of her crew, and her mission has one heck of a lot to do with it. I hope Karben's lot have tracked down their own leaks at their camp out by *and* that they still have a tight grip on that pal of Jecks that was nosing around our site at the Warren. But where are Ma and Grammy? I thought they were here to help."

"Organising the neighbours, I think. Maybe asking if there had been strangers in the neighbourhood asking about her or us. Or snoopers."

"Just as well we're not paranoid; well at least I'm not," Linen said. "But the cab's due soon isn't it? We need to drop Ma and Grammy off before we head out to our transport stop."

All four were collected together soon afterwards. Magenta and Corona had indeed been visiting the neighbours to ask after snooping strangers but no one had seen anything. The younger women were relieved, knowing that the occupant of Unit One at least would have kept a weather eye on any comings and goings. It was with some amusement that Copper and Linen realised that Magenta had sent for a private armoured cab for their onward journey to the military dock off the Orbital Route.

"I'm only glad we don't have another leave before our final postings," Copper told her friend as she climbed aboard. "I don't think I could take it."

* * *

The transport designated as their ride back to basecamp was smaller than the usual bus that ferried batches of recruits hither and thither and was berthed in a secluded corner of the dock, to which the two were directed from the guard post. Although the vehicle did not physically sport their names, the two realised it was theirs when a familiar form strode out of the nearby office.

"Colonel Moritz!" Linen exclaimed. "We thought you'd be aboard your ship."

"I have business at Beagle Basecamp," was the reply. "Hop in. We'll have a chat on the way."

The chat was more or less a dissection of the problems that had bedevilled much of their leave. Both trainees were relieved to hear that Jecks' sidekick out at the Warren was still in secure hands and that two moles had been dug out of the ground at the nearby military base camp. With little left out, Copper and Linen were honest about both their experiences during and after their sojourn at their research site and their conjectures about the same. It was the former that brought up the subject that had given her some food for thought.

"It strikes me that there must be moles or at least a few bad eggs in Law Enforcement as well, as it was *their* ex-apartments that Jecks was originally holed up in. Unless *he* was an ex-law officer?" Copper posited.

"Very astute, and he was," the colonel informed them. "But he'd also completed military training, with two years in Ground Ops. He got out as he knew he wasn't promotional material, being too much of a troublemaker and hardnosed with it. Which of course caused disciplinary problems in the Law Enforcement Service, but recruits are hard to come by. He'll be found, but until he is, you two keep your heads down."

"We're unlikely to be doing anything else back at base," said Linen ruefully. "When do we get our postings?"

"When your assessors think you're ready and or when I send for you," was the dry reply. "But it won't be too long now."

"Just as long as Lieutenant Gadget Blazells isn't posted to the *Drake*," Linen grinned. "He's smart but he's got a streak of bad temper in him and a superiority complex we don't want to see more of. And he's scared witless of Copper."

8: BASEWORK

Beagle One Basecamp was quick to usher the transport through once the guards at the gate realised it was housing a colonel of the Fleet. It was not particularly late in the sol, but Copper and Linen found that they were not the first of their cohort to return from furlough. After a quick trip to drop their belongings off at their quarters, they headed into the mess. The first people they recognised were Blazells, Dingle and Zills.

"Looks like Foxy and Zills are still a twosome then," Linen chuckled. "Does Blazells realise he's being a gooseberry?"

"I'm sure Zak Zills would put him right if she thought he was," Copper informed her. "But I expect we'd better be polite. What made you tell Colonel Moritz that Blazells wouldn't be a good bet for the *Drake*?"

"Would you want him as a shipmate?"

"Nope. So let's hope she heeds you. But grab your caff and then we'll head over: they've seen us."

Zills had only just come into the mess, they found out, and had noticed the two of them alighting from their transport. She had already imparted the information to her two colleagues and all three were curious.

"So who was the top brass?" the jovial Zills persisted. "She had a colonel's ranking insignia, as far as I could see."

"You've got very good eyesight then," Copper temporised. "Where were you that you could make that out?"

"In the guardhouse talking to Joe Fells; he has a brother with Fleet Security, so I was pumping him for info. The surveillance screens were all operational and I spotted you. You can see your hair from half a kilometre away," she explained to Linen. "Once Joe figured a piece of brass was heading in and he hadn't been informed, he thought he'd better call it in."

"He must have been told, surely, if she was expected?" queried Copper.

"Not he; nor had his boss. They figured it was some sort of unscheduled inspection. But who was she that you two were able to scrounge a ride?"

"A colonel of our acquaintance; and that's as much as you need to know," Copper told her with half a look at Blazells.

"Oh come on…" Zills insisted.

"I suggest you don't probe. Or I'd have to tell the colonel that you were asking after her and her business, and then she'd have to have you taken out and shot." It was said with humour but Dingle was looking at the pair in a perplexed manner.

"But on another note," Linen interjected, her gold-flecked eyes sparking in mischief. "Just what were you two doing in the BC Hotel on Tuesol eve?"

"Cocktails," Zills put in swiftly. "But I suggest you don't try to probe, or we'd have to take you out and shoot *you*."

"Fair deal," the redhead laughed as she turned to the others. "Did you get as far as the Leisure Dome, Blazells? We were there earlier this sol, but we didn't hang around."

"I don't see that's your concern," was the sour retort.

"Please yourself," Linen shrugged. "How did you like the Plaza Hotel?" she went on to Dingle. "I haven't been there in years, so I don't know how it goes these sols."

"It was okay," Dingle told her. "Though I didn't stay but the one night; I moved across to the Pallas Hotel as they had rooms free there and it's handy for most things."

"What about you, Blazells? Did you move out too?"

"Why don't you mind your own business?" was the response.

It was evident that the lieutenant was not in a frame of mind for banter and Linen soon realised that it might have something to do with the loss of his best buddy's adulation, which seemed to have transferred to Ensign Zak Zills, with whom Dingle was exchanging glances.

The party was interrupted by the advent of a bunch of new arrivals: evidently another transport of trainees had come in and had disgorged its occupants, who were now on the lookout for company and caff. A handful settled down at the adjoining table and looked over. Ensign Bass Ferret was quick to congratulate

Copper on her suggestion of Giordano's as a party venue. Most had, it appeared, had a good time.

"Seen the internal message board yet?" he added. "You have a message outstanding that's marked urgent."

"We're still officially on furlough until morrow-sol," Copper announced irritably, but tabbed up the link at her table's console to check if Ferret was pulling her chain. "I have," she added to Linen. "It'll be Captain Max Meltdown, I bet, about that little dispute over Isidis on Satsol. He'll want to know who and where and why. Bet he'll say he knew it was me and it was a test."

"What little dispute over Isidis on Satsol?" Blazells asked curiously.

"It's not your concern," Linen told him sweetly. "Why don't you mind your own business?"

"It *is* Captain Meldyn," Copper sighed, raising her eyes to heaven. "Well, he can damn well wait."

"So what gives?" demanded Ensign Bonny Skate from the next table. "You met Captain Max the Melt over Isidis? What in hell were you doing?"

"Outflying him," grinned Linen. "Him and his tight schedule and straight beam. We were in a civilian transport and Cop was at the helm," she added ingenuously for the edification of their fellows. "He breached flight protocol; she set him straight and he didn't like it."

"I was in the right. What the hell way is that to teach trainees, flouting regs to show off?"

"Maybe it wasn't a trainee he was up with," Linen suggested.

"His private business I don't need to know," Copper told her as their companions began to question them on their presence aboard a civilian transport over the Isidis plain.

The two sidestepped the inquisition ruthlessly, mildly amused by the furtive baffled glances between Blazells and Dingle. Talk soon turned to the exploits of their comrades not yet returned. It seemed that most of the trainee cohort had spent their leave in some sort of dissipation or another, mostly centred on the attractions of Beagle Central. Copper and Linen escaped before long back to their quarters and their unpacking.

"We've done it now," Copper remarked. "They'll be talking about us behind our backs and Blazells will no doubt fill them in on what he thinks he knows, even though I told him to keep his mouth shut or else."

"You reckon? I think you scared him pretty effectively and Dingle will rein him in. But young Foxy and Zills the man-eater still look to be an item; wonder how long that'll last?"

"Until she captures a post in some security position and he's assigned somewhere else. She's made for security and as she's basically honest, good luck to her," Copper replied. "But Max Meltdown? And I wonder what Auntie Elle's business is around here, apart from keeping her eyes on us?"

"Maybe recruiting for the *Drake*?" Linen suggested.

* * *

Early Frisol found all the trainees back in harness and under gruelling physical instruction from the gritty and inflexible Sarn't Biskott and the acid-tongued Senior Fitness Instructor Chi, who were adamant that all should be put through their paces. It was in the gym that the tattoos that Copper and Linen had acquired on leave were seen and several positive comments received from their mates. The sharp-eyed Biskott, who was no fool and had been around several blocks several times, also noted the tiny licence tags that the two wore around their necks on the chains that carried their visible Fleet idents.

"So it's not only tattoos you two have been picking up," he remarked wryly, lifting up Copper's ident with his swagger stick and studying the smaller tag. "PPF licence, if I'm not mistook."

"You're not, sir," she replied, slapping the stick away and raising a challenging eyebrow.

"If you brought the hardware on site, I'm surprised you got it past gate security."

"We were in an armoured Fleet transport and in company, sir," she shot back. "And gate security doesn't tend to question a Fleet colonel on the way in. Maybe they should in future."

Biskott tilted his head and grinned maliciously at her. "Maybe they should at that," he responded, before bawling out orders for the next drill.

The next assignment for those of their group with relevant skills was flight simulation exercises followed by practice in real craft. Copper and Linen, along with Blazells and Dingle, had been allocated the Ares-Class Mark IV training shuttle as their ride. Copper had responded to Captain Meldyn's link earlier and had been assigned an interview with him before take-off. Her three colleagues had been ordered to wait on the observation deck whilst the meeting took place in one of the nearby briefing rooms. It was evidently a short dialogue for the trio were called only ten minutes later for the obligatory pre-flight briefing. Copper was grim-faced and Meldyn looked infuriated.

Dingle was appointed flight captain for the ride, with Blazells at navigation and comms; Copper and Linen were assigned the weapons and the surveying and mapping positions respectively. The trip was scheduled as short, a straight course west of north beyond Darwin, Beagle's westernmost Dome, with no landing and no drone target practice scheduled. Twenty five minutes later, the four trainees were allowed to depart for the hangar and were soon aboard their designated shuttle.

"Blazells, you keep your ears pricked for anything coming in over the comm: Captain Meldyn looked severe and that often means trouble," Dingle began. "Milkstone, we've been told we won't have target practice this trip but I'm not betting on it, so have our targeting systems online and our weapons ready for deployment. Lyrican, make sure what you see is what's down there. Everyone, web in and stay sharp."

"Aye, Captain," Linen responded with a wink at Copper.

It seemed that Flight Captain Dingle was out to impress, for he verified their ready status with Control as he performed the pre-flight safety checks and was set to taxi out to their take-off pad the second permission was granted.

Once in level flight, the ensign seemed to breathe more easily and demanded updates from his three crewmen, advising that they keep him posted on anything they noted. As the minutes ticked away and nothing but the reddish terrain below seemed to be visible, Blazells began to show a little restlessness.

"What's Captain Meldyn playing at?" he demanded. "These flights are supposed to test us and we've seen nothing yet."

"Testing our patience maybe," Linen told him. "Most flights are probably as boring as hell most of the time. And I sure as shells haven't seen anything not on the charts. Anything to shoot at, Cop?"

"Nary a thing. But check your flight screen, Captain Dingle,

I'm reading a blip at two three nine mark six, just on the edge."

"Got it," he confirmed anxiously. "It's getting closer; we should have a visual shortly. It's certainly airborne and heading this way. It may be a small shuttle but it's reading unregistered. I'll try to raise it."

"It may be a very big missile," Linen suggested as Dingle requested an ident on the incomer.

There was no response to their hail as Copper called out that her targeting had definitely identified it as a small, very fast craft and not a test drone of any kind encountered before.

"Captain Max testing us on a novel situation?" Linen asked wickedly, aware that their comms were almost certainly being monitored.

"No," her friend said decidedly, trying to hide a smile. "Got a visual yet? She's catching up on your side and I bet she flies a parallel course."

The small red-hulled fighter, its twin fins sharp against the sky as it banked to come around them, passed at a speed that left Blazells and Dingle almost breathless.

"One-man fighter," Copper announced. "Military. I wasn't aware there *were* test flights scheduled and I *did* check the boards for other craft from our base. We're the only scheduled flight at this time."

"Smartarse," Blazells muttered.

"Belay that," Dingle ordered as he repeated his hail. "This is Training Flight Six-Five-Six-Eight out of Beagle One Basecamp to unregistered aircraft in north-east quadrant sector twelve nine four three: please identify yourself, over."

"This is Red Bravo Two Niner on unscheduled manoeuvres in this area. Enjoy your outing, trainees; you have priority over me, out."

"Got the vis evidence?" Copper asked her companion, trying not to laugh.

"You're capturing visual on an unscheduled military flight?" Dingle demanded.

"You're damn right I am, how in hell do we know they are who they say they are?" Linen replied. "Are you activating your targeting eyes, Milkstone?"

"Targeting, aye," Copper confirmed. "Just in case. She *is* one of ours, though," she added. "A small flyer for atmospheric as well as short-range space flight; one aboard, but one false move and I *will* let loose with virtual fire. And if that's ineffectual, I'll use the real McCoy."

"Maintaining our course as planned," a rather shaken Dingle informed his crewmates. "The blip has veered off. Just looking us over, I guess."

"I guess," Linen chuckled, eyeing Copper, who smiled back: both had recognised the voice. "Keep your eyes peeled, Cop, lest we *are* in the firing line for drone target practice."

In the event, nothing disturbed the remainder of the flight and the four and their craft returned to basecamp on schedule. The trainees made quickly for their assigned briefing room for the obligatory debriefing with Instructor Captain Max Meldyn once their shuttle had been checked in.

The suave Captain Meldyn was as perturbed by the strange encounter as Ensign Dingle, not having been able to find out anything about the vessel or its business in the area. He had plenty to say on the responses of his trainees, however, and all four were rapped for lack of follow-up in their contact with the small ship. Dingle's lack of control over his crew was criticised and Linen's gathering of visual data was praised, but Copper was singled out for rebuke for her positive targeting of the craft.

"Why didn't you argue it out with him over the targeting?" Linen demanded as the four were making their way to the mess.

"Because he's not worth the waste of breath," Copper said shortly. "He didn't want to know why I did it anyway; he just wanted to show he was watching every move we made and to take a cheap shot at me."

"And what did you tell him that he had a face like fury at our initial briefing?" the redhead went on.

"That he was wrong and I was right. *I* think he was annoyed that we had others aboard as witnesses. He did figure it was me, he said; he also said that it was poor protocol to quote MAT Procedures to another pilot, but that's minewash and I told him so. Flight priority regs are there for a reason and where's the point of us having to memorise them if an instructor can flout them as he sees fit?"

"You didn't tell him that?" Dingle interjected.

"You're damn straight I did. He was pissed."

"We could tell," laughed Linen. "I bet he *did* have some unscheduled drone practice lined up as a surprise, but he was outflanked by the appearance of that flyer."

"Who the hell was it anyway, and why didn't they identify themselves?" grumbled Blazells.

"It was military, unregistered as far as we could tell, and who are *we* to quiz a competent and possibly high-ranking member of the Service?" Copper told him. "Some of those manoeuvres were pretty classy, so whoever was flying that fighter could fly."

Over their caff, the four evaluated their flight's more unusual aspects, calling on sundry crewmates to join in, until summoned by the chronometer to their next task, a technical flight lecture. It was past noon by the time Copper and Linen could have a private conversation as they collected their gear for an hour of combat simulations.

"Nice of Auntie Elle to look in on us," Linen began. "I bet she knew Max the Melt was monitoring very syllable; hence the allusion to priority – if we *had* priority over her. But how did she find out the nitty-gritty of the flight over Isidis?"

"We mentioned we'd taken turns at the helm and we *had* a lot of action after that, if you recall," Copper reminded her. "She'd want to know every detail and it probably came out then. But as for priority: if she was on unscheduled manoeuvres, *that* would be her equivalent of training, probably keeping up her flight hours. So with four of us to one of her, we have priority."

"Glad you're on top of it," Linen admitted.

"On another matter," Copper continued. "I had a link from Ma Kellyn about her apartment info-sheet: she's done it and has sent it through. I'll have to print out an interactive plas-film as I don't want it linked to me. You reckon I should just put the sheet next to the staff info panel and let them work it out? I can add Ma's link to it."

"Good idea; that way, Max Meltdown for one won't connect it with us. We can put a copy by the trainees' panel as well, as some of our lot may very well be assigned locally. But let's get on: I want a decent sim seat."

✳ ✳ ✳

The ensuing sols passed in the usual whirl of study, technical, flight and weapons exercises and physical fitness drills. Copper and Linen had heard little from outside apart from the news that the long-delayed launch of MDMC's newest and most expensive supra-light starship, the *SS Fearless*, was set to go ahead to great acclaim. The actress Alecta Lattim was to press the appropriate button at the launch. The ship's mission was classified however, and her heading unknown, Linen's friend Quartz Craterhouse informed them.

Colonel Moritz had not been in touch with the two since last they had passed her during their training flight; they assumed this was down to keeping them out of the notice of undesirables such as Jecks and his nasty buddy. Majorelle had likewise heard nothing of her aunt, but supposed that duty aboard the *Drake* was keeping her busy. Trisk had linked in once or twice: *he* appeared to be in the throes of setting up and organising the laboratories and stations assigned to him and his friends aboard the *Drake* but had not elaborated on his duties or mentioned his commanding officer. The two had called Mik Mack to find out what was happening over at their erstwhile site, but he had received orders to keep communications to a minimum and was unable to pass on any information regarding the outcome of the security breaches at the Warren, which was in a state of virtual lockdown. Even Spook seemed to be maintaining his distance, Copper told Linen, and she was beginning to miss his company.

It was just before the only free half-sol that the trainees were entitled to per sevensol that the order was issued that every member of Class Alpha Zero One report to their main lecture room for mandatory briefing. There was some grumbling at this curtailment of their leisure time, but most of the cohort was in hopes of word about their looming final appraisals, gradings and postings, as rumour had abounded ever since their return from leave. Copper and Linen trooped in with the throng and slid into their favourite seats.

The news imparted by the basecamp commandant was to the purpose: all present were to undergo final appraisals over the next five sols, interspersed with their usual drills. At some point after that their postings would be allocated. Any future training needs would be assessed and assigned during the same period.

Their remaining duties were to be outlined by Sarn't Biskott and all were dismissed to his charge: whatever they had planned for the rest of the sol would have to wait.

"Aren't we supposed to parade up and down our main drill hall in our uniforms for the gratification of friends, relatives and assorted dignitaries or something?" Linen demanded as various comings and goings allowed a chance to chat. "We've been threatened with it."

"I hope not, if it's like the usual official College graduation," Copper told her. "Expensive to travel to for any kin that want to see the show and then we set off for our postings hell knows where and they never see us again."

"Class Alpha Zero One of Beagle One," Blazells snapped from the row in front of them. "The pride of the Fleet Academy and they haven't even organised our send-off."

"I don't want one," Copper informed him. "All I want is a uniform that doesn't itch and escape from endless drills."

"You'll have that once we're assigned our ship," comforted Linen. "But for now, here's the Sarn't, and you can bet he's not here for our good."

"So you think you're headed for a ship of the Fleet?" Blazells sniffed deprecatingly over his shoulder. "You'll be lucky."

"You can bet your bottom credit we will," Linen shot back with a glance at Copper as Sarn't Biskott yelled for order.

The gist of their instructor's message was that most of their physical sessions from here on in would comprise practice for their passing-out parade, in just over two sevensols hence. Dress uniforms were to be collected from stores and maintained in readiness for a full dress rehearsal, once the requisite drills had been imprinted into their brains and could be completed in their sleep. Three attendance permits would be issued to each trainee to give to family or friends for the ceremony, which would take place in the reorganised main hangar. Assigned transports from the military dock on Evolution Avenue to the basecamp would be available and all refreshments would be provided in the mess later, but trainees' invitees would be obliged to make their own way to Beagle and fork out for their own lodging once there. Dismissed.

"Damn and hell and blast!" Copper exclaimed. "Nice of 'em

to give us plenty of notice! None of my lot will come over from Pathfinder, that's for sure."

"But they'll be there over the holo-link won't they?" Dingle asked. "My people are out at Mars Two and Savich, and I guess one or two will make it."

"I won't be holding my breath for a show, even a virtual one, though they now know I'm here," Copper murmured grimly as she shrugged, earning her a friendly nudge from Linen.

"Ma will certainly come, and so will Grammy; she'll hotfoot it over from Deep Two. We'll have to let Majorelle and Lofty know for sure, and tell them to pass it on to Ma Kellyn or we'll never hear the end of it. They can view the virtual link-up; and so can the rest of the folks at Lowell and the Warren, 'cos Mik Mack's been asking. Auntie Elle might turn up as well, you never know," she added in a low voice, laughing. "She's the one responsible for us being here after all. And maybe Trisk could commandeer a ride with her."

"Lor' help us, that's all we'd need," Copper protested crossly. "I don't want to parade around a hangar to a blaring racket, saluting all and sundry, just for a free feed and a pat on the back from a bunch of top brass. And Thars had better not let Lomax Gratikule or the Waterbone in on it or we'll have Thulia gushing unstoppably over the comm for hours and Waterbone here to eye up your legs."

"MDMC still pays our way as part of our ongoing research," Linen reminded her quietly as the clamour around them rose and the seats began to empty. "We owe them."

"We pay in the damn reports they keep asking for."

"We haven't had a demand for one for a while."

"Don't count your asteroids; once we're done here it'll start again, no matter what else we'll be doing," the redhead was told. "But enough already — let's go find these damn dress uniforms as most everyone else seems to be heading off to do the same."

"Including Blazells and Dingle. Probably just as well, Blazells was paying close attention to our chat. Hope the dress uniforms fit a bit better than our usual. Why they take our measurements I don't know; they don't seem to use them," Linen complained.

It was on the way to the stores that Copper's wrist-comm let out a cheep. She checked it briefly and gave a small chuckle.

"Ma Kellyn. I'll check it later as we're still officially on duty."

"And as we are you shouldn't be wearing that comm; it's not standard mil issue," her friend announced righteously.

"Can it; you're wearing yours and they're more military than anything any quartermaster's store can come up with. Now that a number of our comrades seem to be keeping us at a distance, no-one will be looking anyway."

"You noticed, huh? I think Blazells *has* been spreading gossip about us, but what he's been saying isn't clear. Though I note *he* still stays close."

"Can't help it," said Copper. "Captain Max Meltdown thinks we're such a good team he always seems to pair us with him and Dingle for flight training. Or maybe Max the Melt knows they annoy the hell out of us and does it on purpose."

The queue at stores for the issue of dress uniforms was busy as trainees passing idents over relevant readers stopped to check the contents of the bundles that appeared in response. The two joined on at the end, where Blazells and Dingle were involved in lively speculation as to the comfort factors of the garments.

"Once we're in these we're real officers, I take it," Zak Zills remarked. "Nice to know a bit of cloth makes such a difference. So when we do hear of our postings? It'll have to be soon, as we've got our end date now. And are we allowed to slap on our new insignia when we do hear, or do we hang fire until we're in our new posts?"

"I expect you report to your nearest stores and get issued with your rig the first sol," Copper conjectured. "Then you get down to it; I don't think you'll be let loose so that your nearest and dearest can admire you in your new uniform before you disappear over the horizon. We're all Fleet officers, so we all wear the same; only the badges and rank pins will be different."

"I heard that we get our postings as soon as we've done with our appraisals, which means before the big parade, maybe next sevensol," Dex Inkle put in as he came to a halt, clutching his new accoutrements to him. "But I'm off to get rid of these and then I'm heading to the mess. I'll see you there."

"I assume we'll wear our rank pins when we march out as newly-fledged officers, Lieutenant Milkstone?" Linen asked her friend playfully, pushing her forward.

"If they hand them over: it depends what's in these bundles being handed out. We'll have to spit shine them and everything else from our teeth to our boots, I expect."

"Aw! You like dressing up!"

"For a party, not to impress a bunch of brass," Copper said grumpily. "It's black! With collar, shoulders and front inserts in Military maroon!"

"That's only for the dress jacket," her friend said, examining the bundle that Dingle had just picked up. "We'll be in our Fleet blues for sol to sol, with inserts denoting speciality or service branch. What's to get het up about over a uniform?"

"That depends on the uniform," Copper muttered darkly as she passed her ident over the reader and stood back to await her allocation. "You wouldn't want to be seen in standard prison issue, would you?"

"You have a point, but our flight fatigues are comfy enough minus the combat jackets. Here we are. Let's go check them out and then find a space to stretch in. And you have that link from Ma Kellyn to follow up."

Back in their quarters the two shook out their acquisitions and held them up critically. The jackets were designed to fit just over their hips; they sported shaped, textured insertions down either side at the front which matched the stand-up collar and epaulettes to which stat ranking pins could be attached. There was a circular Mars Service patch on the left front displaying the insignia of the Fleet Academy, with its wings and star above the motto 'Lux in Tenebris' that showed Beagle One as the relevant training station. A gold Mars Fleet insignia pin was fixed on the right breast and there were two hidden pockets. The regulation trousers matched the jackets and were essentially standard issue but for a dark red stripe down each outside leg.

"At least the jacket more or less fits," Copper announced, shrugging into hers and fastening up the front placket. "I expect we have to wear this white vest underneath. What's with the embossed patterning?"

"Search me," was the response. "But we're all going to look real cute in the caps. They haven't taken my hair into account; I'll have to braid it and leave it down my back. Have you got your lieutenant's stat pins?"

"A four-pointed star with a bar either side, so that's second lieutenant. And cuff bands to match. Well, it's one up on most of our cohort, they'll be ranked ensign and have the single star. Except for Blazells and Spelspar for some reason, possibly due to friends in high places, for neither of them have anything more than standard degrees," Copper stated. "But let's see what Ma Kellyn wants: I doubt if it was a social call."

"What gives?" Linen demanded as her friend began to laugh softly.

"She's had two bites from here on the strength of the info-sheets we stuck up. She doesn't say who they are, but one's a senior instructor, apparently. Even credit says it's Max the Melt. He'd fall for the cosy and private accommodations with high security whatever-it-was that Ma was touting."

"On another note, did you know there's a medal for best trainee from each cohort? As we're the only ones graduating this bout, it'll be one of our lot. As we've both scored high for most of our classes, we should be in there with a chance. You more than me I have to say – you're much better at the physio than I am, not to mention the various parts of flight training."

"Not if my favourite instructor Captain Max Meldyn has a say in it *and* he will have," Copper snorted. "He was severely put out over the Isidis affair…"

"But your record states that you've completed each flight to schedule and on target and that you've missed nary a one of his virtual combat drones in flight sims or actual flight, even though he's been known to boast that there's never been a trainee could best him. Okay, you've been pasted over your actions on some flights, but so have we all, *and* it's been logged. He's not our only flight instructor and then there's the rest: classwork, drills, weaponry, teamwork, leadership and all that hokum."

"I don't score high on teamwork for sure," Copper argued. "But considering the teams we've had, is it any wonder? Oh, who cares, let's get on over to the mess and see what everyone else has to say about the latest stuff."

* * *

The latest stuff occupied most of their waking thoughts over the next sevensol. With their usual working sol stretching from wake-up at oh seven hundred hours to off duty at twenty one hundred hours, with only two hours total break-time during the period, the trainees were finding the endless drills and classwork both tedious and tiring. Their one free half-sol at the end of the stretch found almost everyone washed up in the mess to play a waiting game: they had been told that the results of their final assessments would be released that afternoon.

The statement in Sarn't Biskott's loud and powerful tones as he stalked into the mess sent most of the trainees to the nearest wall station to call up their final grades. Copper and Linen were among the throng and found themselves in the wake of Dingle, Zills and Blazells, all trying to commandeer consoles.

"Way to go, Cop! High scoring on most of the assessments!" Linen congratulated. "What do these highlighted marks mean?"

"Main award in the subject," Dingle clarified. "Zak's got the prize for unarmed combat skills," he added proudly, linking his arm through his mate's.

"Good for you, Zills!" Copper applauded her. "We knew you would, you're way ahead of the rest of us as far as that goes."

"What about you, Dingle? Any awards?" Linen grinned, as she tabbed up her own record.

"Only a mention for teamwork," the ensign admitted. "But you don't get a medal for a mention; you only get listed in the graduation roll. The medals are doled out at the parade and you have to step out, get it given and then rejoin for the final march-past as fully-fledged Fleet officers. We'll have to practice that, now we know who's got what. And then we get the drinks and nibbles and then we say goodbye to all our instructors and each other and then we can leave, thank hell. But you've got a couple of highlighted items, Milkstone: what's the deal?"

"Navigation *and* piloting skills!" Copper exclaimed. "I really thought Max the Melt would spoke my wheel on flying: he and I do *not* see eye to eye."

"He doesn't have the final say, I'll bet: Commandant Okenite is the ultimate authority and Oke's no doubt been keeping an eye on everything," her redheaded friend declared. "But there's another note here – what's that?"

"Top trainee of the cohort," Dingle read out. "Good for you, Milkstone: you must have come near the top in a few things."

"That's my girl!" Linen enthused. "I just got two mentions

for outstanding work. What about you, Blazells?”

“Oh, Gadget got the top prize for leadership skills, didn’t you?” Zak Zills beamed over at the unusually silent Blazells.

“I did,” was the sour retort. “So when do we hear about our postings?” he continued. “It’s about time it was organised: they must have known our expected gradings as they keep tally all the way through.”

“Can’t wait to get out, huh?” Linen asked him.

“We’ve been here long enough. With all these new ships we hear about getting ready to leave on this massive exploration drive, there must be a lot of spare berths for junior officers.”

“You don’t get assigned to a brand new starship straight out of boot, officers or not,” Zills laughed. “Most of us will be up for further training before we’re let loose aboard any starship, so I guess that means a few spells of on-the-job prep at land bases or on short-range training or mission ships.”

“*You* might be,” Blazells retorted. “Who’s for another caff or sparkle juice? It’s our half-sol and as we’re stuck on this damned base, we may as well make the best of any leisure time we get.”

“We may as well,” Copper observed to her friend. “The next sevensol will be endless drill practice or sim sessions, now we all know what’s what. But where do we pick up our postings? They sure as hell won’t be flashed up on the message boards for any dustbagger to read.”

“Oh, the link’s sent directly to our ident tags and we shuttle off to the main rec hall; they have stations set up there that issue the information to each recruit privately,” Dingle assured them as the group wandered back to requisition a table. “I heard it from a guy out of Mars Six basecamp that I met on furlough; he was hanging fire at Beagle ’cos he was waiting for transport to his new station out on Arcadia – or so he said.”

“Arcadia?” questioned Zills. “There’s a no-fly zone around that station and who knows what goes on there?”

“Logistics,” Linen said briefly. “Organisation of supplies to and from the Fleet. Trisk told me,” she added to Copper. “You for caff?”

“I’m always for caff. But this is going to be a *long* sevensol.”

* * *

The following several sols were extremely long, with parade

practice taking up two hours every afternoon. All medal winners were compelled to carry out and refine their award collection drill interminably and were thoroughly jaded with it by the time the call went out that posts had been allocated and all trainees should report to the main recreational area for assignment.

"Now for it," Copper whispered to her friend as they joined their colleagues in the walk to the rec hall at the outside edge of the main dome.

The place had been transformed; where once the perimeter had been taken up with seating and comm consoles, there now were enclosed stations, each of which would seat one individual, with private screens that could be activated as desired. Several of their instructors were on hand to direct the recruits to a booth and advise on the means of obtaining their own data.

"Go on," Linen said, her eyes crinkling up in amusement as she pushed Copper before her. "I'll hop in once you're done and then we'll see what we and all our buddies are going to be in for over the next however long it'll be."

Copper slid into the station, swiping her ident tag across the relevant slot. She placed her palm on the reader plate, intoning her name and Service number. As she replaced her tag chain inside her shirt, a small screen lit up and a data chit slid out of a slot to the side of it; the latter contained all the details she would need for taking up her new appointment, including the timings. She slipped the chit into an inside pocket as she read the details on the screen. A frisson of excitement ran up her backbone to finish at the nape of her neck and she was engulfed in a warm, ethereal hug. It was Spook's way of saying congratulations. Her face was one beam of delight as she slipped out of the booth and made way for her friend, giving a double thumbs-up in the passing.

"I take it you're happy with your post, Trainee Milkstone?" Sarn't Biskott barked at her elbow.

"Yes, sir. I'll wait until Lieutenant Lyrican's finished and let you in on it – if you're interested."

"Should I be?"

"Oh yes."

Biskott set off to point a couple of eager interns in the right direction but returned in time to see Lieutenant Lyrican and her friend dance a mad waltz with each other.

"Well, let's have it: you both seem to have got what you wanted," Biskott said dryly.

"Posted to the same ship, sir," Copper stated enigmatically.

"Ship? So the powers that be think you don't need more on-the-ground training, do they? And the same ship, eh? Lor' help your crewmates is all I can say. So what's the lucky vessel that'll have the pleasure of your company for her next cruise?"

"The *MSS Drake II*, sir," Linen smiled impishly at him, her eyebrows raised as if daring him to comment.

"The *what*? How in blazes did you engineer that? You'll be expecting me to salute you, once you've passed out. You'd best go tell your mates, so they can bring you back down to Mars for a while."

"I doubt many of them will realise exactly what the *Drake* is," Copper said wryly to her friend.

"Don't be too sure: we're Class Alpha Zero One, the cream of Fleet Academy. They'll know she's the Class ship of the new squadron being spit-shined at Phobos Station II Space Dock for out on the edge exploratory. One or two will be seriously pissed. But now it's official, I feel really shivery, as if we're just about to jump into a very big, deep freezing pool."

"You, me and Spook make three. And here's Blazells with a sneer fit to fry us. He must have got a good one."

"Well?" the lieutenant asked mockingly as he strolled up with Dingle and Zills on his tail. "Keeping it a secret or are you going to let the planet in on it?"

"No secret," Linen told him with a shrug, raising her hands, palms outward. "We both got posted to a ship of the Fleet. The same ship."

That took him aback a little. "Not receiving further training before assignment, then? Neither am I, as a matter of fact," he informed them with a patronising smirk.

"So come on, let us know," Copper urged.

"I've been posted to the *MSS Lithium Star*," he announced proudly. "I don't expect you've heard of her."

"The *Lithstar*!" Copper and Linen exploded simultaneously, beaming at one another in extreme glee.

"An Explorer Corps mid-range cruiser," said Copper archly,

an amused flicker in her eyes. "Way to go, Blazells, she's one big ship. Her last mission was a mapping and space safety cruise out at the edge. I knew she was in for overhaul but I thought she'd been reassigned," she added in feigned uncertainty to her friend.

"She *was* in orbit over Lowell and was scheduled for refit, but that was ages ago," Linen agreed. "Remember us to Lieutenant Commander Floris Fludge and First Lieutenant Erkal Chokatti if they're still aboard her," she went on, laughing up at the confounded Blazells, whose jaw was dropping.

"You *know* that ship?"

"And some of her crew; we last saw them at Lowell Leisure Dome, but that was months and months ago. The *Lithstar* had been recalled from her ongoing mission, but obviously we can't tell you why," Copper stated matter-of-factly.

Dingle was equally as perplexed. "What ship did you two get?" he croaked eventually.

"The *MSS Drake II*," Copper acknowledged, trying to sound offhand although her heart was jumping in what she assumed was gratified pride – and relief that Blazells, who was preserving an outraged silence, had not somehow managed to capture a berth aboard the *Drake*. "We have a sevensol after we pass out here to get our gear in order before we join her. We'll be science officers, given our credentials. Where are you posted, Dingle?"

"Korolev Station, for ground-based training," was the rather dismal response.

"I got the Station Security Office at Olympus Mons Support Squadron HQ," Zills put in. "I wanted shipboard, but once I've done my stint there I can request another posting. At least we're both still on Mars," she added to the still-downcast Dingle.

The majority of their colleagues were happy and excited at the prospect of an end to the restrictions of basecamp and the chance to shine in other settings. Very few had been given off-planet postings and several had been assigned further training. The latter included Ensigns Skate and Ferret, who were destined for a small fleet training section attached to the Astronavigation and Spaceflight Sciences Centre at Viking One College.

"Only a couple of months," Bon-Bon Skate declared. "But after that, it'll be a ship, I'll bet. So we may see you up there, one of those sols. Pity we can't celebrate our postings in style, but once we're done, we can have a ball!"

"You bet," Copper agreed. "It's been an age since I've tasted some really good ale."

"We can hit Lofty's once we're back at Lowell," Linen said soothingly. "Martian Minewater, and I bet he and Majorelle won't let us pay for a drop. But we'll have no time for a ball once we're done here: it's a quick turnaround and we'll need all the time there is to sort our stuff out at Lowell."

* * *

The need for haste had followed everyone around, for time had zipped by, with much having had to be crammed into little. One delight for Copper and Linen had been a tentative request from Majorelle and Lofty for the opportunity to watch the two at their passing-out. As they had six permits available between them, they had had no hesitation in advancing two, along with the offer of a berth at their Beagle home unit down Road Five. Ms Firewall had agreed to stay with Corona for the duration and the latter's friend Phoebe Orphistene had also been invited. The spare permit they had passed on to Dingle, who seemed to have numerous relatives intent on shuttling in.

Copper had been heartened to receive the news that her blood kin intended to view the ceremony by virtual link-up. It was more than she had expected from her short contact with them on the subject, given their former blankness rather than pleasure at her change of career tack. She and Linen were also pleased that friends at Lowell, the Astrobiology Field Dome and at the Warren field site would be watching.

"Walls are going to be alive with faces," Copper predicted as the two were making final preparations, having arisen very early on the great sol. "We'd all better be step perfect or else."

"We will be," Linen groaned. "I march in my sleep. I wish it was over, and we were breathing the air of Lowell again."

"We soon will be," Copper sighed. "Let's get some breakfast down before we suit up and then get our gear stowed and ready for shipping out. Magenta's arranged travel-cabs for us from the military dock so we can go straight back to ours with Majorelle and Lofty to freeze for a bit before whatever your Ma has organised for later."

"It won't be much: I warned her we'll be bushed. But she's

booked someplace or other for dinner. The stuff they'll supply here after the show won't dull our appetites."

The final breakfast in the mess of Beagle One Basecamp was a cheery affair, with most of the trainees having fallen out of their cots to fill up before the ultimate wash and brush up and the donning of the dress uniforms. Back in quarters, there was much coming and going out of friends' billets to borrow pieces of kit and to seek confirmation that everyone looked their best. Bulletins from outside delivered by helpful service hands let the trainees know that the crowds had begun to arrive and that the whole place was set up and ready to go.

By the time the cohort had been marshalled into its drill lines and marched to its starting line, the virtual musicians had begun. The group passed down the entrance corridor and with due fanfare proceeded into the main hangar. The demonstration drill and march-past was completed without a hitch and as the order to stand was given, the whole unit stopped simultaneously, eyes front. The address was given by Commandant Walt Okenite, the trainees inducted as fully-fledged officers and the prize-winners ordered one by one to step forward, collect their awards and resume their places for a final review by some of the invited top brass that were seated in the centre of the front semicircle.

It was as Copper was assuming the *attention* position and had allowed her eyes to flicker over the row of senior personnel that adorned centre stage that she caught the very amused glance of Colonel Elle Chryse Moritz. Maintaining her posture, she waited patiently whilst the colonel, in company with a couple of others, stepped down and at the invitation of the Commandant began a review of the new officers.

"Congratulations, Lieutenant Milkstone," the colonel said as she halted, one of Okenite's adjutants stating Copper's rank and name at her elbow. "Three awards I see," she noted, eyeing the medals around Copper's neck. "You'll be an asset to the *Drake*."

"I hope so, ma'am," was the rather facetious response. "I'm looking forward to it," she added with a grin.

"To what? The work?"

"That – and the release from bondage here."

"I see. Good. Carry on, Lieutenant."

"Yes, ma'am. Thank you, ma'am," Copper responded as the

colonel set off down the row.

Once the requisite dialogues were over, the parade reformed and was marched off, to the rapturous applause of the audience both present and watching from the viewscreens around the ground. Once the cover of the corridor beyond the main hangar was achieved, the ranks broke like water over a dyke and there was an unholy race for the nearest comfort stations.

"The chow should be set out in the mess," Linen panted to Copper as she extricated herself from the logjam around her. "The crowds will be directed there eventually by camp ops staff but everybody will be catching up with their virtual guests. Did you see any of our people on the vis-screens?"

"No; I was too busy trying to keep my mind on the next step even to look up. Did you see them?"

"No. Let's get back to the hangar and have a look-see, before we get caught up with our bunch here," Linen directed, linking her arm through her friend's.

They joined several like-minded colleagues and set off back down the corridor, capturing Lofty and Majorelle en route. That pair had been close enough to the exit to make a quick getaway but turned back obligingly. The screens around the large hangar space were still lit and those viewing from a distance were no doubt being entertained by the ongoing spectacle. It was Linen who spotted their friends from the Warren, and waved cheerily up at the relevant screen, miming her thanks. Mik Mack was almost dancing as he returned the greeting. Several techs of the Amberline Group at the AF Dome, along with Silver Yarrow and a couple of PhD students had made time to put in virtual appearances and Lowell was represented by Thars Amberline and his exec Avrom Elath, along with a number of students, including Noa Dunelm and Syriana Steefens.

"No Mariner or Alessa in sight," Copper noted, referring to Professors Mbolon and Aclarke, the second mentors they had been assigned for their PhDs. "Too busy with their undergrad work, I guess."

"That's College life, but we'll see them in a sol or so. Look!" Linen called out delightedly, still busily waving. "It's Malachite!"

"We had the link set up specially," Lofty beamed shyly from behind. "We thought it would be a nice surprise," he went on as one or two of the irregulars from Amaloft's Diner peered over Malachite's shoulder to see what was going on.

As the two expressed their appreciation and looked around at the sea of unknown faces, trying to distinguish any more that they recognised, Copper gave a small snort and tried to form a smile, although her face was creased in what Linen recognised as bitter but resigned disappointment.

"Thulia," the redhead grated in an undertone as she returned the extravagant greetings. "Who let her in on it?"

"I'm afraid I did that," Majorelle confessed. "She linked me and asked: she'd heard of the ceremony from her boss, I think, and wanted to know when it was."

"She'd have been able to find out from Service channels, it's not secret information," Linen consoled.

"No," Copper agreed. "Anyone can find out the dates and times; even the Waterbone, though I don't see him anywhere. But you need authorisation to link in, so she must have swung it somehow. But where are your folks? I'd have thought they'd have got here by now," Copper went on to Linen.

"They've been captured by Colonel Moritz," was the reply. "They're over there. I see Aunt Phoebe's there too," she added as she signalled to Phoebe Orphistene, who was standing on the edge of the group looking a tad out of place.

"I did see Auntie Elle on the reserved seats," Majorelle said, turning to look. "She nodded over but I didn't dare disturb her; I didn't realise this kind of thing was one of her duties."

"Somehow I don't think it usually is," Copper stated wryly. "But let's go interrupt and then head in for the free feed. And then we can get out of these uniforms and head on home."

"You have a lovely home unit at Beagle," Majorelle enthused. "Your Grammy met us at the spaceport yestersol, Linen, and took us straight there; and she and your Ma picked us up and brought us out here. You have a wonderful family."

"That she does," Copper agreed with a twist to her mouth, earning her a squeeze on the arm from her friend.

"They didn't show?" Linen whispered as the quartet threaded their way across the erstwhile parade ground.

"Couldn't see them; the screens were ordered by location, so they should have been on the Pathfinder link," was the hurt response. "There *were* one or two blank screens, so maybe the link failed or they had to cut off."

"You know you've always got me. But here's Grammy and Ma – and Phoebe!" she added more loudly, as the pair were met and enfolded in a warm embrace by Corona Lyrican, who let loose with a torrent of joyful greetings.

Magenta pushed in to hug them unmercifully and lash them with her ever-ready tongue. Phoebe Orphistene held out a hand to both but was quickly hauled into the family group. Majorelle had greeted her aunt effusively and was in earnest conversation, whilst a tongue-tied Lofty brought up the rear, smiling shyly whenever his partner caught his eye. It was some time before they could regroup and make their way through the throng to the mess and the refreshments set out there. The place was alive with personnel, visitors and ambling servo-mech units, the latter having been pressed into service as extra drinks trolleys.

Very little was achieved apart from making inroads into the rations and breaking off now and then to greet friends and ex-instructors and bid them farewell. The noise precluded serious discussion, but loudly bellowed introductions were called out across the large room and many were the promises of keeping in touch and class reunions at some yet to be settled future date.

"Who's the top brass at your table?" the spruce Lieutenant Blazells inquired of Copper when the two met at a service hatch where fresh sustenance was being doled out.

"Our new commanding officer," she returned levelly, raising an eyebrow. "Didn't you recognise the insignia of the *Drake II*?"

"*That's* the captain of the *Drake II*?"

"The commanding officer and she's a colonel. The *Drake* is the Class Ship of the new squadron, after all. And she's about ready to go. We have a sevensol's breathing space before we ship up. How about you: heard from the *Lithstar*?"

"Yes," he said shortly. "I'm joining her soon."

"She got her mission yet?"

"That's classified information."

"Meaning you don't know," Copper surmised. "Well, good luck with that. We'll maybe see you on the flipside, down the road a ways."

"Maybe," he responded tartly and turned away.

"Got caught by Blazells, I noted," Linen twinkled up at her on her return. "What did he have to say?"

"Not much. It seems he's joining the *Lithium Star* in a few sols but it sounds like he doesn't know what he'll be doing. He's still peeved that we were assigned to the *Drake* and he got the *Lithstar*, given he got the leadership prize. He thinks it gives him the right to the most prestigious posting."

"So you think you've got the most prestigious posting, do you?" Colonel Moritz demanded, selecting a titbit from the plate Copper held out.

"Naturally we have, ma'am," Linen told her, eyes creasing in glee. "We're the best, or at least, Cop is. I didn't capture any prizes, bar mentions for navigation and flight skills."

"Mentions for outstanding abilities in those fields," Copper corrected her. "There can only be one medal in any category and you came pretty close."

"*You* copped them both, though, not to mention one or two mentions."

"That was brilliant, Copper!" Majorelle put in brightly. "Your folks must be *so* proud."

"Talking of flight skills, I see Captain Meldyn has just come in so I expect I'd best go and say goodbye. Excuse me."

Majorelle's face fell as Copper stood abruptly and marched off. "Did I say something wrong?"

"Cop's people didn't show," Linen told them quietly. "They said they would link in over the vis-screens but we couldn't see them. I'm going to check the logs to see if they did try – in fact I'll do it now."

"Belay that, Lieutenant," Colonel Moritz cut in. "Best leave it," she added. "That's for Lieutenant Milkstone to do, not you."

The elevated eyebrow warned Linen that argument was not something she should try. She articulated her accord in a low voice as Majorelle's empathic tears began to well and Magenta growled "Damn them!" in a carrying voice.

"We'd actually best get all our farewells over and done with," Linen sighed. "And then we get changed and catch the shuttle bus to the transport dock. Hope our uniforms aboard the *Drake* are a sight more comfortable than these, ma'am," she went on to the colonel in an attempt to lighten the atmosphere before her friend returned.

She need not have worried: Copper was actually grinning as she resumed her place. "Guess what!" she demanded of Linen. "Max the Melt actually boasted to me that he's got a home base in Beagle Central, as his posting here on a semi-permanent basis has been confirmed. This'll knock your socks off, Majorelle: he's got one of Ma Kellyn's apartments in that block she purchased out on Skady Lane. I tried to sound impressed, but I had a hard job to keep from laughing."

"So he was one of the two that bit!" Linen cried. "Figured," she added as she explained to their friends some part of the dealings they had had with Ms Kellyn over the apartments.

Twenty minutes later and with most of their goodbyes said, the two new officers made their excuses and headed for the last time to their quarters to change into civilian attire, return their uniforms and gather their kitbags. By the time they had made their way back to the mess, Colonel Moritz had departed for somewhere unspecified and the others were ready to move. The whole party made their way out to the waiting transports and bundled aboard in company with a number of their fellows and their kinfolk.

Magenta had made arrangements and two travel-cabs awaited them at the crossover. One was scheduled to ferry Ms Firewall, Corona and Phoebe onward and the other would take Copper, Linen, Majorelle and Lofty out to Road Five and home. The cabs had been paid in advance and as theirs drew away, the two rookie officers sighed simultaneously.

"It's been a helluva sol," Copper smiled wearily into her friend's eyes.

"One helluva sol," Linen agreed. "Like old times, in a way. We had a lot of helluva sols out in the field," she explained to their two friends. "But once we get back, we relax for a few hours before we head out to the dinner Ma promised. She's booked the Carnelian Crucible."

"Good; we won't have far to walk. It's opposite the entrance to Road Five," Copper told Majorelle and Lofty. "It's lit up at night like a holo-pyrotechnics display, so you can't miss it, and the food is really tasty."

"It's so good of your family to invite us," Lofty informed

Linen. "But Majorelle and I will pay our share."

"You will not!" the redhead told him sharply. "Grammy's already signed the tab; she can afford it and this is her thanks to you for coming all this way to see us. Phoebe will be there too, though her new partner won't, but it'll be a proper send-off."

"We'll have to pack our traps for our flight out morrow-sol," Copper reminded her friend, stretching luxuriously to ease the tension in her neck. "Back to Lowell! It's been a long time."

"And a long road," Linen added, smiling over. "But here we are at our place, and the start of our next adventure. After you, Lieutenant Milkstone, ma'am!"

9: STARSHIP

Copper and Linen looked up affectionately at the familiar façade of Lowell College main entrance as it shimmered in the glow of a late afternoon sun filtering down through the rad-shielded and plas-protected Dome roof. The multi-coloured crystalline shards of the huge plas-glazed portals that depicted the crossed shovels and red mortar-board within a gold shield that formed the Crest of the University of Mars had represented their life for the past several Mars years and would now only do so at a distance.

The previous evening had had its own heady glory as the new lieutenants were wined and dined by relatives and friends who knew they were not likely to see them again for a very long time. Copper was in sore need of such companionship, although her own family had belatedly apologised for missing her passing-out parade owing to some unspecified problem with the linkage.

Both Magenta and Corona had risen early to see the two and their Lowell friends set off from Beagle spaceport on the first flight out. Majorelle and Lofty, with their usual generosity, had insisted that the pair stay at their home unit for the duration of their time at Lowell. Malachite had met them at the spaceport and ferried them to Coblentz Street and the comfortable living quarters behind and below Amaloft's Diner.

Time being at a premium, Copper and Linen were obliged to spend as much as possible of it at College. There, they planned to meet up with old friends and organise the work to be done to transfer as many of their samples and other research necessities as possible to the *Drake*, where they were destined to carry on with their Lowell work as well as become familiar with their new duties as science officers in Mars Fleet. Crossing the well-known Lowell threshold with a sigh, they stepped into the coolth of the large and airy hall and made for the nearest elevator. They knew that their chief mentor was in residence and intended to make their first stop-off at room twenty three on sub-floor six.

Avrom Elath, Professor Amberline's exec, was seated in his habitual chair in the outer office and rose to greet them, treating both to a warm hug and the offer of caff, as Thars was off on a spree. The exec was quick to send a message to inform his boss of the new arrivals, however, and bade them sit and tell him about their exploits, many of which he was sketchy about.

"News doesn't filter down from the Warren," he told them. "Too much is going on out there that Thars doesn't want spread around here – you know what some people are like."

"We can't enlighten you," Copper said firmly. "We haven't been out that way for a while and we have quite a bit to check up on with Thars."

The latter was certainly true, as no word had been received in relation to their adventures from anyone at the site station apart from the few hints from Mik. They had also not heard anything concerning the missing twosome from Beagle Hospital's secure wing, leading them to suspect that the fugitives were still at large. Thars, once he had returned to his office, had little more to pass on other than that the Warren was still locked down, as was the military base next door. The highly mortified Personnel Unit of Lowell College was urgently revising its recruitment system and things were proceeding more smoothly.

The professor escorted the two to the stores where most of their samples were lodged, to assist in the decisions on what should be transferred to the *Drake* and what should be left. As far as Copper and Linen were aware, their mission would take them away for ten months, but the schedule had not been set in stone and was liable to change without warning. The helpful Dr Trisk Addystone had sent on information as to the dimensions of available storage space in ship's labs and suggestions on what not to bring aboard.

As Copper was climbing into a lab coverall, she was framing her own opinions. Once in the large main store and faced with a rack of their own sample tubes, she gently suggested that they major on tubes, sample sleeves and boxes from the Glory Hole rather than their upper site of the Dragon's Nest. Linen flicked a quick glance at her friend: she knew what had prompted the proposal. She nodded in accord and urged her friend to sort and choose while she and Thars found a trolley to stack the selected items until they could be crated for transfer to their ship.

"We can get Trisk to give us the lowdown on the best way to get them shipped up: they'll have to go through security and who knows how many checks before they're allowed aboard," Linen smiled at their mentor as they made for a nearby trolley bay. "But as we have bucketloads of data from the Dragon's Nest, we won't be short of work to do on that in any spare time we might have."

Thars Amberline was no fool. "Your lower site was breached by those thugs and *that* nearly put a stop to the whole operation down there," he said softly. "There's something close by on the military side that's at the bottom of it and that's why we've been having all this trouble, not to mention the camp of troopers on our doorstep. And why you and Copper seem to have been hauled into all this."

Linen stopped short. "I can't confirm or deny," she told him honestly. "But we're doing our best to work it out and hopefully keep our people out at the Warren as safe as possible. I suspect we *will* be constrained as to what we can and can't report to you and to MDMC as our main research sponsors but we'll keep you updated as far as we *are* able. That's all I can promise."

"That'll do," he smiled gently down at her. "Just you two keep yourselves safe in that great big tin can out there."

Copper meanwhile was running rapid ungloved fingers over the array of tubes before her and quickly making her choices by unlocking each of the relevant containers from its allotted space. When the other two returned with the cart, she indicated those for abstraction and the three began to load. Once the trolley and its cargo were locked down, the trio made for one of the smaller storage areas to collect a number of sample sleeves that the two had not yet analysed, although with Thars in tow, both Copper and Linen were hard put to pretend some sort of reasoning for what they considered pertinent examples. The sleeves they added to the trolley, which they then secured to their implanted idents only.

"We seem to have quite a haul," Linen noted, scratching her head in perplexity. "And we still have the high security cells to check. We'd best stop now and do a quick run-through morrow-sol. We'll have to tip a few back in store, or Colonel Moritz will do it for us. Trisk *did* say we had a lot of space, but I don't think we're expected to fill it before we leave orbit."

"That's a job for later," Copper agreed. "For now, we have a few people to drop in on, or they'll never forgive us. And here's Freeman for a start," she groaned slightly as a well-remembered form strode up, grinning all over his face.

Lab tech Freeman Osk, his silver-blue spangled boots visible beneath his enveloping coverall, greeted them cheerily and spent the next five minutes telling them how much they had been missed and of the various rumours still rampant as to why they had signed up. They did not enlighten him, escaping as soon as civilly possible. Thars helpfully let them know that Freeman and the lately-graduated Aurora Maquie had formalised their status and were in the throes of arranging their legal pairing. Aurora was presently at her own home in Viking One, but several other erstwhile colleagues were around and expecting to be visited.

"Here come Captains Lyrican and Milkstone!" Noa Dunelm called out as the three entered the Amberline postgraduate study suite. "Everyone to attention!"

"Oh Lor', he never knows when to stop," Copper grumbled in an aside to Linen.

"Play it to the hilt, kiddo," her friend advised as she waved.

Noa hopped up smartly and saluted the approaching duo as Thars stepped over to talk to a disgruntled Mockle Ellund, who was sulking by the entry to the tri-dee simulation suite.

"Stand easy, trooper," Copper ordered in her best Colonel Moritz tone. "I expect you're the wiseacre responsible for that mock window set up," she added, gesturing to the feature with an inclination of her head: it had been programmed to show a comic military duo saluting one another.

"Might have been," he grinned.

"Your lack of talent has obviously improved somewhat," was the rejoinder. "So how are things with you and your partner?"

Noachis was quick to fill them in on his and Syriana's latest doings, although their other colleagues were obviously itching to know more about what had been going on out at the Warren and the next steps for the two new officers. One or two were also eager for an invite aboard a starship of the Fleet. Every hint dropped was severely quashed and Thars eventually recalled the pair, leaving the others to their conjectures.

"What's with Mockle?" Linen demanded as the door closed behind them. "He doesn't look to be a happy bunny."

"Thesis trouble," Thars said briefly. "How long are you two going to be around? The guys want some sort of banquet as a send-off for you and are expecting the Group to cough up. If I make it a divisional seminar I can organise it, but you'll have to sing for your supper by giving a lecture."

"Not on our work aboard ship, we can't," Copper told him. "We could dredge something up and add in a bit on our recent research, but that's about it. We have a maximum of three sols, here so it would have to be Thursol at the latest, and *not* evening as we leave to join our ship at oh seven hundred on Frisol."

"Understood. Why not use the tri-dee stuff you presented at MDMC's self-congratulatory knees-up at Viking One months ago and change the script? No-one here apart from me has seen it and it's pretty spectacular. Half an hour will be sufficient."

"Done," Linen agreed for both of them. "But we've had a long and busy sol and we're due at our friends' place for an early dinner, so we'll say goodbye now. We can catch up with Mariner and Alessa and anyone else we've missed morrow-sol."

The professor agreed, and bidding them farewell, he set off for his own office. The two watched the receding back.

"We'll have to be in here sharp and organise our gear before the rest of the place is fully awake," Copper said decidedly. "I'd like another rummage in the main stores to see if we've missed anything that we – or Spook – think we should take, and dump the stuff we don't want without eyes and ears prying."

"You'll be lucky; all the labs and stores are festooned with recording cams that'll follow our every move. They were put in after our last break-in troubles away back: the one that Mizzle Chert at the behest of his handlers had his inexpert hands in."

"Then we act like responsible students and say nothing that can't be safely overheard. And as for our lecture, we show the visuals and we wing it; we know enough about our site to do that and they won't be expecting the wisdom of the ages."

"Anything for a free feed. Must get Avrom well-primed on

the food and drink," Linen beamed. "But let's get back to base; I for one am seriously tuckered out."

* * *

Tuesol dawned brightly and Copper, Linen and Majorelle set off for Lowell College. Their friend had an early lecture and was in no way averse to a cosy gossip on the way. By the time they reached the Main Building several more early risers were visible and the heating had been turned on. Bidding Majorelle goodbye the two set off to their postgraduate study suite on lower level six. They found their task-desks still arranged as they had left them, probably because MDMC was still funding their research was Copper's opinion. That and the fact that no-one was prepared to face the trouble they would be in if Linen came back and found aught disturbed.

Dutifully firing up their long-abandoned comms stations, the two cleared their outdated links and left notifications for their second mentors to arrange meetings before setting off for the Amberline storage facility. They had several sample cartridges lodged in the high security storage cells there that they wished to abstract, as well as checks to carry out in the main stores. They chose the latter place first, and suitably attired in the compulsory coveralls, they sauntered in.

"No duty tech here, but our trolley's where we left it," Linen noted as she strolled over to its docking station.

Copper stiffened visibly. "But it's been disturbed: this is *not* how I left it, even though the trolley's still locked to our idents," she said in a low, angry voice, her gloved hand poised atop the stack. "Touch nothing until we get the security visual: I think there are a couple missing."

"You sure?"

"I'm sure," Copper responded as she turned slowly, her eyes scanning as her hand stole into a pocket to abstract the small scanner on a chain given her by Colonel Moritz.

She passed the device to her friend. "Check the local area," she ordered, ungloving and unzipping her coverall to reach her inner clothing.

Linen's eyes widened as Copper removed her PPF and undid the safety catch. "What the frock's up?" the redhead hissed in an undertone.

"Hover-cams are inoperative," was the terse response. "All of them. Get your gun; whoever the hell's supposed to be on security watch is going to get blasted for this."

"*If* they're awake," Linen replied softly. "Remember Mik…"

"Believe me, I remember," her friend said, still scrutinising the area carefully.

Slowly, she raised her weapon and took careful aim, letting loose a pulse of energy. It crossed the gap between her and a small hover device that was suspended just inside the store entry, shattering it into fragments.

"There's another stranger in the corner above the info-bank and it's scanning this way," Linen informed her friend. "They know we're here or it's programmed to lock onto motion."

As the second hover-cam exploded, Linen widened her field. "Nobody outside or in the immediate vicinity," she noted. "But we can't risk trouble: the undergrads will be heading in by the bucketload soon."

"So will the usual staff," Copper pointed out. "That includes the techs and the department security bods. Trouble is going to be headed this way right now. In fact, here it comes."

"I concur," said Linen as she hauled out her own weapon. "Two of them."

"Shoot first," Copper directed, throwing one of her gloves as far as she could towards the back wall. "They are *not* friendly."

The two hunkered down behind their trolley, both reminded of their previous run-in with armed and hostile infiltrators at the Warren station. Seconds ticked by and as beads of sweat trickled down Copper's forehead, she began to see in her mind's eye two approaching individuals. One was operating a scanning device.

"Dammit!" she breathed, tightening her grip on her gun and sliding further down towards the floor.

The intruders slid quickly through the door, weapons poised for action. The leader gave a signal and both aimed their rifles at the serried ranks of tubing in the furthest section, opening fire with practiced rapidity. They ran forward, letting loose energy bolts that ruptured both racks and sample tubes. Copper and Linen rose in unison, unleashing PPF bursts at their opponents' legs, bringing the pair down. As the gunmen dropped, the two sped across the space between them. Copper stamped viciously on the hand of one of the duo as he tried to raise his rifle. Linen kicked the other in the face.

"Get those damned guns away from them!" Copper snarled, aiming a boot at the large phase rifle carried by her quarry.

Linen obeyed as a high-pitched whine began to echo around them. It was the evacuation alert and, moments later, a squad of security personnel could be heard at the entry.

"Don't move!" one powerful voice commanded.

"Wasn't planning to," Linen retorted, holding up both her hands in compliance as she turned to look at the armed group.

Copper maintained her stance, weapon and eyes directed at the two on the floor. "They'll have more weaponry on them," she informed the newcomers in a loud voice. "But you'd better get the emergency medical service, they'll need it. And the law: this one at least is a fugitive from Beagle."

"Who the hell are you two?" the powerful voice demanded as its owner strode over.

"Amberline students," Copper snapped back, looking up at the tall form quizzically. "And who the hell are you? *You're* not regular Lowell College Security – you're far too efficient."

"None of your business," was the retort as the leading guard removed his helmet to reveal a close-cropped head of dark curly hair and startling blue eyes that scrutinised the twosome intently before eyeing their handiwork. "You've made a mess of them."

"They were attempting to make a mess of us," Copper told him curtly. "We got in first... again," she added pointedly.

"You're the two that had all that trouble over at one of the field stations out on Isidis," the man conjectured astutely.

"That's us," Linen grinned. "You've heard of the incident?"

"I was briefed," was the laconic response. "Check these two out and get the medics," he ordered his team. "And get that damned racket cut, I can't hear myself think."

The two students looked at one another questioningly as the alert in the immediate vicinity muted and the various members of the squad jumped into action.

"Another branch of Magenta's marines?" Copper hazarded as a terrified face appeared around the door.

"Come on in, Freeman, it's safe enough," Linen called over as she returned Copper's multi-scanner. "Don't you believe in following evac procedures when an alert's called?"

"Oh, is that what the noise and the lights are about? What's happened? Somebody smacked up my task-station in the small store and it's a disaster area. What the..." His voice failed as he took in the destruction and the bodies on the floor. "Oh Lor', all the samples! That's months of work!"

"Not ours, fortunately," Linen muttered. "They were way off beam," she added as she cast an enquiring look at her friend.

"Emergency trauma team on the way, stat," one individual called up from his kneeling position on the floor.

"Situation contained," another reported. "This and the local security office down the corridor seem to be the only breaches."

"*Seem* to be?" Copper demanded trenchantly. "I suggest you make certain before you cancel the alert."

She deactivated her PPF, motioning her friend to do the same, and replaced it in her inner pocket. "I want to check out our samples to see if they've been tampered with *and* our secure storage lockers; and everything else we have here. Nothing gets shipped out until we know it's safe and secure."

"One moment, ma'am: you're not touching anything until we've made our investigations," the team leader interrupted, his eyes raking Copper intently.

"That's lieutenant. And our time here is short, we have a ride to catch and I'm not about to hold up a flagship of Mars Fleet just to oblige Lowell College Security, or whoever the hell you are. Lieutenant Lyrican, you're with me."

"Affirmative, ma'am," Linen responded formally as Freeman Osk stared open-mouthed at the pair.

Barking an order at his second, the man escorted the two over to their trolley. Copper immediately activated her scanner and began to probe. Assured that it was safe, she unlocked the vehicle to pull out the top tube, running her scanner and her hands over it carefully as she read the label. As Freeman Osk had trailed the trio, she instructed him to fetch another trolley for transfer of the remaining samples.

"I want to check each tube to make sure none have been interfered with and I want to find out which ones have gone AWOL," Copper said to her friend. "But we need to lose at least a third anyway; if we choose carefully we should be able to get a fair sample and maximum coverage. And we should go over our other racks again, just to make sure we haven't missed anything of note, or any more tampering."

"Just who are you two?" their tall follower demanded evenly.

"You give us your credentials then *maybe* we'll give you ours," Copper countered. "As I've already told you, we're Amberlines; and you're not the usual Lowell site security detail, you and your band of troopers over there. We have implanted idents, so you know damn well we have every right to be here."

"Right to be in Lowell College: that doesn't necessarily mean you have the right to be in here. Or to tote those firearms you were using, *Lieutenant*," he retorted emphatically.

"Oh, they're legitimate," Freeman assured the man as he reappeared hauling a trolley. "They're two of our top students."

"Can it, Freeman," Copper ordered. "Go find Thars and get the details on what's happened to our own people. And as for you: I don't know who or what you are and until I do, that's all the information you're getting," she announced, looking him squarely in the eye.

"We're security. I'm Locksmith, that's my team, and that's all *you* need to know," the man said with a quirky smile.

"They were brought in after the trouble out at the Warren," Freeman volunteered from the sidelines. "As extra security for the Enviro-Sciences Department; a private firm, we were told."

"Ex-military?" Linen guessed as her friend's eyes narrowed warily, evidently not convinced.

"Who brought you in? It sure as hell wasn't Lowell College Authorities or MDMC," Copper snorted as she hefted another sample tube, handing it on to Linen after careful scrutiny.

"It's probably none of our business," the redhead grinned at her, stacking her burden carefully as she threw the stranger a sly glance. "Go, Freeman," she added to the still-hovering tech.

Osk had no need to go anywhere, as Thars, in defiance of the still-sounding but muted evac alert, sped through the entry at a run, calling out to know what the blazes was going on. Two of the usual divisional security personnel were on his tail.

"Are you all okay?" he demanded.

"Fine, Thars," Linen said equably. "The bastards who burst in here and tried to kill us are not, however."

The professor stopped dead. "You what?"

His students quickly brought him up to date, the unfamiliar security guard listening to every syllable. Thars Amberline was not happy. The additional security had been brought on board just over three sevensols previously, after the professor's frank and highly detailed report to his departmental head and the College Authorities and his demand for more protection for his students from what appeared to be highly dangerous elements targeting his team and its research. The Astro-Environmental Sciences Division stores had been breached yet again despite the surveillance measures brought in after a small incursion several months ago. The extra security personnel recently drafted in had evidently not been sufficiently effective and given the outcome, the stakes now were higher than previously.

Meanwhile, a medical team had appeared and the two injured felons were being strapped into gurneys under the sharp eyes of a couple of the security guards. The alarm had ceased its wailing and heavy footsteps in the outer corridor implied that other actions were being carried out. One of the team came over to report to his senior that the only other local break-in apart from Osk's small store had been the security office, where the overnight operative had been left unconscious and all the cams reprogrammed to show an empty central Amberline store.

"And where the hell were you when all this was going on?" the professor demanded of the leader.

"We've been spread over campus," was the short reply. "It's not just your division that's been targeted; there was a report of a small explosion at the hydro domes and a dangerous leak in the biogenetics lab. Once the people on the spot realised that both incidents were not as serious as reported and probably put-up jobs, we figured something big was going down. And this place was the obvious target, given your previous problems. We picked up the weapons discharge on our own security nets and got down here as fast as we could."

"Not fast enough," Copper put in. "But those two must have had help: our trolley had been disturbed when we got in despite its being locked to our implants and personally coded to us, but there was nobody here. Those two were coming back for more, their scans told them somebody was here and they came in ready to use weapons."

"So how come you two weren't cut down the second they appeared?" the senior guard demanded.

"We took steps," Copper snapped brusquely. "Our samples had been disturbed, I saw that the secure cams were immobile – none of them shifted to monitor us – but there were a couple of rogue hover-cams looking our way. So we scanned the area and picked out those two on approach. There was nowhere to run, I flung my glove over by the wall as a decoy and we took cover behind the trolley. They had evidently figured we were in here from their scans. They didn't stop at the door but made straight in, firing at the place they thought we were hiding – their mistake. We took them down: villains toting weaponry like that you don't argue with."

"But why did they do it?" Freeman wailed.

"People want what they think we've been finding down at the Warren; *this* is another attempt to get it," Copper told him. "Our stores were broken into months ago, remember; that's why all the new cams were put in place then. Much good it did," she added scathingly. "But there's insider knowledge here, there has to be. How did they know our stuff was here and was going to be moved? How did they breach it?"

"I want those questions answered too," Thars told them. "But for now, we need to get this place checked out, our people checked over and Law Enforcement in to deal with it. You say you recognised one of those two?"

"We ran into him at Beagle," Linen explained. "He and his pal Jecks were sprung from the hospital and have been on the run. I think a few people would like a word with him."

"Jecks!" Thars exploded.

"Another story," Copper put in. "We have work to do. We still have to find out where the hell our missing tubes have gone. As they're coded to us, we may be able to track them if they're still around. If not, then our samples are out there and who knows whose hands are on them."

"*And* the samples we have in our high security storage cells," Linen reminded her. "We'll have to see if those have been filched as well."

* * *

The clean-up of the central store was unavoidably delayed to allow a thorough examination of the scene. Copper and Linen refused to be budged and worked through. As far as they could tell, their only missing items were two of their sample tubes. At a quiet moment the redhead brought up a couple of topics that had been taxing her. How, she asked, had Copper known that something was amiss in the first place; and how had the two interlopers missed them, having scanners that were no doubt top of the range? Copper answered her questions in one word.

"Spook."

"That I figured, but how?" Linen continued. "Okay, you'd have picked up on the trolley, but how did those two miss us?"

"He interfered with their scan readings," her friend told her. "At least, that's my guess. He gave me the clue to slinging my glove as well."

"The chief security guy didn't quite buy that part of your story," Linen stated. "Who are these people anyway? A private firm? Sounds likely, doesn't it? And I can't imagine that MDMC or its lackeys are at back of all this trouble either – MDMC pays our disburse after all and calls the shots to some extent. Maybe it's Mizzle Chert's string-pullers? They're a nasty bunch, what we guess of them."

"There's more than one outfit out there that wants a piece of the action," sighed Copper. "Colonel Moritz told us that a long time ago. And as we *are* essentially deep into the action, we're targets. But you carry on here: I want to track down our missing tubes and I have the feeling they're not too far away."

"Spook has a feeling you mean. But you're not going without me: where you go, I go. We can lock this down, since the place is still swarming with investigators. Where do we start?"

"Techs' common room; one of the insiders has to have had access, or even *be* one of the techs. And then student hang-outs – Mizzle was over at Bio-Ag. But we'll see…"

The two commandeered Freeman Osk as their passport into the techs' common room as the premises were normally out of bounds to non-technical staff. Chief security officer Locksmith had already set a couple of his people to going over the place as he had had his own suspicions but they had come up empty. As Linen was pondering where she would hide objects as large as the two missing tubes, it was Freeman who suggested a possible answer.

"If it was me," he said, "I would stow them in one of the divisional high security cells. Some of the cells are large enough and it's a short distance to transport them. But you'd need to be able to get into them in the first place."

"Easy, if you're a tech," Linen pronounced as she exchanged a glance with her friend. "So we check them out, see which ones are locked to the idents of people we know and bust open any that are not."

"You can't just bust open secure cells!" Freeman said aghast. "That's against regs!"

"So's trying to kill us and stealing our stuff," Linen told him. "And it doesn't stop some. Let's check the register and go."

The still-twittering tech was dragged off to the info station in the secure storage room to check the logs. The cells were used to preserve important, rare or classified samples from prying eyes. Copper and Linen had a couple signed out to them for the rarer samples that they had extracted and which had not been sent on elsewhere. Rapidly matching the idents with a list of their own staff and students, it was quickly apparent that no cell had been requisitioned by any other than their own.

"So that leaves us where?" Linen groaned. "Good idea, Freeman, but we're out of luck."

Copper, quietly musing, held up an interrogative finger. "Just one second: these three cells here next to each other are marked down to Aurora. But she's finished her PhD, so would she sign out secure cells to leave samples she wouldn't need again unless she'd planned to come back here and do more research on them? Her stuff wasn't classified anyway, as far as I remember, although she was finding some interesting bits and pieces."

"I helped her clear up after she'd done," Freeman told them, turning wide eyes on Copper. "She'd nothing in here. But let's see the dates… these were signed out just a couple of sols ago!"

"So someone's got hold of a copy of Aurora's ident: *that* smacks of a tech to me. But how would it work? She's not a current student," Linen frowned.

"Her contract's in place up to the end of next month, so she'd still be on the register," the tech told them. "She finished a few sevensols early," he added in pride.

"So let's find out what they're hiding," Copper told the other two, marching along to the relevant lockers.

"Hadn't we better call security?" Freeman asked.

"They're watching," Linen told him, waving up at a cam in the corner. "Your gun or mine?" she added as Copper was running her hands over the first of the three storage cells as if to check for anything untoward.

"Seems to be locked to an ident right enough," was the calm response, the tone telling her friend she had sensed something. "Can techs get into these cells in an emergency?" she suddenly demanded of Freeman.

"The powers that be certainly can," observed Linen dryly. "They did it to us way back when we found our first flake of interesting material and Lomax Gratikule of MDMC was quick off his butt to commandeer it."

"We techs can't, not without security here," Freeman replied hurriedly. "And a heap of authorisation."

"Then I suggest we get it," Linen said. "It'll take a lot out of our armaments to get through that. And we don't have much time or spare charge-caps."

Even as she spoke, Locksmith and a crony appeared around the portal. "Just what are you three at?" he challenged.

"We think our missing tubes might be in one or other of these three secure cells," Linen told him.

"And just how do you figure that?"

She told him, enlarging on Freeman's part in the deduction and omitting to mention that Copper was already pretty sure: she had picked up on that from her friend's body language. In as short a time as it took to find Thars and obtain the relevant clearances and the security override for breaching secure stores, Locksmith had the whole of sub-floors four through six sealed down, with no one allowed to leave or to come in. Where he got the additional people to maintain the cordon he refused to say.

The six in the small space of the secure storage room let loose sighs as thorough scans told them that the first cell under investigation had not been booby-trapped. The appropriate codes were input and a master ident slotted into the emergency access aperture. The outer cell door unsealed with a hiss and was pulled open by Locksmith, who quickly unlatched the inner.

"Yours, I take it?" the security chief demanded of the two students as he pulled out a large sample tube. "There's another in there as well," he added, reaching in.

"Ours," Copper confirmed as she checked them both. "But we only have two missing from the main store as far as we know, so what are the other two cells hiding?"

"Let's find out," Locksmith announced.

The first of the adjacent cells contained three small sample cartridges that the students recognised only too well as theirs; both held fragments of what they knew were alien artefacts. There were also small cartons belonging to other postgraduates with study sites out at the Warren. Copper and Linen exchanged glances with each other and Thars.

"Looks like one of our smaller cells has been cracked open as well," Linen said. "That's where we had these stored. So some sticky-fingered felons have been very busy. But when and how; and how many more have been ransacked?"

The third storage unit was stacked with sample sleeves and cartridges, many of which were also familiar.

"These ones are ours," Copper said. "That means our secure storage cells along the way there have been emptied. But that doesn't track: they *must* have known we would come along here to get our stuff and discover the breach."

"Maybe they were dumb enough to reckon all this would tie us up long enough that they could get away," Linen suggested.

"Jecks' buddy? Not likely, he's a nasty piece of work and clever with it. Let's check our cells."

"Somebody's had quite a party in there with a small explosive device and a lot of gunk," Linen observed once Locksmith and his team had forced open the first of their cells. "Not reading what should be our stuff, but then maybe I wouldn't, given it's all over there."

Copper shrugged. "We've got what's ours, but the other guys will have one helluva lot of sorting and salvage to do."

"You're telling me," Thars interjected, looking shocked. "I want to know what went down in the central store as well — I've only heard part of it," he went on to his two students.

"We need to take what's ours for the *Drake*," Copper said

shortly. "We'll cut to the bare minimum, but we're running it fine. Half the sol's gone already and we had meets with Alessa and Mariner – they've gone by the board."

"Every damn lecture and meeting has gone by the board," Thars told her. "The whole department's in an uproar. Do what you have to and get your samples cleared. I'll help and we'll talk on the way. Where the hell you'll store your stuff until you leave I don't know."

"*We'll* worry about that," Copper told him. "I'll commandeer a shuttle if I have to."

Linen gave her a quizzical look but said nothing. Locksmith raised a searching eyebrow, his mouth twisting up in a sardonic grin as he scanned her closely, but all he said was that he and his team would carry out a thorough search of the area.

With Thars and Freeman assisting, the two cleared out their chaotic gear and left the security personnel to their work. They carried the containers through to the main store and to a free patch of bench space for sorting. The professor was given a summary of the morning's happenings as they worked. Copper and Linen were then left to it as the other two had a mountain of their own problems to sort. An hour later the duo decided that they had done enough, secured their loaded trolley and set off to a study carrel for a lunch-break and a private talk.

"You'll commandeer a shuttle?" queried Linen, spinning in her chair, a cup of caff in her hands. "How and from where?"

"I suspect there may be one with our name on it at Lowell spaceport already," Copper declared. "Colonel Moritz will have been brought up to date as all this relates to our mission aboard the *Drake*. And whatever Locksmith claims to be, he's not your average private security bod. I sense something else in him; he knows a helluva lot more than he's letting on, including about us. But we're no doubt being overrun by the Law and the Press by now, so we'd best ship out earlier rather than later. We've handed over quite a few pertinent finds to Colonel Moritz and her team anyway – which now includes Trisk – so we'll see most of *them* again at some point."

"But that means any samples we leave here will be targets," Linen objected.

"As will our site at the Warren *and* the military site next door, and every other blasted site on Mars that's generated results, including around Lowell," Copper said. "We can't cover every base, that's Mars Intelligence's job; Karben and her playmates in other words. All we can do is try to plug the leaks *we* have. *We're* being targeted because we have links to high-ranking people and are soon going to be beyond the reach of the troublemakers that are trying to grab a piece of the action. I'm sure I got most of the important bits from our samples, but I strongly suspect that once we're out in the great dark yonder we'll have more to take up our time than bags of rockery."

"We *are* supposed to be doing our PhDs based on our site," Linen reminded her friend. "MDMC won't keep ponying up the credit unless we produce results on what we're supposed to be doing in relation to that."

"We'll get it done. Let's finish up here, find a private nook and thoroughly sort the samples we need to take. We'll find out the latest about the situation here and then see about transport for our kit. I think we should aim to get it aboard morrow-sol."

"And what about overnight storage here?"

"Mr Locksmith can do a night-shift," was the curt response. "I'm sure he's got it covered in any case."

"You and me both. I'd get Spook to keep watch on *him* if I were you."

* * *

Lowell College was almost back to its usual tranquil state by Wedsol, as Copper, Linen and Majorelle sallied up and in via a side entry. Majorelle had contacted them the previous sol to find out what had been going on: she and her fellow students had been ordered home when the lock-down had come into effect but she had realised that her friends were on the wrong side of the blockade. She had been pacified by their calm demeanour and their story of plenty of routine to keep them occupied.

Various updates on the previous sol had included the news that the intruders were comfortably locked up in a high-security medical facility. Copper and Linen had been a tad surprised that their own actions had not resulted in interrogation but as the College Authorities seemed to be playing down the seriousness of the incidents by blaming a technical malfunction for most of the disruption, they accepted the situation with little more than sceptical shrugs. The efficiency of the new security team had resulted in the detention of two rogue techs and a student, who had all been spirited off somewhere, but that was about all they could find out.

The two Amberlines had decided to keep a low profile lest any more adventures befell them. They chose the super tri-dee sim suite as a suitable base of operations: they were familiar with it, it had not been requisitioned by anyone else, it was secure and once within, they had control of the door. With the efficient Avrom as go-between they had communicated with both Alessa Aclarke and Mariner Mbolon whilst packing and securing every sample carton they would be taking aboard the *Drake*. They chose to wrap most of their tubes and stacks of cartridges in film copies of the *Goodwitch Guide to Mars' Mission History*, a handy tome for foiling any clever scanning ops. A surreptitious link to Trisk aboard the *Drake* using Copper's wrist-comm had elicited the information that a shuttle would be available when they needed it: the colonel was fully cognisant of the events at Lowell and their aftermath.

With their feelings of urgency increasing, the two had agreed that a trip to their ship that afternoon was the best option and had accordingly made arrangements. Linen had had the brilliant idea of asking Lofty for a loan of his Spirit Hover for the trip to the spaceport: it would be speedy, discreet and almost effortless. Their friend was delighted to be trusted, offering Malachite as pilot and himself as minder. Copper and Linen therefore found themselves more rapidly than expected marching alongside their trolley towards a small departure area specifically set aside for private and other craft. There they were perforce obliged to bid their escort farewell, but promised to catch up with them later.

"So where the hell do we go now?" Linen demanded in a low voice as the panel closed behind them and they were faced with a fairly large space with rows of ordered seating in the centre and several apertures around the perimeter. "The ramp to our shuttle should be through one of those doors, Trisk told us."

One of the few forms that were lounging on the central seats rose and walked towards them. He was dressed in Fleet uniform and both recognised him instantly. It was Locksmith and he was sporting the insignia of the *MSS Drake II*.

"Lieutenant Kit Locksmith, security chief of the *Drake*," he grinned at the pair. "I'm here to escort you to your ship."

"Why am I not surprised?" Copper looked up at him with a wry smile as she pointed to their trolley. "Lead on Lieutenant, this is our gear."

"This way. I understand you've both been aboard before?"

"We have, some while ago, but I expect things have changed somewhat since then. This must be our shuttle," Copper stated as the ramp ended in an irised opening into a small pressurised hangar in which a pristine craft that looked like a larger version of the Ares-Class Mark IV four-man shuttle was berthed. It bore the badge of the *MSS Drake II*.

"It is. Let's get your trolley secured in the aft cargo bay. You can both sit forr'ad with me, there's plenty room."

"I expect there is," Copper replied as she and Linen pushed the trolley across the open space.

Locksmith unlatched the bay and the two Amberlines hauled the equipment aboard, securing the webbing before hopping out and around the side of the craft.

"I can take her up, if you like," Copper called after the man as she followed him aboard, her friend on her tail. "I *can* handle a shuttle."

"But you haven't actually docked one aboard a ship of the Fleet before," Linen murmured in her ear as she settled her kitbag more comfortably over her shoulder and climbed up.

"Sims," was the reply.

Locksmith acknowledged the offer with a small chuckle and once on the flight deck he strapped himself in, waiting until the other two had stowed their personal bags and done likewise.

"You're not officially crew yet," he told Copper. "So *I* take her up. Maybe next time," he added, his blue eyes twinkling.

The shuttle was given clearance almost immediately and the two newest crew members of the *Drake* braced themselves for the shock of take-off as they were crushed down into their seats by the accelerative forces. Shortly afterwards they were free of the lower atmosphere and heading for the massive mesh of light and metal that was Phobos Station II Space Dock. In one of the numerous lacunae hung the sheer hulk of the massive *Drake II*, docking struts holding her in place whilst an army of repair and construct bots swarmed over her metallic hide.

"Looking good," Linen observed to her friend. "Bit more polished than last time. She'll be on the tail of MDMC's new boat soon then, since the *Fearless* is still apparently in process of showing her fancy lines and classy uniforms to the upper ranked MDMC lackeys that run various asteroid mining stations."

The *SS Fearless* had launched over a sevensol before and was reportedly headed on a shakedown cruise that would take in a number of MDMC locations en route to system edge.

"*Fearless*," Copper grunted. "*Pointless*, more like."

Locksmith laughed quietly as he expertly brought the small craft into one of the *Drake's* huge front bays, manoeuvring her into her assigned docking station. Waiting only until the inner bay doors had sealed and their station lights showed green, the three were quick to disembark and request permission of the duty officer to come aboard. Once checked by the watch officer they made their way through the mandatory security field to find a familiar face awaiting them on the flipside: Trisk Addystone, resplendent in a pristine uniform, saluted all three smartly and then leaned over to give the Amberlines a hug.

"Welcome aboard!" he grinned. "Heard you'd been up to no good again."

"How?" Copper demanded.

"I keep my ears open for news of Lowell; I heard something was up so I made enquiries," he told them. "I told the liaison officer I'd show you about, since you're not officially supposed to report for duty until Frisol. I'll give you a hand with your gear – we can go directly down to the labs and get it all into storage. Bet you'll be glad to have it off your backs."

"In which case, I'll get on with a few things I have to do," Kit Locksmith announced. "Let me know when you want to get back planetside; tonight, I expect?" he asked Copper.

"Yup. We have a lecture to give morrow-sol," she informed him. "We promised Thars. Thanks for the ride, by the way."

As Locksmith departed with a smile and a nod to the three and the promise to see the two students later, Linen looked round. "No Colonel Moritz?" she asked their friend.

"She doesn't meet and greet every new crewmember that

comes aboard," Trisk admonished, laughing. "She's got rather a lot to keep her busy. But once your gear is stashed, I can show you to your quarters; they've been assigned. You'll have to link in with the first officer to get your clearances, but he's okay and he knows you were headed up."

Trisk seemed to be familiar with his surroundings and soon the three were several decks down and towards the central area of the ship, where a reasonably large office close by the main astrobiology lab had been assigned to them.

"I'll get your names on the door panel when you're officially signed in," he promised. "But first we get to stores, just here. I'll stash the stuff under my ident. Then I suggest we get on up to the exec's office and get you set up. Even though you're a couple of sols early, you should be able to pick up your badges. I'll just let Captain Helmis know what we're up to."

The two newcomers began systematically unloading and stacking their samples in the place pointed out by their colleague as he put the link through to the first officer of the *Drake II*, Captain Merris Helmis. Neither Copper nor Linen had met the captain, but they had heard of him through Trisk.

"The captain says he'll meet us in the exec's office – that's where he's located officially, though he's mostly on the bridge when he's on duty," Trisk explained. "And once you're in the system, you should upload the ship's spec into your solid idents, which are basically wrist-comm units; there *are* info-points all over the ship, but it's handy to have your own map."

"And then we see our quarters," Linen nodded cheerfully. "Hope they look as good as the specs you sent us down."

"And then the officers' mess?" Copper added hopefully.

"You and your stomach," her friend laughed as they dutifully followed Dr Addystone, who enlivened the journey by pointing out various points of interest along their route.

The trio passed several officers on the way, most of whom appeared to know Trisk. The exec's office was close enough to the bridge to be handy and their friend buzzed at the entrance, waiting until the door panel slid across and a voice called out "Come on in". After introductions, during which the two new officers were unusually silent, Captain Helmis took their hand prints and passed over their idents, explaining that these also operated as the comm units for the crew of the *Drake*. Each ident was fashioned as a thin tight bracelet with a flat oval face sporting a sliding key that allowed voice-operated comms. Once attached, the ident bonded to its owner, the linkage providing locational data when required to relevant ship's stations.

Copper grinned amusedly at Linen. "Magenta's handiwork," she said a low voice.

"Looks like," the redhead agreed.

"You both know Ms Firewall of course," Helmis smiled. "I was briefed," he added at the questioning glances. "You're required to wear your idents when on duty; otherwise it's up to you," the captain went on. "I'll no doubt see more of you when you formally take up your posts on Frisol. You can collect your uniforms and other kit from the quartermaster. Dismissed."

"Aye, sir," they responded jointly as they turned and made their way out of the office.

"Looks quite young to be a captain," was Copper's summing up. "Especially of a ship like the *Drake*."

"He's not in command, the colonel is," Trisk reminded her. "Some officers with the rank of captain would object to having to defer to a senior officer aboard a ship of the Fleet. But let's get you your uniforms and then I'll show you to your quarters. You're on deck nine, section thirty four, next door to me. You'll find the berths comfortable."

Copper had other things on her mind. "He was briefed," she said. "So was Locksmith. How many more of this ship's officers have been briefed about us?"

"Quite a few," Trisk grinned. "But let me introduce you to Major Tiff Tuffet – he's the quartermaster and considers every piece of ship's property as his own..."

Half an hour later Copper and Linen, after a few hot words with Major Tuffet over the newly supplied uniforms, boots and regulation weaponry, were taking their first look at their new billets on deck nine, section thirty four. Crew quarters twenty four and twenty six were next door to one another and close to Trisk in twenty two. The spaces were identical, a smallish main room giving on to sleeping and hygiene units. A comms desk, seating and a small table with drawers inset underneath made up much of the rest of the space, with handy shelving attached to the bulkheads and storage lockers set in. A kitchen area to one side was flanked by a snug booth for dining.

"Well, at least I can have you over for dinner," remarked Linen as she dropped her bundle on the low couch in her new quarters. "Four could squeeze around *that* table as long you don't mind somebody else's elbow in your soup."

"This is high class accomm," Trisk informed her, laughing. "I'll have you know I persuaded the exec's office to assign you these as soon as I could – some of the others in this section are smaller or oddly shaped. Want to see mine? I've decorated and changed it around a bit. You can requisition stuff from ship's stores or bring your own. And then you'd maybe best head on down as it's close to twenty two hundred back at Lowell. We'll leave the mess and the tour for another sol."

The two agreed with alacrity, linking to Locksmith to apprise him of their schedule for return. Their friend's billet was similar to their own but less clinical and certainly warmer. After a rapid rundown on the source of his extra accoutrements, Copper and Linen agreed that they had better pick up their own needs and make for the bay and their shuttle planetside. Now that they were officially members of the *Drake's* crew they had decided to take their regular shipboard uniforms down with them in order that Lofty and Majorelle could see them in their finery. It would also be useful to be in uniform for return aboard, they reasoned, although secretly both were more than keen to gauge the effects of their outfits on the denizens of Lowell Central.

* * *

Thursol began with a large breakfast at the Amaloft-Moritz place. Their hosts had insisted on this luxury as the guests had a very busy schedule, having done little more the previous eve than drop into their beds in exhaustion. With Osterley snuffling around, Copper and Linen were unanimous in preferring to don casual workasol wear for the first part of the morning. They planned to aim for College and set up for their mid-sol seminar and then head back to base to change for the event.

Thars had contacted them with the news that the place was settling down, although it would be a long time before the large store would be back to normal: a number of their colleagues had lost valuable samples and with the lockdown still in operation at the Warren, life would not be easy. The two were only grateful that their most important materials were now aboard their ship and everything else pertinent to their site had been stored in the deepest recesses of Lowell College with more security attached than that accorded the President of Mars on one of her visits to the southern hemisphere, according to Kit Locksmith, now out of Fleet uniform and tying up loose ends in divisional security.

Lowell College Main Building was humming when the two bid goodbye to Majorelle and made for sub-floor six and their study suite. Many of their usual associates were absent, no doubt clearing out in the stores. The duo was grateful: their task was to empty out their own study booths, as these would be needed by new students, an apologetic Avrom had told them.

"We're used to it by now," Copper consoled the exec when he came by to see how they were coping and to inform them of the timing of their presentation. "We had to move out of our accomm in Lowell when we shipped out to Beagle and that was a struggle, with all the gear we'd accumulated over the years we've been here. Luckily we had Linen's Grammy's place at Beagle to store stuff," she added. "And we have our friends on Coblentz Street here that are always willing to help out. We'll miss the place though – and the company."

"You'll have plenty of time to say your goodbyes," Avrom told them. "You won't be on long: Thars insisted, as you'd not had time to prepare, what with all the problems we've had. I think most people are amazed that you're still going ahead with it. Quite a few are turning up – the Amberlines here and all their mentors for a start."

"Then we'd better move it," Linen said, shooting a smile at him. "We can take all this to Lofty's when we head back to change," she said to Copper. "We have to look the part," she explained to Avrom, "So we'll see you back here later."

"Look the part," Copper echoed once the exec had strolled off. "You mean get into our uniforms to impress the locals."

"Exactly. We may as well get as much fun out of them as we can; we only have until morrow-sol."

"Lor' don't remind me: I'm all of a shake and so is Spook. I'll leave my weather station for the next person at this desk; I doubt I'll need it on the *Drake* and I can't be bothered sending it back to stores."

It took little time to prepare their presentation in the seminar room allotted and the two were soon on their way to Amaloft's Diner, bulging carryalls in hand. Once rid of their baggage and freshly attired, they paraded their gear for their friends' benefit. Lofty insisted on capturing a holo-pic for memory's sake and with Malachite at his back, waved the pair off up the street.

Few people appeared to be impressed by the sight of the two uniformed individuals marching purposefully down Mine Street and across the Public Gardens by way of the narrow paths that led to Lowell College. The mid-sol light filtering down through the plas-crystal of Dome roof was hazy, as if a windstorm was in the offing, and they decided to make for Beta Block and thus through to Main Block. They encountered no familiar faces until they reached the entrance hallway of the main campus building, where the first person they recognised pulled them up short. He was interrogating an info-point and seemed as shocked to see them when they strode up.

"Mizzle!" Linen greeted the gangly form before them. "What are you doing here?"

"I'm still doing a Master's in Advanced Agro-Sciences," was the apprehensive reply.

"And what else are you doing?" Copper demanded, less than politely. "Greensands Minerals still providing your disburse and asking you to perform their so-called commissions?"

"You're in uniform," he noted dazedly.

"You haven't answered my question. I suggest you do it now or we haul you in for questioning," Copper advised.

"You what? I can't tell you anything!"

"Then you're coming with us," was the abrupt response as Copper grabbed hold of his sleeve, slapped his hand away from the console he had been manipulating and pulled him towards the nearest elevator.

The man was too dazed to protest. Linen raised her hands in perplexity but closed the info-link and trailed them into the lift, where Copper ordered sub-floor six. It was as her friend towed her quarry along the corridor towards the stores area that Linen realised their endpoint: they were headed for the local security office. Mizzle had also by this time figured what was to come and made a futile attempt to release himself. He was rewarded by a sock on the ear and bundled through the door.

"Locksmith about?" Copper demanded brusquely.

"I'll call him in," a man that both girls recognised as one of the new team responded, eyeing their uniforms.

Kit Locksmith stepped through the door moments later, by which time Mizzle had been attached to a chair by restraints and Linen was systematically going through his pockets.

"Naughty boy," she reproved, shaking a finger under his nose as she pulled out a small handgun. "Not a nice toy to be playing with. And I bet you don't have a licence for it. Now this scanner is a doozie, mil issue but with the ID marks removed. Where on Mars did you get it?"

"We don't have time, we're on a mission," Copper reminded her. "Mizzle Chert, supposed to be doing a Master's degree in Agro-Science, broke into our stores away back but not charged. He was searching College schematics of the lowest levels via the info-point next to the elevator in the main hall. He's funded by an outfit called Greensands Minerals and has some *very* nasty friends. He's all yours," she added as Locksmith's blue eyes shot wide at her tone and he inclined his head quizzically.

"Copper…" came Mizzle's agonised voice.

"That's lieutenant," she snapped. "Goodbye."

Linen smiled ruefully, shrugging expressively at the security chief and his crew before turning and following her friend from the office.

"You realise he outranks us?" the redhead said in a low voice as the two set off to their allotted seminar room. "You okay?" she added in response to the silence that met her question.

"Yup. Life never seems to let us alone, does it? Our last sol and we run into Mizzle Chert. Locksmith will be able to pull up the data on him, as the colonel was well aware of his activities."

"*Lieutenant* Locksmith," Linen corrected. "But the Mizzle was left loose before, probably deliberately," she continued. "So why are his operators still using him? They must realise he's as dim as a doorknob."

"No idea. But let's check all's ready for the show, ourselves included. I see Avrom's got the eats laid out next door."

* * *

Their uniforms proved a sartorial success with their audience and the tri-dee sim of the Glory Hole, once the projection had been fired up, caused gasps of admiration. Thankful that they had spent some time recently at their site, the two could reel off the impressive aspects of its structure and the more mundane of the finds that had already been reported to MDMC with little effort. It was Thars who finally called a halt and announced that questions could be asked of the two as the assembly enjoyed the catering so capably organised by Avrom.

Two hours later and the hoarse duo had regretfully to decline further festivity at one of the local hostelries. They were called back into the main seminar room and amid the cheers and applause of their fellows, were presented with small tokens of appreciation in the form of geodes as Thars made a farewell speech, ably seconded by Alessa Aclarke and Mariner Mbolon. The professor had decided that they would head back to his office to finalise arrangements for the reporting of their work for MDMC from the *Drake* and shepherded the pair out of the room and into the peace of the hallway outside. Copper took the opportunity of thanking him: she for one was grateful that they would not be escorted off the premises by an ardent mob of friendly well-wishers.

Thars himself was sincerely affected as he bid the two a final goodbye, with much handshaking. They had elected to make their way without company up to ground level for a good look around the campus at which they had spent so much of their life over the past few years. A stroll around the grounds led them to the Plane Tree and a mug of caff for old times' sake.

"We'll be back," Linen promised. "We can look into one or two old haunts around Dome and then head back to Lofty's – I bet they'll have something planned."

10: FIELDING FLAK

Kitbags in hand, Copper and Linen stepped off the ramp of the shuttle that had taken them up to the *MSS Drake II*. They had more baggage to collect from the cargo bay, but both halted for a moment to take in their docking station and the surrounds that would become more familiar over the coming months. The lack of a welcoming committee surprised neither: with the ship due to depart in the very near future, few personnel had time to greet rookies. Having saluted the duty officer smartly and been given permission to come aboard, they presented their idents for validation and for logging into ship's systems. Formalities completed, their pilot called them over to collect their gear. As the two complied, he advised them to report to the exec's office via one of the local comm-ports on the flipside of the security exit whilst awaiting the arrival of the liaison officer who would guide them through checking onto the ship.

"So here it starts to get interesting," Linen smiled, having sensed that her companion was more than a little anxious.

Their last evening planetside had been spent with Lofty and Majorelle in their family unit; Malachite had joined them for the excellent fare and the session of nostalgia. The two new officers had also received several farewell links from various associates who had somehow got wind of their imminent departure. Ma Kellyn was one of them and Majorelle had to admit to telling her. *She* had passed the news onto her pet tenants, Maressan Chengi and Jenika Grass-Tephra at Road Eleven, and to Linen's ex-Landlord Pa Grunwalker. How Thulia and Wolff Waterbone had found out was anyone's guess, Linen surmised, but Mik and Ambrose had left messages, as had Captain Kezza Brownpelt.

"Well, we'd best report in and then wait for whoever's to show us around," Copper said at last, their pilot having made off. "There's a comm-station over there."

The two headed over to one of the many consoles set around the light blue-grey bulkheads that made up the space beyond the several docking stations that led from the main bay. A number of operatives in service coveralls were at work, diligently poking probes into side stations and down hatches scattered across the deck. The new officers were cheered when their idents let them use the station but the exec and his subs were evidently busy elsewhere as a routine acknowledgement was all they received.

As they waited, the two examined the insignia of the *Drake*, displayed on opposite sides of the roughly square area, no doubt to welcome incoming visitors and crew. Several passageways led off in diverse directions and locational information was marked on info-screens incorporated into the bulkheads. It was while they were discussing the various uniform colours of the visible personnel that they were hailed by a cheery voice.

"Hello, you must be Lieutenants Lyrican and Milkstone! I'm Tany Melucca, the duty liaison officer. Welcome aboard!"

Copper and Linen turned; the duty LO was a short individual with dark red hair and dazzling teeth. As her insignia indicated that she was a first lieutenant, the two saluted – they had been practising in their spare time back at Lowell and had almost got the gesture down to a fine art.

She returned the salutation with a nod and announced that as the pair had already been assigned quarters, she would escort them there to dispose of their kitbags before reporting to the exec's office, where all personnel matters were handled. There, they would be officially cleared to operate aboard and receive their orders and assignation to their relevant work centre.

* * *

The next several hours were a whirlwind of orientation to the ship, appointments with the chief medical officer and his staff, an introduction to the recreational facilities and a stop-off at what was now their science unit on deck five: it was arranged over sections six through nineteen and it was there in a side lab that they found Trisk deep in some analysis or other. He was quick to call a halt and offered to take over the tour, as he was about due to break for lunch. Copper for one was relieved: Lieutenant Melucca was an exhausting guide that reminded her far too much of Magenta Firewall. And lunch sounded like an excellent idea after the prodding and poking she had undergone in medbay, not to mention the implantation of a permanent locational ident that could be activated if necessary.

There were two officers' messes aboard the *Drake*, Trisk told them. With the number of crew aboard and the vagaries of duty stints, they were needed. Both were run on the principle of grab a tray, grab your food and find a space, with scant regard given to rank in most cases, though it was always wise to err on the side of caution: some officers could be tetchy. The pair was also advised to wear jackets for forays into the mess, or at least standard uniforms: informal workasol gear or fatigues were not acceptable attire. Trisk smiled as he spoke, however, and led them to the mess closest to his office and labs: it was on deck four and easily accessible by elevator or by one of the numerous ladders that linked the decks at salient points.

Lieutenants Milkstone and Lyrican gazed around at the space and were reminded a little of the mess at the Warren: a selection of tables and booths of various sizes, with food stations set along one side at which to select the chow that the galley staff had decreed the choice of the sol. There were more comfortable eating spaces for snacks and chat, with armchairs set around low tables, over by the wall, but a separate officers' lounge next door was provided as relaxation space, as were other entertainment facilities in dedicated areas close by, including a small theatre.

The place was relatively busy despite the early hour for lunch and as Trisk was hailed by one or two shipmates, he took the opportunity to introduce the duo around. Amongst a sprinkling of senior officers the two discerned Lieutenant Commander Faela Khilph, the nav-officer who had been their guide the first time they had set eyes on the *Drake* months before. As they had had no glimpse of the colonel since boarding, they wondered if she would make contact over the short break time. She had a private mess for distinguished visitors, Trisk told his friends, but she rarely used it and was in the habit of stopping into whatever mess was handiest at the time, usually the one on deck four.

In the event, Colonel Moritz did not put in an appearance and Copper and Linen decided that the remainder of duty time might profitably be spent in organising their gear in the office that they would be sharing with Trisk, and capturing lab space for their own researches. They were thrilled to find that their names had been added to the door panel below Trisk's and that the office door opened to their crew idents.

"Most doors do," Dr Addystone informed them. "There are very few off-limits places to officers, just private quarters other than your own, weapons stores, secure stores, some parts of engineering and medbay, places that have complex equipment and so on. Local comforts are thataway. Once you've got your task-stations set up, we'll retrieve your samples from my store and set up stowage for your stuff that only you and a few choice others will be able to access."

"Others? What others?" Copper demanded as she sat in her allotted chair and swivelled round to test it.

"The colonel and Captain Helmis; security people with the right clearances, Chef Locksmith for one; and me, as I'm your senior. Not to mention one or two others. You'll have to catch up with the other senior SOs but we're all involved in different things, so they won't bother you much. The chief science officer is Dr Ossy Inkscree and he's ranked lieutenant commander, but he's okay. We'll call in before we head to our main lab," Trisk went on, his lopsided grin widening as his eyes twinkled.

"Inkscree!" the other two exploded.

"I thought you might recognise that name. Yes, he's a nano-engineer and he's Opal's brother. Isn't Mars a small place?"

Commander Opal Inkscree was the co-pilot of the Scuttle, one of the two main Amberline transport craft, and the three knew her. Ossian Inkscree turned out to be a large man, a genial chatterbox with a hearty handshake and a loud voice that belied the intelligence and wit lurking behind a pair of very shrewd eyes. As she looked cannily at their new colleague Copper had a fleeting vision of a mission that she and Linen had carried out on behalf of their sponsors, MDMC, many months before which had in part led them to their present position.

"Miniaturised stealth surf-sci bots," she said into a pause. "Are you in charge of them, sir?"

Dr Inkscree looked at her, startled. "I was told you two were sharp," he laughed. "Yes, the mini stealth surface science bots that may or may not be deployed on our upcoming mission are my responsibility. I know you two have handled them and had some role in suggesting improvements. We'll have to talk about it later. But you'd better get on with organising your own space. I understand you have a lot of your own work to carry out."

"That we do, sir," Linen put in. "Where next, Trisk?"

Their friend led them in the direction of the main lab and the adjoining stores where he had temporarily stashed their samples. The three spent the next hour transferring all their tubes, sleeves and cartons to a series of secure storage lockers signed out to the new science officers. That done, they checked out the facilities available to them in the lab that they would use most of the time. The two were heartened to find a couple of top-grade bio-geo-chem sequencers, as well as sundry sample and data analysis consoles that were rather superior to those they had been used to in Lowell and at the AF Dome's labs. There were also several small tri-dee sim stations in a dedicated side lab.

"Do we have a super tri-dee sim suite somewhere?" Copper demanded of their friend as she looked around.

"Just where do you think you are, Lowell College?" Trisk demanded jocularly. "Not round here but there *are* very superior tri-dee test facilities for various bits of kit on the engineering decks that are capable of hard-holo projection, though you need the data for the actual projections. Doc Inkscree's in charge of one of those."

"Huh," Copper grimaced. "They'll be for those damned surf-sci bots, I'll bet. I wonder how many we have aboard and what's planned for them. Planetary drop?"

"Dare you to ask the colonel!" Linen grinned.

"I would if I could but we've not seen hide nor hair of her since we checked aboard."

"That'll change," Trisk chuckled quietly. "She did drop a link saying she'd catch up at some point. She's rather busy, with the ship due for her official launch in two sols."

"Two sols!" Copper and Linen looked at one another.

"Nobody tells us anything," Copper grumbled.

"Get used to it," Trisk told her. "It'll be a bit of a send-off, with media attention no doubt. And we're still not up to scratch with installations *and* we don't have our full complement yet. That's why Captain Helmis hasn't been around. He figures you two can handle yourselves without much extra help."

"Yes, he was briefed. Inkscree was briefed, Locksmith was briefed, half the damn ship was briefed. We've got a rep already and we've been aboard less than a sol," Copper complained.

"Oh stow it, Cop! You know you love it really. And we'll always have the option of seriously winding up our crewmates and getting away with it," Linen twinkled.

"Oh go throw a glass-candy at the two moons why don't you?" her friend told her in exasperation. "So who's launching the *Drake* in two sols? Galaxia Sandbar?"

"I hardly think so," a voice at their backs responded dryly and all three turned to find Colonel Elle Chryse Moritz.

"Good afternoon ma'am," Copper gulped, her head rearing up, unsure of whether she was supposed to stand to attention as she had seen Trisk out of the corner of her eye snap upright and give a dutiful nod.

"Welcome aboard," the colonel greeted them. "Apologies that I wasn't able to meet you personally earlier, press of duty. Finding your feet?"

"Yes, ma'am," the newcomers responded in unison.

"Good. Lieutenant Addystone, take a walk; I want a quiet word with these two."

"Aye, ma'am," Trisk replied laconically and strolled off.

"I hear you had quite a time of it yestersol. Trouble seems to follow you two around like a pet hound," the colonel observed.

"You were briefed," Copper sighed. "Mizzle Chert… what in blazes was he up to anyway, ma'am?"

"Checking out where you two had stashed the samples you didn't bring aboard," Colonel Moritz told her. "As you figured, no doubt; although I expect the samples you left behind are not particularly interesting."

The commanding officer's eyes narrowed as the two traded glances and shrugged. "You appear to have an uncanny knack of hitting upon fractions containing traces of alien artefact without using scanners or other assists even when you're not in direct contact," the colonel went on sharply. "You in particular, Lieutenant Milkstone. Care to tell me how you do it?"

"Was Lieutenant Locksmith keeping an eye on us while we were carrying out our final sort late Tuesol?" Copper enquired suspiciously. "I'm sensitive to the stuff," she hurriedly went on as the expression on Colonel Moritz' face told her she was close to overstepping a boundary. "I get a frizz when I'm close to artefact material even if I can't see it. That's how I figured..."

"The ship," Linen put in quickly, nudging her friend lest she blurt out some indiscretion about Spook. "Out at the Warren: you knew something big was there. I felt it too, once you'd got it pinpointed. But you're way more sensitive than I am. That's how you know which sample tubes are liable to contain artefact material; and how you're able to make the surface patterning on some pieces shift," she added adroitly.

"Another of your talents," the colonel observed shrewdly, aware that something had passed between the two. "And we *do* have that artefact aboard, the one that you dug up at your lower research site some time back and were able both to operate *and* to lock to you, but we'll deal with that later. To bring you up to date: your friend Mr Chert is now in custody and undergoing questioning as to his sponsors and the work he's been carrying out for them. The authorities have not been able to find your assailant Jecks; he's covered his trail too well. As to your other problems, Military Intelligence has a handle on at least two of a number of suspected operations that have their beady eyes, and want their greedy claws, on ways and means of getting a piece of the action as far as making actual alien contact is concerned."

"You mean they know that conclusive evidence of past alien incursion on Mars has been found and hushed up and all this launching of ships to find new resources is a blind to find out more because there is reason to suspect that there are aliens out there right now, ma'am? And they think that the kudos of being the first to make contact would give them not only massive prestige and a hands-up on the alien organo-technology they're trying to steal from here, but a heap of credit into the bargain?" Copper asked, trying to clarify her thought processes.

"That's what some believe."

"Not realising that some of said aliens might be really nasty and are as likely to blow them out of space as to extend a few friendly tentacles or whatever?"

"I think you miss the point, *Lieutenant*," the colonel said levelly. "Ways and means of getting a piece of the action include incursions not only into your and our research sites, and others where alleged alien artefacts have been uncovered, but strikes on personnel that seem to be – sensitive – to the materials."

"Like us and Trisk!" Linen put in. "Is that why he accepted a position aboard the *Drake*, ma'am? I remember him saying ages ago that the military was interested in him but he wasn't up for it; though he took the funding that was offered at the time to further his research. But after that he joined the *Drake*. He *did* suggest that he'd had some trouble with nasty people but didn't elaborate…"

"Belay that, Lieutenant. I expect you've had your orders," Ms Moritz went on. "Your duties now include detailed analyses of the samples from your Warren site and of samples from other sites that we have aboard; Lieutenant Addystone will give you access to those. You will report *any* reactions you experience when in contact with the samples immediately. You'll also be expected to assist with other science duties aboard, including stints at the science stations on the bridge and elsewhere, and in deployment of scientific probes and instrumentation as required for our ongoing mission. Clear?"

"Yes, ma'am," the two chorused.

"You have a question, Lieutenant Milkstone?"

"Deployment? Does that mean the army of surf-sci bots that Dr Inkscree seems to have in his pockets?"

"He told you that?"

"I guessed," Copper admitted.

"They may or may not be deployed," the colonel informed her. "It depends on other issues."

"Like what the *Sapphire Sunset* finds, I expect," was the blunt and unthinking response.

"What! What do you know about the *Sapphire Sunset*?" the colonel asked dangerously.

"We met a couple of their new crewmen out at Beagle when we were on leave from College, before we joined up," confessed Copper, regretting her slip. "It was on that sol you gave us our civilian stat pins. In fact, we had a drink with them in the BC Hotel that eve, when we ran into Mizzle Chert's sponsor… and the fun we had after that: chases across Beagle Central, Grammy Magenta's marines, *your* assist to take him down…"

Colonel Moritz sighed in vexation, folding her arms. "You did *not* mention meeting officers from the *Sunset* and extracting information from them on their mission; and I saw the pair of you the very next sol. *That* was when you told me that you suspected that the alien ship that you two had helped locate was manned, Lieutenant Milkstone. You suggested that the signals we were picking up might be from a functioning life support unit. For all our months of study we were never able to verify that and we still have not been able to fully penetrate the ship's hide: it's sufficiently active to repair any breaches we can make."

She paused for a moment, thinking, her eyes boring into the duo in front of her. Copper began to feel a frizz of anxiety that communicated itself to Linen, and her friend turned to her, eyes widening.

"You two, my office, now!"

"Yes ma'am!"

It took several minutes to gain the quiet and security of the colonel's office, which was next to the bridge on the flight deck, the uppermost part of the ship and five levels above the main decks. The officer's grim face and steely eyes suggested that whatever was in store was going to be less than pleasant. Once within the small space, the two were ordered to sit at the briefing table, from where the colonel informed her first officer that she was not to be disturbed unless there was an emergency and then slapped the local info-console into life.

"Interesting," was the result of the examination of the data readout. "I am regularly updated on the outcome of the work out on Isidis, next to your site, as it obviously impacts on this ship's mission. There was a change in the signal output from the alien craft that MI is investigating early this sol, almost exactly at the time that you two came aboard. In fact it decreased. The coincidence did strike me then. The signal hasn't changed since. And I *now* recall, Ms Milkstone, that you told me at the meeting after the incident at the BC Hotel, that you felt, how did you put it, that you had a sort of affinity with some other mind that reaches out to you for a brief time and then vanishes? Akin to the intuitive resonance that seems to exist between the two of you but it was colder, more distant? I dismissed it at the time as the result of the head injury you had sustained. But events since then have suggested that there's a lot more to you than meets the eye, Lieutenant, much more than I know and suspect. You *will* enlighten me and you'll omit nothing. Remember, you are now a serving officer in Mars Fleet and as such you are required to uphold the constitution to which you have sworn allegiance."

Copper bit her lip. "Yes ma'am," she responded. "This may sound a little incredible, but…"

Hesitantly, she began with the injury she sustained in the rockfall triggered when Amberline techs had tried to breach a new tunnel that was adjacent to previous exploratory diggings, the lurid dreams that began soon after, and the finding of their first fragment of alien artefact that had inexplicably caused the now-familiar but intangible twitchy sensation when she handled the material. It was after the meeting with Karben and Bilkitt, Copper reminded her audience, that she had admitted to both Linen and the colonel that she felt an increasing edginess that was alien to her nature and she could not explain: all her medical tests had shown that she had nothing physically wrong. Her unease was increased by her instinctive reaction to the complete artefact found by Malachite under Lofty's cellar, which had been subsequently handed over to the colonel, and Linen's growing conviction that ever since the head injury, Copper had become more intuitive, irritable and impulsive. Once she realised that she *was* sensitive to alien material, she deliberately set out to find more in their samples by using her ability rather than her tools. At that point the two Amberlines put the newfound skill down to Copper having been exposed to the material more than her friend, and becoming sensitised.

The colonel had been nodding as the account advanced and interrupting with points of clarification, but her brow remained clouded and Copper was beginning to fear that she might be in for a spell in the brig, as the next significant event had been the discovery of a large slice of alien material with strange surface markings: the two had used a discussion of it to mislead Karben and Bilkitt of Outer Mars Ops into believing that they were about to publish their speculations when they realised that the two MI officers were bugging their conversation. *That* had resulted in an irate Colonel Moritz demanding explanations and the first inkling that Copper had had that there was an alien ship buried out at the Warren. It was as the two were analysing the new sample shortly afterwards that Copper was profoundly shocked by the surface striations on the piece moving in response to her touch – a fact that they had at first concealed from the colonel.

It was after this that a foray into the Glory Hole had caused inexplicably strong reactions in both Copper and Linen and led to the in-depth site analysis that indicated the presence of an alien ship buried beneath their location. It was at this point that Copper had also realised that the military were interested in the alien artefact material, as it was able to self-repair by a replicative process that Mars science had been trying to achieve for decades as a skin for deep-range starships such as the *Drake*. A chance remark by Magenta Firewall not long afterwards that she was involved in the production of new tech led Copper to speculate that the *Drake* was not a one-off but the class ship of a fleet, a notion she had shared with the colonel when the latter met them at Beagle to hand over their civilian auxiliary stat pins.

"We met the officers from the *Sapphire Sunset* just after that ma'am; the incident at the BC and its aftermath you know of," Copper went on. "We were relaxing afterwards when I began to go over what I had been feeling down the Glory Hole, crawling over the floor... the ship beneath our site was different to the others your people had found, it had something..." she looked upwards, her hands working as she evoked those feelings.

Once more she was back below the surface of Mars, crawling over the rock-strewn cavern floor, soaking up the sensation of sharp, ecstatic frissons of charge shooting through her body and shaking her to the core. Her eyes glazed as the feelings became more palpable and seemed to wrap her round in a blanket of pure emotion.

Copper came to with both Linen and the colonel at her side, shaking her back into reality. Her friend was swearing fluently and assuring their commander and the *Drake's* chief medic Dr Kynedd Faerin that she had seen the reaction before. Faerin had set up his medi-scanner and was sweeping Copper from top to toe, a puzzled look on his face.

"I'm getting nothing, she's perfectly normal; there's increased alpha, mu and gamma wave brain activity but that's not unusual in a relaxed state. How do you feel?" he asked his patient.

Copper took a deep breath and pondered the question for a moment. "Fine," she admitted. "What the hell happened, why are you all looking at me?"

"You were out for at least ten minutes, Cop," Linen told her.

"Shit!"

"That's what I figured."

"I want you in medbay for tests," the doctor informed her.

"Like hell," was the mutinous response. "There's absolutely nothing wrong with me, as your own readings have proved. I'd like a caff, though," she added suggestively. "Interrogation gets tiring after a time."

"I can see discipline is going to be a major problem with you two," the colonel barked, but she seemed to have lost her stern expression. "Lieutenant Lyrican, fetch three mugs of caff from the side station. I will personally escort Lieutenant Milkstone to medbay once I've finished with her, Doctor, but meanwhile you're dismissed."

"Not the brig, then," Copper announced brightly as he left.

"I'd quit while you're ahead, Cop," Linen advised, depositing a mug by her elbow. "Your caff, ma'am. And mine. I need it. And you: will you stop scaring the living sol-lights out of me?"

"Can't help it," Copper told her. "It's not my fault."

"You can't go blaming everything on Spook."

"If you two have quite finished," the colonel interrupted. "A ghost running around the Warren? I joked about that after your trouble at the BC Hotel. Are you seriously trying to persuade me that you both believe there *was* an alien entity aboard that ship below your site and it was brought out of suspended animation when its ship was disturbed?"

"Yes we do, ma'am," Copper said hesitantly, grimacing at her friend, who mirrored the gesture but remained silent.

There was a pause as their commanding officer regarded the two doubtfully. "You're no fools, either of you, or you wouldn't be here. You also believe that this entity mentally reached out to you, that it was sentient and that you felt that it was afraid, Ms Milkstone?"

"Yes, ma'am."

Colonel Moritz' eyes narrowed. "I suspect there's a lot more that you've not told me," she added harshly. "You'd better start by explaining what you think happened, both to you and to this intangible entity you believe contacted you."

* * *

An hour later and an exhausted Copper, with additions from Linen, had brought the colonel up to date with all that had taken place from the time that she realised that she had some sort of enduring linkage to Spook, including the events in which she was sure his warnings had saved their skins. As Linen had once pointed out, Colonel Moritz was seriously vexed that she had been kept in the dark over a number of issues, but Copper was unrepentant. The colonel had given the impression that she was sceptical over the contact and had they pressed the matter, there was the possibility that others might find out and be sufficiently interested to cause them serious trouble, given that MI seemed to have been breached and there were a significant number of very nasty people interested in the subject.

This plain speaking caused the colonel's green eyes to flash dangerously but she admitted her initial scepticism and nodded. "I see. So you've now told me everything, both of you? There's nothing you've left out?"

The two exchanged glances, frowning and pondering, but it was Linen who spoke first, her face lightening in a smile. "You forgot about the tattoo!" she exclaimed to her friend.

"If you think I'm about to show off my butt, you've another think coming, lady!"

"I swear I'll have the pair of you in the brig one of these sols! What in blazes is this about a tattoo?"

As Linen made haste to explain, the colonel sighed irritably. "You've been here less than a sol and you've both done enough to warrant a disciplinary! Let's get you to medbay, Lieutenant Milkstone; but nothing to Dr Faerin about your Spook just yet."

"One thing does puzzle me, ma'am," Linen admitted as the trio made their way below decks and towards the main medbay. "If Copper reckoned she could make the marks on that piece of alien tech move because her sensitivities had increased due to Spook, how come Trisk, to name but one, can also cause marks on some alien tech to move?"

"Just how do you know that Dr Addystone had that talent?"

interrupted the colonel.

"We figured, ma'am," Linen told her. "After you said you'd seen the effect before but you *didn't* follow up on the fact that Cop had the knack. So you must have had someone close to you who could, and that had to be Trisk. So does *he* have his own resident alien?"

"He'd better not," Ms Moritz grunted. "Or that'll be three of you in the brig."

"Five if you include two Spooks," Copper said. "Ma'am…"

* * *

"We never did find out who's launching the *Drake* two sols from now, if it's not Galaxia Sandbar," Linen said to her friend over their dinner trays in the officers' mess on deck four. "But we can ask Trisk; here he comes with a stranger in tow."

The stranger in tow turned out to be Lieutenant Ash Goff, a geologist and part of the science group aboard. He seemed to be a friendly individual and not averse to talking about himself, but he was more interested in the happenings in the colonel's office earlier: that event, its length, and the advent of the chief medic had not gone unnoticed. He was told politely to mind his own business but both Linen and Copper were subliminally aware of the glances of more than a few fellow crewmen who were no doubt similarly curious.

"They'll get used to you," Trisk grinned, aware of the tension at the table. "But as to who's launching the *Drake*: some bigwig of an admiral from Fleet HQ in north eastern Utopia Planitia, as far as I understand. I don't think they want too much of a media party. She'll launch us from her shuttle just off space dock, we'll slip our moorings with the usual fanfare and then she'll come aboard on inspection. So we'll all have to be kitted out in our dress uniforms in case she stops by our departments."

"Lor' does that mean itchy necklines?" Copper demanded.

"They're not as bad as the ones in Bootcamp," Trisk assured her. "But the briefing will be despatched ship-wide in advance. Just make sure you're doing something interesting but nothing you want to be recorded in case she's got her press crew on her tail. And then, thanks be, we should be able to head out on our mission. About time," he added.

"I thought we weren't fully manned and our installations

hadn't been completed," Linen put in.

"They'll be done and all aboard that are coming aboard or the colonel will want to know why," their friend laughed. "But once you're done here, want to sample what's on offer in the officers' lounge next door? Half the off duty guys in here will be heading that way."

"What about the other half?" enquired Copper.

"Private entertainments, links from home, buggy races along the engineering decks, the gym, visits to the ship's enhancement salon, toenail clipping, billet redecoration; you name it, they'll be doing it," was the reply.

"Private entertainments?" Linen queried.

"Card school to name but one," Trisk told her. "The rest I'll leave to your imagination."

"Where's the bar?" Copper wanted to know.

"Officers' lounge, but don't go expecting alcohol, you won't get it," was the grinning reply. "Only the colonel or chief medic can sanction that, and it'll be on celebration sols only, *if* you're lucky. Tuffet keeps a supply in stores, but he won't issue to rank and file and that includes us. We may get a taste on off duty time when we launch but we'll see."

The officers' lounge was a large space populated by various booths, tables and relaxed seating, a few tri-dee sim stations and vending facilities. The bar stretched along part of one bulkhead and a number of slots for checking comms with a modicum of privacy decorated another. There was access from thence to a separate theatre for live entertainments and holo-flic viewing.

"Use your idents when you order at the bar or use vending slots. Extras outside normal rations are charged and you can call up your mess bill from any info-point. The credit's subtracted from your pay," Trisk explained. "These tables all have info-consoles, so if you want to check up on most things, you can do that from here; though I wouldn't check anything too personal, you'll have an audience."

Their evening of casual chat with Trisk and Ash Goff was interspersed by innumerable comings and goings. Copper and Linen found that they were not the most recently-arrived crew, as several bemused individuals had been taken under the wings of longer-serving fellows and were being hauled about to be introduced. Captain Helmis stopped by to have a few words, as did Chief Engineer Themis Sage and her sidekick Lieutenant Oaky Grimsson. Trisk and Ash pointed out one or two other notables of their acquaintance but as their colleagues were by that time so full of new names and new faces, the information was refusing to register. Four musicians had set up in a corner and were treating their shipmates to a cacophony of sound that led Copper to declare that they sounded like a quartet of cats having a barney in a bandstand.

"Two of them are on the ents comm, so I wouldn't say that too loudly," Trisk cautioned as he activated a suppression screen to cut the racket. "Entertainments committee," he elucidated. "They organise concerts, musical eves, that sort of thing. And they're the ones that decide what holo-flics will be shown in the theatre. They're always on the lookout for new talent," he added suggestively.

"They'd better not look at me," warned Copper. "I'll have enough to do just keeping afloat in all this."

"But you can sing, can't you? In the shower at least?"

Linen was meanwhile fiddling with their table's info-console and working out what she could do with it. She had discovered that she could call up any links that had come in for her and had decided to do just that. An exasperated hiss told her friend that the redhead had found something she wished she had not.

"What's up?"

"You'll never guess who's just left me a link – first sol aboard and he sticks his oar in!"

"Wolff Waterbone," Copper said matter-of-factly. "It always is when you use that tone. What's he want, a report on the work you've done so far?"

"Just a sec, I'll check the audio… he requests a personal link to discuss the work I *will* be doing," Linen huffed, outraged. "From the privacy of my quarters in case there are sensitive matters to discuss!"

"Wants to see what you look like in Fleet uniform is what he wants," her friend told her. "Leave it 'til sol after morrow and record a message in your dress uniform, buttoned to the brim, and tell him you can't call personally as there's a fleet admiral on inspection and it would be most inappropriate, but you *will* let

Colonel Moritz know that he linked in with that request and you'll take an advisory from her. *That* should send a flea up his trouser leg for him."

"Good idea," Linen nodded as Ash Goff looked at the pair in shocked surprise. "Want another drink anyone?"

"I've had enough for one sol and I want to record a link to Mik Mack before I hit the sack; I promised I would," Copper responded. "And I suppose I'd better check my duty schedule for morrow-sol as well."

"You're in the labs," Trisk told her. "You're to report to our office at oh eight thirty, so breakfast in time for that. I'll be in the mess around seven thirty. You'll be given a sevensol or so for getting used to the place and all the kit you'll be using before you start your training assignments."

"Training assignments for what?" asked Copper.

"For manning ship's science stations, including the bridge: we all have to do stints. I've done one overnighter so far, but that's been that. Once we're out in the great beyond, there *will* be more opportunities. Training's not bad," Trisk went on. "It's usually two or three hours at a time with an instructor, slotted into your normal work schedule and then a supervised duty-watch or two once you're considered competent."

"What about other training?" she persisted. "On shuttles for a start: we've both got pilot's wings, so we should be in for regular instruction and flight."

"Then it'll be sims I should think," their friend reckoned, his brow creasing. "You can't be let loose while the ship's in flight; and I guess you won't be qualified to fly fighters if there's some checking out to do. Link to the Personnel Office, it's next to the Exec's on level four, just below the flight deck. Jinn Limlite is the training liaison officer – he should be able to tell you."

"Chill," Linen enthused. "I'll head on in as well and put in a credit's worth to Mik, or he'll be thinking we're neglecting him."

"Give him my regards," Trisk put in. "And everyone else out at the Warren. I haven't heard of them for a while."

"Will do; see you morrow-sol."

The two rose slowly and made their way through the throng to the nearest exit. Copper looked at her friend as they made the passageway.

"Been a helluva sol," she remarked.

"And this is only the start," Linen replied in a low voice. "Spook glad to be aboard a ship again?"

"You figured he was here?"

"Yup. I noticed you were looking over your shoulder at the end there, as if there was something round your neck. Are you relieved that Colonel Moritz knows at last?"

"In a strange way, yes. And so's Spook. I think he now feels he has free range to wander all over the ship."

"Lor' don't tell the colonel that: I doubt she'll be over the two moons about it."

"Not much she can do. But he may give us a heads up on anything going on, if we need to know about it," Copper said enigmatically.

"If we have infiltrators aboard, you mean. Or if something turns up that might spell trouble," Linen surmised.

"Exactly. But we can head to mine and make the link to Mik. Anyone else we should leave a message for?"

"Grammy and Ma. Not to mention Majorelle and Lofty. But we can leave those for a while; they won't be expecting a blow by blow account of our first sol at the end of it. And I want to check out the shower and the other trappings that my quarters are blessed with. I guess if we want our favourite drinks on tap we have to order the stuff from stores and we'll be charged?"

"You got me. But normal rations come free, so I shouldn't think caff will be charged," Copper guessed.

"You hope. But excess water will, so you'd better watch your shower timing or you'll be left soaped up with no way of rinsing off."

"Thanks for that: I'd just come next door to borrow yours."

"That would really make our shipmates talk," Linen laughed. "Especially if you were dressed in nothing but a towel."

"Enough already. Deck nine," Copper ordered the elevator. "Does this tube come out near section thirty four?" she asked her friend. "I'm disorientated."

"If not, we get the horizontal or we run. We probably need the exercise anyway."

"Speak for yourself! But here we are — we're not too far off in fact. This way."

Copper led the way to her billet in twenty four and invited her friend in. "D'you know, I've almost forgotten what it looks like," she confessed. "I've not been in here since I dumped my kitbags first thing. It's much smaller than my old place at Ma Kellyn's and it's drab, but at least the sleeping unit's separate."

"You mean there's a sliding screen. Doesn't seem to have the facility to change the wall colour," Linen remarked, examining the various controls next to the door. "But I guess you can hang holo-pics and things. Trisk had one or two hung about his place, as I recall. Did you bring your mini hard-holo projector of your blue dragon my Ma gave you, and the holo-pic of Beagle in Darklight you got at the Leisure Dome?"

"I brought my dragon, but not the holo. You can order stuff up at ship's stores, I guess."

"You'll be lucky; deco for blank bulkheads will be way down the inventory of essentials."

"We're still in dock, they can order up, surely," Copper said as she made for the comms desk and sat down. "Pull up a chair and come on over; we'd better get the settings on this sorted."

"I'll share yours," Linen announced after a fruitless tugging at the single armchair. "It's fixed – to prevent it flying about if we lose gravity or are sent spinning into space upside down, I expect. Does your chair move?"

"There's some slack to it, but it's secure as well; I suppose they have to think of these things. But the comms unit is regular voice-controlled, so I guess I just tell it to start visual and audio recording…"

* * *

A little time later and the links were made, the two deciding that they may as well make all their planned communications in one fell swoop. The launch briefing promised by Trisk came in whilst they were still at the console; attached to it was the dress requirements and the timing of the state visit by Admiral Vexilla Stannum to the departments designated for her inspection. The latter included theirs, with a note to the effect that all relevant personnel should expect to be quizzed on their roles and their current assignments.

"Our rep precedes us," Linen announced facetiously. "But the colonel should be there to deflect any flak."

"Huh! Auntie Elle will leave us to deflect our own flak if this admiral decides she wants a run-down on our ops. But it's late and Spook's hinting gently that he wants a look-see around the ship on his own and wants me settled before he sets off."

"You what? He's now telling you when to hit the sack? Even my Ma never did that and she was pretty strict."

"Your Ma strict? That's a fib, Linen Lyrican…"

"That's Lieutenant Lyrican," Linen grinned. "But Spook's getting out of hand if he's now telling you it's sleepy time. He may be older than you by millennia but he's no call to tell you what to do in your personal life. That could get really out of hand if he doesn't like the company you're keeping – if Ash Goff asks you for a date, for example."

"We'd *both* say no to that," Copper interrupted. "And where d'you go for a date aboard a starship, apart from somebody else's quarters?"

"Theatre for a holo-flic, officers' lounge for a party or some fun, buggy races along engineering, sneaky assignations behind the greenery in hydroponics, a sortie through the 'tween decks spaces, a hot date in one of the iso-labs in medbay or in one of the shuttles… this is a big ship, there must be plenty of spaces to get lost in."

"You actually have a point. I must get Spook to memorise his way around and if ever I get lost he can be my handy guide."

"He's already that. But as we have our wrist-comm idents, why not upload the ship's spec into them as Trisk suggested? Local info-points might be out of commission one sol and then we'd be sorry. And though our ship's idents *are* comms units that work as ID and location pins, I don't think they're much more, given the capabilities of a typical space-trooper, so we'd best upload the spec into our own wrist-comms that Grammy gave us as well."

"Morrow-sol," Copper told her friend firmly. "I am *seriously* tired. One sol aboard and we've already been interrogated and threatened with the brig by our commanding officer, I've been poked and prodded and psych-tested to the limit and half the damn crew seem to know who we are. You want a choc?"

"Spook okay with that is he?"

"If I had a cushion in here, it would be heading in your

direction, lady," Copper said crossly. "Go sit on the sofa and I'll work out how to squeeze a couple of Chocó-crèmes out of the damn dispenser."

"Affirmative, ma'am. And then I'll head on home to my cosy little billet next door. I'll call for you at seven twenty morrow-sol and we can head on up to the mess for breakfast and to find Trisk. He can show us the ropes as far as a typical sol's duty goes."

"Done. And get your feet off my sofa, I've only had it a few hours."

11: RAINBOW ROOKIES

Copper and Linen ambled casually towards the officers' mess on deck four. The former was still tired as she had spent some time the previous night in sorting and stowing various pieces of kit. She had been pleased to find a thermo-clean unit at one side of her catering area and had made use of it, she told her friend.

"Like the hair," she went on, eyeing the redhead critically. "Looks neat and shouldn't dangle in your cereal."

"It doesn't normally," scolded Linen. "But I thought I'd best start to tie it smartly as practice for this Admiral Whatshername that's stopping by for the launch morrow-sol. Have you tried on your dress uniform yet?"

"Nope, just hung it away. Should I have?"

"It's a tad more comfortable than the ones we had at Beagle Basecamp but I wouldn't recommend it for a sol in the lab. In fact I'm planning to ditch *this* jacket once we get into our office; it's like wearing a hug from Grammy."

"Thanks for that image: I'd just about blotted Magenta from my mind."

"Welcome. How did Spook enjoy his tour around the ship last night?" Linen enquired in a low voice.

"Didn't mention a thing," was the bland response.

"Very funny. What was *your* impression of *his* impression?"

"Contentment, oddly enough. But we shouldn't mention him in public: I don't think Auntie Elle would like it."

"Our commanding officer catches you calling her Auntie Elle in public and *she* won't like it," Linen reproved as the two turned into the mess, their eyes roving the space to find their friend. "There's Trisk over at the chow console. Who's that with him?"

"Don't know but she's wearing second lieutenant's pips and sporting a hand-weapon. The insignia's familiar. Security?"

Copper was correct in her assumption and Trisk introduced the stranger as Lieutenant Tawinna Brown, one of Lieutenant Kit Locksmith's juniors.

"Call me Tawny," the tall young woman beamed. "I've heard all about you two."

"Most people seem to have," Copper admitted ruefully. "Are you permitted to carry a weapon on duty?"

"Yes, so most of us in security do. It's force of habit: you can get posted to a lot worse than the *Drake*. And as I have some weapons drill first thing, I thought I'd bring mine along."

"We've got lab drill," Linen announced as she collected her rations and loaded her tray. "We haven't actually discussed what we'll be doing straight off."

"Checking out the lab apparatus with samples we've analysed already to make sure we get comparable results would be a good start," Copper advised. "And making sure Gerald and Gemima are up to scratch. We've never used them aboard a ship before."

"Who are Gerald and Gemima?" enquired Brown curiously.

"Our MEDICs," was the reply. "Not standard in security, I guess."

"Not standard in most places," Trisk put in with a wide grin, going on to explain the instruments, their multifarious uses and their many quirks as the quartet found a table and settled down.

Over the meal the two rookies quizzed their companions on protocol and routine aboard ship, as well as domestic matters such as how to ensure supplies of Chocó-crème for the drinks dispenser and the best way to order goods from stores. Copper was also more than interested in how she could reserve time on the tri-dee test facility in engineering. As Trisk had stated it was capable of hard-holo projection, it would be useful for the work they had planned for their Warren site materials. She had already worked out that there was no high-spec super tri-dee simulation suite for crew leisure, as Thars Amberline had once jokingly suggested. Trisk advised her to check with Ossy Inkscree, who was responsible for one of the two suites, and arrange a visit.

Back in their office, the two new lieutenants soon found out that their task-desks had been programmed with the necessary data to begin logging routine analyses as they carried them out. They had agreed to begin with data runs on material brought up from Lowell as a means of familiarising themselves with the gear. The tube they chose had already proved a fruitful source of alien material and by sifting out various fractions to retrieve finer particles in line with the colonel's instructions that such detailed analyses were part of their mandate, they could use any standard finds made and conclusions drawn to bulk out the reports to MDMC that they were perforce obliged to prepare. The data could also be used as a basis for the publications that were a necessary part of their Amberline research work.

It was refreshing to be able to commandeer a bio-geo-chem sequencer without locking implants to it and Copper and Linen were impressed by the speed of analyses at the science consoles. The tri-dee sim stations in their attached side lab were simple to operate and the two soon decided between them that that was where they would station themselves for the expected visit by Admiral Stannum, with a carefully selected section of their lower site set up and corresponding samples being run through the analyser. Gerald and Gemima would be on standby with holo projector ports ready if awkward questions were asked.

"You can talk through the holo if she does stop by and I'll run the samples," Copper informed her friend. "You're a much better smooth talker than I am and sure as shells the colonel won't be putting her credits'-worth in."

"You'll be analysing samples the *Lithium Star* brought in from the edge," Trisk told them, having overheard the plans. "I've a few tubes under high security that the colonel wants examined as a research priority, which means you start now."

"Why haven't you been doing them if they're such a priority then?" demanded Copper, folding her arms and attempting to look intimidating.

"I've had *this* place to put in order and my own work to get through," was the smiling response. "Our labs and office were moved up here from deck ten, remember. And with the number of external ops teams we had aboard, it wouldn't have been a wise move. We're now clear of non-Fleet personnel – I hope."

"You have a very good point," she admitted wryly. "But how many sample tubes make a few? If I remember aright, our old buddies Fudge and Chocolate of the *Lithstar* said they'd found only a few *pieces* of practically unidentifiable space junk, as most of the rest was still stuck to the rock that took the *Griffon* out. That doesn't sound like a few tubes, it sounds like hardly any."

"That was Chocolate and he wasn't exactly the top ace in the deck," Linen reminded her. "He also said they'd been ordered to collect a heap of samples to bring back, once Fleet Command figured what their prelim data was saying; and then they had to hot-ship it back to Lowell for all sorts of meetings. They were a couple of officers off the *Lithstar* that we met in Lowell Leisure Dome a while back," she explained to a mystified Trisk.

"They told you that? They should've been thrown in the brig. And they were called Fudge and Chocolate? They were pulling your chains."

"Not exactly," Copper admitted. "I called them that behind their backs. They were Lieutenant Commander Fludge and First Lieutenant Chokatti; and they didn't exactly *tell* us much…"

"Cop listened in on their private chat in a café in Lowell and as it was a tad interesting, we made their acquaintance," Linen enlightened him. "Mind you, they shouldn't have been talking shop in a shop in any case so it was their own fault. We found out more over dinner at the hotel and then passed it on to Auntie Elle, um, Colonel Moritz. Well, she made us, really."

"Enough already," Copper interrupted. "So we have a bundle of *Lithstar* sample tubes aboard. But I've to report any reactions I have to any materials I find right away," she added hesitantly.

"I've been briefed on that and *I've* been ordered to do the same," Trisk disclosed. "We cross that bridge when we come to it. But don't mention it to any of our fellow science officers: this aspect of our work here is one of the reasons we're sharing our office and this lab, as both have been finished to a higher-than-usual security spec. That intact alien device you found down your Glory Hole we also have, by the way, but we only use it on the colonel's say so. I've been authorised to grant you both immediate access to the *Lithium Star's* samples, and a collection of fragments that the *Wayfinder* found, and as we're alone I'll do that now. You get into the stores on the basis of your implanted idents only."

"You mean not our wrist-comm idents?" Linen queried. "I thought they were the same, more or less."

"You can't talk to your implanted ident. But I bet Magenta

had a hand in the implants," Copper opined. "Sounds like a security feature she's integrated. But there are samples here the *Wayfinder* brought in way back? Why do we get access to them?"

"We're rare and precious," Trisk laughed quietly. "Why do you think we're all here aboard this ship at this particular time?"

"And on this particular mission: why did I even imagine we were here for our own good and not the good of The Service?" Copper sighed. "Well, let's get it done: it must be nearly break-time and I need a caff."

* * *

Caff-break in the mess proved useful as the two met Training Liaison Officer Jinn Limlite and were able to enquire about their further instruction in various aspects of duties as officers of the Fleet. A number of pilot sims were available, but the *Drake's* fighter pilots had priority. Weapons and stations drills and other exercises would be fitted in as applicable. If the two lieutenants would link him their list of preferences, Jinn would see what he could do. He already had a list of the training they were required to complete. A wary Copper asked for the definitive record: she had assumed that she had left most of the rigours of Basecamp behind and was darkly suspicious that physical training would form part of the schedule.

Once back in their office the projected visit to the tri-dee sim test facilities in engineering was brought up. Ossy Inkscree was called; he proposed a whirlwind tour, as he had other pots to stir in view of the imminent launch of the *Drake*. The two and Trisk sauntered along to the chief SO's office as if they had all the time in the sol, to find him barking orders at one of his staff, who was giving as good as she got. She was ordered to scarper as Trisk informed Copper and Linen that the stroppy one was bioengineer Elyssal Halsen. He introduced the lieutenant to his friends on her way out.

"Can't stop, maybe catch you later. I've heard about you," Lyssa Halsen called somewhat throatily as she set off at speed.

"Who hasn't?" Copper bawled after her.

"Right you two, let's move it," Dr Inkscree announced. "I expect you've used a hard-holo tri-dee before?"

"We have, sir," Linen responded.

"Well the one you'll be shown is for work only, no larking

about on holo-beaches or calling up hot dates at private cafés."

"We've got better things to do," Copper remarked.

"And you don't have the requisite data," Trisk added in the background.

"And that also," Linen chortled as the four made their way to the elevator for the ride into the depths of the great starship.

The *Drake's* engineering decks extended over a massive area in the lower part of the ship and the two rookies could see why buggy racing was a popular pursuit during quiet times. There were a few crewmen in engineering blues working at bulkhead compartments. The many side entries evidently gave onto other sections, but a view of the mighty engines powering the *Drake* that spanned the mid-sections of several of the lower decks was denied them. Dr Inkscree led them through various doors that separated parts of main deck twenty, carefully sealing the area behind them. The hard-holo projection test facility that was their endpoint was through a door marked with locational data and dire warnings to keep out. An external board gave the existing status of the suite, which was currently non-operational. Inkscree opened the door by raising his hand-implanted ident to the reader plate, informing them that if the place was in use they would have to request entry clearance.

"There *will* be a schedule set up once we're in transit," they were told as they stepped inside, the door sealing smartly at their backs. "You book time here and it'll show on the extern board. As you can see, the facility spans a couple of decks. That station houses the controls for the central projector plate and the ops manual. There are two ops chairs, so the two of you can use the controls in comfort..."

"Or you can call up a holo-chair," Linen put in, examining the main station in interest. "Wonder if the ops manual has the same annoying voice as our one at Lowell did?"

"Controls look similar," Copper conceded, sitting down in one of the control chairs. "Data ports are standard but there's more to this than our one in Lowell. We have auxiliary projector plates for one. They'll be for novel bits of kit, I expect: you can maybe build up a tri-dee sim from scratch rather than feed in stored data. We'll need to do a training run or two. We can use the Glory-Hole info, it's more than comprehensive and much of it was got by those pesky surf-sci bots, so we should have no trouble in persuading the ops system to accept it."

"You hope," Linen told her as she sat alongside and began running swift fingers over various regulators.

"And you thought you were here to teach them something," Trisk laughed over at Inkscree.

"This place has a few tricks up its sleeve," was the sardonic response. "Just don't get too comfortable. I'll clear you for using this suite, all three of you, but you'll have to wait in line; and if there's priority usage declared then you give way. Clear?"

"Aye, sir," Linen responded.

"Milkstone, are you listening?"

"Aye, sir," was the somewhat absent response as Copper ran her fingers instinctively over the comms control that allowed users at the ops manual station to communicate with anyone on the other side of the secure door.

She called up the viewer and tapped the image of the reverse of the exit. "Who's that hovering out there?" she demanded.

"We'll find out," said Inkscree with a questioning glance as he strode over to the door, the others following.

"Can I help you?" he asked the surprised individual at the threshold.

"Just testing the reader plate," the lean man in maintenance tech fatigues responded with a smile. "Everything shipshape for the launch morrow-sol is the mission."

"Like hell it is!" a furious Copper hissed, pushing past the chief SO and raising a closed fist to smack the man in the face.

He was faster than she and as her blow glanced off he pulled her through the door, spinning her round and into the bulkhead. He had unsheathed a weapon, aimed and fired before the other two men could react, but Linen, throwing herself past them at ground level, grabbed the tech by one leg as he made to run. He was caught off balance and fell. Inkscree and Trisk were upon him in seconds, the superior weight of the former bearing him down. Linen clawed for the man's weapon, twisted its setting viciously to heavy stun, aimed deliberately at his chest and fired. She then spun on her knee and crawled to her friend's side.

"We need a medic!" she screamed at the other two. "Get an emergency team down here now! And get security to throw that frocking bastard in the brig!"

Notwithstanding his superior rank Inkscree obeyed, tabbing his comm link and issuing orders as Trisk came over to assist Linen. The shot had caught Copper below her left shoulder and a spread of burnt and blackened jacket showed that the impact had been severe. She was totally unresponsive and Trisk quietly surmised that a stunning beam had been part of the bolt.

"I know," the redhead gasped shortly. "A frocking Personal Protection Firearm A03 and set to full power. Oh Cop!"

A brace of primary assist techs came sprinting along the deck and threw themselves down, demanding the particulars as they unfolded a medi-scanner and began to pull it out. Linen, barely aware than some alarm was sounding around them and that an illuminated line of holo-arrows had appeared on the bulkheads, responded with a harshly abusive tirade against the unconscious assailant as she pushed them away. It was Trisk's persistent but gentle command to let the professionals handle the situation as he enfolded her in his arms, drew her away and kept her pinned that brought Linen back to a juddering calm.

Another primary assist tech had appeared from somewhere and was attending to the still-insensible gunman. Inkscree was briefing a newly-arrived security officer when a team headed by Kit Locksmith raced up, the chief demanding details.

"Get that bastard searched and locked up!" Linen ordered, still shaking.

With a penetrating look, Locksmith nodded once and turned to examine the prone figure, probing fingers searching his clothing and the gear he had been toting. As the security chief removed another gun and a scanner and ordered two guards to keep weapons trained on the suspect, a trauma team headed by Kynedd Faerin thundered down the deck, Colonel Moritz on their heels. The chief medic took command, issuing orders as he unpacked equipment and slapped hypo-shots into his patient. Minutes later, Copper was on a gurney, its emergency systems operating, and being prepared for the trip to medbay.

There was a groan as the man on the deck began to come to. That was enough for Linen, who lunged up swearing fluently and demanding to get at him. Trisk and the colonel between them kept her pinioned and immobile, the commanding officer using the voice of authority to compel obedience.

"I think they both recognised him," Trisk said quietly as he briefly imparted the events that had led to the outcome to the colonel and the security chief.

"Lieutenant Lyrican? You know him?" Ms Moritz demanded.

Linen turned haggard eyes on her. "It's Jecks," she said dully. "The hair and the face have changed but the eyes are the same."

"Jecks! Are you sure?"

"Yes, ma'am. Cop was sure…"

Colonel Moritz shook her head. "How did she know there was someone outside the door?" she enquired quietly.

"Don't know. Spook, I expect. Only he wasn't fast enough this time…" Linen turned her face into Trisk's jacket and began to shake uncontrollably.

"I'll deal with this," the colonel said grimly. "Trisk, get her to medbay; you *will* comply, Lieutenant. I'll be along later. Inkscree, you secure the tri-dee suite. Locksmith, you're with me."

"Aye, ma'am," all four responded.

The muted alarm was still sounding through the engineering sections as Trisk helped Linen to her feet and guided her along the passageway to the nearest elevator. The gurney with their friend aboard was already distant, its path cleared of personnel by sign and voice commands at every junction to give it right of way. The two made their way slowly, interrupted by none: those crewmates they passed were acutely aware that something serious had arisen and forbore to intrude. Medbay was its usual scene of well-ordered calm. Word of their approach had gone ahead, for Medical Officer Dr Amber Embertz was on hand to escort Linen and her friend to a side bay.

"Where's Cop?" was Linen's first question.

"Lieutenant Milkstone," Trisk elucidated for the doctor's benefit.

"Under the best care this side of the asteroid belt," Embertz told her. "She's undergoing surgery and we'll hear as soon as possible. Meanwhile let's have a look at you."

"There's nothing wrong with me…"

"Let me be the judge of that," was the level response. "It *is* what I went to medical school for."

Linen was too emotionally exhausted to argue and submitted

quietly to the scans and prods with the various instruments that the doctor deemed appropriate. Trisk slid discreetly out of the door, to reappear some minutes later with two mugs of caff. The two sat quietly on, in obedience to Embertz' instructions to remain until called for.

* * *

It was a movement on the other side of the glazed viewport of their bay two hours later that caught Trisk's eye; he looked up to see Colonel Moritz regarding them with shrewd eyes. Linen, following his glance, started up. The colonel made her way in, gesturing the two to continue seated.

"She'll be fine," she said before either could utter a word. "A fractured rib and lung puncture, muscle and skin damage, but Dr Faerin is confident that she'll be back to light duties in a sevensol or so."

"How the hell did he get aboard?" Linen demanded bitterly. "And how the hell did he know Copper was here?"

Colonel Moritz sat down. "To answer your first question: he came in on someone else's ticket. He's been surgically altered to resemble the person his ident says he is, a tech that was among a squad recently assigned to the ship. Having been in the Service before, Jecks knows his way around. The obligatory med checks were done on the ground, where he got hold of the other man's ident, his personnel records and a very clever skin sheath of his hand print. He also wore lenses but they cause him discomfort: that's why he wasn't wearing them when you met him. Chief Locksmith found them and various other pieces of kit in his quarters. We don't know what's happened to the tech whose place he took. As for your second question: he couldn't have known Ms Milkstone would be assigned to the *Drake*. He knew of the ship and her mission and *his* mission was probably either infiltration or sabotage, or both. We'll find out. Once he realised you two had come aboard, he no doubt had another motive for setting up snoopware in various places, including the tri-dee test facility, which is what he was doing when you disturbed him."

"But how did he know *we* were in there, ma'am?"

"He didn't: your visit was unplanned. Once he gathered that there *were* people in there, he tried to find out who you were. Ms Milkstone clearly realised someone was outside. She recognised him more quickly than you did, I think," the colonel surmised.

Linen nodded. "She knew; she was mad and was about to punch his lights out. But he was faster. Once he'd clocked it was Cop, he was out to kill. It was lucky he only had the PPF A03. It's a dangerous enough weapon, but if he'd had that phase rifle he had at the Warren, he wouldn't have missed…" Her face twisted in pain at the memory. "I want to see her."

"Later," Colonel Moritz commanded. "She needs rest. The doctor will let me know when I can see her and you'll be next in line. Go get sorted out and then get something to eat, both of you. You're excused duty for the rest of the sol. But you *will* be expected to be in post for the launch morrow-sol. And you will *not* discuss what's happened with anyone. I'll see you both later. Dismissed."

"Aye, ma'am," the two chorused as they rose and made their way out of the bay.

"Have a shower and change into fresh gear," Trisk advised as they made their way in the elevator down to deck nine. "Then knock on my door and we'll head up to the mess."

"I think I'll just stay in my quarters, if you don't mind," Linen sighed wearily.

"That wasn't a request, Lieutenant, that was an order," Trisk responded, his usual lop-sided grin reasserting itself. "As your senior officer, I'm telling you that you're having a late lunch with me. In the mess. Don't forget your jacket."

"Aye, sir," she said with a watery smile. "Pulling rank…"

The two met up as agreed and made their way to the officers' mess, fielding one or two attempts at conversation en route. They collected their trays and sat together and Trisk slowly drew the story of the adventures at the Warren as far as they related to Jecks out of his companion. He had heard the bones of the events from Thars Amberline and the colonel but figured that a retelling would ease Linen of some of her obvious tension.

"It was the eyes," Linen finished. "They're an odd shade of light grey and they followed us about, which creeped us both. That's what made me ask for checks on him from Mik Mack in the first place."

Trisk shook his head slightly. Some things were not adding up for him and he thought for a moment or two, chewing on his food. "Spook," he said eventually. "Who or what is Spook?"

"Don't even go there," he was told harshly as Linen raised a warning finger. "You'll have the colonel *and* me on your back."

"Fair enough. If you're done, why don't we go for a stroll through the gardens?"

"The gardens? There are gardens aboard?"

"Well, hydroponics and testing beds. We do grow some food aboard; research for the self-sustaining long-distance starships that will head out one of these sols. And it's used in the galleys. Some of that stuff on your plate is fresh."

"This ship never ceases to amaze me. I guess it beats sitting around waiting for a call and I want something to take my mind off what's happened. I sure as hell hope Chief Locksmith starts cranking up security big time."

"It'll happen, the colonel will see to that. Come on: I'll show you round the places you miss on the scheduled orientation to the ship you get when you first come aboard," promised Trisk.

Linen assiduously logged the visits to the gardens, the stores, the galleys, the weapons ranges and the various storage areas for racing buggies and other sports kit, as well as the therapy salon, where the crew could have a massage or have their hair styled, or any number of relaxing treatments.

"You thought it was all work and no play, didn't you?" Trisk grinned down at her. "It's just…"

They were interrupted by a link to Linen's comm unit. It was Colonel Moritz, informing her that she could pay a quick visit to Copper in iso-bay four of the main medbay. With one look at her companion, she confirmed and set off at speed. In a short time the two had made it to deck six. The colonel and Dr Faerin were there to meet them and lead them to the appropriate bay.

"Five minutes and no more," Faerin warned as he pointed through the viewport. "And don't be upset if she can't answer questions: she's still woozy from the effects of the anaesthetic."

"I'll wait here," Trisk told his colleague tactfully. "I'll knock the window when your time is up."

Linen nodded and stepped through the door. Copper was supported semi-upright in a life-support cradle and was attached to several tubes; a bio-monitor on the cradle flickered as various readings changed to show her ongoing condition. Although pale and with a face drawn in pain, her eyes lit up at the approach of her friend.

"You okay?" she demanded.

"Isn't that what I'm supposed to ask you?" Linen returned, a wash of relief flooding her as she sat down and patted Copper's hand. "I wish you'd do as you're told. I've told you before not to scare the willies out of me by your antics. You never listen."

"That's a fib. I always listen. I just don't always do what I'm told."

"You can say that again."

"I just don't always do what I'm told," Copper repeated obediently.

"You're asking for a smack, you are."

"Promises, promises."

"Oh, Cop!" Linen sighed, a touch tremulously. "The fizzing universe seems to have it in for us, doesn't it? You doing okay?"

"Sure am. Doc Faerin says I'll be out of here in a sevensol. I told him I wasn't staying here that long, I've got things to do — we've got things to do. I want to get my paws on those samples from the *Lithstar* and the *Wayfinder* for a start. I'll have to pass up on the launch though. Not that I'm bothered, I can watch it from here. You could watch it with me?"

"Can't," Linen said briefly with a lift to her shoulders. "The colonel wants me and Trisk in post for the whole shebang. And it was an order, not a request. But how can you watch the launch from here?"

"This thing here's an info-point. Look, you can call stuff up on it. This is a news channel… and there's ship's business, with a few things about the launch and a list of what's on…"

"Keeps the patients out of trouble, I expect," Linen guessed as she examined the screen and called up a few links. "Useful where you're concerned, that's for sure. Where's Spook, by the way?" she went on in a lower voice as she deactivated the device and pushed it to one side. "Trisk suspects something — he asked me outright who Spook was. I had made the mistake of saying he probably alerted you to someone outside the tri-dee sim suite door when the colonel was quizzing us and he evidently picked up on it. Sorry."

Copper looked at her friend in compassion. "No worries,"

she murmured softly. "He's not here just now. I think he's off on a mission of his own, sniffing out any other undesirables that we might have aboard."

"You what?"

"I think he was pretty upset at what happened over Jecks. At least, that's the impression I got when I came to. But my head was a ball of wool at that point. Still is," she added sighing. "Not sure quite how I feel, really."

"Oh Cop, don't cry!" Linen rose from her chair in concern as the tears trickled down her friend's face.

"Can't help it," Copper responded weakly. "I'm tired is all, just very tired. And doped to the eyeballs. The colonel asked me if I wanted my folks informed…"

"What did you tell her?" Linen breathed.

"That you were my folks, you and Corona – and Magenta. And Majorelle and Lofty, come to that. I think she thought I was out of it," she sniffed noisily.

"Bet she didn't. Let me wipe your face for you or people will think I've upset you. There you go, that's better. Hey, did you know we have a therapy salon aboard? You can have a massage, have your hair done, all sorts."

"It makes sense: this is a massive ship with a big crew. Six months in space and we'd all look like a bunch of vagabonds if we didn't. Why is Trisk banging on the porthole?"

"My five minutes are up. That's all I'm allowed. But I'll be back later. You look after yourself; and tell Spook to look after you, or I'll be having words with him."

"I'll let him know. Don't worry, I'll be fine." Copper's face creased in a weary smile. "Say hi to Trisk."

"I will." Linen leaned over and gave her friend a kiss on the cheek. "Be good," she said.

"Now you've done it: people will think we're an item."

"Don't give a damn. See you later."

Copper raised a hand to wave at the two on the other side of the viewing port. They waved back cheerfully and turned away.

"How is she?" Trisk asked concernedly, once out of earshot.

"Trying to pretend she's fitter than she is," Linen told him ruefully. "I can read a bio-scanner. She said hello, by the way."

Colonel Moritz captured the pair on their way out of medbay

and diverted them to a side office, ordering them to sit. Linen repeated her conjectures with regard to Copper and queried the real state of affairs.

"She took quite a hit. But she *will* recover, don't worry. Jecks has been removed planetside and matters are in hand; security has been upped and the recruitment office at Pioneer II, where all the relevant checks were supposed to have been carried out, is being turned inside out. You will not of course discuss this with anyone, either of you, and that includes Admiral Stannum, even if she asks you directly. You're on her tour route, although her press-team will *not* be accompanying her."

The colonel went on to list the duties the two would have on the morrow before dismissing Trisk. She then turned to Linen.

"Your opinion on Lieutenant Milkstone's mental state?"

"I'm not a psych counsellor," Linen declared, but continued hurriedly at the glint in her commanding officer's eyes. "But I think she'll do all right, ma'am. She's not panicked and wanting to head back to Mars, she wants to get on with the work we came here to do. As do I. We're safer here than we would be on Mars anyway, *that* much is clear, which is no doubt why we and Trisk were drafted in the first place. But if Jecks managed to get on board so easily, it strikes me that others like him may have slipped through the net."

"That's my problem, not yours, Lieutenant."

"It *will* be mine if Cop ends up as the mark of some other creep's targeting eye," Linen retorted, looking around warily.

"Belay that, Lieutenant. And this place is not bugged, believe me. Now, a comment you made earlier: you suggested that this entity you both refer to as Spook somehow informed Lieutenant Milkstone that someone was outside the door – that's why she activated the external viewer."

Linen nodded. "Yes. I don't know if he recognised Jecks as the one we tangled with earlier, but Cop knew it was him."

"How much control does Lieutenant Milkstone have over this Spook of hers? Are there risks to my ship? And if so, how great are they?"

"With respect ma'am, aren't these questions you should be asking her?"

Colonel Moritz sighed. "You walk a fine line, Lieutenant. But

I don't intend to put more strain on Lieutenant Milkstone than I can help at the present time. And you're closer to her than anyone else and you know the full story. So?"

"To be honest ma'am, I don't know how much control Cop has over Spook, and I don't think she does either. But may I ask where the questions are tending?"

"You tell me."

"You're worried you may have an uncontrollable alien entity aboard that could endanger the ship," Linen speculated. "I don't think so. But Spook's here now and even if *she* was compelled to leave the ship, he wouldn't necessarily follow. So you're stuck with him. Cop *can* call him up and he seems to be around her a lot of the time. But he does go off on his own, as far as we can tell. And that's as much as *I* can tell you, really, ma'am."

"You mean that's as much as you *will* tell me. How strong is this link between the lieutenant and this Spook?"

Linen shook her head. "I'm sorry ma'am, I can't answer that. As far as I'm aware, it seems strong, but how can you measure it? I've no idea of Spook's structure, his nature, his essence..."

"But you call it *he*."

Linen gave a short laugh. "We agreed that he should be a *he*, is all. *I* don't know. But I can't speak for Copper."

"You mean you won't."

"All right, I won't. I don't think you should be quizzing me about Spook behind her back, ma'am."

"That's enough. This ship and her mission are my priorities and if you have information that impacts on those, I want to know about it. Now. Or you *will* be in the brig. And then off my ship. Both of you."

Linen looked at the steely green eyes in alarm and shrugged helplessly as she realised the score. "Ma'am, I really *am* in the dark over this. I feel Spook around now and then, but I get the impression it's only when he lets me. Copper *can* call him up and as far as I'm aware, he comes. He warns her of trouble and I sense that there's some sort of... emotional link. Whether it's gratitude for easing his loneliness or a hope that through her he'll find another of his own or get back home, I have no idea."

"After being buried for millennia in a ship under the surface of Mars, I hardly think he'd have a home to get back to," the colonel remarked.

"If *that's* the case, ma'am, why were your people at the site next to the Warren logging incoming signals of unknown origin that were being picked up by space-based ships and stations? You said at the time that it was speculation on our part but if these signals *were* directed towards Mars, they must have been directed at someone or something: the alien ships that we know are buried on Mars are the obvious targets."

"These incoming signals have been picked up for decades, as I think Lieutenant Milkstone pointed out at the time. The recent increase in their intensity was the reason for our concern."

"So Spook's people or whoever is sending the signals doesn't give up. Let's hope they *are* Spook's people and friendly," Linen added, "Because if they're the ones that *may* have caused Spook's lot to hide their ships under Mars' surface in the first place, we could be in a lot of trouble. They'll know now that Mars has the know-how to send ships out, possibly after them. They probably figured we had the tech after the *Griffon* was sent out… Maybe that's why she was taken out?"

The colonel shook her head. "Ms Firewall was right: you two are hotshots. And both of you seem to have vivid imaginations. And you are quite cleverly deflecting me from the questions I want answered. Does this Spook that you clearly believe exists pose a threat to my ship? And if so, how great is that threat?"

The green eyes narrowed and Linen knew from experience that her commanding officer was beginning to be very annoyed. She took a deep breath to steady herself and looked across.

"I can't say for sure, ma'am. But I don't think he does – I've never sensed any hostility from him and I'm sure Copper never has. He's saved our butts a couple of time and as Cop once pointed out, he gets scared. That implies a friendly sentience that worries about himself and about us. He gets anxious about Cop, I'd swear to that. He turns up when she's worried or upset, I know that much, even when she doesn't call him."

"So it, or he, is probably by her side, or at least around her now?" the colonel speculated. "If that's the case, there may be a way to detect it."

Linen looked away self-consciously. "I did once think I saw a slight mist or vapour round Cop's head and shoulder area when

Spook was about. I scanned with a MEDIC and the scanner you gave me but got nothing. I wasn't sure if I was seeing things. We were in our lower site and near his ship," she explained. "We reckoned he may have been able to generate a visible form when he was close to his ship but we couldn't prove it and neither of us has seen anything like it again."

"She's in medbay and that's where many of our top range bio-scanners are," the colonel mused. "Why are you shaking your head?"

"One, if he was around, I'm sure he'd figure what you were at. Two, he may not actually *be* near Copper at the moment," she squirmed, a rueful smile on her face.

"What the hell are you trying to say, Lieutenant?"

"When I was with Cop just there, she was certain he wasn't near. She said she thought he was off on his own trying to sniff out any other rogues that might be on board."

"*You what?*"

"That's exactly what *I* said, ma'am," Linen shrugged. "She got the impression that he was upset over the Jecks thing, but she did admit that she was feeling really lightheaded."

"So there's a disembodied alien wandering around my ship like some sort of vigilante, tracking down troublemakers?"

"It does sound unlikely when you put it like that," admitted Linen. "But ma'am, Spook is *real*. We've had occasion to be grateful to him. We'd both have been damp spots on the ground long since if it hadn't been for his warnings."

"So you're saying that this entity is aboard my ship, there's precious little I can do about it, but it might even be useful?"

"That's about the gist of it, ma'am."

"You will not breathe a word about this to anyone. Are you clear on that, Lieutenant?"

"Absolutely, ma'am."

"One thing: if there's something that comes up that I should know about, you *will* inform me immediately. You're dismissed. Get out of here."

"Aye, ma'am."

Linen obeyed with alacrity, sliding out of the door and in the direction of the closest outside passageway. She was breathing deeply and slightly shaken. She gained the nearest elevator and slumped against the wall as it began to sink. It was as she was marching towards her own quarters on deck nine that she was confronted by Lieutenant Ash Goff.

"I hear you've been to see Lieutenant Milkstone," he greeted her. "What went down? We heard there was big trouble and she took a hit. Security's been swarming over every deck like a cloud of flies over a cake. So come on, give me the lowdown."

"Get out of my way or you'll find my boot so far up your arse it'll come out of your mouth," she hissed at him.

The angry eyes glaring up into his face nonplussed him for a second, but he stood firm. "I *am* your senior, you know. So why don't we…"

"You heard the lieutenant; back off," ordered the firm tones of Dr Trisk Addystone as he emerged from his own quarters.

"I don't need you to fight my battles for me," Linen asserted hotly.

"I know that," her friend agreed. "But the colonel *will* have you in the brig if it comes to fisticuffs, no matter how much he provoked you. You as well, Ash, *once* you'd been released from medbay," Trisk warned.

"Only trying to be friendly," Goff returned, holding his hands up, palms outward in token of peace. "I'll see you both around," he added as he sauntered off trying to look casual, whilst Linen stood, hands on hips, watching darkly.

"He's all mouth and twitchy nose," Trisk said. "And he's not the only one. Want a caff? You look as if you've been hauled over the coals."

"I want a jug of Lofty's best Martian Minewater," she told him. "If you can arrange that."

"I've got a buddy in medbay; I could give it a try?"

"I thought only the colonel or chief medic could authorise alcohol?"

"My buddy *is* the chief medic," was Trisk's laconic reply, accompanied by his habitual grin.

"Lead on, Lieutenant," Linen replied. "I've just come from there and I don't really want to go back, but if there's promise of a mug of ale at the end of it, I'd follow you into hell."

"You must have got some toasting. I thought the colonel was handing out cookies and sympathy."

"I should be so lucky. And don't even ask or I'll be forced to punch your nose for you."

"I won't; I know you too well."

* * *

Later on that evening, Linen sought and gained permission to pay her friend a short visit. After quickly setting up a privacy bug, she looked around to ensure that no obvious eyes were upon them. Despite the colonel's strict warning not to breathe a word about the events of the sol or the conversation that they had had, Linen was not about to leave Copper in the dark.

Quickly, she brought her friend up to date on her exchanges with their commanding officer. She was convinced that Copper would be next in line for cross-examination over Spook and did not want to leave her unprepared. Linen then hid her bug and moved on to the events afterwards.

After the exit of Ash Goff, she and Trisk had made for the inner area of medbay and the chief MO's office. Dr Faerin was nowhere in sight but one of his staff directed the pair to a small monitoring hub, where they found him busy at some station. He waved them over once they had caught his attention.

"He was looking through your files," Linen told her friend. "I caught an eyeful as he flicked off. He assumed that Trisk had brought me because I had a problem," she laughed wryly. "We soon put him right. And he *can* dispense a nightcap if he deems it appropriate. We went back to his office and had a shot of scotch each. And then another one," Linen confessed. "So he *is* a man to cultivate. I mentioned Lofty's finest, but naturally he had none of that on tap."

"Maybe he can order in before we leave dock?" Copper asked with an attempt at joviality.

"I wouldn't suggest it," Linen advised, looking at her closely. "And let's face it, as great a guy as Lofty sure is, his home-made Minewater isn't exactly the best ale on the planet."

"Don't tell him that or he'll be very upset and Majorelle will set Osterley on you as a penalty," she was warned. "But I could do with something. This place is deadly and with all these tubes and monitors, I feel as if I'm only half-human. And it hurts."

"How are you feeling at this very moment?"

"Weepy," Copper admitted. "And seriously sore; I think my

meds are wearing off. Spook flits in and out, but I'm sure he's on some scent or other. I don't know if he's found something."

"Dammit," Linen murmured.

"What?"

"The colonel ordered me to let her know of anything that came up that she should know about, on pain of throwing me into the brig. So if Spook's off on a trail, she'll want to know, even if you don't know what it is."

"Well, you can tell her now: she's just turned up outside the door. I can see her through that porthole and the doc's with her. And I don't expect he's got a bottle of hooch in his pocket."

The colonel's errand was a brief discussion with Lieutenant Milkstone; the chief MO had come in to ensure that his patient was both fit and willing to be questioned. Copper agreed on the proviso that Linen remained, both as a witness and as back-up lest the talk lead her into some indiscretion. Colonel Moritz was granted half an hour and no more, and Dr Faerin departed.

"I expect you've already briefed Ms Milkstone on our talk of this afternoon?" the colonel said shortly to Linen as she looked from the one to the other.

"Yes, ma'am."

"Despite the fact that I ordered you not to breathe a word to anyone?"

"Yes, ma'am. But Copper's…"

"Enough!"

"Don't shout at Linen, ma'am, it's not her fault," Copper put in. "I'm the one that started all this, after that damn bang on the head down the Warren. I…" her face creased in pain and her bio-monitor let out an alarmed beep.

"Oh Cop, don't cry!" Linen started up, a hastily extracted medi-wipe in her hand.

"I'm not," was the ragged response as her back arched and her hands clenched in a spasm. "I… shit, damn, hell…"

The colonel's hand hit the emergency button as the wipe in Linen's hand fluttered in a shifting of air around the life-support cradle. A tenuous wisp of flowing vapour wreathed around her and Copper closed her eyes, slipping down with a sigh.

Dr Faerin pounded through the door demanding to know his patient's status. Linen pointed wordlessly to the bio-monitor: its wildly fluctuating readings were almost off the scale. The MO immediately began to manipulate the cradle's controls, his eyes flickering back and forth towards the monitor. As the other two watched, the flashing lights calmed and the traces began to settle into the green zone, registering stability. Faerin swiftly hauled out his own medical scanner to verify Copper's condition.

"What the hell happened, Elle?"

As the colonel described Lieutenant Milkstone's seizure and its aftermath, Faerin look a touch incredulous. "You saw what?"

"Lieutenant Lyrican, I expect you saw what I saw?"

"Yes, ma'am."

"Care to explain what you think it was?"

Linen looked up at her commanding officer; her eyes flicked over to Copper and then back to the colonel. "Colonel Moritz, Spook; Spook, Colonel Moritz," she intoned softly.

"It's still here?"

"He's still here," Linen confirmed.

"How *is* the lieutenant?" Colonel Moritz demanded of her chief MO.

"Readings are normal and she's asleep. I've increased her pain relief and her sedatives. I'll post a watch on her. No more interviews until I say so. What's still here?"

"I'm posting a security watch on her as well as a med watch," she alerted him. "No-one but your team gets close. Any changes and I want to know. Lyrican, you're with me. Once you're done, Doctor, we'll all talk in your office."

Well-versed in most aspects of her ship, including the chief medic's office in medbay it seemed, the colonel lost no time in availing herself of the drinks dispenser to call up two mugs of caff. One she placed in front of her subordinate. She sat down at the table with the other and quickly made a link to security to order the watch in medbay. She was finalising the details when Faerin stepped through the door. He collected his own drink and sat alongside.

In the short silence as the three regarded one another, Linen pulled her privacy bug out of her pocket and set it on the table, methodically activating the device. As its blue ring of light swept around the space, she folded her hands demurely but her glance at the colonel was challenging.

"I've told you before that this place is not bugged," Ms Moritz said evenly, with a glance and half-smile at Faerin.

"With respect, ma'am, things change; you've already dug one rotten apple out of your barrel and you've a ship to launch on the morrow. Not much time left if there are others and they plan to act before you do."

"I expect you're armed as well?"

"Yes ma'am: PPF, non-regulation but I *am* licenced to hold it. And I note no alarms have gone off anywhere to tell me I shouldn't be carrying it – even in medbay."

"What do you do in your spare time, security back-up?" Dr Faerin demanded.

"Belay that, Doctor. Good point, Lieutenant. I suspect that this is going to be a long night."

In as few words as possible, the colonel brought her chief medic up to speed on the apparent alien entity aboard ship and its relationship to his patient. She insisted that no records of any kind be kept of the phenomenon or its seeming links to Copper, but wanted additional scans made on a regular basis with every medical tool available, including instruments under development for the mission ahead. Linen had the nagging suspicion that the colonel was still unsure of Spook's existence, but was surprised that Ms Moritz seemed to be hinting there were devices under test for the detection of alien lifeforms. As she was about to ask for clarification, the commanding officer abruptly demanded to know Linen's take on her friend's spasm and what had led to it.

"She complained of pain before you came in, ma'am," stated Linen bluntly. "Weepy and seriously sore is how she described herself; she felt her meds were wearing off. She mentioned that Spook had been flitting in and out and she assumed he was on some trail, but she didn't know what. *I* think he wasn't around when I stopped in, but she *did* get upset over your questioning of me and that's when it all started. I reckon he picked up on it instantly and flew back to check: she said before that she felt he was extremely upset over the Jecks incident and I guess he was attuned to any changes in her. It was once we saw what we saw that the readings began to stabilise."

"I think you'll find I had interfered at that point, Lieutenant," Faerin put in.

"Don't agree," Linen contradicted. "The readings had already started to normalise before you'd finished for one thing, and for another, how many sedatives and analgesics do *you* know that start acting on a patient so immediately?"

"Are you trying to suggest that this – whatever – can *physically* interact with a human?" the doctor asked sceptically.

"I'm not trying to suggest anything, Doc; I'm stating my view of what I think happened, as ordered."

"That's enough," interrupted Colonel Moritz. "You said this Spook of yours was on some trail? What, where and why?"

"I've no idea, ma'am; neither has Cop. But I want permission to stay by her overnight in case something turns up."

"Negative, you'll stay in your quarters and you'll be called if the doctor thinks you're needed. That *is* an order, Lieutenant."

Linen pursed her lips in annoyance but continued calmly. "How many people know of the attack on Cop, aside from the crew at the scene and others like Ash Goff that are nosey?"

"Too many, I suspect," the colonel returned. "I informed Ms Firewall of the assault but it will have gone no further by her."

"I'm amazed she didn't commandeer a shuttle and head up here to get Jecks out of your hands and into hers, ma'am: she'd sort him out."

"No doubt. What's this about Lieutenant Goff?"

"He demanded the details from me after I'd been to see Cop in medbay that first time: he knew she had been hit and where she was. I threatened to kick his butt. Trisk put a stop to it and hauled me off for a drink to calm me down."

"I can verify that, Elle," Faerin stated. "He hauled her in here. But my people know how to keep their lips buttoned: we sign up to that in med school."

"Won't stop others checking up on med logs and any other data they can get their paws on, if they have malice in mind and realise that there are some things and people aboard that would be useful to them," Linen cautioned. "In fact, that might be a place to start. If there *have* been data enquiries, security should be able to pin down the originators – sir."

"Mr Locksmith has all that in hand," the colonel said as the doctor noted that for rookies, Linen and Copper had caused more trouble in two sols than most would in six months aboard.

"That's as maybe," Linen began, pausing suddenly to clutch the colonel's arm and point to her privacy bug: the blue circle that denoted all clear had changed to a delicate pulsating pink.

Colonel Moritz rose slowly. Linen pulled out her gun, passed it to the colonel and then detached her scanner to begin a sweep of the immediate surroundings. Faerin stepped over to the one-way window of his office to check outside; he nodded fractionally as he caught something.

"Let's all have another drink," the doctor said, signalling with his hand to the spot. "I'll set them up."

As the colonel and Linen burst out of the office together, a figure in tech fatigues started up from the med-station she had been using. She realised immediately that she had been caught red-handed and turned to flee, letting go the equipment in her hands. A stunning beam caught her and she dropped.

"Good shot, ma'am," Linen commended as she stepped over to the fallen tech, Faerin on her heels.

"Don't recognise her," the doctor was saying as a noise at the door caused them all to turn.

Kit Locksmith stopped dead at the sight of the group. "You beat us to it," he announced. "We're searching her quarters."

"Another bad apple," Colonel Moritz remarked, handing Linen's weapon back to its rightful owner. "How many more?"

"We'll have them," the security chief assured her. "You two, search her and then get her into an interview room, pronto," he added to his team.

"Just one minute," Faerin interrupted. "She's not going anywhere until I say so."

Linen left them arguing and returned to the doctor's office to retrieve her bug, which was still showing pink. She picked the device up and sauntered back into the main area to scan the station that the tech had been working on. A small flat button attached to one side of the viewscreen grid seemed atypical. She pointed and made a cutthroat gesture to Kit Locksmith, who had caught her eye. Between them, they examined the appliance. The security chief pulled a small sharp knife from a pocket and eased the button from its anchorage. He was familiar with the device, for he carefully scraped away a small section, inserted his knife point into its innards and pushed. The pink of Linen's privacy bug faded and its usual blue reappeared.

"Somebody listening in, Chief?" she asked Locksmith.

"Not now," he told her. "But if it's just been planted, she'd have had to have the controller on her. She's been aboard for almost a month, ma'am," he added to the colonel. "Standard log checks showed she'd been in regular contact with some surface link over that period – identical call sign but the location moves. One of my team noted that she called at precisely the same time every three sols and checked it out. They seemed to be standard link to home messages, but every so often a set of holo-images would be transferred up here."

"Orders?" Colonel Moritz barked.

"That's what we read it as, ma'am. Pity we didn't pick it up sooner. We're trying to locate her planetside contact and decode the holos. But her record's clean: she joined the service a year ago, assigned to a small sweeper rig and then to a planet-runner as engine-tech. Not outstanding but competent enough."

"Keep checking. Any more?"

"A couple of leads; I'll keep you updated."

"Do that. Lyrican, you get on back to your quarters and stay there. You have an early start morrow-sol."

"Aye, ma'am."

12: SPUN STARLIGHT

Linen awoke to the sound of Gerald's alarm, which consisted of a shrill whistle followed by a stream of abuse about laziness. She threw her thermal cover from her as she ordered him to cut it or she would deactivate him. He grumbled inconsequentially for a moment or so before subsiding. She paused to look around, every sense alert, but there had been no calls overnight and her link to her comms desk in the main apartment was blank. She had left the screen door of her sleeping unit open for a rapid sortie if need be, but there had evidently been nothing to disturb her. It was early and Linen yawned widely as she made for the shower. She had planned a quick breakfast and a trip to medbay to see her friend before reporting for duty.

A rapid turnaround and she was soon set for sol. There were still no messages apart from an updated schedule of Admiral Stannum's tour of the *Drake* and the responsibilities of those who would be in the firing line. A quick request to medbay for news of Copper was met with the stony reply that she was not authorised for that information and should go through a senior officer. She told the disembodied voice precisely what it could do with itself and left for the mess.

"Not in your best bib and tucker for the high jinks?" Trisk enquired as he caught up with her in the queue.

"Nope. Might spill the chow."

"What's the beef? You seem annoyed about something."

"Found an armed man outside my quarters when I left them a few minutes ago," Linen said in a low voice, raising her light-flecked eyes to his face.

"You what? I didn't see him. Who and what was he doing?" Trisk questioned equally quietly, although no others were near enough to hear.

"He was a security guard Chief Locksmith had posted. Don't know if it was on orders from high or not, he wouldn't say, but he'd been there all night. As if I can't secure my own billet!"

"Do you secure your own billet?" her friend asked curiously.

"No. But I will from now on, if I can get the gear. I'll ask Kit Locksmith when I chew his ear over the guard; I'm sure he can spare something."

"Good luck. How's Copper?"

"Medbay won't tell me, so that's another set of ears to chew. I'm heading there after breakfast and then I'll get kitted out for the shindig. We have a couple of hours before launch, according to the schedule. Where are we headed first, once we're out into the deep dark yonder?"

"Lagrangian Four Orbital Dock, to catch up with the rest of our squadron, I think. We were the first out, but they must be near ready to launch as well," Trisk told her.

"What does Fleet Command do with a complete squadron? Shoot them out of dock one at a time like balls from a squash-ball server, with a handy bigwig to throw a holo-bottle, give each one a name and bless all who fly in her?" Linen queried.

"No idea, I'm not an expert. There's Tiff Tuffet, he's career military and has been around a few blocks, why not ask him?"

"Because you may recall he bit my face off for asking for classier boots that looked fit for purpose when first I got my kit is why: we're not the best of friends."

"Oh, he'll have got over that. Besides, if we sit with him, you won't have to sit with Ash Goff."

"I wouldn't anyway. But after you; you can field any flak."

Major Tuffet could not enlighten the two as to the launch of more than one ship at a time, but sundry grumbles about the imminent launch of the *Drake* served to pass the time until their plates were cleared. Linen was only grateful that the major did not enquire over the events of the last sol and the rumours that were inevitably circulating. She could feel other eyes on her over the entire meal, and despite her usual extroversion she was in no mood to spin yarns in order to yank her shipmates' chains.

"Off now," she informed the two once done. "See you in the lab," she added to Trisk.

"Hi there," said a voice at her elbow as she marched out of

the door.

"Busy," she responded shortly as she sidestepped Ash Goff.

"I just wanted to apologise," the lieutenant replied. "I didn't mean to upset you over your friend."

"Apology accepted; bye."

"Are you off to see her now?" Goff persisted.

"Go away and mind your own business or I'll take back the acceptance and file a complaint against you for being a pest," Linen retorted. "That'll be after I poke you in the eye and kick you up the butt, by the way, Lieutenant."

Her irritation carried her swiftly into the elevator and then along the passageway to medbay. By the time she had dealt with two inquisitive medical personnel and a security guard, she was ready to bite the head off Kynedd Faerin, who intercepted her on the way to iso-bay four.

"Colonel's orders," he told her. "And they apply to you as well as everyone else, Lieutenant. So you go through my office every time you want to pay a visit to Lieutenant Milkstone."

"Aye, sir," Linen replied resignedly. "In that case, would you be kind enough to escort me to Copper and tell whoever is holding up the bulkhead outside to let me in?"

"Come on," he responded.

As they walked, the doctor informed her that her friend had spent a comfortable night and was making good progress. Linen responded that she only hoped that Mr Locksmith had triple-checked the guard he had posted on Copper and everyone else involved in her care.

"Including me, I take it?"

"Yup," she said abruptly. "Especially you, Doc. Thanks for the scotch the other eve, by the way. What's your line in ale?"

"You tread a thin line," he grinned down at her.

"So the colonel keeps telling me. But Cop likes a good mug of ale and I'm sure it would aid her recovery – and my nerves."

"You do your job, Lieutenant, and let me do mine," Faerin laughed at the twinkling gold-flecked eyes. "But we'll see… ten minutes and no more, and I *will* be checking."

"Aye, sir."

Linen left him talking to the guard at the door and stepped through. Copper was awake and grinned cheerfully enough.

"How's it cooking?" the redhead greeted her.

"Just done breakfast, if that's what it was," Copper replied. "Some sort of cereal mush, toasted bun with cheese-sub filling and caff that's as weak as water."

Linen smiled into her friend's face, but was acutely aware of its gaunt look and deeply etched lines of pain that had not been there before. Copper's eyes looked tired and red. Impulsively, the redhead took her hand as she sat alongside.

"Spook had better be looking after you, or I'll have his non-existent hide," she told her.

"He is. The colonel called in earlier, just for a few minutes, as did Locksmith, asking about Jecks and my involvement there. He said they found another bad guy. Wonder how many more?"

"Spook not found that out? He's slacking."

"He's on the case. I had a link from Magenta, by the way: a bunch of holo flowers, advice on keeping up my strength and an apology for not being able to send up a crate of goodies. And on shooting first and asking questions later if I see something I don't like the look of."

"That's Grammy," Linen chuckled. "I'm surprised she didn't fly up personally to take this place apart."

"Bet she tried," Copper said. "I asked the doc if I could start some of the training we're supposed to do while we're aboard — a lot of it will be getting used to the science stations and so on, so there must be sims I could practice on."

"What did he say?"

"He said give it a sol or two and if I still feel the same he'll get Jinn Limlite to call by to discuss it."

"Just don't go asking for flight sims, they'll shake you to hell and back," advised the redhead. "But on the subject of the doc: he now knows about Spook. And the colonel implied that there may be a way of sensing him, or at least aliens, with instruments we have aboard; but she wouldn't spill the details, so I'm not much wiser. But before the doc starts shouting time's up, what can I bring you to make life in this box more bearable?"

Linen had very little time to do more than make a list, for Dr Faerin shooed her out after the specified ten minutes. With a wave, she set back off to her quarters to change into her dress uniform for the rigours of the sol and to pay a visit to Copper's place next door to pick up a few items requested by her friend.

Trisk was setting out his schedule of work in the office when she strolled in at eight thirty. He had decided on the samples he planned to analyse and advised Linen to do the same. His main task would be a run-through of several fractions from one of the first sample tubes filled by the *Lithium Star*. A preliminary analysis of much of the material had been carried out in military labs back on Mars but Trisk had not been granted the results of those initial investigations.

"I expect the colonel has the data," he told Linen. "With orders not to release it until we report, no doubt."

"But that wastes time," she argued. "Though I suppose it means that later researchers start without pre-conceived ideas of what they'll find."

"It also means that other eyes or noses where they shouldn't be won't get a clue as to what's already been uncovered..."

"And make off with the samples... when I signed up to this, I expected excitement, mystery and suspense. I didn't have cloak and dagger high on my wish list," Linen sighed.

"Comes with the territory," Trisk smiled. "You should know that by now, given all we've been through. So you'd better hop to it. Here's the list of what I have."

The first part of the sol passed quickly as the two prepared their rapid-analysers and other equipment and set to work. The launch ceremony of the *MSS Drake II* was being broadcast ship-wide and they knew that at the appropriate time they would be expected to stand by and salute as the great starship slipped her moorings and slid out into the greater space beyond Phobos Station II Space Dock, to the acclaim of the watching audience.

Linen had examined the schedule closely and knew exactly when the shuttle carrying the admiral on inspection was due to intercept the *Drake* and come aboard. She reckoned she would have a good half hour between launch and arrival and on that basis had contacted Faerin to request a visit to Copper in time for the ceremony. He had returned her link a little later with an affirmative. She let Trisk know and his eyes crinkled in laughter.

"You'll get thrown in the brig one of these sols. We've all been given our posts and yours is here."

"I know, but you'll cover for me, won't you?"

"This once," he promised. "But be back here in good time. And don't forget, after we wave Admiral Stannum goodbye, it's drinks all round. The colonel has sanctioned a few drops of the best for all off duty crew and we won't be charged for it."

"I'd best make sure Cop knows – a fortified caff will set her up for the night."

"You'll be lucky. Just make sure you're back here in time."

Copper was not surprised to see her friend as the doctor had let her know that Linen planned to stop by. She had set up the info-point and had linked to the ship's channel that was set for the launch. As they waited for the main event, Linen handed over the booty she had brought from Copper's quarters and outlined the plans for the sol and the research that she and Trisk would be carrying out.

"Lor' that's a lot of brass!" Linen interrupted herself as the viewers set to capture the occasion swung into action. "Where's the colonel?"

"On the bridge, I hope," was the dry reply. "She's in charge of this mighty vessel, so she'll have to make sure she doesn't hit anything on the way out. Wow, that's what she looks like all the way round! I hadn't realised there were so many sections to her hull. Here come the speeches… that must be Admiral Stannum aboard her shuttle, but who are all these other uniforms?"

"No idea; but quiz the info-point if you want to know, I'm sure it'll tell you," Linen said. "There are more than a few other shuttles and ships standing by. Hope somebody's got them all marked on some grid somewhere; we don't want the new paint on our hull scratched on the way out."

As the two watched, the voice droned on, wishing the *Drake II* and her crew a safe and successful voyage, a safe return and continued prosperity in all her future endeavours. The holo-fizz bottle was loosed and it smacked in a shower of stars against the mighty *Drake's* hull. As the docking struts that held her secure were released one by one, a thunderous fanfare echoed over the audio systems and everyone in sight on the various viewscreens saluted, to the sound of cheering from the many stations that were linked in.

Both Linen and Copper straightened to attention and saluted likewise as the images coalesced and the bridge of the *Drake* was visible, her commanding officer standing ramrod straight, her hand to her ear in the customary gesture of respect.

"Auntie Elle's got a lot of gilding on the uniform," observed Linen as she dropped her arm. "Bet it itches round the neck. But now we're officially an active ship of the Fleet, I'd better scoot back to my post or I'll be thrown in the brig. Can't say it *feels* like we're moving," she went on as she gave her friend a hug. "I'll be back in a while and tell you how it went with the admiral – that is, if she does call in for a chinwag."

"Just wait 'til we get to near light speed. But be good, or at least be careful," Copper advised. "And on that note, I want you to take this with you: Magenta gave it me a while ago. And thanks for watching the show with me," she added tremulously.

"Just keep your chin up, kiddo and I'll see you later," was the parting instruction as Linen shot out of the door.

* * *

"The admiral's shuttle's on the way over," Trisk greeted the redhead as she sailed in. "Nobody missed you, but you'd best be at your station when the tour starts. She's headed for the bridge first, then medbay and then engineering. We're near the end of the schedule, but there's no saying she won't change it."

"I just hope nothing exciting decides to pop up just as she comes in," Linen responded. "I'm setting my deep probes for traces of alien organo-tech or similar. After all, that's what we're meant to be looking for in the samples and there should be something, given the hoo-hah over them in the first place."

"Maybe," Dr Addystone replied. "The stuff I've analysed so far has had precious little of interest. The scraps I did extract are bits of the self-rep material that have been found on Mars and other places, including in samples the *Wayfinder* brought in from rocky planetoids out at the edge way back. I suspect that on the initial trawls through the bulk samples, anything that looked interesting was removed, and it'll only be the tinier pieces that we'll have here."

"But we *will* have samples that haven't been deeply probed, surely?" Linen argued. "The *Lithium Star* is one big ship and she must have brought back quite a lot of stuff, despite what some of her crew said. There can't be the military resources on Mars to analyse everything brought in at such a fine scale."

"Good point. We don't know how far the analyses went," Trisk agreed. "Or at least I don't."

"Damn Military Intelligence!" Linen grumbled. "One half never knows what the other half is up to most of the time. How they get anything resolved… but I'd best get on. And I want a caff break before all the fun starts in here…"

All the fun started three hours later, by which time Linen was in sore need of lunch. The colonel, with the admiral and a brace of aides, stalked in through the lab door. The two officers had been warned by colleagues along the way of their approach and were thus busy at their respective analysis stations, but stood to attention to be presented. Admiral Stannum ordered them to stand easy, instructed her assistants to keep watch outside the door, and then began an informal chat on the work in which the scientists were involved. Trisk's outgoing manner encouraged enquiry as he enlarged on the nature of the tri-dee images of the samples under analysis. The admiral had been briefed, for she introduced the subject of alien artefacts and the search for more and bluntly requested information on the most advanced that had been found. Trisk, with a quick glance at his commanding officer, pulled up the holo-image of a small object that spun slowly in the air above his station.

Linen recognised the iridescent, reddish-green flat oval with a circular aperture at one end and ridges along the opposite edge: it was the device that Copper had found in one of their sample tubes from the Glory Hole. She looked anxiously at the colonel as the piece continued to rotate and a prickly sensation that had begun at the nape of her neck and was crawling over her scalp made her feel increasingly uneasy. As the admiral called for an explanation of what they were looking at, Linen shook her head slightly, turning as if by compulsion to her own station.

"Damn!" she hissed silently to herself as she unobtrusively moved a small batch of sample cartridges to one side. "You pick a great time to show up!"

Behind the stack, a small silver-coloured cone encircled by two fine blue crystal bands was glowing softly. As Linen's eyes widened, a semi-translucent holo-note spread from the device across her console, figures and directional symbols changing as they became clearer. Colonel Moritz had been alerted by her officer's agitation and was aware of something amiss: she tabbed her wrist-comm and spoke quickly into it.

Several things happened at once: as the admiral demanded to know what the hell was going on, Linen pointed silently to the exit and her own ear. Trisk pulled a weapon from a concealed drawer and sounds of a scuffle beginning outside were disrupted by a burst of fire that buckled the skin of the door.

Both science officers were on their guard, but it was Trisk who spotted the hover-cam detaching from an upper corner of the lab. He fired quickly and the device exploded in a shower of flak that took a fair chunk of bulkhead with it. Linen had pulled her own PPF from a pocket and quickly scanned the vicinity. Kit Locksmith burst in, pulling up short at the gun in his face.

"Friend!" he called out and Linen quickly changed her aim.

"We got two at least, ma'am," the security chief announced. "Just as well we had them all under surveillance."

"Explain," Colonel Moritz ordered.

"One of the admiral's aides was carrying a bug, possibly unknowingly; it was activated just after you got to the lab, by a timer, I reckon, to cut down on the chances of our picking it up. And we caught one of our own tailing your party, so we tailed him. As for that tight-beamed signal we picked up earlier: its source is a small commercial cruiser just off our port bow. The receiver's in one of our outer bays but the signal's rerouted from there, so I have one of my team tracking it both ways, from source to end point. Given the mess in here, I guess this is the end point, but there may be others. Though I suspect whoever's behind this now knows we're on to them and they're half way to Jupiter by now."

"You said two at least," the colonel pointed out.

"We also have a suspect from the admiral's shuttle: one of the non-Fleet press-officers. She was trying to inject a data chit into a comm-station in the arrivals area: we had to let the crew through the security field to stretch their legs and grab a caff, as we knew the tour would be a few hours. She's in the brig."

By this time Admiral Stannum had picked up sufficient data to know that she had been kept in the dark over several aspects of her visit and was furious. Colonel Moritz pulled no punches: being very aware that she probably had a few more scallywags aboard the *Drake*, she had ordered security to keep a tight rein on everyone and everything and had ordered the whole party tracked from the time they boarded. She had likewise revealed nothing about unauthorised signals being directed towards her ship that her security had picked up, or the measures she had ordered for her own crew's protection.

Linen was by this time also aware that there must have been systems put in place to protect both her and Copper without her knowledge. Unaccountably, a cosy chat that she and her friend had had many months ago with her family, after a fraught field trip to the Warren, came into her mind. She recalled Magenta Firewall jokingly mentioning a hover-cam the size of a cookie crumb and looked around warily but saw nothing. It was as she was trying to fathom the source of the thought whilst listening to the two senior officers that she sighted a tiny wisp of vapour out of the corner of her eye. As it drifted towards the admiral and condensed at one spot, she realised what she was seeing and its likely association; it gave her such a jolt she jumped visibly.

"Something, Lieutenant?" enquired the colonel.

Linen opened and shut her mouth like a virtual goldfish and bit her lip.

"Out with it!"

"A hover-cam the size of cookie crumb," she said slowly as her eyes narrowed, her head tilted to one side and her finger pointed. "It could be disguised as a ranking pip…"

"What the *hell* are you insinuating?" Stannum spat out.

"Precisely," Colonel Moritz interjected. "Explain yourself, Lieutenant Lyrican, or you *will* be escorted to the brig."

Locksmith had caught the exchange and the implication and hauled out his security scanner. "With your permission, ma'am," he said shortly, raising the device and moving it gradually in the admiral's direction.

"I'd have a few sharp words with your tailor, ma'am," he said slowly. "How did you pick up on it?" he added to Linen, who shrugged in perplexity. "That central pip's a miniaturised spy-cam of some sort."

"That's preposterous!" Admiral Stannum was red with wrath. "Let me see that!"

She unzipped and hauled off her own dress jacket, slapping it down on a nearby console as she snatched the scanner out of the chief's hand. After a thorough examination, she pulled the offending pip off the uniform and set it carefully apart.

"Heads are going to roll over this!" she threatened, resuming her outfit. "And I want a few words with you," she told Linen. "How in hell *did* you figure it?"

"Dr Addystone, escort Lieutenant Lyrican to her quarters and stay with her for the present; I'll see you shortly. Admiral, *I'm* the one you'll be having words with, in my office. This tour is at an end. Locksmith, tidy things up here, especially that minicam, and get the Admiral's crew back to their shuttle. I'll catch up with you later. Dismissed."

"Yes, ma'am," the officers of the *Drake* intoned as the three of them turned on their heels.

"I hope you're escorting me via the mess," Linen told Trisk as they quit the lab. "It's way past lunchtime and I'm starved."

"You really know how to rock the boat," he responded with a twinkle in his eye. "How *did* you spot it?"

"Mind your own business. Mess?"

"Let's go."

"Has the colonel appointed you as my guardian?" Linen went on. "She seems to keep asking you to keep an eye on me."

"Not officially. Serendipity, I expect."

"And the band played believe it if you like," was the sardonic reply. "What a mess out here! Wonder where they've stored that aide with the bug in his pocket, or wherever?"

"Don't care; just mind your feet."

"I left Copper's bug detector in the lab – Chief Locksmith better not have made off with it," Linen went on.

"You were going to chew his ears off over the guard he posted outside your door," Trisk reminded her. "You can add it to your list of beefs with security."

"Whatever; just lead me to lunch…"

* * *

Linen and Trisk were seated cosily in the former's quarters, having eaten and changed thankfully into regular uniform, when there was a buzz at the door. They had linked to Copper via what they hoped was a secure channel and were in process of bringing her up to date on the happenings in the lab. Linen cut the link quickly with a promise to call back.

"It'll be Colonel Moritz," she guessed. "She should be at the helm of her ship, not making house-calls. Enter," she called out as she and Trisk stood up.

"So I should be at the helm of my ship, should I?" was the greeting as the door panel slid across.

"I thought our quarters were soundproofed!"

"Never assume anything, Lieutenant. May I sit?"

"Of course, ma'am. Sorry, ma'am."

"At ease, both of you. And the *Drake's* at station-keeping in high Mars orbit until we dispose of our unwanted guests and clear up a few security matters, so the bridge can do without me. Your take on the Admiral's visit…"

As the two science officers gave their opinions and surmises on exactly what they thought had happened, the colonel listened carefully and questioned succinctly. Trisk was then sent back on duty. Linen had expected as much and so ordered up two mugs of caff, carefully setting them on her small table.

Colonel Moritz regarded her junior officer shrewdly. "Point one: where did you get your very clever bug detector and why did you set it? And point two: just how did you work out that the ranking pip *was* a disguised spy-cam?"

"Point one, ma'am: Copper gave it to me earlier this sol as she figured it might be useful. She got it from Magenta Firewall ages ago. And point two: Spook, but there's more to it. When Trisk was showing the admiral the holo of that bit of alien tech we found out at the Dragon's Nest, I had a really strong feeling that I should check the detector, which I did, and you know the outcome. Then for some peculiar reason, a chat that Cop and I had with Ms Firewall months and months back jumped into my head. Grammy was joking about trails that could be followed by a hover-cam the size of cookie crumb and I know it fazed Cop at the time. I guess that Spook had warned her of the problem and she was trying to alert me through him, but how in blazes she or they did it I don't know; all I do know is I saw a thin trace of mist close to the admiral's neckline – just like we saw round Copper when Spook turned up in medbay the other sol but much finer – that focused in on the central pip. It seemed to glow slightly, and I realised what the score was."

"I *did* suspect that this Spook had materialised, but this manifestation of its, or his, talents is something else. You realise that if you *had* been wrong, you would have been in the brig?"

"*Now* I realise, ma'am: at the time, all I could think of was that we could be in trouble."

"On another note... this bug detector that Ms Milkstone gave you. How come it was with her in medbay?"

"I brought it to her from her quarters. She asked me to bring along one or two things," Linen confessed uncomfortably.

"When you visited her to watch the launch, no doubt."

"Yes, ma'am."

"And just how many other articles did you pass on to her?"

"A few," Linen admitted. "Not weaponry," she added, seeing where the question was leading. "Just her holo-dragon and her MEDIC: *that* contains the bulk of our Lowell research data that we need to produce the reports that MDMC expects. Naturally, we'll pass everything through your office before we send it out, ma'am. And another couple of personal things…"

"Like the bug detector."

"Yes, and the scanner you gave her last year. She'll be able to do more in a sol or two and she's hoping to be moved out of the iso-bay, or at least off that life-support cradle. She wants to do some training to keep her mind and her hands occupied," Linen added in support of her friend's plans.

"I'd heard," the colonel replied. "I'll sanction it if the doctor concurs; you can tell her that when next you see her, no doubt later this sol. But meanwhile, you'd better get back on duty. Thank you for the caff."

"You're welcome, ma'am."

As the commanding officer strode through her door, Linen breathed a sigh of relief. She had expected a penalty for leaving her post in the run up to the launch. She hauled on her jacket and set off quickly to her office and the remainder of her work.

Trisk was in the lab tidying up the task-stations and trying to avoid the security personnel that were sifting through the debris. The blast that had heralded the demise of the intrusive hover-cam had caused some damage to one bio-geo-chem sequencer and two sample analysers as well as the upper bulkhead. Linen consoled him with the fact that the side lab with the tri-dee sim stations was still intact. That thought caused her to pause and regard her colleague in disquiet. Trisk caught the implicit notion and pulled out his hand-held scanner. Linen extracted her own device and followed him into the attached room. The two began a systematic scan of the small space.

"Hell's teeth, these bastards seem to have been busy," Trisk sighed in exasperation. "Hey, you two! In here!"

As a head peered around the door, Dr Addystone pointed aloft. "Damn well hidden, but there's another of those hover-cams up there. I suggest you inactivate any volatiles before we have a repeat performance of the earlier big bang."

"It's not active, so whoever planted it isn't around with the controls in his or her hand," Linen surmised. "You'd best let the chief know as well. I want a word with him anyway."

Kit Locksmith appeared a few minutes later. "When you get fed up with your work in the science department, care to put in a few duty spells with security, you two and Ms Milkstone?" he asked them.

"Only if you let me have that bug detector back," Linen told him. "I note it wasn't where I left it. And stop planting security guards outside my door at nights."

"That was orders," the chief shot back. "Nice piece of kit, that detector. Where did you get it?"

"It's Copper's and my Grammy Magenta Firewall gave it her. And I want it back. You want one, you request it of Ms Firewall. But on your own head be it. Just warn me when you do, so I can be there to watch the fur fly."

"I've met Ms Firewall," was the dry rejoinder. "But good call; I'll have my teams scour every lab and secure station we have."

"And other sensitive places. Weapons stores, food stores…"

"Thanks for that wisdom, Lieutenant. We'll take it from here. You can pick that bug detector up from my office whenever."

"Back to work," Trisk grinned. "After our caff break."

"And a visit to the chief's office," Linen added.

* * *

Post dinnertime found Lieutenant Lyrican at her friend's side in the iso-bay discussing the latest in their own department and elsewhere. Linen had brought in a couple of small dispo-cups of some alcoholic beverage that she had persuaded Dr Faerin to dispense in deference to the occasion of the launch, as Copper had missed out on the free hooch in the mess.

"Our crewmates are going to be avoiding us like the plague in case we attract even more trouble and they find themselves in the middle of it," was Linen's opinion as she raised her cup in a toast.

"Or seeking our company for precisely the same reason," stated Copper, reciprocating the gesture. "Drama merchants that *want* to be in the middle of things and hope we're it."

"At least we can hide in the office or in the labs," her friend comforted. "But the latest searches have come up clean thus far and I got a good look at Chief Locksmith's office when I went to pick up your bug. I tell you, the whole ship must be decked out with secure-cams and the output of most of 'em shows up on the viewscreens in main security. His office looks through to it; it's like a never-ending holo-flic. It would drive me doozy."

"No it wouldn't, you were born nosey," Copper disputed. "But enough already. At least the latest batch of bad guys is off the ship and Admiral Stannum's back on planet shaking up her own people. Locksmith's got the place buttoned up tighter than Ma Kellyn's lips when she's peeved about something. Talking of Ma, she left a link for me and a present of a holo-pic of Altair looking smug. She hopes we'll have a pleasant trip and passes on her compliments to Colonel Moritz."

"You didn't, did you?"

"I did; the colonel came by just shortly before you came in to ask how I was and stayed all of two minutes. Locksmith had been in just before that to ask about the detector Magenta gave me. We're set to break orbit at oh eight hundred morrow-sol."

"That's *Lieutenant* Locksmith – he ranks you. And nobody tells me anything round here," Linen complained as she took another sip of her drink.

"I just did, but don't you go passing it on," warned Copper. "I want out of here but Doc Faerin says no, until my meds are reduced to at least half… Mind you, this stuff helps."

"Cop, you were hit only yestersol; it must seem longer, stuck in here, but things don't turn around overnight, even with a few mil of booze mixed in."

"The rib fracture's been fused, the lung puncture's sealed; the medics say the skin and muscle injuries will take longer, but I'm on the mend," her friend said rebelliously. "And I'm sick of this place, linked up to these tubes as if I'm incapable of functioning on my own. I feel like Spook did in his life-support system."

Linen was startled. "How do you know how Spook felt in his life-support system?"

"I don't," Copper admitted uncertainly. "I'm not sure where that popped up from. Did you know that we have heaps of life-support systems aboard, in case things go belly-up? Life-tubes are located in the 'tween-deck areas in lower engineering, the hangar bays and on the flight deck next to the bridge. Not that anyone in them would last long in the cold of space, but if you can't get to an escape craft, they're there."

"How d'you know that?"

"I'd been conning over the ship's spec in between sorting the Warren data that can be massaged into a report for MDMC if Lomax Gratikule or the Waterbone start to bawl and I spotted them, so I asked *Mr* Locksmith about them when he called in and he told me. I've got Gemima started on the outline report for MDMC already, by the by. Doing something proactive beats twiddling my thumbs or watching endless info-flics."

"Chief Locksmith told you, did he?" Linen asked shrewdly. "Before I forget, Colonel Moritz said she'd sanction training for you if the doc says you can. She told me to tell you."

"Why didn't she tell me when she stopped by?"

"If she was only here two minutes, she'd hardly have time. And you'd have started bending her ears on what training you'd like," Linen told her. "With Spook as back-up, you're a lot more pushy, not to mention impudent, that you used to be."

"Thanks for that. I'd like to be at the main science station on the bridge when we do break orbit. That would be something."

"We'll both need a lot more training before we're allowed to man any of the bridge science stations solo. Or even in tandem with one of our seniors."

"I expect. Wish I could have a Chocó-crème to go with this whatever it is, I haven't had one in an age," Copper mourned.

"What, they don't do intravenous Chocó-crème in medbay?"

"Hah, hah. Go chat up Doc Faerin if he's still about…"

Dr Faerin was absent and Linen could not persuade the duty

medical officer that her patient would benefit from a mug of the beverage, but caff was authorised and the two sat sipping in contented harmony until Linen was ordered out for the eve.

* * *

Moonsol at zero eight hundred hours found the majority of the crew at their assigned stations, and the remainder at some viewport or other, or on the observation deck that spanned part of levels two and three. Linen and Trisk were among the latter. As the mighty *MSS Drake II* bid farewell to Fleet Control and the helmsman directed her immense bulk away from Mars orbit there was a muted cheer from the watchers. The space between ship and planet increased at a rapidly accelerating rate and Linen waved as Mars turned into a small dot and was finally lost in the immensity of starlight. A muffled thrumming was the only clue to the movement of the ship through space.

"Wish I was on the bridge," Trisk muttered to his friend.

"You and me both. But we'd better get into the lab and put in a good sol's work or the colonel will want to know why not."

It was a strange feeling to be aboard a ship of the Fleet on a mission to the outer reaches of the system and Linen mused on how she had come to be in such a place as the two made their way down to the science section. The mechanics of the journey itself, the build-up to a velocity close to light speed that was possible partly as a result of the mathematics of one of her own forebears, flitted through her brain and she raised a mental toast to her great-grandmother, Curiosity Lyrican Lear-Grange.

Their priority work for the next several sols was, as Trisk had mapped out, to begin a thorough analysis of their share of the samples that the *Lithium Star* had brought in from the edge. Dr Addystone instructed Linen in the abstraction of the specimens from the high security cells in which they were stored and to which she and Copper had access, and the means of securing them in their lab itself when the officers had business elsewhere. He also disclosed the specifics of the advanced security systems in place in their office and main lab and their activation.

"Pity they weren't primed when the Admiral was nosing around yestersol," was Linen's decided opinion.

"Questions would have been asked," Trisk pointed out. "Just make sure they *are* operational at all times. And be grateful for the high-spec strengthening of our bulkheads – that exploding cam would have taken out more than just a chunk of our roof and we would have been peppered with a lot more than bits of flak if it hadn't been in place. We might have been sharing a space in medbay with Copper."

"It was *so* dangerous?" Linen demanded.

"It was. Naturally, we don't know that."

"Naturally. So, surface scans, deep probes and sectioning?"

"Stick to the non-invasive techniques for the moment," Trisk directed. "We'll have sols of this ahead of us, even when Copper gets back to the lab. How was she earlier?"

"To be honest, I thought she looked worse than yestersol when I linked. She said she was fine, but she would."

"Did you speak to the doc?"

"Dr Faerin wasn't there and I wouldn't, on an open channel, and they probably wouldn't tell me anyway. But I'm going to stop by later. I've requested a visit, but I'll head along whether I get an affirmative or not."

The following hours were occupied in routine sample sifting, analysis and data logging, with only one short break. By a late lunchtime, Linen had had enough and was only too pleased to shut up her station, store her gear and head down to medbay, where she had approval to call. She had little to tell her friend: neither she nor Trisk had found anything worth reporting.

"A few tiny shreds of the organo-matrix that we think makes up the hull of alien ships like Spook's, but that's been it – and as you know, Trisk is sensitive to the material, but not so much as you I don't think," the redhead conjectured.

Copper was tired and acknowledged as much, but had one or two snippets to impart. She had drafted their next report to MDMC on the basis of the backlog of sample analyses they had stored in their MEDICs' memory matrices: she had discovered that by patching through to the superior data facilities of the *Drake*, she could carry out trawls of several accessible as well as restricted data sources for similarities or differences to their own findings and using Gemima, produce a succinct summary. And as they now had permission to use data that had been acquired by the octet of miniaturised stealth surface science bots with which they had been entrusted in a test mission whilst they were based at Lowell College, they had the material to produce later reports with little effort.

"Meaning we can concentrate on the ship's mission and the work the colonel has given us as priority," Linen nodded.

"You got it. We send out reports now and again to pacify the EMMS Office and thus MDMC, and keep Lomax Gratikule and his chums off our case. But I suggest we give it a sevensol or so before we despatch our first report from up here, unless Thars starts hinting. We haven't heard anything from our lot at Lowell or the Warren, have we?"

"No. I didn't want to contact them again until you were back on your feet," Linen admitted. "You know how things get taken out of context. But they'll figure we're finding our way around and I doubt they'll press for a while. Though I *did* send a link to Waterbone informing him that the colonel had vetoed personal links to discuss work aboard ship and that *all* personal comms were monitored in any case. That should put paid to any more of his antics."

"You'd better hope comms are not being monitored if you're telling fibs about the colonel behind her back. But did you wear your dress uniform for the link?" Copper wanted to know.

"Of course; and I borrowed your medals for nav and piloting and stuck them on my chest to give him something to eyeball," Linen added, her own eyes twinkling in amusement. "I'll return them, I promise."

"You'd better," her friend growled. "Or I'll restrict your access to my quarters. You watched us leave orbit?"

"Yup, from the obs deck. But you cut down on the work you're doing on our reports and have a rest, for frock's sake; I *will* do my share, once I've worked out some sort of rota for the stuff we're supposed to be doing in the labs. And we'll have to organise another trip down to the tri-dee sim test facilities in engineering to check out how to set up the hard-holo of the Dragon's Nest accurately: I bet we still have a few surprises in our sample tubes. If you're okay with that?"

"Well of course I am," Copper stated matter-of-factly. "I've thought long and hard about the Jecks incident and I'm sure as shells not going to let that weasel scare me out of doing what I have to aboard this ship. Besides – we're aboard the best ship in the fleet. We have facilities and possibilities here that we could only dream about at Lowell. When we were mere undergrads at College, how could we have seen that one sol we'd be aboard a starship on a deep space mission? Okay, getting into space was one thing we could have aimed for, but it would have been the mundane commercial stuff…"

"There's nothing mundane about space travel, commercial or otherwise," corrected Linen. "But at least we're not space sick. How long are you going to be stuck in this bay, do you know?"

"Another sol at least, though they've cut some of my meds. They only let me off this damnable couch for minutes at a time but at least they don't have to unhook various bits from my anatomy any more: the med-patches take care of pain relief and healing. But the monitors are set to continuous scan, so I can't scratch an itch without an alarm going off. I'm having a meet with Jinn Limlite to discuss my training needs later and I've had Ossy Inkscree and Captain Helmis both stop in already, *and* Kit Locksmith: he'd come to check details with his security guard, so he said. You'd think they'd be busy in their own units with the ship in flight," Copper huffed.

"Well, Helmis *is* exec and responsible for personnel, Inkscree is chief science officer and technically your boss and Locksmith is security chief," her friend told her. "Any more visitors apart from them and the medics?"

"Nope, but Trisk has asked to call. So did Ash Goff, but I told Dr Faerin to tell him no way."

"He just wants a piece of what he thinks is the action," Linen surmised. "How's Spook?"

"Under the bed."

"What!"

"Got you! No, he's… actually, he just turned up. He must have heard you, or sensed that you wanted to know about him. I think he's exploring the ship on his own account; it's bigger than anything he's travelled in."

"How in blazes do you know that?" demanded Linen.

"I get the feeling. I also get the feeling that he tends to leave us on our own when you turn up."

"So now he's decided two's company and three's bad manners? Or doesn't he like me anymore?"

"Of course he does, he just being discreet. And he thinks that you're capable of looking after me, so he can head out on his own," Copper grinned.

"Aw, that's cute... You're winding me up, aren't you?"

"I am. Can't help it, this place is driving me doozie, I feel as if I'm under surveillance all the time with that porthole open to anyone that looks in and all this gear. I need a bit of privacy."

"You *are* under surveillance: this is medbay, you have to be," Linen pointed out. "It'll be the same when you're moved out of the iso-bay. I guess you'll get one of the side bays off the main surgical unit?"

"No idea. As long as I can get up and walk about a bit or at least have a turn in a physio booth. There's nothing wrong with my legs. What is it?"

"Are you talking to Spook?"

"He's twitchy about something," Copper said, puzzled. "Just a sec..."

She closed her eyes, tilting her head to one side as if listening. Linen took the opportunity to scan her friend's face. She looked drawn and pale and the grey medical fatigues did nothing to help. Suddenly the redhead sat bolt upright: the filmy wisp of vapour that she had come to associate with Spook was wrapped around Copper's shoulders in some sort of ethereal hug. As the latter's eyes slowly opened moments later, Linen mutely raised her hands, palms upwards, in a questioning gesture.

"That hidden hover-cam in our side-lab," Copper explicated. "There are a couple more that security's missed... maybe you'd better pay Kit Locksmith a visit?"

* * *

Ten minutes later and Lieutenant Lyrican was sitting calmly in the main security office on deck three awaiting Lieutenant Kit Locksmith's return from some mission in engineering.

"About time," she greeted him as he tramped through the door. "I haven't had lunch yet and I'm starved."

"What's so urgent you need to speak to me personally?" he asked with a lift of his eyebrow.

"Your office," she told him with a challenging look.

Once in the chief's own space, Linen unfastened her small multi-scanner from its chain, and began a systematic sweep of the space. "I suggest you do the same," she told Locksmith.

"You what?"

"Just in case. Given there's another of those well-hidden and very nasty exploding hover-cams in main security. It's behind an upper bulkhead opposite the door, and high enough to catch a good view of who's coming or going. It'll take out a fair chunk of your viewscreen wall if it does go off," she told him equably. "And then where would you be?"

"If that's the case, how come you know about it?" was the suspicious enquiry.

"No offence, Chief, but the colonel I will tell, not you. But trust me, I'm sure of it. *This* place reads clean."

"I'm glad to hear it. But this hover-cam: is it operational?"

"You got me: I don't know. But you're sure we still have one or two moles aboard, aren't you?" Linen probed.

"No comment," was the dry response. "I'll assume that the cam's there and *is* active, for now. But I'm not bringing the colonel in; if there *is* someone with a finger on a trigger, that's likely to set them off. You said you were hungry: want to go get some lunch?"

"I'm game. You'd best let your buddies next door know."

"Will you stop telling me how to run my department?"

"*You* were the one that suggested I pull a few shifts with security if ever I got fed up with science," she returned.

"I take it back, in your case at any rate. Let's head on down to the mess. Hey, Pete! The lieutenant and I are off to grab a bite; keep an eye on things here," Locksmith called through the door to one of his deputies. "Okay short-stuff, move it."

"You're asking for trouble," she told him. "Bet I could take you out with one hand behind my back."

"Bet you couldn't," Locksmith riposted.

"I could: the hand behind my back would be holding onto a fully-charged PPF. You wouldn't see it coming."

Over lunch in a near-empty officers' mess, Locksmith could not prise out of Linen the reasons for her certainty of the device hidden in his own headquarters or for another in the hangar bay where the ship's small fighter squadron was based, but had figured by enquiries after Copper that she was also aware of the dangers. He reiterated his advice against bringing the colonel in, as that would arouse suspicion if any of those who had been involved with the devices were still aboard. Linen had other ideas and once back in her own office, contacted medbay with the request to talk to her friend to arrange a visit once she was off duty. In a roundabout way, Linen enquired after the timing of other visitors, principally Colonel Moritz. Copper caught the subliminal message.

* * *

"Kiddo, have I got news for you!" was the cheery greeting as Lieutenant Lyrican bounced through the door of iso-bay four at the end of her exhausting work-sol.

"Wouldn't be our chum, Thulia, would it? I think we got the same message," was the reply as Copper set up her bug detector.

"It is," Linen agreed as she piloted a seat closer. "How she engineers these things I don't know. What do you make of it?"

"I recall many moons ago that Thulia and Wolff Waterbone tried to extract information from us on the work going on down at the Warren and we suspected at the time that MDMC and the Press in the form of Stellaria Firedrake were behind it, given the snoopware the pair of them were toting. Maybe this is one more attempt to dig up information about what's going on, but this time in relation to our mission here. You put a spoke in Wolff's wheel by telling him our comms were being monitored; maybe somebody's now trying to launch a parallel strategy in hopes we won't notice and will let things slip to our old and valued ex-colleague from Lowell," Copper suggested. "Maybe somebody should tell whoever's orchestrated it that the value we put on our erstwhile college pal isn't what *she* thinks it is. But here's the colonel; we'll have to pass this story on as well. Good evening, ma'am."

"I see you're here, Lieutenant Lyrican."

"Deliberately, ma'am. Things have come up."

"Why am I not surprised? How are *you*, Ms Milkstone?"

"Itching to get out of here, ma'am."

Colonel Moritz was quick to spot the detector and listened carefully as the two provided her with the details of the hidden hover-cams that Spook had suggested were *in situ*. The pair found that Kit Locksmith had not been idle, for he had located both mechanisms, neither of which was operational, and they were now in pieces in a highly secure store in his office. The colonel had been apprised of the finds in a routine briefing and had guessed that there was more to the story than Locksmith was telling on an open channel.

The news from Thulia gave them food for thought, although Copper and Linen were both more amused than otherwise. The ecstatic link that they had received from their former colleague Ms Numbridge was to the effect that she had been removed from the Triton Unified Bio-Base Scheme, of which she was the marketing officer, and seconded to MDMC's Planetary Survey Missions venture, the astrobiology arm of which provided much of the research funding for the Amberline Group and supported both Copper and Linen as PhD students. The unctuous Wolff Waterbone, lately promoted, was now Thulia's immediate boss.

"The TUBBS project operated through the EMMS Office at Viking One but it's never been up to much and I don't think many take it seriously," Copper told the colonel.

"Except Thulia," interjected Linen with a laugh.

"With *her* on our case, she'll be on the link every other sol demanding this, that and the next in her usual flashy style, in the hope that we won't notice she's logging every nuance of our response. *And* she'll have every photon of the record scrutinised by some expert she has on call. She's ditsy but not brainless and will step on any stone that she thinks will get her to the top of her career ladder. Or anywhere else of note."

"Including over the top of Wolff Waterbone," Linen put in. "But who's pulling her strings? MDMC has its own ship out here but I bet its bigwigs want to know a lot more about ours."

"They'd be better picking on one of our sister ships for long-distance snooping," was Copper's opinion. "They're built to the same spec but the *Drake's* the flagship, and she's the pick of the squadron and has the cream of Mars Fleet as crew, mostly."

"Thanks for that," the colonel remarked dryly. "Though we still have one or two miscreants aboard by the look of things."

"Will the rest of the squadron be setting out along of us, ma'am?" Copper wanted to know. "I note we're headed for the Lagrangian Four Orbital Dock, but there's been no word on other Fleet launches from there."

"You're keeping an eye on ship's business, then? No, our

mission is solo: this *is* our shakedown cruise after all. The rest of the squadron is rigging for launch over the next two sevensols, so this is a courtesy call only."

"And a means of preventing any dustbaggers from guessing how important our main mission is," Copper noted astutely.

"Perhaps," Colonel Moritz said. "It's also a strategic position from which to set course and build speed. Keep me informed of anything else that seems important. I'll be seeing you both."

"Aye, ma'am," they chorused as their commanding officer took her leave.

"No doubt Thars will have been informed of the change in executive structure at the EMMS Office," Linen sighed. "We'll have him on the link next. Colonel didn't stop long…"

"She never does, given she's a starship to command. And as we're turning on approach to dock, she's needed on the bridge."

"We're here already?"

"Course we are: have a look," Copper invited as she turned her info-station. "*That's* what a squadron of starships in dock looks like."

An immeasurable net of light extended into the distance, criss-crossing space and blotting out the stars. Enmeshed within were the massive forms of a dozen simulacra of the *Drake*, each one attended by a swarming army of bots completing final outfitting. The dazzling display rotated as the *Drake* turned for her final approach, settling into her allotted bay with a gentle thrumming as the docking struts spread out to meet her hull and lock her in.

13: SPUN MOONDUST

Two sols later the *MSS Drake II*, on a heading that would take her in the direction of the asteroid belt in the next phase of her initial cruise, was readying engines for the velocity increase that would herald the induction of her main drive. The crews on the bridge and in main engineering were holding their breaths as the initiation phases passed one after the other. Elsewhere aboard the mighty starship the duties of the sol continued as usual.

"I like the new accommodation; it's a little less clinical than that iso-bay," Lieutenant Lyrican observed as she breezed in to visit her friend. "What in blazes have you got set up there?"

"A sim of the secondary bridge science station," Copper said to her. "I'm trying to get the hang of it. Long-range scanners are incredible, I can read the atmospheric composition of that small moon and we're not even close."

"Never mind that; I've brought you lunch."

"Isn't lunch supposed to be delivered by responsive medical assists and comprise all the vitamins, minerals and whatever that I need to consume for healing and healthy recovery?"

"In general yes, but this is a special delivery courtesy of me and a little sweet-talking of Dr Faerin," Linen said wickedly.

"What's in the dispo-cup?" her friend asked curiously.

The redhead set down her piled tray and carefully loosed the cup from its inset, handing it over with the order not to spill.

"It's ale!"

"It is – not exactly Albany Export Red, but a good imitation. The doc keeps a stash handy. I had a chinwag with him yestersol eve and persuaded him that it would be just the thing to set you up. He wouldn't authorise any for me, even though I suggested I was in dire need," Linen shrugged.

"So the soulful eyes and the adoring smile didn't work then?"

"Not on Faerin they didn't. In fact he told me to save them up for Kit Locksmith. Ever since I had lunch with *him* the other sol, people have been making suggestive comments and treating me to winks. Trisk thinks it's hilarious, but knows different – so does the doc, I suspect: *he* was winding up my prop. But try this for size," she added, lifting a large covered platter and disclosing its contents.

"Cream-sauce steakfry!" Copper raised puzzled eyes. "How on Mars did you manage it?"

"Had a word with Cookie in the deck four mess and he and his team produced it. You're quite a celebrity, you know. I think word's got round that you were injured in the line of duty and people are impressed," Linen nodded. "But this is a one-off, it won't happen every sol," she warned as she disinterred her own plate and sorted out the cutlery.

"You are the best," Copper told her as she set to with relish. "It's almost as good as Chef's special at Lofty's."

"That's my girl; you eat up and enjoy. And once you're out of this unholy place, we'll make an appointment at the therapy salon; it's on deck eight and not far from Tiff Tuffet's hangout near ship's stores. I could do with a massage and face-make and I bet you could too. We may as well use the pay that we won't be able to squander otherwise."

"Things are getting back to normal," Copper noted, snorting wryly. "You spending my credit for me before I even get it."

"You'd best just get on and get well; we need you back in our lab. As *our* lab science stations are the best aboard, one or two of our colleagues think we're one up on them and are pressing for a share. Ash Goff for one."

"He's a geologist, we're astrobio," Copper said crossly. "And we need the specialist equipment there for our own research, as it spans so much. He must have his own rocks to play with and his own work – isn't he supposed to be sampling asteroids as we fly by? How are you getting on with the *Lithstar* samples, by the way?" she added, ramming in another forkful.

"Don't speak with your mouth full," Linen reproved. "And slowly; I think Trisk was dead-on when he said whoever did the initial run-throughs filched any sizeable bits and the stuff in the tubes we got aren't as representative as they should be. Though there may be some yet that haven't been given more than a cursory scan, as heaps were probably brought in. And we have some pieces that the *Wayfinder* brought back to analyse as well."

"I'm hoping another sol or so in medbay will do it," Copper disclosed. "I've had a few spells in the physio suite and done okay. I'll be strapped up, but I should be able to sit at a station and carry out routine tasks. Physical jerks I'll have to miss out for a while, but walks along the lower engineering decks should fit the bill."

"You'll have company," Linen warned. "Trisk and I thought we'd better have a run to keep fit late yestersol, so we linked up with Tawny Brown. I tell you, the number of people we passed on the move down in engineering! I was nearly creamed by one idiot in a racing buggy. In fact, I got a holo of the beast to pass on to Avrom, once I'd chewed the ear off the pilot of the darn thing. She was an engine-room tech. And I ranked her, so she was mortified, once she figured."

"I'll bet. But you'll have to butter Cookie up and persuade him to keep this on the menu, it's superb."

"I'll pass on your compliments. I can't stay long though: I've a session of weapons drill after lunch. I think the Training LO thinks we all need to be kept up to scratch, as I've had one or two other sessions marked down over the next sevensol or two and so has Trisk."

"Orders, I expect. And you have to keep the crew occupied or they'd get up to all sorts of mischief. I mean, what do the medics do when there are no patients?" Copper asked.

"There are always patients: with a crew this size, there *will* be a few hypochondriacs and given the speed of that frigging buggy along the deck, I'm surprised there aren't a few broken bones about," Linen declared. "But I expect medics have surgical sims and that sort of stuff to keep them up to date. Heard any more from the colonel on what's been going on about Jecks and the other dustbaggers that have been routed out?"

"No, but I expect she'll be more than busy with the ship now en route. I *did* have Kit Locksmith in asking about the hidden hover-cams. He figured that I'd had a hand in finding them and was trying to find out more. He brought me some Chocó-crème as a bribe."

"Hah! He is one savvy article. He waylaid Trisk as well. Tell him nothing; tell no-one anything in fact. Spook around?"

"No; I think he's off having fun somewhere. But your wrist-comm's barking at you, so I expect you'd best get on with your sol. I'll clear this lot up and get back to my sims."

* * *

It was forty eight hours later that Lieutenant Milkstone bade a thankful farewell to medbay and made her way back to her own quarters, which seemed eerily unfamiliar, as she had spent so little time there. She was still officially on sick-leave and so had time to sit and look around her, to take stock of her current situation and await Linen, who had planned to call in on the way to the mess for lunch.

Very little had happened over the past two sols apart from the progress the *Drake* had made from Mars: the ship was now about to negotiate the main asteroid belt, after which a short stopover at Jupiter Station was scheduled. News from home had followed the crew and Copper and Linen had several messages, amongst which was one to each from Thulia Numbridge. The link suggested that EMMSO's latest recruit was taking her duties seriously, as she had asked for a personal update to their last report by return. She had evidently also been assaulting Thars Amberline's ears as he had sent a memo advising them to ignore the request and divert all information relating to their research via his office as usual.

By the time Linen appeared at her door, Copper had changed into her standard uniform, had made a couple of comms links of her own and had mapped out her itinerary for the next few sols. The latter included a phased return to duty, as sitting about in her small billet appealed to her not at all.

It was gratifying to be greeted courteously by a number of crewmates as the two made their way up to deck four and the mess. Copper was mystified, as some of them she did not know.

"Told you that you were a celebrity," Linen archly informed her. "But we can sit with Trisk once we grab our chow. I bet you're glad to be back to normal."

"I don't know what normal is," Copper replied. "I didn't get the chance to find out. Huh! No cream-sauce steakfry!"

"This isn't the BC Hotel or Lofty's on a Frisol eve," she was scolded. "The rule here is shut up and eat it, even if you're not sure what it is. And most times, it's better not to ask. I note that you had the holo of Altair set up in your quarters."

"Yes, I sent a return message to Ma Kellyn just before you came in, so I thought I'd better have it in full view. He may as well stay there, next to my blue dragon. I'm trying to personalise my space, but given the limited stuff available in stores, and its cost, it's a slow process."

"There *are* one or two amateur artists among our crewmates: ask them to do you a piece," Linen suggested. "Or capture an image of the view outside, if you're so keen. I've put that holo of you in the dark red gown with the silver net overlay that the mysterious Mr Midnight of Coblentz Street in Lowell altered for you into a holo-frame and set it over my comms desk: I still had it on my wrist-comm and it's turned a few heads in its time."

Copper's jaw dropped. "You what! You little minx!"

"It'll be a talking point," Linen reasoned. "And we sure used it to good effect once or twice back at Beagle when we were trying to pick up information on what various parts of the Fleet had been up to, including the famous *Lithium Star...*"

"And look where that got us: a whole heap of trouble, then drafted into said Fleet; and now we're halfway to the edge of the frocking Sol system!"

"What, arguing already and you're only just out of medbay?" Trisk Addystone greeted her cheerfully. "That won't do your blood pressure any good."

"Keeps her mouth exercised, though," Linen joked as she sat down and began to rearrange her tray.

"Did you hear the latest?" Trisk went on in a quiet voice as he leaned towards the two.

"Spill," ordered Linen.

"Ossy Inkscree's been told to deploy a batch of mini surf-sci bots in a fly-by of one of the larger peripheral asteroids. Just a test, so I understand; he's surveying likely candidates at present. But as you two had something to do with pre-testing the bots, he'll be calling on your expertise."

"Who told you?" demanded Copper.

"He did: he spoke to me at breakfast, but as there was a lot of coming and going in the lab earlier, I haven't had a chance to let you in on it. He'll be by the lab later but said to keep it quiet for now. Some of his other people are in on it, so they know about it. Lyssa Halsen for one: being a bioengineer, she has a handle on several of the probes used for bio-mapping and such like. But not Ash Goff," he grinned at the two.

"Just as well," Linen announced darkly.

"And the colonel made it clear that we were required to assist in probe and instrument deployment and other technical stuff in keeping with our capabilities," Copper reminded her friend.

"Which definitely includes those bots," the redhead smiled toothily. "As we had such fun with a bunch of them in our Dragon's Nest."

"Lor' we only had eight," Copper groaned. "Wonder how many a test deployment requires?"

"Best come along to the lab with us and maybe find out," Linen smiled in response. "You can sit and advise while we do the usual round, if you don't feel fit for strenuous stuff."

"I was planning to get some work done: it beats sitting in my quarters watching a holo-Altair making faces at me and pawing thin air."

* * *

A spry Dr Ossian Inkscree found the three science officers in the main astrobiology lab and seated at stations there when he strolled in shortly after lunch. The trio had little option but to halt their work and Copper, who had elected to screen a sample tube, the original contents of which had been gathered by the *Lithium Star*, was put out. A trawl through the store housing the units had produced an uneasy prickle as she ran her hands along that particular tube and she was keen to know the reason. She paused in piqued curiosity, however, when she saw the sizeable pack that the chief science officer had slung over one shoulder. It looked vaguely familiar.

Inkscree was carrying a smoothly-contoured case with a wide carrying strap, which he slipped off, dropping the case carefully onto a side bench. Copper looked over at her red-haired friend.

"It's a tad bigger than the one we had," she said. "How many of the little sods are nested in it?"

A raised eyebrow greeted the remark as the doctor undid the catch on the container. He used his implanted ident to operate the lock, leading the other three to speculate that the contents were security-tagged. The case split neatly into two, each half of which contained an array of small metallic green convex shapes, like a set of flat round eggs in shallow nests.

Linen ran her eyes over the collection in rapid calculation. "I estimate there are thirty two, unless these are only top layers."

In response Inkscree began to operate a holo-pad that he had retrieved from the nest. As the others watched, each upper layer of case-half rose to reveal a lower section in which another set of convex buttons sat demurely.

With one glance at Linen, Copper hauled her MEDIC from her station and ordered a scan of the case and its contents, after intoning a coded instruction.

"You won't be able to scan them with that," Inkscree told her complacently as he continued his manipulations.

"Want to bet, sir?" she responded boldly.

Gemima reported that she was detecting data exchange within the target device between its sixty four component units and that each one had initiated surveillance of its environs and was emitting probe beams.

"I see they still glow that cute green when they're operating," Linen remarked. "That'll make covert use of the little sods a tad difficult, as I think we pointed out once before. And as Gemima can still scan them and analyse their operation, alteration of their ident nano-coding obviously wasn't part of the upgrading." She grinned maliciously at Inkscree.

"What exactly *was* improved on the basis of our initial report on their case of set up, use, data acquisition, depth of analysis and so on?" Copper put in. "Are they still as vulnerable as they were, since my MEDIC can detect them? Do they still ignore your orders and do exactly what *they* want when they set out on their little sorties – sir?"

The chief SO had been looking in exasperation from one to the other. "I was warned you two would be trouble," he said at last. "I assume your MEDIC can track them because it has their original ops data in its memory matrix but their security coding *has* been enhanced. We programme and control them from their nest or from whichever science station they're assigned to; and their ops factors we set within strictly specified limits."

"Good luck with that, sir," Copper interjected.

"This nest will be transported via a control pod that will be dropped into whatever environment we choose and the bots released when we've scanned the surroundings and deemed it appropriate. Once they've completed their pre-set mission, they will return to the nest with samples and data, re-nest and be returned aboard for data retrieval."

"I'm assuming we *will* be able to access their data as they're scanning?" Copper asked. "Lest they're damaged or destroyed on the surface or in transit?"

"The data is relayed to the central ops unit within the nest and from thence to the ship..."

"But we'll be able to tell from up here whether or not they're operating individually, won't we?" she persisted, eyes narrowing.

"Yes we will, our detection systems have been enhanced."

"I thought as much," Copper nodded to Linen. "The flights we detected overhead when we had a nestful of the little spit-shrikes down the Glory Hole – *somebody* up there was on survey to see if they could detect bot ops and data from a distance. It sounds like they couldn't, at that time, even though they were supposed to be detectable by specialised sensors and even though our MEDICs had no trouble picking up their signals."

"So we'd better have a look at the little sods at work. I take it they still scramble about on their lanky little legs," Linen grinned in return.

"Dr Addystone, lock this place down," Inkscree ordered, ignoring them as he began further manipulation of the holo-pad.

Trisk, who had been an amused observer of events, released a side panel on the bulkhead by the door and flicked a switch. A green delineator line spread around the lab perimeter and once complete, a short beep indicated lockdown.

"Clear," he announced. "A warning outside will say testing in progress, no admittance," he told his two friends. "But *this* lab has shielding most others don't."

As they watched, each bot within its hollow began to vibrate, the green glow becoming stronger. Suddenly the whole nest was a mass of movement as each device sprang up upon six spindle-thin legs, quivered for a moment and then sped off, almost faster than the observers' eyes could follow.

"They're still fast," Copper breathed. "I assume they choose their own target area based on their initial area scan, sir?"

"Affirmative," Inkscree confirmed.

"Why choose our lab for this test?" Linen enquired. "Hoping they'll find another hidden hover-cam?"

"I've planted a couple of test pieces for detection that the doc doesn't know the nature of," Trisk smiled at her.

"You what? When?"

"When you weren't around," he shot back.

"When I went to pick you up for lunch, Cop," the redhead reckoned. "Or at early break: I noticed you'd disappeared. What did you plant?"

"Wait and see," was the laughing response.

They waited. The spider-like forms scuttled at speed over the bulkheads and then slowed to begin what appeared to be careful examination of each surface, disappearing beneath task-stations and pieces of equipment and in and out of crevices and service units, their frail legs having no trouble in negotiating the various surfaces. As one of the devices shot up her leg, Copper let out a small scream.

"I hate it when they do that!"

"They should be able to scan us from distance and generate a tri-dee image," Inkscree declared. "They're programmed not to interact with animate targets."

"That would be us," Linen winked over at her friend. "Either they're ignoring instructions or they think you're not real."

"Maybe I'm not; maybe I'm a figment of your imagination," Copper returned. "How much data's being captured?"

"Rather a lot; would you look at the data stream…"

Dr Inkscree had programmed a short operations window of ten minutes of surface scans only and at the end of the time, an automatic recall order was issued. With breath-taking precision, each bot began its return, the whole cavalcade becoming several streams that made for the nest in an orderly fashion. In a matter of moments, every nest-space bar one was filled.

"You've lost one, sir: it's probably found an escape hole and is off to party on its own account," Copper informed Inkscree. "I told you they do their own thing when your back's turned, and even when it isn't."

The chief SO hissed in irritation and began an in-depth scan of his surroundings. "It's in that sample tube and it's locked in!"

"Test successful then," Trisk announced. "I coded it to close when the far end was contacted and it has."

The doctor eyed his science officer in annoyance. "You were supposed to plant test specimens."

"There's one at the end of the tube," Trisk replied. "Only the bot couldn't get back to report it. But if the data has been sent to the nest, a record should be there."

"It's fuzzy," Inkscree noted. "The probe beams were set to surface scans and can't fully penetrate the tube wall."

"So if a bot's lost, we may not know what's happened to it or if its loss signifies an unknown danger. It should have a means of emergency ops if it falls off the register or we lose its data," Trisk advocated.

"You'll have to boost scan depth," was Linen's contribution.

"Why didn't all its little friends run to its rescue?" Copper wanted to know. "They're cluster-enabled after all. 'All for one and one for all' is their mantra, isn't it? And they *can* sample the environment they're supposed to be scanning, as we know only too well, so they could maybe dig it out."

"You don't want to sample an unknown system: who knows what you'd bring back that might infect the ship. But what if one gets lost and doesn't make it back and the rest can't find it?" the redhead demanded.

"It's recorded as missing in action and the others award it a medal and hold a memorial service for it," her friend told her.

"Will you two button it!" Inkscree snapped. "Okay, what *did* you plant at the end of that tube?"

"A highly reflective platinum mirror and a tiny sample of alga I got from hydroponics," Trisk responded with a grin. "The bot will be looking at itself and registering organic life."

The doctor returned to his scrutiny of nest output. "This will take a lot of analysis to pinpoint what else you planted. It was supposed to be sufficiently unusual to raise a query…"

"It is."

"Just a sec… very funny. Where did you get it?"

"Dr Faerin: he keeps a supply. But he wants it back," warned Trisk. "It's very rare and precious, just like us."

"What is it?" the other two demanded with one voice.

"A bottle of very old scotch. It's under this BGC sequencer," he announced, patting the edge of the holo-grid screen of the bio-geo-chem analysis station at his elbow.

"That would certainly raise a query if it showed on a routine probe of an asteroid," Linen agreed.

"That's what I figured."

Dr Inkscree was less than impressed by his senior science officer's antics but had to agree that the tests had shown a few minor snags that would have to be surmounted before asteroid drop was attempted. The four dissected the results obtained and discussed means of improving the whole assembly prior to its scheduled deployment.

"I want a break before we get back to what we're supposed to be doing," Copper announced to her two colleagues when the chief science officer finally quit their lab. "I'll lock this tube back in store before we go."

"You can leave it here, nobody will run off with it," Trisk was certain as he retrieved Dr Faerin's precious bottle.

"I'll lock it in store," was the decided response in a tone that caused Linen to look at her friend suspiciously.

"Something?"

"Not sure. But I want to be fortified before I start."

"And your shoulder hurts, doesn't it?"

"Yup."

"Then increase your meds," Linen counselled.

"Nope; I want to be fully awake."

"We're in for some fun," Linen told an openly curious Trisk. "Let's refuel in the mess. I expect we'll see the colonel at some point, as she hasn't been by for a few sols and Dr Inkscree will certainly brief her on the outcome of the bots' lab test."

* * *

After a quick break, the three resumed their places in the lab, Copper having dug out her chosen specimen tube. It took some time to sift out and run through the more nondescript matter, although several fragments of what was more metal than rock appeared to give her some disquiet. She separated out a few fragments of blue material and set them to one side on her task-desk, calling on her friend to check her conclusions.

"It's reading as alien artefact material all right: organo-matrix, definitely synthetic, with pico-coding I can't decrypt. And it'll be capable of self-replication no doubt," Linen concurred, scanning the small shards. "But it's blue, like that stuff you found in the contract stuff we did for Mars Gov Defence Department, way back. We couldn't find a match for it in any of the databases we had, but you sure didn't like it and neither did… we passed it straight on to Colonel Moritz," she went on hurriedly. "She was aboard the *Drake* at the time, wasn't she? And she said that they had found miniscule traces of similar blue material in the past, among the wreckage of the *Griffon*."

"Which is what this tube contains," Copper said. "It's from the *Lithstar*. It must be one that hasn't been pre-analysed, or it's not been done thoroughly, because these pieces are small, but I'd hardly call them tiny."

"Scanners won't have been programmed to react specifically to that stuff," Trisk told the two as he came over. "And those *are* quite small fragments. It's been reported in the past but I've not seen any until now, though I've heard of it and seen sims."

He picked up one of the small splinters to take a closer look but dropped it quickly back into the open cartridge on Copper's task-desk. "I don't like it," he said, his eyes opening wide.

"That's the reaction I had," she told him. "I felt I shouldn't even touch it, though I couldn't say why. But it's not the end of it, I'm sure," Copper added, shivering convulsively as she turned back to her station.

She tilted the tube, allowing a small trickle of rockery to slide into her analysis tray. Carefully she sifted through the material, intending to send it through her analyser. She checked suddenly, her hand a fraction above the assemblage. Quickly she picked out a thin sliver about the size of a large thumbnail, scrutinising it closely before dropping it hurriedly onto the desk.

"Aah! I felt that through my glove!" she gasped, holding her right wrist tightly in her left hand. "Dammit, that tingles!"

She leaned slowly back, stiffening, still clutching her affected hand, her eyes glazing, hardly aware that Linen, exchanging a startled glance with Trisk, had grabbed her friend's wrist and was pulling off the thin protective glove. Copper's right hand was turning blue, whether from the pressure of her left or some other factor, Linen did not know.

"Get Faerin up here – him, no-one else!" she ordered Trisk. "And then shut that – whatever it is – into a sample cartridge."

Trisk was quick to comply; he also set the lockdown on the door to prevent unwanted entry by others. Linen meanwhile was attempting to bring the frozen Copper back to reality. She recognised the symptoms and realised that Spook had stepped in quickly to protect her friend from some threat. A thundering at the entry moments later told the three that aid had arrived. The chief medic demanded details as he systematically examined his patient's face and hand, loosening the wrench-like grip.

As the blue tinge began to fade from Copper's right hand, a dark mottling became perceptible at the tips of her thumb and forefinger. Faerin grabbed a hypo from his kit and slapped it to her upper arm.

"Hold that hand still," he urged Linen as he quickly brought out a dressing and moulded it to the two discoloured digits.

"What the hell is it? Will she be okay?"

A shuddering sigh from Copper told her friend that she was recovering as the doctor systematically swept his medi-scanner over the affected area.

"Surface skin cells are partially destroyed, but that seems to be all; the lower epidermis is intact and I don't detect tracking of any toxic agent. The skin should recover."

"Cop! Cop! Are you okay? What in blazes happened?" Linen demanded as Copper's eyes blinked rapidly and she groaned.

"Damn thing frocking stung me," was the thick response. "Felt my whole hand beginning to go numb, but…"

"But Spook got in quick," Linen finished. "But I don't get it," she went on, raising troubled eyes to Trisk, who had turned back from some operation at a comms console. "*You* touched the other blue fragment, but you weren't affected."

"I didn't touch *that*," he replied. "I used forceps to lift it into the cartridge. We'll need to analyse it. It may be different."

"Let's give you the once over," Faerin went on to the still-shocked Copper. "I'm giving you another shot of pain relief and I want you back in medbay for a thorough exam."

"I've just got out of that place, I'm not going back!"

"You'll do as you're ordered, Lieutenant."

"Try and make me!" was the rebellious retort.

"I'll have the colonel make you," she was told.

"Colonel Moritz is on her way," Trisk calmly announced. "Any reaction to alien tech was to be reported immediately," he reminded Linen. "I linked to the bridge and she's confirmed. I'll get this piece set up for a closer look and we'll see what makes it different to the other pieces we've met with thus far."

The colonel made good time and was soon with them and in possession of the facts. Trisk had been busy and had set about capturing as much surface detail of the alien shard as he could. He had just brought a tri-dee image of the fragment into focus above his task-desk and was magnifying it when Copper let out a short gasp and clutched her friend's sleeve.

"Rotate!" she instructed. "Those markings! Do you see?" she demanded of Linen.

"I see…"

"Hell and blast and damn… oh frock…"

As Trisk enlarged the pattern that had caught Copper's eye, the colonel examined it closely and then turned to her officers.

"You recognise these markings? You've seen them before? Where?"

"It's partial, but it's the same, isn't it?" Linen asked her friend as she studied the holo. "This is the edge of the diamond shape, with swirls through and around it. Bring up the colour, Trisk. It's a dark blue with solid pink. But what the hell does it mean?"

Copper shrugged. "Wish I knew. All I *do* know is I don't like it, it's dangerous if not deadly and it sends shivers where sol don't shine."

"What is it and *where* do you know it from?" Colonel Moritz repeated sharply.

Linen raised an enquiring eyebrow. "Cop?"

"My butt," Copper said wearily.

"Lieutenant!"

"It's all right, Doctor: I think I know what Ms Milkstone is trying to tell us. Are you sure?" the colonel asked.

"I copied it to my wrist-comm. And I sometimes see it in my dreams at night, so I'm pretty certain. But I'll check."

As she spoke, Copper twisted up the jewelled unit she always wore beneath her sleeve and spoke into it. In response, a pale holo began to extend from the unit across the task-desk.

"I've tried to fill in extra detail, but it's not exactly as I see it in my mind's eye," she went on. "But that's as close as I can get. It's similar if not the same, isn't it?"

"And you have no idea what it signifies, apart from a sense of danger, which now seems to be substantiated?"

"Affirmative, ma'am."

"Will somebody start making sense around here?" Faerin implored. "What *is* that material, how did it do what it did and what do those marks mean?"

"The blue stuff *has* been reported before but I don't recall any in-depth on it, or references to patterned bits," Trisk said. "But there have only been a few fragments and most of those were off-planet in origin. I could make a start on trying to find out why it caused that reaction in Copper," he offered. "I'll need the med data, Doc, but I can start by trying to analyse it with the best we've got."

"Do so. But this stays under wraps," Colonel Moritz warned. "I want the remainder of the *Lithium Star's* and the *Wayfinder's* samples examined as soon as. Your own sites will have to fit in around that, but your lower site will have priority," she added to the other two. "But as for that pattern, Lieutenant Milkstone: perhaps you'd like to enlighten Dr Faerin and Dr Addystone."

* * *

"Well," Trisk began to Linen a little later, as they began to secure their lab. "I did wonder about this mysterious Spook, but I never figured an alien entity. And you're both sure?"

"Oh we are," the redhead confirmed. "And we've now got the colonel convinced. I'm not so certain about Doc Faerin, but I bet he checks Cop's tattoo, now he's got her in medbay. I'm a bit worried, though: if Spook went to all that trouble to warn her about that pattern, there must be a very good reason why. But let's shelve it for now. There's a concert at twenty hundred in the officers' lounge, so what say we head there after dinner, if you've no other plans? Copper should be done in medbay by now, so I'll head along and see."

Copper was indeed done and itching to be free from the clutches of various medical personnel. She grumbled quietly to her friend as the two made their way along to their quarters to make ready for dinner.

"And we *will* have to make those joint links we promised to all and sundry," she went on. "We owe Lofty and Majorelle, Mik Mack, the Prof, Ma Kellyn and hosts more. They'll think we're ignoring them."

"We've been ultra-busy," Linen soothed. "And we can't make links at the drop of a hint; there are shipboard procedures to be followed."

"You make it sound so reasonable. I'm just wondering what else is about to happen. Things do, to us."

"On that note, as Trisk now knows about Spook, that's one less thing to try not to let slip and *he's* doing the work on that patterned piece of tech. But we'll have to be around for the test-drop of the bots. I hear Ossy Inkscree and Lyssa Halsen are doing overtime in the tri-dee facilities in engineering to sort out their little quirks. Have you figured out why Spook's so keen we know about that pattern?" Linen went on in a lower voice as the two stopped at Copper's quarters. "I get the impression he's sticking close at the moment."

"You're right, he is; but no, I just get a feeling of danger, but I don't know if it's to him as well as us, or it was to him or his people in the past."

"What exactly are his people? Like him, able to discard their bodies or life-support units, or is he special?"

"Special he is," Copper said tenderly. "He's still around for one thing, and I can't think that many, or any, of his kind are. But this isn't the place to discuss it – bulkheads may have ears and we still have one or two subversives about."

"You're getting paranoid; you need your dinner is all. Go sort yourself out and I'll call back in a few minutes."

Linen was as good as her word and the two soon found themselves in the queue in the officers' mess, casting disgruntled eyes over the chow on offer as they loaded their trays. Once in a small booth, they were joined by Trisk and Kit Locksmith, the latter having been briefed on some of the events in the lab. The security chief acknowledged that he was having trouble keeping up with the two. He declined their invitation to join them for the concert however, having some matter of his own to arrange.

* * *

It was some time later, as the three were approaching Trisk's quarters, where Linen and Copper had been invited in for a nightcap, that the latter, obeying a subliminal hint from Spook, raised her eyes to the bulkhead above the door. She stopped, pointing a finger.

"What's that?" she demanded, indicating a small half-dome that resembled a lidded eye that was situated between her entry and Trisk's. "I think it's a teeny cam and I can't think whether it was there before. None of the other doors close by have one."

"Are you sensing danger?" Linen asked practically.

"No – just curiosity."

"Then let's get in and call security," Trisk suggested, studying the apparatus carefully before opening his door. "It wasn't there before, I'd swear it. You speak to them," he ordered his friends once he had put through the link. "I'll organise the drinks."

Kit Locksmith responded almost immediately to Linen's curt request for a word; the chief was in his office and was surprised at the call. He was even more surprised when she asked outright if he knew anything about the cam installed between the two doors, with its beady sensors scanning the passageway outside.

"Was that what you were arranging when you knew we were at the concert?" Copper put in suddenly from the sidelines.

The response was an exasperated snort. "You lot don't miss much. Yes it was: given your problems earlier and objections to armed guards outside quarters, I want a specific watch kept on various parts of the ship, and like it or not, that includes crew decks – all of them, as a matter of fact. You want to argue about it, you take it up with our commanding officer. Have a very nice evening, what's left of it."

"Want to come over for a nightcap, Chief?" Trisk called out, holding up a bottle of something that was not standard issue.

"On my way," was the quick rejoinder. "I came off duty an hour ago…"

"Okay, why did you do that?" Linen demanded of her host.

"Somebody will notice him; they'll also notice that we three came in here, given the cam above my door. So I thought we'd give any nosy dustbaggers on watch something to gossip about. Including why Kit Locksmith seems to like hanging about with us. Some people still think it's you."

"You're asking for trouble," Linen told him in an undertone. "And some people are way off beam: Locksmith's not interested in *me*, as you damn well know. But where did you get whatever's in that bottle?"

"Don't ask; just drink," she was told. "We've all had a hard sol and we deserve it. Only don't tell anyone else."

* * *

The following three duty sols were spent mostly in the lab, with brief forays into the office to catch up on links and other business. Copper and Linen found that they had been assigned training spells on bridge station simulations, most of which were scheduled for their off duty time, to their joint dismay. They put it down to the urgency attached to analysis of the contents of the sample tubes from the *Lithium Star* as well as the collection of pieces from the *Wayfinder* and the suspicion that the colonel wanted one of them on the bridge when the test drop of the small battalion of mini surf-sci bots was made. They had heard intermittently from Ossy Inkscree and Lyssa Halsen of their progress in adjusting the bots to render them stealthier and less prone to get lost, leading them to assume that their deployment was imminent.

Trisk's in-depth analysis of the flakes of blue alien organo-technology so far dredged up had provided little insight into what had caused him and Copper to experience negative effects when in close proximity to the material. The patterned shard he had worked out was somehow different to the other specimens, with far more densely-packed material at atomic levels, possibly within a lattice structure of novel molecules. The nature of the unknown moiety was indefinable but it seemed to be capable of reacting to animate matter. Further partially-marked pieces had been pulled out of the same sample tube and were added to the collection and as far as Trisk could tell, it looked as if the motif was part of a larger but less destructive whole and sat slightly proud of the base material, as if it had a purpose independent of its substrate.

Despite busy sols that left little time for contemplation, there was time enough for Copper to analyse her experiences since she had come aboard the *Drake* and to commune with Spook on a number of the mysteries still extant. That there were still a few people on board pursuing their own interests or those of others, she was sure. Of the threat that they posed, she was not so certain. She said as much to Colonel Moritz, who had paid a visit to the lab one afternoon to check on progress. As far as the function of the raised pattern on the alien material went, she felt that it was some sort of active device, operable only by specific means and designed to deter intruders from breaching whatever it protected. Once as much data as possible had been garnered from the samples, it was Copper's view that they use the tri-dee sim suite in engineering to visualise what they had and attempt to build a more coherent picture.

The colonel agreed in principle, but she had more immediate tasks on hand for them. The testing site for the surf-sci bots had been chosen: it was a rocky body, one of the larger asteroids in the section of Belt through which they were passing and it had a tiny satellite of its own. The *Drake* was already slowing to match speed with the object of choice and drop was scheduled for sixteen hundred hours the following sol. Copper and Linen were told that they would be on the bridge jointly manning the secondary science station. Dr Inkscree would be in control of the primary console.

"Lor', we'd best put more practice in on science station sims then," was Linen's contribution when she heard.

"You can have the rest of the sol to get on with it," Colonel Moritz smiled. "But morrow-sol, you're with Dr Inkscree from oh eight hundred hours onwards for equipment set-up."

"Yes, ma'am!" the two replied in unison.

"Congratulations," Trisk said sincerely when the colonel had disappeared. "You'll like bridge duty: it's chill."

"Then give us the lowdown for a start," Copper begged. "I wouldn't want to make an ass of myself even if nobody was watching. With the colonel in the hot seat, I *really* want to be up to speed."

* * *

The bridge of the *MSS Drake II* was a fascinating place to the rookies when they finally stepped out of the rear elevator and into it at thirteen hundred hours at the back of Ossy Inkscree. It was large and quasi-circular in shape, with duty stations and data consoles arranged to left and right. The command unit with its pair of seats and attached ops boards was raised and set towards the rear, with two duty stations to right and left in front that Copper and Linen knew were comms and navi-helm positions. The commanding officer's duty office was close by the elevator. Facing the command unit on the far side was a large holo-grid and a holo projection point was sited in the upper bulkheads.

"Bigger than the *Explorer's* bridge," Linen whispered to her friend. "But no helpful signs to tell you where your station is; and I bet you won't get a turn in the command chair."

"What's the *Explorer*?" Ossy Inkscree asked curiously, having caught the exchange.

"A holo-ship that Copper commanded out at Beagle Leisure Dome on our last leave," Linen told him. "I was first officer. It was good fun."

"Welcome to the real planet," was the rather dry response. "Reporting for duty, sir," he added to Captain Helmis, who had the conn.

"All set?" Helmis asked, nodding acknowledgement.

"Aye, sir. The components are nested and the case is secured within the control pod for deployment at sixteen hundred."

"Good. Report to your stations."

"Aye, sir," the three echoed and turned to the right and the science positions.

Having used science and various other ships' stations in drill sims both aboard the *Drake* and at Beagle Basecamp, Copper and Linen were used to the layout, which was standard for most large Fleet vessels, but the company of their crewmates around them gave added impetus to the tensions that both felt as they relieved the duty officer at the secondary science console.

"Do we share the seat?" Linen whispered to her companion as she took in the arrangements.

"No," Copper murmured in return. "You fold out the spare and lock it in place. They think of everything here. It's under the station top. I'll just lock my ident to the position so it knows I'm here. But now we're on the bridge, we're authorised to use any of the positions as the occasion arises."

"Any position?"

"Yup – in case there are problems and any other officers go down. That way, the main stations are always manned as far as possible in an emergency, at least until more help arrives."

"I don't recall that as part of my sims," Linen grimaced as she retrieved and set up her seat.

"It wasn't; I checked it out as I was curious and it seemed to be the obvious way forward in an emergency situation."

"Just don't go jumping into the command chair if Captain Helmis faints, is all," Linen cautioned as she logged herself in.

"Will you two sort yourselves out and check the status of the control pod for our current mission," Inkscree interrupted. "I'm reading her ready to go. We're coming up on the target asteroid and we'll be holding station-keeping once we get into position. You copy that?"

"Aye, sir," Copper responded. "I take it Lieutenant Halsen will continue to monitor from your lab?"

"Yes; she'll make sure that the data streams from each of the units and the control are reading loud and clear and will conduct ongoing analyses, as Addystone will be doing in your lab. We need as many eyes and ears as possible on the job so that we can capture maximum data *and* spot any glitches that might hamper future missions. Follow ship's progress on the auxiliary monitor here… that's us, and once the control pod is deployed, you can follow it down."

"On it," Copper said briefly as she called up the relevant data with practiced fingers.

Linen looked on in some bewilderment: her friend was much faster than she was and she felt as if her world was faintly out of kilter. It was then she realised that the duo was in effect a trio: Spook was close. Copper looked over and sensing the upsurge of emotion, gave a reassuring smile and winked.

"I'm used to it," she said quietly. "You want to start checking the nest's ops parameters? They'll come up on monitor three. Make sure you take careful note: I want to store them in Gemima later," she added in a whisper.

"You got it," Linen replied, reflecting the smile as her world reasserted itself. "What are the conditions the bots are being dropped into?"

"Here," Copper answered, tapping the output of one of the screens. "I'll call up the holo: a small, barren ball of rock, hardly any gravity but it has one satellite. There are surface features and crevices that go deep into the matrix, so those will give the bots something to explore."

"They're ready for it," her friend told her.

Copper was moving her hands over her screen, calling up the features of the target body in tri-dee. For some reason her hand strayed to the tiny moon of the asteroid and a small tingle shot up her arm. She paused, puzzled.

"What is it?" Linen demanded, sensing the change.

"That's not a natural satellite," was the slow response. "It's a captured piece of space junk."

"Are you sure?"

"Fairly certain: it's semi-faceted and looks like a splinter off a larger piece of something. Sending out probe beams…"

"What you got?" Inkscree questioned, alerted to the action.

"Suggest we also deploy bots to the orbiting body," Copper said as she turned to him. "That's not a natural moon, and it's reading semi-organic."

"You what?"

"Organo-tech?" Linen enquired.

"Maybe…"

"I concur," Inkscree agreed, eyeing his own screen. "Captain, we have an anomaly," he called over to Helmis, who promptly stepped down from his chair to head over.

Once informed, Helmis tabbed the local comm. "Colonel Moritz to the bridge."

The colonel was in her bridge office and walked in moments later. "What have you got?"

"We've identified an irregularity orbiting the asteroid," the first officer replied, gesturing towards the relevant monitors.

Copper enlarged on her findings, bringing up as much data as her probe beams could impart. She linked to her own data sources and ran a comparison with the known pieces of alien technology identified so far.

"It matches the red-green pieces found by the *Wayfinder* and *Lithium Star* in that it's what we think is more highly developed tech than the artefacts found originally on Mars, though we *will* need to confirm dating," she informed her listeners. "But if that's the case, we have a big problem…"

"How so?" the colonel asked interrogatively.

"We're in the asteroid belt – close to home in other words. The pieces found by the *Wayfinder* and the *Lithstar* were out on the edge. Looks like whoever they are or were made it closer in than we thought, maybe even as far as Mars. *This* would not have drifted in from the edge over the lifetime of known tech."

"That's quite a can of worms you've opened up there, Lieutenant," the colonel told her.

"Speculation on my part, ma'am, but it fits. Though I would like to have answers to a few questions about which I'm not totally clear."

"Go on."

"The pieces of alien tech found by the *Lithium Star*: just how much of it was the blue material that we've come to regard as hazardous? Or was most of it like the greeny-red material that makes up the bulk of the alien tech on Mars? As we've not been granted access to the results of the previous analyses of *Lithium Star* samples – or the *Wayfinder's* come to that – and have done precious little of our own and uncovered even less, it's difficult to come to any conclusions. Especially as we think that the samples we've looked at so far are *not* representative and some potentially significant pieces have been sifted out."

Colonel Moritz looked down at her. "There was more than one type of alien material found in the samples; several in fact, but there were only two identified as self-repairing and hence believed to form part of the skins of space-faring vessels or of valuable devices such as tools or weapons: one construct, the bulk of the relevant material, was similar to the reddish-green substance that you found at your site and that has been found elsewhere on Mars; the other was the blue matter that both you and Lieutenant Addystone seem to have a marked aversion to. The original reports said minute traces. Later reports have given revised estimates, but still very small amounts."

"And both were believed to be upgraded versions of the originals found on Mars, ma'am?" Copper asked.

"That was one view – the consensus in fact. But you suspect the samples we have in store have been selectively separated out? Why?"

Copper sighed, closing her eyes for a moment to make sense of the mental pictures she was seeing in her head. "I can't say why, ma'am," she told the colonel. "But it could be argued that not only are our ex-resident Martians trying to return home, but some others with mischief in mind are also returning?" she went on as she looked up.

The colonel shook her head. "Very questionable reasoning, Lieutenant, but I dare say you would find one or two who would agree with your interpretation."

"So whatever happened to the *Griffon*, at least two other vessels or constructs were involved, or are part of the puzzle?"

"Not necessarily: it's feasible that both the blue and the red-green types of self-repair material form part of the one whole."

"No it isn't," Copper said decisively. "Spoo… the ship buried under the Warren doesn't contain any of the blue stuff."

"You're sure?"

"Yes ma'am."

The colonel inclined her head in silent acknowledgement. "Where does that leave us as far as bot-deployment goes?" she demanded of Inkscree.

"We go," he said. "But I agree that we should deploy several individual units to survey that chunk of matter: it's sizeable and with sufficient gravity that the bots should be able to get a toehold. And as the main body has several deep cracks, fissures and gullies, there may be additional recoverable pieces there."

"Good point, Doctor. But we still go on schedule, so you'll have to deal with the logistics of either releasing bots from the nest en route to the asteroid or sending down a separate unit."

"Aye, ma'am."

* * *

The following two and a half hours were spent manoeuvring the great ship into position and in working out how to separate a discrete number of bots from the nest. Inkscree and his two juniors, with support from Addystone and Halsen in their own labs, quickly reprogrammed the control pod for a drop at the orbiting piece of junk, where sixteen individual units would be released from the top layer of the nest. Some neat recoding by Halsen allowed the detached bots to operate as an independent taskforce but maintain contact with their nest remotely. The remaining forty eight units would operate as the second brigade for their survey of the asteroid itself.

Once at station-keeping the point of entry into asteroid space was confirmed and environmental scanning set in motion. As all read clear, pod drop proceeded to schedule and five pairs of eyes kept a constant surveillance on the incoming streams of data. Separation of the sixteen units and their attachment to the captured lump of space debris was achieved effectively. Copper had been charged with maintaining control of that operation, with Halsen as her back-up, as data was being relayed directly to the *Drake* rather than via the central operating unit of the nest. The other three were controlling main asteroid deployment.

"It's by far the largest lump of hull that I've seen," Science Officer Milkstone reported to the colonel, who was leaning over her shoulder.

"Hull?"

Copper gulped. "Yes, ma'am, I believe so. It looks similar to some of the hull plating of Spook's... the ship buried out at the Warren," she went on quietly.

"Which you've never seen."

"Not *directly*," was the uncomfortable reply. "In my head," she added for clarification. "And I seem to know intuitively."

"I see. If this is a piece, there may be more pieces nearby, pulled in by other heavier bodies."

"That's so, ma'am, but we'd have to spend months combing the Belt if we wanted to search – which would alert others that there was something worth searching for."

Colonel Moritz smiled briefly at that and raised an eyebrow. "In your opinion, would it be safe to bring that piece aboard?"

Copper's eyes widened, a frizz of apprehension shooting up her spine. "I'd want a lot more data before I brought anything else alien aboard this ship," she told her commanding officer. "And even then I'd keep it somewhere we could get rid of it without harm to ship or crew."

"Carry on, Lieutenant," ordered Colonel Moritz, turning to the primary science station where Inkscree and Linen were keeping tabs on their own nestful of investigators, who seemed to be industriously burrowing into every nook and cranny of the spinning rock below.

"I have them set specifically to detect alien artefact material," Linen responded to the colonel's questioning. "But so far we've got nothing. *If* any loose pieces were brought in via that orbiting shard or in space dust, we haven't found them yet."

"Which suggests that the artificial moonlet was captured way after it detached from the mother body," Inkscree put in. "And scoured clean of anything before it got this far."

"You're capturing *all* the data in real time?"

"Yes ma'am, even the sample analyses of traces brought back to the nest. Asteroid composition is as expected, no surprises. Just our luck we happened upon one with a synthetic satellite."

"I wonder," the colonel responded with a sidelong glance at Copper, who was diligently scanning every shred of evidence her small team of bots was sending in.

* * *

A couple of hours later, Dr Inkscree announced the mission a success and issued the recall order for the bots. Initial data scans had revealed that even within the fissures and clefts of the rocky body beneath them, no traces of material non-Sol system in origin had been found. More painstaking analysis would be carried out as the *Drake* made her way outwards, but Inkscree was satisfied that the equipment had performed well and was in a fit state for future planned missions. Copper and Lyssa Halsen had between them scrutinised every scrap of data brought in by the subset of bots and the former at least had come to the conclusion that the large chunk of alien matter orbiting the asteroid was a piece of hull that had been blown off a somewhat larger whole and *that* whole had been a ship. The piece itself, set up in rotating tri-dee at Copper's station, was sponge-like in cross-section, with reinforced struts holding the structure firm. One surface appeared to be almost seamless, and Copper suggested that this had been the outside layer exposed to space.

After a great deal of deliberation, the colonel decided that it would be useful to bring the chunk of debris aboard the *Drake*: it was about a third of the size of a small shuttle and could be stored in one of the great ship's outer landing bays. The area could also be sealed off completely and high level security set in place. The cost in time would be minimal and could be made up easily. An added advantage was that various science teams aboard the ship could employ the extra time in scans of nearby asteroids to determine if any other traces of what might be alien material had been netted. Copper and Linen were two of those assigned the task and remained on the bridge at their stations as they thoroughly swept the surrounding space, whilst engineering and security personnel prepared the berth for the wreckage and worked out the means of bringing it aboard.

The salvage operation was almost complete when the comms officer, uttering a curse that could be heard across the bridge, turned to the command chair, a hand to his ear.

"Ma'am, incoming distress call!"

"Put it on amplifier and let me hear it!" the colonel barked.

"Aye, ma'am…"

"This is Mars ship *SS Fearless* to all ships in area! Mayday! We are under attack…"

14: SEARCHING FOR SOLBEAMS

Most of the bridge crew sat frozen in amazement, mouths open in shock as the distress message rang out again. Colonel Moritz had jumped to her feet, her face a study in disbelief.

"What in hell! Get me a visual link to that ship and find out where she is!" she ordered. "*Fearless*, this is the *MSS Drake*, what is your situation?"

In moments the dishevelled face of the captain of the *Fearless* materialised in the main holo-grid. The bridge crew of the *Drake* could hear the dull thuds of what may have been impacts on the MDMC starship's hull registered by her external sensors. The captain reported that they were under fire from an unidentified enemy, the source of which was a nearby asteroid. The *Fearless* could not pull away as her main engines had taken direct hits and a restraining tractor beam from the surface was holding her. Return fire had resulted in increased bombardment by some sort of high-energy bolts from the rocky body.

"We have you on our screens, we're on our way," Ms Moritz responded, scanning her own boards as she resumed her chair. "You're not far from us; we'll be with you in twenty minutes."

A request for speedier relief was ignored as the colonel began to issue a staccato stream of orders to her crew to rapidly wrap up their current mission and prepare to make headway. Calling battlestations, she ordered her weapons crews to stand by. The science stations were directed to scan the area into which they were headed for any signs of activity or unusual materials.

Information relayed from the *Fearless* suggested that she had been making a detailed investigation of the rogue asteroid, listed as Helixus, at the behest of MDMC Acquisitions, as potentially valuable resources had been indicated by routine remote scans. The large body was less than ninety kilometres in diameter in its widest aspect and was dotted with deep crevices and craters but Captain Si Vendor was strangely reticent as to the resources that the body and its small moonlet were suspected of harbouring.

"Even credit says it's alien tech," muttered Copper to her redheaded friend as she worked her boards.

"Alien tech that fights back, then," Linen frowned.

"You'd think the *Fearless* would have done a few deep scans from distance before she got close," was Copper's opinion. "But the first hits get her main engines, even though she was running shielded? That smacks of malice aforethought, high intelligence and *very* sophisticated scanning gear."

"In which case it's maybe very smart baddies from Mars that got there first and didn't want to share the goodies with anyone else until they could extract them," Linen suggested. "So they set up defences in hopes that they could sneak back later with the proper bits of kit. But how do you figure she was shielded?"

"We'd have detected her. And home grown villainy doesn't fit: if they were so smart they would have been able to get at any goodies, or they would have had the nous to hide their signals from anybody taking a peek. And they have a restraining tractor that can hold a ship that size? Now *that's* high tech. You getting anything? If there *is* something down there and MDMC knew about it, they would have had to detect it without getting shot at, which suggests unmanned probes at distance that didn't set off what's firing at the *Fearless* now."

"Nothing that could be alien tech, it reads as standard, but we're too far yet; I get nothing unusual in the immediate vicinity either, but there might be something well-hid."

"Will you two quit speculating and keep your eyes on your work," the irritated voice of Ossy Inkscree cut across the chat.

"I'm getting ion trail signals; the *Fearless*, I guess. What was her angle of approach?" Copper demanded. "We don't want to come in on the same beam if there's something close by pointed in this direction."

Inkscree opened and closed his mouth and exchanged rueful glances with their commanding officer, who had come over to check the results her science stations were producing. "Ion trails," he repeated.

"So her shielding isn't as effective as she thinks it is," Linen put in as she confirmed the readings.

The colonel ordered her tactical staff to follow up the results and prepare evasive manoeuvres for potential hostile attack. She also ordered a course change and the *Drake's* weapons stations to run hot: she was taking as few chances as possible.

Copper had by this time confirmed Linen's readings that the approaching asteroid and its surrounding space read outwardly regular. The *Fearless* had reported that the offensive was easing and she had managed to pull back a little. Her angle of approach and her actions prior to attack were relayed to the *Drake* and caused Colonel Moritz and her first officer some puzzlement: she had moved in on a direct line and so close that she could practically drop anchor. Vendor was uncooperative and refused to explain his mission any further.

"Doctor!" Copper rapped out abruptly at Inkscree. "I'm reading synthetics deep within the body of Helixus. Confirmed as semi-organic and similar in constitution to the self-replicative materials we've seen before."

"Which ones?" That was the colonel, suddenly at her elbow.

"The reddish-green material, comparable with earlier samples found on Mars; I read it as pre-dating the piece we have aboard now, ma'am," she added quietly. "The good guys?"

"That remains to be seen, Lieutenant. How much and in what form?"

"Approximately twelve percent: as if the asteroid was blasted out systematically to take these emplacements... no wonder MDMC was interested... and that the *Fearless* was sent in to have a really good look, she being the latest ship they have."

"Emplacements?" Ms Moritz jumped on the word sharply. "What makes you say that?"

Copper, realising that she had made an unconscious blunder and that it was Spook rather than she that had called it, bit her lip. "Look at the structures we're picking up, ma'am," she invited. "These vertical shafts are regular and seem to be lined with cell-like depressions; and these rounded rectangular areas here are reading as semi-organic: the control centres?"

"Go on."

"High energy readings that I can't quite make out... but the structure may have a defensive rather than an offensive purpose:

the last line of defence before Mars? A sentinel post from eons ago, maybe one of many but the rest long gone? Something with hostile intent gets close and it's programmed to take it out?"

Colonel Moritz shook her head. "I don't buy it," she said softly. "Even supposing it was still active after all this time, it wouldn't recognise a human starship…"

"But if said starship is attempting to extract the material, it might be construed as invasive: *Fearless* is pretty close to that rock… And she's reporting incoming fire from that source."

"Which is confirmed," Inkscree interrupted. "But it's some sort of pulse energy salvo, not projectile… it's powering down."

"Confirmed," the officer at the main tactical station echoed.

"*We* don't," the colonel said briefly. "We go in at full alert. Get me an update on the state of the *Fearless*…"

The starship had taken quite a pounding but casualties were minimal. By the time the *Drake* reached the stricken ship and stood off at a safe distance, the assault had all but ceased, the restraining beam having released the vessel, allowing her to limp to beyond the danger zone. Her captain requested immediate escort to the nearest MDMC-run base for repair, obviously reluctant to have a ship of Mars Fleet investigating the situation.

"Get all you can on what's down there without provoking a hostile response," the colonel told her science team. "Liaise with tactical on positioning. We'll drop a couple of orbiting probes as we leave. Engineering, make ready to tow the *Fearless* to MDMC Mining Station Robert Ball: they'll be able to get emergency assistance there. Stand down battlestations, but maintain alert status. Merris, coordinate with Vendor on getting his ship ready to head out. Comms, patch a link to Fleet HQ through to my office, priority one."

A chorus of assent arose from the various bridge stations as the officers complied. The colonel returned to the bridge a scant ten minutes later to find her first officer locked in civil but steely argument with Vendor over the deployment of science probes above the target asteroid. The latter was insisting that probes from the *Fearless* were already preparing and that Mars Fleet had no business in interfering in a civilian concern, MDMC having staked a claim through the proper authorities over mining rights.

"I'll remind you, Captain, that you called for help," Helmis told the man. "It's a little late to start dictating the type of help you're prepared to accept. Station One, drop your probes."

"Aye, Captain!" Inkscree called out. "Probes away!"

"Make ready for departure," Colonel Moritz instructed. "All tight?" she enquired of Themis Sage at main engineering.

"Aye ma'am; we're locked on."

"Make ready to drop probes!" Vendor charged his own team.

"Belay that, Captain," the colonel stated equably as she took her chair. "This area is now under military authority. Mars Fleet is despatching a science vessel to investigate the nature of that asteroid and she'll have an armed escort. MDMC Central will be informed, naturally. All stations, prepare to move out."

The tactical stations of the *Drake* were watchful but it was Copper at her own post who noted the drop amongst a drift of detritus that trailed the MDMC vessel as she slowly manoeuvred out of the purlieus of the strange asteroid.

"Ma'am, the *Fearless* has let loose a pair of science probes among that waste aft of her," she called out in a high voice.

"Confirmed!" a couple of other voices cut in as the *Drake's* commanding officer jumped to her feet.

"Weapons station one, take out those probes! Captain Vendor, you have explaining to do!" she exploded at the face on the viewer as she made contact.

"I had my orders," was the unrepentant response, but there was no move to order additional probes.

In the most astringent of terms, Vendor was instructed to take no more actions in respect of his late mission and warned that his comms would be monitored.

"Think he'll comply?" Helmis asked the colonel as she cut the link.

"He'd better," she responded darkly. "Good call, Lieutenant Milkstone," she added to Copper as she headed over. "Did you suspect, or was it just your usual knack for picking things up?"

The dry tone and raised eyebrow suggested that the colonel suspected additional aid. Copper shrugged, giving a tight smile and the merest nod of acknowledgement.

"The *Fearless* jumps straight in and starts digging, gets into trouble, bawls for help and then complains when she gets it," she returned. "And then tries backhand tactics? She should have been called *Feckless* or even *Spineless*. But why dump your waste when you're on the first leg of a shakedown cruise and haven't had time to accumulate any yet? And in a super-spec ship that should be able to reprocess body odour? It didn't stack."

"You should stick with the Service," Ms Moritz advised her. "You'll make a formidable commander one sol."

"I think you already are," Linen whispered to her friend as the colonel moved away. "But what's up? You're jumpy about all this, aren't you, or Spook is?"

"Later," was the only reply.

Linen turned back to her console.

* * *

The MDMC Mining Station Robert Ball was attained before long. She had been well prepared for the advent of the *Fearless*, for two transports bearing what were presumably spare parts for the battered pride of the MDMC exploration fleet were in orbit. By that time those science officers who had stood watch on the bridge and in the labs were off duty and in the mess, sipping hot caff and discussing in low tones the happenings of the sol with a couple of their curious crewmates.

Copper and Linen were giving little away: they knew Colonel Moritz well enough to know that she would not approve gossip or conjecture. Using evening appointments at the ship's therapy salon as their excuse, they quickly finished their light rations and made for deck eight.

"The whole damn ship now knows we've encountered alien tech and that that's what we're looking for," Linen complained on the way. "Our comfortable perspective that we're too far off the beaten galactic track to be in danger from whatever might be out there has now got seriously off beam and the whole system will be set for invasion."

"Doubt it," her friend said dubiously. "*We* know, as part of the Fleet and thus Mars Gov, but who else out there, apart from some MDMC big shots and a bunch of smart-arsed villains has any clue?"

"The Press, academics like Thars Amberline, consortia other than MDMC – whoever's at the back of Greensands Minerals for a start – and that's probably only the nose of a very large dog, and a Martian one at that."

"You're making me depressed, stop it," Copper said shortly as they turned into the salon. "This session had better make me feel like a million credits or else."

"Gossip," Linen whispered. "Best place for it here and it's quiet at this time of night…"

The only rumours abounding in that neck of the ship was that the attack on the *Fearless* was probably a put-up job and that some nasties from Mars, Earth or elsewhere were responsible. The two were quizzed mercilessly about what had happened on their watch, but would not be drawn. As they made their way back to their quarters, Copper gave vent to her irritation.

"It was like being at that dinner with Waterbone and Thulia, when they were trying to get the lowdown on why the military were digging out at the Warren and what it had to do with us and our work: *they* even bugged the conversation."

"At least that won't have happened here," Linen consoled. "Or at least if it did, Spook would warn you. But we put a spoke in their bugs with ours, if I recall. Let's have a Chocó-Crème at yours and a little chinwag of our own: I'm not in the least tired."

Linen was keen to know why her friend was so edgy over the incidents earlier in the sol and what it had to do with Spook, but whilst they had been on duty, a batch of incoming messages had been received, two of which bore urgent tags.

"Thulia Numbridge! In her new role as our project link and the ears and eyes of Wolff Waterbone! Well, she can wait," Copper announced testily as she called up a couple of Chocó-Crèmes. "But what does Thars want?"

Professor Amberline had linked in to alert them that he had been contacted by Lomax Gratikule over the reports that they had supplied recently to EMMS Office on the work done on the Glory Hole. Gratikule felt that their work, thorough as it was, did not go far enough into the structure of their lower site and was pressing for more in-depth analyses: he had gone as far as declaring that EMMSO planned to sponsor a new team to begin an exhaustive excavation. Thars had vetoed the idea on the basis that such intrusion would destroy the integrity of a site that had been clearly designated a unique scientific structure and should be preserved as such. Gratikule was insistent, as if his buttons were being pushed, and had ordered the professor to begin recruitment at once. Thars was deeply concerned, for credit to begin work on the long-promised surface access tunnel from the Warren station out to the research site had just been agreed. The two looked at one another with wide eyes. Copper spoke first.

"They know the military's found an alien ship below our site and they think things are happening. I wonder if something was triggered when the *Fearless* breached those asteroid defences and its protective systems woke up. Spook's ship would have been warned… but *this* link would have taken time to reach us."

"The initial probe that suggested alien tech," Linen surmised, raising a finger. "Something had a look, the systems woke up and sent out an alert to anything that could receive."

"*That's* why Spook was anxious," Copper realised. "And why the assault on the *Fearless* was called off, once we took a hand."

"Called off? Are you saying *Spook* powered down weapons and released the restraint beam? And that his ship alerted him?"

"That's what I'm saying," Copper confirmed. "I'm almost sure of it. But if Spook's ship *did* receive some sort of alert…"

"How many other listening systems did, ones not leftover from eons ago," Linen finished. "We'll have to tell the colonel. I know she's not in charge of the military dig close to the Warren now, but this smacks of infiltration that involves MDMC, given they want to dig down through our site. Our site!" she spat out angrily. "That's *our* PhD research Gratikule and his associates are trying to undermine, and they're funding it!"

A chime at Copper's comm interrupted them: it was Trisk, requesting their presence in their office. He only winked when asked the reason and told them to make their way pronto.

"Colonel's there," Copper said briefly. "She wants to know more about what went on earlier. We've left the vicinity of that MDMC station, so she can leave the bridge to lesser mortals."

"Is she always on call?" Linen asked conversationally as they prepared to set off. "It's very late."

"Goes with the territory, solbeam," was the answer. "She's in command so she always has to be available."

Copper was right: Colonel Moritz wanted more information on events around their rescue of the *Fearless* and the veiled hints that the alien entity loose aboard the *Drake* had a part in them. The two junior officers were thus bidden to relate all they knew, suspected or guessed. Copper's belief that Spook was not only aware of the defensive systems they had encountered but had inactivated them to protect the *Drake* startled the colonel.

"If this Spook of yours can deactivate alien technology that's a threat to my ship, it's a useful ally to have."

"That's not all, ma'am…"

The colonel sat back, steepling her fingers as she digested the import of the information from Thars Amberline. She was clear, however: their current mission was their priority and everything else was the concern of Mars Gov and Military Intelligence. And as for their PhDs, the two had sufficient samples aboard that they would have no problem completing them creditably. And even if MDMC saw fit to pull the plug on their support, the Service would certainly see them through.

The immediate duties of the *Drake's* science officers involved the large chunk of alien material brought aboard; it was to be rigorously analysed and comparisons made with all the data they had garnered in relation to alien tech thus far, as well as the inbound stream of information relayed from the two probes left in orbit around the asteroid. The latter would soon be out of range, but the colonel had ways and means of having the data passed on by the ships even now en route to the area.

"What?" Copper demanded of Trisk, whose glance had fastened on her face when a halt had been called to the briefing. "Come on, you've had an idea."

"Just a suggestion, if you're agreeable, ma'am: why don't we use that operational alien device that you two found at your research site out at the Warren to analyse that massive lump of tech that we brought aboard? It's locked to you, Copper, and I would like to see it in use."

"Not without testing first!" Copper interrupted. "I only really used it the once and it freaked the hell out of me."

"*I* tried it and it stung me," Linen added feelingly.

"I agree it must be tested," Colonel Moritz said, "But firstly on material that we are familiar with. I'll sanction it; but I want Dr Faerin in on testing and it *will* be done under high security."

"Don't I get a say?" Copper muttered rebelliously.

"You're here to obey orders, Lieutenant Milkstone," she was reminded. "I use all the tools I have available and that device is one of them."

"And you're another," Linen added. "And that scanner, or whatever it is, beats anything similar the Service has … I think."

"That remains to be seen," Ms Moritz stated. "Meanwhile Dr Addystone, you set up the testing. Keep me informed."

"Aye ma'am!"

"Thanks for that, buddy," Copper said severely to Trisk once the colonel had left the office.

"You're welcome. But we've been looking to get that scanner into use for a while and this seems the best opportunity: the other similar piece that was dug up under your pal Lofty's place at Lowell is back on Mars and never did work, as far as I'm aware. But we'll have time for this testing now we're back on course. I know you two have a load to do for your PhDs as well as the stacks we have of *Lithium Star* materials, not to mention the bits from the *Wayfinder*, but we can fit it in."

"And we sleep when?" Linen demanded.

"When you're not working, training, eating or talking," was the cheery rejoinder. "Welcome to life aboard the best starship in the Fleet."

"Huh! Well, technically we're off duty and we still have links to catch up with," Copper reminded her redheaded friend. "So I vote we do that now, just in case Thulia has something up her sleeve or down her front that might be related to all this. Then we'll see."

Trisk agreed to catch up with the two in the mess for a late supper and set off to return to his current concerns. Copper and Linen made tracks to review their additional comms links in the former's quarters, beginning with the one from Ms Numbridge.

"The cheek!" Copper exploded after careful scrutiny of the communication from the EMMS Office.

"We relay it via Thars as usual." Linen raised her shoulders in a casual shrug. "I told the Waterbone that our off-ship's comms were monitored and that our esteemed commanding officer had banned personal links to discuss our work aboard. Maybe he thought that we'd think Thulia hadn't been told and we'd let slip all our secrets anyway."

"Then he's dimmer than we know he is," Copper snapped. "But it's tempting to let slip misinformation just as a wind-up."

"I don't recommend it," Linen chuckled. "Remember the time we tried that with our erstwhile adversaries Karben and Bilkitt of Outer Mars Ops, because they were listening in on our talk? Colonel Moritz was livid then. Now we're under her direct command she'd have us in the brig, and she *will* find out..."

"I suppose you're right," Copper sighed. "But a personal link immediately on receipt of hers to go over what she reckons our latest Glory Hole samples show, given that she's reading things into our last report that are *not* there? And does she think we can conjure up a supra-light link to EMMSO on a whim?"

"We'll have to respond; her links are worth that much, just for the amusement value."

"But we could wind her prop up just a tad; I suggest we produce an itemised reply going over each of her points in turn and have it tagged as having passed through security's hands on the way out. I'll get Gemima on the case. You can sweet-talk Kit Locksmith into providing the relevant tags. And then we copy her link and our reply to Thars."

"Agreed," said Linen. "But I'll let *you* sweet-talk the chief, he'll listen to you. And then we head to the mess and eat. But we'd better see what Mik, Majorelle and Ma Kellyn have to say, they've all left comms."

By the time the two had finished all their personal links, they were more than ready to socialise. They found Trisk, cheerful as ever, ahead of them in the mess and once they had found a quiet table, he relayed the details of what he had put in place for the testing of the alien scanner that his two friends had unearthed from their site on Mars. He had booked time in their assigned tri-dee sim suite in engineering: its hard-holo projection facility would be useful to see what came up. He had chosen a sample tube originating from the *Lithium Star* that had yielded a couple of pieces of the reddish-green alien tech but none of the blue material that had caused reactions in himself and Copper. Dr Faerin had been briefed and would be free two sols hence at oh eight hundred for the testing. Kit Locksmith had agreed to allocate a couple of security guards and would have the sim suite and its surroundings monitored for the duration, as the chief himself explained when he joined them at their table.

* * *

The three science officers had collected their materials from stores and were set to meet Kynedd Faerin outside the tri-dee sim facilities entry on deck twenty. They had breakfasted early and were looking forward to the task in anticipation, and a little anxiety in Copper's case, as she had not been back to that area since her run-in with Jecks and its painful consequences. Linen was toting Gerald as back-up and all three officers were armed.

The external board indicated that the suite had been booked to Dr Addystone for four hours and in token of his punctuality, Faerin was already there, flanked by two of Locksmith's hand-picked guards, who would secure the entry. Trisk raised a hand to the reader plate and the door slid open. He stepped into the extensive facility and made for the station that controlled projection and ops, followed by the other three. The door slid shut and locked.

"I have the data from the initial scans of this tube," Trisk told the doctor, pulling a data chit from a pocket as he dumped the sample tube on the station top. "We extracted the scraps of organo-tech we found in it, so this is just the leftover rubble as far as we know and we have its structure and composition. I've got the alien pieces here as well and the sims we made, so we should be able to set them up if we need to. But first, Copper: tell us what happened the first time you used the alien device."

"The only time," Copper corrected, perching herself on the edge of the ops station. "We were in the lab at Lowell and I had realised that something big was in the tube that I'd hauled out from store. I figured what it might be, as we'd seen one before – one that had been dug up from under our friend Lofty's diner on Coblentz Street," she explained. "We passed that one on to Colonel Moritz at the time."

"It's still non-operational, as far as I know," Trisk confirmed.

"Well, this is the one from our site," Copper said as she held up a chunky flat ovoid, lustrous and red-green, that fitted into her hand.

There was a circular aperture near one end into which she slotted the thumb of her right hand, remembering the first time she had held the alien device. Her fingers spread out and curled around its ridged far end, grasping it as if it was a hand weapon. She pointed out the spiral marking etched into the flat surface of one side of the device to Faerin and explained that when she had touched it, the pattern had changed subtly and a miniscule energy shift had been detected. Nothing had happened when she first ran the tool across a sample tube, even when she tried to picture its contents. But once she had relaxed, she felt a tingle spreading up her arm as a visual of the gritty matter within the tube materialised like some sort of hazy holo-projection from the upper edge of the device.

"And that's when I dropped it like a hot chipper and refused to try it again," she told her audience.

"I did," Linen confessed. "I pointed it in fun at Copper and it stung me."

"Served you frigging well right," her friend snorted. "It might be a very clever scanner, but I sense it can do damage as well. We passed it to Colonel Moritz as soon as we could."

"Without telling her you could operate it," Trisk reminded her. "She was rather put out when she found out."

"She was furious," Copper admitted. "But I hadn't figured at the time that it had bonded to me: *you* figured that. Or so you said. I still don't know if it has, I haven't held it again 'til now."

"Well, it's not nipped you or sent a shock up your arm, has it?" Linen put in.

"No; but it actually feels like it's *mine*, somehow. Difficult to explain, but it feels like something I'm used to using. It's quite a peculiar sensation," she went on.

"You reading anything, Doc?" Trisk asked Faerin, who had been paying close attention to his medi-scanner, which he had focussed on Copper.

"Nothing to cause anxiety so far: rise in heartbeat, adrenalin rush, increase in sweating… symptoms consistent with fight or flight, but that's it."

"Then best get on with it," Linen encouraged. "Try scanning the tube, Cop, and see what happens. I've got Gerald set up to scan for the energy shift we got the last time."

Copper stood, directing the instrument towards the tube that Trisk had set down on one of the projector plates of the control station. Almost casually she ran a finger of her left hand across the spiral design on the flat body of the device; she could not feel the texture of the motif against the silkiness of the scanner but she was subliminally aware that the pattern had altered. A slight hiss from Linen caught her ear as the latter detected the expected energy shift. Slowly, a haze began to emanate above the device, forming into a tri-dee image of a mass of varisized particles, ranging from less than dust to fragments the size of a small human hand. Trisk reached out and lightly shook the tube. The image wavered and broke apart, reforming to the shape of the contents within the cylindrical container.

"But how do we capture the data?" muttered Trisk in an undertone. "We see it, but we don't know the composition…"

"Wait," Copper told him as the whole began to expand until it filled the space around the four watchers.

"How far can this go?" demanded Faerin, turning to follow a holo-chunk of rock that flew past him.

"My readings are showing that we are capturing visual data at atomic level," Trisk announced. "So we'll have the structure and should be able to extrapolate. But best not let it get outside the tri-dee suite or you'll freak the crew," he went on.

"It won't," Copper promised. "But Spook reckons there's something… This tube *is* actually one that was aboard the *Lithstar*?" she queried.

"As far as I'm aware, yes," Trisk said. "Why?"

"Because it will have been down on the rock that holds the remains of the *Griffon* and what we think are bits of at least two other discrete forms, possibly vessels…"

"Not necessarily: automatic coring or scraping would get the samples out and then the material would be shunted into tubes for storage by vac-grabbers and sorters, possibly aboard the science pod that was sent down to bring the stuff out. Storage aboard the *Lithium Star* would have been in the extern holds initially, they wouldn't have brought anything into the labs until the science officers had checked the lot for any potentially hazardous materials."

"Pity they didn't check their own gear," Copper said, her eyes narrowing as she shifted her hold on the alien device and drew it carefully across the surface of the tube, her free finger caressing the swirling pattern on its flank. "Look at the exterior of this thing: this patch of deep scoring here is raised rather than incised, as if something has been trying to fill it in or repair it."

Linen looked askance as a holo-bubble of visual information expanded outwards. "Are you trying to say that when this piece of kit was close to what was left of the *Griffon* and whatever else was down there, *something* attached to it and tried to fix the scuff marks on it?"

"Well look at it. Trisk, what are you getting?"

Trisk had pulled out his own MEDIC and was going over the area that Copper had pointed out. "It reads similar to alien organo-tech that we know is capable of self-replication, but it's subtly different – as if it has somehow tried to meld with *our* tube and failed or been halted. It's inactive at any rate and it's a very small area. Your Spook picked this up?"

Copper nodded. "I guess. We should check some of the other *Lithstar* tubes."

Faerin had been studying his own readings closely. "Enough for this session," he told her. "You've been losing energy and you're showing increasing signs of exhaustion."

She sighed and complied, lowering the device. The vast holo around them snapped off like a light.

"Damnation, that's unnerving!" Linen exclaimed. "But now we think that this alien organo-tech we've been finding once was able to fix stuff other than itself? So why did it stop?"

Copper bit her lip and slumped down into one of the ops chairs. "I think it needs input to do it – from a sentient source."

"Oh shit!"

"That about covers it," Trisk agreed. "We have a few hours in here still, so why don't we interpret the data we captured and build up a tri-dee sim of the tube contents – and the tube – that we can interact with, as far as possible. It'll be useful as training to use this place. I'm not up to scratch on it as I'm not here often enough. You okay with that, Doc?"

"As long as you've got caff on tap; I want to do more scans of Lieutenant Milkstone in any case, to figure out the nature of her bonding to that device."

"Good," Dr Addystone grinned, commandeering the second chair, his fingers scampering over the station regulators. "Linen, you take that auxiliary projector plate and start on the tube: you can use the actual as a base rather than the data from the alien scanner and then we can do a comparison."

"Aye, aye sir!" the redhead responded impishly. "But first I'm going to call up more seats."

* * *

"Essentially, organo-tech self-repairs by extracting pieces of its surroundings that are compatible with its own base structure. It can do that as long as the repair sequence operands within the structure still function and these are built into the material itself, instructors if you like, which recognise damage and tell affected moieties at subatomic levels what to do: thin out or expand their structure to fill gaps, for example. The hull of the *Drake* works on a similar principle; not as effectively, but it can heal damage to itself that isn't too extensive," Trisk explained as he pointed out the repaired scar on the holo of the sample tube that he had called up.

Colonel Moritz glanced quizzically across the table at Copper as she took in the implications. The party was seated in one of the briefing rooms off the science labs, discussing the events of the early part of the sol.

"So you think that detached pieces of this organo-tech can operate independently, providing certain crucial systems within itself still operate?" the colonel demanded of Trisk.

"That's how we read it, ma'am," he agreed. "And quickly, I would imagine; else how could this tube have been repaired? It must have been in contact with a section of organo-tech that recognised a breach and began to fix it – but as the tube was not of its own type, it made a poor job."

"Lieutenant Milkstone, what's your take on this?"

"*I* suspect it needs guidance for automatic repair of non-self material," Copper said quietly. "I think it needs sentient input. I checked that scoring: it went more than skin deep, it punctured the tube. And something fixed it – why, I don't know."

Linen looked closely at her friend. She might not know, but she had some idea, was the redhead's surmise as she looked into Copper's eyes. That idea, Linen guessed, would cause a furore. She shrugged imperceptibly, raising an interrogative eyebrow.

Colonel Moritz caught the exchange and impatiently viewed the pair. "What?" she snapped.

"You reckon someone tried to hitch a lift?" Linen asked.

"Maybe," Copper grimaced. "But did they make it?"

"What the hell are you suggesting?" the colonel barked.

"Pure conjecture, ma'am. But if some unidentified entity *did* survive similar to what brought the *Griffon* down, it would look for an escape. Perhaps we should examine any other tubes that came directly from the *Lithium Star* and maybe someone should check the *Lithstar* herself?"

"You're in the realm of fantasy!" Faerin burst out, with a quick look at the colonel. "I've read the reports, the *Griffon* was creamed, they couldn't scrape her up, and presumably any other ships involved suffered the same fate. How could anything, even alien, survive?"

"Spook," Copper said shortly. "His life support system kept him going for millennia and he could leave his organic body."

"You think," Colonel Moritz said sharply. "You don't know for certain."

"No ma'am, I don't. But I don't have another explanation."

"And no-one's been able to penetrate the hull of that ship under the Warren to find out *and* as far as we know, it's intact. Believe me, judging by the mess left of the *Griffon* and the other objects that collided with that bit of rock, very little would have survived the impact."

"And now we're headed out that way," Copper frowned. "But how big was that piece of rock, actually, ma'am? Large boulder, asteroid, planetoid? Has it a name?"

"We have a partial tri-dee sim of it," Ms Moritz stated calmly. "It was built up from the data that the *Lithium Star* collected. The body can be classified as a minor planet: it's about eight hundred and fifty kilometres in diameter at its widest, so it's big. It's chiefly rocky but has an icy outer sheath. As far as we *now* guess, including your input Lieutenant Milkstone, we have three impacts in one area. No full scans were made outside the crash zone: the *Lithium Star* was recalled too quickly and few aboard realised quite what they had. The world was tagged Lux Noctis."

The other four looked at her and then at each other in silent consternation.

"So *that's* our mission," Trisk croaked at last. "Check out that planetoid for what's on it – what the *Lithstar* may have missed – without falling victim to whatever's down there ourselves?"

"Planetary drop of surf-sci bots on a massive scale," Copper announced to the table at large. "I remember your saying that when first we heard we'd been chosen to test the little sods," she added to Linen.

"*Part* of our mission," the colonel corrected. "I'll authorise your access to the relevant tri-dee sim data and priority use of the sim suite. But you *will* check up on all the rest of the tubes that came from the *Lithium Star*, on the QT and with security support. Deal with Mr Locksmith, no-one else."

"Ma'am?"

"Yes, Ms Milkstone?"

"Where does the *Sapphire Sunset* fit into all this? Didn't she head out to the edge with a large human and cargo payload, and she has FTL drive, doesn't she? Search for alien artefacts over a very large area of space, or drop nests of bots off at short range? And what of our sister ships? They were set to launch just after we did and *Drake II* Class Explorer ships don't come cheap. They must have very special missions."

"What sort of missions?" Ms Moritz enquired dangerously.

Copper lifted her shoulders expressively. "Posturing? Look at the ships we have, we can take you on and then some?" she suggested. "Or are they there to cover our backs and expand our remit to more of the worlds out on the edge, or elsewhere?"

"You *will* make an outstanding commander one sol. But you need to learn to curb your imagination," was the dry response. "You'll accompany me to the bridge: we'll be initialising the supra-light drive shortly, so you may as well gain from the experience. The rest of you, get back to work. I expect constant updates on what you find."

Copper had only time for a startled exchange of glances with Linen before she was ordered to accompany her commanding officer to the bridge. Once there, she was assigned one of the science stations with the instructions to keep careful note of the changes in the surroundings of the massive starship as the main drive was primed preparatory to the slow increase of speed to near-light velocities, which would eventually take the *Drake* beyond the orbit of Neptune and on a heading for the Kuiper belt, where their objective of Lux Noctis lay.

* * *

"What in blazes prompted the display?" Linen asked of her

friend much later, in the comparative privacy of their lab. "Our sister ships are there to cover our backs in case we hit trouble? They're out to show what's out there that we have the power?"

"It seemed reasonable to me," Copper grumbled. "But the colonel's giving nothing away. Though she hinted she wants me on additional training in ship's ops, which will eat into my free time. Not that I have much of that."

"Oh stop bellyaching; I'll sign up as well. We've come this far together so we may as well keep on the same track. What does Spook have to say to all this?"

"He can't talk, can he? But I sense he's – content – at the turn of events."

"We checked a couple more of the *Lithstar's* tubes," confided Linen. "We used the data we got in the sim suite to validate, but so far nothing. You really think something like Spook made it off one of those two ships that we think hit the same rock as the *Griffon*?"

"I'm beginning to doubt it myself," Copper conceded. "But Spook was seriously excited for a short time: hopefulness that one of his own is out there somewhere maybe. I've been trying to understand just how he operates as a non-physical being, but I can't. The nearest I get is that his kind were physical and some of them were altered to cope with the rigours of space travel, hence the life-support system that I assume kept *him* alive under the Warren all that time. But what they were doing on Mars ages ago, why they were trying to make it habitable by altering the extant organic life there, I don't know. Or why they were forced off – by other hostile forces maybe."

"We need a break: this sol seems to have gone on forever and we're both way over duty time, so we halt now," Linen decided. "I could seriously down a mug of Lofty's finest. Think we should call into medbay and see Kynedd Faerin? He *is* our best buddy now, after all."

"I'd take advice from Trisk, he knows the doc better than we do," Copper told her. "As the ship's now accelerating on course over the next month or so we should have a window of quiet time to get on with what we're supposed to be doing."

"You mean we won't be woken in the middle of the night to hop into our riot gear and prepare to repel boarders?"

"You got it; let's go see Trisk. I have some Amberline news, by the way, that I'll share with you both."

"If it's about the new post-grads, we know: Thars copied us in on the link as well," Linen stated.

"Wait and see," Copper replied mysteriously.

Their gregarious friend was in the mess and at a table with Lieutenants Ash Goff and Tawny Brown. They had just missed Oaky Grimsson, they were told: he was off to commandeer a racing buggy for a sprint along the engineering decks with some playmate from main engineering.

"Enjoy your stint on the bridge?" Trisk asked Copper as the latter sat down with her tray.

"I can imagine it would get boring after a while," she said evenly, not committing herself; in fact she had been exhilarated, but had no intention of sharing that with anyone but Linen.

The officers ate their way through their rations with no more than ship-talk and one or two digressions on life back on Mars and it was not until an hour later that the two had the chance to broach the subject of a little additional fortification.

Trisk was more than keen but suggested a halt at his quarters, where he could put a link through to Dr Faerin. The upshot was that the four gathered comfortably around a table in the senior MO's office, caff mugs in hand that were not filled with caff.

The latest news, that two postgraduate students sponsored by MDMC's Extra-Martis Missions Survey Office were to be recruited explicitly to carry out additional research at both sites currently being studied by Copper and Linen, had been linked to the three ex-Amberlines. Thars was clear that the details of any future projects required justification; he was strongly opposed to any interference in either the Dragon's Nest or the Glory Hole, but was in danger of having his other MDMC support cut if he refused to cooperate, as MDMC held ownership and mining rights to the site.

A few snippets of gossip that Copper had picked up from contacts at her old home on Road Eleven off Flagstaff in Lowell during a short break in her quarters after her stint on the bridge had led her to request permission to link supra-light to Thars Amberline for a private chat. Permission had been granted.

"The colonel agreed to an immediate supra-light link?" Linen interrupted. "How did you swing that?"

Copper smiled broadly. "Told her the reason: to ensure that I got to Thars before he was coerced into taking on whoever the Waterbone considered appropriate to tramp all over our site and fawn all over his feet. And to make sure that Thars snapped up a very suitable pair of diligent PhD students."

"So who gave you the lowdown on these students?"

"Ma Kellyn."

"Ma Kellyn! She told you where to look for new postgrads for the Amberlines?" Linen was thunderstruck.

"So who are these two spanking new PhD students that will be tramping all over your sites?" Trisk asked, his eyes twinkling.

"A couple of geologists, newly got their degrees from Lowell; good ones at that: a Grade One and a Grade Two. They've got astrobiology as part of their degrees, they work well together, they live locally and they're about to get legally paired," Copper elucidated. "And their new apartment's in Halley Street, close to where you used to live," she said to Trisk. "It belongs to Ma Kellyn and she's letting them have it at a *very* decent rent, since the pairing will be out of *her* place on Road Eleven. She's over the two moons 'cos she'll have a front seat at the ceremony."

"Maressan and Jenika!" exclaimed Linen. "Bet Jenika was the Grade One."

"She was," Copper confirmed. "And as Maressan's uncle is the renowned Dr Marku Chengi of Marsgem Exploration, he of the Chengi mineral extraction technique, he's got background. And Jenika's a Grass-Tephra, another well-known name in Mars circles. Waterbone will have nothing to argue with. Jenika's as straight as a die and won't stand any nonsense…"

"And Maressan will do as she says; and he's one of your old buddies that's always looked up to you," Linen finished. "Thars has agreed, I take it?"

"He *did* check their records first, but agreed. Ma mentioned in her link that Jenika had put in for a PhD place in Geosciences and that Maressan was hoping for an offer through his uncle for a place in Marsgem's Lowell office, but naturally a PhD with the Amberline Group with ready-made support *and* an immediate start will blow anything else out of the water. I don't know for sure if they'll accept, but I'm betting they will."

"And if they do, will Thars let on that you recommended them?" Trisk enquired shrewdly.

"That's up to Thars, I'm saying nothing. But if it helps his cause and ours, he may."

Kynedd Faerin was eyeing the trio in amusement. "I can see why you were all considered hotshots," he told them. "You're worth your weight in ale. But why bother about your research sites back on Mars? You're all here now."

"That's what started all this for us," Copper told him. "And we have a very special site that's of great interest to Mars Gov and that has a bearing on our mission; it's one of the reasons we brought so many research samples aboard."

"And Spook's ship is buried below our site," Linen added.

Faerin looked dubious. "Now it has a ship?"

"He always had," Copper retorted. "And stop calling him *it*. I know you're not totally convinced he exists, but why don't you just humour me?"

"Cop!" Linen exclaimed warningly. "We might be off duty but the doc outranks you, remember?"

"Doesn't outrank Spook," was the peevish reply.

"That's a very small ship he has – had," Linen reminded her gently. "So he could hardly have been an admiral. But why are you suddenly so cranky?"

"That was a small scout or fighter he was in, not his main vessel. And I've had a long sol and I'm tired…"

"Liar, you're full of fizz… what gives?"

Copper closed her eyes, took a deep breath and shivered. "The universe just shifted," she announced. "Something's up."

"It can't be," Linen contradicted. "It was fine a few minutes ago. Engines probably just shifted into a higher gear as part of our acceleration process."

Giving the lie to her words, a siren began to sound outside in the main medbay. As all four rushed to the door, they could see the flashing lights of the amber alert that denoted all hands to duty stations.

"*Now* do you believe in Spook?" Copper hissed belligerently.

"Can it, Lieutenant," Faerin replied, pushing by her to catch a member of his team and call for details.

"Something's up in engineering: parts of it have been sealed off," the nurse tech reported. "No note of any casualties, but we're calling in back-up, just in case."

"Good. You three get to your stations. I'll see you later."

"Aye, sir," they chorused, suddenly in duty-mode, and made for the exit at a run.

Controlled chaos existed elsewhere; many of their crewmates were also in motion, some pulling on parts of their uniforms.

"Nice to know we're efficient," Linen panted. "Maybe it's just a drill?"

"You wish. Let's take the ladder; we're not far from our own labs here," Copper urged.

She led the way to the stairwell that linked decks five and six and was close enough to their own sector to be useful. By the time they had linked into ship's comms requesting an update on the current situation, the alert status had reduced to yellow.

"So they know what's up," Trisk noted wryly. "But they're not telling. How bad is it?" he asked of Copper, who was busily calling up specs of main engineering.

"Worse than they think," she said grimly. "Get Locksmith on the comm: while half the ship's busy trying to track down what's up on the engineering decks, what's the bet something else is about to go bang just under our noses?"

15: HANGING FIRE

The data recorded by various engineering stations indicated that as the *Drake* had drawn more power for a second acceleration, a minute flaw in a crystal segment of one of her main drives had grown to a crack. The partial pressure drop sensed by the ship's safety systems had caused immediate drive shut down, sealing of the local area and initiation of the alert. A leak in an adjunct coolant chamber had also registered. There were no casualties and the situation was being contained. The chief engineer had ordered a full main engine diagnostic and the ship was flying on her auxiliaries.

Trisk knew Copper sufficiently well to realise that she was in earnest and put the requested call through to Kit Locksmith. He was already asking why the flaw had not been detected sooner, despite the shakedown nature of their cruise. Every micron of the drive should have been scrutinised before primary initiation, was his opinion, he told Dr Addystone.

"It probably was," Copper put in darkly, looking over. "And why a coolant leak at exactly the same time? I've checked the engineering logs: the chambers were all checked just before acceleration shift and read as safe."

"How did you get access to the logs?" Locksmith growled.

"The dimglow in charge hasn't coded them as classified."

"You go telling Lieutenant Commander Sage she's a dimglow and she'll have you tied to the reactor core!" Linen warned.

"Commander Sage isn't responsible for secure-coding logs, I am," the chief retorted wryly with look at Copper. "But are you hinting at a sinister motive for slowing the ship and tying the crew to their duty stations?"

"Standby," Linen corrected. "We're down to yellow alert."

"Good," Copper snorted. "I want to check out our chunk of

alien moonlet that's hanging fire in outer landing bay four. It's still under high security, I take it, Chief?"

"It is. What the hell do you want to check it out for?"

She glared at his face on the screen, daring him to challenge her. "I've got a feeling."

"And on that basis I release a team to escort you to the outer reaches of the aft section of the ship while we're on alert status and have slowed to part-speed?"

"You do. I'll go through the colonel if I have to."

The security chief regarded the three on his viewscreen; Trisk nodded slightly and Linen shrugged noncommittally.

"*I'll* inform the colonel," he said. "Suit up in protective gear and call by my office. I'll assign you guards I can trust and warn the detail near outer bay four that you're on your way."

The three made for their own quarters to don the necessary kit and equip themselves with weapons; they trusted security but felt better for having their own arms. They also stopped by their lab to pick up extra gear. Locksmith had chosen their escort and gained permission for their sortie by the time they reached his office and before long they were navigating their way to the aft exterior portion of the ship.

Outer bay four encompassed docking space for at least two standard shuttles and was huge, rearing overhead. Banks of task-stations were set along light blue-grey bulkheads, with recesses between that led to storage and service areas. Hatches giving on to various facilities cut the deck at intervals. The three and their two escorts were permitted through after their idents had been verified by security personnel at the door. A secure-arc field had been set up within the bay and a disembodied voice informed them that they were being scanned by cams from every angle as the door sealed smartly behind them.

"Not taking any chances, then," Linen murmured, eyeballing a hover-cam just out of reach that had decided to follow them.

She waved at it, and it executed a neat dipping action.

The large chunk of alien material that had been brought on board sat within its own security field, which showed as a bluish haze around the mass. Copper called for more lighting and the whole space brightened. Now that they could see it clearly, its reddish-green outer colouring and iridescent sheen proclaimed it to be related to the alien tech with which they were familiar. Its inner sponge-like construction, with thicker support struts set in a uniform pattern to hold the whole in place, was of a similar colour but less burnished. The three researchers spread out and began to circle the jagged bulk. The seamless face that Copper believed to be the exterior and exposed to space was smooth but faceted, making it look angular. Some compulsion made her reach out to touch it through the field but Trisk and one of the guards pulled her back before she could make contact.

"We scan first," Trisk announced firmly. "Colonel's orders. No-one's been allowed near it apart from the team that brought it in and the security personnel that set the defence systems."

"And it's been under constant surveillance in main security *and* by the detail posted outside ever since," one of their escort put in.

"Fair enough," Copper agreed, removing her favourite bug detector from a thigh pocket and setting it up purposefully.

"We need to get your Grammy Magenta to produce more of these," she said at last, having placed the conical device on her palm, and watched critically as its two delicate blue crystal bands pulsated, indicating that its sensors had locked onto something. "And sell them to Mars Fleet: security *here* sure as shells could use them," she went on as an informational holo-note expanded out and sharpened into focus.

"Source?" Linen demanded practically, quickly unsheathing her PPF and unlocking it, her eyes darting around the space.

Their two escorting guards had drawn weapons likewise and had assumed a back-to-back stance. Trisk was reading the data.

"Down that deck hatch," he said quietly. "That one next to Lyrican's left foot," he added for the convenience of the guards.

Even as he spoke there was a rumble beneath them and he found himself sprawling face down, Copper's forceful hand in the small of his back having sent him over. She had let fall her bug and dropped to one knee, gun in hand but aimed skyward whilst the other three had directed their weapons to the hatch.

"Up there!" she screamed, letting loose with short bursts of wide-angled fire at tiny target drones that no doubt held more than stings in their tails.

"Can't even see the blasted things!" Linen panted at her side, having crouched down alongside her friend and a cursing Trisk Addystone, whose nose was bleeding. "Here comes back-up," she went on as a heavy thunder at the door heralded assistance.

"Got the things!" one of the two guards announced as the shooting ceased, wiping sweat from his brow.

"Did you?" Copper asked scathingly, rescuing her detector as she clambered to her feet. "I guess the bug under the hatch was destroyed when whoever's responsible realised we'd located it – but they must have access to *your* security surveillance systems."

She pulled out a small probe on a neck-chain and began a methodical sweep of the immediate area, carefully scanning the settling dust that was the remnants of the target drones.

"Auntie Elle's scanner, I see," Linen whispered, coming up behind her. "Still not an instrument to touch it, is there?"

"I figure if there's a military link to *this* tech, it'll be able to tell us," was the terse response. "It's linked to practically every mil database there is and now we have full access."

Linen eyed her askance. "You don't think..."

"Hush, later. Here's Kit Locksmith, better late than never. His hand-picked security team can fill him in."

"I'll come and visit you in the brig," Copper promised the chief once he had been briefed by his own team and had come to get their report. "I'll bring cookies. From what I can gather from the debris, the drones were packing enough sleepy juice to have us out for a sevensol. They were probably there to take us down and make you think that something in that piece of space junk was responsible, so that the colonel would order all work to cease on it and whoever planted these things could move in at leisure. Slowing the ship might just have been a distraction to cover this; or maybe not. I would keep looking and trust no-one. Especially your high-level security team: there *must* be a mole in your department that helped set this up and you'll need to locate it."

The blue eyes twinkled at her. "*If* the colonel doesn't throw me in the brig over this," was the rueful rejoinder. "I'm glad as hell you're on my side. Care to speculate on who's the mole, since you seem to enjoy telling me how to run my department?"

"No thanks. I just want to get on with checking that our stuff's not been interfered with. So I'd be grateful if you'd gather up your bits and pieces and do what you have to, Mr Locksmith, sir. You okay Trisk, or do you need a medic?"

"I need a reminder to keep out of your way when there may be trouble in the offing," he grinned. "Next time just shout. Or pick a softer spot on the deck to aim my face at."

"Here's the colonel," Linen warned. "Bet we've just made her sol for her."

"The chief can explain: it was his team that muffed it," said Copper with a swift glance in his direction. "I want a closer look at our piece of alien hull."

"Thanks," Locksmith responded laconically as the other two shrugged and followed Copper as she set off towards her goal.

"You're totally convinced this is part of a ship that belonged to Spook's people, aren't you?" Linen questioned in a low tone after an exhaustive remote analysis of the huge chunk of debris.

"I am and I want to take samples. I'd also like to send some of Dr Inkscree's surf-sci bots through the superstructure: we can only do so much from out here without touching it and I don't want to give anyone who may still be eyeing us on the sly any reason to think it's safe to approach."

"It might be safe for you," Trisk observed astutely. "But for anyone else?"

"You got me," Copper admitted. "I don't think it's been got at and I don't think it'll react negatively to you or Linen, but how far its organo-systems are still operative, I can't say."

"Can Spook?" Linen asked archly.

"Haven't asked him."

"You think we're still being watched by unfriendly eyes?" Trisk went on quietly.

"Maybe: that's why I'm not risking using the alien scanning device. Here's Colonel Moritz."

"I hope you're not expecting a medal and a party, Lieutenant Milkstone?" the colonel remarked as she reached the trio.

"No ma'am. I wouldn't advise it in any case: it'll just make the crew think they've been in real trouble. Play it down and they won't worry so much."

"Thanks for the advice. Play down what?"

"Someone wants this," Copper gestured to the piece of hull. "And badly enough to risk the lives of your officers."

"That would be us," Linen put in.

"Belay that, Lieutenant," Copper ordered crisply. "Why slow the ship? I think…"

"Slow the ship? You're saying you suspect that our situation in engineering was a deliberate set-up that relates to this?"

"*This* is known about ma'am, as is the body that the *Fearless* was ordered to investigate, so you can bet the information's leaked out and is in several ears by this time. And a lot of nasty people out there would like a piece of the action. You suspect we may still have one or two infiltrators aboard, ma'am? Ones who haven't shown their hands and who have high-level access to *our* systems, given they got past Mr Locksmith's security. I assume you reported *this* find to Fleet HQ, where there's more than likely to be infiltration and thus the risk of sabotage?"

The colonel regarded her with asperity. "You don't mince words, Lieutenant."

"Admiral Stannum was compromised," Copper pointed out. "And you've suspected leaks in Intelligence for some time."

"What've you got here?"

Copper brought her up to date on the nature of the drones as far as she could work it out: they were set to target moving lifeforms and deliver a powerful sedative that would incapacitate the victim. She suspected that they also included some kind of anti-detection device or they would have been picked up before.

"Depends who was doing the looking," Linen interrupted.

"Good point," her friend conceded. "They must have been deployed from above, but they may have been in the overheads for sols, if not longer. Who would know?"

"Security should have known," the colonel retorted sharply.

"They must have been well-hidden; but Mr Locksmith will know what to look for if they *have* been shielded," Copper said decidedly.

"How many more small areas may be shielded?" Trisk asked. "The *Drake's* one big vessel and security can't check every micron. If there *are* traps in place but inoperative at present…"

"Internal scanners," Copper cut in. "Every deck's got them. Configure them to look for what we know so far to be the type of materials in these drones, in the hidden cams we had trouble with earlier, anything not standard. This *is* the most advanced ship in the Fleet so we should be able to secure it.”

“Watch it, Cop: Mr Locksmith will have you drafted into his department before you can turn round,” Linen warned jokingly.

“He’d be better off liaising with Dr Faerin: if there *are* more of these damn things around, the doc’ll need to have a response in place. And we need to get on with our analysis of this before anything else tries to disturb it. What say we get a solid medical iso-bubble set up around it? There must be one in stores for field deployment on away missions, surely. It would cut out a lot of trouble if it was set to our and emergency idents only.”

“And would raise a bucket of gossip among the crew,” Linen said, shaking her head. “You’re just too keen to get your paws on this.”

“Before someone else does. I don’t like having to look over my shoulder every five minutes in case there’s a gremlin waiting to leap at me.”

“You’re still jumpy,” the redhead surmised. “Waiting for the next bang under our noses?”

“Enough,” Colonel Moritz ordered. “You stop work on this until this place is secured.”

“With respect, ma’am, this place was supposed to be secure, and *still* we were hit. No disrespect to the chief, but until the perps are found, and maybe not even then, he can’t guarantee it *will* be secure when his team is finished. So why stop work?”

“Are you questioning my orders, Lieutenant?”

“No, ma’am, merely asking a question.”

“Noted. *You* will note that our alert status is now amber. So finish up here, head back to your duty stations and process the data you have so far, including these drones. Link your findings to me on a secure channel and I will pass what I deem necessary on to my senior officers. Dismissed.”

“Aye, ma’am,” the three replied smartly as their commanding officer turned on her heel and stalked off.

“You know Cop, you’re getting a tad too high-handed with our fellow officers, including the colonel,” Linen told her friend blithely as she began to wrap up her gear. “If you don’t watch out, she’ll think you’re trying to commandeer her ship.”

“Very funny.”

“I’m being serious. Have you listened to yourself? Or are you too busy listening to Spook?"

Copper gave her friend a sidelong glance as she stowed her own equipment. "Just what are you hinting at?"

"You're too close to him, overprotective even. Let him be: he's way older and wiser than you and unlike you he can't be hurt, at least by our kind. Let's get along to the lab and have a caff; I sure as hell need one and so do you. Trisk, you'd better get your nose fixed, it's still bloody. We can leave this place to Chief Locksmith and his people; they won't risk touching that chunk of tech and we've done all we can."

* * *

Back in the comfort of their office, Copper spun in her chair to face her friend. "You really think I'm turning into a tyrant and it's down to Spook?" she asked uncertainly.

"I wouldn't say tyrant – but you did tell me to hush up and you did argue with the colonel when she told us to stop our work for the duration. Bossy boots, maybe."

"Same thing."

"Not quite. But you've let slip a thing or two: the ship under the Warren wasn't Spook's main vessel? He can power down or take out hostile weaponry without a physical presence? Just who or what do you think he was before he was Spook and how can he do it?"

"Position of authority," Copper said. "I feel he's been in command of some sort of space-faring vessel *and* he's learned some of the ops of part of the *Drake*, because he can anticipate me at the science station."

"He can actually tell you what to do?"

"It's not like that: I feel I know what to do intuitively and much of it's down to my link with him. How he can physically influence systems I don't know. It may be energy manipulation, like some sort of force field?"

"Whatever it is, we'd best get on with data analysis, especially those drones: the colonel will want to know ASAP, especially if there *is* a mil link, like you hinted up in the bay," Linen told her, rising. "Let's get the tri-dee sim up and running next door."

Copper followed, collecting the high spec instrument that the two referred to as Auntie Elle's scanner. She swiftly linked it to one of the tri-dee sim stations and began to transfer the data from her sweep of the scattered remains of hostile drones whilst Linen used cam-footage to build a holo of a complete unit. Trisk sauntered in with a med-patch over the bridge of his nose and watched critically as the elements were brought together and a complete sectioned holo of a target drone was built up.

"Can't say I've seen that design before," he declared. "Nasty looking thing, isn't it?"

"With an explosive delivery system," Copper noted harshly. "It could have caused serious skin damage as well as knocking any one of us out for hours, even though we were in protective gear. Now let's just correlate these…"

After several minutes had passed and diverse classified and secret databases interrogated, Linen turned with eyes wide. "The colonel's going to be seriously pissed over this," she breathed. "When do you plan to tell her?"

"Right now," was the response. "She said secure channel: I'd better suggest she takes it in her office."

"Well suggest it *politely* or you'll be telling her from the brig," Linen advised. "We're still at amber, so I guess things haven't quietened down much."

"What gives?" Trisk demanded.

"These drones are mil issue and as far as I can tell, they've not been subverted for alternate usage," Copper stated. "One at least still has its tag of origin in place – the biohazard labs out between Fleet HQ and Korolev Station."

"They're ours and they were programmed to take our people out?" Trisk said, shocked.

"Looks like. I'd better link the colonel."

Linen was correct in her appraisal: Colonel Moritz was more than disconcerted by the news, so much so that she left Captain Helmis in charge of the bridge and made her way down to the science facilities, collecting Locksmith on the way. *His* teams were working overtime in every section of the ship, reinforcing restricted sections and re-coding logs and sensitive equipment.

"We'll have the inside of this ship locked down so tight a flea can't jump but we'll see it," he assured the commanding officer.

"What about the outside?" Copper flatly enquired. "Any approaching ship could release a micro-breaching pod and with a ship this size, you'd be hard put to detect it. The *Fearless* could have stuck one on us and would we know?"

"Cop!" Linen interrupted in a low, cautionary voice.

"What in hell's a micro-breaching pod?" Locksmith rapped.

"A breaching pod's a powered device that can be directed to latch onto and penetrate the hull of a vessel or similar and release whatever it's carrying, be it personnel, equipment or an arsenal the size of a shuttle. A micro version could release a few million microbes that could wipe out the crew of a starship."

"Cop!" Linen repeated more loudly.

"I bet Magenta Firewall's got the blueprint of one in a back pocket," Copper added belligerently. "One that can crack the hide of a ship like the *Drake*, even with her self-healing hull."

"Don't think we haven't thought of that kind of attack," the colonel interrupted. "But a micro-breaching pod, if such a thing exists, wasn't considered. Our external sensors have overlapping ops fields, so we should be secure – but I *will* order a scan, just in case. What else have you got?"

"We didn't check the exploding bug under the hatch, ma'am, we left *that* to security," Copper stated with a sidelong glance at Kit Locksmith. "But here's the spec of a complete drone as far as we can make it out. This design hasn't been released for service yet, so it's still a prototype."

"Which means someone or some people can get their hands on military technology before it's passed as acceptable for use in any field that needs it," Linen said shortly. "That's worrying, since it's got this far out and has been encoded for hostile use against Mars Fleet's own."

"I've liaised with Dr Faerin," the chief cut in, looking at the colonel. "I suggest he runs standard med checks on every single crew member but looks for signs of surgical intrusion or similar that's not in their records. And we don't advertise the schedule; crewmen are told on the sol. That way, if we have compromised personnel aboard, or impostors, we'll have a good chance of finding them. The doc has to run regular med checks anyway, and it'll be one way of filling time as we head out to the edge."

"Good call: I'll sanction it," the colonel agreed. "Tell him he can start with me and the rest of the command staff. Let's finish up here; I have to get back to the bridge."

The colonel had not long departed when the amber alert was

reduced to yellow and an announcement over the comm let the crew know that the situation in engineering had been contained and the *Drake* was now resuming her course. The three science officers were grateful that they could now leave their duty posts but were somewhat puzzled as to how a crack in a crystal drive unit could be so speedily repaired. Events in outer landing bay four were also evidently being played down, for no mention was made of the security breach there.

Once in the mess and with plates of rations before them, the trio found that news of the security incident had spread, for Ash Goff was quizzing a non-cooperative Tawny Brown at the next table whilst various other crewmates listened in. Trisk's patched nose caused Goff some merriment until Copper informed him that she had dealt it and there was plenty more where that came from for over-inquisitive crewmen. His smile froze at the look on her face and he let the matter rest. Tawny winked at her: she knew the story.

* * *

In Linen's quarters later, the redhead looked seriously at her friend as she dealt out the after-dinner caff. "You've changed."

"So have you: you've never had a tidy billet in your life, but this place is immaculate. What's up?"

"Stop changing the subject. You were more than short with Ash Goff; I know he deserved it but you hardly had a civil word for anyone else. You're stressed, but something's eating you."

"It's all this trouble, especially since we've been aboard the *Drake*," Copper confessed. "I bet the first *Drake* didn't have all this flak to contend with. But I suppose as she was unmanned, any scallywags stowing away on board would have got what they deserved. But I just get the feeling it's not over yet and we're in for some very big and nasty surprises before this mission's over. I hardly like to tell the colonel that forces within and without are undermining us every step of the damn way."

"I think she's got most of the picture, she's no fool," Linen comforted. "But what do you mean *forces* within and without?"

"Things bigger than we are, a whole lot bigger – you told me a while ago that the colonel had hinted there were devices under test for alien lifeform detection, remember? What sort of alien life and where are these gadgets and who's testing them? Are they looking for Spook?"

"Too many questions. Why don't you ask the colonel? All she can do is bite your head off and throw you in the brig. But seriously, she did only suggest it and I may have picked her up wrongly. But you have a good point: if there *are* sensors being tested, *has* someone been detailed to scan the ship for Spook? And if so, who?"

"Trisk," Copper nodded. "He's the obvious one, he and Doc Faerin. I'm too close to Spook; you're too close to me. But they won't find him: he can leave the ship if he wants, like he did when he deactivated those asteroid defences and took out that restraining tractor beam."

"Doesn't that mean that aliens of a similar nature could do the same?" queried Linen. "Where would that leave us?"

"In a heap of trouble. But all this is pie in the sky, we don't know if there *are* aliens out there and if there are, what form or forms they're able to take and if they're hostile or friendly."

"Come on, Cop; you wouldn't be in this much grief if they were friendly and just waiting to shake our hands or whatever they do to say hello. You and Spook think there's something out there and it isn't friendly and there are threats from in here and back on Mars as well. But are the threats here and at home of human origin or is there something more sinister going on?"

"How the hell would I know?"

"Don't snap at me," cautioned Linen, brow furrowing. "You have some inkling and it's got you seriously scared. I can tell."

"I'm telepathically linked to Spook, and there's a physical link to him at some level, according to Doc Faerin; Spook's a goody, for want of a better term..."

"Oh shit! If there are hostile forms out there, or on Mars..."

"That have the same capability," Copper continued, "*They* might be able to link in a similar way to a human that's not on our side – or who maybe can't prevent such a linkage."

"But that won't be the case on Mars, surely?" interrupted Linen.

"I don't know – we *did* find traces of that blue material that both Trisk and I are averse to on Mars and we can be sure it's hostile alien tech, in view of the other evidence we have. I know it's been there for millennia, but then so has Spook."

"In a complete ship," argued Linen. "There's been no other whole ship – oops! We suspected that there was one found out near Lowell, but no-one would confirm it, although the colonel did let slip at the time that there was evidence of other ships elsewhere on Mars. But no, there would have been more than just traces of the blue material found and Colonel Moritz said that very little was ever recovered. Perhaps we'd best get on with checking out the rest of the *Lithstar's* tubes and that tri-dee sim of the rocky body that we're heading for – she did say we'd be given priority access to the tri-dee sim suite and we've been forbidden to get on with our examination of the alien lump of stuff in outer bay four."

"I guess. She told us to liaise with Kit Locksmith on security support and keep it quiet. And when we are supposed to get on with our own researches, I don't know. Let's check with Trisk and see if he wants to be in on the tests of the *Lithstar* tubes."

"He'll be too busy searching for Spook," Linen grinned. "But later: we're now off duty until morrow-sol."

* * *

Kit Locksmith, despite his own tight schedule, called into the science office for a briefing with Copper, Linen and Trisk. The latter was keen to be in on analyses of sample tubes originating from the *Lithium Star* and felt as his colleagues did, that they had best complete that task before starting the next. Locksmith listened sagely and decided that Lieutenant Tawny Brown would be assigned as their back-up. He would brief her himself and send her along, he told them.

Copper's immediate anxiety once the chief had left was the use of the alien scanner. She felt she wanted to test it again but was aware of the personal cost in energy and was also aware that Dr Faerin had not been able to ascertain precisely how she bonded to the device and was chary of its use as far as she was concerned. In the end she decided that she would wear a medi-tag for the duration, which would be set to monitor for specifics and sound an alert if her readings exceeded safe levels.

There were several tubes originating from the *Lithium Star* that the three researchers had not yet analysed. These were dug out of the store and locked in a cabinet in their lab for ease of access. As the colonel had granted them priority call on the tri-dee test suite down in engineering, the trio had no hesitation in commandeering the facility for the next few sols. The engine decks in any case were still undergoing thorough searching by Kit Locksmith's teams and were off-limits to all but security-cleared personnel, so they expected no trouble for their spell of duty down there. They found out through Tawny Brown that the fractured crystal unit had been switched for one scavenged from one of the auxiliary drives. The flawed section would be abraded to remove the fault and would then be reset into the auxiliary. That the initial fracture had been deliberately induced was the theory that Chief Locksmith was working to, although most of the *Drake's* engineers were sceptical, given its material durability, its relative inaccessibility and the danger to anyone near that part of the main drive whilst the ship was in motion.

It would be simple enough to induce the flaw, was Linen's opinion, expressed to Brown over a caff break in the office. Any mineralogist with the requisite knowledge and the relevant tools could scratch crystal at distance: a gem-quality microtome beam guided by a premium targeting eye would do it, or even a guided drone, although the latter loose in the main drive of a starship would be bound to be picked up by system monitors.

"Engineering's been continuously monitored since the initial acceleration phase," Brown informed the three science officers. "Any such incursion would show up. And how do you figure that a micro-whatever beam would work?"

"It cuts very minutely and very precisely," Linen explained. "We've used larger versions to cut through rock; our obsidian corer works on that principle," she nodded at Copper. "And my Ma's a fine jewellery artist – *she* can cut the hardest gemstones very accurately. And would routine monitoring pick up a nearly invisible beam, especially if it was projected from distance?"

"The main drives span a couple of decks, but unless a beam had a clear path there would be other damage," Copper argued. "So security should start looking for that."

"The chief probably is. He'll have Commander Sage on his back until he finds out exactly what happened," Trisk put in.

Brown's forehead creased in concentration. "You finish your caff and wait for me," she instructed. "I'm going to have a quiet word with the chief."

"You've got Tawny going with your invisible beam," Copper informed her friend.

"That was the idea. But while she's away: she doesn't know about Spook, so I guess we keep him out of the conversation. But you make sure you have him as back-up while you're using that scanning thingy. It still freaks me. And I vote we get these analyses done as quickly as possible, even if it means eating into our off duty time."

"Off duty time? What's that?" Copper enquired archly.

"Sometimes I wonder. But if Spook's around the tri-dee sim suite, Trisk had best not scan for him using that alien lifeform probe that he and Faerin are testing," Linen finished tranquilly.

Trisk looked at her wryly. "You what?"

"You heard. You've got some sort of device. And the colonel has you testing it by looking for Spook, hasn't she?"

Trisk could not deny it. "How did you figure?"

"We're smart. We also figure that if you start using it, Spook will scoot, you'll get nowhere and we might be in trouble."

"Unless you bring him into the experiment," Trisk suggested.

"Ah! That had not occurred to me."

"It had to me," interrupted Copper. "But any scans are under Spook's rules and *not* in the tri-dee test facilities. We get the rest of these and the *Wayfinder's* pieces analysed pronto, we get on to our analyses of the big prize in bay four and then we start on the partial tri-dee sim that the colonel has of our target location."

"Ma'am, yes ma'am!" Linen sang out. "Any other orders?"

"You're asking for a poke in the eye, lady," Copper told her sternly. "The last *Lithstar* tubes you two looked at produced not a thing. There may be no more surprises but I'm itchy. Where in blazes is Tawny Brown?"

"On the comm," Linen replied, taking the link.

The lieutenant had called in to say that she would meet the threesome down in engineering, outside the main entry on deck twenty. Linen confirmed and raised her eyebrows at her mates. "Let's get the *Lithstar* tubes we'll be working on this session."

In short order the three made their way down to the lower decks and the tri-dee testing suite assigned to them. To no-one's surprise, both Brown and Locksmith were standing by. As their use of the facility was listed on its external board, Copper raised a hand to the reader plate; the door opened smoothly and all five sailed in.

"People will think we're passing secrets," Trisk mentioned to no-one in particular as he dropped the tubes he was carrying onto a side counter close to the central projector plate station. "Best call up more seats."

"No need, I'm not hanging about," Locksmith told them as he faced them squarely.

"So why *are* you here, Chief?" Copper asked, eyes narrowing. "You found something?"

"One of my hawk-eyed team found a tiny pinhole through a bulkhead; we've now found a matching hole through a deck plate on the far side. You follow the line and you get to a drive buffer shield that protects sections of the main drive…"

"Including the crystal segment that was fractured," finished Copper. "But a targeting eye through a bulkhead: how would it work? Unless it was based on very classy remote sensing tech or linked into the security cams that monitor the lower deck mid-sections at all times. You *must* have a leak in your department or a mighty smart villain who can get into your monitoring systems, Chief."

"I'm working on it," he retorted. "And you lot are too quick by far. But we'll smoke out the troublemaker."

"Try your best sharpshooter," Trisk suggested jocularly.

"That would be me," Locksmith winked. "And I'm not the guilty party or parties. But why sabotage the main drive?"

"To delay the ship; I told the colonel," Copper said. "But it hasn't worked as we're back on course. So whoever is up to no good will try again, and soon, if they're after that piece of tech in bay four and want to get it before we're too far out to catch up. What has the scan of the ship's outer hull shown, if anything?"

"Cop, you're doing it again," Linen cautioned in an amused aside. "The chief ranks you, or hadn't you noticed?"

"We don't have one of your imaginary micro-breaching pods attached," Locksmith told Copper, smiling quizzically into her face. "Nor are we being followed by anyone that we can detect."

"Maybe they have an invisibility cloak?" Linen suggested.

"Or they're not following us, they're up ahead," Copper said sardonically, with a lift of one eyebrow.

"Can it," they were ordered. "Especially you, Ms Milkstone. I suggest you get on with the job you have in hand. Anything untoward and you call me directly," he ordered Brown. "I'll be in the vicinity."

Once the door had closed, Trisk transferred one of his tubes to a projector plate. "We can start with this. I'll set up the medi-scanner. You want to get your gear organised? We'll have all our MEDICs as well as the internal banks here capture the data …"

When everything was in place, Copper removed the smooth, burnished device that was the alien scanner from her pack and fit it securely to her hand. Tawny Brown watched curiously as she aimed it over the intact tube that Trisk had set down, sliding a finger of her free hand across the body of the instrument.

"Working," Linen whispered from behind, checking her own readings.

"You're good to go," Trisk agreed.

Relaxing into her task, Copper felt the tell-tale prickle begin to spread up her right arm; she was aware that Spook was close and took a deep breath as a fuzzy holo began to emanate from the scanner, becoming more distinct as the contents of the tube were probed and analysed. Time trickled by as Copper made the conscious effort to limit the extent of the projection and home into areas of the container that she felt to be important. Slowly moving the scanner across the body of the tube, she settled eventually on an area near one end.

"Got something here," she croaked to her companions. "It's not dangerous, but I'm sure it's organo-tech – I'm getting to recognise the sensation. Not much and it's small."

Linen had pulled out the military-issue multi-scanner given her by Colonel Moritz and prepared to corroborate her friend's readings, but halted as the holo of the fragment Copper had found was picked out in high definition.

"Frock me, we're getting its fine structure!" Trisk breathed. "It seems to match the previous stuff at sub-atomic levels as far as I remember. Slow down a bit," he added. "Your adrenalin levels are increasing and so's your temp. Can you tell if it's active at all?"

"Not sure," Copper said thickly, concentrating. "Don't think so, it's long past any functionality. That's about it for this tube, I reckon: there are no repairs to the tube itself that I can detect, but it *has* been scratched a bit."

She sighed as the insubstantial image switched off abruptly.

"Interesting," Linen observed. "The holo flicked off but you still have a hold of the scanner and your finger's still on its ops area. But did our MEDICs and the databanks here get all the stuff we wanted?"

"Should have," Copper told her. "There was a transfer of data, I felt it."

"If that's the case, we'll be able to flash through these sample tubes," the redhead asserted, eyes sparkling. "If we can use that gizmo on our Warren samples we can speed up our fine analyses no end. Can you teach it to write our reports for us as well?"

"Don't be a flooshy!" Copper said sternly. "But let's have another tube before I get too tired."

Three tubes later and Copper called a halt, backed by Trisk at the medi-scanner. She was excessively tired, but realised that as she was becoming more familiar with the alien tool, she could control it more effectively. As far as the researchers could work out, their auxiliary kit had logged most of the collected data.

"Lockdown, lab and lunch in that order," Linen twinkled. "I could demolish a cream-sauce steakfry with greens and chippers like Lofty used to serve. I miss Chef's cooking."

"But not his temper," Copper reminded her.

"So you reckon if you keep the holo contained to a smaller area, you use less time, energy and data storage?" Trisk asked as he deactivated his MEDIC and stacked the tested sample tubes.

"That's about it. We don't need to deep-probe the mundane in the samples, just any significant artefacts; and I feel I can zero in on anything of interest fairly accurately. And it *is* less tiring than last time," Copper admitted. "But we can leave the untested tubes here for now and come back later, if that suits you, Tawny?" she added to Brown.

"I'm yours for the whole sol," she smiled. "It beats pounding the decks or eyeing endless cam footage. But I have a game of squash-ball set for this eve, so no late shift, if you don't mind."

"We can accommodate that," Linen beamed. "We have flight training sims that Jinn Limlite kindly organised for us to fill up our off duty schedule: it was someone's bright idea."

"Auntie Elle takes no prisoners," Copper muttered as she wrapped up Gemima and stowed her in a pocket. "You set?"

The other three were more than ready to tread the path that would end in the officers' mess and a hearty lunch.

* * *

The afternoon found the trio of friends and their attendant guard on the way back to the tri-dee unit. Engineering was still under containment and security checks had to be undergone en route, to Copper's annoyance: she was impatient to return to the facility, having had a sensation of immediacy all through lunch.

Once locked in the suite and with systems operational, Trisk hefted the first tube onto the projector plate. As before, Copper activated the scanner and set to work, barely pausing to allow her mates to initiate their own instruments. She shook her head slightly, knowing that the material under test was not the source of her strange disquiet. Subliminally aware that Spook was close by, she took a deep breath and doggedly swept the length of the cylinder, without waiting for the holo to form and stabilise.

The next two tubes were equally unproductive but it was obvious to Linen and Trisk that their colleague was holding one back. The penultimate cylinder she spent more time over: its outer surface sported a hairline fracture filled by minute dust particles, no doubt from the rocky body that was the source of the sample matter itself, but the breach had not disturbed the tube's integrity. The three scientists scrutinised the area closely but nothing of note was apparent.

"Here we go then," Trisk said, hefting the final tube onto the counter. "Let's just check that all cams are operational. The medi-scanner's showing you're within safe limits Copper, but in the upper zone, so be careful. Tawny, how's our secure status?"

"Expecting trouble?" Brown asked with a raised brow as she swept their environs and checked her attached arsenal. "We're clear," she continued after a moment.

Copper was exceptionally careful in her close examination of the final sample tube. After a taxing ten minutes, noting she was becoming more and more tense, Trisk called a halt. She brushed him off, knowing she was close to something.

"You stop right now or I turn off the power," he threatened. "And I get Doc Faerin to ground you…"

"It may be Doc Faerin we need to get down here," was the cryptic response.

"Cop?" Linen demanded, having picked up her tension. "It's more than just the usual tech, isn't it? We have a fragment of the red-green stuff," she stated, fingering her own MEDIC. "But that's pretty standard now. It shouldn't pose a threat," she went on for Brown's edification.

"Look," Copper elucidated, nodding at the structure that she was homing in on, visualising ever finer details of its structure and bonding. "Linen, get the surface bio-comp of the piece at sub-atomic levels if you can."

"On it," the redhead responded promptly. "Definitely typical organo-tech but with additional elements: flecks of some sort of biofilm coating, I think. I'm capturing the data... what do you figure we have?"

"Back in the lab later – I want to complete this tube to make sure we have nothing else like this."

"You're running it fine," Trisk warned. "You're exhausted."

"Button it," she told him.

A seemingly endless fifteen minutes later and Copper flexed her rigid shoulders with a sigh. "I think we got all we could. We get this lot back to the lab under high security and we lock it up until we can go over it at pico-level. I want that morsel removed as soon as and subjected to in-depth analysis. And I want Doc Faerin there when we do."

"You want mayo on that?" Lieutenant Brown demanded.

Trisk and Linen knew better than to quiz Copper on what she thought she had found and the four secured the sim suite as quickly as possible before retracing their steps to deck five and the lab. Their guard was more than curious but maintained her position as escort until all four had reached their destination.

"The chief wants a debriefing," Tawny Brown announced after checking in with security. "If you're okay to carry on here, I'll love you and leave you. He'll no doubt be in touch."

"I bet he will," Linen grinned. "Thanks for the escort. We'll see you around the mess. Now, Lieutenant Milkstone, ma'am," she went on as the door closed. "What in blazes do you reckon those bio-coating scraps that seem to be fused to the flake of organo-tech are?"

"I think they're more than organo-tech… Hard-holos are okay but we need the finer details of layers, structure, bonding, and cell and nucleus composition, what's left of it…"

"Cell and nucleus composition?" Trisk demanded. "Are you saying there's cell-like structure that's *not* an organo-tech mix?"

"I'm saying it may be an organo-tech mix that's more organo than tech," was the reply.

"As in tissue?"

"I wouldn't go that far."

"Just how far would you go?" Trisk persisted, his normally smiling faced creased in concern.

"I need a caff."

"Answer the question, Lieutenant, ma'am," ordered Linen, talking her friend by the arm. "Dr Addystone…"

Copper shook her off, turning away.

"Cop!" The redhead looked concernedly at Trisk, raising her shoulders and shaking her head in perplexity. "You don't think they're fragments of body tissue?" she continued in a low voice. "Oh Lor', you don't think… the *Wayfinder* only found traces of the reddish-green alien tech but the *Lithium Star* found the same stuck to the what was left of the *Griffon* – not to mention teensy bits of that blue alien stuff, if I recall. You don't think these bio-flecks can be remnants of the crew of the *Griffon* do you?"

Copper looked upwards, sighing. "No, I don't think that. That's why I want Doc Faerin here when we analyse them."

"Not human?" That was Trisk.

"Not human."

16: KICKING HEADS

The following sol found the three science officers painstakingly sifting through the grit of the most recent *Lithstar* tube they had examined. Prudently opting to keep their notions under wraps, they had deftly fielded queries from Chief Kit Locksmith, whose curiosity had been raised by Tawny Brown's report. Choosing also to ignore the colonel's order that all tubes from the *Lithium Star* were to be examined with security standing by, the trio had locked down the lab and were holding siege.

The first part of the sol was gone before the run-of-the-mill material had been filtered out and set aside. A methodical run-through was then made of the remainder and a number of small batches reserved for deeper analysis. The fragment of greenish-red matter that had sparked Copper's concern was disinterred, securely coded and locked away whilst testing of the earmarked samples was underway. That nothing unfamiliar turned up was no surprise to the three, but several tiny splinters of synthetic organo-matrix was identified by the lab analyser, as well as metal and plas residues that could conceivably once have formed part of the skin of a starship. Trisk was set to find and decipher any nano-encrypted signatures in the latter whilst Copper and Linen tested, evaluated and logged the remainder.

It was well after noon when a persistent buzz at the lab entry alerted the trio. Ever-cautious, Copper toggled the viewer. She released the door with a muttered oath to allow an irate Colonel Moritz to stalk in.

"When I say I expect constant updates on your findings, I mean it," she began without preamble. "You spent yestersol in the tri-dee sim unit in engineering and I've heard nothing. You've locked yourselves in here and refused Chief Locksmith access. Your report, now."

Trisk as the senior officer took it upon himself to give their commander a quick rundown of the findings from the session in the sim facility, leaving the discovery of the interesting piece of artefact material until the end. Copper's conjectures he did not reveal but the colonel was more than aware that something was being held back. She pressed for details, having obviously been informed via her security chief that the presence of Dr Faerin would be necessary for the analysis. A wrinkled brow and sharp nod were the only expressions of surprise at the inference that the biological scraps coating the piece might be alien in origin as she watched the holo of the structure captured in the sim suite rotate above the bench top.

Copper was watching the colonel, revolving one or two ideas in her head. "This isn't new to you, ma'am," was the sum of her musing. "There's been suspicion of alien bio-remains before."

"Astute of you," Colonel Moritz said. "Military Intelligence has been aware of similar for some while, at a couple of the sites on Mars where alien technology has been found."

"Outer Mars Ops," guessed Linen. "Our chums Karben and Bilkitt for two; they're the cream of the MI crop after all."

"Belay that, Lieutenant," ordered the colonel, although she probably shared the redhead's view of her former subordinates. "What else?"

The breakdown of Trisk's analysis of the plas-metal residues that suggested the hull of a ship was sharply queried: he had confirmed their origin as the *Griffon*.

Copper was still eyeing their commanding officer: there was something in the air that she had not quite fathomed. Aware of the scrutiny, Colonel Moritz turned at last.

"What *is* it, Lieutenant Milkstone?"

"Something's up – out there." She nodded towards the door. "Did you post guards outside our lab?"

"Chief Locksmith did," the colonel answered harshly. "As he has in several sensitive areas, *Lieutenant*. Why?"

Copper swallowed, aware of her protocol gaffe. "Apologies, ma'am. I mean, are we in trouble? I sense unease, as if the ship's at a state of alert without the alert, if you catch my drift."

Colonel Moritz shook her head slowly. "You three are maybe better off locked in here," she said at last, as she looked around.

"We're not being bugged," Linen put in brightly, pointing to Copper's pet detector on the edge of the desk. "But we haven't had lunch, so I expect we'll have to come out soon."

"We could order in?" Copper suggested, trying to lighten the mood and failing miserably, judging by the icy expression on the colonel's face.

"You two go get something to eat; Ms Milkstone, stand fast."

"Aye ma'am," all three chorused as Trisk and Linen swivelled on their heels to obey the command, leaving a mortified Copper wondering what was in store for her.

"Sit," commanded the colonel as she pulled out a lab stool for herself and one for her junior officer.

"Yes ma'am."

"You have a problem with discipline, Lieutenant Milkstone. Your tone to senior officers often borders on disrespectful."

Copper bit her lip. "I'm aware of it, ma'am, often too late to correct it. Linen's pulled me up on it," she grimaced. "I have no explanation and no excuse."

"Apart from your friend Spook?"

"That's a possibility," she acquiesced as she glanced into the green eyes, in which she thought she detected understanding.

"I've read reports on your work from Dr Addystone and Dr Inkscree, and on your training from your instructors. Your flight and weapons skills in particular are outstanding; you've taken to the duties of a science officer on the bridge seemingly naturally. Your lab work is remarkable but you acknowledge external assistance."

"Yes ma'am," Copper said warily, uncertain of where the talk was leading: the commander of a starship on active service did not routinely carry out staff appraisals and the unscheduled tête-à-tête was unnerving her.

"How close are you to this Spook of yours?"

"Very, I think. I *do* think he's very close when I'm in taxing positions such as the bridge, but I can't tell how much I'm being influenced. I feel I'm on auto-pilot at times and he's guiding my actions. But not often," she added.

Colonel Moritz nodded. "I once said that your Spook would make a useful ally: it seems to recognise threats to my ship and be able to deal with them."

Copper's eyes widened. She was beginning to suspect where the colonel was going. "There *is* something wrong out there, ma'am and you think it's linked to our work here, the piece of alien tech we have in bay four and our ongoing mission?"

"*One* of the reasons I require constant updates," was the cool reminder. "If you *are* going to command a ship of your own one sol, you'll have to realise that. I've had a word with Dr Faerin. I want you to connect with this Spook of yours under controlled conditions in medbay and with its support see if you can find out what seems to be eluding security – if you agree."

"Spook's already scanned several areas for more explosive or dangerous devices but hasn't located any," Copper disclosed as she nodded her consent. "I take it that security hasn't tracked down the people behind the sabotage in main engineering or the attack in bay four, ma'am. Have there been other incidents?"

"Yes," she stated bluntly. "Attempts at least. So we still have infiltrators or worse aboard and I want them. Chief Locksmith's hands are tied by a possible plant in his own department. There will be no more work carried out on that alien technology in bay four until I'm sure it can be done as safely as possible. We have a mission and I intend to carry it out without interference from other agencies."

"Aye, ma'am."

The colonel nodded, satisfied.

"Ma'am? Will Dr Faerin be using the probe that he and Trisk are developing to detect alien lifeforms on Spook while we're trying to figure what's going on?"

"Dr Addystone told you about the probe?"

"No ma'am, we guessed and asked," Copper admitted.

"I might have known. Report to medbay at twenty hundred hours – you'll find you have a routine med check scheduled at that time. Meanwhile, no word of this to anyone, especially Ms Lyrican, or you *will* be up on report. Go get your lunch."

"Aye, ma'am."

∗ ∗ ∗

"Did you get fried?" Linen asked sympathetically over a plate of chippers in the mess.

"I appear to have a problem with discipline," Copper sighed. "If the colonel's noticed it, it must be getting bad."

"It is," Trisk confirmed, laughing. "*We* can put up with it as we're your friends, but you might find that others won't."

"Well, there's one thing the colonel could do that will help," Linen announced gleefully. "You could suggest it to her and see how she takes it."

"And what's that, smartarse?"

"Promote you. Your next step should be first lieutenant but she could hike you up to lieutenant commander: that would put several noses out of joint, but you'd be less likely to be put on report for insubordination."

"Thanks for that, friend. But I'd better eat up and we'd best get back to work. I have a routine med check at twenty hundred hours, apparently. I wonder if Doc Faerin's free to stop by if we begin analysis on that chip of green-red stuff we have in the lab lock-up?" she added quietly, lest others were earwigging.

"You'll be lucky," Trisk informed her. "I have *my* med check at nineteen hundred, which successfully interferes with my plans for dinner and I'm sure I'm not the only one. So the doc'll have his hands full, as will most of the medbay staff on duty."

"I've not been told of mine yet," Linen grumbled. "Though I do have a flight sim programmed in for twenty thirty, so I'll be busy. But who does routine med checks on medbay personnel? Bet they'd find it easy to fiddle their own records."

"Lor' don't go opening that can of worms," Copper begged. "I'm sure Locksmith's got it covered in any case."

"*Lieutenant* Locksmith," Linen corrected her. "He ranks you."

"So does Trisk but I don't call him Lieutenant Addystone. Hell, I do need to mind my tongue, don't I?"

"Finish up and let's hit the trail. We have lots to keep us busy if the Doc can't spare us an hour," Linen advised. "You chat him up, Trisk: he's a good buddy of yours."

Trisk's chat-up was to no avail as the doctor was far too busy to take time out to assist in any analysis but suggested Medical Officer Amber Embertz as a substitute: her previous post had been aboard a long-range starship of the Fleet and she was more familiar than most with unusual materials. The doctor's face as he told them raised a suspicion in Copper, and her first question to Dr Embertz as she sailed through the lab door was to ask to which ship she had previously been assigned.

"Why do you want to know?" Embertz enquired, smiling.

"Wasn't the *Lithium Star* by any chance?" Copper asked.

"It was," admitted the doctor. "This post was a promotion and I jumped at it – as you would, the *Drake* being what she is."

"Yes, a new ship for *all* the crew," Copper noted, a quizzical look on her face. "And the best-equipped in the Fleet to boot, so let's get on with it."

The doctor was given a quick run-through of the finding of the organo-tech fragment and the readings that suggested that the patchy film coating it was biological in origin and potentially non-human, given internal structuring and gross composition. The sample in question was soon set up in a tri-dee sim station in the side lab and various probes and recorders activated to capture and extrapolate the data. As the physical features of the surface were enhanced, the arrangement of sub-elements caused some head-scratching by Embertz.

"There are characteristics here no human cell has ever had," she admitted. "It's as if these cells are more densely packed than your average mammalian type and there are surface constituents that are new to me – although they may be damage, or infection by parasitic factors."

"Have you seen anything similar before?" Copper asked. "I figured an organic tissue base but with some added tech, hence these inclusions here and here."

"I've not seen anything as clear as this, but on the first trawl of samples in labs aboard the *Lithium Star*, there were organic moieties that had the bio-specialists dancing up and down. But *they* didn't think to call in the medics to lend a hand; I only know because I got caught up in the discussion and went for a look-see. But we were recalled too quickly to go into it in any depth and I had my own duties."

"*I've* seen something similar," Trisk said into the subsequent pause. "Not in mammalian cells but in pollen-like grains. I'm sure these inclusions are close to what I found in the augmented grains I found in my samples during my first PhD over at Wells. There were features within the grains that weren't natural as far as I could tell," he explained to Embertz. "So I began to look into it, figured they'd been engineered somehow and went on to base my second PhD around them."

"And other things," Linen added dryly. "Including alien tech. But you reckon Cop's right, Doc? This stuff's cell-like and the remnants suggest some type of unknown but DNA-based tissue that's been altered by the addition of novel technology?"

"I wouldn't stake my reputation on it, but it seems a feasible explanation," the doctor said. "But if this was once living tissue, there's not enough left of it that you could work out what kind of being it was part of."

The advantage of being aboard the *Drake* was that the latest technologies as well as the latest databases, both military and civilian, were available. Despite these aids, the only records of organic remains logged as alien seemed to be those mentioned by the colonel as having being found by Military Intelligence on Mars. Even there the data was sparse, classified as restricted and with no tri-dee images available.

"Interesting that MI hasn't got a record of anything like this being found in the *Lithstar's* samples," was Linen's opinion.

"Maybe they weren't told," Copper said grimly. "There were leaks suspected, so if our chums Karben and Bilkitt *did* find out, they maybe didn't add it to their database lest nasty people had access. That kind of data would certainly set ears flapping and eyes popping in certain circles. I take it Military Intelligence was first on board when the *Lithium Star* docked at Lowell all those months ago, Doc?" she added to the medic.

Embertz was puzzled. "You seem to know a lot about the *Lithium Star*," she observed.

"We met the dazzling Lieutenant Commander Floris Fludge and his mate the slightly dimmer First Lieutenant Erkal Chokatti when they were in port for some top brass meeting about the finds," Linen grinned up at her. "We were out at Lowell Leisure Dome completing our flight quals at the time. And MI was certainly there."

"You're right we came into Lowell," admitted Embertz. "But I don't know about MI – as a humble medic, I had other things to do."

"Like look for a new berth," Copper put in. "But you reckon we can't go much further with this as it is, Doctor?"

"That's my opinion. I doubt you'd get better even if you had more of the sample, unless it was a sizeable chunk."

"Thanks for your help in any case," Trisk told her as she made to leave. "We'll report this to the colonel as soon as we've got the lot logged," he went on to his colleagues. "She wants an immediate update."

"Well at least we have medical confirmation that this is not human," Linen shrugged as the door closed. "What do we do now? Lock it up and look for more?"

"I'll see if we can use the new alien lifeform probe we've got under test on it," suggested Trisk. "But later: I have my routine med check soon and I want something to eat beforehand."

"Dr Embertz said that there were organic fragments that had the bio-specialists of the *Lithstar* dancing up and down in the first trawl of the samples they scraped up from that planetoid they found," Copper argued. "There may be more tubes with similar – we've only found one…"

"So?" queried Linen. "We only got a share of the *Lithstar's* tubes, so maybe we were just lucky with this one."

"Maybe," her friend conceded, "But there may be more in tubes we haven't analysed yet. How many are left?"

"Only two from the *Lithium Star*," confirmed Trisk. "They're still in the lab lock-up. Now we know what to look for, we can programme the parameters in and help ourselves a bit, unless you want to use the tri-dee and your special scanner."

"Not with security breathing down our necks I won't – but as the colonel hasn't *insisted* we get them back on board, we can maybe forget she said we were only to work with their support."

"Another thing," Linen put in. "The samples Trisk and I checked when you were in medbay: we did them thoroughly but did we miss anything that you and your scanner might find?"

"No," Copper said reassuringly. "I'm sure I would've picked up on it. I could run my hands over the tubes if it would make you feel better," she offered. "You're one damn good scientist, and so's Trisk. You're neither of you going to miss out on something important."

"Thanks for the vote of confidence, Lieutenant, ma'am. But just to humour me, *please* go over all the tubes again. If I *did* miss something big, the colonel will have my ears on a plate and my butt in the brig. You could always do a quick run over the final two *Lithstar* tubes as well, so we'll have some idea if there's a surprise waiting for us when we do the full whizz-bang on them morrow-sol."

* * *

Much later, and in some trepidation, Copper made her way to the assigned station in medbay for her appointment with Dr Faerin. She was not surprised to find Ms Moritz there. How the colonel had contrived *that* without arousing suspicion, Copper was not about to ask and greeted the two equably. Having spent the previous half hour in her own quarters calming herself down and making a positive link to Spook, she supposed she was as prepared as she would ever be to face whatever was planned. She did have something of a shock when the colonel announced that they were awaiting another member of staff and moments later Trisk Addystone strolled through the door.

"So that's your new probe," she greeted him sardonically, pointing to the carton slung over his shoulder. "Is there anyone else with an invitation to my private and confidential med exam that I should know about?"

"Belay that, Lieutenant, or you'll be examined in the brig," the colonel warned. "Set your equipment up, Doctor and let's get on with it. Is all the recording gear in place?"

"Yes, ma'am. Lieutenant Milkstone, you know the ropes for the usual medi-couch testing, so hop up and we'll start with that – I may as well have a current baseline."

Once the routine medical and psychological procedures were complete, Copper transferred to a diagnostic chair and prepared for the connection to Spook. The colonel and Trisk had been setting up their own apparatus as she had been busy with Faerin and she turned to find them fine-tuning a hologram of the ship's spec set out above a nearby console.

"Locational data," Trisk explained.

"I know."

Copper clamped her teeth together to stop herself saying more, aware that her tension was showing as irrational irritation, for she knew instinctively that Trisk had been able to pick up some clue to Spook's presence on his new probe. She drew a deep breath, settled into her chair and suddenly felt lighter, as if a mental load had been lifted from her. The feeling increased, until she was buoyed up in a cloud of tranquillity. She closed her

376

eyes, knowing that not only was Spook around, he was as close to her as he had ever felt.

"I'm getting a physical connection!" the surprised voice of Kynedd Faerin announced somewhere off her left ear.

"Confirmed," Trisk intoned.

"Can you hear me, Lieutenant Milkstone?" That was Colonel Moritz at her other side.

"Yup," was the somewhat dreamy response.

"*Yes ma'am*," corrected the colonel astringently. "You know what you're here for?"

"Yes ma'am: a thorough sweep of this ship, deck by deck, to determine hidden dangers in whatever form they take, including humanoid," she stated tranquilly, opening her eyes and gazing intently into the green ones of her commanding officer, which were examining her in some concern.

"Humanoid?" Trisk queried. "Strange choice of word…"

As her eyes slid to the side and towards the nearby console, it seemed to Copper that in her mind's eye she was a part of the holo of the *Drake* and knew every atom of her. Launching out from the bridge, she felt her consciousness spreading out like a translucent cloak, becoming thinner and more insubstantial as her perception stretched. The whole ship, from the sensor and weapons emplacements of the upper hull to the outermost skin beyond the lower engineering decks, was part of her being. The exec's office and personnel unit on level four, the observation deck spanning levels three and two, the secondary bridge on level one above the main deck… all were visible.

"Kynedd, is she all right?" That was the colonel, who was staring keenly at her junior officer, whose eyes had glazed over.

"Her readings are within normal parameters; in fact similar to those I logged when I was called into your office when she lost consciousness and you couldn't rouse her; but this time, she *is* conscious. I judge from her readings that she's able to maintain a link to this Spook of hers *and* communicate with us."

Faerin was correct and Copper was more than aware of what was going on around her, but she had other concerns. Despite her intuitive awareness of the vessel in its entirety, she knew that Spook, with his deeper understanding of human-kind restricted to her and the relatively few people with whom she had contact, had limits. He had a functional knowledge of the ship and had explored much of it, but the quest that was now required would test him. To Spook, this was an alien vessel and he could only search one section at a time.

"That's where you come in," the colonel told her when she voiced her disquiet. "Your Spook may be able to home in on substances and devices that shouldn't be there – he can use your extensive knowledge in that field – and you'll be able to use your own intuition on the human element."

"*If* they're on duty," Copper pointed out. "But anything alien to us and he may recognise it."

"I appreciate that. Go through the most populated parts of the ship first; leave docking and fighter bays, main engineering, stores and the like for now," Ms Moritz ordered. "You got me?"

"Aye ma'am," she responded, her nose twitching as she tried to refocus her thoughts.

After several minutes, over which she figured aloud the areas she and Spook between them had screened, she checked, rose and walked over to the holo projection, where the image had frozen on deck three close to the central security facility. To the watchers it seemed that a thorough scan was taking place as the holo homed in on the main security office, where virtually every visual aspect of ship's security could be examined via the banks of viewscreens around the bulkheads. They could not see what was happening but it was obvious that Copper could as she noted that the duty officer was furtively perusing an ents channel on a side monitor, although the chief's office was next door and overlooking the scene.

A comprehensive scan that left Copper exasperated brought nothing more to light and the search moved on through decks four and five and thus to the science facilities, with its auxiliary services located along the inboard sections. The difficulty with science sections six through nineteen was that much of the alien material brought aboard the *Drake* was housed there and was hence of interest to Spook. The colonel ordered the search curtailed on the basis that as Spook was there much of the time anyway, anything suspicious would have been picked up.

The doctor was primarily interested in the trawl through the main medbay services on deck six. The facility spanned sections eight through thirty and was base to a number of personnel as well as some of the most sophisticated equipment aboard. One anomaly that aroused Copper's concern was a secured store just outside Faerin's own office in the centre of his domain: it was unlocked and its alert light was blinking redly. As she reported the situation and pointed to the relevant position on the holo, she felt the sudden shift in tension within the room.

"It's the store the new probes are kept in and it's implant-coded to me and Trisk only," the doctor stated. "I take it you locked it when you took *that* one out and brought it here?"

"I did, it showed green. And I checked the other two: they were still in there and cased as we left them," Trisk confirmed. "No-one else was around at the time. But if someone broke in, why leave it unlocked when we'd be sure to see it?"

"They were disturbed or they wanted us to see it?" hazarded Faerin.

"The unit's been badly damaged," Copper informed them. "I don't see anything else and no-one's near there now."

"Just too late then," the colonel sighed. "Dammit. We go on if you're still fit. I'll have *that*, and that duty officer in security, checked later."

Despite the order to bypass the stores on deck eight, Copper felt a strange compulsion to linger by one entry, adjacent to the therapy salon. The latter was quiet, only a couple of crew having treatment at the hands of the resident technicians. But behind the sealed compartment, which could be entered from the salon itself, was something that was causing Spook unease. A familiar prickle began to slide up her arms as she struggled to decipher the jumbled imagery she was receiving from her alien sprite: whatever he was picking up, he had seen it before but whether it was alien or human, Copper could not tell. Suddenly, she jolted.

"Close to the piece of hull in bay four!" she hissed. "Those drones that were set to take us out! Were internal scanners ever configured to look for the materials that were part of them? And if so, were all ship's areas included in any searches? There's some link to that storage compartment there, I feel it."

She felt little more, for a wave of nausea overwhelmed her and she felt herself falling. The colonel and the doctor caught her between them and lowered her to the deck. She was out for only moments. It was Trisk who realised what had happened.

"Spook's gone," he said. "It must have been a sudden break of the physical and mental link."

Faerin verified the loss of contact and reported that Copper's physical parameters were returning to normal. His patient sat up groaning. As far as she could work out, Spook had had a sudden awareness of danger in close proximity and had shot off.

"Like what?" Trisk demanded.

"Like someone doing exactly what you're doing," she told him after a second or two. "Scanning for an alien lifeform."

"Whoever stole those probes was damn quick!" the colonel said angrily. "Unless there are similar detectors aboard we're not aware of. Enough for now, we've plenty to be going on with. I'll want a rundown on what you think you saw on deck eight. The therapy salon! Who would think to look there for subversive activity – if it exists," she added. "But for now, we head to your office, Doctor. I want to know what the hell's going on."

Faerin's office was a few sections further along and the four lost no time in heading there, the colonel calling Kit Locksmith to meet them. As Copper had noted earlier, the locked store outside had been breached, and with such force that it could not be reclosed. Both probes had gone. Copper immediately pulled out her small scanner and set it to monitor the surrounding area. Trisk meanwhile had set the probe he carried to detect similar instruments and was able to inform the colonel that one was operative in iso-bay six of the main medbay facility: they had in fact passed that room on the way in.

"You three stay back," the colonel warned, swiftly turning on her heel and colliding with the security chief, who had appeared at the entry. "Arm your weapon," she ordered him as she pulled out her own sidearm.

Copper hauled her own PPF from a thigh pocket, unlocking it quickly, but felt little alarm. Indeed there was no need, for iso-bay six was empty, apart from one of the missing probes, which had been activated and thrown on the couch. Locksmith quickly scanned the room but reported no evident tampering. Faerin was using his own authority to scan for intruders in the medbay facility as a whole, but could find no evidence of alerts in any of its sections or units.

"Not that it was likely," he grimaced. "Crew can come in at any time to the designated areas and most of the corridors are designated spaces."

"Missed again!" the colonel snapped angrily. "Whoever it is, they're one step ahead and probably realise we're on to them."

She stalked over to an information console, and after perusal of schematics of the surrounding deck areas, she instructed her security chief to get together a team of his most trusted aides, with orders that a covert raid on a specific section of medical stores on deck seven would go down at twenty three thirty. He was puzzled, especially when she informed him that she would be part of the team. Copper and Trisk swapped glances, drawing their own conclusions. They were summarily dismissed with the injunction that they keep silence on the doings of the past couple of hours.

* * *

The two science officers made their way to the mess, where a few off duty fellow crewmen were enjoying late snacks. Copper had a link awaiting her from Linen, who had finished her stint in training and was in her quarters. As she tabbed her wrist-comm shut, she pulled a face at her companion.

"She'll figure something's up," she noted. "She'll pester me."

"Too bad," Trisk commiserated. "We have to hold our hush until we're given the all-clear or until the whole ship knows what's gone down. But mind your tongue in here: I bet even the walls have ears."

"Or at least a couple of Kit Locksmith's hidden cams," was Copper's reply as she leaned her chin on her fist and drew a deep breath. "Lor' I'm tired. But..."

"But what?"

"Deck eight's above deck nine," she said softly, a frown creasing her forehead. "And deck nine's..."

"Mostly officer crew quarters," Trisk finished. He pondered for a moment. "But not only surveillance by a person or persons unknown might be possible... those drones that came from above us in bay four..."

Copper's eyes blazed as she took in the implications. "Frock, you have a point! How many more are planted in compartment overheads? The 'tween-decks run everywhere and auto-drones could be set to scout them. I only hope the ship's sensors have been reconfigured to sniff out every trace of that knock-out potion that was part of the ones that almost got us."

"We shouldn't be discussing this in here," he cautioned.

"Tell me about it. But here's Linen. Flight sims go okay?" she asked her redheaded friend.

"Middling," was the smiling response. "How was your med check? You were a while. Or were you up to no good down in medbay?"

"Mind your own business, nosey," Copper told her. "Grab a caff, we'll finish ours and then let's head in – I'm bushed."

"That must have been some med check. Ale didn't form part of it, did it?"

"I should've been so lucky. Get your caff."

Linen was shrewd and knew quite well that something had happened, but had the sense to talk of nothing but the mundane until the three were safely installed in Copper's billet. The latter deployed her privacy bug and to the surprise of the other two, set up a secure perimeter field, paying particular attention to the overhead area, and the side vents that provided air and links to power and other systems.

"You realise you're scaring me witless, Cop," announced Ms Lyrican as she helped herself to her friend's caff and cookie supplies. "What gives?"

"Can't tell you, we're under orders," Copper stated crisply. "No nagging. Trisk, check your comm-link and see if you have anything. Linen, forget the rations for now, I'm linking into my main system."

"Nothing here," Trisk declared. "You?"

"Ship's gone silent, no alerts," Copper noted. "But you two, get to your quarters and haul out the best you have in weapons and armour and then get back here: I have a nasty feeling some balloon is about to go up not a million clicks from here and I want to be prepared."

"Can I use your hygiene? You are *really* scaring the socks off me, Lieutenant, ma'am."

"Get on with it, Lyrican!"

"Aye, ma'am! You'd think she was in command of a frigging battle-boat," Linen added conversationally to Trisk as the two sped out of the door.

"*I* need to use the hygiene," Copper muttered to herself as she dug out a protective vest and slipped it over her shirt. "Now where the blazes are my spare power packs?"

The other two returned within a few minutes, both sporting defensive clothing. Trisk had a phase rifle.

"Where in hell did you get that?" Copper demanded.

"Stores, ages ago: I got it for training and nobody asked for it back, so I didn't return it."

"Fair enough."

"Cop, what *is* going on?" Linen demanded. "You two know something I don't and you're seriously worried. Is Spook here?"

"Yes, he came back. We can't tell you what we *think*'s going on – and we only suspect, we weren't told… but Spook reckons a whole lot more's in the wind and he's seriously alarmed."

"You think the colonel and the chief are in for a surprise?" Trisk demanded. "If so, they should be informed…"

"Which would no doubt inform anyone else with half an eye on them. The chief's no fool, he knows that whatever he's been told is only part of the truth, because the colonel suspects a leak in his department as well as elsewhere and can't risk letting slip what she's got planned. But that puts *her* at risk."

"So we step in. I wish you'd tell us before you set us up to be the heroes that ride in and save the sol," Trisk said indignantly. "Where are we off to on *our* midnight jaunt?"

"There's the door," Copper shot back equally hotly. "You don't want to come, go right on back to your little bed and listen out for the big bang."

"Shut up, the pair of you! Listen to yourselves!" Linen burst out. "Cop, for frock's sake, tell me what you know or think; it's a bit too late to be spouting orders and secrecy."

"Colonel's ordered a raid on some med stores on deck seven: they're above the therapy salon and its lockup and that's her real heading. There's a hatch and ladder going down close by. But I bet you anything that the station she used in medbay to visualise the schematics was checked after she left; so whoever's at back of some of the trouble aboard will be ready."

"So what do we do? We can't make a difference to a bunch of trained and armed security personnel even if they are headed into an ambush. I agree with Trisk, she should be warned."

Copper hesitated, warring notions in her own mind causing her some ambivalence. "Dammit! Okay, I'll make a short link to her private comm and cut it immediately… Milkstone to Moritz – you're headed into a trap, take care. Out."

"Well that was short and sweet. But if there's no trap, you'll be spending the next month in the brig," Linen warned.

"Cut it. I'm practically wetting myself and so's Spook."

"Where are *we* headed?" Trisk insisted.

"Down – deck ten. Spook's convinced there's trouble from that direction and it's linked to what the colonel's headed into."

"We are going to look *so* conspicuous walking the decks in our riot gear, even if it is late," said Linen.

"Spook's clearing the way," was the enigmatic rejoinder.

"Just what's our destination?" Trisk asked suspiciously.

"Armoury."

"I figured. Well, I've made my will, so let's get on with it."

The trio slid out of Copper's quarters and into the empty passageway beyond. She led them quickly to the closest ladder linking deck nine to deck ten, adjuring them to keep quiet. The main armoury of the *Drake* was some way along the deck, but as very few other active stations were housed in the area, the place was untenanted at that late hour.

"Fully arm your weapons," Copper ordered.

"Are you kidding? We could kill someone!" Linen hissed.

"That's what *they'll* do to you if you miss," she was told shortly. "They'll be more than protected – better than us, in fact. You stay behind me, both of you."

"How in hell do we get into the armoury? It's off limits and must be secured by energy fields or worse," Linen persisted.

"Shut up and let me think! I'm making this up as I go along!"

Copper was sweating: her input from Spook had moved into high gear and she could almost smell the danger into which she was leading her friends. She pulled them into a small alcove that housed a block of info stations and held up a hand for caution. Trisk hauled some tracing device from a pocket and after a swift examination of their immediate area, whispered harshly that he was picking up no life readings other than their own anywhere near or within the highly secured armoury just beyond.

"Then they're shielded," Copper responded in an undertone. "We wait here until the colonel's raid starts up top – that should be their signal for whatever they have planned. Spook reckons there's at least three of them…"

The minutes ticked by as nothing happened. Copper's every sense was striving to understand what was going on through the bulkhead that separated them from the armoury but there was some blockage that even Spook found hard to penetrate. Linen pursed her lips in enquiry as zero hour closed in, her hand-gun raised, and Copper realised in a flash what was about to happen.

"We go now!" she hissed, slipping out to the passageway and towards the armoury door. "Blast it open!" she ordered Trisk.

He wasted no time, his phase rifle making short work of the locks and seals. The place was lit but apparently empty, racks of small weapons behind tamper-proof plas-glazing glinting dully from the walls, and cases of larger arms lining the bulkheads. As Copper hurled herself into the shadow of the nearest cabinet, a small skitter of sound from the edge of a detached unit beyond them caused her extra-attuned ears to prick and she felt herself being physically pushed sideways. A beam of light shot towards her and caught the glazing of the cabinet, causing it to shatter in a cascade of crystalline fragments. Figuring the situation at once, she rained fire at the spot from which the shot had come. Three hazy outlines flickered like translucent holos, two more streaks of energy crossed the space between them and she heard Linen scream as her own protective vest took a searing hit and she was flung backwards.

"Take them down!" she yelled, crawling back up. "Armoured chameleon suits!"

She ducked behind the arms case to slot another energy cap into her firearm, rolling out across the floor a second later and firing blind. As their three opponents went down shooting, their suits flickering as their chameleon capacity was lost, she was on her feet and heading for them, Trisk's warning shout ignored. Her right boot met the faceplate of the first rogue she reached and she kicked until the full-faced helmet he was wearing came away. As Trisk, at her back, stamped on the hand of a second who was reaching for an abandoned weapon, she repeated the manoeuvre on the next, releasing the helmet catch.

"Put them to sleep!" she ordered her white-faced friend as she pulled the third helmet off and kicked a couple of beam weapons out of harm's way.

"Too late!" her target spat, stabbing upwards with a small blade he had flicked from somewhere, just before a bolt from Trisk's gun rendered him unconscious.

Copper spun, scouring the cases around her for what she instinctively knew she would find. A blue winking light gave her the clue and she raced for a grey armoured box attached to one of the silos that housed the small torpedoes that were standard issue for armed shuttlecraft. Fear gave her hands speed as well as dexterity and she tore the primitive energy housing apart to remove the primer for the explosive device that had been set to blow the silo. She smashed the timer and pulled out every attachment she could see to make certain the thing was dead.

"Don't see anything else like that and nothing's showing on my scanner. Linen swears she's okay, a phase-beam graze to her arm," Trisk reported shakily.

"Are *you* okay?" Copper demanded as she straightened up and looked at him.

"Yup. Here comes back-up: Tawny and her troops."

Lieutenant Tawny Brown was accompanied by five guards, two of whom she ordered to check out the suited individuals on the deck and the others the surroundings.

"How the blazes did you three get here and how did you figure?" the security officer demanded.

"Later," Copper replied sharply. "I want to see Linen – and I want a look at *them.*"

An expletive from one of Tawny's squad caused them all to turn. "Spokes! Fergalla Spokes!"

"You what! One of us!" hissed Brown.

"One of your moles," Copper said evenly, looking down at the three unresponsive faces. "Make sure you completely disarm the bastards."

She made her way over to the entry, Brown at her heels, to find Linen, who was clutching her arm and trying to look blasé.

"Hurts like hell but I'll live," the redhead replied to Copper's concern. "How did security work it out?"

"No idea, but I bet the colonel had a hand in it. We'll no

doubt find out at the debriefing that we'll all have to attend before this sol's over."

"Isn't this sol already over and it's morrow-sol now?"

"I'm heading to medbay with Lieutenant Lyrican," Copper informed Tawny Brown crisply as she slipped a supportive arm around her injured friend's back. "Let them know we're on our way. I'll leave you this mess to clear up. You're with me, Trisk."

"Aye ma'am," he replied, his usual grin reasserting itself as he winked at Brown, whose eyes widened at the tone. "I'll retrieve our weapons."

"I was worried I'd killed somebody," Trisk confided as the trio made their way swiftly to the nearest elevator. "Those suits must be near impenetrable. What the hell are they and how did you work it out?"

"Later. We get Linen fixed up and then we get the doc to prescribe a restorative."

"Double scotch for me," Trisk told her as they marched their friend along the passageway and into the medical facility.

Faerin was still on duty and medbay was close to chaos. He was assessing those coming in and barking out orders to his harassed staff. He halted long enough to inspect Linen's injury and told them that although no general alerts had been sounded on the colonel's orders, five targeted attacks over and above the response to the planned raid had gone down across the ship in the space of the past hour and he and his people were picking up the pieces. Colonel Moritz herself was not there but word was that more casualties were on the way in from decks eight and ten and engineering had been particularly badly hit.

"Ten would be ours, there's three more wounded and they'll need to be locked in iso-bays and kept under guard," Copper informed him. "Bastards! Synchronised attacks to tie up security and compromise the colonel's raid on the deck seven stores, I'll bet. Look, Doc, you've got enough going on here. I've got my General Health Qualification: just point me to a work space and tell me where I can get a primary assist kit or similar and I'll deal with Lieutenant Lyrican. You can send in any minor injuries once she's patched up. I'll log everything and Trisk will assist."

"I'll take every pair of trained hands I can get. Use that bay behind the screen over there: everything you need should be in the cabinets. You need advice or additional meds, ask one of the nurse techs at the dispensary station out front, I'll clear it."

"Aye sir. Trisk, you're with me. Stow our gear in a safe place and get your hands under the steri-wash."

"Aye, aye, ma'am!"

Copper was cautious enough to call up options for treatment of phase-burn on the medi-comp attached to the station at her post and began, ordering Trisk to find the appropriate sprays and delivery hypos. Linen bore her handling stoically, uttering no more that the odd expletive. She was soon comfortable, a soothing compress encircling her upper arm and a med-patch delivering pain relief, but refused to be packed off to her billet, deciding instead to observe.

To Copper's amusement, but not to his, her next patient was Ash Goff, who had been with a friend in one of the sports kit storage areas on deck twelve, checking out his racing buggy. An explosion in a store close by had taken out part of the bulkhead and he had been blown off his feet and hit by a shard of flak. The friend had towed him into medbay. Goff was livid that he had been passed on to Copper rather than a nurse tech, but was sufficiently shocked by his experience that he submitted to her ministrations. His leg wound cleaned and sealed, he was advised to rest and ordered out.

After another three cases of minor cuts and burns had been dealt with, a pause in traffic led Trisk to suggest a short break for a caff before more came in. He made for the edge of the screen that gave their station some privacy to check on the seats outside, returning hurriedly with a quirky look on his face.

"One more," he announced. "This way, ma'am."

"You three never cease to amaze me," was all Colonel Moritz said as she stepped behind the partition.

One appraising glance told Copper that their commanding officer had seen some action: her face was covered in cuts, her protective armour was scored in a dozen places and much of her uniform was tattered. What appeared to be a phase-weapon burn had sliced through her upper left arm, and it was bleeding.

"Ma'am, you need more than primary assist," she told her. "Trisk, get a medic in here pronto."

"Belay that, Lieutenant Addystone. The medics have enough

to do. I'm sure *your* skills are sufficient, Lieutenant Milkstone, you've assisted in dangerous situations before."

"Hardly at this scale," Copper was impelled to point out as she hauled out a whole-body medi-scanner. "I'll get this plate-armour off first, ma'am, and see what's underneath. Trisk, get a pain hypo set. You're not allergic to any meds, ma'am? I don't have access to your med-records."

Once the officer had been scanned and Copper was assured that there were no underlying complications, she administered the hypo and began on the burn to the upper arm. It was at this point that Dr Faerin stuck his head round the screen.

"Getting on all right, Lieutenant?" he enquired.

"Fine. If you're free, Doc, a check on what I've done would be appreciated."

"I'm putting you in for advanced GHQ training," he told her as he examined her work. "It'll be useful on away missions. I called by to update you, Elle," he added to the colonel. "We've accounted for all the casualties: nine with serious but not life-threatening injuries, twelve that will need to spend some time in here and the rest are walking wounded. Locksmith's directing his troops in person: he's refused to keep off his fractured leg but he'll do okay."

"How many in confinement under guard?"

"Seven: three from the armoury, another three from your party on deck eight and one from the big bang in engineering. Chief Locksmith reckons the other incidents were set to go off automatically but he's not discounting the idea that there may be more loose mischief-makers with their fingers on buttons," said Faerin. "The worst hurt would be the three from the armoury. One has a fractured skull from a heavy blow."

"That was mine: I kicked his helmet off," admitted Copper as she continued to seal the cuts on the colonel's face with her steri-closure gun. "In fact, I kicked two helmets off; the second one must have had a thick skull."

"I'd like to see the secure-cam footage of exactly what went down in the armoury," the doctor disclosed.

"Doubt you will: those bastards probably fixed the cams."

"Maybe not, Cop," Linen put in. "They were invisible, the cams wouldn't have picked them up, surely."

"They would," Trisk contradicted. "Motion sensors would have worked out there were intruders even if they'd knocked out the outside sensors."

"Please can we discuss this later," Copper said tiredly. "Once you're patched up to the doctor's satisfaction, ma'am, I vote we adjourn to his office and have a small refreshment. That bottle of scotch you let Trisk hide in our office for Doc Inkscree's bots to find would do, Doc," she added mischievously.

"I'm keeping that to toast your promotion," he told her. "Or your incarceration in the brig, whichever comes first."

"This ship doesn't run on votes, Lieutenant Milkstone, and don't you forget it," Colonel Moritz reminded her. "However, suggestions I listen to. You four head to the doctor's office. No argument, Kynedd, you have a very capable second. I'll join you once I've checked up on all my people in here and had a word with Chief Locksmith."

"You also have a very competent second, Elle," was the doctor's wry response.

"Who's on the bridge on duty," she said, slipping off the couch. "Dismissed."

17: MYSTERIES

The bottle unwrapped by Kynedd Faerin was not his treasured very old scotch, but it made a reasonable substitute and he and the three science officers whiled away the time by an exchange of information on what they had pieced together of the latest incidents. As well as the armoury, there had been attacks on an auxiliary drive unit in main engineering, an energy pack store on deck twelve, one of the hull weapons emplacements and in two of the fighter bays. There had been no casualties from the latter as emergency containment systems had immediately locked in, but the damage was extensive and would require refit. As for the raid by security on decks seven and eight, all Faerin knew via Kit Locksmith was that the hatch to the ladder between the two decks at the point of operation had been booby-trapped, but the trap had caught out one of the guilty parties.

The colonel was able to further enlighten them when she walked in later. She had changed her original plan for the raid by security and had made for her target via deck nine ten minutes early, sending a second team to deck seven with orders to block escape routes but not to engage otherwise. The one infiltrator on watch at the therapy store entry had had no time to sound a warning to her fellows but her weapons fire alerted them and they blew the charges they had planted at the hatch to prevent the ladder's use by security. They had tried to run but one had been caught in the blast and the other wounded. All three had been prepared to fight their way out: the upshot was a number of injured security personnel and another crewman who had got in the way.

"So they knew what you'd planned and they knew when, ma'am," Copper mused. "What I don't get is why they risked what they did: they *must* have known they wouldn't get away with it, even if they'd managed to surprise you."

"They know they have friends in high places, maybe?" Linen suggested. "Send them off for trial and suddenly they disappear, like Jecks did not long after he was pulled in the first time."

"Some very high-tech sponsors," was Trisk's contribution. "Those armoured chameleon suits: I've never seen anything like them before, they blended completely into the background and my scanner didn't pick them up. Lucky your Spook did. How in blazes did you know where to shoot?" he asked Copper.

"Instinct," she said. "I'm fond of my skin and I'd like to keep it in one piece."

"I want to hear the whole story," Colonel Moritz demanded.

Once she had been briefed on the action in the armoury, she let them know that preliminary sweeps of the deck twelve area, the weapons emplacement on the hull and the fighter bays had indicated that drones similar to those used in the outer bay four attack had been used. The newly-instigated regular scans by internal ship's sensors had not picked them up, so they had either been well-shielded or they had been very recently planted.

"But why all this trouble all the way out here?" demanded Linen. "What could they – whoever they are – gain?"

"Preventing or delaying the ship reaching her destination and carrying out her mission would help any less than honest outfits out here in getting first dibs on whatever's going," explained Copper. "And will sow seeds of dissention back home if word gets out. It's one of the oldest tricks in the book. There's a lot of taxpayers' credit locked up in Mars Fleet and the launch of a new wave of ships of the *Drake's* class won't be popular in a lot of places. This type of incident will be hailed as a failure of Mars Gov to organise anything for the protection of Mars."

"Ever thought of going into politics?" Faerin queried as he topped up her glass.

"Hell no, I'd shoot first to prevent them asking questions," was the retort. "But as for those attack-drones: we should get *our* engineering techs to produce a set of auto-drones and send them through all the 'tween-deck spaces to hunt out any strays that ship's sensors haven't found. If Mr Locksmith hasn't got a set in his back pocket already."

"I'll bear it in mind," the colonel said dryly. "Good work, all of you."

"One thing," Linen queried. "The therapy salon: was one or more of the bad guys you caught part of that team, ma'am? I wouldn't like to think that someone who'd had their hands in my hair had the same hands in some very nasty muck."

"That's confidential at present, Lieutenant. As is everything we've discussed here and all that's happened over the past few hours, and you *will* keep it so. We've all had a long sol. Back to your quarters and get some sack time. You'll all be on duty for your next scheduled shift."

Taking that as a dismissal, the three science officers drank up, thanked the doctor for his hospitality, nodded formally to their seniors and made for the door.

"Lor', how to plant a mole in security," Linen said softly as the trio gained deck nine and their own section. "Have several at different times: any mole masquerading as a therapist could bug a crewmember and remove the bug when he or she next came in for a treatment. How in hell would they know?"

"How would anyone be so dim?" Copper returned.

"Ranking pips," was the rejoinder. "It worked on Admiral Stannum, didn't it?"

"You got me. Come on in for a choc, you two; I need one."

* * *

The following sol brought a host of rumours wafting around the mess on deck four. A hobbling Ash Goff stopped by to pry a few facts out of Copper and Linen, who were eating breakfast quietly in a corner. Given short shrift, he set off with pursed lips to annoy someone else.

"It'll be round the ship that you were in medbay in the early hours wearing armour and toting a hypo," Linen grinned.

"I'd taken my protective vest *and* my jacket off!"

"Yes and they were sitting on a chair with our guns and you were in a burnt and torn undershirt flecked with blood – which wasn't yours, I take it? Or was it? Copper Milkstone, are trying to tell me you were injured and you didn't let on?"

"Only a few scratches and they didn't hurt at the time: lucky for us those thugs weren't toting more than regular phase rifles. But keep your voice down, people are earwigging."

"Let them. We did good."

"And we'll be up on report if we're caught boasting about it in the mess or anywhere else. Here's Trisk looking chipper."

"All set for the last two *Lithstar* tubes?" their colleague asked genially, setting his tray on the table. "We'll have plenty of time for analysis now we're en route to Jupiter Station and a longer stopover than planned."

"How d'you know that?" Linen demanded.

"Met Oaky Grimsson on the way up and we traded a secret to two: engineering's in for a bunch of repair and refit. At least Fleet's *got* the supply-station off Europa: as Jupiter Station has a high civilian population, most of their outfits will have first dibs on stores that their own syndicates have shipped in. According to Oaky, Fleet HQ's sending out repair drones and supplies for us, including something very special, via high-speed auto-ship. She's on her way even as we speak. I heard that Colonel Moritz was up all night scorching several ears on a supra-light link to the high and mighty."

"The joys of interplanetary! And how long will we have to hang off Jupiter before refit's done?" Copper sniffed. "And what's this very special cargo? Who's supplying it and the repair drones? The biohazard labs on Vastitas Borealis between Fleet HQ and Korolev?"

"You've got a suspicious mind," Linen informed her friend. "But Arcadia Station controls Fleet supplies, so final packing's done there and will be up to speed. But there's Kit Locksmith looking like death warmed up and limping. Bet he didn't get much sleep either," she went on as the security chief waved over on his way to collect his rations.

"Maybe he'll stop by and reanimate the gossip about you and him," Trisk laughed. "It's gone a bit quiet on that front."

"*His* eyes are set elsewhere and he's got better things to do at the moment, as do we: back to the labs, people. The quicker we get the *Lithstar* analyses done, the quicker we get back to other things like our PhD research. I've almost forgotten what we're supposed to be doing. You could lend us a hand there, Trisk: you're more experienced than anyone we know in that respect. In fact, I've just had a terrific idea," Linen beamed, her eyes wide, as she shoved her tray into the clearing hatch.

"Brilliant!" Copper enthused. "Would Thars go for it?"

"Are you reading my mind again? Go on, what was I about to say?"

"That Trisk would be the perfect external examiner for our PhD theses: he's got three for a start, two of which are Lowell; he's worked out at the Amber Warren site; he's here, he's smart, with impeccable security credentials and loads of publications to his credit; and, he's an all-round nice guy."

Linen sighed in exasperation. "That about covers it."

"And I agree with every word," Trisk twinkled. "But I'm one of your best buddies, which would invalidate all the rest: bias and all that."

"You wouldn't be biased," Linen disputed. "You're far too honest for that. We could suggest it to Thars when we link the next report. Ossy Inkscree could stand in as second external."

"Desperate to be doctored?" Trisk questioned roguishly.

"We've done enough hard labour and produced more than plenty reports to warrant two PhDs each," he was told. "And we've published two Mars-shattering papers *and* presented our work at a couple of high-profile conferences to boot."

"I'd be honoured," Trisk announced with an impish wink as they all rose. "But for now, we've *other* jobs on hand."

* * *

Their lab was empty and as they had left it. Copper had the previous sol, at Linen's request, quickly gone over the samples that her two friends had examined without her input. She had sensed nothing doubtful but had been a little hesitant to handle one of the remaining two tubes, leading her friends to surmise that something interesting might turn up. Eschewing the use of the alien scanner, the three rapidly but thoroughly ran over the first of the containers. While hard at work they wondered if they might have a visit from the colonel, but no-one disturbed the tenor of the morning. The ship was at yellow alert, the doings of the previous sol warranting such a heightened security status, and their crewmates were no doubt all warily wondering what would happen next.

"All done!" Linen announced finally. "I vote we break for an early lunch before we start on the last one: I need refuelling if nobody else does. We're still at yellow, so we don't have to hang here. Let's get on up to the mess and see who's about."

Very few were about the mess but Tawny Brown sat down with them and let them know that all had been quiet since the arrests of the early hours. The colonel and Kit Locksmith were eager to jettison their apprehended felons and had planned to offload them at Jupiter Station, although the place had no long-term detention facility. The mid-range cruiser *MSS Swordfish* was on her way in from a mapping and safety mission, however, and they were hoping to transfer the prisoners to her and have them transported to Mars for trial.

"Saving the brig for Copper," Linen surmised. "You must have violated half a dozen regs by organising a raid, breaking into the armoury and shooting down your fellow crewmen."

Her reward was a slap on the head from her friend and the advice from Tawny that she had better keep her voice down, as those not directly involved in the fracas were to be kept in the dark as far as possible. The four included Ash Goff amongst those to be kept ignorant despite his link with the troubles, and when he hove to for a gossip Linen denied his request for more information on the basis that he was still too lightheaded to understand plain language.

"Who dislocated *your* funny bone?" she enquired with a lift of her eyebrow as he gave vent to his displeasure by a tirade of personal abuse directed at Copper and her treatment of him. "If you want to sue him, we'll be your witnesses," she added to her friend as Lieutenant Goff stalked off.

"He must have a crush on you," Linen declared. "He keeps coming back for more even though you've choked him off so often. Of course, after your promotion, you'll rank him, so he'll not be able to point his forked tongue in your direction."

"Promotion? What promotion?" Brown demanded.

"She's pulling you chain – and mine," Copper sighed wearily.

"Come on," the redhead continued jauntily. "Colonel Moritz will *have* to promote you once she lifts this embargo on what can and can't be leaked. After word gets round of your brave actions in defence of ship and crew, she won't be able to do much else. Goff's probably already plotting to dine out on what *he* knows."

"Can it, Lieutenant. Back to work, both of you. Our analyses won't do itself and the aforementioned colonel wants updates on a regular basis, remember?"

"Aye, aye ma'am."

Copper rolled her eyes heavenward and gave up.

* * *

Trisk hauled out the final sample tube from the *Lithium Star* and placed it carefully on the task desk to allow Copper to run gloved hands over it before a scan of the whole was attempted.

"There are scratch marks here," she noted, "And there's dirt embedded. I know the *Lithstar* was recalled urgently and was in a hurry to get back to Mars but you'd think they'd have cleaned this up before they stacked it in their hold, or the teams back at Fleet HQ would have given it a wipe before they ran tests. I'll get a scrape from it and we can check it: Spook's in a tizz."

"Bio-traces we have," Trisk announced as he glanced at the output from various instruments. "I'll pull up the data from our bio-coated flake of red-green stuff and run comparatives: I think there are similarities."

The tiny amounts of matter extracted from the surface scores of the tube provided little evidence that the organic residues within it were comparable to the bio-matter coating the material from the earlier sample and Copper sighed in exasperation.

"Inconclusive: as far as I can tell it might as well be bits of some jarhead's lunch. Let's sort through the stuff in the tube a speck at a time: I don't think we've run out of surprises yet."

One surprise turned up an hour or so later when a chunk about the size and shape of a thumb rolled out of the tube and into the analysis tray. Linen's remark that it maybe was a thumb was met with a sharp reprimand and the command to reset the probes for analysis. Trisk had already extracted his MEDIC and was inspecting the piece.

"The organo-tech that we know can self-replicate, but with inclusions of *our* tech: just like the stuff filling out that area of deep scoring in the tube we looked at down in the tri-dee sim suite with Doc Faerin. But there's more – we have remnants not a hair's breadth off that bio-coating we found on our little flake of red-green stuff. The data's stored in my MEDIC: it's reading as tech-enhanced DNA-based material, in other words what we're assuming is some type of organic tissue, and more than we had before, by the look of it."

"So it might very well be a thumb," Linen sniffed. "Maybe

it's one of Spook's cousins?"

"Very funny. But Spook's still here and he *is* quite excited, though I can't quite work out why."

"He's not scared, is he?" Linen asked.

"Not that I'm aware of. Why?"

"So it's likely to be the remains of a friend rather than a foe — if it *is* the remains of something that once could caper about. But if it is, it may be that the *Lithstar* did pick up a hitchhiker, only this is all that's left of it."

"To extend this bizarre conversation," Trisk cut in. "If this *is* a remnant of the organic part of an alien being like your Spook, maybe the incorporeal part is still aboard the *Lithium Star*, if it *was* capable of separation from its organic self, like Spook."

"We should check in with the sour-faced Lieutenant Blazells and see if he's got a disembodied alien friend," suggested Linen. "Bet he won't have many others."

"Behave yourself," Copper scolded crossly. "We'd best get all we can from this, check the rest of the tube, and then update the colonel on what we've found, but not on what in a different universe might be the case. We can leave a link as she'll be up to her ears: we're still at yellow alert though it's been mighty quiet outside. I'll get the alien scanner on this lot. It'll take a bit more time, but I can handle it now without a medic breathing down my neck."

"Trust me, I'll still be breathing down your neck," warned Trisk. "The colonel will have my butt in a sling if I don't — I'm still your superior officer."

"For the moment, First Lieutenant Trisk, sir," Linen laughed. "But we'd better lock ourselves in, in case we have intruders that will wonder what in blazes is going on."

* * *

"Maybe its self-repair mechanism's developed a fault," Linen stated calmly. "It maybe needs an overhaul."

"It's not the only one — my self-repair mechanism could do with an overhaul," Copper groaned as she rubbed her neck.

The alien scanner had snapped off, its tri-dee projection gone so suddenly that they had all jumped, but a small collection of tiny fragments of what Trisk figured was DNA-based material fused with alien technology had been found.

Dr Addystone had been eyeing his friend critically and noted that her eyes were tired and she winced as she moved. "D'you know what I think?" he asked. "I think that the scanner is now so bonded to you that it knows when you've had enough and shuts down. Or your Spook's aware of how exhausted you are and has frozen it. In any case, I'm calling a halt. You've had enough. Linen and I will finish this tube and you can sit and supervise. Then we're off duty, whatever happens. There's been nary a word on current status over ship-wide comms, so I guess all the trouble is being cleared up on the QT and we all hang fire until we know what's happened."

"Done and done," Copper agreed wearily. "I'm bushed."

"I can tell," Linen said sternly. "We'll be paying medbay a visit as soon as we've done. You're still hurting from last night and I want one of the medics to look you over."

"Who made you my guardian angel?"

"I did, years ago when first we met at Lowell. Goes with the territory, kiddo, get used to it. It's what friends are for."

"Thanks. But just get on with all this. The sooner I see my dinner plate, the better-tempered I'll be."

The other two set to with a will and soon had the remaining contents of the tube fine-screened and analysed. Nothing novel was found, to their shared relief, and the whole was wrapped up, safely coded and stashed with its fellows. The extracted scraps were placed in sample cartridges and stacked in the lab's high security storage locker. Copper had busied herself with collating the information to be passed on to the colonel as briefly as possible and soon had the relevant link copy ready.

"That's that," she announced finally. "Dinnertime!"

"Medbay time," Linen corrected. "You come quietly or Trisk and I'll carry you. Your call."

Medbay was rather calmer than at their last visit. Copper's case was articulated at the reception point but Faerin must have been checking incoming, for he appeared just moments later from a side bay demanding to know what the hell had happened now. He was furious over her lapse in reporting her injuries the previous sol and speedily hauled her in for examination. He was even more irate when he saw the extent of the bruising caused by the hit her protective vest had taken and by a cut to her upper arm where the knife of her last adversary had bitten deeply and she had done no more than slap on a therapeutic dressing. He cleansed the injured areas, applied supportive med-patches to the bruising and sealed the cut, in the interim giving vent to his irritation about patients who thought they knew better than he did.

"You ignore injuries like these, you end up giving me more trouble in the long-run," he snapped. "It'll be recorded in your med-file and sent up to personnel – so Captain Helmis will be on your back, as he's the exec. And maybe the colonel as well, as you didn't mention *this* in the account you gave her of what happened."

"This is the thanks I get for helping out," she said resignedly to her friends. "Maybe next time I won't."

"Blackmail doesn't work with me," the doctor said. "There, you'll hold together for now. Get off my couch and go get your dinner. I'll send you a check-up link, which you will *not* ignore."

"Aye, sir," Copper sighed as she complied, hauling on her undershirt and jacket. "Now for the mess: I'm famished."

"You and me both," Linen sighed as they marched out. "The rest of *this* sol we chill: it's back to routine morrow-sol."

"Check your link, Ms Lyrican," Faerin called after her. "You have a med check at eleven hundred tomorrow."

"Lor', I thought you'd given up on those!"

"Dream on," was the retort. "Just be there."

The trio found the mess a little more populous than they had earlier and judging by the number of stares and the rising hum of conversation as they entered, news had percolated through.

"Shit!" Copper groaned as someone began a slow handclap that rose to crescendo. "Just ignore it and get our chow."

"What happened to the ban on gossip-spreading?" Linen wanted to know.

"You can't keep a good crew down," Trisk enlightened her. "Look out for the inquisitives that want the gory details."

The first of these was one of the galley crew, but he was choked off thoroughly by Kit Locksmith, who was ahead of the three in the queue and still looking exhausted.

"You look like hell, Chief," Linen apprised him. "Not had a break, apart from the leg?"

"Very funny, but no, though you three look energetic enough after all the kerfuffle you took part in. Just done your shifts?"

"Not exactly," Linen told him, flicking a glance at Copper. "Had another chore. We'll let you in on it if you'll join us for dinner."

Locksmith's eyes lit fractionally and he agreed with a smile. Linen *did* let him in on it, to Copper's irritation, but her friend's real reason for the invitation was to find out how much more the chief knew than they did. He was far from deceived but was sufficiently sanguine to know that they would find out anyway, and once the noise had died down and the four had captured a table, he opened up. The colonel had been granted approval to transfer all the prisoners to the *MSS Swordfish* at Jupiter Station: a prison ship would rendezvous with the *Swordfish* to pick them up for transport to Mars. The *Drake* herself would resupply at Europa and ship out as soon as all her repairs were complete. Most of the bad eggs had been routed out and life should be quieter from here on in was Locksmith's opinion, but Copper's idea of sending auto-drones through the 'tween-decks to hunt out stray rogue drones or other malevolent devices was under discussion – the chief *had* heard of such hunt-and-intercept gear but the *Drake* did not come with a ready supply.

"Link to Magenta Firewall supra-light," Copper advised him. "She could probably send you a set of blueprints by return."

"Or you could assign Ossy Inkscree's surf-sci bots to carry out a search and destroy mission," Linen recommended lightly. "I bet they can be reprogrammed to do that."

"You'd have to reprogramme Dr Inkscree first," Copper told her. "He'd never agree – they're for our mission after all," she added more quietly. "And *I* want them for a look-see through that chunk of whatsit in bay four."

"Which is *still* out of bounds," Locksmith told her, his blue eyes searching hers. "Repair crews are working flat out to fix as much damage as they can, but until we're shipshape, certain areas are under restriction: the hits we took were quite bad."

"*That* you don't want to spread around," Copper warned with a slight shake of her head. "Crew's jumpy enough as it is."

"Yes, but they know *you're* here to jump in and save their butts if things get too bad," Linen grinned at her.

"Stow it, Lieutenant Smartarse. Go fetch me a dessert, I'm still hungry."

"No you're not, you're just grumpy. Serves you right for not letting on about your injuries. At least the chief *let* the doc fix him up before he ignored orders to keep off the leg."

"I'll get us all something sweet," Trisk cut in. "*You* certainly need it," he notified Copper.

He returned with their orders and the news that the luxury goods he had coerced out of the galley crew would not be charged to mess bills. They all had celebrity status, apparently, which amused Trisk no end. As he doled out the confections, he invited Locksmith to spill more beans but was summarily told to check ship's current status. Trisk did so immediately, using the table's info-point, and found that as well as the outer bays most of engineering was closed to all but relevant personnel and parts of decks seven and eight were also off-limits. All departments were to have their logs secure-coded afresh and new security systems were already being put in place. *Those* were classified but there should be no overt changes to the sol-to-sol running of the ship.

"How many villains *are* being shipped out?" Copper asked.

"Eleven to date, but the ones we have may be persuaded to name any associates," Kit Locksmith answered her wearily. "Or the locations of stashes of auto-drones and other gear – like your missing probe," he shot at Trisk. "I have a couple of my people and one of the ship's psychologists on it, but I'm down quite a few and we're stretched; so are other departments, so we might be assigned more crew from the *Swordfish* or from Jupiter or Europa stations, but I don't think the colonel's keen."

"Don't blame her," Linen put in. "You never know who we might be landed with. And surely we've enough crew to reassign some to other areas as and when needed? What do our fighter pilots do when they're not training or flying for example?"

"Man auxiliary stations and keep their craft and their bays in trim. And for now they're on repair detail, helping the repair crews wherever they're needed. But to repair, you need materials and those we don't have an excess of. But I'll have to hit the trail; I still have one or two things to finish up."

"Need a hand?" Linen asked brightly.

"No thanks: given the trouble that follows you three around, I'll take my chances on my own."

* * *

Copper's first task the following sol was to test her bonded scanner to check if it was operational; she found that the device had returned to normal and was inclined to agree with Trisk that it had sensed her exhaustion and cut out – not a useful attribute in a tight corner, she observed to her friends, but she was sure there must be some method of overriding it. However, as the tri-dee facility in main engineering was off-limits, the device was the most efficient way of analysing the small sample collection from the *Wayfinder* and the three agreed that it was their priority task: the PhD research that Copper and Linen were supposed to be carrying out would have to hang fire a little longer.

Very little had been heard from Thars Amberline or MDMC about their Mars-based research, leaving them to surmise that the professor had his hands full. They knew that Jenika Grass-Tephra and Maressan Chengi had been appointed as the new PhD students at their erstwhile site, but nothing more. Even the normally effusive Thulia Numbridge had not taken the trouble to assault their senses with a standard link, although her name had been included in a short request from Wolff Waterbone to Linen that some communication would be welcome.

The sample cartridges holding pieces that had been found by the *Wayfinder* on her collision-reduction mapping cruise were small but the contents had the advantage of being the results of previous sifting and analysis by military scientists; they therefore comprised fair amounts of the reddish-green alien material that was by now familiar to the three scientists. The *Drake* had been granted custody of the samples as reference materials for any similar that might be recovered during her current mission.

Linen looked critically at the four units that Trisk had hunted out from the secure store in their lab. "You could walk out of here with those in your pocket and no-one would be any the wiser," she noted.

"Wrong," Trisk told her. "They have secure-tags that would alert the chief SO to their whereabouts, and believe me, Ossy Inkscree would not be impressed if you headed for somewhere that wasn't strictly within bounds. But we know more or less what's in them, so hopefully we won't have any surprises."

"Want to bet?" sniffed Copper. "This is us, remember: the universe has always got surprises up its sleeves for us, or hadn't you noticed?"

"Point taken. But we can spread these out on the analysis tray one cartridge at a time and we should be able to see pretty clearly what we have. You got your scanner, Copper?"

"Aye, sir. Let's get at the first one."

The first packet contained fragments typical of the alien tech with self-replicative capacity, but also one sizeable shard lacking that ability, the like of which neither Copper nor Linen had seen before. It was paler in colour than the other pieces and the two wondered if it could have come from a ship's interior. Trisk told them that similar material had been recovered on Mars but in very small quantities; *he* had come to the conclusion that it was quite rare and the repairable substance was more likely to make up the bulk of alien ships.

Copper wrinkled her brow, concentrating. "I've got an idea," she announced. "Separate out that larger pale piece and let me at it with this thing…"

As she directed her scanner over the fragment that Linen had isolated from its fellows, she stroked the area of the device that was its operational centre and closed her eyes for a moment.

"What gives?" Linen whispered, checking her own readings. "Waiting for a genie to pop out?"

"Hush it," Trisk ordered softly. "I think I know where this is going…"

More tense than usual, Copper felt the tell-tale tingling begin to seep up her arm as Spook made his presence felt. Her breath was ragged as the holo of the sliver under test slowly formed at the edge of the scanner, enlarging and increasing in complexity as it took structural form. Trisk grasped Linen's arm as, piece by piece the image expanded, building into something that was not part of the original. Time ticked on as, sweat sheeting off her, Copper blinked rapidly and concentrated her efforts to build a whole from the fragment.

"It's working!" Trisk breathed as he peered more closely at the vaguely octagonal image on the bench. "Capturing – we can maybe make a tri-dee solid from the data."

Linen had picked up the medi-scanner from the side and was monitoring her friend. "Let it go, Cop, it's taking too much out of you," she warned. "Your heart rate and blood pressure are at danger level. Spook, put a stop to it," she instructed as Copper ignored her.

Spook had also chosen to ignore the command as there was no halt, but as a minute trickled by and Linen was being forcibly restrained by Trisk, what looked to be edges to the shape began to appear.

"Almost there!" the senior science officer said.

Moments later Copper relaxed her grip and stood straight, the scanner's image snapping off as she disengaged it. "Got it?"

"We got it," Trisk confirmed. "Way to go, Copper! But what the blazes is it?"

"There you got me," was the weary reply.

Linen narrowed her eyes at her friend. "How many times do I have to tell you not to do that to me? I thought you were about to collapse in a heap on the floor. And you're no help!" she rounded angrily on Trisk. "And neither was Spook. What the frock was he playing at?"

"Spook knows what he's at, he wouldn't have let her go too far," Trisk soothed, taking her arm.

The redhead shook him off. "Hah! So you say, Dr frigging Addystone! You wanted the whole shebang and if Cop suffers for it, well too bad!"

"Shut up both of you and give me a hand," Copper hissed through clenched teeth as she reeled against the table.

Still seething, Linen immediately slipped an arm across her friend's back and helped her to a seat. "Get Faerin or Embertz up here," she ordered her senior. "I'll be registering a complaint with the colonel."

"No you won't," Copper told her. "But we got it, and I now know I *can* do it, at least at a small scale."

"That's what frocking scares me," Linen announced grimly. "You managed to reproduce an image of a whole article from a small part of it — what if you're tasked with doing the same to something the size of a shuttle? It'll kill you!"

"Whatever this scanner is, and I seem to be finding out more and more of what it's capable of, it must have the imprint of what *that* once was in its memory matrix and recognise it from the piece I scanned: each molecule or composite of the whole thing must contain its own blueprint, I think. But I need a caff."

"Doc on the way?" was the only rejoinder, aimed at Trisk.

"I caught him in his office, he'll be along."

"Good. And that fiddling hard-holo box will probably turn out to be an alien hairbrush or something equally mundane; all that effort for basically nothing!"

"Will you cool it?" Trisk said sharply. "Copper's fine…"

"And where did you do your medical training?"

"I swear if you two don't stop arguing, I'll smack the pair of you!" Copper threatened. "Where's my caff?"

"In the dispenser, and there it stays until the doc's seen you," Linen told her.

Faerin turned up a couple of minutes later, by which time the remaining contents of the first cartridge had been checked by Linen and Trisk under Copper's eyes, deemed unremarkable and cleared away. His first words were to Lieutenant Lyrican.

"You have a med check at eleven hundred, which is in ten minutes from now. You *will* keep the appointment. And what the hell have *you* been up to now?" he demanded of Copper.

"*You* tell him, Dr Addystone, and don't leave anything out," Linen muttered rebelliously as she made to leave. "I *will* check."

Once in possession of the facts, Lieutenant Milkstone was examined and given a short dressing down by the chief medic. He was satisfied that no lasting hurt had been done but insisted that any attempts to repeat the procedure be carried out with medical attendance just in case, which in effect meant not any time soon, as he could not spare the staff. He also insisted in the face of Copper's objections that a brief report be linked to the colonel. Trisk agreed with him: as the senior science officer technically in charge of the lab, he knew that she would require information on any matter that had a bearing on the *Drake's* main mission and the latest trial certainly fitted that bill.

* * *

Linen returned half an hour later bursting with the news that another arrest had been made, bringing the total number of outlaws to twelve. Kit Locksmith had been in medbay to have his leg examined and she had collared him in a quiet corner. He still looked like hell, she confided to her friends, and had been ordered to rest the leg for at least three sols. He was being fitted for a prosthetic limb support in order that he could still rule his roost in security and chase up any backsliders. She had invited him to join them for lunch, she told Trisk and Copper, as a means of finding out any other juicy titbits of gossip.

In the event, Locksmith was not particularly informative. He had little to pass on other than that Copper's victims would all recover and that she was not likely to be charged with the use of undue force in their capture. Copper was shocked: the thought that she might face repercussions over the means she had used to break into the armoury she accepted, but that she might face disciplinary procedures over her actions to protect herself and her friends from their adversaries had not occurred.

The trio heard more later from Colonel Moritz, who stopped by their lab in the afternoon to discuss the latest findings. The threesome that had planted the charges in the armoury had been planning to head out to one of the outer cargo bays as soon as the coast was clear, to be well away from the blast when it occurred. As two were registered as maintenance techs and the third as a systems engineer, they would have had every right to be there. How or where they had been recruited and trained and how they had infiltrated Mars Fleet the colonel did not know, but she had been in contact over a supra-light link with Military Intelligence and had passed on the information and part of the story to one of her reliable ex-colleagues, Lieutenant Colonel Toxi Karben. Colonel Karben recalled both Copper and Linen, the colonel told them, a twinkle in her eye, as she left the lab.

"So Karben's a good guy; I bet you're disappointed," Linen chuckled, making a face at Copper.

"There's good and there's good," was the wry retort. "But we'd best get back to work if those last two cartridges are to get analysed. The colonel wants it done before we go off duty and the results copied to Dr Inkscree. And she's threatened us with more arms training! You'd think she'd have realised I can tell one end of a phase rifle from the other by *this* time."

"I think she's more concerned with the uses you put your boots to," Linen told her. "Kicking dustbaggers in the head to knock off their helmets is probably considered a bit too drastic."

"Needs must. Bet she's only trying to keep us out of mischief on the road to Jupiter Station."

"Just let's get the next cartridge out. I hope there's nothing in it we need to fire up your scanner for or the doc'll have our heads for handball. And believe me, I'll be first in line to gab if you try it. Are you listening, Dr Addystone, sir?"

"Ma'am, yes ma'am!" Trisk responded as he made for the analyser. "*You* just make sure you capture all the data."

The third sample container was on a par with the one they had examined after lunch and comprised a collection of pieces of typical organo-tech interspersed with crumbs of rocky debris. A small shard that appeared to have a smear of biological origin overlying it was separated out and stored apart, but testing was reserved until later. The last cartridge was also standard in that nothing out of what was now passing as usual was discovered. It was with something akin to relief that the three wrapped up their work for the sol and made to their respective billets to change for their evening amusements.

* * *

Copper was less than amused to find a message awaiting her on her comm when she reached her quarters. It hailed from Ms Thulia Numbridge, was coded urgent, and was a demand to be brought up to date on project work immediately. It also hinted that early completion of her research analyses was requisite. The directive had come in via supra-light, implying that MDMC was upping the ante as far as its students on board the *Drake* were concerned. Linen called through moments later to announce in vexation that she had received similar from Wolff Waterbone.

Copper was adamant during the council-of-war that she had called in the mess: copy the details to all their mentors, charge MDMC for supra-light priority linkage and set their MEDICs in train to write up everything they held in relation to their two Warren sites to date that could be passed on. The samples they had brought out from Lowell could be analysed in their main lab, as outer bay four and the tri-dee suite were still inaccessible. Trisk could be roped in as adviser and he could be named as co-author on a couple of papers that could be drafted on what the two had achieved so far, if he would help write them.

"Colonel's going to love us," Linen complained. "Aren't we

here to work on mission science and the furtherance of Mars Fleet as a highly necessary part of Mars defence, to up the glory of Mars and justify the use of billions of Martian tax-credits that a lot of our fellow-citizens think might be better employed in cleaning the streets and upping Dome heating?"

"MDMC is topping up our pay and living allowances, don't forget," Copper said.

"How could I, with the Wolff-boy reminding me on a regular basis? But I don't recall any MDMC credit finding its way into my personal account lately, do you?"

"Haven't checked; I haven't had the usual notice, though, so you may have a point. Here's Trisk; let's see if he's up to helping us out for a share in the fame and glory that will indisputably follow from our publications, given our contact address will be a ship of the Fleet."

Trisk was certainly up for it: he had never heard of scientific publications coming from officers actively serving aboard a ship of Mars Fleet and considered that they might have a first, if the work was up to the rigorous standards required by the *Journal of Archaeoareography* or whatever prestigious diffusion outlet they decided should be chosen. They spent a happy hour debating the best way forward until they were pulled into a wrangle at an adjacent table over the upgrading of security and access to ents channels. That was sufficient to prompt Copper to make her excuses and head for her billet on the plea that she had several links to return. Her real reason, as she disclosed to Linen, who had chosen to accompany her, was that she wanted to check if the latter's observation that MDMC had not coughed up the latest disburse due them was accurate.

Some time later, and with mugs of hot Chocó-crème in their hands, the two looked enquiringly at one another.

"You were right," Copper conceded. "I should've had my last disburse ten sols ago at least and it's not appeared. That makes things interesting, doesn't it? MDMC hasn't shelled out our dues, so by my reckoning, they've no call to go demanding data at the drop of a link from their hirelings."

"May I remind you, Lieutenant, that we've done precious little on our Lowell work while we've been here and MDMC has essentially paid out for that lack of work. So we *do* owe them a little at least. I suggest we note the absence of our support in the links to Thars, Alessa and Mariner but carry on with the analyses and reports at high speed, as we've agreed with Trisk. That way, we'll have done more than enough to warrant what we *have* been paid. And anything over and above: well, if MDMC won't pay, we have the whip hand of them, which means that we can push ahead and do things our way as regards our PhDs."

"Thars is our senior mentor," Copper argued. "And Lowell is part of the parent body bestowing our degrees. So we'll have to abide by the guidelines. But we can chew Trisk's ears: two of his PhDs were given by Lowell, so he'll have all the lowdown on what's required, how you have to organise things and what we need to do – and how much of it."

Linen's face creased in a smile. "Methinks we're rewriting the rule book over that. How many PhDs have been completed aboard a starship of the Fleet?"

"Precious few, I'll warrant. We can check up."

"Not now; we'd best get those links done that we said were waiting. I owe Majorelle and Lofty, and Mik Mack to name but two. And I guess Ma Kellyn and Maressan and his Jenika will be on your list, especially as the last two are now stomping all over the Dragon's Nest and the Glory Hole. I expect they'll have to see our reports as well?"

"Thars' problem, not ours," Copper returned. "For now, get your feet off my sofa or I won't get you another drink. We'll do double acts for our joint buddies; that'll save us time."

"Including Ma Kellyn," Linen cut in. "I rather enjoy driving her doozie."

* * *

The ensuing ten sols brought the *MSS Drake II* ever closer to her target of Jupiter Station. She had built up speed to make headway but had necessarily to cut back well before she closed in for orbit. The high-speed unmanned ship carrying her repair drones and stores was also on course and heading in but would be several sols behind her. Thus much but little else had been disclosed to the crew and the pace of duty had been quiet but watchful. The seeming lull gave those who had been involved in the recent goings on a chance to relax a little; nothing else that could remotely be construed as sabotage had occurred.

The general slackening had not extended to the three science officers down in their office and main lab on deck five. Copper and Linen had almost forgotten the obligations of their research work on the samples brought from Lowell and found to their chagrin that in checking their stores, they had numerous tubes and cartridges still swathed in film copies of the *Goodwitch Guide to Mars' Mission History*.

"You called this the bare minimum," was Linen's complaint to her friend as she surveyed the collection. "I vote you use your Spook scanner on them and we do this as quickly as we can. There weren't *that* many examples of alien tech in our previous tubes, and your handy skills should be able to hone in on the right areas in these, so we should be able to run through them. Trisk, if you would be an absolute gem and skim over our last couple of reports to MDMC's EMMS office and figure what we can include in a publication," she had implored their senior. "If we at least have a draft to send out on the pollen moieties and other plant stuff, it should light up a few eyes. We have the tri-dee eye candy that we put together in the super-sim suite at Lowell, so I'll dig that out and that can be added. And at least Stellaria Firedrake and her like can't get to us out here over our Mars-shattering results."

"I have my own duties, but I'll clear it with Ossy Inkscree, *if* you make me third author on your papers. I'll even give a hand with your samples," Trisk had agreed, and the deal was struck.

The trio had consequently put in extra hours on the Lowell material, and Copper and Linen had cleared their report backlog to MDMC, sending the results off via a super-fast link to Thars Amberline for checking and forwarding to Lomax Gratikule and his EMMSO underlings. All three had, however, found that they had been assigned training sessions in various ship's disciplines that ate into their scant leisure time. This Linen put down to Copper's earlier observation that certain senior parties aboard the *Drake* were ensuring that they would have no opportunity to get into more trouble during the ride to Jupiter.

Having had enough of hard graft in the lab, they were in the office polishing up a very rough draft of a paper they intended to submit one afternoon and debating whether they should halt for a stroll to the mess and a change of scene when a call came through for Copper. It was from Captain Helmis, who wanted to see her in his office immediately, on a priority matter. His composed but serious face gave nothing away.

"Damn!" she protested once she had affirmed "It'll be about my actions in that frocking carry-on down in the armoury and in medbay. I thought they'd forgotten all about it. Doc Faerin *did* threaten to record my non-reporting of injuries in my med-file and send that to personnel as well. And now here's Captain Helmis requesting my immediate presence in his office. One reprimand coming up, I guess. Don't leave for the mess without me – I'm going to need a massively large caff when I get back – if I get back."

18: THE ROAD TO JUPITER

Copper stalked into the office almost an hour after leaving it, looking slightly bemused. Her two friends had already had a caff break and had elected to carry on working on the paper in her absence, figuring that completing another section or two might cheer her up. She made no answer to their joint appeal for news, other than raising her shoulders, pursing her lips and asking for a large caff. They had barely reached the dispenser when a buzz at the comm indicated an inward call for Copper, this time from medbay.

"Bloody hell, I'm more popular than a pay rise!" she snapped as she headed to respond.

"You had an appointment to have your injuries checked out, Ms Milkstone: you were due here twenty minutes ago," the face of Kynedd Faerin reminded her sternly.

"Sorry, Doctor, I had an urgent meeting with Captain Helmis come up and I'm just back. I'll be along right now. Can I bring Linen and Trisk with me? I got news that I'm a bit shook up about, and as they had a part in it, they should be in on it."

There was a pause as the chief MO digested the information. "Okay, bring them along but be quick. And remember for the future that I'm *not* your diary or your messaging service: you should have notified us."

"Aye, sir."

The other two looked at their friend in perplexity.

"What gives, Cop?" Linen demanded.

"Tell you in medbay. The doc's waiting and he'll be spitting quarks if I don't show. Don't worry, it's not *bad* news – I think."

The other two exchanged glances and shrugs, but obediently hurried along behind her. They made the medical facility with little trouble and Copper soon found herself in a small bay and in the hands of Dr Amber Embertz. Faerin had elected to stay outside and chat to Linen and Trisk and they were trading ideas on what might have occurred when Copper returned with the update that her healing was progressing as expected.

"In your office, if you don't mind, Doctor," she requested formally when asked what in blazes was up.

Once the four were seated around the table and the privacy sign lit on the door, Copper bit her lip and looked around them. Linen's concerned glance and the reassuring hand on her arm brought an impish grin to her face, however, and she exchanged an affectionate glance and a wink with her friend before her eyes came back to Faerin.

"You might recall, Doctor, that a while ago you told us that you were saving that rare bottle of scotch you have to toast my promotion or my detention in the brig," she said levelly. "Well, you'd best get it out – Captain Helmis and Colonel Moritz just told me that on the basis of my actions in that sabotage attempt in the armoury, and my help in medbay, I'm to be promoted to first lieutenant."

Linen's jaw almost hit the table, but her subsequent whoop could be heard through the reinforced office door. "Way to go, First Lieutenant Milkstone, ma'am! Oh, Cop, I'm *so* happy for you and you so deserve it!"

"Damn you, Lieutenant," Faerin chuckled as he rose. "But congratulations, all the same."

"Nice one, Copper," Trisk twinkled, taking her hand in his, subjecting it to a hearty shaking and following his actions with a shy kiss to her right ear. "Where and when's the party?"

"On board and once we get to Jupiter. But it's confidential for now: the colonel told me I could tell a chosen few, but that's all. She cleared it with her senior personnel people and pushed the paperwork through. I guess she had a few arms to twist or butts to kick."

"And I'm sure she didn't," Kynedd Faerin smiled as he set out his precious bottle and four small tumblers. "You're only having one each," he warned. "You're still on duty, as I am, and I want to keep a *little* of this for future festivities. Hell knows we need them. Please be upstanding!" he ordered. "To the health of First Lieutenant Copper Milkstone! May her next promotion be long in coming – I'm not made of rare and expensive scotch."

The others stood also and Copper returned their salutations by raising her own glass. "The captain didn't include you two in the promotion, even though you were part of it," she told her two friends. "And Lor' knows what difference it'll make, apart from pay. A heap more training, duty shifts elsewhere and even more pressure to get results, I expect..."

"You'll find out soon enough," Faerin laughed at her. "Drink up and get the hell out. I've a shift to finish and you'll have as well. We'll open this again when you're given a medal or made commander."

"Promises, promises," Copper beamed. "Thanks, Doc, I feel a lot better now. It was more than a shock: I was expecting an ear-bashing."

"Still need that large caff?" Linen enquired as the three made for the security of their lab and a private celebration.

"I'm still fizzing, so maybe not," Copper said wryly. "Let's finish that frigging draft, chuck it in the direction of Thars and company and then head in for an early shower and dinner. I hope chippers are on the menu, is all."

* * *

Chippers *were* on the menu when the three met for dinner shortly afterwards and they were able to eat their meal in peace as the place was quiet. They spent some time looking over ship's updates at their table's info-console and found that repairs to most of the less-damaged areas were complete. On calling up her duty schedule, however, Copper found to her disgust that Jinn Limlitc had programmed in a series of flight sim sessions over the next three mornings of an hour each.

"Oh seven hundred!" she griped. "I'll have to leave breakfast until after that, I can't fly on a full stomach!"

"It starts now," Linen snickered in a low voice. "Promotion costs and this is the first bill. But I put in for extra flight training as well, so I'd better see if there's a sim station with my name on it before I gloat too much."

"Huh! He might have told me in advance!"

"He's probably only been told himself that you're to be put in for it. Bet it was the colonel's idea – I see I haven't been set up yet, but I guess it won't be long coming," the redhead went on. "Never mind, I'll eat your breakfast for you and Trisk will help. Though I'm on weapons drill at twelve hundred, so he's not forgotten me either."

"Look out, here's your best friend Ash Goff," warned Trisk. "He's got a full tray and he's heading over."

"Told you he'd got a crush on you, Cop: looks like he can't help himself," Linen smirked.

"Then I'll help him," was the reply.

Goff was indeed homing in, but it was only to ask Trisk for help in some project that he and Lyssa Halsen had been handed by Ossy Inkscree concerning examining asteroids for bio-signs. Copper viewed him narrowly as he sat down at Trisk's invitation and came to the conclusion that the request was an excuse. Goff was evidently alone, bored and seeking company, especially such company that seemed to live on the edge: the story of the attack on the armoury was apparently still the sensation of the sol and he wanted details. Linen fabricated a few for his benefit that caused her friend to smack her head and tell her to behave.

"You two don't act like officers in the Fleet," observed Goff in a loud voice, frowning. "It's a wonder you get away with it. Everybody notices."

"Then everybody should mind their own frocking business, and that includes you," Copper retorted, to the amusement of Kit Locksmith, who had just commandeered the table adjacent to theirs.

To deflect antagonism, Linen, oozing sympathy and mockery in about equal doses, enquired after Goff's injured leg and the upshot of the explosion on deck twelve, particularly in relation to his prized racing buggy. The lieutenant was resentful: repairs had been rapid to deck fabric, but stores were refusing to supply the means to restore his vehicle, which had sustained damage.

"Ask the pilots that have been drafted into engineering," Linen advised brightly. "They may be able to get their hands on a few bits and pieces, and the tools that go with them."

Goff's face lit up at the notion: it had not occurred to him. Pushing her advantage, the redhead managed to steer him in the direction of Oaky Grimsson at a nearby table, as an engineer that might help with the identification of the relevant pilots.

"Thanks," Copper said shortly to her friend. "I just wanted

to check on the flight sim station I'm to report to morrow-sol: I have a feeling… hah, I hadn't imagined it," she went on as she called up the relevant link.

"What?" the other two demanded in unison.

"It's not a shuttle sim I've been assigned to, it's a short-range fighter sim. Wonder whose bright idea that was? And why?"

"Easy," Linen said softly. "The colonel's, and because she's testing your mettle for reasons best known to herself. She keeps threatening you with a future in the Fleet and she's upping every aspect of Fleet training that you'll need as an officer destined to rise through the ranks."

"I'm a scientist, not a frigging battle-bucket commander!"

"I wouldn't go calling the *Drake* a battle-bucket, you'll have half the crew up in arms," Trisk put in, laughing.

"That'll be a problem, with the armoury out of commission," Copper countered, smiling back as her sense of reality kicked in and the funny side of the situation struck her. "But if I'm to be up at the crack of sol, I'm sure as hell not doing anything more strenuous tonight than relaxing. Sifting out more bits of self-rep tech from endless tubes of rockery from the Warren can wait."

"You chose those tubes for a reason, Cop," Linen pointed out in a low voice. "Maybe all the pieces in them are parts of a jigsaw of some sort and we can link them all together and make a useful device: something that would write up our PhDs for us would be ideal."

"Something that would keep you in order would be better," Copper rejoined equally quietly, suspecting that one or two ears were tuned into their chat. "But you have a point, solbeam: the tubes are mostly from the Glory Hole and the sample areas were close together. The bits we're finding *may* be part of a whole; though I suspect they're more likely to be parts of a bigger part of a whole," she went on wryly.

"No doubt, but you're talking shop, stop it. Let's talk about our crewmates: they sure as hell have plenty to say about us, and they'll have even more soon enough," she added mischievously.

* * *

Early next sol Copper reported to the relevant training suite and headed over to the check-in station for her assignment. She was less than surprised to see that Colonel Moritz had come in before her and was suited up for training.

"Ma'am," she greeted the commanding officer equably.

The colonel was also destined for a spell of short-range flight simulation, she told Copper. It was essential that all officers with flying experience keep up their hours and thus their expertise. The *Drake* was particularly fortunate in having the resources to allow a wide range of skills to be honed and simulations were an ideal means of gauging aptitude for further training in relevant areas. With an enigmatic smile that made Copper wonder what was in the wind, the colonel left her to it and strode off to seek out her own test station.

A pilot instructor was on hand to demonstrate the interior of the two-man training fighter and go through flight drills. Copper would learn her initial skills in that setting before being allowed the use of a simulation of the type of one-man fighter that was used aboard the *Drake*. That fighter model was the latest off the production line and as such was the best there was, she was told as her instructor pulled up its spec. Copper examined the design closely: she recognised the outline of the red-hulled, twin-finned craft. It was similar to the one that Colonel Moritz had flown when Copper, aboard the Ares-Class Mark IV training shuttle out of Basecamp with Foxy Dingle at the helm and Linen and Blazells aboard, had spotted her all those months ago. Copper recalled the later reprimand by Captain Meldyn for targeting the craft as it buzzed them and smiled to herself.

"Atmospheric flight as well as space, then," she noted. "Do we need that on a deep space mission?"

"You never know what you might find out there," she was informed. "Lock in your ident and let's go."

That first hour in the bucket seat of a fighter was gruelling. Her instructor had obviously been told to put her through her paces to see what she was capable of, Copper suspected, as she tottered out of the sim and made for her quarters for a shower to slough off her fatigue. She found her two friends still in the mess when she rolled up there shortly afterwards.

"Saved you a seat," Linen announced, indicating. "Get your chow, tell us how it went and then we'll tell *you* something."

The news that Linen and Trisk were eager to impart raised a chuckle from Copper. Trisk had found out from Lyssa Halsen that her brother's ship was also due in at Jupiter Station within a sol or two of the *Drake's* arrival. First Lieutenant Erik Halsen was a flight engineer aboard the ship that was taking over from the *MSS Swordfish* in her mapping and safety mission; it was also an Explorer Corps mid-range cruiser and was their old friend the *MSS Lithium Star.*

"I hope her ETA's a sol or two after ours, especially if we get time to swop a word with Second Lieutenant Gadget Blazells," Linen laughed quietly. "Maybe you can invite him to the party?"

"Hush," Copper cautioned. "There are flapping ears about. Let me get this down me and then we'd best get to the lab. Lor' another two sessions of early flight sims will kill me."

"Good grief, just look who's walked in!" Linen breathed in return. "The colonel, and she's heading over…"

Colonel Moritz had stopped by to commend Copper on her prowess in her first sortie in a fighter sim and to let her know that her promotion would be announced as part of a general notice on the various commendations that were to be bestowed in the aftermath of the recent troubles. Apparently all three of them would be on the list as having performed over and above the call of duty. The commanding officer left as quickly as she had arrived, leaving the three looking at one another in surprise.

"Don't often see the colonel in here at this time," croaked Trisk. "But why is she informing us personally and not via the usual channels?"

"What *are* the usual channels?" Linen asked. "This is all new to me. At Beagle Basecamp, we just checked the handiest info-station to call up anything from this sol's menus in the mess to our final gradings and awards. Remember Blazells face when he found out you'd got the medals for navigation and piloting *and* the best overall trainee of our cohort," she reminded her friend. "Though our postings notifications *were* private."

"Ship's info channels are available to all crew and updated as and when required," Trisk said. "I suppose the colonel wanted us primed that we'd be mentioned. I see she's having her rations in here at any rate. But it looks like your news will be out before we hit Jupiter orbit, if it's to be pinned onto the honours list."

"Great!" Copper sighed. "Let's get into the lab: I really want to break the back of the bulk of the Glory Hole samples or it's going to take forever.”

* * *

It was two sols later that Copper met her two friends in the mess after another arduous session in the training suite. She was greeted by the tidings that the anticipated commendations list had been posted ship-wide via the *Drake's* crew info bulletin.

“Hah! That explains Ash Goff's sulky face as I came in. He's figured I'll rank him; though not you, Trisk,” Copper responded as she sat. “But cheers to you two on your commendations. Do we get some formal bit of plas-paper or a brass button?”

“Check your personal link log,” Linen ordered. “There's to be an official knees-up on the observation deck in two sols time, before we hit Jupiter orbit. I guess we'll all have so much to do then that it was decided to hold the party in advance. The order is dress uniform and a line-up of all those due to be honoured. There's a few of us, including Kit Locksmith. Nobody honours the colonel, though she deserves it more than most for taking control of the affair without flaking *and* keeping us all on an even keel.”

“We get a holo of our commendation to decorate our wall,” Trisk elucidated. “And it's mentioned in usual Fleet despatches, so the folks back home will get to know about it.”

“That'll only make them worry about us,” Copper observed. “Your Grammy will be climbing the walls to find out what went down,” she added to Linen.

“No she won't; she knows the score. Though you're the only one listed for promotion, but as we've only been shipboard a couple of months or so, I guess there hasn't been time to tally the merits of all those on the up-ladder to the top,” the redhead added jauntily.

“Hah, hah. But if MDMC's Accounts Department finds out, maybe it'll pony up the credit we're owed. Thars hasn't got back to us, but I guess it takes time to kick the great and the good of EMMSO up the behind. You going to finish that biscuit? If not, hand it over: sims are hungry work, especially when your tutor's bullied you into volunteering for extra time on solos.”

“You're going on solo sims already?” Trisk demanded. “I was in a dual cockpit for ages, but then I don't have the knack. I think they've given up on me, I'll never make a pilot of more than a slow shuttle-bus.”

“Useful at the Warren, unless they’ve constructed the tunnel from the station to the site that was promised us way back when we were just rookies,” Linen told him.

“None of us will be back at the Warren, except as visitors,” Trisk predicted ruefully. “We’re Fleet scientists now and we’re stuck with it. Come the end of our contracts, you think they’ll let us go without a fight? In your dreams!”

“They can’t prevent us leaving,” Copper said stubbornly.

“You won’t want to, kiddo,” smiled Linen astutely, crinkling up her golden-brown eyes. “You’ve taken to Fleet life like a shuttle-duck to a puddle, in spite of your claim to the contrary. Okay, you’ve been influenced, but you’re finding the *Drake* is every bit as home-like as Lowell College once was. You need the comfort of an organised existence, even if things go belly-up every so often, just to keep you alert.”

“Stop psychoanalysing me and finish your rations,” she was told sternly. “Alert! Scared out of my wits and wondering what the hell we’re doing here more like.”

“Lab work,” Trisk put in. “Back to the grind, shipmates: we have samples to analyse. And as they’re all yours, you should be grateful I’m giving you a hand.”

Copper and Linen were more than grateful for any help and Trisk was doubly useful, having a greater depth of knowledge than the two on some of the biological scraps originating on ancient Mars that were turning up within their Amber-Warren samples. With the data the two had amassed from sorties with the surf-sci bots in the Glory Hole and which they had approval to use, their analyses and interpretation were proceeding apace and being slotted into their theses, the progressing of which comprised a part of their usual tasks at the end of almost every sol in the comfort of their own billets.

* * *

The threesome had spent so much time and overtime in their laboratory that the evening of the awards ceremony came upon them surprisingly quickly. Despite the last-second scramble, and dazzling in dress uniform, they stood in line with their fellows to receive their commendations from the colonel. Such honours were generally bestowed on Mars by a Fleet bigwig, but in long-range starships, formal festivities brought a welcome interlude to the tedium that could be an aspect of shipboard life, although this was not the case on the *Drake*, many of the crew thought ruefully. Copper was a little unsettled to find that the ceremony was being recorded for posterity and was likely to figure in many links back home, but heartened to know that the exotic food and drink provided for the event was gratis and not an added extra to her mess bill. The notice of her promotion was last on the list, but all she was required to do was to stand up, collect her new pips and acknowledge the applause.

"Way to go, First Lieutenant Copper, ma'am," Linen beamed as she slapped her friend on the back upon her return to the ranks to listen to the final speech by their commanding officer, which was mercifully brief.

Those invited to the soiree comprised only a portion of the ship's crew, as many were on duty, but the remainder were given free rein to stop by and many such made their way over. Copper had not realised just how well-known she and her friends were and as a respite from the seemingly never-ending parade of well-wishers, she walked over to the massive viewing portal that gave the observation deck its name. The speed of the ship made no difference to the immensity of space and she breathed deeply, her hand outstretched towards the vast expanse beyond.

"Trying to catch a star?" a voice said at her elbow.

"Not exactly, Chief. A minute's peace is all."

"It gets you, doesn't it?" Locksmith observed, smiling at her. "Pulls you in. Once you've seen it out there, everything else is second rate. I'll leave you to your peace: enjoy it while you can."

Copper's peace lasted no more than sixty seconds. She was claimed by yet more shipmates and was finally rescued by Linen, with Kit Locksmith and Kynedd Faerin in tow. The latter had strong-armed Tiff Tuffet to deal out some good quality liquor from his stores and the major and Trisk were over in a corner guarding it. As Tuffet's domain had been close to the action at the therapy salon, he had had the turmoil of Locksmith's people tramping all over his place, but the security chief had smoothed his path and Tuffet was grudgingly grateful.

"Spook giving you a hug?" Linen whispered in Copper's ear a little later, when her friend had failed to respond to a question.

"Bone weary," she told her. "We worked our socks off all sol and we've worked our mouths and ears off all eve. And I don't know what's in this, but it's making my head sing."

"I know what you mean: the eats haven't really mopped it all up. Back to mine," Linen said softly. "I've some Oxypep tabs looking for a use. Aboard ship, they've never been necessary."

* * *

Early next sol Linen called in for her friend on her way to the mess. As they trod the deck, the redhead admired the twin four-pointed stars each side of the neck of Copper's uniform jacket.

"They're holding up my head," was the moaning response. "Thanks be I've no flight sim scheduled; I'd best order a bowl of stodge to keep me going until I know where my brain is."

"Spook doesn't warn you when to hold back on the booze, then?" Linen asked as they collected their trays.

"He did: I didn't listen. Wish I had, though: we've got *some* sol coming up."

"He knows what we're going to find when we scan those bits we pulled out and set aside?" the redhead whispered sibilantly.

"I figure. But shut up until we've done here. Don't see Trisk, he's maybe not awake yet."

"We left him with Doc Faerin, if I recall; they were both still holding glasses up last night. Though I noticed the colonel left early, wise woman, and so did Kit Locksmith."

"Then it's you and me, kiddo, just like the old sols. Let's eat up as quickly as we can and get the hell out of here, too many eyes and ears," Copper observed.

After breakfast the two stopped off in their office to quickly scan their personal links and then made for their main lab. Once there they hauled off jackets and set to, both MEDICs handy, several probes in operation and Copper's alien scanner ready. Their target for the sol was the close scrutiny of as many of the fragments of self-replicating alien technology that their Glory Hole site had yielded. These they had painstakingly removed from the rocky matrix materials and other fine-grained scraps that made up most of their collected materials. Their private intention was to produce a comprehensive assessment of the alien pieces and add them as an appendix to their theses, which could be handily excluded from the copies that would be passed to their sponsoring body.

With a light-grid representation of a sector of the Glory Hole projected from the largest tri-dee sim station in the adjacent side lab, they called up the areas of floor from which the pieces had been gathered. Copper had recollected correctly, for the sample areas were adjacent and situated at the far side of their small cavern, below and beyond which was the site of Spook's ship.

"I'm getting freaked," Copper confessed to her friend as they sorted the relevant cartridges on their bench space in the main lab. "I think it's Spook. Maybe I should use the alien scanner to try and extrapolate these bits as a collection? It might give us the clue as to their potential origin as a single larger piece."

Linen looked mutinous. "You tried that not long ago and nearly gave me a seizure," she said sternly. "On one condition: if I say stop, you stop, whatever Spook is telling you."

"Agreed. Our tests are all showing that the pieces are near identical structurally and mostly the red-green stuff we've come to associate with the typical material that practically everything alien we know of is based on."

"That will be because it's the only stuff that's survived," said Linen. "Everything else will have deteriorated and disappeared over time. We're talking millennia here, not just a few centuries. Trust you to go picking up an older alien entity," she continued.

"Frankly, I don't think I could handle a young one," Copper told her. "Just imagine a teeny with the talents Spook has! How in blazes would you keep it in order with the insubstantial equivalent of hormones racing through its system? But enough already, we have work to do."

With a routine check to confirm the security of their lab, the two spread the contents of each cartridge into separate, labelled analysis trays. Copper had sorted these into a close array that seemed logical to her, for some reason she failed to understand, and with the alien device fixed firmly in her right hand and a finger of her left tracing a circling path on the side of the device, she began to relax into the attitude she knew was suitable for its operation.

"Spook's seriously fizzing," she murmured. "This should be fun."

"Maybe it's one of his favourite toys," Linen hazarded.

"Just capture the data!" she was ordered. "The secure cams should record externals and our other scanners are operational."

"Aye ma'am; but just don't forget I'm scanning you and I *will* render you inoperative if you refuse to stop when I say so, first lieutenant or not."

Copper's only response was a grunt as the customary tingle spread up her arm and the faint holo began to materialise at the edge of the scanner, expanding to take in the total bench section and intensifying as each piece underwent some sort of scanning by the device. Linen gaped as the image of each individual part seemed to shift, spinning and twisting in the space above the bench, drawing apart from its fellows and then moving together, above or below the plane of the image until the whole was a kaleidoscope of motes swirling about in a frenzied spiral dance. Copper blinked the sweat out of her eyes as she concentrated on forming a complete picture of what she was seeing as each piece began slotting into place.

"You're getting it!" Linen murmured huskily, mesmerised by the sight. "Auxiliary instruments capturing data; medi-scanner readings still within safe zone, but you're close to upper limits."

"Acknowledged," Copper confirmed gratingly as she strained to maintain her arm level and the data flow steady.

A few minutes later and the image wavered and broke before it suddenly vanished.

"We got most of it," Linen verified. "Good work, Cop. And it's a *thing*. Spook's diary?" she suggested. "Or his lunchbox?"

"You were right," her friend admitted, ignoring the remarks. "It was a frigging jigsaw, more or less. I think there are only a few odd pieces that don't fit, but which ones among this lot I don't know."

As she gestured at the collection on the bench, both became aware of the insistent buzzing at the lab entry.

"Best see who's at the door," Linen announced. "The lights have been flashing for ages. Whoever it is might be a tad upset."

Their visitors were Trisk and Colonel Moritz. Trisk's absence at breakfast had not been due to overindulgence the eve before but an early meeting with the colonel. Whilst both grasped the need for security and the colonel had not used her authority to enter, they were annoyed that their call had gone unanswered for so long. The explanation that followed mollified them a little and both waited whilst the accumulated data was integrated into the bank of instruments that had been deployed to capture, analyse and extrapolate it into the tri-dee image of whatever the alien scanner had produced.

"So what is it?" Linen asked at last.

"Search me," Copper sighed. "It's about as clear as the last one we got: that octagonal piece from the *Wayfinder's* stuff."

"The colonel has seen the report," Trisk apprised them. "We think *that* was a complete piece of alien technology, or at least a representation of it and this seems to be another, but you don't look as exhausted as you were last time you tried that trick," he added to Copper.

"Most of the pieces were there, I think, unlike the single bit of non-rep stuff we had from the *Wayfinder*," she guessed.

"And you're getting more used to the Spook scanner, or it's getting used to you," Linen commented. "You're certainly more at ease each time you use," she told her friend. "Spook's not holding your hand, or whatever he does, quite so often."

"How in blazes do you figure that?"

Linen shrugged. "I get a feeling. But that doesn't mean that you go trying it on any old piece of alien tech without a standby medic: the bits from the *Lithium Star* with what might be organic tissue attached or the lump of tech in bay four for example," she warned. "Whatever your orders," she added, noting Trisk and Colonel Moritz exchange glances.

"You're sailing close to the wind, Lieutenant," remarked the colonel coolly. "But I've no intention of exposing any of my crew to risk unnecessarily, believe me. Let me see what you have here thus far."

The appliance from the Glory Hole, whatever it was, would have been fairly small, based on the holo-representation that floated above the projector port of the console that Copper had activated. It was about double the size of her alien scanner and the colonel confirmed that *she* had not seen anything similar among the larger pieces of alien material that had come within her authority whilst working with Military Intelligence. The piece appeared to be a flattened and rounded rectangular case banded by what looked like green metallic studs around its widest edge. There was no obvious operating toggle, opening or markings on it.

"Recorder of some sort?" Linen suggested. "Maybe you push those buttons round its middle or talk to it?"

"Won't work on a holo," Trisk said sagely.

"Very funny. What's your take on it, Dr Addystone, sir?" the redhead returned.

"Alien equivalent of a MEDIC?" was Trisk's contribution. "But as the Spook scanner can do that, I shouldn't think so."

"Did the Spook scanner actually belong to Spook?" Linen wanted to know. "We found it just above where his ship was buried after all."

"Don't know; I never asked," Copper retorted as she circled the holo. "But as a non-working one was found under Lofty's cellar out at Lowell, I guess they were usual bits of kit."

"Or we were just very lucky," her redheaded friend replied. "They were made of the self-rep stuff, as this mainly is. But the on-switch of the scanner is that design etched into its flank: this doesn't seem to have that, unless the holo hasn't picked it up."

"Hmm," Copper muttered to herself as she continued her tour of the holo. "I still can't figure what this is – but – and it's a big but – if my scanner *did* recognise what that piece of non-rep stuff was part of and could replicate its image from a fragment, it seems as if the base structure of alien technology somehow incorporates within itself its entire schematic. Like cloning: you only need a few cells that include the instructions for generating a whole being and you can grow one – *if* you have the right mix of constituents to hand and the right growing media and so on."

"Some alien technology, maybe," Trisk said. "I can't imagine that you could produce a whole ship from a piece of hull, for example, if you just stuck it in the equivalent of an incubator and fed it the right building blocks."

Colonel Moritz had let her junior officers talk, a wry smile on her face. "Speculation is everything," she noted. "But you don't know what you have or what its purpose is. For the moment, keep thinking about it, but as long as it doesn't pose a danger to my ship, it's not your priority: our mission is. I'm having outer bay four cleared and secured as we speak and you'll be three of the few that have access, at least until we reach Jupiter Station.

You'll be notified when you can get in, but you *will* have security back-up: get Chief Locksmith to arrange it. Meanwhile, you two finish up your Lowell samples as quickly as possible and work on finishing your theses. All the facilities of the *Drake* are at your disposal as far as data and instrumentation goes and Dr Addystone will assist with advice. Anything related to alien technology or similar that has not come to my notice before I want to hear of; the mundane I do not. Clear?"

"Yes ma'am!"

As the colonel disappeared out of the door, Copper turned to her friends. "Break for lunch," she said. "We deserve it."

* * *

All three had decided to check on updates to their personal links on the info-console at their table and once in possession of their rations, Linen waded in.

"News from Thars!" she exclaimed. "It's copied to you, Cop, so let's see what he says: it's not marked private or confidential, so I'll just call it up…"

Thars Amberline's message was direct: Noachis Dunelm and Syriana Steefens had both completed their PhD theses and had successfully defended them at their assessments.

"I bet Thars won't be finding them posts at Lowell," Linen laughed flippantly. "They'll probably end up hired by Mars Gov and will turn into Waterbone or Thulia clones."

"At least they won't be annoying Mik Mack or Ambrose or the other guys out at the Warren," was Copper's contribution.

"There are your friends Mr Chengi and Ms Grass-Tephra for that," Trisk grinned.

"Mik will keep those two in order," Linen prophesied. "But what else have we… Grammy's demanding an update on status, *if* we can provide it. That means the folks at home have heard that something's been going on out here, but they won't have got the latest, that'll take time to get back. There's nothing that could be an urgent note from MDMC Accounts on our lack of financial support. So we do as the colonel suggests and power through with our theses in that case: we have more than enough data to complete them twice anyhow."

"I think you'll find that our esteemed colonel issues orders, not suggestions," Trisk enlightened her, laughing. "But as I've been ordered to give a hand with advice we'll get on it, between training sessions. I've a few overnighters at the science station on the bridge looming, and I bet you two won't be far behind."

"More flight sims for me, and Doc Faerin's put me in for the advanced GHQ," Copper sighed, her shoulders drooping.

"A General Health Qualification's a good tag to have, even if it doesn't pay extra; I might put in for it," Linen said, her eyes crinkling up in anticipation. "Useful for away missions."

"And you think you'll be on one of those if we find anything interesting where we're going?" Trisk asked. "You'll be lucky!"

"I can't imagine there'll be a queue in the shuttle bay," Linen responded. "Away missions tend to be dangerous."

"Which is why experienced crew usually make up the teams," Trisk elucidated. "Which means not rookies like you."

"Hah! We've done okay up to now!"

"In triplicate – or as a duo in your case. You really think the colonel or the captain would order you two or the three of us down at once if there was a need? Not how ships operate."

"Excuse me Dr Smarty-pants, this is also *your* first mission, so don't come the experienced spacer on us," Linen told him.

"Eat your lunch," she was ordered. "Then get back to work."

* * *

Back to work over the next few sols meant finalising analysis of their Lowell samples and processing quantities of data. Trisk had found that dark-watch on the bridge gave him free time enough to check over what his friends had worked on to date and tweak their output into something that could be published; he had two papers in outline at the end of four sols, just as the *Drake* was on final approach to Jupiter Station.

Copper and Linen had completed all they intended of actual research and were drafting their theses in between training stints and setting up for their planned foray to outer bay four. Kit Locksmith had advised Copper over a shared caff break that an escort he could not spare and until he could, she and her friends would have to hang fire. This sat ill, but as Trisk was spending his morning hours catching up on sleep, they had little option.

"MEDICs are rare and wonderful things," Copper sighed towards the end of this time. "And Trisk's one is as batty as a box of quarks, but they're all three churning out stuff at a rate I have trouble keeping up with."

"As long as it's useful stuff," Linen declared. "They can see correlations that I can't, and it's annoying that a box seems to know more than I do. But hey ho! Now I know how Trisk *did* manage to get three PhDs, if he had this sort of help."

"He put in the hours and then some," her friend answered. "Thars wouldn't have selected him otherwise. But I bet we have more data each than Noa and Syr had between them. I know we had the advantage of those thrice-damned surf-sci bots and Auntie Elle's scanners but we worked extra sevensols and gave up furlough to get through our work."

"There, there, little Cop! Don't get your hair in a knot over it. I'd suggest a trip to the therapy salon, but everybody seems to be avoiding the place like the plague these sols. I feel sorry for the virtuous down there: they must feel unloved. Why don't we see how they are and schedule a session? Even if there was still a mole amongst them, they wouldn't dare tangle with us."

"Go ahead. At this moment I wish I was back at the Warren and down the Glory Hole. At least it was peaceful down there, most of the time."

"When people weren't aiming to kill us, you mean? But you don't really: you're just over-tired. Hey, d'you think we get leave when we dock at the station? It *is* a base after all and technically under military jurisdiction, though it *is* part-civilian."

"Heaps of stores, eateries and salacious bars there won't be," Copper told her. "And with a crew this size, you'll be lucky to be at the top of any list for time off. I pity Captain Helmis: one of his jobs as exec must be organising crew rotas. And as a few of our shuttles need overhauled, how do we get down there?"

"Orbital docking ports," Linen said blithely. "We'll be linked by pressurised tunnel to more than one transfer point, so we can just walk off, as long as we have the relevant bits of attached or implanted metalwork and the permission. Every sensor in the place will know who we are and where we are, so there'll be no place to hide," she continued melodramatically.

"Shut up and just get us a massage and a face and hair make or something. I've no drill or training listed this eve and neither have you, so after our shift here will do, if they can fit us in."

* * *

The therapy salon had moved quarters and now inhabited what had once been storage further along deck eight, no doubt to allow Chief Locksmith and his sleuths the opportunity to take their former quarters apart bolt by bolt. The two found only one other customer, Liaison Officer Tany Melucca, in the place. She was having a little dazzle added to her hair, she informed them casually. Copper groaned inwardly; she had met Tany a couple of times since coming aboard and found her banter exhausting. The chatty Lieutenant Melucca turned out to be the least of her worries. Her session was nearly done when a chirp of her comm unit heralded a priority message from Captain Helmis. She was ordered to report to the bridge at twenty two hundred hours, where she would assume the secondary science position as the *Drake* made into Jupiter Station.

"Aye, sir, twenty two hundred, confirm," was all she could croak out as her jaw dropped in dismay; she could almost feel him laughing in the background.

"Lucky you," Linen congratulated her.

"Who are you kidding? No sleep for me tonight then, and I've been up since the crack of sol working in the damn lab!"

"Just make sure you don't fall asleep at your station," Linen warned. "You can bet the colonel will be in the command chair and Captain Helmis alongside."

"Bet it was the colonel's idea. And why in hell can't we dock at some reasonable hour," Copper grumbled. "And why me?"

"Newest first lieutenant aboard," her friend explained. "Goes with the pips, and at least your face will match your uniform: the guys have done a good job."

"Yes, I'm *so* relaxed," was the ironic retort.

She thanked their therapists nonetheless, and tottered off for her evening meal with Linen in tow. If she was destined to pore over a science console for much of the night, she was damn well going to do it on a full stomach, she announced.

The mess was remarkably busy and it looked as though there would be an audience for the docking, as it was a rare enough spectacle. Linen promised to be among the throng on the obs deck, if she could commandeer a space. All Copper wanted was a quick dinner, a quick shower and a short time in which to prepare herself mentally for her task. Her friend's dry assurances that she would be one of the smallest cogs in the almighty wheel that was the *MSS Drake II* and no one would notice her fell on deaf ears. With Ossy Inkscree as chief science officer no doubt next to her and several senior ship's personnel manning the main bridge stations, she would be in some sort of light, even if it was only reflected, was her opinion, and she was seriously apprehensive.

* * *

"Reporting for duty, ma'am," Copper's voice was steady as she stepped onto the bridge at precisely two minutes to twenty two hundred hours.

Both Colonel Moritz and Captain Helmis were in post; the former responded by a nod and invited Lieutenant Milkstone to assume her place. The bridge of *MSS Drake II* was familiar now as Copper had spent a couple of night watches there and had taken part in frequent sim sessions to accustom herself to the layout and equipment of the science stations and various others. She mentally reviewed her colleagues as she trod over to her position, noting Lieutenant Commander Faela Khilph alongside Lieutenant Bell Kivian at the navi-helm console, with Lieutenant Flax Dyxin at comms. Engineering, weapons and tactical at her side of the bridge were manned, although she observed in some relief that the emergency medical station was unoccupied. At the opposite side, the second weapons station was crewed, as was ops, but environmental and security and both auxiliary positions were empty. As she sat, Copper was amused to see a breathless Tawny Brown, with two others at her heels, race in through the rear elevator. Tawny made for security as the other two slid in at environmental and operational management stations, relieving the current ops officer.

Dr Ossy Inkscree was manning the main science console and greeted her cordially, advising that she lock in her ident, charge up her station and assess the current status of all ship's science sensor arrays under her command promptly. Although still more than an hour away from docking, it was as well to have all such sensors under direct bridge control and not tied up by science officers elsewhere aboard. Not that they would dare this close to docking, Copper thought to herself as she complied with a smile and an affirmative.

There was time to look around and contemplate what this spell of duty would mean to her record, Copper mused as she automatically inspected her monitors and established the status of the external sensors that told her what was going on beyond the immediate environs of the vessel. Her business at her post in general was to monitor shipboard scientific activity, maintain active links to the ship's data sources lest they were needed and to keep track of conditions and activity outside the ship; she could also scan other vessels or external bodies and initiate drop and tracking of scientific probes for a number of purposes.

As the *Drake* was on final approach to her destination and manoeuvring on thrusters to assume her position alongside the massive spinning structure that was Jupiter Station, a thrill that was almost palpable rippled through the bridge crew and the watchers who had commandeered the best views from the observation deck. The final command to set for station-keeping had just been given when the comms officer let out a cry.

"Picking up a distress call to Jupiter Station, ma'am!"

The colonel started up. "Put it on amplifier, let's hear it!"

"Aye, ma'am…"

"*MSS Lithium Star* to station Jupiter! Mayday! We're being pulled off course… energy spike of unknown origin. Our main engines are failing to compensate…"

"All hands battlestations! Helm, prepare to disengage. Get us a direct line to her reported position and punch it, Ms Khilph. All stations, get me everything you can on what's going on out there," the colonel ordered brusquely.

"Jupiter Station is responding," Dyxin at comms called out. "She's preparing to despatch two small scouts but they're poorly armed. Jupiter requesting our aid: we're the only large vessel in, ma'am."

"Confirm we're on our way and tell them to hang on to their scouts – we'll call if we need back-up. Raise the *Lithium Star*, comms and get their status. Tie yourselves in people, this will be a rough ride."

"I'll say!" Copper muttered to herself as she set her sensor arrays to their widest spread to capture every available piece of data she could, to the sound of pounding feet as duty officers sped onto the bridge to man every last station.

"Tactical, long-range sensors to maximum and ready tractors; make sure our shields are up to full strength. Weapons stations, all defensive systems on line and heat them up. Get the fighters to their bays, Number One; we may not need them but I want them on standby."

"Aye, ma'am," Helmis answered.

"Make sure your engines are up to it, Chief: we may have some close manoeuvring to do."

"On it," Themis Sage responded briefly as Colonel Moritz again demanded the status of the *Lithium Star*.

A crackling voice echoed from comms. "We're being pulled off course by an unknown force, diverting as much power as we can to engines to compensate. Triangulating source of energy — it's definitely moon Elara!"

"What? Comms, get confirmation of that. See if you can set up a supra-light link and get me visual!" the colonel ordered. "Helm, steady as she goes but make speed."

The minutes ticked by as the *Drake's* speed increased and the links were made. Copper rapidly recalibrated her long-distance sensors to increase their operating efficiency and then began to scan ahead to where she expected to find the first signs of the stricken ship. She was fizzing with excitement but a small corner of her mind was busy with some inkling of unease.

"*Lithium Star* on the comm!" announced Dyxin from his station.

Seconds later, the face of Captain Mortin LeFlynn emerged from the main holo-grid. He looked grim but the bridge of his ship seemed to be intact. The *Drake's* bridge crew were aware of strange creaks that may have been the *Lithium Star's* engines straining to cope with the forces pulling her off course. LeFlynn was checking the output of something on his board but looked up to acknowledge Colonel Moritz and immediately gave orders for his ship's readings of the situation to be sent on a tight beam to her vessel.

"Receiving," Ossy Inkscree announced from his station.

As the distress call had stated, the *Lithium Star* had suddenly been assailed by an energy beam of unknown configuration that had appeared without warning. It had captured the ship in some sort of restraint field and begun to pull her off course. LeFlynn's crew had tracked the phenomenon back to its source as the ship had fought to maintain position, but the strain had seriously drained her main and auxiliary engines and reduced her power. The tractor's origin was now verified as the distant Jovian moon Elara. The *Lithium Star's* inward trajectory would have taken her across Elara's orbit but not in close proximity to the moon.

"We're on our way," the colonel advised as she scanned her boards. "Helm, increase our speed. Science and tactical stations maintain long-distance scans: I want to know what's out there and if that source is capable of sending out a second beam. This seems like an uncanny case of déjà vu," she added.

"I've got ion trail traces – working out precisely where she was when the tractor hit," Copper announced. "If we keep her between us and the beam on approach we may be able to avoid attack. Elara's not an enormous body, though there may be more than one source there."

"Coming in on the same line? We're a tad larger than the *Lithium Star*, Lieutenant," Inkscree pointed out.

"Smaller target if it can't visualise the whole vessel," Copper clarified as the colonel released her seat restraints and came over to check the science stations' outputs. "But there may be probes linked to it dispersed over a large area that are keeping an eye on anything approaching *and* other sites capable of engagement."

"Tactical, keep a close eye on developments and prepare to move if we find ourselves a target; weapons stations, targeting eyes in three hundred and sixty degree sweeps, I'm not taking the chance there's more than one source of whatever's got hold of the *Lithium Star* or that anything else untoward is scanning," the colonel ordered.

Copper had set up a spec of Elara, which was now rotating above her console. It was a small, dark world that reflected little light. She checked its structure carefully as something niggled at the back of her mind. The small moon had been charted as comprising mainly carbon, she reported. Carbonaceous silicates, other common rock and mineral types and a small quantity of water ice made up much of the core, but no in-depth scans had ever been done. Its structure was similar to its neighbouring moons, which were all believed to be captured asteroids…

"Asteroid!" she muttered. "Just a sec, that's it… Let's pull up the spec of that asteroid with the organo-tech inclusions that caused the *Fearless* trouble when she started getting too close."

The chief SO was quick to catch on and began to modify his own boards to make sense of the data that the *Lithium Star* had garnered. "No specifics," he rumbled. "But their data's patchy."

"Let me see," Copper said suddenly. "Patchy," she mused. "As if bits of the moon's surface are shielded?"

"Blanks in the data don't imply shielding, other things can interfere with sensor readings," Inkscree disputed. "And they could only get a partial visual due to their angle of approach."

"Granted, but they should be able to extensively visualise the surface and they haven't. But there's something else: they were pulled off course from much further out than the *Fearless* when she reported problems – *that* suggests they were detected as they passed a certain point that triggered something and I don't for a second imagine it was coincidence that they passed exactly the spot where some handy probe could pick them up."

"You're suggesting that there may be some sort of operative detection network set to sense traffic in the area?" the colonel asked. "Not logical: there have been spacecraft through this area for decades – the *Wayfinder* for one – and there's been nothing reported before, as far as I'm aware."

"We haven't had this level of interest in alien activity before, ma'am," Copper pointed out. "Not to mention the increasing numbers of spacecraft, known and unknown, that are making forays into space in the hopes of finding something of profit, especially of alien origin. Back on Mars, I recall my visit to the military base next to the Warren: part of it seemed to be set-up to receive and monitor comms of unknown and potentially alien origin being received on Mars. And weren't there Fleet ships out here then, ma'am, relaying signals that had been detected?"

"You and Ms Lyrican challenged me with that later on," the colonel remembered wryly. "You'd both noted the volume of incoming comms from orbital stations at our base and guessed that unidentified signals were being relayed by the Fleet ships and space stations picking them up. You also suggested that certain parties were likely to be building explorer-type vessels on their own and stealing the tech to do it, hence the troubles at your Lowell lab with break-ins and thefts. As Lieutenant Lyrican pointed out at the time, things seemed to be coming to the boil. So what's your take on the present situation, Lieutenant?"

"Maybe some well-hidden and long defunct defence systems are waking up – or being woken up – because of the outflux of ships and hence the increase in movement further out from the densely habited areas. And of course the actions of the *Fearless* in attempting to penetrate that asteroid awoke something there – I take it there has been no word from the science vessel despatched to check it out, ma'am?"

"Not yet. But you're implying that potentially there are more ancient *alien* defences out here that are now on alert because of increased activity and the aggressive action of the *Fearless* against such a base?"

"Speculation, ma'am. But the *Fearless* was attacked and now the *Lithium Star* seems to be in the same position, only they didn't provoke the response, as far as we know. That smacks of escalation to me, ma'am."

The colonel's green eyes narrowed as she scanned the data at Copper's station again. "No previous in-depth scans, ever?"

"None recorded, ma'am. So my guess would be ancient tech that *was* shielded, since the inclusions within the asteroid the *Fearless* went in to investigate were similar to the materials we know about – replicative and so able to withstand the rigours of being locked within a body in space for millennia. We'll know when we get readings from Elara and do a data comparison – we have enough of our own data to do that."

"Keep on it. Current status of *Lithium Star*?" she went on as she made her way back to the command unit and her chair.

"Still losing power," Helmis confirmed, scanning his boards. "We'll be up with them in fifteen minutes, but we'll be cutting it mighty fine. And support from Jupiter Station is way behind."

"Get us more speed, Chief, but be prepared to break off if we meet trouble," the colonel ordered Sage. "Tactical, use ship's long-range sensors to scan any local objects that might pose a threat if they're hostile and helm, plot evasive manoeuvres to avoid. Tactical and engineering, enhance defensive shielding and make sure our tractor systems are up to full capacity as we may have to pull the *Lithium Star* out of trouble."

"*Lithium Star* reporting incoming fire!" yelled Dyxin from the comms station. "Phase-beam weapon, pulsed salvo. Their main engines have taken a direct hit!"

19: JUPITER STATION

The *Drake* picked up speed at her commanding officer's behest, the red alert siren screaming as the ship sped on at full-tilt. The implications of the hit on the *Lithium Star's* main engines were clear in most minds on the bridge: she would no longer have the power to prevent the tractor beam drawing her in and much of her remaining energy would have to be diverted to the shields to deflect the incoming weapons fire. As the embattled ship shook under a second salvo, the shaky visual of her bridge in the main holo-grid shimmered and faded. The *Drake's* tactical stations were ordered to set up a tri-dee visual of the surrounding space in the overhead grid and plot the course of the action as soon as they were within visual range.

As the overhead holo-grid extended down into the well of the bridge, Copper glanced up, tightened the restraints holding her to her chair and turned back to set every science sensor she had to its fullest extent. "Dammit, Spook, do something!" she hissed through clenched teeth.

Quite suddenly, Copper was aware that Spook was no longer close by, but some compulsion made her link to Linen over her wrist-comm and demand her location. As ship's status was red alert and battlestations, Lieutenants Lyrican and Addystone were in their main science lab. Both were surprised at the summons.

"Listen," Copper commanded. "That lump of organic tissue we found in the *Lithstar's* sample tube – the thumb-sized piece: get it out of the high security storage locker and get all the data we have on it. Leave the sample out, let the data run."

"You what?" demanded Linen.

"Just do it, dammit! Now! Milkstone out."

"What in hell are you doing?" demanded Ossy Inkscree from the main science station.

"Hunch," Copper responded.

Five minutes slid by as Dyxin at comms wrestled with his controls in an effort to establish a link to their fellow vessel, the holo starfield in the overhead grid shifting as the *Drake* pushed onwards towards Elara. Through a sudden static burst, the voice of Captain Mortin LeFlynn could be heard harshly requesting confirmation of something as a visual was at last achieved.

"Affirmative, Captain: unknown energy weapon has ceased fire and tractor beam reads as weakening," a voice responded.

Colonel Moritz called for a review of the situation from her own teams before she requested an update from LeFlynn. The *Drake* was now close enough that her stations were able to verify the *Lithium Star's* readings: the assault from the surface of the moon was no longer in progress, although the tractor beam could now be detected.

Copper was quick to run comparisons with the data collected during and after the *Fearless* incident. "Energy signals detected from Elara match those recorded from unidentified structures on asteroid Helixus. Composition and relative size of Elara also very similar to Helixus," she added.

"We're in range," Lieutenant Vespoltz at the tactical station on her left announced.

"Don't bring us in too close, helm, I don't want to provoke further hostility," the colonel ordered. "Engineering, prepare for towing the *Lithium Star* to Jupiter Station: she won't make it on her own. Science stations, set every sensor you have on Elara, I want to know what in blazes is capable of pulling a starship off course from distance and then trying to shoot her out of the sky – and halting ops when *we* turn up. Ready a couple of probes to drop into orbit as we move out. Captain LeFlynn, what's your status? Can you manoeuvre away from that moon?"

The captain of the *Lithium Star* replied in the affirmative and thanked the *Drake* for her assistance, immediately ordering his bridge team to get some space between his ship and Elara. As the large ship slowly turned away and out of the small satellite's sphere of influence, the last vestiges of the restraint beam that had captured her cut off. Almost immediately, another surge of energy visible as a stream of photons from Elara shot up.

"What the hell!" half a dozen voices exclaimed as the *Lithium*

Star was enveloped in what appeared to be a diaphanous white cloud.

"It's a scanning beam of some sort!" Copper called out. "It's penetrating the *Lithstar's* hull. It's non-hostile."

"And how the hell do you figure that?" Inkscree asked icily.

"I'm not reading any further injury to ship, systems or crew," Copper responded mildly. "I've set some of my auxiliary sensor arrays to monitor her and she's fine. And she's still moving away from Elara. Scanning has ceased," she added more loudly.

"So I see," Dr Inkscree noted sardonically, indicating the tri-dee image in the holo-grid, where the ship was now free of the strange cloud.

The *Drake* slowly hove alongside the battered *Lithium Star* in order to deploy her tractors. The science stations of both ships had been set to gather every piece of information they could on the moon and the structures that were apparent to closer scans beneath its surface. Colonel Moritz had ordered a stand down to amber alert but left her first officer to direct the flight to Jupiter Station: she intended to notify Fleet Command of the latest incident at once.

Copper worked closely at her station, fielding questions from the senior SO. He was no fool and had realised that his junior officer knew more than she was telling and that something was biting her. That something was anxiety: Spook had not returned and she wanted to know why. In the past, when she had been uneasy or afraid, he had by some means sensed it and made his presence felt. Now she sensed nothing and she feared for him as much as for herself. That he had taken part in the action with the *Lithium Star* by inactivating the attacking systems she was sure, just as he had done to protect the *Drake*. All she could do now was try to work out the nature of the materials wedded to the bedrock of Elara, and of the structures below its surface, by analysing the streams of data her arrays were gathering. She was fast reaching the conclusion that the shielding defending the moon and its installations was superior to that of the asteroid. She had doubts whether this was down to chance or had been a deliberate bolstering of defences as a reaction to the actions of the *Fearless* at Helixus. If the latter, there must have been some data exchange between the two sites. So how many more were out there and in the network or open to comms breach?

"Same as Helixus!" she breathed at last and with a sense of relief. "Vertical sections drilled down into the substrata, regular recesses carved out, and they're reading part-organic. I guess this plexus area must be the central coordination point."

"Base material?" Inkscree demanded.

"Material is reading as the earlier version of alien organo-tech that we know of from Mars. But there's more been blasted out than there was at Helixus: about eighteen percent of the mass. And the shielding's greater."

"So it's another one of these defensive posts and it's been activated?" queried the chief SO, looking at her.

"That's my reading…"

They were interrupted by Captain Helmis giving the order for probe drop. Inkscree turned back to his console to ready the probes just as the colonel emerged from her duty office. Copper inhaled deeply and smiled as she continued her extraction of the last vestiges of data from the small moon below them: Spook had returned and she could sense a warm glow of satisfaction, as of a job well done – and something else.

"Fleet HQ thinks we seem to have started some sort of chain reaction with these unprovoked capture and attack tactics," the commanding officer noted to her second as she regained her seat. "They're getting jumpy."

"They should try sitting in our seats," Helmis responded. "Probes away! Let's get the hell out of here, helm: direct line to Jupiter Station, and don't forget we're heavy in the beam with the *Lithium Star* at our side."

"Aye, sir."

"At least when *we* show up, the action seems to tone down a little," Helmis continued.

"That's exercising the minds at HQ somewhat. They seem to think it might be our superior firepower, but that's hardly the case: the *Fearless* is a pretty large ship and was equipped with all that MDMC could throw at her, including massive weapons arrays. Let me have a look at what we've got," Colonel Moritz said, hauling an operations board across and tabbing the screen to call up the specs from her science stations.

"And how many other bodies are out there with that kind of

tech hidden inside, I wonder," the first officer queried.

"Let's hope we're not going to find out the hard way," was the dry rejoinder. "Alien fever is already gripping Mars media and a number of channels are positing invasion scenarios."

She pushed back her board and stepped down, heading over to the science positions. There, she propped herself against the secondary station with arms folded and looked down at Copper.

"Interesting turn of events, Lieutenant Milkstone: a situation similar to Helixus in that a restraining tractor is followed by high energy pulse fire. First catch your prey and then destroy it."

"Not quite, ma'am," Copper dared to contradict. "A well-shielded ship flies in and begins a close system scan, and that was *after* MDMC had probed remotely and detected enough of interest to despatch the *Fearless*. The remote probe may have alerted the systems on Helixus that they had been scanned; the arrival of the ship must have triggered something, but we don't know if the *Fearless* was just scanning or had sent in probes for a closer look. *That* may have activated the tractor, but the first hit gets her main engines? That was some targeting. It may be that disablement was the tactic, but the *Fearless* returned fire. Catch your prey to find out what it is as it's trying to find out what *you* are, and then disable or destroy it when you realise you don't know, just in case it's bent on your destruction."

"You reckoned last time that the first exploration by MDMC alerted the hardware on Helixus that it had been surveyed and the system was sufficiently advanced to activate some automatic alert, which was picked up by various stations and ships. But it can't have been the first alert, as we've been picking up strange signals for years, though perhaps not for the same reasons," the colonel mused. "But this encounter by the *Lithium Star*: she was much further away from Elara, and yet she was intercepted. As if she was recognised as potentially hostile."

Copper nodded and voiced her theory of data transfer from Helixus to Elara and perhaps to other linked sites: some form of early warning system that not only alerted but updated the core data of connected sites, enabling the recognition of threats from outside and identifying the ways to deal with them. That systems planted millennia ago throughout the Sol system were becoming active seemed clear, but given their power and their nature, they were more than a match for human starships.

"But they haven't downed one yet – as far as we know."

"No ma'am," Copper responded, aware that there was some other agenda behind the colonel's remarks. "But they *have* used deadly force to good effect."

"Which bodes ill for the likes of us," Ossy Inkscree put in. "If we're headed out there and more of these bases are hidden on various bodies that we might be exploring – we *are* looking for alien tech after all."

"Let me see the data the *Lithium Star* transferred – the visual as she was being pulled in, when that weapon on Elara opened fire," Colonel Moritz commanded.

The three watched the holo above the main science station as it revolved and expanded, the moon coming ever closer and its surface showing a marked similarity to that of Helixus. Copper slowed and enhanced the initial pulse of the destructive beam to enable a closer scrutiny of its source: it seemed to emanate from one of the vertical shafts that pierced the rocky body.

"It's very high energy but fuzzy, as if there's some shielding or data-scrambling in effect that's blurring readings," she said.

"Several cavities, but only one firing," Inkscree noted. "But where's the source of the tractor that's pulling the *Lithium Star*?"

"This one," Copper pointed. "I wonder if each shaft has a specific purpose, or if each one's set to use whatever is needed at the time. But there must have been some scanning device in operation in the vicinity that clocked the *Lithstar* on a close vector and warned the systems on the moon."

"Or their long-range scanning capability is phenomenal," argued Inkscree.

"Move on to when the *Lithium Star* reported the weapon had ceased fire and the tractor beam had begun to power down."

Copper did as she was bid, feeling a trickle of anxiety down her back as Inkscree eyed her closely and turned to check his own station. "Before we came into range, ma'am," she admitted.

"Just after *you* contacted Lieutenant Lyrican in the lab," the chief SO cut in. "When you told her to get some sample that had come from the *Lithium Star* out of secure storage and leave it out; and something about running the related data? A hunch, you said."

"Aye, sir."

"You've got explaining to do," he told her.

"Let me hear it," the colonel ordered, her eyes narrowing.

"It was that lump of tech-enhanced DNA-based matter that we figured might be some type of alien organic tissue, ma'am. It caused – excitement – at the time in the lab," she said quietly, with a glance at Inkscree.

"Why leave it out and run the data at such a critical time?"

"Ma'am, I'd rather not say at this point."

Inkscree exploded quietly at his station as the colonel looked searchingly at her science officer. "Dr Inkscree, take a walk but not off the bridge. Ms Milkstone, you have two minutes."

"We found the chunk of alien tissue in the *Lithstar* sample; Spook was seriously excited but *not* scared. We figured it might be the organic remains of an alien like him: we did suggest as much to you, ma'am, when we reported it. Trisk suggested at the time, jokingly perhaps, that the non-organic part might still be aboard the *Lithstar* if the original was able to separate its non-organic from its organic body, though we didn't pass *that* on to you. But I'm beginning to suspect he was closer than he knew. When the *Lithstar* was hit, I mentally yelled at Spook to do something; *he* vanished and some instinct made me tell Linen to fish out the sample and run the data. I don't know why but I think it was Spook running some checks of his own."

"Are you seriously telling me you think there's another alien analogous to your Spook aboard the *Lithium Star*?"

"It's a possibility, ma'am. It might be worthwhile paying the *Lithium Star* a visit when we reach base. It looks from the data that the power drop on Elara began before we re-established contact with her but after I asked Spook to take a hand – but that's not all…" Copper shuffled uncomfortably in her seat.

"Out with it."

"When Spook came back, I felt he was really happy with the outcome. I don't know why, but it was almost physical and for some reason, I kept sensing Linen… Lieutenant Lyrican. So I'm wondering if he *has* found one of his own kind. And then the scan of the *Lithium Star*," Copper went on, her fingers to her lips as she reflected. "I suspect it might have been an attempt to capture the complete spec of a human starship."

"For what reason?"

"There you have me; but if the control hub of the structure has *that* data stored in its memory and it comes across another similar ship, it knows its parameters – and its capabilities."

"Massive speculation – but if these bases are linked, and that *was* a scan to capture the spec of the *Lithium Star*, then any ship that comes close enough to one may be a target; and with the sophistication of the set-up, the weapons could be configured to take it down before it knew what hit it."

Copper was shaking her head. "I disagree, ma'am. The scan had no effect on the ship or the crew, as far as I could tell, and Captain LeFlynn reported none. And there was no hindrance to her moving out of Elaran space."

"So?"

"I think Spook convinced the intelligence of the system that we pose no threat and our ships can be safely ignored."

Colonel Moritz looked at her closely. "That is one hell of a theory to take on trust. I'd like it confirmed," she said slowly. "I think you and your Spook need to find some way of exchanging specific information. But this stays under wraps."

"Lieutenants Lyrican and Addystone…"

"Will be told when and if I say so."

"Yes ma'am."

A call from comms that Jupiter Station was on line and the colonel was requested to respond cut the conversation, much to Copper's relief. She turned back to her station, glad to be rid of the feeling that she was the sole repository of more information than she was comfortable with. She was convinced that the scan of the *Lithium Star* was a deliberate act and that the result would be less trouble for Mars Fleet in the space lanes. The downside was that such a respite would also benefit MDMC and any other greedy concerns that wanted in on the spoils of alien booty that might be out there. In light of the troubles that she and Linen had faced ever since they had found that first piece of alien technology in their samples whilst they were still working with the Amberline Group, there were a few such outfits around, no doubt with clout and credit enough to launch starships of their own on clandestine missions. There had been commercial ships on exploratory operations to search out potentially profitable resources far from home since such ventures had been possible.

Whether it was the result of their conversation or the data that indicated that nothing was pursuing them from Elara, the colonel ordered the alert status of the *Drake* reduced to yellow. The bridge crew had perforce to remain in station, but it meant that others not required to be on duty could stand down, albeit it on standby. Copper knew Linen and Trisk sufficiently well to realise that they would still be in the lab and no doubt following as much of the action as they could from their own stations. She had a task for her friend, but as Dr Inkscree had resumed his station, she was reluctant to make the link.

With the *Lithium Star* in tow the *Drake* took over two hours to make Jupiter Station, but as she manoeuvred into her final position alongside the base and could at last release her fellow vessel into the safe arms of the docking struts of one of the repair berths, her bridge crew breathed a collective sigh of relief.

* * *

Copper was not released from duty until an hour or so later, when her first thought was breakfast. She linked her two friends to invite them to join her, more to avoid the inquisitive than as a need for congenial company. She was grateful that they made it to the mess before she did, for even the galley crew began to probe the second that she and Tawny Brown joined the queue. The security officer seemed to have much more energy than her colleague, for she directly launched into an abridged account of the action with two of her security colleagues, but Copper was not in the mood for questions.

Once seated, she informed Linen and Trisk that they would be brought up to date as and when Colonel Moritz deemed it appropriate and refused to provide more than the very basic details. She did, however, bring them both into her confidence as regards her suspicions that Mars Fleet and MDMC were not the only bodies with interest this far out into the Sol system and with a look at her redheaded friend, suggested that she contact Magenta Firewall and ask her to investigate what was happening as far as the launch of private outward bound exploratory ships was concerned. The name Greensands Minerals Mining Corp might be dropped into the mix, Copper suggested.

Linen gazed at her friend intently. "I remember ages ago, just before Grammy knocked our socks off by arranging a tour of the *Drake*, where, by the by we were drafted, that Majorelle mentioned a couple of missions due to launch about the same time as the *Drake*. One was MDMC and we now know that was the *Fearless*. The other was a commercial venture being built at the lunar construction dock by linked interests, to search out novel mineral resources, allegedly; one of the outfits was a Greensands Archaeology. *That* caught Majorelle's attention."

"And ours," Copper added. "Greensands was a bunch we'd never heard of until we found it was sponsoring Mizzle Chert's research though Mars Gov's Postgrad Educational Scheme; and Mizzle turning up was the start of big trouble for us, including robbery and violence," she clarified for Trisk's benefit.

"With Grammy's marines and Colonel Moritz coming to the rescue at one point," Linen remembered, smiling. "So you want to know who's out here and what they're doing, if possible, but you can't tell us why?"

"That's about it."

"Why Grammy Magenta?"

"Because Magenta has more fingers and toes in more pies than Mars Gov and she's savvier and sneakier than anyone I know. I bet she'd be able to find out more about underhand dealing than the icy Colonel Karben's lot at Military Intelligence; and *her* office won't have spies in the cellar."

"You have a point and she'll be tickled by your opinion; I'll see what I can do. But what if *our* comms are monitored?"

"She's your Grammy and you link to her often. And she's known aboard the *Drake*. She was responsible for much of our comms systems for a start – we were the damn lab rats that she tested them on, remember?"

"And for which we had good reason to be grateful," Linen said jauntily. "Our necklets and wrist-comms saved us no end of credit. I'll link to Grammy later. We two are due back on duty in an hour, according to our schedules – they don't take account of red alerts and the human need for sleep, it seems."

"I'm heading for a shower and some sack time," Copper yawned. "But I'll see you both later."

Once back in her billet, refreshed and free from distraction, Copper set out purposely to link to Spook, whom she knew was with her. She realised that the colonel's way of thinking required specific information in relation to the future and Copper knew Ms Moritz well enough to know that she would want results sooner rather than later. Copper had received very clear data in the past but as mental images of locations or past occurrences, and as feelings or impressions that she assumed were akin to those her alien friend was picking up. But how to understand such perceptions as the answers to explicit enquiries about the future was problematical. The test set up in medbay with Faerin, Trisk and the colonel at hand had resulted in a measurable physical link and had shown her some small part of what Spook was capable of: she had felt then as if she was almost merging with the non-physical bubble that was the essence of the *MSS Drake II*. She therefore drew her robe around her, snuggled down into her sofa and sucked in a long lungful of air, relishing the lightness and sense of wellbeing that surrounded her.

* * *

A few hours later a loud buzz awoke Copper from a pleasant dream. It was Linen with the news that she had sent the link to Ms Firewall and that she and Trisk were headed to the mess. Orders from on high had come through to the effect that as the *Swordfish* was still two sols away and repairs and resupply to the *Drake* would take fourteen sols, shore leave for the crew would be arranged as soon as possible. Approval to utilise the facilities at Jupiter Station would be granted on application. Linen urged that the two get their bids in early and request the same timeslot. Copper groaned, eased into her uniform and made ready.

A bubbly Lieutenant Lyrican had already appropriated a table by the time Copper had collected her rations, and she slumped down beside her and Trisk, flexing aching shoulders.

"Fell asleep on the sofa," she replied to her friend's solicitous attentions. "How can you be so cheerful on no sleep?"

"Tough Mars Fleet training," she was told. "And a few winks that I caught in the office: Trisk stood guard."

"I didn't, I nodded off," he admitted. "But not before I'd locked the door and set it to alert me to intruders. Eat up, it's hot and it's all that's left. Galley crew's planning a major restock when we make the supply station off Europa but we'll pick up a few stores and finish all repairs and crew transfers here."

"Crew transfers? What crew transfers?" Copper demanded.

"Getting rid of our trophies in the brig, mostly, according to Tawny," Trisk disclosed. "Chief Locksmith's sorting it out and our Personnel Unit's hunting around for a few additions to the *Drake's* crew, but nothing's settled."

"Lor', as long as Gadget Blazells hasn't put in for a transfer!"

"He and his leadership skills prize," Linen put in. "He won't, it's too early, and as he knows we're aboard the *Drake*, it may put him off, especially as you beat him to the top prize for best of cohort. And the colonel *has* seen him and most likely knows our opinion of him. She was at our passing-out parade at Beagle Basecamp," she reminded Trisk. "Blazells is a second lieutenant aboard the *Lithstar*. I expect Lyssa Halsen's got her name down for leave already, as her brother's aboard that ship."

"We won't be poaching crew from the *Lithium Star*," Trisk consoled. "They may have to hang around for complete repair but they're still on an outward bound mission: they were to take over from the *Swordfish*, remember."

"As long as any we get are certified good guys," said Linen. "We need some peace to get on with our work."

"We'll get it," Copper promised, a quirky grin on her face as she tucked in to her lunch.

"I'll hold you to that," the redhead responded. "But for now, leave applications…"

Although not technically on duty, Copper accompanied her friends to the lab to put in a few hours work. For some reason she was itching to finish as much as possible of her thesis. With that behind her, she felt she could devote more time to duties that should be occupying her aboard ship. She had subliminally realised that Linen had read her correctly and she had taken to Fleet life as surely as she did to her student sols at Lowell. She felt the comfort of an ordered but ever-changing system that had sufficient slack in it to allow freedom from pure routine.

Indisposed for physical work, Dr Addystone was catching up on various links and intercepted a message from Prof Amberline in response to the reams of data that the three had sent on to Lowell. As MDMC in the guise of Lomax Gratikule was urging early publication and hinting that such action would stimulate MDMC Accounts into coughing up overdue expenses, Thars had decided to recast their two papers himself and send them off to the editorial section of the *Journal of Archaeoareography* in hopes of acceptance. His two recent acolytes, Ms Grass-Tephra and Mr Chengi, had both put in stints at the Warren and had acquitted themselves well. The military base alongside their site on Isidis Planitia was still active but very little interchange had taken place with them. It also appeared that EMMSO rep Ms Numbridge was bombarding the Prof's office with unreasonable requests for some of the samples that Copper and Linen had left in storage in Lowell's Enviro-Sciences Department. She had not been accommodated.

"Cheek!" was Copper's response. "Tell Thars that Maressan and Jenika have first dibs, as they're working our sites anyway; and as *we* won't be in the neighbourhood to foil any requisition, better them than anyone else."

"Agreed," Linen twinkled. "Add our salutations to Mariner, Alessa, Avrom and anyone else you can think of at Lowell. We'll link to Mik Mack and the guys at the Amber-Warren later."

"He likes what you've done on your theses and he's sending on hints for improvements. I'd ignore most of them, you're both doing fine," Trisk advised. "And he's congratulating all of us on our commendations and you on your promotion, Copper: word must have got through to home, then. Who's for a caff?"

"I've an appointment in medbay," Copper shrugged. "So I'd best get along for that. I'll have one when I get back."

"What gives?" Linen enquired. "I thought you'd been given a clean bill of health over your hits."

"GHQ," she said briefly. "To discuss advanced training. See you shortly."

Linen looked across at Trisk as the door closed. "That was a fib. What's she up to?"

Copper was up to a short trip back to her own quarters and then a visit to Kynedd Faerin in medbay. The doctor was just back on duty and she caught up with him a section away from his usual duty station. She had not told him in advance what the meeting was about but once they had reached the outer area of his office, she halted and removed a scanner from her pocket.

"I'm not bugged," Faerin observed ironically.

"I know. I'm not looking for bugs," she replied, heading to

the protected locker that had been breached some time before.

"And that store has been repaired and its security upgraded by Lieutenant Locksmith personally."

"I know. Can you open it, please?"

"Not before you tell me what this is all about and why you need to get into it."

Copper looked him squarely in the face. "I had a dream."

Faerin sighed. "Sarcasm gets you nowhere, Lieutenant."

"Okay, a hunch then, that I think Spook had a hand in. I just want to check it out before I go annoying the colonel or security with it. This secure locker of yours is supposed to be tamper-proof and you stored those probes in there that you and Trisk were working on. Are the two remaining ones still there?"

"No; and their current location is not your concern."

"Fair enough; but I can't tell you any more until you open up."

"If this is a wild goose chase…"

"At least the colonel won't be on my neck," Copper finished as the green light of the store changed to red when the doctor placed one hand on the door seal and the other on the unit top.

The door slowly unsealed and Faerin pulled it fully open to reveal a few stacked boxes. Copper asked him to remove them as she got down on one knee, scanner at the ready, to sweep the inside of the compartment. Puzzled, she swept again.

"Can the floor of this space be removed?" she asked.

"No idea. I'd assumed it was sealed down."

The two poked and dug for a few minutes, trying to lever the floor of the locker up. Copper rose to her feet, tapping her lip. Abruptly she made for the closest info-console and called up the schematic of the whole side section of the area.

"Ah – the fascia along this whole section of storage can be disengaged at either end; it's just clipped in for ease of access to the conduits behind. I'll get this side, you get the other."

"This had better be worth it," Faerin grumbled, complying.

In seconds the fascia board had been removed and the space beneath the wall-hung units revealed. The doctor had unearthed a flashlight from somewhere and was directing the beam along the length of myriad linked circuits. Copper held up a hand as the light illumined the space below the bulk of the secure store.

The two looked at one another as they realised that a package, closely mimicking its surroundings, had been rammed into the opening. Copper swept it with her scanner before slowly and carefully pulling it out by a corner.

"Not set to blow up in our faces, then," she said archly. "It must be very smart tech, my scanner can't penetrate it and it's chameleon wrap, it's changing to match the deck."

"But you know what's in it, don't you?"

"I have a notion. But it might be wise to get Mr Locksmith down here, if he's on duty."

Locksmith was on his rounds and reached medbay minutes later. Once up to date with the situation, he scratched his head.

"How in blazes did you figure?" he demanded.

"Can't tell you, Chief, but I thought you'd best be here when we open this up."

"*I* think we'd better get this up to security and open it up in a safe place," he argued, looking quizzically at her.

"It'll be fine," Copper replied confidently, having felt the rectangular carton and studied it thoroughly. "But you'll want to look at this wrapper up close. Can your scanner get through it?"

"Nope. Stealth tech, I guess."

As Copper unpacked the item from the layers of chameleon fabric that enshrouded it, the two men looked at one another.

"Well I'll be!" Faerin exclaimed, as he realised what they had found. "My missing probe!"

"My guess is it was shoved there to be picked up later, only whoever stashed it didn't get back to recover it," Locksmith said, slowly, regarding the two.

"It must have been stuck here some time after the break-in," Copper surmised. "It would have taken too much time to get the fascia off, wrap this up, stow it, replace the board and then make off with the other probe."

"I'll have a couple of my guys give this place another sweep," Locksmith sighed wearily. "They'll thank me for it," he added ironically. "But we're headed back to my office and we need to bring the colonel in on this. And I'll need your probe, Doc."

"Take it; but I'm not coming, I have my own mountain of work to shift. Keep me up to date on what you find. And have your team check in with me first."

"You got it."

* * *

"No Ms Lyrican?" queried the colonel as she walked through the security chief's office door to find Lieutenants Locksmith and Milkstone examining the probe's wrapping.

"As our talk on the bridge was to remain private, ma'am, and this relates to it, I thought it best to keep her out of the picture. She would have picked up on it," Copper responded. "If she hasn't already, that is."

The colonel's eyes widened. "I see. Well, let's hear what you have and what you think's been going on. And then, Chief, I'd like the use of your office for fifteen minutes, if you please, for a few words with Lieutenant Milkstone."

"Aye, ma'am," he agreed, with a searching look at Copper.

The two briefed the colonel on the happenings over the past hour, and after a short question and answer session, Locksmith was dismissed and ordered to take a break.

As the security chief stepped out, Copper removed the small thick metal cylinder that was her favourite privacy bug and set it down on the main console, activating it at a touch. The blue light ring radiated outwards, scanning, and she paused, aware of the amusement emanating from her superior officer.

"Taking no chances, I see; but I think Mr Locksmith has the sense to check his own office every sol. You've contacted your Spook I take it, and that's how you found the missing probe."

"Yes, ma'am," Copper confirmed and went on to describe the link she had attempted after her duty on the bridge.

She recalled her sensation of oneness with the alien entity that shared so much of her time and space and her attempts to ask him specific questions expressed as mental words rather than pictures or sensations. She had strained to physically hear rather than mentally see Spook's responses, but was forced to confess that she got nothing other than a slight ringing in her ears. She had persisted as long as she could stay awake and was at last certain that Spook had understood her enquiries over the action at Elara and its consequences for the *Drake*, the *Lithium Star* and Mars Fleet in general. As far as she could work out, there *was* a sequence of linked outposts scattered across the Sol system that had, millennia in the past, been the eyes and ears of entities that had set up some sort of station on Mars with the intention of colonisation, Earth already having a population of primitive sentients that they had no wish to displace. The posts had been used as intelligence gathering and defensive centres to give early warning of threats to the home planet. Abandoned when Mars fell apart under the onslaught of forces intent on plundering their superior technology, the outposts had endured because they had been well-shielded, with the majority of their functional systems held within the rocky bodies chosen to house them. As to why the ancient systems were now waking up and coming back on line, Copper had not been able to work out, but she was sure that the recent upsurge in exploration by human starships, made possible by advances in innovative technologies, was not the whole story. She had sensed disquiet in Spook over that and suspected that some of the recent increase in signals posited as alien that had been intercepted by ships and stations of Mars Fleet, and probably others, were related in some way.

"Invasion scenario," the colonel interjected dryly. "But where does that leave the safety of our vessels?"

Copper smiled briefly. "Spook, I think, managed to connect with the intelligence software of the central coordinating system on Elara and has altered it to recognise as non-hostile ships that are similar to the spec of the *Lithium Star* – and hopefully us, though I didn't pick up on that specifically. Given the system linkage that seems to be in operation, other active posts should receive the message. But I can't figure if any such will ignore any passing ship, or will attempt communication."

"That would be awkward."

"The bases must be so far apart that I can't see it would be much of a problem, ma'am," Copper differed. "Their comms range is so superior to ours that unless a ship passed really close, any message wouldn't be picked up."

"I hope you're right. Well done. But what about the alien sample and data run you asked Lieutenant Lyrican to organise?"

"That I haven't figured: *we* weren't scanned, so it can't have been a means to trigger some response in the tech on Elara. I think it was some agenda of Spook's that's not quite clear to me. But on a related note, ma'am: Linen and Trisk are no fools and by the expression on Linen's face when I headed to medbay, *she* wasn't convinced I was up to what I said I was."

"Now that the missing probe has been uncovered, there will no doubt be speculation as to who and what and how and your name will be in there somewhere. You'd better bring them up to date. I'll deal with Dr Faerin and Mr Locksmith. Meanwhile, as you've had a busy sol, you'd better take a break – all of you."

"No disrespect, ma'am, but shouldn't you take your own advice? You've been on duty longer than I have and with no respite," Copper ventured as she collected her bug.

"Get out of here, Lieutenant. That counsel can only be given me by my first officer or my chief medical officer and you're neither," the colonel informed her crisply, but she was smiling as she said it.

"Aye, ma'am."

"My office free now?" a voice asked at her elbow as the door to main security slid open.

"Colonel's still in there, but I'm sure she'll be out ASAP, Chief," Copper said with a quizzical half-smile.

"Like a caff?" Locksmith enquired with an uplifted eyebrow. "The colonel *did* tell me to take a break."

"I *would* like a caff but I have to get back to my office: I've got something to do before I can take a break."

"Maybe later," he persisted.

"Maybe later," she agreed as she turned, feeling his eyes on her back as she made for the elevator.

Copper made for her lab, where her advent was hailed with relief by her friend. "Where in blazes have you been? I checked with medbay and was told to mind my own business."

"Long story, which I am now authorised to pass on to you two, but no-one else. Is that clear?"

"Ma'am, yes ma'am!" Linen responded, saluting.

"Cut it, or I won't tell you. But let me get at the dispenser, I *really* need a caff. After which we can hit the mess if you like, as our respected commander has authorised off duty for us."

"Way to go, Cop: you must have impressed her – again."

* * *

Jupiter Station was an immense mass of metal and plas-glass, the central part of which rotated to maintain gravity at a degree comfortable for human existence. A chain of outer docking bays supported the starships which called in on their way to and from their own missions and other ports of call. The bays were linked to the main station units by transfer tubes to ease the passage of loads and people. Copper and Linen, having secured their leave, were among the third company from the *Drake* to head out station-side. Trisk had elected to take his leave later, as he had some buddy to meet up with that was due in on the *Swordfish*.

As Linen had deduced, a flexible pressurised exit tunnel was attached to the outer section of one of the smaller shuttle bays; it linked into a crossover node and thus to three transfer points, two of which were passenger-carrying transport tubes. With their implanted idents updated to allow them access to most of the amenities of the station, the two joined the line awaiting the next tube. Their ride, when it did turn up, reminded them of the monorail that plied the upper levels of Lowell Central Dome, except that the lower gravity required that they hang on tight. The views were certainly different, as the blackness of space and the massive view of part of the outside hull of their own ship looked nothing like the superstructure of a habitation dome. They also caught a glimpse of the *Lithium Star* in the distance and the scoring on her hull that showed where her main engines had come under fire.

"Ah, I see she's linked to a transfer section," Linen pointed out. "So there are probably a few of her crew on station as well. Wonder if we'll meet any we know?"

"You mean Blazells; or Fudge and Chocolate, if they're still aboard."

"I do, and it would be a hoot. But as we only have twelve hours, we'd better make the most of them. I'm not sure where the most entertaining places are to hang out, but I guess there will be a servo-mech or two advertising the best bars."

"And they'll all be lying," Copper told her. "But we'd better not start any brawls or all our gold stars for good behaviour will be wiped off our records."

"I doubt we have any: I bet you're down for insubordination for a start. You still haven't quite got the knack of being civil to your fellow officers, or even your superior officers. But where do we get off? We seem to have been travelling for a lifetime."

"This place coming up's called Precinct One. There're a lot

of bodies heading for the tube exits and they don't all look like they're due on their next shift. Some must be off duty station personnel, by the look of the uniforms."

"Talking of uniforms, we do look smart and your pips are standing out like diamonds. Been polishing them?"

"Very funny," Copper retorted, although her friend was not a million clicks from the truth. "Let's grab a handhold and make for the doors or they'll shut before we get there."

Precinct One, as a handy info-point informed them, was the centre of all that was current aboard Jupiter Station. Linen had decided that a useful stop would be the small café with outside seating just over the way, where they could sit and spy out the lie of the land whilst imbibing the general ambience of the place. They found chairs and ordered at Café Crème's table menu-vid. The caff appeared moments later at the hands of a cheerful acolyte, who required direct payment. Copper tendered a credit chit whilst her friend began a conversation designed to extract as much local gossip as possible on who was about and why. As the chat proceeded, the two automatically eyeballed the various places of interest pointed out and took in the directions to other areas that might be worth a visit.

"So crew from the *Lithstar* are in, the *Swordfish* is due sol after next and Fleet personnel on shore leave are renowned as big spenders," Copper summarised when their waitress left them to attend to other clients. "The locals are cannier with their credits and rumours have been rife about alien intrusion in Sol system space, but most locals here thought it was utter hogwash until the *Lithstar* was attacked just off the local beacon."

"That's about it," Linen agreed. "Except we don't visit Soapy Jim's as it's a dive that only rough and tumble dockworkers use. We should give it a go."

"Later: I want to visit the market on level six, if it's full of the tasteful merchandise she said it was."

"You have enough junk in your quarters, you don't need any more," Linen told her. "And we can't send stuff home this far out, it would cost six months' pay."

"Who said I was buying? But if it's where visitors go and it has places to eat there that'll no doubt be cheaper than here, we should look. We may as well do the tour anyway; they have an

ents hall, sports suites, hydroponics gardens and an officers' club where visiting officers are welcome – that would be us."

"Hey, you're right, it would. And if Gadget Blazells is on shore leave, you can bet your blue dragon he'll stop off there."

"I might see him later, if the colonel *does* visit the *Lithstar*," Copper said unguardedly.

"You what? You're getting a trip to the *Lithstar*?"

Copper halted, cursing herself. "Keep your voice down! The chat the colonel had with me on the bridge, when I hinted that there might just be another alien entity aboard her. I also hinted that it might be worth her while to pay a visit to the *Lithstar* – she didn't pick me up on it, but if she went ahead, she would need me there to verify anything of that nature we came across. I didn't say to you and Trisk, because she's not got back to me. Maybe she thought I was going too far."

"These sols, you always go too far," Linen said resignedly.

"Look, I'd no intention of holding out on you. Truth be told, I'd forgotten all about it after the fun of finding Trisk's missing probe. But it may come to naught, so for frock's sake, say *nothing* to anybody."

"Not even Gadget Blazells?" Linen asked, her eyes crinkling up in mischief.

"Why do you say that?" Copper began, but paused, looking around: Linen's tone and a feeling had alerted her.

"Over by the power stanchion, where the holo-flic theatre entrance is," the redhead nodded. "He's with another officer – a first lieutenant, by the pips. He's spotted us!"

"It's your hair. You've let it loose and it stands out like a flare in a fireworks factory. Stop waving!"

At Linen's mimed invitation, the two officers over the way advanced, Blazells obviously alerting his colleague to the identity of the seated two.

"Well met, Gadget!" the redhead smiled engagingly, ready to turn her usual charm offensive on the unsuspecting unknown. "We obviously knew the *Lithstar* was in station, but what a small galaxy!"

"Lyrican and Milkstone," was the salutation, as he indicated the two to his friend. "This is Lieutenant Leo Skyller."

As that seemed to be the only introduction that Blazells was prepared to make, Linen invited both to sit, ordering up another two cups of caff. She then began questioning their ex-colleague and his friend as to the state of their health after the action their ship had seen, kindly informing them that Copper had been on duty on the bridge of the *Drake* at the time and thus was part of it. This was enough to draw Blazells' eyes that way and they widened as they caught her shiny new pips and the slide on her jacket that denoted her rank.

"You've been made first lieutenant already!"

"As a consequence of outstanding action over and above the call of duty, after some trouble aboard, but naturally we can't give you details without the proper authority," Linen informed him ingenuously. "We had the ceremony aboard ship."

"You had a special ceremony aboard ship?" asked Blazells.

"Hardly," was Copper's response. "It was just at the end of a general knees-up."

"The finale," Linen corrected. "But I'm surprised you didn't hear about it, Gadget; I know it was mentioned in despatches, because we both had congratulations from home."

"You *both* had?" the lieutenant repeated, somewhat blankly.

"There were a handful of commendations," Linen explained blithely, raising her shoulders. "But here's your caff. Tell us all you can about the trouble aboard the *Lithstar*, and if our old friends Floris Fludge and Erkal Chokatti are still with you. We remember *them* from your ship's stopover at Lowell more than half a year ago."

Fludge and Chokatti were still serving aboard the *Lithium Star*; the former had been promoted to full commander and was now chief tactical officer. As to the interception by the strange energy beam, Skyller could tell them little and Blazells even less, as both had been at their own duty stations at the time. Blazells was now a junior flight officer and was currently training on weapons; his friend was in supply and logistics. In return, Linen reminded Blazells that she and Copper were science officers, the result of their College background at Lowell, and were thus busy most sols in the labs aboard the *Drake*. Both had manned the bridge science station and were subject to the usual rounds of flight and other training.

Lieutenant Leo Skyller seemed friendly enough but not much

of a talker. Gadget Blazells was a little less aloof than he had been at Beagle but seemed aggravated at the notion that his two ex-colleagues had made it slightly further than he had. None of the three had heard anything of others of their cohort and how they were progressing, but no doubt they would come across one or two of them in the future, Linen suggested as she sipped her caff. After a round of talking, where the two officers from the *Lithium Star* seemed to unbend a little and had been induced to describe their life aboard a mid-range cruiser bound on a mapping and space safety mission, they were interrupted by a chirp from Copper's wrist-comm.

Copper had time only for one startled look at her friend as she quickly tabbed up the link and confirmed her identity.

"Moritz here. I need you aboard, Lieutenant. I'll meet you in shuttle bay twelve in one half hour. Out."

20: NEW FRIENDS

When your commanding officer demands your presence, you do not sit around gossiping, Linen was quick to point out to their two acquaintances as Copper shot to her feet with an oath. She was all too aware of what this summons possibly meant and bid a hasty farewell to Linen and the two from the *Lithium Star*. The redhead had a small inkling of what was in the wind and elected to accompany her friend as far as the tube stop.

"Thanks be there's a comfort station in shuttle bay twelve, I'll need it," Copper muttered as the two marched swiftly off. "How many are headed out on this little spree, I wonder?"

"Think it's a trip to the *Lithstar*?" Linen queried.

"I do. I doubt the colonel would have intruded on my leave for anything else: she's not unreasonable. I'd like to know how she fixed it up with LeFlynn and how she'll explain me. But it was my idea in the first place, so I guess I deserve all I get."

"It's *Captain* LeFlynn, and don't you forget it," warned Linen. "Here we are and good luck. I'll see you when you get back; just link me and we can meet up. If you get back, that is. I'll scout out the good places around here."

"Just don't get into trouble. See you later – I hope."

Copper had a few minutes in hand to refresh herself before her assignation. She espied the colonel heading her way shortly after taking up a visible stance just inside the entrance to bay twelve. A shuttle was prepping for launch, which she assumed was theirs. The colonel was not alone: she was accompanied by Chief Engineer Themis Sage and Security Chief Kit Locksmith.

"Lieutenant Milkstone," she greeted Copper. "Let's go. As you've probably realised, we're heading to the *Lithium Star* for a meeting with some of her senior personnel to discuss what went down during her interception and subsequent release by that automated station on Elara that we think is alien in origin. Your part is to contribute to the scientific aspects of the briefing, as you are more than familiar with similar alien technology and you were in post on the bridge of the *Drake* at the time. You can pilot the shuttle over: they're expecting us."

Copper had only time for a thrill of horror before she found herself following her senior officers into the shuttle. She could see Kit Locksmith smiling amusedly out of the corner of her eye and she gritted her teeth in determination. Her annoyance at the security chief carried her up and into the craft, and she settled herself in and began flight safety checks equably. The fact that the colonel had chosen the co-pilot's seat did little to mitigate a growing anxiety, however, but trying to imagine herself back at Beagle with Dingle and Blazells behind her and Linen alongside, she succeeded fairly well. The hours of shuttle practice in the sim suite aboard the *Drake* had better pay off, she thought to herself grimly: piloting a shuttle in a confined area of space was not the same as piloting an atmospheric craft back on Mars or in a virtual cockpit, however similar the controls.

Whether it was the calming influence of Spook or her almost automatic reflexes, Copper made the short trip competently and docked as requested in one of the outer landing bays of the crippled *Lithium Star*. Captain Mortin LeFlynn was there to greet them with his first officer, Commander Helma Gannet, and his chief of science, Dr Texel Ruddin. The introductions passed in a flurry and Copper soon found herself and Ruddin bringing up the rear of the small party as it made for one of the briefing rooms close to the bridge of the *Lithium Star*.

The colonel and the captain had met before, it transpired, and Copper soon worked out that it had been at the stopover of the *Lithium Star* at Mars, when the finds of rock and remnants of alien technology had been delivered to Lowell Leisure Dome and into the competent hands of Military Intelligence. Copper had only minutes to digest the information when another officer known by sight to the colonel turned up: Commander Floris Fludge, the chief tactical officer. He had been on the bridge during the attack, and on her previous mission he had been involved in the recovery of the samples that were now known to include relics of the *MSS Griffon*. Fludge was more surprised to see Copper than she was to see him but nodded composedly to her as he fell in alongside.

The *MSS Lithium Star* was much smaller than the *MSS Drake II* and her spec was less advanced, despite her recent complete overhaul. Her passageways were narrower and the decks seemed cramped to Copper, used as she was to the larger proportions of her own ship, but she paid close attention to the commander as he pointed out various points of interest. She kept him occupied by asking what she hoped were pertinent questions but she had not forgotten why she was aboard.

The briefing was an ordered affair until the colonel brought up the troubles she had aboard her ship with deliberate sabotage and enquired if the *Lithium Star* had been subject to similar. The senior officers looked at one another and Captain LeFlynn, after a brief pause, admitted that one or two incidents had marred his mission thus far, but his security had handled it. Kit Locksmith caught Copper's eye: it seemed that the spate of disruption to Mars Fleet was more extensive than Command was prepared to acknowledge. When LeFlynn had been brought up to date on the level of infiltration of the *Drake*, he was visibly shocked. That the *Swordfish* would transport the prisoners was less of a surprise: his own two were to be handed over to her also.

The colonel had requested that her chief engineer be allowed to examine the damaged engineering sections, whilst she and her science officer would like to see more of the ship, especially the laboratories. Her security chief would liaise with his opposite number aboard the *Lithium Star* on security measures. Copper found herself attached to Dr Ruddin whilst Locksmith was left with Commander Fludge for company. As Colonel Moritz had served aboard the *Wayfinder*, she was more than familiar with ships of the Explorer type, which left her junior officer with the opportunity to examine the science and related storage facilities in that section of the *Lithium Star* in relative peace. Lieutenant Milkstone was left in no doubts as to her task, as the colonel proposed that Ruddin clarify the search and recovery systems for sample-grabbing from the rocky worlds at the edge and edify her lieutenant as to the most effective means of operation.

Copper *was* deeply interested, for although the *Drake's* gear was advanced compared with that of the *Lithstar*, she had never seen it. She was due simulation exercises in such equipment use, but they had been deferred until closer to the time when she might be expected to apply them. One thing she did pick up on was that pieces of alien technology were still aboard the *Lithium Star* and that they were larger than the normal run of fragments she had encountered to date. They were locked in secure storage and Ruddin made no mention of them but she was positive. She also had a hunch that Spook was making a sortie of his own, for he was nowhere close.

The visit ended with an exchange of files on the structures scanned on Elara and the transfer of data relating to the asteroid with similar technology from the *Drake* to the *Lithium Star*. The latter was destined to spend at least twenty sols at Jupiter Station but LeFlynn was sanguine she would be fit for duty after repair. Kit Locksmith was given the job of piloting the shuttle on her return trip, to Copper's relief and his perception of it, as he had winked at her in evident enjoyment.

A swift debriefing back on board the *Drake* left Copper with the feeling that she had not heard the last of it by a long way. Themis Sage reported that the hits to the *Lithium Star's* engines had been extremely precise and designed to knock out salient systems without causing extensive damage elsewhere in main engineering. Security was not as stringent as that aboard the *Drake*, Locksmith stated, but the team had most of it sewn up tight. The two senior officers were dismissed to their duties and Copper was left to explain her impression of the science unit. She was hard put to clarify her opinion that Ruddin was not as open as he might have been about their previous mission, given the nature of the *Drake's* current assignment, but she admitted to her strong intuition that alien tech was still aboard the *Lithium Star* – as was a presence vaguely parallel to Spook.

Spook had returned just before the order had been given for the crew from the *Drake* to head back to their shuttle. He was seriously excited and the images that Copper had had, again of Linen, was strongly suggestive that he had found a friend, or at least an entity similar to himself, and it was non-hostile. She had sensed *something*, she disclosed to the colonel, but she was unable to resolve the feeling into anything akin to what she sensed when Spook was near. As far as she was aware, whatever it was had remained behind on the other ship.

"Why?" The colonel's question was sharp.

"Perhaps it's waiting for an invitation?"

The commanding officer's steely gaze was uncompromising and Copper continued hurriedly, "I don't know, ma'am. I only sensed it briefly, which makes me think I might have imagined more than was there – and it wasn't quite like Spook, but I'm used to *him*. It's maybe a matter of trust, or of loyalty to the ship that in a sense was its rescue – or just plain fear. Spook was certainly afraid when first I realised he was there and real."

"I recall you saying that this Spook of yours was scared when you told me of it out at Beagle. I didn't quite believe you. And now you think that there's a presence aboard the *Lithium Star* that's similar?"

"I think that's what I'm reading from Spook. The question is now, what do we do about it?"

"I suspect there's very little that *can* be done. You finish your leave, without revealing the details to Lieutenant Lyrican, at least off-ship. As to any alien technology aboard the *Lithium Star* – that cannot be proved. That goes no further. Dismissed."

"Aye, ma'am. Thank you, ma'am."

* * *

Copper made haste to return station-side, tabbing her link to locate Linen. Her friend acknowledged almost immediately and told her she would meet her at the exit to the transport tube.

"Four hours!" was the greeting when Copper stepped off the tube to find Linen leaning patiently against a nearby stanchion. "What in hell took so long?"

"Briefing, visiting, debriefing," was the terse reply. "I need a caff and some food, I'm starved. What have you been up to?"

"Met Lyssa Halsen and her brother, Erik. He's training to be a fighter pilot but he's a flight engineer and works mostly on the *Lithstar's* shuttles. But he's done his stint in main engineering: he was there when the ship was under attack. He didn't see much, but says there wasn't a lot of damage in his section; it was the main engines that took the worst."

Copper nodded. "Let's find an eatery. What's a good one?"

"I had lunch in the RedStar Bistro and it wasn't worth linking home about, so we won't go there. We could try the Disposable Cup over by those offices: it doesn't seem too busy."

"Maybe there's a good reason," Copper murmured pointedly, following in her wake.

Neither had cause for regrets as the café provided adequate food and drink at affordable prices and their uniforms elicited courteous attention. Copper was still too unsettled over her visit to the *Lithium Star* to indulge in much light chat, and her duty there and its aftermath she refused point blank to discuss. Linen on the other hand had much to disclose on the deficiencies of Jupiter Station as a base to which one would wish to be posted. For a start, if it *did* come under attack by anything or anyone, it couldn't exactly remove itself from the danger zone. It was also home to a surprising number of civilians, as trade concerns had had a hand in setting it up in the first place. The ents facilities were superior to the *Drake's*, Linen admitted, but not much else, although there was a dark underbelly to the place, judging by the various remarks from some of the resident personnel that she had spoken to, that sounded quite exciting if cloak and dagger was to your taste.

"We've tasted that kind of action far too often for comfort," Copper told her. "We're on leave, so let's make the most of the remaining time we have."

"Don't you get extra for having been called away on duty?" Linen queried.

"We're in the Service," her friend reminded her dryly. "We don't get overtime pay when we work twenty hours straight."

"Then let's go get some holo-pics to send home, to let them all know back on Mars what a great life we lead aboard a ship of the Fleet," the redhead advised cheerily. "There's no point in splashing out on souvenirs, we'd just have to store them in our quarters for the duration."

"And you might find yourself buying trouble," Copper said cynically but quietly. "If this place is as riddled with subversives as everywhere else seems to be."

That provoked a raised eyebrow. "That's not what you said earlier when you wanted to visit that market on level six."

"Things change; drink up your caff and we'll hit the trail and take in more of this ambience the place is famous for."

"Soapy Jim's?" Linen suggested. "It's on level five."

"If you must, but if you get into a fight, don't expect me to jump in after you."

In the event, Soapy Jim's was denied them as some problem had resulted in the place being closed until investigation by local security was complete. They therefore headed for the market on level six, where stalls were crammed together and light-fingered felons were a speciality, as far the waitress they had spoken to in Café Crème earlier was concerned. Copper took the precaution of ensuring Spook was close enough to alert her to trouble, but the only such they found was Ash Goff, with Tany Melucca in tow; *they* had just come from the officers' club and were looking for more entertaining company.

"Boring as hell: the only new faces were a few bright sparks off the *Lithium Star*," Tany enlightened them. "And this place seems no better. We're for the holo-flic theatre: want to come?"

Linen quickly declined on behalf of them both, having a wish to see the officers' club and the kind of people frequenting it. They found it on level three and most of the personnel in view were part of the military corps of Jupiter Station. Linen looked in vain for their former acquaintances Floris Fludge and Erkal Chokatti among the sprinkling of *Lithium Star* crewmen but was unlucky. With a wry glance, Copper told her she was asking too much of coincidence and if they *were* on leave they would be somewhere more salubrious. After discovering that the caff was free, she warmed to the place and collected two mugs. The duo elected to sit alone, although a few officers bearing the insignia of the *Drake* were about. There was a handy info-console that would display a holo-tour of the station if relevant idents were presented and it seemed a more comfortable way to see the sights than pounding the decks.

An hour later and Copper was of the opinion that if this was leave, Fleet could keep it. She was not of a mind for the dubious amusements provided by the local bars, the events and activities on offer were lacklustre and their fellow officers tedious. Linen knew exactly what was bothering her friend.

"It's Spook, isn't it?" she whispered. "He's around and he's bored or anxious or something."

"Yup. Let's finish this mediocre caff and head out."

Once the two had regained the wider spaces of Precinct One, Copper was more forthcoming. "He wants to set off on his own and doesn't want to leave me," she said.

"Aw, how sweet!"

"Very funny. I think he's set on a trip to the *Lithstar* for a call on whatever he thinks is on board there."

"There's something aboard the *Lithstar*?"

Too late Copper realised her slip. "Keep your voice down, for frock's sake or you'll have me court-martialled!" she hissed in an urgent undertone. "You didn't hear that. I'll tell you back aboard the *Drake*. How much time have we left?"

"Until we're back on duty morrow-sol, but we shouldn't stay here that long," Linen replied equably. "It's twenty hundred shipboard time. You want more shopping, eating or drinking?"

"To be honest, I'd rather be back in my quarters with my feet up and a mug of hot Chocó-crème," Copper confessed.

"What, no ale?"

"No ale. If you want one, I'll come along, but I feel I need a clear head."

"Well, as you've piqued my curiosity no end, I'd better come back with you. Besides, this was supposed to be *our* leave and you've been away for a large chunk of it. I missed you. Or at least your narky little ways."

"Thanks. We'll have a last look around, but I'm not going to be recommending Jupiter Station as a must-see for any travellers out this way. I've had better trips to the medi-centre at Lowell College for my bi-annual check-ups."

* * *

The following sol saw a return to duty for many of the crew of the *Drake*. After a breakfast enlivened by Kit Locksmith, who stopped by ostensibly to talk shuttle-handling with Copper, the two science officers set off to their lab. As the auto-ship from Fleet HQ was about due, the two felt that with the business of organising equipment and supply transfer, as well as the ongoing repairs to the ship by specialists from Jupiter Station, the colonel would be far too busy to pay them a visit. Accordingly, they had decided to tie up various loose ends in relation to their theses, Trisk being on leave for the sol as the *Swordfish* had made port. Their friend had left them his MEDIC, Barking, to augment the vast stores of data held by their own devices and to aid them in producing outlines that would meet the conditions of doctoral thesis submission to the University of Mars.

Copper had brought Linen up to date the previous evening on the events aboard the *Lithium Star* and her notion that their suspicions were perhaps correct that an alien entity had survived trouble out on the edge in the past, as Spook had on Mars, and was aboard their sister ship. The colonel would no doubt want more corroboration of that. As to the instinct that sizable pieces of alien tech were held aboard the *Lithium Star*, there was little they could do but speculate. Ruddin had been evasive, but there was no disloyalty in him, Copper was sure.

Linen suggested that another visit to the *Lithstar* with the alien lifeform probe put together by Trisk and Faerin might do the trick, but telling them that an alien may have hitched a ride from the crash site of the *Griffon* all those months back and they wanted to check it out would probably not go down too well. She was rewarded by a slap on the head and the instruction to start work or it would never be done: the data amassed by the initial batch of surf-sci bots they had been inveigled into testing in memorable sorties through their research sites at the Warren was now legitimately theirs to use as they would and they should take full advantage. Spook had in any case abandoned Copper, who suspected he *was* off on a quest to the *Lithstar*.

The first interruption to their labours came with the notice of a supra-light link to Linen from Magenta Firewall. The redhead decided to receive in the lab to save time and comms put the call through immediately. After a quick appraisal of the two by Ms Firewall, she cut to the point: her discreet enquiries had ferreted out that a high-spec exploration vessel, built under the strictest commercial security out at the lunar construction dock, had successfully completed her initial space-trials and was ready for launch on a shakedown cruise. Of those companies involved in its commissioning and financing, the names of Greensands Archaeology, an offshoot of Greensands Minerals Corp, and an outfit entitled the Nanedi Valles Extraction Consortium had floated to the surface of the depths of intrigue that Magenta had plumbed. The two officers were staggered.

"I recognise *both* those names!" Copper gasped.

"I thought you might," Magenta grunted. "They're smaller fry, but there are a couple of other outfits that I'm familiar with that have less than respectable credentials and bigger pockets, but one or two genuine investors as well. It's a sizeable venture and it seems to have attracted a lot of credit, though I haven't been able to find out what promises have been made on the returns and prestige expected."

"Nanedi Valles," Linen repeated. "That dustbagger that tried to fleece Ma Kellyn out of her uncle's inheritance way back had dealings with them – and so had you, Grammy," she went on.

"I did, and they didn't get away with it," Magenta responded tersely. "I couldn't get a hold of any names, but it looks like there's at least one other high-spec ship headed in your direction on the lookout for unique mineral reserves, so they say. Worlds out on the edge that initial probes suggest are repositories of rare and precious commodities," she snorted. "Not to mention that other credit-spinner, traces of sentient alien life, especially if it's up to date and flying a ship that would make yours look like a worn-out garbage scow."

"First dibs on alien life flying a starship might be last dibs," Copper interjected mildly. "I doubt if any such out this way are interested in just saying hello and handing over bundles of new tech for outfits like Greensands to make credit out of."

"Cynic," Magenta returned. "But I'm now transmitting what I found. I've sent a copy to your commanding officer, by the by: I thought she might be interested, given our links in the past."

Linen acknowledged receipt, grimacing at Copper over the last remark of Ms Firewall. The two, however, exchanged a few more pleasantries and then signed off, sighing.

"That's put a few shuttle-ducks among the greenery," Linen remarked. "The colonel will wonder why we're interested."

"It *is* part of our mission," Copper reminded her. "And anyone out to find alien tech, especially working alien tech, now probably is aware that there *is* some out there that may be worth the pocketing. And as the military is very interested and has despatched the *Drake*, not to mention her sister ships that are even now heading off into uncharted territory, they'll figure the incentives are as high as the risks and worth the gamble. And as the bases we've encountered may not now defend themselves against human-built starships, there may be troubles ahead. No, it's better that Colonel Moritz knows we have competition that's not liable to be over-friendly if we do meet up face to face."

"No commercial ship could take on the *Drake*, no matter how high-spec," Linen said plainly. "She's the best of the best – and with an advantage no other ship in the Fleet has. Or should I say three advantages?"

"That's debateable, if you're referring to us. And I suppose Fleet will despatch a ship to Elara and any other potential bases reported and set up strings of monitoring probes. But busy or not, we may see our glorious leader, so we'd better start moving. I want this thesis out of my orbit: I'm so frocked off with it I could scream."

"We could get our MEDICs to order everything as required by the UMars awarding body and fill in the blanks," suggested Linen wickedly. "Gerald and Gemima know us better than our blood kin, I bet."

"Yes; so well that they'd squeal and we'd be defrocked, or whatever happens to devious students. They have the outline locked in, we fill in the blanks we've got data for, which is all of it, and then *we* sit down and make sense of it. And then give the whole lot to Trisk and ask him nicely to make rude comments about our arguments and conclusions – he can extract any juicy bits to add to any publications he has a mind to submit. I'll even let him be first author, just to get this lot out of my hair."

"What's the rush? We have a whole mission to get through and no doubt plenty of down time, once we're out there and powering up to near-light velocities."

"That'll happen," Copper snorted. "We have our chunk of hull in outer bay four to play with, not to mention the stores of alien tech we've squirreled away in high-security storage that we should check out *and* the hard-holos we made of what we have pieces of. And then we have training schedules coming out of our ears: I've three flight sims over the next ten sols booked in mine for my off duty time."

"Not to mention a skim over that partial tri-dee of the chunk of rock that's our final destination, for this leg of our mission at any rate. Okay, you have a point. But I need a break: I want to check my personal comms, as I'm sure I've still seen nothing of what MDMC Accounts owes us, despite Lomax Gratikule and his empty promises."

"All the more reason to finish this and MDMC can go hang. We were promised that Fleet would give us every support to finish our stuff off if our sponsors came up short, I recall the colonel saying half an age ago. Let's lock up and head to the mess, I'm sick of it here."

The mess was alive with rumour, chiefly about the arrival of the *Swordfish* and two civilian cargo vessels. Speculation as to the assignment of additional crew to the *Drake* was rife but no-one seemed to know if it was on the cards. Kit Locksmith, whom Copper and Linen had joined in a corner booth at his request, was hoping for a few more for his team, but only on the proviso that he had a hand in selecting them. He also had information that the *Drake* would not be leaving her berth at Jupiter any time soon: as her repair schedule was tight her supplies from Europa station would be shipped across, and Kit was adamant that his people would be at the receiving end to scan every crate and scrutinise every manifest.

Linen meanwhile had called up her personal link log and to her annoyance found that no credit from MDMC had appeared. A short note from Thars informed them that he had sent several complaints in that direction but was none the wiser. Thulia had taken it upon herself to explain at some length that a lag in the arrival of their project reports at the EMMS Office was the root of the problem and would the two please link supra-light for an in-depth discussion with her and Mr Waterbone at their earliest convenience.

"Inform Ms Numbridge that she can go pee up a rope at her earliest convenience," Copper growled. "And tell her I said so."

"You got it," Linen grinned, as Locksmith chuckled quietly. "I'll tell Thars not to worry, as we're getting paid here and we're finishing up our theses ahead of schedule anyway, as we've so much data we're drowning in the stuff – and we have sufficient publications to submit as part of them, if we get the last couple accepted. If Noa and Syr could achieve doctoral status on the basis of what they didn't do at Lowell and the Warren, we sure as hell can on what we *did* do."

* * *

Despite their initial confidence that the colonel would be too busy to catch up with them, Copper had been right and they were somewhat chagrined to find her at their lab door a couple of hours later. She had skimmed over Ms Firewall's input on the new commercial ship and its links to Greensands Minerals. Also expecting that Lieutenant Lyrican would now be well-informed on what that had gone down aboard the *Lithium Star*, she had stopped by to find out if Lieutenant Milkstone had been able to garner any more on the situation aboard that ship.

In the event, Copper was able to report that Spook had spent time aboard the *Lithium Star* and had returned in a state that she sensed as content, overlain by a restless flurry. This, allied to his rising anxiety, she could only ascribe to the presence of a second alien entity akin to himself aboard the ship. The colonel was sceptical but Copper was sure that Spook's main concern was what was going to happen next: having found a being of his own kind after so long, he was irresolute as to how to proceed.

"Simple," was Linen's decisive opinion. "The *Lithstar* keeps its own and they're both lonely, or we get two. It seems unfair on the *Lithstar*, but then Spook gets a buddy, which will aid us in the long-term. Maybe they could both be put on the payroll?"

"Can it," Copper advised her friend. "I suspect there's very little we can do, ma'am," she went on to the colonel. "I *am* fairly sure there's another entity aboard the *Lithium Star*, but as I can't link to it and my sensing it at all was only a fleeting feeling along with images of Linen I got through Spook, all we can do is let Spook know it won't be unwelcome aboard the *Drake* and see if that probe that Trisk and Dr Faerin developed can pick up on it. It can on Spook, and I bet those two have refined it since…"

"It can on Spook?" Linen interrupted. "How do you know?"

"Because it's been tested," Copper told her. "Don't ask," she added.

The colonel was far from happy about the idea of *two* alien entities on the loose aboard her starship, but sanguine enough to know that there was very little that she could do about it. She demanded to be kept updated on anything relevant and ordered the two to carry on with their current work. She was keen to have them finish everything related to Lowell College and begin full time on what they had signed aboard to do.

"She seems to forget that we signed up on the proviso that we *could* carry on with our PhD research aboard the *Drake*," Linen muttered rebelliously when the coast was clear. "And now she reckons it's getting in the way of our real work?"

"Well it is," Copper frowned. "I want an end to it, and if we can get it off our backs sooner rather than later with every help we can get, I say go for it. We've worked our socks off for the data we have and the analyses we've done. We've put in more hours each than Noa and Syr have jointly on theirs, in far less time, and we've been chased, robbed and shot at in the process. We damn well deserve to have it all wrapped up."

"Yes ma'am!" Linen exclaimed, recovering her good spirits. "Hey, if we have the doings here, who confers the degrees?"

"In absentia, back on Mars. Magenta can pick them up: that should set a few ears aflame and annoy the authorities no end. Why don't we put it to Thars, with Trisk's agreement, and see what he says? If MDMC's refusing to cough up for us, at least he can dun them for supra-light links on what Maressan and Jenika are doing, as they *are* using our ex-site and do of course require communications with us."

"Bet the Glory Hole's been stripped half-bare by this time," Linen said glumly.

"*I* don't," Copper returned. "Maressan's a tidiness addict, so he's probably cleaned the place out and polished the facets of every embedded crystal. It'll be like stepping down into a hall of mirrors and he'll make you wipe your feet before you do."

"But what's the news on Spook's ship? We've heard nothing from the colonel on what's to do under our site, where the great and the good of Mars finest have been working for months on end. They've maybe managed to breach it by now."

Copper looked at her friend and shook her head slowly. She raised her head and closed her eyes, as if she was listening to something. A few moments passed, the only sound in the lab the gentle murmuring of background ops.

"What is it, Cop?"

"It's locked down," her friend sighed at last. "And if by some means somebody did force their way past its defences, it would self-destruct."

"What! Wouldn't that set off a marsquake or something? The power in it must be phenomenal."

"But controlled: internal meltdown, with containment. There would be warnings and anyone successfully breaching the hull would be in no doubt that it was about to blow and run for it."

"How can you know that?" Linen demanded.

Copper shook herself back into full consciousness. "Saw it in my mind's eye."

"So Spook shows you mental holo-flics whenever you want to know stuff; what does he do as a side-line, sing you songs?"

"Back to work, Lieutenant," she was ordered. "But I suspect the mil research out on Isidis has been put on a back burner for the moment: remember the number of incoming signals being picked up while *we* were there? Relays from ships, stations and all degrees of bases in-between? The levels must be near off the scale by this time, given what we've been involved in thus far, not to mention the *Fearless*, the *Lithstar* and Lor' knows how many other vessels that have kept quiet or haven't made it back. And now we know it's probable that stations like the ones on asteroid Helixus and on Elara *are* relay posts, how many more are out there…"

"And why are we up to our necks yet again?" Linen seethed stormily. "You're right: the sooner we get our Lowell research out of our hair, the sooner we get back to the real reason the *Drake* is out here and why we and Trisk to name but three were drafted in as part of her crew."

* * *

By the end of the following sol, much of their research work was in order and Copper and Linen were populating the outlines of their theses with relevant data, inferences and conclusions. Trisk had agreed to lend his hands, his brain and his MEDIC to the task and a link had been transmitted to Thars Amberline to enquire after the process of completing and submitting such a body of work from a starship of the Fleet. Trisk had sent a note on his own account proposing himself and Dr Ossy Inkscree as external examiners. The appointment of Lowell-based assessors was Thars' concern.

"Comms will have a field sol with the supra-light links we'll have to make," was Linen's opinion as she slapped a final data chit into Gerald's reader port. "Not to mention the simulations in glorious tri-dee that will have to be part of our stuff. We took the trouble to generate them, so we're frocking well going to use them to their fullest extent."

"Dr Inkscree will thank us for that," was Copper's view. "We can use that tri-dee spectacular of the Glory Hole we created for our presentation at Viking One when we were still learning our trade. It blew the socks off the audience there, so it should open a few eyes here and back at Lowell – though most of our lot at Lowell have seen it, because of our farewell seminar there."

"You deserve medals for the work you've done," Trisk put in with his usual lopsided grin. "But on another note, Copper: I've had words with the colonel, or rather, she had words with me. She wants me to set up one of the probes that Kynedd and I developed to scan for non-physical signals that might be alien life and link it to the whole-ship scanning system in security. She wants a deck-by-deck scan done, beginning morrow-sol, without alerting anyone to what we're at. There *will* be a number of areas we can't scan – engineering for a start, as they're in the middle of refit – but she told me to ask you for advice on the matter."

Copper sighed deeply. "I suggest you start in the secure store here," she told him. "And you can start now, if you've a mind, without linking to security. I've no doubt it'll read positive."

As the other two looked at her in stunned amazement, she gave a wry smile. "Spook came back an hour ago turning mental somersaults. The colonel more or less agreed he could bring a friend aboard, so he took that as an invitation and did. Say hello to Spook Two, or whoever he – or she – is."

"Or she?" asked Trisk.

Copper made a face. "Search me. I don't know if Spook's male, female, both, neither or something completely different."

"If neither, how do you get more than one?" Linen queried.

"The equivalent of amoebic splitting? A piece breaks off and hey presto, a new Spook? I've never asked. It's a tad personal, don't you think?"

"As *he's* able to access your every mood and physical sense and go beyond up close and personal, I'd say you'd every right," her redheaded friend informed her. "He can feel what you feel and when *you're* personally involved, so's he."

"Too much information!" chuckled Trisk. "And please note the time: we were off duty more than an hour ago. You two are holding me back and I've no intention of beginning more work right now. But what's Spook's buddy doing in the secure store?"

"Hiding," Copper replied. "Wouldn't you be, especially if you knew you could be detected by inquisitive aliens with scanners?"

"Aliens in the cupboard: what next?" queried Linen.

"Dinner on the table," she was told firmly. "It's mess-time and I need some sustenance."

The mess was humming, as not only had vital repair work begun on the *Drake*, major resupply was underway, both from the auto-ship and from Europa station, which had sent out rigs, equipment and operatives. Some of the latter were busy aboard, to Locksmith's annoyance, as he had been assigned no new security personnel to keep them in order both on and off duty. Officers' messes were posted off-limits, but other leisure areas were not and some visitors were taking advantage, the security chief informed the three as he hauled in alongside for dinner. Transfer of all prisoners had been completed, however, and the brig was now empty, which was a relief, Locksmith admitted. He was also pleased to report that among the supplies for his section were a selection of the latest security auto-drones, which he intended to use as roving monitors for 'tween-deck and other surveillance purposes. They could also be encoded as hunter-interceptors, he remarked to Copper, winking roguishly.

Themis Sage and her teams were apparently more than happy with their own stock of repair drones and had already deployed some to tackle the trickier jobs in main engineering. In response to Copper's less than subtle questioning, the chief did admit that the new gear had originated from Mars Defence Department's biohazard labs out near Fleet HQ, but both the facility and Fleet Intelligence were acutely aware of the problems the *Drake* had faced with subverted drones from that source. The equipment had thus been more than rigorously tested and his people were repeat-testing their way.

"So how long do you reckon before we're due to head out?" Trisk asked of him.

"Ten sols tops – we may get out earlier if we can persuade the riggers to work double shifts," Locksmith grimaced. "Why?"

"We have a lot of mundane work to get through and now will be the best time. With strangers on our doorstep, we don't want to be tackling anything too sensitive," Trisk said, gesturing at his companions.

"I think our own research work might be seen as sensitive, Lieutenant Trisk, sir," interrupted Linen. "We sure as hell went through plenty to get it, and there are those out there that would like a piece or two of it – as we know to our cost."

"We keep it locked down in our main lab; it's secure enough, wouldn't you say?" was Trisk's expressive response. "The chief could always post a guard."

"Like hell!" Copper broke in, well aware of the direction of her friend's conversation. "We're almost done anyway. The drafts should be ready to send on to Thars in a sol or two and as for our samples, we lock them down tighter than the armoury. And then we start on our other assignment in bay four, civilian or other intruders notwithstanding. And you owe us a guard for that, on colonel's orders, Chief," she reminded Locksmith. "As Tawny Brown's worked with us before, she'd be ideal."

"I don't tell you how to run your lab, Lieutenant; don't you tell me how to run my headquarters," Kit replied with a hint of amusement, his blue eyes twinkling.

"You sure as hell keep your beady eyes on what we do get up to," was the retort. "I remember you setting up that secure cam outside our quarters."

"That was for your security, Lieutenant."

"Or your peace of mind?"

"And that also. But I have to go. I'll no doubt see you later, all of you. Enjoy your eve."

"Enjoy!" Copper repeated, looking up at him as he stood. "I have a flight sim in an hour."

"If that's not enjoyment, what is?" he winked as he stalked off.

Linen had been watching the exchange in high glee and recalling others had come to the conclusion that it was time to let her friend into her assessment. When the chief had made his way out of the mess and the door had closed behind him, she turned to face Copper.

"Kit Locksmith has a soft spot for you, Cop, a *very* soft spot," she said with a knowing grin.

"Shit! And I thought I was imagining things!"

"Is it reciprocated?" Linen asked slyly.

Copper considered for a moment, pursing her lips in mock concentration. "He's tall, good-looking in a rugged sort of way, very nice blue eyes, amusing when I've shared a caff with him now and then, straight as a die, nice butt…"

"Please!" Trisk interjected in a pained voice.

"But he almost certainly has a string of admirers he can call on for company…"

"Don't think so, he never has time," Linen interjected.

"…and I have no intention of being on the end of a string," Copper continued severely.

"Or even the first bead on the string?" Linen demanded archly.

"Or even the first bead on the string. End of conversation."

: PROBING PROBLEMS

An hour after breakfast the following sol found all three science officers in their lab. Trisk was busy recalibrating his probe with data transferred from Kynedd Faerin whilst Copper and Linen were arguing over the placement of the numerous tri-dee extras they intended to submit with their respective theses.

"For pity's sake, just set in links and list them numerically at the end!" their friend implored. "And make your summaries as short and comprehensible as possible – and no amusing inserts, nobody will be impressed, least of all me."

"Aye, sir!" Linen agreed. "If Thars hasn't replied by the time we're done, I vote we send them on in any case and he can pass them on to whom he likes. Too bad if we ruffle some feathers."

Copper acquiesced as she was too tired to do otherwise. Her fatigue was partially the result of her toils the previous eve on a very taxing fighter simulation, but the main cause was that she was subtly aware that Spook was using her as a testing ground for the introduction of a responsive human to his new friend, who was still frightened and still hiding in the secure store. She confided as much to Linen and Trisk, who were sympathetic. One alien around your neck was trouble enough, they figured; two were just plain worrisome.

Trisk let out a short crow of success. His readjusted probe had not only been able to pick up a trace of what he believed was Spook, but it showed a distinct second signal that he put down to the presence of the second entity.

"Spook's just by you and his pal's in the secure locker," Dr Addystone explained. "Which means this probe can penetrate one of the most protected areas aboard ship!"

"Very good," Copper said. "But if you and Dr Faerin have come up with that between you, no offence, Trisk, but so could someone else. I'd report it to the colonel."

"She'll also want to know why you didn't report that Spook brought his buddy aboard yestersol," Linen reproved. "She did say that she wanted to be informed immediately of anything related to the situation."

"She wanted to be kept updated; it's not the same thing," Copper contradicted.

"She won't recognise that distinction and you know it," the redhead said sternly. "I'd send a link now and say you suspected it late last eve and Trisk has now more or less confirmed it. And don't go passing *that* data on to Dr Faerin over an open channel, Dr Addystone, sir," she advised Trisk.

"I won't; I'll ask him to come up here. He's been working on some other aspects of this on his own account and says he's got some new data that he'll pass on to us. I'll see if he's available now – medbay wasn't too overwhelmed last time I was in."

Copper had completed her circumspect message to Colonel Moritz by the time that Dr Faerin had traversed the level from medbay up to their lab. He listened patiently to his colleague's update on the modifications to the new probe and the outcome of Trisk's recent scans. He was mildly surprised by the news of a second alien entity aboard and concurred with Linen that the colonel ought to have been informed the previous eve that one was suspected. He further suggested that Copper try to link to it via Spook: he wanted to take readings for his own records, the reason for which he would explain. He also requested that both Linen and Trisk quiet their minds and try to feel the presence of either or both entities. Linen, he knew, was often able to detect the presence of Spook at a subliminal level.

The three were puzzled by the appeal but complied, pulling their lab chairs over to the secure store and resting quietly whilst the doctor ran his scans. They were still sitting in silence when a chime at the door advised them of a visitor. It was no surprise to see Colonel Moritz step over the threshold, as she was able to breach any space aboard her own ship, but Faerin's warning hand halted her and allowed him to complete his readings.

"Anything?" he demanded of his subjects.

"No," Trisk said immediately, shaking his head.

"I *thought* I got a hint of Spook," Linen admitted. "I was trying to see that mist I've seen before when he was around, but I couldn't. It's maybe not apparent all the time. But I'm sure I did get some sense of him. But nothing else."

"Lieutenant Milkstone?"

Copper sighed, hunched her shoulders and with half a look at Colonel Moritz, nodded. "Spook's certainly here; and so's his friend. And he's still too scared to come out of the store. I can't figure why, we can't see him. But why me? Why in blazes me?"

"I can tell you why," Faerin said quietly. "There's a genetic link. I've been analysing that lump of so-called thumb that you found in one of your samples – Trisk gave me access – and trying to work out if it has anything akin to a genetic code. Its dissimilarity to ours makes it tricky, but one thing I did pick up on was a short sequence of multiple-stranded nucleic acid that bears some resemblance to a tiny section of redundant coding that occurs in a very small pocket of the human population. My reading is that in the very distant past, some alien DNA, for want of a more accurate term, was incorporated into the human genome. And you, Lieutenant Milkstone, must be one of the few individuals recorded that has the relevant coding. Naturally, there's no telling what proportion of the population possesses the sequence as there's no way of testing everyone and relatively few have been examined down to that level of detail. But you have and you're one," he said, looking at Copper.

"But how could it have got there, unless…"

"Aliens had visited Earth," the doctor continued. "As they had ships fit for space travel, they probably did, but were less than careful over contamination, perhaps."

"But genetic material!" Linen exploded. "That suggests some sort of physical contact at least."

"Not necessarily," Trisk pointed out. "Exposure to an alien disease that shared some of the same genetic characteristics of the actual alien might do it."

"Are you saying Cop's ancestors might be related to a virus?" Linen demanded.

"I'm hypothesising," Trisk informed her mildly. "It may have been a friendly alien trying to lend a hand in fixing up an injury and using organo-tech to do it – organo-tech *does* have organic components within it. Or even just inadvertent exposure to alien organo-tech. You recall that piece of blue material that had such a drastic effect on Copper in the lab a while ago, and me to a lesser extent? A friendly version of that which heals rather than harms *might* have that effect. And that tube…"

"When you have all quite finished, perhaps you'd better let me in on what is going on," the colonel interrupted icily. "And you have some explaining to do, Lieutenant Milkstone."

"Oops! Brig might have a new occupant before long," Linen muttered under her breath.

Half an hour later and Colonel Moritz had been fully briefed on the current situation. As had been surmised, she was angry at not having been informed of Copper's suspicions that a second alien entity had come aboard, but a slight shake of Faerin's head warned her to go easy on her officer. His and Trisk's current concern was how to link the probe into security's whole-ship scanning system without alerting half the personnel there that something alien was suspected.

"Why don't you just link your probe to the *external* ship's sensors?" Copper suggested irritably. "Then you can patch that into internal systems without raising hackles or anything else. And we'll be prepared if we come across anything untoward out there. I mean, it's standard practice to link our science scanners to the extern relays when we want to search for specifics en route, isn't it?"

The discussion had been going on around her and she was extraordinarily tired, so much so that Faerin had covertly turned his medi-scanner on her and was keenly perusing the result.

"Good idea," Trisk agreed slowly.

"Are you okay, Cop?" enquired Linen anxiously, well aware that her friend was upset as well as exhausted.

Copper put her hand to her brow, her head drooping as she inhaled deeply. "Oh, dammit," was all she said as she leaned back in her chair.

"Oh, oh," Linen breathed, hopping out of her chair to stand by her friend. "Now you've got two, haven't you? I sense extra frizz around you."

"It's worse than that," Copper sighed. "I now know why he, she or it is so scared it keeps hiding in the cupboard."

"Lieutenant?" queried the colonel.

"Say hello to Baby Spook."

"What!" was the exclamation of all four.

"Well, Spook Junior," Copper amended. "I think it's a young one – Spook's been showing me images of myself as a teeny, hiding in my room when I'd been out of bounds or broken fam unit rules and wanted to escape the penalty; or just hiding from the usual ragging from my older brother – he had a hard fist."

"Hell, Cop, you never told me that!" Linen was aghast.

"Past now. But that means that the ability to detach from its corporeal body must be part of the life cycle of Spook's people. I'm assuming Junior *is* one of his kind. But why would so young an entity *be* aboard a ship that crashed, unless… oh hell, unless it wasn't a military ship, but some sort of transport…"

"Civilian?" asked Trisk. "Or maybe military ships were family-oriented?"

"Or it was a refugee ship," Linen added. "But Cop, this is sheer speculation on your part, surely?"

"I don't know, but the poor creature is scared witless, *that* I do sense."

"Doctor, this is your sphere of expertise," observed Colonel Moritz. "It's way beyond me."

"She thinks she's right and we *are* picking up two entities – and they *are* slightly dissimilar," Faerin responded.

"So I've now got two disembodied aliens running around my ship," Ms Moritz sighed in exasperation. "Lieutenant Milkstone, keeping control of our extraneous crew members, if that's what they are, is up to you. They will not, I repeat not, interfere with the running of this vessel in any way. Is that quite clear?"

"Yes ma'am. But with all due respect, if they wanted to, I'd hardly be in a position to stop them."

"Exactly. And that's where you come in, Doctor, Lieutenant Addystone: your new probe design seems reasonably effective. I want you to work on improving it further, in order that if we come across lifeforms similar but not the same as our residents, we may have some means of detecting them and in the long term, possibly restricting or incapacitating them. And link one of your probes to our external scanning relays as Ms Milkstone suggested: our sensors are far-ranging and rigged for internal-external linkage for routine analyses. But our internal scanners also still need to have the facility to sweep for your two friends, or any other similar, Lieutenant: if for some reason *you* are out of contact, we will need to be able to know where *they* are."

Copper was less than pleased at the thought of finding ways to harm those similar to Spook, but appreciated the logic in the colonel's orders, and acknowledged her compliance, as did the others. After delivering a few more directives, the commanding officer left them to it. The four looked at one another and gave vent to their irritation. The deck-by-deck scan was still required to be completed by the end of the sol and Kit Locksmith had been informed that Faerin and Trisk would require access to his domain at some point. Work on additional modifications to the probe design could be done once the relevant linkages to ship's systems were in place. Copper and Linen were less vexed by disruption to their routine but the former was concerned that her new role as minder to an unknown entity might bring her more problems than advantages.

Linen gave her friend another morsel to digest later, when the two men left them to begin their own endeavours. Dr Faerin had carried out a rapid scan on Copper to ensure that she was fit to carry on, expressing his concern that she was pushing herself too hard. He had requested that she stop by his office in medbay later in the sol for another quick appraisal.

"What's so funny?" Copper had demanded of the redhead, who was chuckling quietly to herself as she set up her MEDIC for another run through the initial sections of her thesis.

"You have a problem, Cop," was the enigmatic reply.

"Tell me about it! Spook, his little orphan, the colonel and one or two others that are breathing down my neck; then there's you. If our new alien *is* a young one, who knows what he or she will get up to, once it's learned the ropes and realises it's not going to be ill-treated or left alone and terrified in the dark! Why are you still grinning?"

Linen grinned more widely, her eyes twinkling. "I think Doc Faerin is interested in you for more than professional reasons."

Copper's jaw dropped. "You what? You're winding me up!"

"I'm worried about you, stop by my place later for a cosy little chat? That was the basis of his approach, wasn't it? You're honoured, as I've heard around that he's not one for playing the field. A few have tried to catch his eye and failed, so I've heard."

"How do you hear these things?"

"I talk to people when you're not listening; last eve, for instance, when you were doing your stint in the flight sim suite. I had a science station ops sim to do and so had Ash Goff – he was put out because he *said* he had his eye on Amber Embertz, but that she'd got a fancy for the doc but rumour had it that the doc was carrying a torch for someone else."

"She's way out of his league and Ash Goff's making excuses so he doesn't feel he's a failure," Copper snorted. "And how in blazes did you induce him to spill that anyway?"

"Oh, I have my methods; and given what I saw just now, I reckon you're the one Doc Faerin's hankering after."

"You're just a meddling minx and I'll thank you to keep your speculations to yourself!" Copper told her crossly. "Lor' I've enough on my plate without you trying to link me romantically to a string of handsome hunks!"

"Aha, so you admit Kit Locksmith and Kynedd Faerin are handsome hunks?"

"Go find yourself some eye-candy to make sheep's eyes at and stop pestering me, Lieutenant Lyrican," she was ordered.

"Don't need anyone else when I've got you," Linen smiled up at her impishly. "But Kit's tall, athletic and handsome in a rugged sort of way; and what else was it you said about him: nice blue eyes, straight as a die, a butt worth a second look? And *you've* been on *his* antennae since we met him first at Lowell. I recall you gave him his credit's worth in backchat and being tallish and athletic yourself – and you can give as good as you get, most of the time – you're right up his avenue. And as for the doc: you're an interesting case if ever there was one, and a scientist to boot. Walking the same line there as well."

"Doctors do not involve themselves non-professionally with their patients, Linen Lyrican. Or shouldn't. Why are you doing this to me? And to yourself," Copper added shrewdly.

"Got to get you off the single track that Spook seems to be leading you along," Linen confessed. "You don't realise how you've changed ever since you hooked up with Spook – or he hooked up with you, I should say. Okay, situation and training have had a lot to do with it, but you're over-confident at times, you're brash, you take risks you shouldn't and you're careless of yourself. In the past you've always been wary of people, thanks to Mizzle Chert amongst others, but now you are definitely of the 'shoot first and ask questions later' brigade. I'm not saying I don't like the new you: in fact I find it rather exciting. But I worry about you, Cop, and I worry what'll happen when Spook takes off for good and you haven't got him as back-up. Because you look on him as back-up, now, you realise? That's one of the reasons you think you're invincible."

"End of lecture?" Copper asked.

"End of lecture," Linen smiled crookedly.

"I won't say there's no truth in it," Copper conceded after a moment's quiet reflection. "I've always been aware that Spook changed me – I thought for the better, actually. And I get bouts of anxiety when I think that one sol he won't be around. And being out here makes it worse, especially as we now know that he's not the only one of his kind around here; and his ship's not the only intact piece of alien tech this side of the Sol system rim either. And yes, I depend on him for a heads-up on what's going down close by, in places we can't get to. I lean on his awareness and experience in command of a ship to some extent as well, though sims are correcting that and his know-how is so unlike ours it's hard to interpret much of the time."

"His know-how seems to be improving," Linen remarked dryly. "How many times has he saved our butts?"

"Lost count. But you *were* kidding about Dr Faerin, weren't you? Because if not, I'll be missing this eve's date with him."

"That'll *really* get him anxious over you. I *was* laying it on a bit thick, I admit; though I suspect him of a slight preference for your company," Linen said wickedly. "But I'm sure he has his reasons."

"Thanks. That makes me feel *so* much better. What the hell's the time? I want a caff."

"Nowhere near lunch-time but we can head to the office for a change of scenery and dial up a couple of mugs. We both need a break from this and as Trisk's with the doc for the rest of the sol, he won't be in a position to help us with our Lowell stuff. Are you bringing your two chums along to keep us company?"

"Don't forget that you can sometimes detect Spook and you reckoned you felt extra frizz when Junior was about – you may have this genetic predisposition that Dr Faerin seems to think I have and you might be ripe for the adoption of a young alien that needs a mother-figure to look up to who'll mentally hug it from time to time," her friend informed her.

"Thanks; that's not what I'd planned for my life. Given the run-around I gave my Ma when I was a teeny, I wouldn't like to think some young 'un could do the same to me."

"It's called poetic justice," said Copper. "I'll ask the doc to haul you in for a complete physical and psychological check-up and then we'll see. You'd make a great parent."

"Who are you kidding? Spook's a very old and wise being, as far as we can tell, and he's helping you turn into a first rate officer that's ripe for a rapid rise through the ranks to your own command. What do I get? A teeny full of tantrums and angst that's scared of its own shadow – always assuming it has one – and all the baggage that goes with it. I'll end up in the brig on disciplinary charges, or scouring out the hygiene facilities."

"No need to call up any parenting advice holos just yet," said Copper glumly. "They're both with me. I'm beginning to feel like a permanent family outing."

* * *

Later that afternoon Trisk Addystone stopped by to inform his colleagues that the probe-linkage to ship's external sensors was to be tested. The probe would be run from a dedicated lab station eventually, with links to both bridge science stations, but that was a job for engineering. Meanwhile, Trisk was planning to plumb one of the modified devices into an existing external scanning relay slot. The linking of a second probe to a console in security that was capable of deck-by-deck scanning was the second means of data collection chosen and was even then being set up by Kit Locksmith, with Kynedd Faerin's input. The initiation of *that* was planned for nineteen hundred hours, Trisk told them.

Copper was concerned. "The scan's to be done then?" she demanded. "Once it reaches here, or wherever *I* am, you'll get a positive result. And as you noted before, your damnable probe can breach the secure store, so if Junior goes back into hiding there, he'll still be picked up. So the chief, with whoever else he wants to take part in the scan, will have to be informed that we have two resident aliens aboard that we know about."

"Or that we've planted test signals to check that the linkage works as it should. The colonel's aware of it," Trisk answered. "She's briefing the chief herself, but just what she tells him we won't be told. As for the rest of his team, they'll be kept out of the loop, and any results that are picked up *will* be logged as test signals we've planted, just in case the records are accessed by anyone. Naturally, the chief will have the records tagged, so if anyone does access them, he'll know about it."

"I still don't like it," Copper said decidedly. "I can't imagine that the colonel would deliberately pull any wool over her chief of security's eyes; which means that Kit Locksmith *will* have to be brought into the picture – and if I was him, I'd be extremely pissed that I'd been left out of it for so long."

"That's the colonel's problem, not ours; it's her ship and she has the right to run it her way. She won't stand any nonsense," said Trisk firmly as he began his installation. "You two want to lend a hand? You can help scan the space around Jupiter Station and help me set the ranges. We want to be able to get as far out as possible. We'll have to let both Jupiter *and* Europa stations know that we'll be running test scans or they'll get their pants in a twist. They can let any civilian ops that might scream in on it. I'll ask comms to send on a link."

"And what happens if we come up positive?" Copper asked.

"We send you out in a shuttle for a closer look," replied Linen succinctly. "You're our resident alien expert."

"There may be something out there so alien that your probe can't detect it. Or something shielded," Copper added to Trisk. "You might be able to peek into our own secure store, but I bet you couldn't get through an all-singing, all-dancing super-spec alien cloaking device."

"If it was all-singing, all-dancing, you'd hear and see it," said Linen with mock seriousness.

"Only if the on-button was activated," Copper replied in the same vein.

"Will you two quit the clap-trap and lend a hand?" requested Trisk shortly. "I want all test results logged, whatever they are, and I want directional and distance data checked as we retrieve it. And set up your MEDICs as well: they may have more in-depth data on any extraneous signals we pick up."

"Alien tech, you mean," Copper deduced.

Trisk ignored her as he linked into the bridge comms station with the request that the two orbital stations and all ships in the vicinity be informed of sensor relay testing. He then began the connection to the external sensors on the hull of the *Drake* that could sweep the area beyond the ship.

"Now we set the specifics," he told the two. "Stand by."

As the sensor waves swept around and beyond the vessel's immediate vicinity, all three watched intently, Trisk correcting to allow overlapping readings to be taken. Even so, with the *Drake* locked in a service dock that was virtually in a stationary orbit around Jupiter, and with repair drones and other equipment swarming over her massive hull plates, there were gaps in her coverage of the area that were becoming apparent. Copper had a sudden thought.

"Who has command of the repair drones? I know a lot of them must be ours, the ones the auto-ship brought in, but are our teams or the station's in control? And how much out there is in other hands?"

"What gives, Cop? You don't think the drones or the repair bots could be compromised, do you?" Linen demanded.

"Hell, I don't know, I'm just thinking out loud. But the data we're pulling in is patchy. Are our relays being interfered with or are some of the sensors inoperative, or is it just a question of automatic switch off as repairs are being carried out?"

"I'll get whoever's at the science station on the bridge to check it out," Trisk decided. "It's Lieutenant Kuillinor, she's on her own."

"She's the botanist, isn't she?" Linen remarked. "Always to be found in hydroponics, nurturing something. Rumour hath it that if you want a bit of home-brew done on the sly, Bloom Kuillinor's your girl."

"Thanks for that wisdom," Copper retorted dryly. "Just keep your eyes on the readout: we have swathes missing from the aft sensor arrays and I can't see that they're offline for anything. I'll check in with engineering."

"You might be better sending Spook out for a look," her friend advised. "He'll be quicker and will probably see more."

"And I'll have the headache of interpreting it, Lieutenant Smartarse," retorted Copper. "It's Oaky Grimsson…"

The young engineer helpfully carried out the requisite checks and confirmed that no sensor arrays were out of commission at his end. Similar information was relayed from Bloom Kuillinor on the bridge. She had informed Captain Helmis, who had the conn. The data that had been garnered thus far had, however, shown no signature that could be interpreted as alien life. Nor were there signs of alien tech, according to Gerald and Gemima, although Copper knew that the *Lithium Star* was once source, and she was only a couple of berths over from the *Drake*. She examined the scans made thus far and worked out that the *Lithstar's* hull had not been penetrated. But Trisk was adamant that he would not attempt such a scan: it would be detected and no doubt there would be a formal complaint made – he had heard of Captain Mortin LeFlynn's reputation for a short fuse and a long memory.

"Wouldn't have stopped *me*," his friend said. "But it's your party, you and Doc Faerin's – who, by the way, wants to see me for a med update later; though he'll probably be too busy with Kit Locksmith in security if he's helping to set up there."

"Two hunks in one office," Linen murmured teasingly from the sidelines and was rightly ignored as Copper systematically began to map the areas of local space being scanned and amplify those areas missing.

"The fields of the aft sensor arrays are where the majority of the missing areas of data fit," was her final assessment. "There are a few blanks elsewhere, but the techs in main engineering are running their own scans on hull integrity and for some reason they have priority: Commander Sage's orders, probably."

"I would think she takes precedence over what's after all an add-on piece of kit testing," Linen agreed. "But what parts of the aft section show the gaps and are there other ship's stations using the external relays for their own purposes? They're not all dedicated science scanners, other ops can commandeer them."

"Very clever," Copper mused. "Note the patchy coverage here, here and here and fuzzy sections here, as if our sensors are meeting interference. There are still *some* operational scanners, or at least ones returning data, over the aft area; but guess where outer bay four is?"

"Frock! Just off-centre of this large affected area! Get Bloom Kuillinor to check for any tie-ups of aft science sensor arrays for other testing schedules," Linen implored Trisk, who had halted his work to look. "And we'd best get the duty rotas of those damned repair teams and see what local outfits are working that area of hull. Ops management should have the data. I assume someone *is* manning ops? And there *are* station repair teams in other areas aboard close by, though not bay four, as that was where one of the coordinated attacks took place, not to mention that little attempt on our skins before that; I think security still has that zone sewn up."

Trisk not only spoke to Kuillinor, but requested that Captain Helmis be brought in on it. The result was that twenty minutes later, both Colonel Moritz and Chief Locksmith appeared in the lab demanding to know what the hell was going on.

The situation being explained, the tightening of the colonel's lips and the sparking of her green eyes gave the others the idea that she was not only concerned but utterly furious, the more so that whatever or whoever was responsible for the abnormalities detected must have somehow been able to circumvent security. The duty officers there had the resources to pick up any covert activity; and there must have been some such from *within* the ship to enable access to the nodes that linked the sensor arrays, *if* that was where the faults lay. There had, however, been no recent node faults or link breakages reported by the monitoring relays which ceaselessly scanned all ship's operating systems.

"So either the arrays are still working but sensing nothing or static, or they're not and there's something been planted to stop the status monitors from detecting it. But the bridge ops station should have picked it up. Who's manning ops at the moment?" Kit Locksmith asked.

"Ensign Charity Wingwarp," the colonel said sharply. "She's young, but no fool. Helmis knows her better than I do, but this is her second posting and I don't for a minute suspect she's had anything to do with this. And your people will have vetted her before she came aboard and presumably again after all the trouble we've had since we left space dock."

"We will have," Locksmith confirmed. "But we'll need to check the nodes linking these arrays *in situ* to see if they've been tampered with, the arrays, and the affected hull sections. This is not going to be a quick job. And there are civilian repair teams aboard ship and crawling all over the hull, not to mention bots and other repair kit out there. Who's monitoring those teams? I guess it must be the central directing office on Jupiter Station that assigns the squads and says who works on them, but they're under civilian jurisdiction, not Fleet or even Mars Gov control. Outer bay four is still under high security and no outsider, or even most of our people, should be able to get into it. But I don't have the personnel to man it nonstop, we have to use our secure cam system and rely on site monitors and my people on watch in the office most of the time."

As the colonel and the security chief made several quick links of their own, the three science officers continued their testing of the external sensor arrays using Trisk's probe and other science scanners that they could link into the arrays. They found that their readings were either ambiguous or that the data was patchy and showing nothing.

"It's clever jamming, is what it is," Copper announced at last, scratching her head in irritation. "I can't figure the source of it, even looking for blocking signals using a comms module."

"Blocking signals?" Locksmith asked.

"It's one way of jamming, and it seems to me to be the way that this might be working," Copper explained. "We send out the probe beam and a very sophisticated sensor picks it up and neutralises it: two opposing waves cancelling each other out, in other words. But it would have to be something that tracks what kind of signal we're sending out on a continuous basis; I've just checked using different wavelengths and various scanning modes, mostly standard, and they're all producing this pattern of gaps in the incoming information that makes the data more or less useless or areas of data ill-defined, so we can't make out specifics. So it looks to me like the arrays are still operative but something is jamming them at very close range, possibly on the hull of the ship. But I don't get it: if our arrays are based on similar tech to the *Drake's* personal comms systems, they should be able to resist practically all forms of jamming known to man, that is if Magenta Firewall had a hand in the designing of them, as she did the comms systems. Even her prototypes could do that, as we know, given Linen and I had the testing of them on Mars. And why do we see this irregular pattern? There's not full coverage, maybe because blanket sensor failure would surely be noticed. Something like this might be put down to systematic repair works being carried out over these hull areas. Engineering and two fighter bays were hit during our spate of malicious disruption and we have a lot of repair work now going on to get us back to full spec."

"What do *you* put it down to?" the colonel astutely enquired.

"Jupiter Station harbouring covert ops that are intent on undermining Mars Gov and any Fleet mission that's being sent out to investigate the alien question, or what people think is the alien question, ma'am," Copper stated. "There are concerns out there that would give their eye teeth to have first pop at finding not only alien tech but evidence – substantiated – of actual alien presence. Comms is one such sign; tech's another and worth a lot more. The cream on the cake would be evidence of an actual alien, hence the speculation and whatever else there is around the stuff found out on the edge, where the remains of the *Griffon*, amongst other things, were discovered. And I bet a whole lot more than Mars Gov is now aware of that."

"You I wouldn't gamble with," Colonel Moritz informed her dryly. "We'll need to get a team of our own out on the hull and see what's going on: if there *are* jamming devices and they *have* breached our arrays, our comms could also be in jeopardy."

Copper shook her head thoughtfully. "I don't agree ma'am; sending a team of our people out will only cause a furore and alert any felons that we suspect something," she explained.

"So what's your solution?"

"Dr Inkscree's bots," Copper suggested after a pause. "They could be programmed for a close-hull survey and won't cause half the speculation one of *our* survey teams would. They could be sent out on a test run to check their suitability for further deployment once we're back on track – or that could be the story. But you'll need to get every repair team there is off the hull and have all our own auto repair drones locked down. And you'll need to have your teams scour the areas around bay four and sniff out undesirables, Chief."

"Cop!" muttered Linen under her breath. "I think you'll find the colonel and the chief have their own ideas and know the best way forward."

"I was asked what I would do and that's it," was the reply.

"Technically, you were not," the colonel reproved. "But now you've begun, go on: I'm listening."

"I'd like to know what kind of jamming is being used, *if* it's jamming, how and when it was put in place – it must be recently planted – and who had the encoding of it, if it *has* been able to circumvent what I assume is partly Ms Firewall's tech; because as you say ma'am, if our arrays *have* been compromised then our comms and hell knows how many more ship's systems are in trouble. *And* where it came from in the first place: it smacks of Fleet issue to me, just like those mini drones that almost took us out, and that suggests that the leak out at the biohazard labs between HQ and Korolev isn't plugged yet, or the gear was filched and brought out here before it came to light. How many Mars Fleet ships have called in here recently, I wonder, before we showed up? Or Earth Fleet or civilian craft that had links with Mars Fleet ops or personnel, overtly or covertly?"

"I'm glad she's on our side," Locksmith remarked to the colonel.

"You and me both," was the laconic reply. "Your conjectures I'll pass on to Fleet Intelligence as soon as I can get a secure link – and a moment to do it. But it's now more than evident that we haven't seen the last of the trouble that seems to be plaguing us; and it seems to have stretched this far out from Mars."

"Funny this trouble started when these two came aboard," Kit remarked, earning him a searching glance from Copper.

"You want trouble, mister, I'll show you trouble," she said.

"Belay that, Lieutenant. We have work ahead of us," the colonel barked.

"Another long night," sighed Linen, squinting slyly at Copper and Locksmith, who were eyeing each other, he in amusement and she in mock annoyance. "Why is it always on our watch?"

"It's what we signed up for, remember?" her friend told her.

"I take it we carry on with the scanning, ma'am?" asked Trisk. "Until Dr Inkscree can set up his bots for a sortie outside, if that's the plan?"

"It seems to me like a sensible plan, and yes: you three *will* help Inkscree in programming the bots for deployment, once we have certain other pieces in place. Meanwhile you will continue to monitor the areas of missing coverage on the hull closely, and see if the pattern changes over the next hour or so. And you will go on with your original schedule of work on making sure your new probe can be used to the best effect when linked to our external arrays. Locksmith, you're with me, you'll have to assign someone else to work with Dr Faerin. Any questions?"

"No, ma'am," the officers responded.

"Just great! Bang goes dinner! You and your big mouth," Linen complained as the door closed behind the colonel and the security chief.

"Lieutenant Lyrican, it may have escaped your notice but we are officers in Mars Fleet and it is our duty to keep our superior officers advised of dangers to our ship or her crew. And by the way, smartarse, we were given an assignment to do, and we've been prevented from doing it well by the interfering dustbaggers that set that – whatever it is – system up out there. Better we get them before they get us – because, believe me, in the end, they would get us," Copper stated ominously.

"You think?"

"Where's our next most important job going to take us, once we've sent our research work off to Thars with a 'please do not return note' on it?"

"Outer bay four," Linen sighed. "And we don't want a repeat performance of what we had to deal with in that quarter."

"It wouldn't be a repeat," Trisk disputed. "Security's ready for that. It would be a new trick and as the last one left me with a busted nose, I *really* don't want a repeat of that, no matter how heroic your intentions were at the time," he added to Copper.

"You'd best cancel your cosy appointment with Doc Faerin," Linen advised her friend. "He'll be far too busy to check you over in his office."

"Can it," she was ordered.

* * *

It *was* a long night, but by the early hours of the next sol the three science officers were glad to note that their assessment of the situation had been justified. A small collection of highly sophisticated minute jamming devices had been removed from the outer hull of the *Drake*, and not all of them from the area immediately adjacent to outer bay four. The colonel had ordered a thorough scan of the hull by as many of Dr Inkscree's bots as necessary for complete coverage. Locksmith had coordinated relocation of repair crews still working on the hull to coincide with bot deployment and at the end of the operation the chief had plenty of jammers upon which to run test scans, and more to the point, to develop means of locating more elsewhere and to foil their working.

Internal scanning deck-by-deck of the *Drake* had brought no lifeforms to light other than those known to be there, and more importantly, no store of the tiny jammers, although certain sections were still too busy with ongoing repairs to be entirely scrutinised. The areas closest to the initial data anomalies were probed minutely and no interference with ship's sensors arrays from the inside had been found: the nodes were intact and no link breakages detected.

Chief Locksmith had scheduled a meeting with his opposite number on the military staff of Jupiter Station; his intention was to coordinate a run-through of everyone who had had access to the outer hull of the *Drake*. He knew the chief of the station by repute and was sure he could be trusted. It was a possibility that additional stashes of the miniature jamming devices might be hidden aboard the station, as well as other apparatus related to covert ops, but locating such would be a headache of major proportions. Much of the station was civilian run and such areas would normally be off-limits to military crews unless there was a really good reason for such incursion. The other problem was that a number of ships were now docked around both Jupiter and Europa stations, from small mining transports to the large explorer ships of Mars Fleet and any one of them could be harbouring undesirables and clandestine equipment.

* * *

Copper and Linen had elected to head to the mess after they had been relieved of duty by the commanding officer. They and Trisk had been commended on their actions and given leave to take a few extra hours to catch up on some sleep. All three had declined politely: Trisk wanted to get back to work on his probe and the other two were intent on completing their theses by any means necessary, and if that meant using their MEDICs and any other equipment they could commandeer to summarise, deduce and speculate, then they were prepared to do so. As the redhead had pointed out, they had enough data to cause much head-scratching and excitement among the elite of Mars' scientific community, as not only had their researches come up with what they deemed conclusively to be pollen-like substances alongside various fragments of other organic matter within biofilms that could be traced back almost two billion Mars years, they had also found slivers of what they had classified optimistically as an opalised wood-like material. Their findings thus definitely hinted at the occurrence of higher plant life on their homeworld at the boundary of the Noachian and Hesperian Periods of Mars' pre-history. Allied to their discovery of the Glory Hole after the marsquake that had left Linen incapacitated, and its subsequent classification as an enormous geode with no precedent on Mars, they had enough to keep any assessors busy for a sevensol just trying to assimilate the implications.

The information garnered by their initial testing of the surf-sci bots for the convenience of both MDMC and Mars Gov, annoying as the work had been at the time, was far in advance of the usual run of the mill or even ground-breaking materials that formed the bulk of traditional PhD outcomes. With the approval of their commanding officer and those involved, they could now include that data as part of their work. The tri-dee visuals relating to their sites were also overwhelmingly complex and Trisk, when called upon to advise on the proper division of data for the two complementary but separate bodies of work, could only say that he was glad he was familiar with much of it, for to start from scratch to try and understand it would take up time – or even brain power, come to that – he did not have.

By the end of the duty sol, Copper and Linen were almost brought to their knees in utter exhaustion. They had given

Gemima and Gerald instructions to check their final drafts for inconsistencies, errors and syntax problems and the two MEDICs had come up with enough to give them two hours of hard toil just to amend the lot. They had shifted and sifted, read and re-read until they were red-eyed, quarrelsome and sore. Some compulsion made the two continue hour after hour until finally both holo-epics were sat in glorious tri-dee above the holo-generators that they had set up to contain them. Trisk had ordered them on a break; too weak to argue, the pair had crawled off to the mess to stoke up with as much protein as their systems could cope with, leaving their friend, who had pleaded business elsewhere, behind. He adjured them, however, to return to the lab after their meal: he would assist in the transmission of the whole body of work to their senior mentor at Lowell. As he had had exhaustive experience in the handover of completed PhD theses, the two were wholly happy to agree and slid off, supporting each other, in the direction of deck four.

* * *

"Something's up," Copper said narrowly to Linen as they approached the entry to their lab after a hearty meal. "There're more than just Trisk at the back of that door. If this is a surprise party, I'm going to bang a few heads together…"

"Only one way to find out," the redhead groaned, waving her implanted ident at the reader port.

Copper had been right: Trisk was there but so were Kynedd Faerin, clutching the remnants of one of his favourite bottles of scotch, and Ossy Inkscree. The colonel was also in evidence: when she slept, neither of the two could fathom.

"Go ahead, press the button!" Dr Addystone invited. "It's all set up. The final versions of your theses are ready to go. And they're damned good, even if I say so myself. Ossy and I are going to be your external assessors; we're waiting to hear who Thars has appointed as internals, but once they see these, it'll be a foregone conclusion."

Copper looked at her friend and both advanced into the lab. At the appropriate point, the two clasped hands and pressed the appropriate toggle that would send their endless months of hard slog into the ether and on the way to Mars.

As their companions applauded, Copper turned to Linen.

"Now the real fun begins," she said. "A journey through that hunk of alien spaceship in outer bay four here we come."

22: MAKING READY

The next several sols saw the *MSS Drake II* refitting to an even higher spec than before. New gear had been sent on in the auto-ship in addition to the auto-drones, much of it ear-marked for security, and it had Kit Locksmith and his team in overdrive. He had eschewed leave to get to grips with the new fixings but was constantly being interrupted by the data streams resulting from an upsurge in security activity on the two nearby bases. The covert jamming of the *Drake's* sensor relays and the likelihood of the culprits hailing from one or both of the facilities had Security Chief Mills of Jupiter Station busy and *his* activity had resulted in the arrest of three suspects and the seizure of more miniature jammers and other infiltration gear, some of it illegal and much of it military issue. He had no authority over orbiting ships, however, and investigations there were proceeding slowly.

Careful inspection of the miniature jammers by security techs aboard the *Drake* had confirmed their source as the military biohazard labs near Mars Fleet HQ, which seemed to put their theft on a par with that of the rogue mini auto-drones that had caused the trouble in bay four. On a more heartening note, the jammers could only operate on their targets at very close range, hence their number and the patchy coverage, and their effects could be neutralised by simple readjustments to target systems. The latter had resulted in the need to update every piece of comms and scanning equipment aboard, which was causing those engineers tasked with the job no end of aggravation.

The goings-on elsewhere on board the *Drake* and off-station had repercussions for the three science officers down on deck five, for without security escort they were barred from bay four and the next part of their task there. The tri-dee sim facility down in engineering was also off-limits and the tri-dee sim stations in their side lab made poor substitutes. On the colonel's orders, Copper had perforce to spend some of her time trying to work out exactly what had come aboard from the *Lithium Star* at Spook's behest, but she was finding it heavy going. She was convinced that the latest entity was young compared to her own attendant alien, but as the being refused to detach from Spook except when it hid in the secure store, which seemed to be its chosen harbourage, she could make out little more.

As Linen had been able to pick up on Spook and had even detected visual clues to his presence, Copper had wondered if her redheaded friend would make a more suitable connection than herself. She had broached the subject with both Linen and Trisk and the former had been cautiously willing, despite Trisk's warning that as Copper had apparently imbibed on more than a subliminal level much of Spook's mature capacity, Linen could find herself losing rather than gaining from an association with a juvenile entity that would have a far less developed outlook and no doubt other propensities.

The three took their concerns to Kynedd Faerin in medbay early one sol, deeming the colonel too busy to be asked for advice. The doctor's speedy response was to order Lieutenant Lyrican in for a thorough physical examination, down to sub-molecular levels, and run the same tests he had on med samples from Copper in order to detect any trace of the redundant coding sequence that he believed enabled the link to Spook. He scheduled the exam for the same afternoon and the three science officers had thus very little time for second thoughts. Back in their office later, Copper digested the doctor's reaction, sifted out a few thoughts in her own mind, and then suggested that Trisk request similar testing. Their friend was one of the few people on record that had the ability to make the patterned marks found on some pieces of alien tech change. Copper had put her own talent in that direction down to her association with Spook, but as it was now clear that other factors may have operated, she was curious as to the link. Linen had tried in the past to achieve the same effect but had been unable to do so. The redhead pointed this out to Copper.

"That was perhaps because I'd already bonded to that piece, although I wasn't aware of it at the time: a pristine marked piece that hasn't bonded to anyone might work."

"Doesn't track," Linen said shortly. "The piece we found in the Glory Hole must have come from something that belonged to someone before it washed up among our samples and you made the marks move there. And then we found that frocking alien scanner; and when I aimed it at you, the damn thing stung me! Then there's the one Malachite found under Lofty's cellar, for that matter; it didn't affect either of us, but we didn't try — we gave it over to Colonel Moritz as soon as we could. But any piece of marked alien tech would have had other fingers, hands, tentacles or you name it on it long before we got to grips."

"The damn thing stung you," Copper repeated. "In other words it reacted to you. It could be one way of testing for this genetic predisposition Doc Faerin thinks some people have and it wouldn't need a lot of invasive medical tests."

"I'll let you tell him. But if you think I can bond to Junior, I'm willing to give it a try. Hey, if we ever get back to Mars, we could revisit Giordano's at the AF Dome and take Junior down to the Cadet Recreation Zone! You think he'd like it there?"

"You're really taking on board what you think it would be like to have Junior as your own alien entity around your neck," Copper told her severely. "If he really *is* quite young, you'd best be careful that you don't turn into the adult equivalent of a teeny in a glass-candy store. Or he's maybe a shy retiring type that'll have you jumping into a closet every time there's a loud noise, as a side-effect of the connection."

"Well, *I'm* willing to undergo this testing that the doc has suggested to see if I have the genetic link," Trisk grinned. "But I make no promises if we find another disembodied alien in our travels out there. Especially as we'd never know where it's come from or where it's been."

"Or even if it was friend or foe," Copper cautioned. "You remember those pieces of blue tech? They were seriously not friendly and you were as averse to them as I was."

"Precisely. And as we're stymied on a lot of the things we'd like to do, we can go over that stuff again very cautiously to see if we can get some clues that would help us in avoiding those reactions if we come across the material inadvertently without protection."

"A good point, Dr Addystone, sir," Linen cheerfully agreed. "You up for that Cop?"

"It's on our list, so we may as well get it done – after a caff break. I need one."

"Done. But I note you've started calling Junior he. Is he a he or a she or a something else?"

"No idea, but we'll have to give him some sort of name. We can't keep saying *it* or people will overhear and wonder what in blazes we're going on about."

The trio returned to their lab after their break and dug out their collection of samples of the blue alien organo-technology. With their MEDICs and a pair of dedicated monitors running as back-up to the usual sensors, Trisk began. He carefully set aside the smaller pieces, picking up each flake with forceps held in gloved hands. The larger shard with the raised patterning he left aside, along with the additional part-marked fragments he had reckoned were part of the same unit.

"Jigsaw," he explained to his colleagues. "I figure the whole of the fancy piece projects above a baseplate or a section of the usual blue stuff that we've found – all these scrappy bits – as if this is some sort of control point or similar. My analysis of the structure is in the database: more packed and folded molecular chains than usual and even its subatomic structure seems denser somehow, but there *is* a logical lattice structure. Some parts just don't compute in any database we have, and we have the most advanced there is in the Sol system. And we know that it's the patterned piece that reacts with living human material; the other stuff just provokes a negative emotional response. And this patterning you recognised, didn't you?" he went on to Copper.

"I did. And Spook sure as hell warned me of it," she reminded him.

"Which is why you have a copy of it on your butt," Linen put in with a grin. "But what does it do when it's complete? I mean if bits of it can have the effect it did on Copper, and you for that matter, Trisk, can you imagine what a whole operative unit would do? Maybe we should keep the parts separate, in case they all come together in some nightmarish dance and link up and then start causing mayhem."

"Thanks for that image. I was feeling quite comfortable up to now," Copper reproved her.

"No you weren't; you're as creeped out as we are," Linen said frankly. "I can still read you like a holo-book, Lieutenant Copper Milkstone, ma'am, whether you rank me or not."

"Well, here are all the bits that have some sort of pattern or marking. We get holos of the lot and run them together, setting them against the design Spook suggested was important," Trisk told the other two. "We'll need a holo of the shape that we can link to the lab gear, so not the one in your wrist-comm."

"If you think I'm going to bare my butt in public, you can think again, mister!" Copper told him acidly as she snatched up Gemima. "I'll be in the hygiene, making another copy!"

"I'll capture a holo of the tattoo, I've seen your butt before," the redhead told her. "How many field trips have we shared thus far? You've got nothing physical I haven't seen before."

"Shout it to the frigging universe why don't you?" Copper snapped in reply as the pair made for the exit, leaving Trisk laughing quietly behind them.

The two reappeared shortly after with the design caught in Gemima's memory matrix. Copper ordered her MEDIC to link the file to the other relevant lab devices and to project it from her holo-port in order that the three could remind themselves of its exact format. As they watched, the almost lozenge-shaped form extruded from the holo-port; it was pinkish and outlined in deep blue, almost as if it was flat, but with a tracery of dark blue whorls and coils meandering through it and around it that seemed to raise it from its base.

"Set it against a background of colour that matches the blue of the majority of the alien tech," Linen advised. "That's lighter than this etched framework and will give us an idea of what this – thing – looks like when it's part of a whole, or at least part of a larger structure."

Copper complied and with a little tweaking the image stood complete as a smooth-edged blue rectangle, the raised pattern seeming to look like a large diamond-shaped pink-filled button with extruding curls of thin piping within and around it. Copper slowly moved her hand towards the image, trying to imagine what it would be like to touch the button, and held position in an effort to feel the result of such contact.

Trisk had stepped forward to pull his friend back, but Linen, understanding what was taking place, clutched his arm and held on, watching carefully. Copper's hand resumed its slow forward progression. She stopped again, and suddenly reared back as if pulled by an invisible string.

"It's a control or ops system, maybe inhibiting entry to a place or a system or something," she said slowly. "But it's not nice and I feel that it hides a few nasty surprises. Maybe it can breach other systems and then start to exert control over them and not in a good way. I was prevented from going any further, even though this is just a harmless holo."

"Spook stopped you?" Linen queried.

Copper gave a quirky little smile. "No. Junior did," she said. "Spook wouldn't have stopped me: he understands what this is and what I was trying to do with it. Junior doesn't. He was scared."

"He's come out of the store?" Linen demanded.

"He's with Spook. And he was interested, as any kid would be. I'm now convinced he's no more than a kid. He *was* scared, seriously scared. If he *was* human, he would have just wet his pants, poor little sap."

"Lor', what the hell has the poor sprite been through?" Linen demanded. "Has he – had he – the equivalent of family? And if so, what happened to them?"

"Hell knows. And now he's got Spook, and us. Frock's sake, when I signed aboard the *Drake* I knew I'd have to explain the alien I had around my neck. I just never imagined in my wildest dreams that I'd end up with a frigging family of them!" Copper spat out. "I'm not annoyed at you," she went on. "It's all right sweetie, I'm just upset at what's happening just now… Spook, for frock's sake, calm him down!"

"She talking to Junior," Linen sighed, raising an eyebrow at Trisk. "You should ask Colonel Moritz for a family allowance," she went on to her friend. "*If* you're allowed to have family aboard a ship of the Fleet, that is?"

"Ensign Lennik Flyte in security has got a virtual dog," Trisk mentioned conversationally. "He sometimes takes it on duty and exercises it along the engineering decks. It's called Fetch."

"That's hardly the same as a teeny," Linen argued. "I don't think anyone aboard has got family with them, though I know Commander Sage has a daughter: she's a junior engineer aboard a Fleet supply ship on the run between Mars and the bases beyond Jupiter."

"How do you find these things out?" demanded Copper.

"Oaky Grimsson mentioned a Lieutenant Merinna Sage he'd met on stopover once at Titan Space Dock, so I asked. He was quite taken with her but was too afraid to ask her on a date as Commander Sage was his boss aboard the *Marco Polo* at the time."

Copper shook her head. "Maybe a junior Spook would keep you too busy to poke your nose in other people's business," she remarked. "But I'm going to need a psych counsellor at this rate, if Junior keeps tugging at my coat tails every time he comes across something that scares the willies out of him."

"Aboard the *Drake*, that'll be at least once a sol," Trisk prophesied. "Maybe you should ground him?"

"This conversation is turning into a third-rate human-interest holo-flic that I wouldn't pay good credit to experience," Copper complained. "Spook, you look after Junior and let us get on with the business of the sol: we have an appointment in medbay in a couple of hours."

Despite the complete holo of the device that had imprinted itself on Copper's consciousness as dangerous, the three had got no further forward in working out what it was or what it was designed to protect or operate. That it was operable by touch was Copper's conclusion, although Trisk proposed that a mental command might be the mechanism of action.

"Lor' it might as well be the key to open a door to a hygiene cubicle!" Copper snapped in exasperation. "Let's leave it locked up – not in *that* secure store – and get on to something else. What about that sample that the *Wayfinder* found, the non-replicative piece? The cartridge it was in *was* supposed to have been gone through by mil experts and we only got it and the other bits as reference samples but you figured it was rare, Trisk and I did manage to expand the piece into the whole that I think it once formed…"

"Yes, and I know where that ended up!" Linen protested angrily. "No, Cop, leave alone!"

"We have the holo now. It's probably a bit of ship interior or some discrete article and so not designed to last as long as hull materials or similar and that's why there's not much of it to find, as I think you pointed out in relation to the finds from our site out at the Warren. But I was sure it was a complete – thing."

"So it's an item with a purpose: a hairbrush, as I said before. And we still have the hard-holo of that thing that you made up from the pieces we collected from the Glory Hole, only in much more detail. But we didn't of course add *that* to our theses in handy appendix form: the colonel would have brained us."

The hard-holo of the unknown alien item deriving from the *Wayfinder* being set up, the three regarded it with interest. It was a flattened smoothly octagonal solid with a pattern of concentric octagons etched into one side that echoed the shape of the item itself. As it was a tri-dee simulacrum, the purpose of the internal structure could only be guessed at. The tools that had captured the data had shown that the internal portion comprised a complex meshwork of interlocking strands and nodules that no doubt had once held data and power to operate the device.

Linen held out her hands, palms upwards. "So what is it, apart from outwardly simple in design? I don't see a crack in it that might suggest it was openable, like a box. It's smooth, apart from the grooves in the upper side."

"As is the fragment of hull in bay four," Copper noted. "Their tech might be so sophisticated you can't see where it opens, but it may come apart or expand, or something."

She began to circle the piece, concentrating. "I can't make it work; it's only a model, it's not real," she said at last.

"You what?" demanded Linen, with a look at Trisk

"I wasn't talking to you, I was talking to Junior."

"He knows what it is?" the redhead burst out.

"It's some sort of data store, for entertainment or instruction or something, I think."

"Like the hard-holo projectors of our dragons?" Linen asked. "But only more complex."

"That's what I figure from what I'm picking up. But at least it's not dangerous, as far as I can tell. But that's not far. I really don't know."

"*Wayfinder*," Trisk mused. "We now know that she picked up debris close to the minor planet where the *Griffon* and at least one alien ship crashed and that's where the samples we have come from. We've no idea of how serious the impact was, or what the ship had done to prevent it or to protect itself. So the original of this could feasibly have come off the alien ship that crashed on that rock."

Linen caught the implication. "In other words, the ship that Junior might have come from. The *Lithium Star* was sent in to sweep that area and she happened upon the remains of the *Griffon*. Which in effect is what really started all this off for us, once you'd worked out that Colonel Moritz had been brought in because of her finds and her conclusions when she was aboard the *Wayfinder*," she went on to Copper. "She was the one that twigged what they had, thus her promotion and her transfer into Intelligence on return, because Mars Defence Department was getting very antsy about the whole shebang."

The three stood pondering the issues for several minutes.

"Well, whatever the heck it is, Spook knows and I can't figure precisely because *we* have nothing remotely like it that he's aware of and can show me to explain. And Junior *is* familiar with it, so it's not a piece of sophisticated scanning gear or a weapon or anything like that," Copper deduced.

"Unless Junior is one smart alien," theorised Linen.

"Given he spends so much time shut in cupboards, he'd hardly be let loose with the wherewithal to shoot at his betters or analyse his surroundings."

"True," the redhead conceded. "We should consult a psych counsellor over him: poor little thing's been through a lot."

"May I be in the same room when you propose *that* to one of the ship's psych counsellors?" Trisk requested.

"Belay that, guys: let's stop for a break and by that time we'll have to head to medbay for your exam," Copper told Linen.

"Linen's med exam: that means her, not the whole troop of us," Trisk cut in. "I'm sure she doesn't want onlookers and I bet Doc Faerin won't put up with it."

"We can ask if you can be examined too – it'll be private, and if we link from here, you don't know who's in the background listening in," Copper argued.

"I think so too," Linen agreed. "Anyway, as you missed your rendezvous with the doc the other night because of the trouble we had with those jammers, I'm sure he'd like to see you again," she smirked.

"You're asking for a smack," was the tart rejoinder. "We'll just pack this lot away and get on with it."

The plan was followed more or less as agreed. Faerin had set up a small side bay to carry out the tests he had planned on Linen and with a little persuasion, agreed that Trisk could be put through the same procedures. Copper he had another plan for. With a nod in the relevant direction, he informed her that as she seemed to have plenty of spare time, there was a new simulation in one of the medbay training suites that she could attempt. As she was still in the process of completing her advanced General Health Qualification, it would be a test of her abilities. The sim itself was not requisite for the advanced GHQ, but it would provide useful experience for the field. He gave her the details and promised to stop by later to check her progress.

"I keep meaning to put in for the GHQ," Linen announced brightly. "But maybe I'll just let you finish your advanced course first and you can tell me how much time and effort I'll have to use up if I carry on with it. Enjoy your sim – I'm sure the doc will put you through your paces when you're done," she added with a wicked wink in her friend's direction.

"Button it," she was ordered as Copper set off.

* * *

The doctor was as good as his word and scarcely an hour later Copper found him at the other side of the viewing window in medical training suite two. She had found the new simulation already set up for off duty medical staff but not in use, and had thus locked herself in. The current platform was field training in dressing phase-burn wounds under cramped conditions and incoming fire using new medical gear that had recently come off the production line at Fleet Medical. The confined space of the training booth was making the work difficult, and she found that the recumbent virtual patient she had to work on was capable of more than just squealing. The programmers had also included two other simulated wounded officers who required attention as well as voices that provided ongoing updates of the conditions under which she was supposed to be operating.

Ignoring the keen eyes observing her from without, Copper continued to work doggedly, remembering to talk to her patient despite his origin off some production line. The new medi-scanner cum treatment delivery system was working well and an advance on the instrument she had used on Linen in medbay after their experience in the armoury. She patched up her patient, checked her previous ministrations on the other two and was immensely relieved when the buzzer sounded that marked the end of the programme.

Carefully resetting the whole, she held up her arm with its implanted ident to the reader to mark the close of her session and stepped out of the suite. Faerin was examining a readout that he had called up of her performance.

"Very good," he congratulated. "You've scored eighty seven percent; that's creditable for a first attempt in someone who's not a medic, even if you are inordinately quick at picking things up. I'll add it to your personal progress log for you to check over at leisure."

"Have you done this programme?" she asked in response. "And if you have, what was *your* score?"

"I have and I'm not telling you, Lieutenant," he retorted. "But I've got other challenging programmes that I have to add to your schedule, so expect more of the same," he went on.

"You *have* to add? Who says?"

"Colonel's orders. Personnel under training should be tested as close to their limits as possible – not only to gauge what they're capable of, but to show them that they *can* accomplish things that they might not think they can."

"Does that include her? And you?"

"Yes to both questions, not that it's any of your business, *Lieutenant*. You're quite like her, in a way: very quick on the uptake and with a streak of stubbornness that stands you in good stead in dangerous situations. But don't let that lead you into trouble. You at least seem capable of getting into trouble at the drop of a hat. And you *will* do those extra training sims."

"Please yourself – sir. But now I need a caff, we didn't take a proper lunch break. How are Linen and Trisk, by the way? All done and it was successful, I take it?"

"Successful in what way?" he asked narrowly.

"They both carry this redundant segment of coding in their genetic make-up, don't they?" she responded astutely.

He paused to look searchingly at her. "I can't give you other people's medical results," he cautioned with a twinkle in his eye.

"They'll tell me later, so you may as well. They both scored positive, didn't they?"

He nodded. "You were so sure they would, weren't you?"

"Yup. Well definitely Linen, and I figured Trisk had to; that's why I suggested he get tested too. You should try it out on yourself, Doc, and see if you have the propensity," she went on, smiling as the two made their way out of the training area.

"I might at that. It's my break time now, how about heading along to the mess for a caff? Your two colleagues will already be there by this time."

Copper immediately recalled her friend's opinion on Faerin's personal interest in her, but as the mess was rather more public that his office, where she presumed he took most of his caff breaks, and Trisk was also a good friend of his, she agreed.

"I really need the walk," she said. "Corralled in that cupboard space in medbay's no fun for any length of time; but it *is* a good sim. There are more in the same set, I take it?"

"Yes – and I'll put you down for every single one."

"Thanks, Doc, you're a true friend," she said ironically.

The two found Linen and Trisk in one of the booths in the mess when they strolled in. Trisk hailed them and asked after Copper's success on her sim.

"Eighty seven percent," she said briefly as she headed off to capture a caff at the chow-line, Faerin on her tail.

"Way to go!" Trisk called after her. "You only got eighty two on the same one, didn't you, Doc?"

"Ninety two," the doctor called over his shoulder. "Smart aleck!" he muttered to Copper.

Back at the booth the four drank their caff and talked over in low tones the results of the genetic tests, the consequences for their research and for their mission and the next steps to be taken. Copper was all for a rapid return to outer bay four and their deep probing of the large sample there, but as security back-up would be required, and also medical back-up if Copper intended to use her alien probe, the likelihood of that before the *Drake* was freed from Jupiter Station and on a heading to the edge was small. Faerin promised to assign a dedicated medic to the project, if he could find one willing, on the proviso that his department had first call on whoever it was. Dr Amber Embertz was the obvious choice given her past experience, but as she was one of his senior members of staff, he would have to check his scheduling.

Trisk reminded Copper in an undertone of her intention to reanalyse the hard-holo of the mystery item that had hailed from the Glory Hole, and its integral pieces, given Spook's interest in it. They could always check if at sub-micro levels any or all of the bits did encapsulate the blueprint of the whole. The original was made of replicative material and was thus probably intended for hard or constant use; as it was rather larger than Copper's alien scanner, it was not something that would be carried as a weapon in a human hand at any rate. It did not appear to have markings apart from the metallic studs around its middle and resembled no more than a box or case. As the colonel had come across nothing similar in her experience amongst things alien on Mars, it was probable that no-one in Mars Military Intelligence had stumbled upon anything like it. And as Colonel Moritz had specifically ordered that anything alien-related be reported to her immediately, it would be another item to be ticked off the list of things that were still to do in that respect.

"Good luck," Faerin told them as he rose. "I have work to get back to in my department and I suggest you get on with yours. And try not to get into any more trouble, any of you."

* * *

Back in the lab, the holo of the alien article from the Glory Hole was called up on an imaging console and the three regarded it critically from all angles.

"Best get a hard-holo of it created with the data we have," Copper said finally. "We've a lot on its internal structure from the way my scanner realigned and configured the pieces, so we should be able to get a relatively accurate mock-up. Not that it will help overmuch as there may be a lot of smaller bits missing and I doubt we'll be able to tell how it was powered."

"Well, we don't have a supply of raw alien tech to make a mock-up of out of that, so it'll just have to be regular plasformic or whatever's available," Linen said thoughtfully

Her friend looked at her, startled, for a moment, as an idea shot into her head, her eyes opened wide and a slow forefinger was raised.

"What?" Linen and Trisk demanded in unison.

"We don't have raw alien organo-tech aboard," she said to them. "But what we must have are repair patches for the *Drake's* hull fabric – which is self-repair to a certain degree. We ought to know: *we* were presented with mil-issue wrist-comms made of similar prototype stuff that they had under development," she reminded Linen. "*And* they were trying to improve it in that lab set-up just outside the Warren, remember, because they knew they had sizeable local sources of real alien organo-tech. We had asked for a tour of the site as Colonel Moritz had just demanded and got a tour of ours."

"*You* asked," Linen recalled. "The colonel was pretty taken aback and suspicious at the time, but she agreed, as we had given her data that more or less told them they'd find what they hoped they would if they looked hard enough and in the right place: *we'd* figured there was a buried alien ship. You came with us on that visit, Trisk and as you'd got your MEDIC and other gear, we reckoned you were hoping for a good nosey about. We hadn't realised at that point that you knew Colonel Moritz probably better than we did."

Trisk concurred with a nod and a smile.

"That set a few cats among shuttle-ducks when we realised they had a massive comms set up and Cop worked out that they were trying to develop their test material into functioning self-replicative hull coating and equip an entire squadron with it. And I had let slip about her making the marks on the tech move and the colonel freaked," Linen went on. "She asked Cop later how far she thought they'd got in replicating the stuff that Spook's ship's hull was made of, when she called in on us at Beagle, just after my Grammy Magenta had given us the wrist-comms. Grammy had said the woman Moritz had okayed them, when she handed them over. We nearly dropped: we'd no idea Grammy had even heard of Colonel Moritz."

"Yes," Copper recalled with a faint smile. "But for now, how do we reset a tri-dee hard-holo copier to duplicate something using a novel and very expensive organo-metal that we probably don't have much spare of as the base material without questions being asked and eyebrows being raised?"

"We ask the colonel on the QT," Linen said briskly. "Then it's her problem, just like all the other ones she has. But for the moment, what can we make of this? We may as well get a standard copy made; it might give us a clue or three. As you're the senior here, Trisk, maybe you could put the request in to the colonel? She did say anything to do with alien technology or similar she wanted to be told about – I figure this fits."

"Passing the buck," grinned Dr Addystone. "I'll get on to it; you two start making the solid from our data."

The device, when it had been replicated, gave them no clues as to its use. Copper had realised that Spook was not close by to help and surmised that he was off with Junior on some mission or other. The science officers scanned the schematics critically. The interior of the piece seemed to comprise a miniature maze of hollows and conduits with myriad screens of the finest mesh separating long runs, much like the safety panels that could be dropped to cut off units of passageway when danger threatened. This led the three to conclude that whatever it was, it was not a box for the storage of precious items or instruments.

The compact and rounded rectangle felt smooth on the exterior apart from the dully metallic protrusions encircling it. Copper was running her fingers around the edge, humming to herself distractedly whilst looking at the expanded tri-dee image of the internal structure hovering above her projection plate, when she suddenly became aware that Spook had returned and was hovering close in some sort of anticipation. And Junior was almost quivering.

"How do you pick up on these things so quickly?" she asked her alien companion aloud as she held the piece aloft. "And what's the fuss about? It's only a replica, it can't do anything."

The other two were alerted by the tone and had realised she was not talking to herself. They stood by as she walked over to their bench and picked up the sample cartridge into which all the relevant pieces of the original had been collected.

"I wonder," Copper mused. "If we can make a tri-dee copier work with our self-rep material, providing the colonel lets us loose with enough of it, could we use *these* bits and pieces on a second run and see if we can get anything close to the original?"

"No way, Cop!" Linen exclaimed.

"Colonel Moritz would never sanction it, Copper," cautioned Trisk. "These are pieces of an alien device, *that* much we've ascertained. If you put it through the tri-dee copier as the base material for its operation, you'll destroy what we have, even if the copier accepted it. As a scientist you must see that it's not feasible?"

"Yes I do; I was only thinking out loud."

"And talking out loud," Linen put in. "Better not make a habit of it or people will think you're loopy."

"People already do," Trisk observed. "But we'll have to wait the colonel's response on the use of our hull repair material. We may have to wait a while; she must still be up to her ears in ship's business. And I'm still not sure it's a good idea or it'll even give us more of a clue as to what this thing does. It won't be complete as we must be missing a lot that either was destroyed or blew away or got lost somehow and we won't have a power source. We don't even know if it *had* a power source or if it even needs one. Or if it's dangerous, once it's operable."

"It's not dangerous, I'm sure," Copper said suddenly. "Junior knows what it is. And I think he now knows it's a model of one and not a real one. Maybe that was what Spook was trying to teach him," she added. "But if we could get what is essentially a complete blueprint of this – and I'll try Spook for that – we *do* have a source of enough alien organo-tech that we could use to replicate it…"

"Yes and where would that be… oh, oh!" Linen breathed. "If you think the colonel will sanction your breaking off a piece of that chunk of whatever it is in outer bay four for a test trial in our lab, in the middle of her ship, then think again!"

"We could get the gear set up in outer bay four," Copper told her. "But how do we break a lump off? It's practically indestructible, as that's how it survived in deep space so long."

"Same way as they make the hull repair patches out of that organo-metallic material for the *Drake*," Trisk said practically. "Secretly. And there must be equipment that can do it. Only I suspect it won't be on the *Drake*. Maybe the repair station just on our doorstep would have it," he added. "Their business *is* the repair of starships."

"But we're top range, just off the production line," Linen argued. "They may have hull plates, or at least we have spares, but will they have the equipment to do much more than just fit them in place? And *our* self-repair stuff is not the same as the alien organo-tech, you know that yourself," she added to Copper. "And the colonel will never let you try it."

"You could ask her," Trisk cut in as he raised his head to see who was buzzing at the entry. "She's just turned up." He hastened to unlock the lab door.

"You have exactly one quarter of an hour to explain what you've been up to and what you want me to authorise," their commanding officer told them as she stepped in. "And it had better be good."

Linen had been right: the colonel refused to consent to any abstraction, use or misuse of the lump of alien tech in bay four as raw material for the construction of a full scale replica of the alien tech that had been recreated from pieces collected in the Glory Hole, no matter how excited their two alien entities were. A link to anyone associated with the Jupiter Station repair teams was also vetoed. Kit Locksmith and his counterpart in station security had tracked down a couple more rogue operatives there and the whole operation was out of bounds as far as the *Drake's* security chief was concerned. Every station technician working on the *Drake* had now been double checked and a reduced and much-chastened team was occupied aboard the ship on the final repairs that would render her completely spaceworthy.

Permission to use raw hull plate material to obtain a replica of the alien article was approved if it was feasible, however, with the proviso that if anything resembling a full blueprint could be obtained, the operation to duplicate the whole would be carried out in a part of the ship that could be buttoned down tight. And that would require the presence of security. Outer bay four was the obvious place, Copper argued, as matters alien were now known to be going on there anyway and would cause less raised eyebrows than somewhere else set aside for the same purpose. She carried her point. As repairs to the bay had been completed, they could now access it.

Their main problem, Trisk believed, would be in persuading the standard lab tri-dee copier to use the novel and very durable self-repair material for the process. But if workable, it would be a useful additional tool for the *Drake's* arsenal — literally, if replica weapons or the like could be made at will. Engineering input would be requisite, was his summing. He was told to find his own engineer to help out but on no account to let whoever it was into what would be the end result of their endeavours. But as it was late, the colonel advised them to call a halt for the sol. No doubt issues would seem clearer on the morrow.

"That's what I call a commanding officer," Linen approved as Colonel Moritz set off for her next appointment. "One who actually orders us off duty. What say we meet in the mess in half an hour? I've got a couple of links to absent friends to make. And I suggest you tell Spook and Junior to take the eve off and do whatever aliens do to relax," she advised Copper. "I bet they need as much of a break from you as you do from them."

Copper did not argue: she feared her friend was right.

* * *

The mess was fairly busy with comings and goings when the three met as arranged. Trisk had been thinking and had decided that sounding out engineer Oaky Grimsson might be a plan, as solving micro-engineering puzzles was one of his specialities. He was also a friend and less likely to require explanations as to what was going on. Copper was by this time more than keen to begin work on the large chunk of organo-metal in outer bay four, now that they were assured that repairs there had finished. Their major headache in that respect was security back-up and the medical cover that Colonel Moritz had deemed requisite if the alien scanner was to be used.

"You approach Oaky, Trisk and see what's to do, and maybe you can persuade Doc Faerin to let us have Dr Embertz at short notice as well, as he's one of your buddies. We two can try to charm security, though they're short-handed, as Kit Locksmith's never tired of telling us."

"That gives Trisk a lot to do on the persuasion front," Linen cut in, trying to sound serious, although her eyes were dancing in mischief. "He may have to take on Commander Sage as well, as she's Oaky's boss. I'll have words with Doc Faerin as I get on well with him. And you can tackle Chief Locksmith – you *did* suggest Tawny Brown after all. Haven't seen him around for a while, but he's probably pulling double shifts: he's way short of personnel, he's had to sort out this last bout of trouble we had with those jammers and he's no doubt had to spend a lot of time station-side over it."

Copper regarded her friend critically, scenting some hidden agenda, but nodded in agreement. "We've only a couple of sols left in dock, as repairs are almost done," she noted, scanning the ship's status logs that she had called up on the table info-point. "I would imagine that all our supplies from the auto-ship and from Europa Station are now aboard. I wonder what the status of the *Swordfish* is: shouldn't she be heading out now with those extra passengers we handed over, to rendezvous with that prison ship? Or is she hanging fire to scoop up the latest batch that station security rounded up? I can't find it here."

"Give it a rest," Linen pleaded. "Other ships' business isn't ours. Enjoy your dinner, for frock's sake. I see there's a concert on in the theatre, according to the holo-board over there; we *could* take that in. It's the Drake Singers."

"Thanks but no: I've had Lieutenant Zennik Chinn trying to persuade me to join them ever since he heard me humming in a weapons drill we both took part in and I've been avoiding him ever since. And Ash Goff's one of them as well and his voice is like the sound of toothache. Besides, I want to go over all we *did* get on that hunk of hull," she added in a low voice.

"Work, it's always work with you," Linen grumbled in mock severity. "You keep pushing yourself and you'll be promoted way above us and end up in command of your own ship, just like the colonel, where even dinner is interrupted by meetings."

She gave a slow rueful smile and nodded over towards a table over by the far wall, where their commanding officer was seated with Helmis, Sage, Inkscree and Faerin, who all looked serious, behind the light haze that indicated that the table's privacy screen had been invoked.

"The loneliness of command, where you don't have the luxury of being able to follow your own inclination," Linen said, her gold-flecked eyes probing her friend's face. "The ship comes first and your life and personal life come second – or not at all. And all those who care about you have to tolerate it and live with the misery it entails."

Copper bit her lip at the intensity in her friend's troubled eyes. "Point taken; I'll try not to let it happen," she promised as she looked away and at her raised mug, her eyes flickering over to where the five senior officers were deep in discussion. The colonel was tapping the plas-film in her hand and Commanders Sage and Inkscree, and Captain Helmis were paying close attention to it. Kynedd Faerin was not: *he* was looking at the colonel with a look on his face she had never seen before.

Copper quickly drained her drink and carefully set the mug back on the table. "So what should we do this eve, then?" she croaked, smiling askance, wondering if her friends had caught what she had. As both were looking at her, she doubted it.

Trisk had his own plans, involving some holo-game with Tawny Brown and some others. Linen thus suggested a relaxing hour in the officers' lounge by way of amusement, as many of their fellows were no doubt there and ready for a chat, followed by a brisk run along those parts of the engineering decks open to traffic as a means of gentle exercise. As her friend had a flight sim scheduled for early on the following sol and did not want to expend too much energy, she readily agreed.

* * *

Copper had a small holo of the large chunk of debris in outer bay four rotating above her console as she scanned the data records that the *Drake* had recorded of the piece before it came aboard as well as the comprehensive remote analysis she and her colleagues had taken. Trisk had gone off to confer with Oaky Grimsson on his help in modifying the tri-dee copier to handle the self-replicative material rather than its usual substance as base matter. Linen had volunteered to sound out Ossy Inkscree on the use of a platoon of his surf-sci bots on a detailed sortie through the wreckage and was in the office trying to contact him. Copper had put a call into Kit Locksmith for an update on the deployment of one of his team with them for the duration of a science session in the shuttle bay, but had no response. According to the duty officer in security, he was due back on duty in a couple of hours, but would then be off-ship for a meeting after that.

Linen returned, semi-successful. "Dr Inkscree wants to know exactly what his bots will be tasked with, so I said he could come along later and we'd show him. He knows you're due for a flight sim shortly, but I'll be here. We don't need all his frigging bots, a handful will do; but he guards them as if they were his private property and scarce as green diamonds. But he's more or less agreed. And he also told me that as ship's repairs are just about complete, there's a final once over to be done by our own people and then we should be ready to hit the space lanes. Sol after next, he reckons, unless orders to the contrary come in."

"Praise be; the quicker we're away the better. But I'd best stow this and get ready for my flight sim. I'm only glad I suited up after breakfast; this having to dress up for the mess is getting to be a pest when you've early drills," Copper grumbled.

"Discipline, Lieutenant, ma'am; it goes with the job. But I'll come with you and take the elevator down to medbay to see Doc Faerin: it'll save my feet. Let's lock this place down."

Copper agreed and the two quickly wound up their tasks. The local elevator was a short walk along and in no time they were on their way. As Linen hopped out at deck six, they heard the pounding of feet along the corridor.

"Wait for me!" the voice of Kit Locksmith hailed them as the man himself hove into view at a trot, wearing a flight-suit that suggested he was heading in the same direction as Copper.

He gave Linen a mock salute as she passed and slid aboard. "Whew! Made it!" he gasped. "Heading down to flight sims?"

"I am, hence the gear," Copper responded. "It seems to be never ending, but the colonel appears to think it's a good idea to have me trained up on fighters."

"You and me both," Kit said as he stated their destination and the elevator began to move. "And as the doc's passed me as fit – well, fit enough that he's authorised flight training – here I am. But you fly a shuttle fairly well, so you should make a fair fighter pilot."

"Only fair?" she demanded archly.

He inclined his head, his blue eyes searching hers. "What's your own opinion of your skill?"

"Fair," she agreed, laughing.

"We should be done about the same time. How about a caff in the lounge afterwards? I guess we'll both need one, and as there isn't a nice bar handy, it's the best we're likely to get."

Copper was immediately wary, but raised a casual eyebrow and shrugged. "Suits me."

He smiled in response as the elevator halted and the panel slid aside. The two made their way amicably along the deck and through the door of the relevant training suite. They made for the check-in station for their sims and found they were the only ones logged in for short-range flight testing.

"After you, Lieutenant," he said, smiling, as he pointed out the applicable units.

Copper nodded in compliance and made for her simulated cockpit, almost ready for whatever the programme chosen by her training assessor was about to produce. She locked down and set the sequence…

* * *

Three quarters of an hour later, and battered by a very testing simulation, she tottered out cursing and snapped the test booth shut. She found Kit Locksmith waiting for her outside.

"You finished early?" she greeted him.

"No, just done. Can't you tell by the crumpled suit and the air of utter exhaustion?"

"You look better than I do… I ache in every muscle," she groaned, flexing her shoulders to ease the tension.

"Here, let me massage your neck and shoulders," he offered, suiting his words to his actions as he stepped behind her and began a powerful manipulation of the affected areas.

"Hey, steady! That hurts!"

"It's supposed to. You'll feel better shortly," he replied, his mouth so close to her ear that she could feel his breath.

Despite herself, she felt pulses of pleasure running down her spine at the deft handling. "That's good," she conceded after a minute or two. "Who taught you that?"

"Martial arts instructor I knew a few ships ago," he said over her shoulder. "He was half my size and could best me in any drill."

She twisted round. "Thanks; I needed that."

His eyes held hers. "You're welcome, Copper."

As her eyes widened at the use of her given name, his face moved closer and his lips were on hers. She moved her arms up to object and found herself clasped in a warm embrace. He was taller than she and stronger and her protests evaporated as her resistance decreased. Suddenly her brain clicked into gear and she pushed him away.

"Back off; this is not the time or the place," she warned him. "I have too much going on around me and so do you…"

"Just tell me when and where the time and the place are: I'll still be here," he promised, his blue eyes twinkling and with a smile that melted her wrath. "Let's get that caff."

"Damn you, Kit Locksmith," she growled into his face.

But her eyes were smiling as she said it.

23: A SHOT IN THE DARK

Copper, Linen and Trisk resumed work in their lab later, with an interested observed in their chief of staff, Ossian Inkscree. He had been briefed on the task that they had ahead of them in outer bay four and wanted to see at second-hand at least, what they had planned. Observing Copper to be twitchy, he pressed to be told the degree of danger attached. She had no hesitation in telling him that it was covered: she had taken the opportunity of her cosy chat with Kit Locksmith in the officers' lounge to ask that Tawny Brown be assigned to them. Kit had agreed, and as Linen had received grudging assurance from Dr Faerin that they could call on Amber Embertz for medical back-up, they were set to go whenever those two officers were available.

Locksmith had apprised Copper that his next job in about an hour was to interview four new security officers, all of whom would be assigned to the *Drake* if they passed muster. They had been drafted from the number that made up the complement of Jupiter Station and their superior had vouched for them, but Kit wanted to make sure himself. He had checked their records, he told her, but records could lie. His mission being successful, he would be in a position to spare Tawny for duty in bay four. The reason for her unrest Copper could not impart to the others with the chief SO around: she had taken time out in her quarters for a couple of tasks, one of which had included asking Spook to accompany Kit down to Jupiter Station and to make his own assessment of the new personnel. Spook had agreed, but Copper now found herself the sole guardian of Junior, who had refused to remain quiescently in his cupboard and was checking out the lab in his own way.

They had no sooner got rid of Inkscree than they found the colonel on their doorstep asking for an update. Copper took it upon herself to explain in depth but succinctly what the plans of the three were, the first part being the programming of the eight bots that Inkscree had sanctioned. Colonel Moritz was no fool and had sensed the disquiet in her science officer; she was also sufficiently astute to realise that the newest addition to the crew might be one of the reasons and firmly demanded the latest on that situation. Copper faced her squarely and outlined Spook's mission, which had resulted in Junior being left loose in the lab, which he was now exploring. As Linen and Trisk traded glances, the colonel eyed her subordinate in some severity.

"You take a lot upon yourself, Ms Milkstone."

"I deemed it an added precaution for the safety of the ship, ma'am; and it wasn't something that I could link you about. And it *was* an immediate concern: Lieutenant Locksmith was headed down there almost directly."

"How did you know that?"

"I had a fighter-sim earlier, ma'am, and so did he. I met him on the way to the training suite," Copper explained, slightly red in the face. "He told me after that."

Linen viewed her friend closely, drew her own conclusions and smiled secretly to herself. The colonel merely acknowledged the information with a nod.

"I see. Let me know the outcome – privately," she told her. "Anything else? Particularly about this new entity that seems to consider my ship its playground."

Copper admitted that Junior, with still-developing skills and insatiable curiosity, might inadvertently attempt to interact with a device in the lab to his or its detriment. He had been restricted *to* the lab, as Spook was able to exert that amount of control over him, but like any young creature, he was testing his limits.

"I see. You *will* remain here until our other resident alien has returned and you *will* ensure that this second entity that we have inherited is kept under control. Dr Addystone, you're with me. Bring your new probe, and have all the data and any hardware relating to the improvements you've effected to hand."

"Aye ma'am," Trisk responded with a quizzical glance at his colleagues.

As the two marched out of the door, Trisk giving a backward glance at his friends, Linen turned to Copper.

"What was that about?"

"What she told us before: she wants the features of Trisk's and Doc Faerin's probe enhanced to the extent that it'll not only detect various alien lifeforms but control them or put them out of action. Junior's got her worried. We now have two aliens aboard, or will have when Spook gets back, but we probably can't stop others getting on board if they want. And we now know there *are* aliens out there. And I still don't know what Junior's capable of, but Spook can interact with hardware and software – and with me physically, according to Doc Faerin. So if Spook and I are somewhere else…"

"I can see there might be a problem. And other aliens out there may not be nice ones," Linen nodded. "And if they can interact with humans the way Spook does with you…"

"Exactly."

"But on another note: I think you remind the colonel of herself when she was younger," Linen said, her head tilted to one side and a knowing grin on her face. "Otherwise she'd have blown up much more at your making decisions about her ship without consulting her – which in effect is what you did. Most commanding officers would have had you thrown in the brig for insubordination at best and mutiny at worst for that one."

"I suppose so: it hadn't occurred. But she's not the only one who thinks I remind them of her," Copper said meaningfully.

"Somebody else thinks you're like the colonel? Who does?"

"Someone not a million clicks from here that carries a torch for her," was the response.

"Carries a torch…you mean Doc Faerin!"

"I do. Why else would he leave his post aboard his last ship – he was chief medic there – to sign aboard the *Drake*?"

"The same reason most of the crew did: she's the best damn ship in the Fleet, we're on an exciting new mission, and let's face it, the facilities here are way better than you can get on most Mars-based stations, let alone on a ship of the line. Why else? And what ship did he last serve aboard anyway?"

Copper gave a sly grin and raised a questioning eyebrow. "Guess," she said.

Linen paused, but only for a moment. "The *Wayfinder*!"

"The *Wayfinder*. I checked her last crew complement earlier this sol, after I'd finished in flight sims and had a caff; and there it was: Chief Medical Officer Kynedd Faerin."

"But what made you figure? Something else must have given it away."

Copper shrugged. "Just a meaningful glance or two, and one or two interactions that I picked up on: he does call her Elle now and again. And I did spend *some* time in medbay after all."

"I'm sorry for him – and for them both, if she reciprocates," Linen frowned. "But the colonel was drafted into MI after her stint on the *Wayfinder*, wasn't she? She had been *Major* Moritz on that ship and it was a promotion for her to Lieutenant Colonel. Majorelle used to figure she was involved in testing advanced tech aboard some new ship on a shakedown cruise after she left the *Wayfinder*, but we found out later it was Military Intelligence. But I expect that's part of their brief, especially the bit she was drafted into – Outer Mars Ops: it deals with any outside threats to Mars, and for outside read alien. Karben and Bilkitt are part of it. But what did she *do* aboard the *Wayfinder*?" demanded Linen. "Whatever it was, when she and her team found bits of alien tech and she figured what they were, she was hauled out, promoted and given the job of finding out even more."

"She was the senior tactical officer, and that means she had charge of the ship's internal and external defence systems, and on the bridge of a smaller ship like the *Wayfinder*, she might have had control of shields, weapons, sensor arrays, probes, tractors and so on, for plotting configuration and positioning of external threats. Counter-intelligence would be one of her main duties as well, hence the transfer to MI, I expect; and I bet she couldn't say no. And *we* know how smart she is: it would've been a short step from MI to command of the *Drake*, given our mission."

"Too smart, maybe," Linen sighed. "But she must have had a degree to be fast-tracked into Fleet and then promoted up the ranks so quickly. I bet her degree was science-based. But when the colonel works out that you've been digging into her past, she's going to fry you."

"She can blame the system for letting me have that much access: it shouldn't have been possible. But as for her degree, I did not get hold of her personnel record, nor would I have even attempted it. But you could be right about her degree: for career military, she has one formidable grasp of the scientific process."

"And I suppose when it was out that Colonel Moritz was the new commander of *MSS Drake II*, Faerin jumped at the chance of Chief MO on a new ship of the Fleet. From the *Wayfinder* to the *Drake* would be a step up as she's a big ship. I'm still sorry for them, for they'd never get time to themselves on *this* ship, with some of the nosey crew we have aboard. And what if she has to send him into a dangerous situation and has to stay behind and wait it out? Lor', it's bad enough when you get into trouble and there's precious little I can do about it, as I've found out more than once. Even with Kit Locksmith in your orbit, at least you and he are able to snatch *some* privacy from time to time," Linen added wickedly.

"Will you give up on that?" her friend retorted irritably. "We are *not* an item and I know better than to make us one, with the likes of you with your ears to my door and your tongue at the ready."

"Hah! And you're telling me he didn't snatch a kiss in the elevator when I saw him hop into it with you on the way down to the training suite on deck thirteen earlier?"

Copper blushed hotly. "He did not!"

"So where did he? In the sim-suite?"

"Mind your own business!" she was told shortly.

"Oh Cop, Cop, Cop! He did! Your face gives you away every time! Be careful! But he's a very nice guy, and with no string of casual amours – I *did* check around the ship."

"You did what? How could you? Why did you? And what's more, how dare you!"

"I've told you before, I worry about you," Linen smiled, but with a hint of sadness in her eyes that did not escape her friend.

"I know. And believe me, Kit and I are not smooching in dark corners and snatching quick kisses in elevators or anywhere else. It was a spur of the moment thing, he caught me off-guard and I did tell him to back off – nicely. He took it well."

"But you sent Spook down to watch his back? Oh Cop!"

"We're still buddies and I'd have done the same for anyone, if I thought it would help the ship," Copper returned doggedly. "We've all suffered from rogue crewmen, we and Kit more than most. But as far as the relationship between Doc Faerin and the colonel are concerned, there are two people I reckon would know more than *I* suspect."

"Trisk for one," Linen immediately replied. "He's a buddy of the doc's and the colonel had *him* hauled aboard even before she captured us."

"So I figured."

"But who's the other?" demanded Linen

"Kit Locksmith."

"What! How?"

"Guess what ship *he* served aboard before he was posted to the *Drake*? Though the *Drake* may have been a promotion for him, as he was second in command in his last post."

"*Wayfinder*," Linen said shortly. "How many more of her crew have we got here? Did they break her up for scrap that they all thought they'd better find new jobs?"

"No idea; I didn't access lists of ships of the line that are on active duty or otherwise. And I didn't recognise any other names on the list. It took me a bit of digging to get into the *Wayfinder's* records."

"I'm not going to ask how. But you're changing the subject in hopes I'll leave it be. Why did you ask Kit Locksmith to back off? You've admitted you like him, at least from a distance; he's a nice guy and now it seems he more than likes you. There *have* been other not so nice guys in your past, I know…"

"Yes," Copper said shortly as a vision of Mizzle Chert and one or two others rose in her mind. "And I was cheated and abused. Never again; I won't risk it, not again."

Linen's face creased in concern. "Never is a dark word. And I'm sorry you think that Kit might treat you in the same way."

"I don't; but I can only go on experience and that's been mine," Copper said, shaking her head.

"Don't go kicking happiness in the face, Cop: you'll regret it down the road a bit. And I'm happy that you've found someone who gives more than a damn about you. And he does, you know: I've seen him look at you."

"Linen…"

"You'll always have me to look out for you, but you need more – more than you got as a kid, more than you had when you were younger. You're too apt to look for people to like you, and you give too much of yourself to the wrong people and they take advantage. Kit won't. But if he dared, I'd kick him to hell and back," she smiled. "The colonel sets great store by him. Why else would she have got him into Lowell security if not to keep her eyes on us? And have you noticed he's suddenly Kit and not Kit Locksmith or The Chief?"

"Stop trying to manipulate me!"

"I'm only trying to make you see sense. But at least you're still buddies. Tell me all about the flight sim suite."

"Go to hell. And stay there!"

"Oh Cop, Cop, Cop!"

Copper suddenly gave a short start and looked up. "Spook's back!"

"Thank frock for that; now we can go and take a break. Tell him to ground Junior and let's get on to the mess for a bite of late lunch, it's getting on. I guess Kit must be back as well, or at least on his way."

"You are asking for one poke in the eye, lady!"

* * *

Kit was not in the mess and neither was Trisk but Ash Goff and Tany Melucca hove in at the back of them and joined their table uninvited. Copper was put out as she had planned to check her personal links. Linen had no qualms over privacy invaded and called up her own to see what had appeared since earlier in the sol.

"Link from Thars!" she announced. "Copied to you, Cop. He's arranged the internal examiners for our theses! Very clever – yours is Alessa Aclarke and mine is Mariner Mbolon! Isn't that cheating, as they both know us so well?"

"Alessa's *your* second mentor and Mariner's mine, so I guess it must be within the rules, as our appraisals will be separate. But don't go expecting an easy ride: Mariner's an expert in cross-examination and I bet Alessa is too and they know our work almost inside out, as it was never off their desks and they were forever in our hair. And as neither one of them was particularly convinced on some of our findings, our arguments will have to impress. It'll have to be done supra-light if it's aboard ship."

"It had better be, as I don't plan to hang around until the end of this mission: I'll have forgotten the stuff by that time," Linen said. "And as we've squeezed two years' work into near one and a quarter by dint of hard work and more overtime than most people put into their entire careers, we damn well deserve to have it recognised."

"What recognised?" asked an inquisitive Ash Goff.

"Our PhDs," Linen explained guilelessly. "We'd been doing them at Lowell College when we were drafted. Didn't you know we'd completed them here and have just submitted them to our *Alma Mater*?"

She was well aware that he had not. Most of their shipmates were likewise ignorant, as given the sensitive nature of their work and everything related to it, it had of necessity been kept under wraps. Their records, had Goff been able to access them, would only have recorded their completed degrees.

"Astrobiology," Linen explicated. "What was your degree in, Ash and where did you do it?"

"Geology, Areology and Areography," he disclosed a little sulkily. "Opportunity College," he added.

The ever-chatty Tany had several questions to ask and much of her own wisdom to dispense and as the two saw any further prospect for private discussion recede, they elected to call a halt and head back to their own office for their after-lunch caff.

"You realise our PhDs will be the talk of the officers' lounge now?" Copper said to her friend as they trod the deck. "Ash can't keep his mouth shut and neither can Tany. What made you blurt it all out?"

"Ash is still soft on you," Linen explained. "Just giving him another good reason to realise you're way out of his orbit. Tany's more his style and at least she's one of the few that can shut him up, as she's more talkative than he is."

"You're *such* a good friend, thank you *so* much," Copper retorted with extreme irony. "But I want to get back to the lab anyway, and see what Spook has got. I don't know why, but I've suddenly got a sort of shivery feeling…"

"That's easy to explain," Linen chuckled.

"Hah, hah. No, it's as if something's not quite right, and I don't like it."

"Here we go again," the redhead sighed. "D'you think Kit's in trouble? Or Junior's caused a problem? Or something else is wrong down on the station?"

"I don't know. And keep your voice down; you never know who's listening around the next bulkhead or how sensitive the deck cams are to the whispered word."

The office was empty: whatever the colonel had planned for Trisk, he had not returned or left a message. Copper accordingly sat at her own desk and tried to quiet her mind, but she was still strangely edgy and shook her head; she was getting nothing new.

"Maybe I should go and see if I can connect to Junior? That might keep him occupied?" Linen offered.

"He's hiding in the secure store again and Spook's here, so no – and I'd rather have you here. Whatever's going on, all I feel is anxious. It's maybe the general unrest Spook's picked up on. We leave Jupiter Station the sol after morrow, at ten hundred hours, I think. That's not a lot of time if who or what's behind some of the problems we've been having is still around. And I imagine they'll be getting desperate by now because they haven't been able to breach us – maybe whoever's paying their bills is so nasty, you wouldn't want to fail or you'd be in worse trouble than if you got caught."

"That's one big can of worms that I don't like the sound of but it's not enough to take to the colonel. It could be that you were missing Spook because you sent him off with Kit," Linen surmised. "Are these new recruits of his heading up with him or are there formalities to be gone through at the station? If so, they'll have to be quick. And surely it's a bit short notice for a career change that takes you off a station and onto a ship that's headed out into the great unknown – or mostly unknown. There wouldn't have been a big line-up of volunteers to choose from, I imagine."

"That was worrying Kit as well," Copper conceded. "That and the risk that there may still be a mole in his department that hasn't been found. As for the new crew, he didn't have much choice. Security is one place that can't run short-handed if we *do* hit trouble and as we've been hitting trouble since even before the *Drake* was launched, he needs all the people he can get."

She leant her elbows on her desk and placed her clasped hands under her chin, staring at the empty holo-grid in front of her. The minutes ticked by and still she stared, finding her mind running more and more on Kit Locksmith than on the prospect of danger for the ship.

"Damn! All I can see is Kit frigging Locksmith! What's the matter with me?" she demanded of no-one in particular, as a buzz at the door caused both officers to turn their heads.

Linen opened it, after checking the viewer. It was Lieutenant Lyssa Halsen and she was toting a glossy little green case. She slipped the carrying strap off her shoulder and held it up.

"I believe you're expecting these?"

"That will be our eight little bots, I expect," Linen greeted her cheerfully. "I recognise the ambience of the ensemble. Do you have a collection of such cases in varying sizes for the distribution of sets of these to deserving individuals, and do said cases have the usual conveniences for data and sample storage, manipulation of the contents and all manner of exciting things?"

"These are a set of test specimens that have been carefully adapted and encrypted for *your* convenience; they're security-tagged and coded to you two and Trisk Addystone only – well apart from Ossy Inkscree and me, as we did the fizzing work on them," was the reply. "They come in this nest, the holo-pad's in there and what the hell you do with the lot is your business, I'm just the delivery girl. Got a caff handy? I've had no lunch."

"Help yourself," Linen invited. "We'd better get Gerald and Gemima up to scratch on them; Trisk can sort Barking out later. I'll go get ours," she added to her friend.

The redhead made off to the lab to fetch their MEDICs. She returned in short order to find Lyssa and Copper sipping caff.

"Yours is there," her friend told her. "Lyssa's been telling me about her brother. She can tell you while I set up a scan. We may as well get started as we'll need it for work later."

With a probing look at Linen, Copper activated her MEDIC and instructed it to begin a scan of the case and its contents, reckoning that as she had updated Gemima with all the data available from the previous bot testing as well as the asteroid drop, the unit would have no trouble.

"It's always work with you," Linen laughed lightly and began to question their visitor on her spell of furlough.

To the surprise of Halsen, but not the other two, Gemima had detected data exchange between the eight cased units and the probe surveillance beams that each one had begun to emit before even the container was unlocked.

"Some things never change," Copper remarked dryly. "And I bet they still glow green in operation."

"You need to see them in the dark," Lyssa retorted, equally dryly. "And where we're going is liable to be dark: space usually is. We haven't actually worked out how to change the light emission," she admitted. "But you're welcome to them. At least it means it's eight less I have to deal with. As they're so high-spec and so highly secure, only a couple of us are allowed to have our paws on them, so we have a fizzing lot to organise. Thanks for the caff, I'm headed for the mess."

"Enjoy," Linen told her as the lieutenant made off. "*We* did, despite Ash Goff and Tany Melucca for company."

Copper rose, snatching up her scanner and aiming it at the door as she activated it. Linen opened her mouth questioningly, hands upraised in surprise.

"Just checking," was the rueful response as she straightened up. "I don't suspect Lyssa of anything bad for a second, but I'm still shivery about something. But she's headed off, so it's okay."

"The sol you start checking up on nice people like Lyssa Halsen is the sol you've got me even more worried than normal. I'd best lock these bots away before somebody else decides to call in. Where's Spook?"

"Still here. And he keeps giving me mental hugs: I can't figure it. I…"

There was another buzz at the entry and both looked up at the viewer, startled. The grim face of Colonel Moritz was visible on the other side and the two made haste to grant entry and stand to semi-attention.

"Your Spook," the colonel said without preamble to Copper. "Is it still on the station?"

"No ma'am: he came back, but I've not been able to work out what he's trying to communicate and I *have* tried. All I know is he's restless, but I have absolutely no specifics and on that basis there's nothing I can report. That's why I didn't link in. I assume that the interviews with the new security personnel have been completed and that Lieutenant Locksmith is back aboard?"

"The interviews were over some time ago, yes. Mr Locksmith did not come back aboard immediately as he had other matters to attend to. However, as of twenty minutes ago he's been listed as missing."

"What?" Copper stared at the colonel in horror for a couple of seconds as a bolt of shock shuddered through her frame and she felt suddenly sick. Her head turned to look down at her task desk. "Why in hell didn't you tell me?"

"That was to Spook, ma'am, not to you," Linen put in, clutching at her taller friend's arm. "Spook's been back for some time, Cop: he must have come back just after the interviews and he may not even know," she added.

"He knew something was up!"

"What's been done, ma'am? I guess a security team's been despatched from here?" Linen asked.

"Yes. And Jupiter Station security's on it. As you reported that your alien friend went down with Lieutenant Locksmith, I was in hopes you would have some additional information."

Copper raised her hands in anguish, shaking her head. She paused for a moment, pondering.

"I'm getting suited up and heading down there and Spook's coming with me – if anyone can locate Lieutenant Locksmith, it's him," she said in a hard, angry voice.

"Cop, cool it. You can't just…"

"Can't I?"

"Copper Milkstone, just you sit still for a second," snapped Linen, steering her to her chair and forcing her down upon it. "You said yourself you kept seeing Kit in your mind's eye and couldn't figure why."

"I thought it was because…" she trailed off, aware that the colonel was listening to every word. "Damn!"

"Now think!" Linen commanded. "Spook was trying to tell you something about Kit."

As Copper subsided and sank back into her seat, the redhead and Ms Moritz exchanged expressive glances. The question in their commanding officer's eyes was answered by a quick nod from Lieutenant Lyrican before she turned back to her friend.

Copper had resumed her former position of elbows on desk but her clasped hands were at her mouth. She closed her eyes tightly as if in prayer, calling up an image of Kit Locksmith, willing Spook to show her what he knew or guessed. Suddenly her eyes flew open, she tightened her lips and her face assumed an expression of extreme concentration. Her hands came apart and she began tapping the desk top.

"Spec of Jupiter Station, high magnification," she ordered as she flicked on the ops system. "Where was Kit the last time we heard from him?" she demanded of the air as the holo-grid lit up and the station's spec appeared.

"Security HQ on level three," the colonel responded, leaning over to see what she doing. "He had a planned security briefing in the main office with Security Chief Mills and his second after the interviews and after that he had a briefing in the personnel office on level four. He made those meetings and was expected back at the station office on level three at fifteen hundred. He didn't make it. Mills couldn't raise him and called personnel and then us. We couldn't raise him either, nor could we find a trace of his implanted ident, which we should have been able to do if he'd met with an accident and was unable to respond. We can only speculate on his disappearance; we don't know if he found out something he shouldn't and had to be silenced before he reported it, or he's been taken for some other reason."

"Damn!" Copper breathed. "So if he's still on station, he's in a shielded location, or his ident's been deactivated or removed; or he's been taken off station. As Jupiter's one helluva big place, we could search for sols and not find him. Which would delay the ship – again. And someone must have been aware of his itinerary."

"A lot of people were," the colonel conceded.

Copper sat, deep in thought, her eyes on the display before her. Her splayed fingers reached out, hovering over the moving holo as she called up location after location. "There are a lot of shielded sections," she noted. "And I bet not all of them are logged in the official spec. There are two reactor cores for a start and any number of repair bays and other service points that contain hazardous materials and have to be protected. And how many private facilities have isolation units for one function or another? A level by level search isn't an option, so logically, shielded sections would be the place to start first; and that's one way of tying security up while other things are going on," she added bitterly. "But he's still on station, I'm sure of it – Spook's sure of it. I'd stop all traffic in or out until we find him."

"You're not in charge," Linen pointed out.

"I'm going down there. Spook's our best chance of locating him. He was close enough to him for those interviews that he should be able to pick up on his signs. And I'll need to be there to direct Spook, and *he'll* get access to areas that I can't. I'll need a protective suit and armaments – preferably ones that station security can't pick up…"

"Belay that, Lieutenant," the colonel interrupted testily. "At the moment you are going nowhere."

"I agree," Linen put in. "If something *has* happened to him and you find out who's behind it, you'll tear off their heads with your bare hands and kick what's left of them into Jupiter orbit."

"Damn straight I will!" Copper exploded, but only to herself. Some caution made her leave the thought unspoken as, ideas already percolating in her head, she clenched her hands above the desk and tried to speak calmly.

"These new security people: did Kit – Lieutenant Locksmith – approve them, ma'am?"

"That's what the meet in personnel was for, I understand," Colonel Moritz clarified. "He told Chief Mills that he wanted to know more than was apparent in their station records before he would endorse any transfer to the *Drake*. Why?"

"Thinking aloud, ma'am: it would be known he was heading to personnel after his security briefing and at what time he was liable to finish. But when was the meeting in personnel set up? Kit told me that he'd checked the records of the new hands but that records could lie before he went across to the station, hence the need for face-to-face with the new people. He may have had some suspicion then that something wasn't right and the talks confirmed it. Did he figure after the interviews that one or more of the files were suspect and he wanted to know why, hence the meet with personnel?"

"You're suggesting that Mr Locksmith suspected an anomaly or missing data, wanted further checks and so asked to meet with personnel?"

"Possibly; I don't know, ma'am. But if the trip to personnel wasn't originally scheduled, whoever planned this must have been in a position to know it was happening *and* had their own pieces in place to accommodate it."

"Lieutenant Locksmith knew of Mills and trusted him, as far as you can trust anyone you don't know personally but I don't know about his second. But if there *is* a leak there, any enquiry about it will raise suspicions. And there must be more than one or two involved, if the chief has been abducted."

"Yes, ma'am. But with respect, this is wasting time. I request permission to head on across to Jupiter Station and without an escort that will raise more than eyebrows. Risk to me is minimal, I'm more than able to take care of myself and I would link back with anything I find."

Colonel Moritz raised her eyebrow in a way that implied that she doubted the last point. She paused in thought for a moment, but only a moment.

"I'll sanction it; but I'm coming with you."

The faces of the two science officers mirrored their reactions to that but it was Copper who spoke.

"Ma'am, you're in command of the ship and too valuable to risk on an away mission like this."

"*You* consider the risk as minimal," the colonel said. "And as you pointed out, *I* am in command here. And I know Jupiter Station rather better than you, in fact rather better than most of my crew. And before you ask, Lieutenant Lyrican, you'll stay on board. You'll be needed to keep an eye on things here, especially our second alien. You're with me, Ms Milkstone. We're headed to the armoury – we've more than just weapons down there."

The colonel turned abruptly to a comms console and tabbed the request that Captain Helmis meet her in a small office next to the engineering research labs on deck ten and thus missed a quirky glance that passed between Copper and Linen, causing the latter to open her eyes wide in mute and furious dissent.

By the time that Colonel Moritz and Copper had made it to the armoury, processed their requirements and then turned into the office to meet the captain, he was already there and in some curiosity as to why he had been summoned. Upon hearing, his reactions were much the same as the junior officers had been. The colonel summarily dismissed his objections and then caused more by telling him that she and Copper would take one of the small transports across rather than use one of the transfer points from the shuttle bays. As they would be dressed in non-standard protective attire that bore no markings proclaiming their link to the *Drake*, and would be toting camouflaged arms, they were less liable to cause undue interest that way.

Helmis had insisted on a secure link to Tawny Brown, the head of their security team on station, to let her know the bare minimum of what would be going down and to have her team on stand-by to be called in if circumstances warranted it. Thus much the colonel agreed to compromise on, to Copper's relief, although *she* had made her own plans without consulting her commander. The latest from Brown's team was that questioning the locals on levels three and four had turned up nothing: no-one had seen a thing, and if they had, they were not about to tell. The security details had been deployed to work outwards from the centre, but as scans would be unable to penetrate the majority of the shielded sectors, it was a slow process accessing those areas. A couple of signals from different places that might have come from Locksmith's ident had been received, but checks there had come up blank.

Shortly afterwards, and dressed in the highest spec protective suiting the *Drake* had available, the colonel and Copper made their way circumspectly to one of the smaller shuttle bays, where their craft had been prepped for departure and the techs cleared out. Copper had sent Spook on ahead to scout out as many of the shielded areas of the station as possible. Helmis had been briefed and was by then in the bridge's duty office, conning over the potential routes Locksmith could have taken from personnel to security and re-checking the vulnerable areas pinpointed by security as points where the chief may have been intercepted. Copper had given Linen the same job and was in hopes that the two would independently come up with similar results, but it was a slim chance. It was just as likely that something had aroused Kit's suspicion and he had decided to investigate rather than call in Jupiter's security, if he had had doubts about them.

Colonel Moritz was to pilot the shuttle to one of the outer ring bays of the base; their mission was logged as a small repair to the craft that required immediate attention, as the *Drake* was due for departure so soon. The crew had other business and would pick the shuttle up on completion of that, was the story. It was only to be hoped that the system checking their authority to come aboard Jupiter was automatic and not human, as the colonel's identity would cause something of a stir. Their arms were registered as military issue and should pass muster. Bearing arms aboard a station like Jupiter was illegal unless the owners were Fleet or otherwise permitted to do so and they *would* be picked up, but argument was unlikely as the small bay to which they were headed was not one that would be supervised by a high-ranking officer who would raise questions.

Once fairly aboard the station and having been hindered by no more than a minor official that the colonel had quelled with a glance, the two began to thread their way through the narrow passageways that linked the local repair bays. Their heading was initially a secondary loading and storage area that skirted one of the control centres for many of the station's ancillary services. By the station's spec, which both had loaded into their wrist-comm idents, there were elevator tubes there that would link up with most of the less densely populated areas.

Copper had meanwhile been concentrating on her own task and was trying to connect to Spook, whom she knew was still scouting the lower levels of Jupiter Station, where most of the larger commercial and industrial sections were located. She had had a fleeting contact that let her know that Spook was aware of her presence aboard, which had led her to suspect that he was following a lead. Copper was jittery: she had another plan afoot and was hesitant as to when she should put it into operation. She and the colonel made steady progress towards their goal: a transport tube that would lead them up to level seven and a small zone of storage lock-ups that served the market on level six above. That had been deemed the nearest area where furtive activity was unlikely to be reported and where protective cubby-holes were commonplace.

Before the two had even reached their target level, Copper was convinced that they would find no trace of Kit. She had been overwhelmed by a feeling of emptiness as she ascended that she knew was not down to the movement of their ride or the expectation of trouble around the next corner. And she was beginning to fear: a trickle of unease was slowly growing within her that she put down to something that Spook was transmitting from wherever he was. She said as much to the colonel as the two stepped out of the travel tube.

The passage in which they found themselves was not empty and the suspicious glances the two met from a couple of dark-clad nondescript individuals as they crossed it and set off down a narrow way that led to a line-up of closely-spaced grey doors caused both to loosen their phase rifles in their sheaths. The slithering sound of some piece of armoury being drawn behind them made Copper spin and she had fired on the leading party before she stopped to think. The other turned and ran.

"Security will have caught that!" the colonel hissed. "We had better make ourselves scarce. This way."

If Copper was surprised at her commander's knowledge of the byways of the station she had no time to express it, for the speed at which she was led along left her no time for more than breath. A small goods elevator that cut across that part of the level to another, followed by a downward journey three decks below, brought them out in a dark tunnel-like place on level ten. Here they stopped, peering into the empty gloom.

"What made you fire?" the colonel demanded.

"He was ready to fire at us," Copper responded breathlessly, her scanner set to wide sweep to check for people or operating cams. "We're clear, but I wouldn't put it past security to have some sort of hover-cam in the local area. If they've detected my weapons fire, they sure as hell will check what transport tubes were operated nearby. Hopefully they'll figure local trouble and don't enquire too closely. I suggest we head to a more populated area and mingle, ma'am. There's the market on level six."

"You never cease to amaze me, Ms Milkstone. Let's go."

By the time they found an elevator and had reached their endpoint they had replaced their weapons and stilled their rough breathing. They were subject to a few curious glances but in the low lighting of the place their dark armoured suiting was hardly distinguishable from the motley attire of their fellows and their camouflaged arms obvious only to the eyes of experience. A slow perambulation among the small booths that made up much of the place gave their eyes time to become adapted to their surroundings and to realise that security was in evidence, some of which was their own. They strolled among the plethora of haphazardly placed stalls, carefully avoiding the company of anyone who looked remotely official. Copper was still tense and drew the colonel over to a small bench space by a wall. She sat down with a sigh, prepared to open up her mind to what she felt was something so close she could touch it.

It was as she was almost absently scanning the nearby stalls that her eyes lit on a series of small painted ceramic-like tiles that were strung, one above the other, up a pole that supported the side of one of the booths. The third tile from the top was mid-blue in colour and sported an outline pattern in a dark shade that she could not distinguish in the light. But the design that decorated it she recognised and would know amongst a thousand others. It was a smooth lozenge infilled in a rosy pink over and through which wound a tracery of curving twists and curls in the same dark outline colour that formed the lozenge. An icy tremor of fear shot down her back and she let loose with a hissed expletive that caused the colonel to turn in concern.

As Copper explained in a short, whispered exchange, she was suddenly aware that they had to move, and quickly. Spook had found something and was urgent that they make their way to his position. She rose as slowly as her anxious state allowed and led the way to the nearest elevator. There was one other passenger there when the panel slid aside but one look at the two faces before him caused him quickly to vacate the space.

"Level nineteen," Copper intoned, the image of the number visible clearly in her mind's eye.

As the tube shot downwards she loosed her phase rifle from its sheath and unlatched the small PPF at her side, with a nod to her commander to do the same.

"Are we expecting trouble?" Ms Moritz asked.

"Don't know, ma'am, but it's wise to be prepared."

The ride took only a short time but in that space Copper had garnered sufficient not to be surprised when the transport tube suddenly juddered and ground to a halt, the metallic voice of its ops system stating a fault, which would be reported. The tube was terminating at level eighteen and all passengers were advised to disembark.

"Damn!" she cursed. "Anything for nineteen is diverted, at least from this transport. We stay aboard and see where it takes us," she went on, quickly punching the overhead cam upwards to face the ceiling. It rotated back and she twisted it off. "Now there really *is* a fault," she said, slipping her rifle out of its casing and unlocking it.

The lift started moving again at normal speed. It was heading down and the two could tell by the sound that it was slowing.

"We're close to contaminated waste reprocessing and a few other large industrial concerns," the colonel noted, checking her wrist-comm. "A lot of shielding and safety systems in place."

"Lucky us," was the dry retort as Copper swivelled her head back and forth, trying to gauge what waited for them outside. She turned suddenly, realising the exit would be opposite to that at which they had boarded.

"Spook," she murmured as she flattened herself against the side wall of the boxy space, raising her weapon.

Colonel Moritz repeated the manoeuvre on the opposite wall as the lift ground to a halt and the exit panel slid aside. All they could hear was the dull throb of heavy machinery and a quiet, tinny grating. They waited. The transport tube, it appeared, was going nowhere. Copper nodded her head fractionally and a second later, both lunged out, automatically assuming a back to back position. The smoke bomb that a silent hand had thrown almost at the same instant was spewing clouds of white, choking vapour, but the lift door closed upon most of it. The colonel raised her phase rifle to fend off a close range heavy gun that was being wielded as a club and then quickly drew back, jabbing upwards. There was a quickly choked-off scream as her brutal thrust made contact with an area of her assailant's anatomy that was clearly not as well-shielded as the remainder. She followed up with a boot to the same place and then a stunning rifle burst.

Copper had taken a vicious slice to her upper arm from some kind of driven blade but her suit had protected her from much of the sting. It was obvious to her that their opponents were, for reasons unknown, trying to make as little noise as possible. She had no such scruple and let loose with a rifle bolt to quickly end the conflict.

"This way!" she urged, an irresistible impulse driving her in the direction of a heavy hatchway that barred one side passage. "Whoever's up to no good down here now knows they've got company."

The colonel narrowed her eyes, nodded her agreement and quickly tabbed her wrist-comm. "Now's the time to call back-up," she muttered.

The massive door was unsealed and Copper pulled it slightly wider. It swung on huge but silent pivots, and she slid through, Colonel Moritz on her heels. The walkway beyond was a dimly lit space of conduit-lined walls and deck-mounted blocks of a dull metal that evoked heavy engineering. They could taste the dust on their tongues and Copper pointed mutely to another narrow way that gave off to one side. She could feel the familiar alien presence close by and as she made for the gap she hauled up her scanner to probe the dim surroundings. They were in a passage with several unmarked doors leading off.

"I'm picking up three lifesigns moving in this direction," she whispered. "They're fast and armed. In here!"

She pulled her commanding officer through a door and into darkness. As she shut the door all but a crack, they could hear pounding feet. The noise passed them and made up the corridor and round into the passageway from which they had come.

"We only have a couple of minutes," Copper rasped in an undertone as she began to move, her scanner active in her hand in a sweep of the nearest doors. "No shielding! Reading three in there, ma'am!" she reported harshly, motioning to one entry.

She moved further down the short corridor, almost to the end. "I don't get any more lifesigns further along here. Spook, where the frock are you now? Is this it?" she demanded in an urgent whisper as she returned to the first door.

With mental pressure that was almost overwhelming, Copper glanced over the narrow entry, her eyes coming to rest on the side-mounted control and comms plate. She pressed what she assumed was the entry pad and waited. When nothing happened she tried a second pad; after a pause, a voice within demanded to know who it was. She put her mouth to the speaker.

"Joe," she uttered in a low, guttural voice.

The distinct sound of plas-metal being snapped back caught their ears and the two realised that weapons were being armed. The occupants were evidently not expecting anyone called Joe.

Figuring attack was the best form of defence, Copper pulled back and blasted the control plate at what she reckoned was its operating point. As the door panel slid aside, she and Colonel Moritz threw themselves over the threshold, one either side.

"It's the frigging cavalry!" Copper yelled, bunching up and rolling as far from the entry as she could, the sound of short-range phase-bursts spattering her suit.

Both she and the colonel were hampered by the awareness that Kit might be close by and were choosing their targets with care. Both had had the advantage of military training and regular weapons drills but their two armed opponents were no novices, had the benefit of familiarity with their environment and were quickly aware that the two they faced had no other support in the wings. They room they were in was a dim, utilitarian place whose corners were crammed with old crates; the space above was festooned with sagging ducting that may have been part of an air recycling system at one time and a table, four chairs and two squat lumpy sofas were the only furniture. Copper's brain mentally reviewed these trappings as she automatically selected a bolthole from which to form her plan of attack whilst keeping her head in one piece.

The duo from the *Drake* had very little time: the three that had passed them in the passage outside would no doubt by now be aware that they had intruders and would be headed back to investigate – and they would be ready to engage. Out of the corner of her eye Copper could see Colonel Moritz move crab-wise across the deck in an attempt to reach a secure spot from which she could cover the entry. Realising in a split second that one of their opponents had also caught the movement, Copper cursed inwardly and spitting out mental orders, she spun, firing blindly, knowing that she was moving into a highly dangerous position.

A couple of stray shots had taken out part of the overhead lighting and hoping for enough protection from the dark she dived towards a jumble of crates that had been stacked across an inside door. She missed her target and caught the edge of the nearest, sending it tumbling and dislodging the ones above it. They toppled over, scattering others. The two bursts of fire that followed her were not the only physical force that propelled her into the stack of overturned plas-metal and again she screamed out a mental directive as ricocheted beams scattered in sparks of light close to her ears. While she cowered against the wall, aware that she had taken a shot in her buttock and that it hurt like hell despite her armoured suit, she checked her rifle: her energy pack was running down. Colonel Moritz was keeping up a barrage to her left, but she knew that the colonel would also be low on power. But they were now down to one adversary, she was relieved to note: there was a sudden silence and from behind one of the sofas a hand loosely clutching a handgun slid out awkwardly. She loosed her PPF from its holster.

They're running out of rifle power, Copper thought fleetingly as her ears caught another sound. The gunfire had momentarily ceased but the door at her back was humming strangely and she could hear banging, as if its access controls were being whacked with a blunt instrument. Almost at once an image arose in her mind's eye and she realised what was happening. Whoever was in there was forcing the door.

None too soon, for the open external exit dimmed as shapes flitted across, wary, unsure of what was within. A staccato tirade from their accomplice inside informed the newcomers that there were two, they were armed and were at the back. It was enough to gauge their chum's position and for the leader to let loose a spray of fire that lighted the space, rattled off the far wall and provoked a return that pinpointed the Mars Fleet officers.

Copper was aware that her wrist-comm was vibrating but she ignored it, trying also to ignore the searing pain of her behind as she shifted, hearing the door behind her give and begin to slide. With one forceful leap she propelled herself sideways to provide the latest arrivals on the outside with a target, guessing that only one would be able to fire through the door at a time. Whoever was in the lead missed by a hairsbreadth and she hit bedrock, returning fire and draining the last from her phase rifle. As she threw it from her to release her small handgun a powerful jolt caught her amidships and she was flung bodily back against the wall. Sliding down in a weird slow motion, Copper glimpsed a strange, clear bright mist wisping up from the deck. Her blurred eyes watered as she tried to make sense of the sight as other shadows darkened the space beyond the outer door. The pain was unbearable and as her vision dimmed, the powerful tones of Lieutenant Tawny Brown echoed in her ears from a place that seemed far, far away.

"Take them down! Take those bastards down!"

24: INTO THE BACK OF BEYOND

She must still be conscious, thought Copper: she could hear low urgent voices hissing like snakes in the crowded, stuffy chamber, the grating sounds of metal against metal as space was cleared around her, the touch of a hand gripping hers and the colonel's sharp tones cutting through, demanding to know where the hell the medics were. The light was growing, battering at her closed eyelids, she was suffocating in pain and her bubbling breath was coming in short gasps. A sudden frisson of heat from below her began to grow and spread, flooding her being with a sensation akin to love and she felt that she was in a light, warm cocoon, knowing Spook was there, protective, supportive and calm.

"You did well, Junior," she mentally reassured the terrified little presence that was agitatedly seeking comfort around her neck, a corner of her mind knowing that her reckoning would come later for drawing him into such terror-filled chaos. At the moment she didn't care: she was too tired.

The station medics must have arrived: the shirring sounds of gear being unpacked were overlain by an authoritative voice that spat out a stream of commands and solid things began to crowd in on her. She felt herself being moved, lifted, constricted as a tight band was fastened across her head, pinning her down. The sharpness of a jab into her upper arm caused her to cry out in pain, convulsively gripping that hand that was still holding hers. She was aware that other teams were doing the same to other helpless beings like her, but she saw them only as shadows at the edge of her mind, dark and hard, whilst she was bathed in a soft clear light so bright it hurt.

She must have cried out again, for a voice calling her name was suddenly close. It was telling her they were going back to their ship, she would be safe home soon. She knew that, for she could hear Colonel Moritz blazing out in cold furious tones to another angry voice that her own people were standing by, but by that time her mind was slipping like tired feet on an icy slope, and she could feel reality slip away like the loosening of her own fingers on that hand that still clasped hers in a tight grip.

"Gently now," were the last words she heard, but they came from very far away.

* * *

There were stirrings in the dark, movements around her that Copper knew must be trying to help but the nauseous, clammy ocean in which she was drowning kept closing in on her and she would drift away into merciful oblivion. She passed what seemed like lifetimes in a half-awake nightmare existence before light broke. She was on her back in some warm nest but she could move under the soft, unrestrictive coverings. The rack of diagnostic scanners overhead glinted and she realised that she was in an iso-bay in medbay but not in a life-support cradle.

"Hello," said a soft voice at her elbow.

She turned to see Kynedd Faerin looking quizzically down at her. He pulled over a stool and sat, waiting. Her voice refused to cooperate; her mouth was dry and sour and she moved her lips soundlessly, but the easy tears could still flow and she could feel them trickle down the side of her face and into her hair. The doctor wiped them away, still waiting.

As Copper's world clicked into some sort of perspective, the memories began to flood in, patchy at first but quickly gathering a coherence that caused her face to twitch in pain.

Her voice was hoarse when she found it. "Kit? The colonel?"

"They're both fine," Faerin assured her. "As you'll be soon. You had a rough ride."

"Tell me about it," she croaked, some flash of insight telling her that he needed assurance as much as she did and that levity was the best way forward. "Linen?" she asked.

"She'll be along soon. She's been in here every sol. As have a few others," he added.

"Every sol? How long was I out?"

"We've been in open space for a sevensol. We stopped over at Jupiter Station for an extra twelve hours, but that was it."

"What?" She paused, taking in the implications. "But what happened? What's the… why did…? I don't understand."

"I'll let your friends tell the story. They'll do it better than I could and they'll have more time. You're not the only patient I have, you know – though you *are* the most trouble."

"You're welcome, Doc."

"Thanks. Think you'd like to be propped up a bit?"

"Sure as hell beats lying flat on my back," she grumbled. "So when's lunch?"

"When I say so," he replied, laughing.

He manipulated her bed controls, carefully scanning both her face and his diagnostic screens, well aware that she was trying to appear better than she felt. Copper breathed more deeply as she found her viewpoint shifting and her small universe expanding. The effort caused a searing, painful spasm across her tightly-constricted chest and she let out a small yelp, quickly stifled.

"That's far enough for now," the doctor said as he fixed her back support in a semi-upright position, judiciously tweaking a couple of controls. "Lieutenant Lyrican will no doubt turn up on the stroke of twelve: she usually does."

"Are you saying I'm turning into one of her bad habits?"

"I'm saying nothing. Like a drink?"

As the eyes returning his intense gaze lit up mischievously, he laughed again. "Water or clear broth. Take it or leave it."

"Something with taste that might help rout out the remains of whatever's been roosting in my mouth for the last sevensol," she told him a little raggedly.

"I'll arrange it; you just stay there quietly and behave."

She watched him leave and as he disappeared past the bay's observation window, she sagged, closing her eyes in relief. Her resistance was flagging, her head spun, she was sore and she felt like a parcel strapped up with too much tape.

Her broth appeared in minutes in the hands of a nurse tech. The nurse stayed to assist. Faerin didn't trust her to eat without help, then, nor without experienced eyes taking careful note of the results, Copper figured. She accepted the situation, grateful for the salt taste of the viscous liquid and the soothing warmth of it flowing into her stomach.

"Thanks," she told the nurse when she'd finished. "Needed that."

"Looks better than the goop they pump into you in critical care," he joked. "Anything else I can get you?"

"No thanks."

"Just buzz if you need anything, the button's here."

"Thanks," she acknowledged with a smile, settling back into her support pillows.

Dr Faerin must have increased her pain relief for she drifted off into a doze and was only roused by someone adjusting her coverings. A familiar face smiled into hers and she returned the smile, tears stinging her eyes at what she saw in that face.

"Doc told us you'd woken up," Linen said cheerily, leaning back in her chair and eyeing her friend critically. "You look just dandy."

"You're a liar, Linen Lyrican; I look like a wet washrag. At least I feel like one. Is there such a thing as a mirror in here? And who's us?"

"No mirror, but I'm sure I can dredge one up. There must be one in the comfort cubicle, but I guess you've too many tubes attached to hop in there? I could prise it off the wall for you."

"Who's us?" Copper repeated with a sardonic smile, electing to ignore the offer.

"The colonel and me for a start. Colonel Moritz was here an hour ago but she left you sleeping. And Trisk." The gold-flecked eyes danced in mischief. "And Kit Locksmith of course. *He's* the one you want to check yourself in the mirror for, I take it? His name *was* the first word you spoke when you came to, the doc said."

Copper flushed in spite herself. "I want to see what they've done to me," she told her friend. "I can't see beyond this corset I'm tied into and it's tighter that Syriana Steefens' purse strings," she said, pulling her upper garment away and looking down her front critically.

"Don't worry, he's probably in his quarters doing the same," Linen told her as she stood up to lean over and peer down her friend's shirt likewise. "Your boobies are locked into articulated cones," she observed gravely. "The whole thing looks like a kinky bodice worn by some exotic dancer in a sleazy nightclub in one of the more downmarket pleasure domes of New Monte Carlo. How's your backside?"

The redhead was treated to a withering glance. "It hurts, much like your face is going to do when I smack it."

"That's my girl!"

"But tell me what the hell happened, for frock's sake. The doc won't, he figures you'd tell it better. We left Jupiter Station sols ago? I was brought up here, not taken to their medbay?"

Linen tilted her head to one side, smiling gently. "I wasn't let into the whole story, but the colonel and Tawny Brown both gave me a version of events. The doc's sanctioned a longer visit, now you're awake; so what do *you* remember?"

Copper reiterated the journey through the byways of Jupiter Station, until the point that she and the colonel had been pinned down in the place on level nineteen. She then recalled the noise at her back, as if the inner door was being forced, just as more well-armed assailants appeared outside.

"I figured it wasn't one of the bad guys, locked up as he was. It *was* Kit, wasn't it?" she asked.

Linen nodded. "He guessed it was the rescue party and they were getting the worst of it, so he attempted to beat the door down – he'd already worked his way loose of his restraints. He still hasn't figured how you knew where to find him, but that's for the colonel to tell. But you reckoned it must be him? So why didn't you help him open the door?"

"With a bunch of armed lunatics just turned up outside loosing phase-bolts and him unarmed and possibly hurt? Don't be a flooshie: as soon as he'd got the door opened, he'd have been blasted to hell."

"But he wasn't," Linen said calmly, watching her friend's face. "The colonel said *you* jumped out all guns blazing to draw the fire and she was pinned behind some crate; but she couldn't work out why they were concentrating on you and not her – and why the bad guy inside the room had stopped firing."

"I remember being hit by a massive energy bolt in my chest – it blew me off my feet and flung me against the wall," Copper said, compressing her lips and looking away from her friend.

"Cop… it was Spook, wasn't it? Come on, out with it. I *will* find out, you know. He located Kit, led you down? But that's not the whole story is it? You set him to protect the colonel, didn't you? She said she felt at times that for villains well-trained in using firearms they were lousy shots. Why were you insistent that you should get down there as soon as possible? What was Spook trying to warn you about that you didn't understand?"

"I'm still not sure," Copper admitted, and went on to tell her friend of the decorative tile she had spotted in the marketplace that bore the alien device depicted on her tattoo. "That may be part of it. But we were followed almost as soon as we left the shuttle bay – so *somebody* spotted us or was monitoring comms and knew we'd come aboard from the *Drake*, and that we were on some clandestine mission, or we'd not have been dressed in armoured suiting and toting weapons. We *had* to check in and the colonel's name's probably well known in a few circles. I took one of them down, and we had to run. But word must have got back to those villains on level nineteen, because it was when we hit the marketplace that Spook was really adamant that we get down there – he'd found Kit, how I don't know, but the guys that had him must have realised that tying our people up on the search for him wasn't working and they'd have to move him – or worse – and were preparing to do it."

"You mean kill him," Linen shivered. "So why did you take Junior down if you thought the stakes were so high? The poor sap's gone back into his closet and won't come out, no doubt 'cos he's still so scared. But you'd *planned* to take him before you left and he *is* just a kid, as far as we know."

"I didn't know how high the stakes were at the time, believe me – Lor' if I'd thought for a second that they planned to kill Kit, you think I'd have stopped long enough even to listen to the colonel? But you guessed I'd taken Junior? I thought so."

"I figured and I used that probe of Trisk's that's linked to the external scanner relays to verify he wasn't in the lab. But why?"

"I wanted him to keep track of our security people because I had the strongest suspicion that Kit's disappearance was a set-up to keep them down there and busy and so keep the *Drake* at Jupiter. It would be as difficult for them to breach a commercial shielded area as it would be for us unless they had clearance – so it stood to reason that Kit wasn't in one. And as our security had received a couple of signals that might have been from his ident but checks had come up empty, I guessed it was them: they must've surgically removed his implanted ident or managed to clone it *in situ* and then deactivate the original; *we* didn't pick it up, and he wasn't in a shielded section."

"Oh they removed it, but not surgically," Linen said bitterly.

"You what? What do you mean, not surgically?" demanded Copper.

Linen realised she had made a gaffe, but went on, as she knew her friend would not be satisfied with half a story. "They'd got him in a transport tube and slapped a fast-acting med-patch on him: knockout stuff. It wasn't very effective but enough to keep him under 'til they got him to that place where you tracked him. They'd disarmed him and were trying to get the implant out with a med-extractor, but they were amateurs. He saw his advantage, put up a fight, got in a couple of punches. They were seriously put out – so they strapped him into a chair and cut his ident out with a knife."

"The bastards!" choked Copper, beginning to cry.

"Sorry, Cop, I shouldn't have sprung it on you like that. Cop, don't cry! Hell, Doc Faerin will have my hide if he thinks I've upset you!"

"It's all right, I'm just *so* tired. You'd think after sleeping for a sevensol I'd be wide awake," she finished with a watery sniff. "He's okay now, isn't he?"

"Still strapped up," Linen admitted. "They kicked him about. You give a helluva lot more than a damn about him, don't you?"

"And I guess the whole damn ship knows by now," Copper snapped, dismayed.

"No, not the whole damn ship; but a few will have worked it out, given what happened after Tawny showed up. But what do you remember after you hit the wall?"

"I heard Tawny's team arrive and I heard the colonel bawling for medics. Somebody had hold of my hand. Spook was there; I think he'd linked physically to me to protect me, because I felt very light and warm and though my eyes were shut, I saw light. Junior was around too and he was terrified. I did try to calm him but the medics were all over me; tying me into a life-cradle, I guess, as it was so tight. I was stuck with a hypo and it hurt like hell – they must have caught the cut to my arm I'd got from that bozo at the elevator. It was dark and stuffy and horrible around me and other things were going on but the light round me was so bright…" Her voice tailed off.

"And?" urged her friend.

"Somebody called my name and told me were going back to the ship and we'd be safe. I think I heard the colonel saying that our people were on standby, but I'm not sure. And that's all. I must have completely passed out. Next thing I remember is the doc saying hello… must be more than two hours ago, I guess. I *was* brought back on board then and not taken to the station's medbay?"

"You were," Linen confirmed. "Colonel Moritz apparently said she'd not trust Jupiter Station's medbay with a hangnail. But I think that's just a story one of Tawny's mob dreamed up."

"You said something happened after Tawny showed up?"

Linen grinned roguishly. "She and her team took down the three at the door, heavy stun. The one still inside and shooting the colonel got and *she* wasn't using stun – he'll make it, but only just. The other one was still alive as well, last I heard. But then the station medics turned up: the place was a shambles, half the lights out, boxes all over the deck, everybody barking orders… They got *you* strapped up first, the colonel insisted on that. More medics turned up, they started in on the other two. They were clearing the space to get you out when one of three outside woke up enough to try and grab for a weapon – the one who'd been shooting through the door. One of Tawny's guys made a grab at him and hauled him up, struggling like hell. But Kit had just got to his feet to let your gurney through and he got a good look at the guy: it was one of the four he'd interviewed topside for the job in security."

"No way! So Kit had been right that things didn't stack?"

"Yes; he's no fool. *That* made him mad enough, but then it must have struck him that this was the guy that had loosed that last shot at you and he completely lost it. Despite the leg and the hand, he let out with a right hook that knocked him flat to the deck; then he jumped him and started turning his face to pulp. Tawny and one of her people had to pull him off and hold him back, but he was still spitting quarks. And according to Tawny, Kit threatened the guy that if *his girl* didn't make it, the bastard would have no place to hide; Kit would find him and – well Tawny didn't mince words, but I'm not going to repeat what Kit threatened to do to him," Linen finished.

"I'm going to smack him!" Copper groaned, closing her eyes in extreme mortification. "The whole of security will have heard by now. But, just a second – you said the *leg* and the hand. What in hell did they do to him? And why did Tawny's lot not set enough stun to keep those bastards down?"

"The leg that was fractured in all that trouble on decks seven through nine, when they blew the hatch; he wouldn't keep off it, remember, and it was still weak. They must have figured it after he'd tried to knock their lights out, so they made sure it was one of their prime targets when they were beating the crap out of him. They did bust him up pretty bad – Tawny was amazed he could stand, much less land the punch he did and have enough energy to blast the guy's ears off after that. But as for the stuns: the creeps were in heavyweight armoured suits, so the stuns were less than effective in keeping them on the deck. Security's learnt a hard lesson there."

"I'll say." Copper sighed deeply, closing her wet eyes.

"You're bushed. Want me to go away?"

"Want lunch," her friend said, opening one eye.

"That's a fib, but I'll arrange it anyway. And I'll come back and feed you."

"Like hell you will."

"I'll bring a mirror and some face-make," Linen promised.

"It's a deal. Go away."

* * *

The redhead was as good as her word; after a quiet dialogue with Kynedd Faerin she returned some time later with a covered bowl, a smart carryall and a nurse assist who was equally laden at her heels. Copper had dozed but awoke to noises in the bay.

"Are we having a party?" she asked somewhat dazedly.

"Nope: we're here to freshen you up; all these dressings and meds are doing everything for your physical health but not a lot for your emotional wellbeing. And you *did* want a look at what the doc and his ever-efficient aides did to you when you were in no position to complain."

"We won't be touching your attachments or med-dressings," the nurse assured her with a smile, dexterously unpacking what looked like a pair of large damp towels and a fresh set of sleep-scrubs with a Mars Fleet medical logo emblazoned on the front pocket. "You okay with the lieutenant being here? I can ask her to leave and get another nurse assist."

"Lor', I haven't got anything she hasn't seen before," Copper groaned, steeling herself to be manipulated.

"The patch on your butt might be new to me," warned Linen as she set her burdens down and prepared for action.

Fifteen minutes later and Copper settled back with a sigh and some relief. Apart from the healing med-patch on her backside, a tight bandage around her upper arm and the support harness for the tubes that dealt with her bodily functions, her only other restriction was the corselet around a section of her torso that covered and protected the area of damaged flesh and bone that had taken the brunt of the phase-burst. The nurse assist told her quite firmly that Dr Faerin would tell her all she needed to know about that, gathered her traps and departed to her next duty, leaving Linen to carry on.

"Lunch next," the redhead said jauntily, retrieving the bowl from a side console.

"I'll be scarred for life, won't I?" Copper moaned desolately.

"There you have me," was Linen's honest answer. "The doc said your armour had fused to your skin, but without it you wouldn't be here. On the positive side, your face is intact – you should've seen Kit when he got in, much of him was twice the size it should have been and the rest was a mixture of strange colours, mostly heavy bruising. The colonel had a few cuts and grazes and Tawny's lot didn't escape unscathed. Kit only got out of medbay two sols ago. He's not back on duty and won't be for a while, though how the doc'll stop him, I don't know."

"I haven't seen him," Copper said a little fretfully.

"He's seen you – he last popped by just before Nurse Tilli and I turned up, but the doc told him to leave you sleeping. And now for lunch. This is all the doc would authorise, but if you're very good and get it down, I might be able to persuade him that you could eat a cream-sauce steakfry in a sol or two. Though he might stop short of sanctioning a mug of ale to go with it."

She uncovered the bowl, abstracted a spoon and dipped into the glutinous mass. "Open wide," she instructed. "Or no face-make," she added threateningly.

Lieutenant Lyrican had evidently been managing things other than comfort, food and prettification, for once Copper was satisfied with her reflection in the mirror, the redhead linked to Dr Faerin and announced that Lieutenant Milkstone was fit for visitors and would he notify Lieutenant Locksmith that he could stop by at his convenience.

"He'll be here in three minutes, I guarantee," Linen grinned wickedly.

"You little minx!"

"I am, aren't I? I'll see you later."

With that, she made for the door, stopping only to wave.

Linen was right: three minutes had hardly passed when a knock on the observation window let Copper know that Kit had arrived. She had prepared a smile to match his, but it vanished in concern at his appearance. He was haggard, limping badly and leaning on a support stick. His left hand and wrist were strapped up and he looked thinner and utterly weary. The tears started to her eyes as her jaw dropped.

"Kit! Are you all right?" she uttered, her throat tightening.

"I came here to ask you that," he responded, his blue eyes lighting up with their usual sparkle. "Can I come in?"

"Damn you, Kit Locksmith, you great oaf. Come in and take the weight off your feet and tell me what the hell you've done to yourself."

"I missed you," he said cheerfully in answer, pulling over the chair and hanging onto its back for support as he set his stick aside and took a good look at her face. He must have been encouraged by what he saw, for he transferred the weight of his injured arm to the side of her bed and leaned over, a roguish twinkle in his eye. "Is this the time and the place?" he asked.

"Damn you, Kit Locksmith," she repeated. "It certainly is not. But the hell with the time and the place," she added in a husky murmur as her smile broke through and her hand reached up to stroke the faded marks of two healing scars on his cheek.

He kissed her long and hungrily and it was she who backed off first, twisting her face away and hiding her eyes on his neck, her arms sliding up to form a barrier to prevent his distracting closeness, pushing him away as if she was afraid he would crush her down. He held her gently, his face in her hair, until she relaxed the pressure.

"Sit down before you fall down," she ordered him gruffly, gathering sufficient courage to cover her confusion and look him in the face.

He did, easing back into the chair and hitching it as close as he could. His good hand sought hers, a concerned smile playing about his lips, guessing the cause of some of her discomfiture.

"I don't bite and I'm not a fly-by-night, Copper."

"No-one said you were, Kit Locksmith."

"Why don't you leave off the Locksmith and just call me Kit," he advised.

"People will talk."

"People do."

That and his deepening smile made her smile back, but she was still acutely aware of the shadows under his eyes and the quick grimaces of pain as he shifted in the chair. Impulsively she reached for the damaged hand.

"What in hell did they do to you?"

"A lot less than they did to you," he said. "Why did you insist on coming after me? They might have… How did you find me anyway?"

"I was worried and I guessed you were in trouble, given your knack for finding it," she temporised. "I thought I could handle it."

A raised eyebrow told her he was far from satisfied with that answer. "And the colonel came too? The commander of a ship like the *Drake*, with a dozen she could call on for such a mission and she took it upon herself? Why? It's unprecedented. I heard she came down to see you not long after I was reported missing, and I bet that wasn't a social call, was it?"

"How did you hear that?"

"I'm chief of security; it's my business to poke my nose into things. And you still haven't answered my questions."

"Is that what you're here for? To interrogate me?"

"I'm not playing that game, Copper," he warned, squeezing her hand as his eyes sparked fire. "I'm here to see you and you damn well know it. But there's something going on that I'm not in on, and I want to know what it is."

She looked down at their clasped hands and then raised her eyes to the diagnostics rack above her. "There are some things I can't tell even you, Kit; the colonel will have to. But there's a lot I still don't understand. Why they did it, for a start. And why they wouldn't have stopped at killing you – whatever the stakes are, they have to be high. How did Jupiter Station's security miss those guys? Two must have followed us from the shuttle bay; then *seven* on deck nineteen… how many more are out there?" Her eyes sought his face, mutely imploring answers.

"The one that got away from you on level seven made for the place I was held on nineteen, so when you and the colonel showed *there*, they realised who you were; but how you got there so fast floored them. I don't think they were aiming to kill you, things just got out of hand. The colonel would have made a far better hostage than I would in any case: the *Drake* would never have left orbit if they'd got her."

"So delaying the *Drake* was one object then; I guessed as much but don't know why."

"How you guessed beats me," he admitted. "And why she came down with you. At least the crew now knows it's got one helluva commanding officer."

"I could have told them that," Copper grinned faintly. "And I suspect you could too. But those guys – the station must be riddled with subversives. Why? What do they gain?"

"There are always massive profits to be made out of civil disorder. And anywhere there are lots of people, those that take advantage are close behind and they're smart, they're clued-up and they can usually find others that are easy to persuade or blackmail. And it keeps the likes of me in business. But these people are something else: they have top-notch gear, they have access to classified data…"

"And you're on med-leave, stop beating your brains over it. But one thing I don't get: how did we get permission to leave? There were crimes committed against our people, against station personnel, *by* station personnel, some of them Mars Fleet… the legal logistics will take months to work out and at least half a dozen will be court-martialled, if not worse."

"And we're on a mission. Colonel Moritz ripped through the lot, told them where to stow any complaints against our people, had the last of our goods hauled in and gave the order to break orbit. As I said, we have one helluva commander. And now you need some sleep. Time and place still okay?" he added slyly.

"Damn you, Kit Locksmith, you great oaf. And you haven't told me the whole story, not by a long way."

"So we're even," he said teasingly, easing himself awkwardly to his feet and leaning over. "And I'll have to come back and tell you the rest later. You take it easy, or else, Copper Milkstone."

He kissed her gently on the lips and turned, retrieving his stick to assist him awkwardly out of the bay. He paused at the other side of the obs window to wave, and was gone.

Copper lay back on her pillows, her brain a disordered mass of conflicting emotion. It was then that she realised that she had not been aware of Spook for some time and wondered where he was, a strange emptiness growing now that she was bereft of his subliminal presence. She shivered, becoming aware that he had in some way sensed her grief and was back, but there was a change: she knew it and was uneasy. In answer, an image of her younger self, weeping and afraid, locked in a dark closet, gave her a clue. Spook was chiding her gently for taking Junior down to the station and he had his reasons. There was a darkness there that had even Spook rattled; and it had scared Junior to pieces. Her mind reeled, screaming at him to explain what it was – she had no idea, she could not interpret the sensations he was trying to impart. She was too tired, too sore and too confused.

* * *

It was hours later that Copper awoke. The gentle undulations of her responsive medi-couch had kept her from much of the stiffness of such a long sleep, but she was parched despite the drip feed that someone had plumbed into her. She was also flat on her back again. A signal must have been sent to the medical station monitoring her condition, for a nurse tech materialised at her side to enquire after her wellbeing. It was near twenty three hundred hours ship-time she was told. She numbly followed orders, was propped up, cleansed and fed. She would feel weepy for a while, the nurse told her. It was a natural reaction to the emotions that had poured in on her after what she had gone through. But morrow-sol things would seem much better. Copper doubted it, but agreed, only half taking in what was being said to her.

She decided that now she was awake, she had better catch up on some of the things that had been happening aboard while she had been out. She pulled the info-console attached to her couch across and began an interrogation of ship's updates and status. They were now well beyond Jupiter Station but she noted that their line would not take them near Saturn. Ship's systems seemed to be up to full spec and no alerts were in progress. On a sudden whim she decided to check up on ship's personnel for a list of the latest additions and found that three new security staff had been added at Jupiter. It thus appeared that apart from the one villain, the other interviewees must have passed muster.

Some compulsion made her look up to see a familiar face at the obs window. Realising he had been detected, Kit Locksmith slipped round the door. He looked better than he had earlier, but his limp was very evident and he still had the stick. His hand had been redressed for he was wearing a different support.

"Why in hell aren't you in your bed asleep?" she scolded him.

"Got better things to do," he replied with that smile that melted her ire. "Had a good sleep?"

Her face must have given her away, for he pulled the chair over in concern and sat down. "What is it, Copper?"

"Bad dreams," she replied with a slight shake of the head.

"About what?" he asked, taking her hand.

"Jupiter Station."

"That place is behind us now." It was said soothingly but it failed to ameliorate her pained look.

"It might be, but the trouble's still there… there's something bad there, Kit; I don't know what, but it's not a nice place."

"Don't think it ever was; but we're on the road to the back of beyond now, and I hope we'll have a peaceful ride, at least for a few sevensols. Give us a chance to catch our breaths and get doing what we should have been doing all along."

"Your three new people working out all right, then?" she asked with a half-smile.

He released her hand and turned her screen towards himself, scrutinising it closely. "You've been checking on ship's business. You're supposed to be resting."

"I've had enough of resting, I need to be doing. Those three new recruits okay, are they?" she insisted.

"They'll do for now. And as you want to be doing, you can tell me more about why you risked your neck to find mine."

"If I need to tell you that, Kit Locksmith, you're denser than a plas-crete donut."

"And why the colonel came with you?"

"Ask her, not me. I didn't want her to come, you know. In fact, I objected."

"So I heard."

"Who told you?" Copper asked curiously.

"Your friend Lieutenant Lyrican. She packs quite a punch, I imagine."

"You've been talking to Linen?"

"She's been talking to me," was the rejoinder, with a quirky smile.

He and the lieutenant had had quite a chat, he told Copper, at Linen's instigation. Once he was visibly back on his feet, she had collared him in a quiet corner and demanded his version of events down on Jupiter Station. He had retaliated by demanding to know what had happened beforehand. What he did not tell Copper was that he had probed her friend for information on *her* – her past, her work at Lowell, her assignment to the *Drake* – and her and Linen's association with Colonel Moritz. The young lieutenant had not been helpful on the prequel to the events on the station or on her and her friend's previous histories but she *had* given him enough information to know that Copper had been hurt by emotional attachments in the past. And Linen had made it abundantly clear that if Locksmith dared hurt her friend in such a way, she would personally kick his private parts so far into orbit he'd never see them again. He believed her.

Copper sighed, closing her eyes: she was not surprised. She could well imagine that Linen would seek to know exactly what had happened or was going on in case she missed something, and to give herself a store of ammunition for any future ploys. As she remembered the incidents that had led up to that last trip down to Jupiter Station, and in her head went over the whole of the mission, from the time that she and the colonel left their shuttle until the darkness descended, Copper sought to pick out any clues that would shed light on the cause of Spook's unease and Junior's terror.

Kit was not the only officer of the *Drake* that had been treading the decks on night watch. As she wound up a long walk that took her along deck six and into the sheltered facilities of the medbay, Colonel Moritz stopped by her chief medic's office to see if he was available and to ascertain the status of those of her crew under his care, particularly Lieutenant Milkstone. As she had thus far been unable to speak to Copper since the latter had regained consciousness, the colonel was in hopes of at least a couple of words. Faerin, she was not surprised to see, was at his desk. He invited her in and rose to fetch a couple of mugs of caff as she outlined her business After a quick rundown on the condition of the rest of his patients, the doctor warned against much conversation with Copper. She had had to be kept under for eight sols; she had only been fully conscious for less than twenty four hours and strain of any sort was out of the question, he told the colonel. He grimaced as he called up the medbay status monitors on his desk console and checked them over.

"She woke up again just before twenty three hundred and had something to eat and drink. She's probably still awake, as I see she has a visitor logged."

"At this hour?"

"Her friends keep late hours," he parried meaningfully. "Just like you. Shall we go see if she's up for a chat? We can always chase away whoever thought it was okay to call."

"You know damn well who it is, don't you?"

The doctor responded with only a smile as he led the way to the iso-bay. The two looked in through the obs window.

"Looks like you're out of luck again, Elle."

Kit Locksmith was still in the chair at Copper's bedside, his head pillowed on his arms, which were resting on her cot. He was dead to the world. Copper, one hand placed protectively on the back of his head, was relaxed into her pillows, eyes closed, also asleep.

"Hadn't you better get him to his bed?" the colonel asked.

"I think he'll do just fine there," Faerin responded, dimming the lights.

* * *

Copper awoke with a start some hours later. She was upright still and Kit had gone, but the nurse that had logged her change in status and come in to check up on her was wearing a knowing grin as he enquired after his patient.

"What time is it?" she asked brusquely, trying and failing to read the chrono on her side monitor.

"Six twenty three," was the reply. "Ready for breakfast?"

"Who are you kidding? Want to get out of this straightjacket and unplugged from all this tubing," she said fretfully. "Want a bath in a real tub with real water; want off this frigging couch."

"Don't want much then," was the response. "I'll make a note and we'll see what Dr Faerin says: his word's law around here."

"You must have other doctors that can give orders."

"You're *his* patient, you do what *he* says," the nurse told her. "If you behave, we might loose you from some of the pipework and let you move about a bit."

"Specify behave," Copper parried.

"Drink, eat and smile, in that order. First you drink."

As she obediently sipped the water on offer, Copper tried to recall the night before and the thoughts that had sifted through her mind as she dropped off. One image kept recurring and she wished it would go away. She was still brooding when the nurse returned to prop her up more fully and set up her tray support.

"Do you always feed your patients this early?" she asked him.

"Only the ones that cause trouble," was the rejoinder. "Let's see what's on your menu. Think you can manage yourself?"

"Of course I can manage myself, I've got a pair of hands and perfectly adequate hand-eye coordination," she retorted curtly as he abstracted her meal from a catering slot on the side wall and locked it to her tray. "Thanks," she added as an afterthought.

"You're welcome, but try the smile. It works wonders and takes years off your face."

"Where the hell did you train? You're mouthy for a nurse," she told him, squinting to make out his name tag.

"Beagle College and then Fleet Medical Corps. And you're a tad contrary for a lieutenant in the Fleet."

"What are you expecting? Yes Nurse Biggs, no Nurse Biggs, three frigging bags full, Nurse Biggs?"

"That would do for a start. Eat your slops and stop griping."

"Take a hike."

"I will when you tell me where *you* trained."

"Lowell College and then Fleet Academy, Beagle One."

"Smart *and* tough," Biggs said, laughing as he tabbed a couple of buttons on her diagnostic panel.

"They breed us smart at Lowell and tough at Beagle. And you're still here. Go away."

"Yes, ma'am!" He gave a mock salute.

"The lieutenant causing you trouble, Nurse?" said a voice at the door, as Kynedd Faerin poked his head around the edge.

"That's an affirmative, doctor," Biggs said, turning to wink at Copper as he pushed the corners of his mouth up with two fingers to signify that she should smile.

"Get the hell out of here," she ordered him.

"I see you're feeling better, Ms Milkstone," Faerin observed.

"How many more do you have like that lippy sprite?" she demanded wrathfully. "And yes I am, so when are you going to unplug me from all this wiring?"

"Axim Biggs is one of our best nurse techs," he rebuked her. "And when I think you're ready. You only woke up yestersol."

"Come on, doc. At least let me get off this couch for a few minutes so I can feel ground under my feet. And have a bath," she added.

"You can have a dip in the buoyant tank and I'll authorise the removal of some of your attachments. I'll also set a schedule of light exercise. And I need to see how you're healing under that burn-guard, and so do you," he added, a little wryly.

"It's that bad?" she demanded, a suspicious flicker in her eye.

"No. Eat your breakfast and then we'll see," he went on as he checked her readings and tweaked a pair of controls. "How's the pain control holding up?"

"Fine," she said shortly, spooning up a mouthful.

Faerin regarded her for a moment and then pulled the chair across to sit. "Liar," he said. "What's eating you, Lieutenant?"

"Bad dreams."

"Not an answer. I want the details."

"Everybody wants the frigging details; I'm sick of repeating them," she rebelliously shot back, but realising that compliance was her best way forward, she began diffidently to speak.

She had pieced together fragments of her own memories and the images and sensations that Spook had been at some trouble to impart since before she set foot on the station with the colonel. The single most repeating symbol was the oddly-shaped lozenge swathed and overlaid in curls and flows. Its dark colour had crystallised in her mind to deep cobalt blue and the pinkish fill now had definite rosy-like overtones that reminded her of some of the sand flats out on Daedalia Planum. She had seen that image in various formats intermittently ever since that memorable sol in Beagle when she and Linen had so light-heartedly waltzed into Ivyleaf Designs for their tattoos. It had been so clear then that she had drawn it out almost without a pause for transfer to the auto-laser that etched it permanently on her skin. And then came the culmination in the sight of that tile in the market on Jupiter Station's sixth level.

Faerin's faint nod suggested that he had heard of the tile but he did not interrupt as she went on with the events after that: the overwhelming compulsion to head down, the certainty of where they were headed, the expectation of trouble that was so soon and so forcibly manifested. One of her main problems had been her inability to work out why Spook was so anxious and why Junior had been so terrified, but there had to be a reason.

"Junior?" the doctor interrupted suddenly and with a lift to his eyebrow, suggesting that he knew more than he was saying. "I understood from Colonel Moritz that you sent your Spook on down but I was given to understand that Lieutenant Lyrican remained aboard, one of the reasons being that she would keep this other entity you think we have aboard under control."

"You know we have Junior on the ship, you and Trisk got positive readings with your fancy new probe," she quibbled.

"Stop prevaricating. You took that young alien down with you. You did not tell the colonel. Why?"

"She would have stopped me. Oh, don't you start!" she said sharply as he opened his mouth. "I've had Linen *and* Spook on my back over it already. I did *not* at the time realise there would be a problem – I set him to follow Tawny Brown's team about, it should have been okay…"

"Matter of opinion," Faerin growled. "But you now know there *is* a problem and what it is."

"Not entirely, but I'm beginning to suspect, and I don't like it. I'm almost scared to fall asleep now in case I have nightmares over it."

"Well come on: you've said enough to give *me* nightmares."

She paused for a second, sighing. "I think there's an alien presence on Jupiter Station and I don't think it's a benign one."

"You need to speak to the colonel."

"I know. There are one or two things I need to speak to the colonel about. But I've not seen her and I can't just request an audience, people would wonder why."

"She *has* been at some pains to see you but has missed you each time, for one reason or another. But one thing: your Spook has so far protected you from a lot of trouble, and more than trouble, from what I've heard. And you're of the opinion that he may have kept you alive until we got you back aboard – and hell knows you were lucky with the burst you took. So why didn't he protect you from that shot, at least partially? From what I've heard of his capabilities, he'd have been able. And he *was* there."

"He was busy," she said shortly, avoiding his gaze.

"Doing what?"

She could tell by his face that he knew, but wanted to hear it from her. "You've been talking to Linen," she challenged. "I set him to protect the colonel, as you damn well know."

"Why?"

"I'm not essential to this ship or any of her crew; *she* is."

Her eyes shifted uneasily away from him as his keen glance raked her, but as she looked back, her air of concerned pity and sympathy induced a sudden realisation in him, for his eyes widened.

"And I've finished this gloop. When do I get off this damned couch for five minutes?" she demanded huskily.

"You risked your life for her and for Kit Locksmith?"

"Wouldn't you?"

"I'll give orders to have you cut loose from most of this and arrange for that buoyant tank. And then we'll see."

* * *

She did see, around three hours later. In the privacy of the iso-bay, which Faerin had sealed from prying eyes, he and one of his wound specialists set Copper up in a frame that would let them remove the supportive casing that enclosed much of her upper half in a tight grip. Earlier, she had been unplumbed and helped to walk the very short distance to the comfort cubicle, and had then been transported to the buoyant tank, a large tub of warm, viscous liquid that supported, soothed and cleansed. It had been a liberating experience. The dressings on her arm and behind had been removed before immersion to allow the fluid to exert its healing properties, but her burn-guard had been left in place, its winking lights indicting satisfactory healing.

Faerin gave her a shot of pain relief, despite her protests, and she steeled herself for the ordeal of having the guard unlatched and peeled away. It hurt and her hands clutched at the bars which surrounded her and held her still. The probes of the medi-couch were busy capturing and analysing data, but the two doctors were more intent on visual appraisal of the wound and on their own readings. After a moment, Faerin spun the holo-grid so that Copper could see what they were looking at. The flesh of her chest was scarred and puckered, a rich metallic blue that extended across her, from just below the top of her breast bone to her lower ribs. It was a large area.

"You'll need more surgery. But it'll have to heal some first," Faerin explained. "It *will* look better," he assured her. "Let's get you strapped up again. This is a softer guard: it's been designed to expand more and will secrete healing fluids to the affected area to maintain its moisture levels and alleviate much of the feelings of tightness. Breathe normally."

She let them manipulate her, looking straight ahead to avoid having to look at the holo. She had the strongest suspicion that they could have carried out the procedure whilst she was under, but for psychological reasons, Faerin wanted her to see it. Left alone to recover after her ordeal, she lay on her back staring into space, waiting for the next bombshell she knew was going to drop. Slow tears dripped down her face and she refused to wipe them away.

An hour must have passed and still she lay. She was aware that faces had come and gone at the observation window that looked into her bay but no-one came near. The readings of her couch and the diagnostics panel above her changed in response to her condition, recording every breath, every heartbeat, but apart from a soft ticking that may have been their operation or the heartbeat of the ship itself, there was silence.

The first noise that disturbed her was Nurse Biggs, enquiring after her fitness and intimating that he was there to assist her with lunch. Her protests that she wanted none fell on deaf ears but did not stop a far from quiet tongue.

"You don't eat, we wire you up again and send stuff into you through a tube," he warned. "And we take away your access to the info-point and tell your visitors that they can't come in."

"I thought you lot were supposed to be ministering angels," she muttered huffily at him.

"All a myth," he told her. "Medbay's run on quiet efficiency, excellent care and the best high-tech on offer, which makes for a rapid return to health for most of our clients. And if our usual tactics don't work on the more stubborn of our inmates, we use threats and blackmail. That usually does the trick."

"Huh! I believe you. Well, as long as it's not slops, I may as well give it a try."

He grinned and called up her food as she wiped her face and began to mobilise her couch into a more upright position.

"You're getting the hang of it," he congratulated as he slotted the tray in place.

She regarded him sideways. "I can fly a frigging fighter, of course I'm getting the hang of it. Go away and leave me to eat in peace."

He did, but returned shortly afterwards to make sure she had cleaned her plate and to remove the detritus. He also brought the news that Colonel Moritz would be stopping by for a chat in twenty minutes, so she had better be ready.

Here it comes, thought Copper, and sighed deeply. Dr Faerin had no doubt been speaking to the colonel and passed on her disquiet over the problems at Jupiter Station – and Junior, she thought, although by this time the colonel must be aware of it. Why had she taken him? It was a question she had asked herself and had come to the conclusion that it was more than just her feeling that there was need for a watch on the *Drake's* security team. Was she beginning to feel the responsibility for the young alien that she had felt for Spook, when first he had intruded on her awareness? Or was it something else, a need to express the child in herself that had been repressed when *she* was young? To put him in a position of trust that would make him feel wanted and give him back some of the self-confidence that had been shattered when he had found himself alone and bereft of all that he knew and loved… Well, that had backfired badly.

"I'm not a frocking psychologist!" she groused as she made herself comfortable for the impending visit.

The colonel and Dr Faerin arrived together and had probably been discussing her, Copper thought, acknowledging their joint presence outside her bay by a nod. Faerin said something to the commanding officer and disappeared. Ms Moritz entered, hailed her junior officer, asked after her current status, and then requested permission to sit. As Copper nodded her consent, the colonel rolled the chair closer to the couch, sat down and slid the package she carried down by her side. There was a short pause before she began. She wanted to hear Copper's version of events, without omission, from the time that the colonel had stepped into the lab with the news that Lieutenant Locksmith was missing.

Copper groaned internally and reckoned she had better leave almost nothing out. Having admitted early in the interview that she had decided to take Junior along, she was surprised that her commanding officer did not flay her verbally at that point. The colonel *was* clearly furious that Copper had not only disobeyed her implicit order that Junior was to be left under Linen's supervision but that the lieutenant had also omitted to inform her of what she *had* done. Assuming that the dressing down was only deferred, Copper continued with her account, responding as frankly as she could to the often very penetrating questions shot in her direction. As the dialogue advanced, it was more than obvious from those questions that Colonel Moritz had interrogated a number of the others involved, including her own security and some of those attached to Jupiter Station. Kit, Linen and Trisk had not escaped either and it seemed that the latter had independently picked up on Junior's absence from his closet soon after Copper and the colonel had left in the shuttle, and had told Dr Faerin of his suspicions.

In the telling, Copper was able to get the answers to one or two of her own questions. The records of the security guard that had tried to obtain a place on the *Drake* and that had turned out to be the recreant *had* raised a suspicion in Kit that had resulted in his foray to personnel. The man's file was too perfect and too short: no-one in security was so faultless that there was not one single remark against them. Chief Mills and his second seemed to be dependable, according to Tawny Brown, but had more or less to take what they were given and with the duty loads they bore on a base the size of Jupiter, which also incorporated the supply station at Europa, both admitted that they tended not to scrutinise every record twice. As for the others that had been detained by the *Drake's* team, all were under arrest and two were in critical care in Jupiter's medbay. It was possible that whoever had been controlling them would find some way to get them out of Mars Gov clutches, but there were enough charges against them to have them locked up for a long time. That there were more infiltrators and their like aboard was certain, but that was a problem for the command staff of Jupiter Station and for Mars Gov's Defence Department.

Just what had delayed the ship for a further half sol was explained by clean-up operations and a thorough search through most of the areas on level nineteen, particularly those related to the elevator section and the place where Kit had been detained. The colonel had also been at some pains to retrace her own and Copper's steps and to work out how the news that they had come aboard in the shuttle had reached the wrong ears so quickly. She also did not disguise the fact that the weapons used against them had been set to more than heavy stun and without their armour any hits may have been fatal.

One question that Copper found difficult to answer was why she had ordered Spook to protect the colonel instead of herself, and the answer that Copper had given Kynedd Faerin was met with a sceptical shake of the blonde head and a keen glance from the green eyes. But it appeared that the colonel had been speaking to Linen and leaning back in the chair, she gave her the redhead's opinion.

"You seem to think you're invincible, Lieutenant Milkstone, especially with your Spook at your back; and given the help it's given you, there *is* some substance in that. But even when you order it, or he, off on something else, you forget that you're not. And even when you realise you're in serious trouble, you would rather risk yourself than risk hurt to someone you care for. You deliberately drew fire away from Lieutenant Locksmith when we were under siege."

"Yes, ma'am," Copper responded, aware that a wash of red was creeping up her face, and also aware that the colonel could have added "and me" to her last sentence.

Colonel Moritz was watching her closely. "Tell me about our new resident alien and what you think it found out down there."

Copper paused to gather her thoughts, picking at her coverlet nervously. She heaved a sigh. "There's an atmosphere on Jupiter Station, like something just on the edge of consciousness, and it scares me – and Spook. And as Junior's so terrified he's gone to ground again, I think it's a threatening one."

"You said alien to Dr Faerin."

"I did and that's what I think – so unknown that I couldn't understand what Spook was trying to tell me. I have absolutely nothing tangible to go on, just impressions that send shivers down my back and haunt my dreams."

Colonel Moritz gave a tight smile. "Nothing tangible," she repeated, reaching down to abstract the parcel she had brought with her. "This might be a start," she said, and began to unwrap the small flat package.

A shiver of recognition ran down Copper's spine even before the item was clear of its coverings: it was the small painted tile from the marketplace stall on Jupiter Station. She recoiled as the colonel held it up.

25: DREAMS AND DARKNESS

Colonel Moritz sat back with one finger to her lip, and regarded Copper with a wry smile. She had rewrapped the tile when she realised the effect the image had had on her junior officer, and replaced it at her side. She continued to sit, apparently deep in thought but ever-watchful. The quiet unnerved Copper and she shifted uncomfortably.

"We'll deal with this later, when you're up and about," the colonel eventually said softly. "I'll have it locked away securely meanwhile. The stall's owner is a regular part of the market and has been for years; he sells on pieces he buys and conveniently could not remember where he got *this* particular tile. I've had it checked and there's nothing inherently sinister about it. And as we've left Jupiter Station, there's nothing we can do in relation to it. But you wanted a word on another matter, Copper?"

The use of her given name startled her for a moment and she stared into the green eyes in some perplexity as she reordered her thoughts. The sympathy she saw in the face looking at her gave her the courage to explain herself.

"It's Lieutenant Locksmith, ma'am: he knows there's more to the story he's been given about what happened down on Jupiter Station and he's been trying to…" Copper paused, embarrassed, "…extract more details. Not in any way forcefully," she went on quickly. "But he's been digging…"

"And what did you tell him?"

"To ask you, ma'am."

"He did," she told her dryly. "He's also been interrogating Dr Faerin, but it's allowable as they're old friends."

"Yes, from the *Wayfinder*," Copper said without thinking.

"I see you've also been digging," the colonel remarked, her green eyes widening in surprise. "But what's your view on what he should be told?"

"I think you'll have to tell him more about Spook, and Junior for that matter, ma'am, and their links to me," she said to her. "He's chief of security: he should be in the know that there are two aliens aboard that aren't in ship's manifest and that are able to interact with at least one crew member, not to mention tech."

"That's also Dr Faerin's opinion. I concur, for more than one reason. I'll deal with it. Anything else?"

"I want out of here."

"That I will *not* authorise: you're not fit, even I can see that. You'll be released from medbay when the doctor says you can, with any restrictions he puts in place."

The colonel stood. "And Lieutenant?"

"Yes ma'am?"

"Despite a certain degree of independence when it comes to complying with orders, you are an outstanding officer. I'm glad you're one of my crew."

Copper gaped. "Yes ma'am; thank you, ma'am."

As the colonel turned and made her way out of the iso-bay, Copper leant back. It had been one helluva sol already and it was only half over. She still had Linen and Kit to face.

Her next visitor turned out to be neither: it was Trisk coming by to tell her that Junior had at last emerged from his hidey hole and was mooching about the lab. He knew, because he had been fiddling with his spare alien lifeform probe and had rigged it to register an alert when either Spook or Junior was about; and the probe could now clearly tell the two aliens apart. He had come along to let Kynedd Faerin know before updating the probes linked into the science and security scanning systems, but as the doctor was too busy duty-wise to disturb, Trisk had decided to come and disturb Copper instead. Linen had been sorting their samples and was at present in the throes of making essential links, but would call later. The two science officers had decided to leave any analysis of the lump of tech in outer bay four until Copper was back in the lab. Apart from which, Chief Locksmith had refused to assign them security back-up. There was hence not much that they could do in that respect anyway, Trisk told her with a sidelong grin.

"Why did you take Junior down to the station with you anyway?" Dr Addystone added curiously.

"Oh, not you as well! Look Trisk, I've had Spook, Linen and the colonel all pestering me about that, so please leave it. And by the way, the colonel will be bringing Kit in on Spook and Junior, so he'll be yet another one that knows. At this rate, by the time we get to the edge, the whole fizzing crew will know that they have two new shipmates and they're not human. And that I have a tattoo on my butt."

"Cranky," Trisk observed calmly. "And you're exaggerating. It'll no doubt get out at some point, but I suspect that point's a long way off. Now I'm here, what can I tell you or help you with? I bet you're getting bored with nothing to do but mend."

"Nothing to do? I listen to lectures is what I do: the doc, the nursing staff, the colonel... And I have to go over the same ground again and again. But get me a paper to work on, or some analysis – or persuade the doc that I can do a training sim of some sort; he's a buddy of yours after all."

"Persuade him yourself! I'm not going to deliberately come in for flak from him – I want to retain privileges."

"Like access to his drinks cabinet, I'll bet."

"You got it. But there must be more we can get out there on the Lowell data. I'll see what I can find," he promised. "In the meantime, I'll go update my probes and give you some peace."

Word must have got through to Linen that Copper was now alone, for barely half an hour had passed before the redhead turned up, brimming with news. One of her vital links had been supra-light to Thars Amberline at Lowell College; the Prof was setting up a few important events, not least the means for the verbal justifications of their theses. He was putting the pieces in place that would allow them the privilege of completing these last required parts of their doctoral works aboard the *Drake*.

Copper was scathing. "That's all I need! Conning over what I need to know for an interrogation on what we did for months and months on a small red planet millions of kilometres away! Does he know I'm in medbay?"

"Yup. I had to let on, as he wanted to speak to you. Naturally I didn't give him the whole tale, but enough to know that if there were medals on the table, you'd be up for the shiniest."

"You're up for a smack, lady!"

"You're in no condition," Linen retorted tranquilly. "Besides, I'm kidding. I told him I couldn't tell him anything, he'd have to ask Colonel Moritz. Grammy knows some of it, by the way — she was on to our engineering people about a tech update she was sending out and she linked to me: she could tell something was up. Heard about Junior, by the way? I gather Trisk was in."

"He was and I did and I don't want to hear any more about it for now; I had the colonel here earlier tearing my ears off. Well, not exactly," Copper admitted, going on to apprise her friend of the details of their commander's visit, and the agreement that they had reached over including Kit in the list of those who knew about their resident aliens. She omitted to mention the last comment of Colonel Moritz before she left.

Linen in return brought Copper up to date on various titbits of news extant around the ship. The crew of Tawny Brown's erstwhile security team had become the most popular people aboard and had been pumped unmercifully by their fellows on what had gone down on Jupiter Station, she told her friend, although Tawny gave the gossips short shrift and Kit tended to bite their heads off. Copper was immediately on the defensive and demanded to know if *she* had been part of the tittle-tattle.

"Sorry Cop, but you know what spacers are. You and the colonel were the leading actors in the whole shebang, with Kit as the feisty victim, so of course you're part of it. I think the upshot is that the crew as a whole is glad you're on their side and not a soul of them would want to meet you or the colonel down a dark alley if they were up to no good. I doubt the news has got further through any of them though — they know better than to mention things like that in any links back home. But some inkling will no doubt get back as time goes on, when one or two things are reported back as general Fleet news."

"What do you mean when things are reported back in Fleet news? What sort of things?" Copper asked suspiciously.

"Things like our PhDs for one. And the folks back on Mars knew about our commendations and your promotion: we had the link from Thars, remember? You got the same link I did."

"That was ages ago and I've been busy with other things since then, in case you hadn't noticed."

"Don't you get grumpy with me, Copper Milkstone! You just want to get up and get busy – you don't like being stuck here."

"They do things to you," Copper complained. "I want done, I want out of this place and rid of…" she plucked at her shirt, looking down. "Rid of this – disfigurement."

Linen's face registered a deep concern. "You've seen what's under there and it came as a shock."

There was no response beyond a non-committal shrug and an averted face. Linen in fact knew, having been forewarned by Faerin, but gave what little comfort she could, including a hug.

"And now I'm going to love you and leave you, as I'd best get back to the lab. But why don't you dim the lights and call up the view from the obs deck? You can link to it and lose yourself in the stars for a bit. The *Drake* in flight is something and we're picking up speed."

Copper looked back at her. "I hadn't thought of that."

Linen knew her friend to the core of her being. "Just as well you've got me, then. You do it. I'll see you later. A lot later."

Linen waited until the connection was in place and then left, dimming the lights outside the bay. She caught one of the nurse techs and let him know that Lieutenant Milkstone was not to be disturbed and asked that the information be passed on to the duty medics. She also found Kit Locksmith, there for his own therapeutic treatment, and advised that he give Copper an hour or so before he called.

"So you're moonlighting in medbay now," he said jocularly.

They traded a few details and by his serious responses, Linen realised that Faerin had also spoken to him. Kit had been called by the colonel however, and that would be an hour out of his schedule anyway, he informed the redhead. She only nodded briefly and disappeared before he suspected that she knew why.

* * *

Linen had been right as usual, Copper thought as she took in a breath so deep it hurt. The starfield did not change with the passage of the mighty ship through it, so immense was it; but she could imagine the forward motion of the vessel as she drank in the inky dark and the myriad sharp points of light that were the stars, their colours sparkling in the endless night of deep space. Sol was far behind them now and would look like a very small but brilliant globe of light against this sight. The view from inside would shift as the *Drake* picked up speed: her own distortion wave would see to that, Copper knew. But for now, she was content to lie back and soak up the peace of this small patch of universe and ponder on the sols to come.

She had almost drifted off when a knock at the bay window heralded Kit. She increased the lighting and waved him in. She had figured that he must have been called in by the colonel and was anxious to hear the outcome. She also had another bone to pick with him. He was quite thoughtful as he pulled the chair over and gave her a quick kiss on the cheek before he sat down.

"I've been talking to Colonel Moritz," he stated, his piercing blue eyes searching her face. "I was there more than an hour. There was a lot you didn't tell me."

"I was under orders."

He nodded understandingly but with a strange quirk to his mouth. "You're often under orders," he said quietly. "I note that you don't always obey them."

"So the colonel keeps telling me," she riposted quietly. "But in that respect we're alike, aren't we? I was told that Linen and Trisk decided not to start work in outer bay four without me. But they wouldn't have been able to, because I also heard that a certain Lieutenant Kit Locksmith had refused to assign them security back-up, which leads me to suspect that Lieutenant Kit Locksmith is back on duty, despite doctor's orders to the contrary and the fact that he's still shuffling about with a stick."

She eyed him interrogatively and he laughed, taking her hand. "You got me," he confessed. "I only stop by to see how things are going and I don't spend a whole watch in there."

Suddenly he was serious again. "But back to your Spooks. You really think we have a couple of ancient aliens aboard and they have something to do with our mission?"

"Yes I do; and we have. And I suspect that neither of *us* would be here if it hadn't been for Spook."

"I probably wouldn't be here if it hadn't been for you," he replied, a catch in his throat. "I heard that you deliberately drew their fire to prevent them getting me when I opened the door."

"Linen," she said briefly. "She told you that."

"And the colonel," he said. "And now you think there's an alien presence on Jupiter Station?"

Copper stared into space, nodding slightly.

"Anything else?" he asked.

"Anything else about what?" she prevaricated.

"There's more bothering you than what happened on Jupiter Station, what you think is down there and these alien friends of yours. What's the matter, sweetheart?"

It was the first time he had used such an endearment, and it shook her slightly. "I saw what's under this," she said, pulling away the front of her upper garment and looking down at the support beneath. "It's not pretty."

"Phase-burn never is," he told her as he stood up and limped across to settle comfortably on the edge of her couch. "As I should know: I've been shot in the past Copper, and believe me, I still have the scars to show for it."

He stilled her protests by wrapping his arms around her and kissing her hair. "If you think for one second that anything like that could change the way I think about you, then you're not thinking straight," he chided her gently.

"It's so ugly… And get off my bed, Kit Locksmith; this is a semi-public place, people will talk."

"I like it when you give me orders, Copper Milkstone," he told her.

"Behave yourself!"

"No," he responded, twisting round to reach her lips.

She fought free, eyes blazing. "Will you do as you're told?"

"No," he repeated.

"Damn you, Kit Locksmith," she murmured. But this time she did not resist.

"You're out of luck again, Elle," Kynedd Faerin remarked a few minutes later as he and the colonel glanced through the obs window.

Colonel Moritz sighed. "So I see. Just one more sol aboard a ship of the Fleet," she said. "I wish *them* luck, anyway."

"Yes; more than…" He bit back what he was about to say.

She was suddenly still for a second and then turned away. "I have something to see to and then I'll have to get back to the bridge. I'll see you later, Doctor."

"Aye, ma'am."

Linen was less circumspect when she dropped in at the end of her duty spell, having watched Locksmith off the premises.

"You and Kit getting up to any hanky panky, as Ma Kellyn would delicately put it?" she asked impudently as she pulled up the chair and sat down. "The crew in security's interested."

"Those nosey dustbaggers in security can mind their own business!" Copper told her shortly. "And so can you, lady! But as Kit's only got one good hand and one good leg and a stick to boot, and I'm still on a medi-couch and wearing a steel corset that you could play a regimental march on if you had a pair of drumsticks and some talent, there's not much we *can* get up to."

"You'd be surprised," Linen grinned. "Or maybe not," she added. "But you *can* get off the couch. How's the butt?"

"You know you're the only one who asks after my backside, apart from the medics?"

"Everybody else is too embarrassed but that's their problem, not mine. Trisk asked me to tell you he'd sent you the outline of a new draft paper on some of our stuff that he thinks might do for one of the less well-known journals."

"Tell him thanks. He'll be making quite a name for himself based on our work," Copper groused.

"He's the one writing it up, I haven't time. But I suggest you go over it; and over the other papers we've done. And over the final copy of your thesis that was sent out to Thars." Linen's face creased in an enigmatic smile.

"What's going on?"

"Our theses have passed muster without any requirements for amendment from our assessors and we're to have our oral examination of their contents in four sols from now, ship-time."

"You what!"

"You heard me. So you'll have to cut the time you spend canoodling with Kit and get working. I hear he's been spinning in his office chair in security most sols, so he's all but back in harness anyway," the redhead informed her friend serenely.

"Damn!"

"You were the one that wanted to be doing something. I'm only obeying orders, First Lieutenant Copper, ma'am."

"Give me the details," she was instructed ominously.

"Frisol, ten hundred hours ship-time, briefing room three of section five, deck five," Linen announced efficiently. "Colonel Moritz thought it would be better to hold the appraisals close to our working space as it would be handy if our assessors wanted to see our tri-dee sims, though they've all seen them before, except for Ossy Inkscree that is. Trisk and I will set the lot up. The colonel's cleared it with the doc that you're okay for the ordeal and that you can be wheeled along for a look at the space on Thursol in case you want anything changed. She was going to break it to you herself, but as you were apparently busy, she popped along and asked me as she had bridge duty. She wanted to give you plenty of warning, I guess."

"Plenty of warning! You call four sols plenty of warning?" Copper choked. "And I've not seen the inside of my quarters for about ten. Lor' knows what state my dress uniform's in, or even if I can still get into it. And I miss my blue dragon."

"Stop saying that or Kit will get jealous of that blue dragon. And calm down for frock's sake; we'll sort it out. If the worst comes to the worst you can wear mufti or even your Fleet sleep-scrubs, nobody's going to complain; or they might, but there'll be precious little they can do about it."

"Mufti aboard this ship? We'd not be able to wear mufti even if we had a swimming pool. And if we did, I bet even our swim scanties would say *MSS Drake II* on them."

"Didn't you bring some of your casual wear when you came aboard?" Linen asked. "Including that nifty little red and silver number with which you often wowed the diners at top-notch hotels like the BC at Beagle?"

"I did, in the misguided expectation of extended furlough at our one glamorous stop-off; not of course realising that Jupiter Station was a top-notch dump and we were required to wear our uniforms in any case."

"You can always wear it for a private dinner with Kit."

"Stop pushing, Lieutenant Lyrican. What else?"

"The reason it's going ahead at such short notice is that Mars is set for a big blow: it's not quite planet-wide but local comms at Lowell are likely to be compromised for some time, even if storm bots are deployed early. And I doubt our mentors will be able to get above the atmosphere to escape it and be able to link into the relevant relay stations. Flax Dyxin's been roped in to deal with that side of things, though he doesn't know why. And I've had it on very good authority that we're not in for a five hour trial each: Doc Faerin has vetoed any more than an hour and a half absolute max for you but I expect it'll be shorter, as will mine. You're up first and I'll have to wait it out in the lab."

"Who's the very good authority?" Copper demanded.

"Trisk: he's not up for a long stint as he knows our stuff inside out; and he's going to get Ossy Inkscree clued-up on it. Hell, I'm scared: are you?"

"At the moment I don't know what I feel. Give me a hand up, I've been stuck to this couch for hours and I need to wash my face."

* * *

The following few duty sols as far as they related to Copper comprised long hours where floods of data came at her from all directions interspersed with short sessions of scheduled exercise and even shorter visits from her friends, who were equally as busy. One authorised foray to her own quarters accompanied by Linen and nurse assist Tilli Chenzen allowed her to organise her attire and renew acquaintance with her belongings. Her dress uniform hung loose: she had lost weight and a good long look in her mirror told her she looked tired and haggard. Faerin had arranged a mobile chair for her that took account of her healing injuries, but she preferred to walk with a support stick.

Briefing room three on deck five was close enough to their lab that Copper could check out both spaces on the sol before the event. That being the case, she and Linen, with Trisk in tow, went through all they would need to have in place. As briefing room two next door to three had been set up as the reception point after the trial as the point where friends and colleagues from Lowell would link in for the expected celebrations, they paid a visit there also. Copper scrutinised all three places with a wary eye, scenting changes she could not quite gauge. It was more than the additional comms relay housings and hospitality stations in the briefing rooms, she knew, and their lab had some new subtle nuance that was not down to the two resident aliens, who now seemed to have chosen that space as their base.

"Security's been upped," she figured at last, looking around their own duty space. "What in blazes for? Our main lab is one of the most protected bits of the ship. It always was, ever since you set it up, Trisk; and *you* were one of the first senior science officers aboard. It was Kit, wasn't it?" she added after a pause.

"It was," Trisk assented. "Dr Faerin told him that as he'd persisted in going back on duty against orders, he'd better not do anything too strenuous. So he's been upgrading his systems as far as he's been able from his chair. It's not just us, it's the whole ship."

Copper shook her head. "System upgrades ship-wide are not going to… just a minute: he's upgraded internal scanners in line with the upgrades that you did to your frigging probes, hasn't he? He'll now be able to pinpoint Spook and Junior!"

"He could anyway; but he'll now be able to look for anything alien that's *not* Spook and Junior," Trisk said softly, taking her arm. "That's the difference. And you're too smart by far."

"Was this his idea or yours?" she demanded suspiciously.

"Neither of us: it was Kynedd Faerin's – I think he thought it would keep him out of trouble."

"Huh! Precious little keeps *him* out of trouble, believe me!" she retorted, although her friends realised she was mellowing.

"We've noticed," Linen told her archly. "And if you would only stop following him into trouble, you wouldn't be wearing a steel corset and med-patches on your arm and butt."

Copper spun on her heel, only to catch her stick and stagger into a console. The other two caught her before she fell, guiding her to a chair and lowering her gently in. A glance from Linen to Trisk was acknowledged and the latter disappeared at a trot.

"That'll teach you not to start getting annoyed at Kit," the redhead laughed gently. "I'll get you a caff, hold still."

She made for their nearby office and returned only moments later with two gently steaming mugs. As she placed them on the work surface, she leaned against the unit and critically regarded her friend.

"You're overdoing it, trying to do too much too soon."

"Who made you my med adviser?" Copper snapped, closing her eyes tightly, secretly concerned at her own sudden dizziness. "I feel sick," she added, hand to mouth.

"Have a sip of your caff, it'll make you feel better," ordered Linen. "It's only the strain of wandering about on that stick and the thought of what's to happen morrow-sol. And finding out that Kit's been up to things behind your back for your own peace of mind – and his," she added, grinning impishly.

"Where's Trisk?" was the brusque rejoinder. "Thanks for the caff," she added more quietly as she reached out gratefully.

"Better?" her friend enquired after a pause.

"Yup. Caff's in short supply in medbay. They seem to have me on various tasteless liquids, mostly water."

"You've got a good Martian tongue in your mouth, so ask: it's the only way you get anything."

"Depends who you ask," Copper grumbled back. "Have you met a nurse tech called Axim Biggs? All mouth and med-coat and thinks he rules the roost."

"In medbay, he probably does, to some extent. Here's your ride," Linen added as Trisk appeared at the entry with a smile, her mobile chair and Dr Faerin with a medi-scanner in his hand.

"I'm fine and I want to finish my caff," the latter's patient objected as the doctor quickly scanned her and ordered her into the chair.

"You can do that in this mobile: it gives you better support than that seat you're on and I'm not about to carry you all the way to medbay. Hop to it."

"All I can do *is* hop," Copper continued to complain as she complied.

She finished her caff to the sound of Faerin's mild reproofs and was unceremoniously wheeled back to medbay and helped onto her couch.

"And there you stay until I tell you otherwise," the doctor announced as he tweaked a few instruments.

"Huh! At least I might get some peace to go over some of my stuff," she griped to herself as he made for the exit.

She was left alone, but not for long.

"I hear you've been causing chaos again, Lieutenant," Kit admonished Copper as he turned in through the bay door.

"Look who's talking; you're a master of trouble if anyone is," she responded. "Trouble knocks on your door, you open up and let it in instead of blasting it to hell. Sit down, for frock's sake."

"You have such a sweet way with words," was the reply as he pulled up the chair. "Ready for the morrow?"

"Don't remind me," she groaned, tabbing off the work she had been conning over. "I'm sick of this; I just want it done."

"You and me both: it's making you crotchety," he smiled as the blue eyes explored her face with a tender intensity that hurt.

Copper bit her lip to hide her concern at his ragged features and the harsh lines around those eyes. "I'm always crotchety; you should know that by now," she croaked, but had to go on, unable to keep silent. "Kit, you're tired; you're doing too much. And you should keep off that leg."

She stilled the retort that was rising to his lips by placing her finger to them. "I mean it. Please?"

"For the next half hour for a start," he smiled. "That's all I'm allowed. Tell me about your sol."

* * *

Copper spent a restless night, waking often to sounds on the edge of hearing that felt like monsters scraping away at the wall beyond her room. She sensed the comforting presence of Spook as an anodyne, but her lurid dreams when she did drift off were jagged nightmares that left her in an icy cold sweat and afraid to close her eyes for fear of what lay behind their lids. The six long hours seemed like sixty, and she was oddly grateful for the early summons that she had requested in order that she could spend her fears and some of her stress under a warm shower.

Nurse Biggs must have been warned against any undue levity, for he was as cheerful and as efficiently quick as before but less brash as he assisted her back to her couch and covertly watched every mouthful she ate to ensure that she absorbed adequate nutrition. On Faerin's orders she was to be prepared in medbay and then transported in her mobile chair to briefing room three. There she could have a word or two with Thars and her second mentor Mariner Mbolon before the business of the sol began, if she so wished. She did not: she had come so far so quickly that she only wanted the whole process ended as soon as possible.

Linen and Trisk were to act as escort and they arrived just as her medical aides had completed their ministrations. The two science officers were in dress uniform and both looked jovial.

"You two are bright-eyed and bushy-tailed," Copper greeted them in an attempt to appear the same. "And very smart! I see you've been polishing your buttons."

"Back at you, Lieutenant Milkstone, ma'am!" beamed Linen with a toothy grin.

"All set?" Trisk demanded.

"As I'll ever be. Thanks for your help, you guys," she added to nurses Biggs and Chenzen as Trisk took control of the chair to manoeuvre it out of the tight confines of the bay.

The journey up to deck five was accomplished easily, with a few glances from passing crewmates who no doubt were curious as to what was going on. Linen whispered to her friend that the matter would be announced later, but that at present only those closely involved were in the know. Copper was taken directly to briefing room three, where she found that the links to Mars had already been made and Thars Amberline and Professors Alessa Aclarke and Mariner Mbolon were virtually present. Both Ossy Inkscree and Colonel Moritz were in attendance from the *Drake*.

"Dyxin's been efficient," she remarked dryly to her friends.

Linen waved up to the three familiar faces looking back from the holo-grid suspended in front of the far wall, gave her friend a good luck hug and a quick kiss on the cheek and told her that she would see her later. The colonel also wished her luck and followed Linen out of the door, which closed noiselessly behind them. Trisk turned her chair and set it behind the console that Copper would use if her examiners requested visual information as part of her assessment. Ossy Inkscree quickly set a glass of water at her side, nodded quietly and took his seat.

As Copper raised her eyes to the vis-link to acknowledge her mentors, she saw with detached amusement that the three on Mars were shocked at the change that must be apparent in her, although she knew that they must have been briefed on her condition. All greeted her warmly, however, Thars indicating that he and Mariner would leave if she preferred it that way.

Copper shook her head and shrugged: she was in such a state of carefully concealed agitation that she scarcely cared less. She was startled by a squeeze of the hand from Trisk alongside her and as she looked into his lively grey-brown eyes, one of them gave an encouraging wink. She winked back and they were off.

* * *

"Congratulations, Dr Milkstone," Alessa Aclarke announced after tabbing a button or two and exchanging a few smiling nods with her fellow assessors. "We won't keep you hanging about with unnecessary chat, as we *will* see you later and I'm sure you want to get back to your friends."

What Copper wanted was a visit to the nearest comfort stall, but she endured the formalities of handshakes from Trisk and Ossy Inkscree with composure and thanked her examiners and her mentors for their friendship, their time and their patience over the course of her studies. There would be a break of fifteen minutes before Linen was due in for *her* assessment; Trisk thus took it upon himself to accompany Copper back to their lab to present her to her commanding officer and her friend as the latest Doctor to grace the long honours list of Lowell College.

The colonel waited only to congratulate her, as she had duty elsewhere, but promised to return later for the joint celebration. Linen's exuberance had broken even its usual bounds and she danced around her friend in delighted joy as Trisk headed back to briefing room three to set up the requisites for his next duty stint. Copper had elected to remain alone until Linen's trial had ended: she needed space for personal reflection and for some quiet time with Spook and Junior. As her redheaded friend left in response to her summons, she took a deep breath and settled down for what she trusted would be an hour of peace.

It was less than an hour later that noises at the door told Copper that someone was arriving. She had expected Trisk or Linen, as they were the only others apart from herself and a few select senior officers that could open the secure entry. She was grateful: her interaction with her two alien friends had given her cause for disquiet and she was tense. It was however, Dr Faerin, there to pass on his congratulations and to ask how she was holding up. The latter was construed to be mere courtesy on his part, Copper guessed, as her medi-tag was no doubt sending out signals that confirmed her status as medically fit and her med-patches had been fully charged earlier in the sol. The doctor satisfied himself that all was well and sat down to chat until the others returned.

"Still waiting for the celebratory," he noted. "I don't expect it will be too long."

There was something behind the assumed easy calm that she could see in his eyes and the smile that was not quite natural.

"Okay, what is it?" she demanded.

"Did you sleep well last night?" he asked.

"No I did not: I had hideous dreams that kept waking me up and I kept imagining that I could hear scraping noises outside my room. Why? *Were* there noises outside my room?"

"Damn!" he muttered to himself *sotto voce*.

Awareness suddenly dawned on Copper. "Drill drones," she said impassively. "I've seen them before and I've used similar so I know their sound. What were they programmed to do?"

He looked at her, startled. "What?"

"You heard me. Your face you might be able to control but your eyes you can't. And they're haunted. What happened?"

"They'd been set to drill through the bulkheads, we think, as a preliminary to whatever else was their purpose."

"We?"

"Chief Locksmith's anti-intrusion sensors caught the noise of the drilling and the vibration after they'd been activated. They may have been under test as they'd no destructive modules in them. His team tracked the first one to medbay and got him up, and he alerted the colonel. They routed me out and we captured it. There were a couple more found soon after: one on level five and another in engineering."

"*Level* five? The bridge? Bloody hell!" Copper was shocked. "But they tracked one to medbay and then got him up? Couldn't they deal with it?"

"Of course they could but he's head of security: the on-duty team knew he'd have had their hides if they hadn't informed him," Faerin stated.

They would, too, the doctor thought, recalling an exchange he had been party to between Locksmith and the colonel just outside the place where the drone had been netted. It had got as far as the iso-wing and the bay where Copper was stationed and both the colonel and Locksmith were of the opinion that it was not a coincidence. They had abstracted the piece and sealed the entry and exit sections of bulkhead with interim safety patches until a team from security could get into them properly, and had retreated to a station just beyond to look at the thing.

"Bastards!" Kit had hissed quietly. "This is a set-up if ever there was one! If anyone does anything to her, I'll..."

"If anyone does anything to her you'll do what?" the colonel had asked.

"Just let's say I won't be responsible for my actions," he had replied tersely.

"So I saw down on Jupiter Station; but I will not condone the use of excessive force. Do you understand me, Lieutenant?"

"Yes ma'am, loud and clear."

He might have understood her, but his face suggested that he might disobey, if the situation warranted it.

"The bridge! *Where* on the bridge?" Copper demanded.

"The commanding officer's office was its target, the security team thinks. But none of them were armed with anything."

"But we're still being undermined so there are still a couple of the bad guys aboard," Copper sighed.

"How did you work it out? It wasn't just bad dreams," Faerin reckoned, watching her closely.

"Spook, just before you came in. He's seen drones now, he knows what they look like and what they can do."

"You and your Spook. But this stays under wraps for now. This is supposed to be a sol of celebration."

"Let's make sure it stays that way," Copper said a tad sadly as she arranged her face, for noises at the entry announced another cause for rejoicing.

"Dr Milkstone, Dr Faerin, may I present Dr Linen Lyrican," the cheerful tones of Trisk Addystone burst through. "Ossy's with the Lowell lot, sorting the last of the admin," he added.

Copper gave the new doctor the praise and the applause that she deserved, but Linen was too old and too close a friend to be deceived and knew quite well that something was out of kilter. Blaming it on the strain of the occasion, she let it slip for the moment and announced that they would head for briefing room two, where a small celebratory had been set out. She and Trisk between them mobilised their friend and escorted her along the passageway, Faerin at their heels. As the briefing room door slid aside, a shower of holo-confetti descended and a storm of applause assaulted their ears from several well-known voices.

Many of the people present were not there in physical form, as they were holo-projections transmitted supra-light from the home planet, but a few solid friends were in evidence. Colonel Moritz had reappeared, with Captain Helmis at her side, to represent the most senior officers of the *Drake*. Kit was there in dress uniform, but all he allowed himself was a wink at Copper as she caught his eye. A soft smile in return was enough to raise sly grins in Ossy Inkscree, Lyssa Halsen and Tawny Brown, but Linen was more subtle and pressed her friend's shoulder.

"Here's to our Dragonets!" the cheerful voice of Mik Mack proclaimed from the link to the Warren: someone had evidently broken out some fizz, for he was holding a glass aloft. "And there's young Dr Addystone! What a reunion!"

Several techs from the station were there, with Ambrose in the forefront alongside Mik; the students currently on fieldwork included Maressan and Jenika, who waved cheerily but Copper was aware that they had noted changes in her that she presumed were not for the better, as the faces behind the smiles conveyed concern. The Scuttle must have been in, for Commander Opal Inkscree was hovering in the background, no doubt hoping to exchange a few words with her brother.

"No Cap Jeffers," Linen noted in an aside to Copper. "But Doctors Noa and Syr must have turned up specially: there *they* are with the Lowell lot."

The Lowell contingent had been enlarged by a number of ex-colleagues of the new doctors and words had to be exchanged with each and introductions made to those of their fellow crewmen from the *Drake* that they could capture as food and drink at each of the three venues was consumed. In a quiet moment, Kit had managed to whisper his congratulations to Copper and plant a discreet kiss on her ear. She could only squeeze his good hand and keep hold of it as long as she dared.

Captain Helmis made his excuses early and returned to duty but the hour soon passed that had been the agreed length of the festivity. Copper was thankful; she was tired, and having caught one or two pointed glances between the colonel and Dr Faerin, realised that the latter had been monitoring her. Others had been equally as observant and no-one objected when the colonel expressed her thanks to those who had attended to mark the occasion and ordered the links broken. She then chased some of her own crew out of the room with the cryptic remark that she would see them later, as Faerin now openly drew out his medi-scanner to thoroughly appraise his patient.

"Back to medbay for you Dr Milkstone, and two hours rest minimum," he instructed.

"But now that the links to Mars have been cut, one thing before you go," the colonel interrupted, with a glance at her chief MO. "At nineteen hundred hours, I'll expect you all in the officers' lounge on deck four; you too, Chief. We have another couple of things to attend to, and as they are more ship-related than College-related, and they will be relayed ship-wide, they are best done there. Dress uniform is requested but not required; but you *will* be properly attired. And now you'd best get back to medbay, Lieutenant."

"I'll take you there, Cop, and see you settled in," Linen stated firmly. "I don't need any help; and that includes you," she added pointedly as Kit stepped forward.

"You're with me, Chief," the colonel directed. "And you, Doctor, I want a word. Lieutenant Addystone, back to work."

"Aye, ma'am," Trisk responded and followed his two friends out of the room. "What gives?" he asked as the door sealed.

"We'll find out at nineteen hundred," the redhead shrugged. "But you need a few hours peace and quiet and help to get out of the glad rags, at least for a time, Cop: they don't get any more comfortable with wear."

"You're telling me; and I wouldn't mind another shower, I'm stuck to this frigging chair."

"I'll arrange it, Dr Milkstone, ma'am. See you in a while Dr Addystone, sir."

Back in the iso-bay, Linen carried out her tasks smoothly and quickly and her friend was soon nestled comfortably into her couch and in no mood for further festivities.

"I didn't think this is what I'd be feeling when once I was doctored," Copper sighed. "I wonder what the blazes is planned for nineteen hundred? Has the colonel given you any idea?"

"Nope, but there will be a few people there from what she was hinting. Dress uniforms? It sounds like somebody's been up to something. I shouldn't think it was another jamboree for us though: that she *would* have warned us about. Now, lady, what's happened? You were fine, more or less, until Dr Faerin showed up. What was it he said that got you rattled? And why are a couple of Kit Locksmith's people just outside this place doing something to the bulkhead?"

"I wonder if this genetic link to Spook's people that we share has a bit to do with the telepathy that Majorelle always swears exists between us," Copper prevaricated.

Linen's expression said plainly that she was not to be put off the scent and she again insisted on answers. Copper realised she had no option and quickly outlined what she had learnt. Linen was acutely disturbed, and much like the colonel and Kit, came to the conclusion that the targeting of this particular iso-bay was no coincidence.

"Spook knew?" was all she said, however.

"He must have: that was why I kept sensing him through the night. He can interact with technology, we know that much, so he wouldn't have let anything happen to me. But I think he still feels the need to maintain his presence a secret, for our safety as much as his."

"If your suspicions are right that there's an alien presence down on Jupiter Station and it's hostile, Spook's hidey hole here may not be as secret as it was," Linen said dryly. "Or Junior's come to that."

"I'm very aware of that. And as more and more people on this ship are beginning to find out about them, it's becoming more difficult to keep the secret."

"Kit isn't more and more, but it'll have to come out sooner or later. Though it looks like we haven't routed out all the bad guys yet?"

"Kit and Colonel Moritz didn't think we had, but I think they reckoned we'd got the worst. Maybe not; or maybe more got on at Jupiter as part of the repair crews and left us a few well-shielded presents before they left that were pre-set to jump out once we were well away. How they would have been able to choose their targets *without* inside help is beyond me, but I don't know what analysis of the drones has brought to light."

"Have you told Kit that?"

"No; I haven't had the chance to speak to him privately. But that's probably as well: he's becoming over-protective."

"Or you're imagining he is," Linen shot back. "Stop over-analysing and just enjoy the fact that you've got a really nice guy that thinks the planet of you – as you do of him. Think I hadn't noticed?"

"Shut up and go away."

"No. Medbay is as much of an escape for me as it is for you. As you pointed out a minute ago, this isn't what we thought it would be like when we'd done our PhDs. We'd figured big party back at Lowell, maybe research posts related to the Warren for us with pay hike attached, sessions of teaching the undergrads a thing or two, having a good time on leave in our own place at Beagle… chasing aliens and being shot at aboard a ship of Mars Fleet was not on our horizon at all."

"At least the pay's not to be sneezed at, since we've precious little to spend it on. But what *has* been planned for later? It must have been set up in advance, or I'm sure the colonel would have cancelled it, given the trouble. That drone found on the flight deck's the one worrying me: set to breach the colonel's office?"

* * *

Copper was adamant that she would walk to whatever was in store in the officers' lounge at nineteen hundred. Linen had left her friend to catch a couple of hours sleep if she could, but had vowed to return in plenty of time to escort her. Copper and her support stick were well attended, for as well as Trisk and Linen, a small coterie of medbay personnel due at the event made up the party, including Kynedd Faerin.

"We look like a very incompetent Fleet Academy passing-out parade," Copper observed wryly as her companions all slowed down to keep pace with her.

"Lor', it looks like quite a party," was Linen's opinion as the group approached the officers' lounge, for several crewmates could be seen making their way in and once through the doors, they could see that many more were already there and vis-links had been set up to other recreational areas aboard.

"There's a table arranged for us all over there at the front, near the grandstand," said a voice at Copper's elbow, and there was Kit, minus his stick and still resplendent in dress uniform.

"Congratulations on your first public date," Linen murmured playfully in her friend's ear as Kit took over at her other side.

"I still have a free hand that's capable of smacking your face, Dr Lyrican," Copper barked in reply.

The table set aside for the three science officers had places set for Kit and Kynedd Faerin and another two empty chairs. It also boasted bottles, one of which seemed to be half empty and looked remarkably like Dr Faerin's prized scotch. As they took their seats, the redhead mused on the identities of their absent friends. Other senior officers seated at nearby tables included Themis Sage, Ossy Inkscree and Faela Khilph.

"Who's manning the bridge?" Copper demanded of no-one in particular. "Most of the crew seem to be in here. And there's a lectern set up just there as if there's going to be a speech or a presentation. What in hell's going on? Do you know, Kit?"

A twinkle in his blue eyes and a half smile gave him away, but he refused to spill any beans. The mystery deepened as Colonel Moritz and Captain Helmis, who had been conversing with one or two others in the distance, made their way over and sat down in the empty chairs. The colonel was carrying a small flat case, which she laid down before telling the two new doctors that she would mention their recent honours as a prelude to the main events of the evening. Small talk filled the time until the bell for nineteen hundred hours signalled the start.

The colonel stood up, took her place on the stand and waited until the noise had died away. She began by outlining the testing time that the ship and her crew had had on the run up to and during their stopover at Jupiter Station, praising their exemplary conduct under such challenging conditions and the successful conclusion of that part of their mission. The evening, for those off duty, was an appreciation of their actions, and also allowed an opportunity to announce a few crew-related matters.

Copper and Linen were not surprised to hear their academic successes revealed as the first of those matters and waved their arms in acceptance of the applause of their mates. The following accolades were more of a surprise, as a number of people were to be singled out for particular mentions for actions over and above the call of duty.

"Bet you're on the list," Linen murmured delightedly in her friend's ear as Copper's jaw dropped in dismay, she having come to much the same conclusion.

There were commendations to be awarded to several of the crew, including Tawny Brown and a few of her team, and Kit, and all had to step forward to collect their handshakes from the colonel. Copper was slightly puzzled that her name seemed to have been omitted from the list, but when the announcement came that the final award would be a medal and citation for outstanding valour, her face began to burn. The pressure of the security chief's hand on her thigh under the table told her that Kit must have been in on the secret, and his was one of the loudest voices as her name was called. Colonel Moritz stepped down from her lectern and walked across to the table as Kit helped Copper to her feet to accept the medal, which her commanding officer draped around her neck.

"We seem to have been here before, Lieutenant Milkstone," the colonel smiled.

"Seems so, ma'am. Thank you ma'am," she responded. "And who gives you *your* medal, ma'am?" she dared to add in a low voice. "You deserve one if anyone does."

"Rank hath many privileges, but awarding yourself medals isn't one of them," Colonel Moritz replied, smiling. "Sit down, Lieutenant, I'm not finished yet."

The applause had died away by the time the colonel had returned to her position to state that the final part of her duty for the eve would concern the promotion of several of her officers. There were two ensigns advanced to second lieutenant and a couple of second lieutenants made full. One of the latter was officer Tawny Brown, to the rowdy cheering of the security contingent, most of whom had already made serious inroads into the bottles on their table. The final promotion was that of First Lieutenant Kit Locksmith to Lieutenant Commander.

As glasses were raised and the cheering redoubled, the new commander waved around the room, raising his own glass in salutation. Copper had called out with the rest, her eyes shining, her hands clasped in delight.

"Oh Kit! You so deserve it!" she beamed at him. "And you knew, didn't you?"

"It's been in the pipeline for a while," he admitted. "Do I get a kiss from my girl as a reward?" he carried on, his head coming closer, both eyebrows raised teasingly above the blue eyes.

"Here?" Copper returned, horrified.

"Oh go on, Cop," urged Linen from the sidelines. "There's nobody watching."

"The whole frigging room's watching," her friend retorted as Kit tilted her chin up and kissed her on the mouth.

"Way to go, Chief!" someone hollered from the background as murmurs ran around the room from several others, few of whom had suspected the liaison between the new commander and Lieutenant Milkstone.

Colonel Moritz closed the ceremonies, ordered everyone to have a good time, and stepped down to join her first officer and the others at the front table.

"You realise you're costing me in rare and expensive scotch," Kynedd Faerin accused Copper in mock annoyance, pouring her out a small glass.

She smiled softly in response, fingering her medal with one hand, her other under the table and clasped tightly in Kit's.

26: BEHIND CLOSED DOORS

It was three sols later that Copper was told she would be loosed from medbay and could return to her quarters, on the condition that she eased herself back into duty lightly and wore her medi-tag at all times. She was also under orders to report for medical checks daily until Dr Faerin told her otherwise. The burn-guard she wore had been replaced after cosmetic skin surgery with a therapeutic support that mimicked her skin and left her feeling and in her own eyes looking more human. The flesh beneath was still puckered and creased but she was more used to her appearance now and at least it had lost the blue sheen that made her look like some sort of semi-robotic medical specimen, she told her redheaded friend, who had come to help her move.

She had been transferred out of the iso-bay the sol after the finding of the drill drone and stationed in a normal bay that, unknown to her, had had additional security measures put in place. The security team assigned to the case was a little further forward with its inquiries but had not arrested the suspect, Kit had told Copper in private: they wanted to cut him some slack to see what else or who else would come to light. It was not someone in security Kit was very pleased to report. He had run every check he could on his own people and was now optimistic that he could trust every last one of them.

When Copper could finally look around her own quarters, she breathed a sigh of relief. With her blue dragon dancing in the background, Altair grinning from his holo and her drinks dispenser well topped-up with Chocó-crème, she felt her small universe was finally returning to normality. She had dispensed with her stick as support but still had a slight limp and moved stiffly. The exercise regime that Dr Faerin had specified she was diligently adhering to but his optional diet she tended to ignore.

Linen had elected to accompany her for her first visit to the mess for a break, as Copper was more a little apprehensive of the expressive looks and comments that would no doubt herald her return to duty. As they turned in through the door she was acutely aware of the many eyes turned in her direction as, with Linen's assistance, she limped over to join Trisk, who was there with Tawny Brown. However, apart from one or two friendly remarks in the passing on her return to fitness, she was left to the comforts of friends, caff and cookies.

Their main science lab was its usual workasol self when the three science officers strolled in after their break and Copper looked around in content, aware that Spook and Junior were close by and the atmosphere was calm. Her two colleagues had evidently been at some pains to set things up for her welcome, for every seat sported a cushion.

"Very funny," she told them, laughing nonetheless. "The butt's a lot better now and I *can* sit down without wincing. But what's on the agenda? I feel as if I haven't done any solid physical toil for an age."

"You haven't," Linen pointed out. "But we now have the go-ahead to use the tri-dee sim rig in engineering for anything we want. We do need to give notice when we head over to bay four though: there's some new piece of hardware that the auto-ship brought in docked there. Commander Locksmith's orders," she finished mischievously.

"We've definitely been assigned Dr Embertz as our dedicated medic and Tawny as our security aide," Trisk told her. "And we have the set of surf-sci bots that Lyssa brought us. *She* says she'll help with analysis if we want," he added. "But I suspect that was just courtesy, because she has enough on her plate with setting up a whole battalion of them for our mission. I saw them in the store – there must be at least a thousand."

"Lor' rather her than me," Copper responded. "But what's the latest on that piece we imaged from the bits we dredged up in the Glory Hole? That flat box thing that you suggested might be the alien equivalent of a MEDIC," she asked Trisk. "Didn't we think of trying to make it up using the lab tri-dee copier and some of the *Drake's* self-repair hull material, if the copier would take it? I remember Spook was excited about the whole thing."

"He was and we *have* been working on it," Trisk answered with a twinkle. "Want to see the results?"

"Results? What results?" Copper demanded. "You got it to work? What have you two been doing behind my back?"

"Well, we'd agreed not to touch that chunk of alien hull, or whatever else is in outer bay four, but nobody mentioned the box, so we thought we'd give you a surprise," Linen chuckled. "Better than a cake, don't you think?"

"I thought you'd been working on our Lowell stuff!" Copper exploded. "You sly scallywags, what did you get?"

"We were eventually able to persuade our little tri-dee copier to believe that the raw hull plate material was suitable as a base material for producing copies," Trisk explained. "I got Oaky Grimsson in – he likes fiddling about with the smaller stuff as a change from the big systems he's usually involved with down in main engineering. He did wonder what the heck we were trying to do, but he knows how to keep his mouth shut, so he didn't quibble when I told him we couldn't let on. The stuff was almost unworkable," he admitted. "It *is* supposed to repair bits of damage or missing patches on the hull of the ship and as it's a self-repair structure that's novel, it's not recognised by most systems, so the copier had trouble accepting it; but Oaky knows a few tweaks and he got it to use the stuff at least. The colonel insisted we had security back up, so we got one of Tawny's guys that she personally vouched for when we had the thing made, but we used one of the smaller engineering test bays rather than outer bay four: we didn't want too many other people in on the stuff we have there and the colonel wasn't keen."

"I don't think we have a complete blueprint of what the box was," Linen put in, "But our holos were pretty good, so we *have* managed to duplicate it. It looks much like the holo, only solid. But whatever it is, we couldn't get it to work so it may not be complete, or it needs sentient input, a command or something, that we have no inkling about. And that's where you come in," she winked. "If you can get Spook to do the needful…"

"Well, let me see it," Copper urged. "Is it here?"

"It's in Junior's secure store. We reckoned it would be safe enough there and might cheer him up – if he's capable of being cheered up, that is," Linen smiled. "The colonel and Kit were okay with it. The chief's quite impressed with the upgrade to the tri-dee copier," she went on. "In fact he figures that if we could make armour or other security assists out of the stuff, it would be worth doing and give us some edge."

"For what? It would use up the supplies of hull repair plating and we have body armour anyway. And what would it call on to self-repair if it was armour? The wearer?"

"I'll let you argue with him over that," the redhead said, snorting with laughter. "But let's have a look; I'll dig it out…"

"The *Goodwitch Guide*," Linen explicated as she unwrapped the article from its swathes of holo-film. "We used it to great effect many's the time back at Lowell for wrapping up our little band of bots, so for old times' sake, I thought I'd give it a go."

The tri-dee copier had captured the reddish-green iridescent colour of the original pieces of the artefact well and the smooth-edged rectangular case felt cool to the touch, the green metallic studs circling its wider aspect standing proud. Double the size of Copper's alien scanner, it was light in weight and there were no markings visible at all.

"We persuaded the copier to take in the data that you two bagged on all the other scanners you had operating at the time, so internally it should be more or less true to form – but the form didn't mean anything to us," Trisk shrugged. "It seemed to be sponge-like or cell-like in shape, with channels and nodes criss-crossing and penetrating the whole structure; we have a run-through holo here," he went on, calling up a moving image on a local console projector plate.

All three watched as the complex image expanded out and the inner structure twisted and turned as the imaging system ran through a mesmerising spangle of twists and turns, with dead ends and through-ways leading to finer and finer conduits within a definite series of honeycomb-like support structures.

"We don't have anything resembling a power source, but I don't know if we'd recognise one if we did," Trisk went on. "It could be that the power source is not some energy cap, it may be movement by the owner or some storage facility that can be topped up…"

"Or light, or spit, or a good shake," Linen put in, holding the device up.

"Very funny," Copper said with a sideways glance. "But *why* is Spook fizzed up about it, unless it was useful to him or it meant something? Junior's recognised it too: they're both here."

"You're the expert," Linen pointed out. "We both tried to activate it and we got nowhere though we've also got the genetic predisposition to things alien that you have," she went on. "But if it doesn't work for you, we could all link hands and try a joint effort? Spook and Junior could join in."

"Will you behave? Hand it over. The material's not the same as the alien organo-tech we've got so we may not get anything," Copper said meditatively, fingering its smooth, flat surface and pressing the band of studs around its edge. "But you know what it reminds me of? It's not the same material or even the same shape, but that has markings around the outside edge that tells us what's on it."

"Well, tell us!" Linen commanded."

"Those mini hard-holo projectors that your Ma gave us with our dragons on them."

"It looks nothing like!" Linen expostulated. "They're half the size of that, they're octagonal and they're made of some sort of yellow crystal stuff."

"Please yourself. But for some reason, I'm seeing my blue dragon and I reckon it's Spook that's sending me the image."

"You're just overly fond of that blue dragon," Linen told her. "Kit's going to be *so* jealous."

"It's very clever of your Spook, if that's who it is," smiled Trisk with a lift to his eyebrow. "What's Junior got to say?"

"He's practically sitting on my knee," Copper grunted.

"Happy families," Linen grinned. "You getting anything?"

"Not yet," her friend replied, continuing to pass her hand rhythmically over the tactile shell of the piece. "I'm still getting the impression it's some sort of hard-holo projector or similar," she murmured. "But it's maybe empty and needs the data to fill it. Wonder what the buttons are for?"

Suddenly she started up, holding up a finger as if something had just struck her. "I think we need to get to outer bay four," she said, sounding vaguely uncertain.

"Why?" demanded Linen.

"We have a very large chunk of alien tech there that I think was once part of a ship. It *is* genuine alien tech, it once must have been active, it may have systems that can still be made to operate and it may just be able to do something with this."

"Was this your idea or Spook's?" Linen asked suspiciously.

"I strongly suspect it was Junior's: he's one smart kid," was the wry response. "He's desperate to see this in operation."

"And how does he even know about the chunk of junk in outer bay four?"

"Search me: I didn't tell him. But I imagine Spook *has* been taking him on tours of the ship. He'll need to know his way around if he's to be one of the permanent crew."

"A crew with two aliens aboard! So when do they start asking to be paid at the going rates?" Linen demanded.

"That's as maybe," Trisk cut in. "But you're one sol back on duty and you're supposed to be taking it easy. And we need Tawny Brown and Amber Embertz as our escorts if we're headed to outer bay four."

"Only if I'm using the alien scanner, I recall," Copper argued. "I won't be. All I want is a look-see."

"Hah! I'd like to hear you argue that out with the colonel," her senior colleague told her. "And as I'm in charge here, you are not going anywhere near bay four without my say so and security back-up, Lieutenant Milkstone."

"Spoilsport," she retorted. "But I'm assuming the colonel has seen this?"

"Yes, and Chief Locksmith and Doc Faerin," Trisk replied.

"Anybody else?" Copper demanded dangerously.

"Now you're being sarky," Linen interrupted. "Only Oaky Grimsson, Ossy Inkscree and that guard Tawny assigned, what's his name, Ensign Kester Murkyles, have seen the whole thing. There were others in engineering and we didn't exactly hide it as we came along, but it's smallish and doesn't look like much, so I don't suppose anyone gave it a second glance."

"With you two carrying it and Oaky Grimsson and a security guard in tow? Don't be so sure," Copper muttered darkly. "But as I have a short trial flight sim this eve, I want to get over to bay four and see what's to do sooner rather than later."

"Then I'm calling for back-up," Trisk said firmly. "And we don't go until it gets here. Which may be some time."

* * *

Sooner was after lunch, for neither Chief Locksmith nor Dr Faerin could spare anyone before that. As Copper had stated that she intended to carry the alien scanner with her lest she felt she needed it, an experienced medic was considered essential and Faerin himself decided to come along. They met the guard that Kit had assigned in the mess, for Tawny strolled over with the comment that whatever they had planned had better be good, as she was off duty but had volunteered when her boss had figuratively twisted her arm up her back. She would meet up with them in their lab at the agreed time of fourteen hundred hours. She also directed them to suit up in protective wear for the trip to the outer part of the ship's aft section.

The three had already decided that outwardly secure or not, they would all wear protection and bring weapons and Trisk had advised Faerin to do the same. They knew that Kit had alerted his people that the trio and their escorts would be heading to outer bay four and had made sure that extra security patrols were operating in the area. The bay had also been upgraded with additional secure cams and a watch would be kept from the main security office on deck three by Kit himself.

A new shuttle was berthed in bay four when the five arrived with their gear stowed in kitbags. Copper was surprised at the unexpected sight, although she remembered that a new piece of hardware had been stowed in the bay. The craft was obviously a combat-shuttle but the design she had not seen before and she gazed at its shiny hull in some suspicion but made no comment. The huge hangar had room for another of the same and more besides and she assumed that as space was at a premium aboard a ship like the *Drake*, it had to be docked somewhere and the most secure bay on the whole ship was probably the best place. The banks of task-stations along the bulkheads, and the service and storage closets between all looked innocent enough, she commented to her friends.

The five were scrutinised by a brace of guards that had been posted at the entry to bay four, their idents verified and their baggage probed. The secure-arc field was already set up and local cams began to scan them the second the door sealed at their backs.

"Chief's been a busy boy," was the only remark that Tawny Brown allowed herself as she deployed her hand-scanner around the whole bay. She pronounced it secure, but decided to subject each of the deck hatches to an additional scrutiny.

"Try your gizmo on this little article," Linen suggested to the security officer as she poked at a hover-cam that had settled close to Copper's shoulder. "Bet the chief's at the other end of it," she added in an aside to her friend.

"Behave," she was summarily ordered as Copper limped forward to look at the great hunk of reddish-green alien hull, iridescent in the harsh light, which the *Drake* had captured, so long ago it seemed.

The massive shard sat within its hazy security field, now well-lighted and also surrounded by an additional security net of airborne mini-cams. The latter opened an area sufficient to let her through and she hopped past them to gaze up at the sight, a monument to Spook's people she felt as she stretched out her arm, palm outwards to get closer to it. She looked narrowly at what she imagined was its internal structure, noting the sponge-like texture and the support framework of uniformly distributed struts. She smiled to herself: the arrangement looked in grand scale very similar to the innards of the small box that she carried in her kitbag. The unbroken though scarred surface, smooth and faceted, that Copper was sure was the exterior hull, was still the same. As she slung her bag more comfortably over her shoulder and stepped out to orbit the irregular hulk, the net of hovers moved in concert and reformed around her. They trailed her every move and she had the odd impression that they were somehow protecting her.

"We can do another scan," Trisk's voice came at her back as she finished her circumnavigation. "No-one's touched it since we were last in here. And I brought Lyssa's bots," he added in a lower voice. "I have the case with my gear. I haven't been able to do more than programme them for a quick sortie, but it will allow them to get some data – and they *have* been updated with all we got from the bots that scanned this thing and the asteroid, as well as Elara, way back. But first things first: you want to break out the box and see what happens?"

"I do; but first this," she grinned, extracting a small tapering device from a thigh pocket.

"Grammy's bug detector," Linen smiled, coming closer to watch as her friend set it up and observed it carefully.

The device sat serenely on Copper's hand, its two blue crystal bands winking in the light. Slowly they began to pulsate, and a holo-note flowed out over her hand and into the air. She viewed the note carefully and then looked around her.

"We are not being bugged by anything that we don't know the source of, as far as I can tell," she announced. "Just let me see… that's it, we're all clear."

"We would have to be," the redhead informed her in a quiet voice. "Otherwise Kit would have somebody's butt in a sling. Our two extra buddies here?" she asked even more quietly.

"Yup," was the response as Copper stowed her detector in a leg pocket. "Now let's see what I can do with the box."

She gently extracted the lustrously gleaming case from her kitbag, dropping the bag to the deck as she slid her hands over the cool smooth surface of the device. She was unsure how to proceed, knowing that several pairs of eyes were watching from various angles. She could feel Trisk's hand on her arm as she slowly extended it, and the box, towards the great bulk of the shimmering metal-like object that stood before her. And it *was* shimmering, a glow that was growing… she could hear an intake of breath behind her and the swish of an unsheathing weapon as Tawny slid her phase rifle from its housing.

"Belay!" she said harshly, extending her arm even further.

"What's happening? Is Cop okay?" That was Linen, her voice creaking with tension.

"Fine," came Faerin's soft reply. "For the moment…"

Copper moved away from the section she had been studying, getting ever closer to one sponge-like segment that protruded raggedly from its base and which seemed to be brighter than the vast bulk around it. As she scanned it closely, various images floated into her mind. It was some sort of power and memory store, she was sure, and she muttered as much to her mates as she deliberately reached out and touched the projecting portion with the box. Nothing seemed to happen and she stood there, waiting, repeating the manoeuvre and watching for any effect.

"No! Cop, don't do it!"

That was Linen again as Copper deliberately withdrew the box and slid it under her armpit in order to draw off one of her protective gloves. She dropped the glove, holding out the box again, but some compulsion made her twist her ungloved hand up to expose her skin to the perforated surface. She flinched as she felt the contact, a fizz that she often felt when interacting with Spook. As a flood of emotion washed over her, she at last realised what was happening: the huge shard of alien technology was using *her* as a conduit to transfer information of some sort to the box. It was having trouble, as the replicative material they had used was nowhere near the same as the original had been and both her arm and the box were beginning to be enclosed within a hazy bluish glow. The minutes seemed to stretch to an eternity, but whatever intelligence was behind the construct eventually recognised enough to confirm a positive linkage and the trickling transfer of data became a torrent.

"That's enough! Cut that link now!" Kynedd Faerin's sharp tones ordered from behind her, but she was too enmeshed in what was happening to pay attention.

"I said cut it!"

The doctor had his own methods of dealing with refractory patients. He quickly pulled out a medi-gun and sent a hypo-shot into her free arm. Distracted, she stumbled back, shearing her contact with the material. Faerin and Trisk caught her as she fell backwards and lowered her to the deck. The doctor was furious.

"Damn you, Lieutenant! Do you *never* obey orders?"

"Oh shut up, Doc," she muttered dozily. "I got it. I know I did. I know what it is."

"Good for you. Do you know what your own name is?" he demanded shortly as he transferred her to another pair of arms that had appeared at his side and hauled his medi-scanner back up and into play.

She cared not one iota: she was drifting off into some warm dreamland with a pair of happy aliens that seemed to be singing songs to her.

"I swear I'll lock her in an iso-bay for a sevensol and not let her out," Faerin threatened.

"I strongly suspect she's not the only one that needs locking up," Linen told him in a quiet voice, breathing a sigh of relief as she realised that her friend's readings were returning to normal. "She's human: I think *they* sometimes forget that."

"I think *she* sometimes forgets that," he said. "The shot will keep her out for a few minutes, but she'll be fine; just keep her still, Chief. I'd like to know what the hell happened."

Kit Locksmith slowly eased his burden into a snug position in the crook of his arm. "You and me both, Doc," he said. "My readings of that blue haze showed an energy surge that made me think the whole thing might blow," he explained, nodding towards the mass of still shimmering junk that lit up the bay.

"So that's why you raced over here like a bat out of hell," Linen said ironically. "She'll flay you for that: she thinks you're over-protective as it is. Oh, don't worry about it," she consoled him as she saw the startled look on his face. "She thinks I am, she thinks the colonel is; she thinks Spook is, come to that."

"Why?" Faerin asked curiously.

Linen smiled down at her unconscious friend and stretched out a hand to stroke her cheek gently with a finger, shrugging expressively. "She imagines that she doesn't deserve people that care about her. She can't see that she does."

"The box has changed," Trisk observed into the silence.

He had picked it up from where Copper had dropped it and was regarding it critically: the band of studs around its middle had changed colour slightly and were an unmistakably brighter green. They were also warm to the touch.

"It doesn't seem to *do* anything," he went on, rotating it in his hands. "But something's happened. I guess we'll have to wait until Copper wakes up."

"You'll wait longer than that, Trisk," the doctor warned. "I won't sanction her touching that or anything else alien until I've given her a thorough check over in medbay. And this incident *will* be reported to the colonel."

"But we've got more work to do here," the senior science officer argued in a low voice. "We'll have to go over that structure with every instrument we've got to see what's changed. And then we have the bots to send through it. We'd hardly scratched surface."

"Then I'll send Embertz across and she can monitor you and Lieutenant Lyrican. *This* one is heading to medbay with me."

"She won't go," Linen informed him.

"The chief and I both outrank her. Believe me, she'll go."

A murmuring from the deck told them that the subject of the conversation was waking up. Kit raised her slightly to let her get her bearings as Faerin scanned her face closely. Her first words were typical.

"What are you lot looking at?"

"You, you ditsy cupcake; what in blazes did you think you were doing?" the redhead asked.

Copper stretched her cramped muscles with a weary sigh and took in her surroundings, seeming a little surprised at the soft glow emanating from the massive chunk of space debris in front of her. She looked up to see Kit watching her, a dry smile of amusement coupled with concern on his face.

"How did you get here?" she asked him.

"Got a pair of feet: I walked. What did you think you were playing at?"

She took in the blue eyes and her brow wrinkled as she tried to remember. "The box: we've still got it?"

"Here," Trisk told her, holding it up. "You said you know what it is? Well come on, don't keep us in the dark."

"It's a hard-holo projector, of a sort."

"A hard-holo projector!" Linen hissed in an irate whisper. "Are you telling us you went through all *that* so that Spook can see holos of his favourite vacation spots or his version of a blue dragon, or whatever else it picked up when you locked it into that lump of organo-tech? We could have given him one of ours if he'd really wanted one."

"Don't be a flooshy, Linen Lyrican," Copper snapped back. "A holo projector that can do a lot more than that; and I said *of a sort*. I need to check it out still, so you'll have to wait and see."

"She will; you're going to medbay and if you don't come quietly, I'll get the chief to carry you," Faerin interrupted testily.

"I'd like to see him try," was the rejoinder.

"So would we all," Linen grinned down, relieved by the feisty tone. "Get the hell out of here, Dr Milkstone. We'll tidy up, collect your stuff and be with you shortly. This thing isn't going away and we can come back later. And Tawny's supposed to be off duty anyway. But you hold onto the holo projector, Dr Trisk, sir," she added to her friend. "I think we *all* want to know what it's capable of."

Copper was helped to her feet and accepted Locksmith's arm as support to steady her as she limped across the deck towards the exit. Tawny Brown was there, directing the pair of security guards and a couple of tech operatives, who were scanning the area immediately adjacent to bay four.

"Anything?" the chief stopped to ask.

"No, sir. It's clean. Apart from the energy surge in the bay itself, nothing's registered out here."

"Lock up after they've finished in there and then get yourself off duty. Thanks for the assist."

Brown nodded in compliance. "See you later," she added to Copper. "Hope it was worth it."

"I think so," was the reply.

"Matter of opinion," Locksmith muttered as they set off along the passageway.

In the elevator heading in, Kit leaned gratefully against the wall, wincing, and Copper realised that his leg was hurting. She looked him in the face and could see lines of pain etched there that should have been long gone. She was concerned and more than a little guilty, having realised that she was the cause of his presence there.

"Sorry," she smiled across at him as he caught her eye.

"What for?"

"Causing you trouble. Again. I seem to be good at it," she sighed, looking away and then back at him. "The leg still hurts, doesn't it? You've been running on it."

"Haven't."

"Liar. You were still winded when I woke up. I could feel your breath and your heartbeat and they were fast," she accused, a reproving finger poking him in the chest.

"That was for other reasons," he replied, catching her hand.

"You two want me to leave?" Faerin interrupted. "I can get off here."

"Can it, Doc. And yes, Dr Milkstone, you cause me no end of trouble. When *will* you learn not to jump into things before checking every angle? And obey orders. If your medical advisor tells you to stop, you do it. I'm serious, Copper."

"Try taking your own advice, *Commander* Locksmith. You were told to keep off that leg. And I don't suppose the hand's back to full working capacity either."

"Playing word games again, Lieutenant? We're talking about you, not me."

The pressure on her hand and the angry spark in his eye told her that he *was* deadly serious and it was concern for her that was making him so. Her anger had risen to match his and her mouth had opened in protest but she stilled it, an overwhelming care for him sheeting her like an electric film. Her eyes misted.

"Damn you, Kit Locksmith."

"You missed the bit about me being a great oaf," he smiled as he put both arms around her.

"That also," she added as she slumped against him and slid her arms around his waist. "You're too good for me."

"I'm definitely getting off at the next stop," Faerin muttered to himself, staring straight ahead.

The trio made it together to deck six and the main medbay and Lieutenant Milkstone was deposited on a couch and bid to lie still for five minutes. She read as perfectly normal despite the events in bay four. The doctor grilled her closely on what she had sensed and felt during the interaction but aside from images of storage units and data chits, and the compulsion that made her touch the sponge-like surface with her ungloved hand, all she remembered was the actual contact that sent the emotive frisson that she associated with Spook down her spine.

Faerin also took the opportunity to examine his other patient and Kit was given trenchant advice on staying off his feet and sent back to his office with a flea in his ear and the promise that he would be kept up to date with what had been uncovered as far as the alien box was concerned, once Copper had had time to see what had happened to it.

Her colleagues turned up to collect her thirty minutes later, with the news that the bay had been sealed down tight and was to be left without further disturbance. They had brought all her gear, including her kitbag. They had also found out that the shiny ship decorating the deck was a brand new combat-shuttle that had been brought aboard at Jupiter Station and was one of the latest off the production line.

"I hope there's a sim of it," Copper replied eagerly. "I'd like a trial flight. I've never flown a combat-shuttle before."

"You shouldn't mention things like that in front of the doc," Linen laughed. "He'll put a spoke in that wheel right now."

"Get off my couch and back to work, Dr Milkstone," was his only response. "You'll continue checking in every sol and I want to be kept up to date on what's going on with your new toy. As will the colonel: I'll be briefing *her* on what happened right now, and I'm sure Chief Locksmith will be doing the same, so expect comeback."

"Aye, sir. Let's go, people, I need some caff."

"What you need is a dose of calm-down juice," Linen told her as they made for the exit. "A flight sim in a combat-shuttle? And I expect you'll want a sortie in the real thing after that?"

"Given the opportunity. But as we're racing through space at something resembling light speed, I doubt I'll get the chance," Copper told her as they made their way along. "But where's the box?" she demanded quietly as soon as the deck was clear.

"In your kitbag," Trisk said. "I thought I'd best keep it out of sight, you never know who's eyeballing us. But what's so special about it?"

"Isn't the fact that it's alien special enough?" his friend asked quietly as they turned into the transport for the ride to deck five.

"We made it using a standard lab tri-dee copier, so it's hardly alien," Linen pointed out.

"Dr Smartarse," Copper retorted, regarding her friend with a critical eye. "It's a hybrid then. But enough until we get to our office. And I'll have a creamy caff once we do, I sure as hell need one. We'd best set the privacy seal so we're not disturbed."

Once in their office, Trisk set the seal as Linen crossed to the dispenser to order drinks and Copper made for her own desk, sitting down heavily.

"Your box, Lieutenant," announced Dr Addystone formally as he dug out the device and handed it over. "It hasn't squeaked once since I picked it up."

"Glad to hear it," she responded.

"But what happened when you touched our lump of alien

stuff? I was scanning and it looked to me like an energy transfer. I guessed massive data streaming through you."

"Good call, I think that's exactly what it was. That projection on the piece of hull was a sort of data and power storage facility and it must have recognised the box as something akin to itself but not quite. I sensed a lot of trouble in the process, but I think Spook was lending a hand to ease transmission. The box picked up power: maybe enough to render it operational. But the data stream felt infinite, as if I was drowning in it. I'm just wondering if the projector now has the capacity to update itself – like our mil issue scanners," she added to Linen. "You know, if there *are* data sources to link with, the thing can update if there's novel information it doesn't hold."

"That's seriously creepy, if we're going to be hunting things alien out there," was Linen's opinion. "But as Trisk's touched it and nothing happened, how does it work?"

"There's the thing: I don't know. But hand it over, and I'll see what I can do," Copper said.

She took the device from her friend. The smooth, burnished surface was oddly warmer than before and she noted the more intense colour of the studding around the edges as she felt it all over to gain some understanding of it.

"It's maybe not touch," she said. "Or maybe…"

"You said it was a hard-holo projector," Linen interjected.

"I think it needs to be told what to show." Copper's face was creased in concentration. "I was so sure… I'll just set it on my desk for the moment… Now let's see."

She stared fixedly at the flat case for about thirty seconds but nothing changed. "I was trying to mentally image something familiar," she told the others. "But zip, zilch, not a thing."

"Drink your caff," Linen advised. "You'll feel better and be relaxed. That's how you got the alien scanner to work after all."

"You have a very good point, Dr Lyrican."

The three sipped their drinks companionably, looking at the box and at each other. It was Trisk who had another brainwave.

"Try turning it the other way up," he advised. "Maybe it has to be at a certain orientation for a holo to show."

"If so, there would be a holo under the desk," Linen stated. "Can't see one," she reported after a series of contortions to peek beneath. "And besides, if the aliens are so in advance of us, they'd have figured that glitch out and fixed it."

Copper in the interim had picked up the piece to examine it again. "It's not exactly symmetrical," she murmured. "The edges are bevelled but there's a slight bias to the whole piece as well and this surface is marginally smaller; that may mean it's the top. And I would swear that the colour's shifted: there's a subtle gradient I hadn't noticed before."

She replaced the box on the desk and regarded it fixedly, her arms crossed, missing Linen's aside that if she made faces like that at it, it wouldn't want to work. After a minute of focussed scrutiny, Copper reached out a hand and began to rhythmically stroke the upper face of the device with her finger, much in the way she operated the alien scanner, easing back into her chair in an effort to relax. The seconds ticked by as the other two waited and watched. Her finger moved to the edge of the box and she continued the slow, rhythmic massage. A buzz at the entry disturbed them and Linen jerked back with an oath.

"We set privacy! Who the hell's that?" she mouthed.

"Colonel," Trisk replied briefly. "Nobody else would dare ignore it. I'll get it."

He unlocked the entry, placing a finger to his lips and eying their commanding officer expressively. She understood and slid in quietly. Trisk set his seat for her and captured another for himself. They continued to watch.

Copper had hardly been disturbed. She knew that Spook and Junior were both there and her fingertip could sense the familiar tingle that heralded the operation of her scanner. The sensation was spreading across her hand, past her wrist, up her arm, and she sighed loudly as an indistinct shape began to grow out of the flat upper side of the device. Copper slowly withdrew her hand, moving back as the shape continued to expand outwards and upwards. The progress of the projection stopped suddenly, its extent blocked by her desk-top holo-grid frame and the whole began to coalesce, becoming denser as it strove to fit the space that seemed to delimit it. With a sudden ripple, it came together into a distinct form.

"We've got one of those," Linen announced to the room. "But not that size."

The metallic blue dragon had gleaming green eyes and scales that shimmered in the light as it began to move, hovering above the reddish-green box.

"Hello, Copper," it said.

"I see you're acquainted," Trisk smiled widely. "I take it that *this* is the famous blue dragon?"

"Scalenyx," Linen introduced. "And if that's all the damn box can do after all the shenanigans earlier this sol, I'd ask for my credit back. But why did you bring *him* up, Cop? How does that help in trying to figure what this thing is capable of?"

"I just knew that this was a hard-holo projector but I've no idea how it works. The data it holds came from that bit of hull so it stands to reason it's alien and thus possibly dangerous if misused. So I pictured in my head a hard-holo that I did know. But this is bigger than the one my own projector is capable of – and *that* has only one holo stored, though it can hold more. But I think this thing is capable of a *whole* lot more, given the extent of the data transfer you recorded, Trisk. But maybe the space it has to expand into from its base unit limits its size."

"Are you saying that if we had an enormous space, you'd get a full-sized dragon?" asked Linen.

"Maybe. But this one's still a projection and he's composed of hard-light energy…"

"Are you sure?" the redhead demanded as the dragon rose a little into the air and flew away from the projector unit to land lightly at Copper's feet.

It stood just above knee-high as it placed its scaly head on Copper's lap and looked adoringly into her face, its tiny forelegs clasped around her calf. She reached down and ran a hand down its spine.

"*Now* I'm freaked," Linen breathed.

The colonel looked at her science officer. "I understand that Dr Faerin and Commander Locksmith are very upset with you, Lieutenant Milkstone: I've spoken to them and they seem to think you still have a problem with discipline. But I see you have results. Does that mean you reckon your conduct was worth the risk of disciplinary action?"

"Yes, ma'am. But I'm puzzled as to how to shut it down."

"You don't want to shut me down, Copper," Scalenyx said.

"You've got two aliens round your neck and now you've got a blue dragon in your lap," Linen said. "Another month of this and you'll have one of the biggest and oddest family groups in the Sol system. You'll need to apply for additional allowances just to keep them. You think Kit's up for handling that?"

"You're not helping, Linen Lyrican. Let me think. I can bring you back anytime," she added to the dragon. "Return to base."

"He's not real," Linen whispered jokingly. "You're talking to a figment of your imagination. And he's still there," she added, leaning over to take up the box.

As the redhead ran her fingers around the studded outside of the contraption, there was a small hiss and she dropped it. As it hit the deck, the blue dragon hopped across, landed on it and in moments had fizzed away into nothing.

"That'll teach you," her friend announced sternly. "He was just thinking about it."

"Much like you then: doesn't obey orders until he thinks it's the right time. And that damn box sent a stun wave into me."

"If you've all quite finished," the colonel cut in, "I want an update from you three on what happened both in bay four and in here."

"Yes, ma'am."

* * *

"The pieces came from the Glory Hole," Copper said to her friends some time later, after the colonel had left the lab, leaving orders that that any new data be linked to her at once. "So the original had been on Mars for a long time, in the area close to Spook's ship. But it can't have been part of the ship, though it was made of the self-rep tech: I don't think it's a standard ship's instrument or piece of gear."

"Why?" Linen demanded interrogatively.

"Because Junior recognised it and how would he know part of a ship or gadget used aboard?"

"He's a kid: kids play make-believe, even alien kids, I bet."

"No," Copper shook her head. "He wants to play with it and I get the impression that Spook's holding him by the equivalent of his coat tail until I work it out. It's maybe an educational tool of some sort."

"Educational?" the redhead said. "It can't be if he's so eager to handle it. What kid wants to be educated when he can jump about here and have fun?"

"Not all kids are like you were. What gives, Trisk?"

"I was thinking: it might help if you let Junior operate it. If he's as young as you think, he'd be liable to use it for familiar things, and that might give us a clue."

Copper thought for a moment and agreed, deciding that the lab was the best place for the trial, as they could set up scanners to capture any detectable output. Once in place, they sealed the door and initiated their gear. Copper set the box in the middle of the floor, ordering the others to move back to leave plenty of space. With a deep breath she began to imagine the young alien playing with the thing.

"Spook gets it!" she breathed. "But I still think he's wary of Junior using it. I don't know why."

All three sat for several minutes silently watching. Trisk had fixed his eyes on the array of recording tools directed towards it, and reported in a quiet voice that energy changes had begun in the device. They knew, because a thin wisp of what looked like vapour was slowly rising. The misty apparition began to expand up and out above the box, the stream of vapour thickening as it twisted and reformed into a hazy, bulbous shape. With a slow ripple, the accretion began to separate into two distinct blobs, subtly different to each other in outline and colour and linked by tendrils of light.

Copper raised her hands to her mouth, concern creasing her face. She began to swear quietly but fluently, realising too late what she had done as the shapes began to manifest. They were not humanoid but extensions that seemed to be a head and four limbs were becoming apparent in each, the latter with tapering extremities that might have been fingers or toes. They were greenish, one darker than the other, but insubstantial.

"Hell, they're his folks, aren't they?" Linen whispered. "What he remembers of them anyway. No wonder Spook was reluctant to let him handle it. Are those darker spots eyes?"

As she spoke, the holos melted away slowly and the box resumed its quiescent state on the floor.

"What happened?" Trisk enquired in a low voice.

"Spook stopped it," Copper said with a muted groan as she

slumped in her chair. "Damn, I should have realised. It picked up my thoughts and produced my blue dragon. And what does Junior want most in the whole frigging galaxy? Damn!"

"At least we can now be reasonably certain that at least two aliens are required to produce offspring, maybe in physical form at least," Trisk remarked. "Which suggest similarities to us at some scale – but as we didn't get the whole hard-holo, we…"

"Oh shut up!" Copper snapped. "When *will* I learn not to jump in feet first before thinking things out? And to obey orders from my superiors? Lor' Kit told me that only a couple of hours ago! And here I go again!"

"Cop, don't blame yourself," Linen urged.

"I was the one that suggested you let Junior try it out," Trisk told her. "Beat *me* up, not yourself."

"I'm responsible for both of them, the colonel made it quite clear. I need to think long and hard about this. I have that trial flight sim soon, so that should let my brain work it out."

* * *

Linen and Trisk were seated together in the mess when they were accosted by Kit Locksmith, who asked to join them. It was obvious that he had something on his mind.

"No Lieutenant Milkstone?" he asked.

"You too," the redhead replied briefly. "You've been trying to contact her and she's not answering."

"What's up?"

"A little trouble in the lab – can't talk about it in here. We *did* update Colonel Moritz as per orders but thought we'd leave you and the doc out of the loop until Cop got back, only she didn't. She went off for what should have been a short flight sim more than three hours ago and we haven't seen her since. We tried to link but no response. We thought she might have come up here, but no. I'm heading to the training suite shortly to see if she's still there. If she's pulling extra flight sims, the doc will have her arse in a sling, as she's supposed to be taking it easy. But you're head of security, so surely you should be able to pinpoint her implanted ident?"

"Not without a damn good reason I can't; though I can pull up the training logs from my office. But why would she want to pull extra flight sims?"

"Lot of thinking to do."

"About what?" Kit demanded, a little anxiously.

Linen smiled mirthlessly. "Our little problem in the lab."

"We can head that way after you've done," suggested Trisk. "She may have got back by that time."

Kit lost no time in dealing with his rations and the three set off. The lab was apparently empty, but on an impulse, Trisk dug out his alien probe and swept the space.

"Junior's in his closet. No Spook," was the result.

In a short time the two science officers had acquainted the chief of the happenings earlier. A rapid review of the availability of flight training simulators indicated that two of the suites were free: it was thus possible that Copper was still there and as there was still no response from her, Trisk elected to stay in the lab whilst Linen and Kit headed down to deck thirteen to check.

"This is getting worrying," Linen announced as their search in all the main training facilities came up empty. "It's going on four hours since we've seen her. But this is a big ship; she could be running the engineering decks, in the gym, on the obs deck, in the gardens, just walking about, in the therapy suite, in the training suites down on twenty four..."

"My office," Locksmith decided.

Back in main security on deck three, the chief liberated his duty officer for five minutes and sat down to commandeer his own station. A quick review of flight training logs showed that Copper had only spent one hour in the sim. Grimly, Kit set to again; Linen was not surprised that he could call up the link to her friend quickly and sat alongside to see the result as the ship's spec was called up on the holo. The two looked at one another as the tell-tale spot of light settled.

Kit was first to speak. "What in hell's she doing there?"

"I told her not long ago that we had leave to use the tri-dee sim suite in engineering whenever, but I didn't figure she'd set it up on her own; and she can't have had time to book." Linen paused, huffing. "I wonder... oh hell! Lyrican to Addystone... Trisk? Check the secure store. Is that damn box still in there?"

A couple of seconds later and Trisk's puzzled voice came back. "It's gone – and so are a couple of other things."

"Bet she didn't leave a note," Linen growled. "Don't worry, I think we know where it is. Meet us at the tri-dee holo projection facility on deck twenty: Kit's called up the current status and it's signed out to Cop. And it reads as operational."

"Oh hell!"

"That's what I figure," Linen told him as she cut the link. "But what in blazes she's set up beats me. Let's go, Chief."

Trisk was already there as the two hove up to the relevant entry. The external board gave the facility's status as operational and under the name of Milkstone. As head of security, Kit had the authority to enter a number of prohibited spaces and the sim facility was one of them. He quickly set his security override to the door reader plate and it hissed open.

The double deck height of the place was almost completely filled by what resembled most of a small craft of some sort. Its hull glowed eerily in the dim lighting and the whole was pulsing, muted sounds echoing through the test chamber. The station that regulated the projector plates and ops was empty of an operator but the system was up and running at full tilt.

"Oh, oh!" Trisk breathed. "What in hell is *that*?"

"Damn! I know what it is… I know *exactly* what it is!" Linen whispered.

27: BEYOND THE BACK OF BEYOND

The gently glowing metallic shell was an iridescent red-green in colour, with clear markings that seemed etched into the surface. The patterns of soft swirls were shifting, undulating and waving in an ever-changing dance, their outlines changing colour as they moved. The sounds from the entity were almost musical, their cadences rising and falling to the tempo of the changing shapes.

Linen clutched Trisk's arm and silently pointed to one of the auxiliary projector plates to the side of the main ops station: the alien box was linked to it by some type of energy field, for it was seated on a bed of light above the plate and the studs around its edge were glowing more brightly green that she had ever seen.

"It looks like it's made of the same stuff as that chunk of metal we have in bay four," Kit grated as he took in the mass. "But it's doing a helluva lot more. What *is* it?"

"Cop was right: that *is* a lump of hull in bay four. And that, Commander Locksmith, is almost what the complete article looks like," Linen said. "It's an alien scout ship, I'd guess by the size. Maybe like Spook's one that's buried out at the Warren?"

"But why's she set it up without telling us?" Trisk asked.

"She locked herself in a flight sim to think, she said. But she must have come back for the box and her other gear: here's her MEDIC and that's the scanner that the colonel gave her. Spook went along with her, so she had something planned. And for some reason, that holo-ship is the result."

"But how in hell do we stop it if we don't know what's going on or what she's doing aboard it – assuming that's where she is," Kit demanded.

Linen seated herself at the station to look over the regulators. "I don't want to touch anything in case I mess up any of the links – I've seen nothing like *that* before," she admitted, pointing to the box. "But she must be in the ship. I guess we wait it out."

"It's still growing into the complete ship!" Trisk breathed. "But this place isn't as big as a shuttle bay – it'll be a tight fit."

The three waited for fifteen minutes, after which the security chief decided that enough was enough and ordered the two science officers to find a way to stop the programme.

"She must know we're here," he argued. "So she's ignoring us or she's in trouble."

"She's in trouble whatever way the wind blows," said Linen grimly, turning to the console. "Trisk, give a hand: we should be able to halt the programme in place. Any regular tri-dee and we could, but that thing seems to be suspended above the deck."

The two worked, quarrelled and cursed for a few minutes as they manipulated links and finally, with a little trepidation, cut the data input to the projector. The surface patterns of the hulk slowed to stillness and the growth that they had noticed halted, the large craft hanging in space like a half-chewed sea creature.

"Now what?" Kit demanded as nothing happened. "How do we get in?"

As he spoke an iris grew in the side of the vessel, expanding into a recognisable entry, with a projecting tongue that formed a slowly descending low ramp. Locksmith started forward but two pairs of arms grabbed him and held him back. The interior light of the construct dimmed as a form in flight fatigues stumbled out, only to trip on the ramp and slide down, landing in a heap on the deck. As she pushed her way upright, the three reached her, Kit and Linen on either side to steady her.

"Whoops! Catch!" the redhead called out as Copper swayed and crumpled to the ground, her efforts to feign fitness and stay erect failing dismally.

Trisk called out for increased lighting in order to view their friend more clearly as Kit supported her back and head. Linen felt for her pulse and heartened by what she found, she nodded quickly at the other two before placing her hand on Copper's forehead to push back her damp hair. One eye opened and Copper looked up at her friend, who sat back on her heels.

"What in hell do you think you were doing?"

"Flight sims," was the mumbled reply.

"Flight sims! I'll give you flight sims!" Linen scolded. "You had only an hour in flight sims. Why didn't you tell us you were coming down here?"

"You'd have stopped me."

"If we'd known this was what you'd be up to, damn straight we'd have stopped you," Linen informed her. "Out with it."

"It *wasn't* planned," Copper revealed. "I didn't mean to spend so much time in the ship…"

"It's like Spook's ship then? The one from the Warren?"

Copper leaned back, sighing. Catching Kit's eye, she smiled and nodded ruefully. "I think so," she admitted. "It's beautiful."

"So how did you do it?" Trisk asked curiously.

"It looked like the box could manifest thought patterns – my blue dragon, Junior's folks. But I was certain it could do more, otherwise why the vast data transfer? So I thought I'd try to see Spook in physical form, to enable better data exchange, maybe prevent another episode like poor Junior. I figured this would be the best place – away from prying eyes."

"You mean ours?" Linen cut in.

"Yes. But I couldn't, I don't know why. And then I thought of Spook's ship, as that's where he left his organic part as far as we know. I thought that this place would be big enough. So I tried the box, but as I'd only ever seen part of the extern of Spook's ship and that was in my mind, I couldn't get it. But that piece of hull in bay four is made of similar stuff and I wondered if it held the blueprint of itself within it, as we suspect a lot of their tech does – and the box had been in physical contact with it. So I called up the data on Gemima and Auntie Elle's scanner and ran it through the central projector. And then I set the box on that auxiliary projector plate and connected the two: the box now has a power source. And then I used the technique I use on my alien scanner to extrapolate holos into free space, but thinking of Spook's ship…"

"I warned you about trying that for something the size of a ship!" Linen barked at her. "In fact I even warned the colonel against allowing you to attempt it! No wonder you're all-in."

"That's enough," Kit counselled. "I think we'd best get you up and out of here. And into medbay for a once over."

"Like hell: the doc'll shoot me."

"He'll have to get in line," Linen told her, still angry. "I have first dibs."

Trisk gave a hand to haul Copper to her feet, looking askance at her as he unhooked her MEDIC and scanner. She was aware of an unspoken question but turned away, testing her strength, hoping she would make it as far as the elevator.

"I'll need to shut down," she said, taking another look at the radiantly gleaming husk.

"Leave it," Trisk said with a quirky look. "The data's in the system, the chief can lock the door to us and security and you'll need it operative to get into it for another session, won't you?"

"You what?"

"You were *inside* that ship as it was regenerating. You're not trying to tell us you were sitting admiring it growing, are you?"

Kit stopped their progress. "What are you suggesting, Trisk?"

"You weren't lying when you said you were doing flight sims, were you? *That's* why you're utterly exhausted." Trisk's grey-brown eyes sparked a challenge.

Linen's jaw dropped as Copper's expression gave her away. "You're kidding! Lieutenant Milkstone, are you saying you were attempting a flight sim *in* that hard-holo crate while you were trying to complete its shell? The colonel is going to kick your butt to hell and back."

"I'm saying nothing. I need a caff."

"You need a sedative is what you need. And Spook needs a kick up the butt: I sense he's behind much of it."

"Later," ordered Kit. "Let's all of us get out of here. You know what time it is?"

The tri-dee test suite was locked down as Trisk had proposed and the four made their slow way to the nearest elevator. Once inside, Copper propped herself against the wall with eyes closed and they could all see how spent she was.

"Deck six," Kit ordered.

"Deck nine," Copper disputed, waking up sufficiently to treat him to a defiant stare. "I need some sleep is all."

"You'll do as you're bid, Lieutenant. And you *will* make a full report to the colonel. I'll be doing the same," he went on, raking her with his blue eyes.

"Aye sir," she responded mechanically, too weak to argue the point further.

"You lot again," was the greeting from the duty officer as the quartet trooped into the main medbay. "I'll ask Dr Faerin about setting you up permanent billets in here."

Copper was pronounced fit enough to return to her quarters but not to duty for at least eight hours and given a protein drink and a couple of shots to restore lost energy. Trisk set off to the lab to return her gear to the secure store, and Linen and Kit escorted her back to her own base to ensure that she got there.

"Shower first," the redhead instructed as Copper initiated her perimeter security field. "*Then* you can have a caff. That way you won't spend an hour in there. Hop to it."

"Hop's all I *can* do. And who made you the boss of me?"

"Move it. Kit will still be here when you're done," Linen continued mischievously.

"That I won't: I have a few things to see to in my office. But I *will* see you morrow-sol," he smiled at Copper, chucking her under the chin.

"Which is only a couple of hours away," the redhead added, winking, as Kit limped off.

Copper sighed and began to strip off her fatigues. "He's still having trouble with that leg," she replied to her friend's anxious enquiry. "I cause him no end of trouble."

"He enjoys it," Linen told her firmly. "You also cause me no end of trouble: you think I'd still be around if I didn't like it? Go get showered and then come and tell me what *really* happened."

* * *

"I *had* wanted to complete that ship in bay four," Copper admitted to her friend. "Some of the data that was transmitted to the box seems to have stuck with me and I was even more sure that it was a ship; and Spook's always known. But Junior's people: their shape isn't quite human but they had what looked like hands or limbs that could manipulate the way we do. Maybe that's why they chose Mars for settling millennia ago: with Earth next door, a planet with proto-humans or whatever, there were similarities and they could make use of the resources there. But I figured if Spook's people were close enough to us physically at least, *if* I could get a hard-holo of the ship, I could get a handle on their tech. It's part of our mission anyway – to see if it poses a threat and if it does, to find a way to combat it."

"So why not wait until we were all back in bay four?" Linen interrupted interrogatively.

"Time, for one; I feel the need for hurry. And we both know what *that* means, we've felt it before. And there are too many in the know about bay four. Whoever was at the back of those drill drones that were found for a start. Nobody's been got for that as far as we know, have they? That's what I had to think about. Then it came to me that the tri-dee testing rig in engineering would be the place as it was big enough, I could lock it down, and if I didn't say to anyone, I could try it out."

"So you just jump in on your own, without a thought to what would happen if you got into trouble?" Linen growled.

"I gave it a lot of thought," Copper disputed. "I knew if I didn't show that you, Trisk and Kit would pile in. But I'm not a fool, Linen: that drone in medbay was meant to get close to me. Of all the sections they could choose, they pick the iso-bay I'm in? And now Kit's close to me, he becomes a target."

"Are you saying that people are starting to figure that there's more to you than meets the eye?"

"People worked *that* out long ago. We and Trisk were drafted to the *Drake* because we attracted trouble from nasty people back on Mars. So did Colonel Moritz for that matter. And now we're here with the colonel in command, and on *this* mission? Those same people now know they were right and that it has everything to do with alien tech."

"So you managed to get the hard-holo of that ship set up? But it wasn't complete when we saw it."

"No; I hoped I could get the whole thing. But it's a complex structure and the data input is massive. I need the interior to be as accurate as possible…"

"So that you can try to fly it, at least as a sim?"

"That's about it. Spook helped, he knew what I was trying to do. So I tested it out for about an hour before you lot showed up, as it was complete enough internally for me to do that. Spook's people can withstand more than we can physically, I think, but that may be down to their protective gear. As far as I can make out, there's a mental as well as a physical link to the controls of an alien ship, even a small one. I've nowhere near got a handle on it and it's killing, but I want to continue."

"Are you going to tell the colonel all this?" asked Linen curiously. "And will she let you?"

"Naturally. But in a private briefing, I won't trust this in any linked report. And *I* think she'll encourage it."

* * *

Copper was right: Colonel Moritz judged that research into the structure and workings of an alien ship, particularly one that seemed to be friendly, was a valuable use of time and resources. The *Drake* was now well into the next stage of her mission and on a fairly even keel, a position that allowed most of her crew to engage in the typical sol-to-sol duties crucial for the operation of a ship of the Fleet. One exception was security, in light of the problems still extant there. The source of the drill drones had not been traced, which implied that others might be aboard, and Kit Locksmith had been authorised to continue to hang fire on capture of the prime suspect in the hopes that he would slip up.

The astrobiologists among the science officers were more than busy. Trisk had taken it upon himself to use his free time on the ship's long-range sensor arrays to sweep for anything resembling alien technology in the area of space through which they were passing. He and his two colleagues had sent the batch of surf-sci bots on a rapid sortie through the chunk of hull in bay four to obtain data that they could analyse, but all three assumed that the box still set up in the tri-dee sim probably held a superior spec of the thing. The three were also scheduled for regular bridge duty in addition to training exercises and drills. Copper had completed her advanced GHQ under the eagle eyes of Kynedd Faerin and thus found that she was obliged to take part in medical sims related to that, much to her disgust.

One matter that Colonel Moritz reminded them of from time to time and pressed for an answer to was the strangely patterned blue alien tech to which Copper had a particular aversion. The small assemblage of pieces that Trisk had extracted from one of the *Lithium Star's* sample tubes and securely locked away had not been touched since his analysis, but that they were a destructive part of some whole was highly probable. The reason for urgency was clear: the closer the ship drew to her destination, the greater the likelihood that they would encounter similar materials and they needed to know all they could. Since the discovery of the tinted tile on Jupiter Station, the subject had become more imperative, particularly as Copper and her alien friends had been convinced that darker alien influences were at work there. No further information related to the incidents on the station had been received other than that the perpetrators of the attacks on the *Drake's* crew had been removed and were headed for Mars, but various parties were arguing over whose responsibility they were. The reason for the attacks had not been ascertained to the satisfaction of either Colonel Moritz or Chief Locksmith, but there was little they could do apart from demand answers.

As the distance from habitable parts of the system increased, the linkage gaps became longer. Likewise, as supra-light comms were restricted in duration, information from home was limited and current news on events related to Mars and the Sol system in general was patchy. However, the crew of the *Drake* had learnt that two of their sister ships, the *MSS En Hedu'anna* and the *MSS Mina Fleming*, were heading out to the edge on different courses, their missions ostensibly being resources survey. The intelligence also trickled down to the crew that those ships seemed to be having an easier time on their shakedown cruises, and had not been troubled by the sabotage that had bedevilled the Flagship of the squadron, although a couple of agitators had been apprehended. The *MSS Lithium Star*, now sound, was continuing on her mapping and survey mission and Mars Fleet science vessels had been deployed around Elara and asteroid Helixus but their results were classified. Two recently-refitted Earth Fleet ships were also heading in their direction, but their precise missions were unknown. Of the MDMC ship *SS Fearless*, nothing more had been learnt. The top-of-the-range commercial survey ship built by several consortia including Greensands Minerals was also out on her first cruise and was said to be scouting for rare mineral resources, but the only other piece of data extant about her was her name: the *SS Morgana Atlantis*.

* * *

Soon after lunch on one quieter sol, the three science officers found themselves together in their main lab with the purpose of examining the set of fragments of blue alien tech brought in by the *Lithium Star*. They had chosen the lab rather than the tri-dee facility in engineering as it would be less conspicuous, and as Copper had decided to use her alien scanner the results were expected to be sufficiently comprehensive. Amber Embertz and Tawny Brown had been ordered in by the colonel as back-up when she was apprised of the situation.

The session started routinely enough, with the pieces under test spread out evenly in an analysis tray and a bank of security and analytical devices in place to record the results. With the alien device in hand and Copper as relaxed as possible as she fingered the operating zone, the three waited for the usual hazy holo to materialise and expand out from the front edge of the scanner. A faint, vapour-like suspension did initially escape the scanner but it rapidly began to spread up and out to encompass the analysis tray and its contents, thickening as it did so into an almost transparent bubble that seemed to remain static but was patterned over with a moving, oil-like haze of colour.

Both Linen and Trisk called out as Copper, unable to move from the spot, could do little but hold onto her scanner and try to maintain her calm. As they and their two colleagues watched, the discrete pieces in the tray were sucked up into a spinning cyclone by some unseen force and arranged and rearranged into a condensing mass, until what had been a collection of variously-sized fragments was now one almost complete and much smaller whole, which then dropped into the tray with a thud. The surrounding bubble popped soundlessly into a mass of fizzing light and disappeared at a dizzying rate back into the scanner.

"Don't touch it!" was the only thing Copper said before she dropped in a dead faint to the deck.

Dr Embertz was quick and calm: medi-scanner in hand, she examined Copper, pronounced her fine and put her faint down to a sudden drop in blood pressure as a result of shock. Copper agreed when she came round a few minutes later – the break of her mental link to the scanner had been very sudden and the appearance of her nemesis as an actual specimen had given her more than a jolt, was her own assessment.

"We stop now," Trisk announced. "I'll deal with *that*."

As Linen collected up the rest of the kit and Embertz and Brown helped Copper to a chair, Trisk carefully scooped up the small, rectangular blue block with forceps, wrapped it in several layers of static film, slid it into a locked case and stowed it in the deepest recesses of one of their least accessible secure stores.

Copper insisted she was fine and once back in their office seemed only to want to sit down with a caff. She rebuffed the efforts of the others at conversation and sat sipping her chosen drink. Once done, she fled the office and Linen and Trisk did not see her again until dinnertime in the mess.

* * *

It was noticed by keen-eyed crewmates that Commander Locksmith had taken a seat alongside Dr Kynedd Faerin and Dr Amber Embertz. Copper, her face set like stone, was alone: she had shaken off the advances of her two friends, who had come in together and now sat exchanging whispers and giving a glance every now and again at her and at the table beyond that which accommodated the threesome.

Copper ate her meal quickly and headed to the exit without a backward glance. Linen rose as if to follow, but Trisk caught her arm and held her back with a whispered comment. The redhead subsided, shaking her head, watching the doorway, her chin on her fist and disinclined for anything else. She was worried.

Around half an hour later Lieutenant Lyrican escaped the mess and Trisk, and having tracked her friend to the obs deck, found her gazing into space. Linen climbed up the metallic ladder to reach the mid-section of the double-level deck and put a hand over Copper's, which was resting on the guard rail across the front of the mighty window onto space.

"You okay, Cop?"

There was no answer and Copper continued to stare into the expanse beyond the ship, her breath coming in uneasy gasps.

"You had a fight with Kit," Linen surmised quietly "So what happened, kiddo?" she enquired. "Want to talk about it?"

Copper sighed and half turned as the pressure on her hand increased. "I was headed back to my quarters after our stint in the lab – I wanted to be alone. I was quaking in my boots and couldn't figure why. Kit was on his rounds, he caught me up. I said a few things, Kit said a few things; I told him how to run his department, *again*. He got hot, I got hot; he pulled rank. I told him to back off and leave me be; he said he thought that might be a good plan for a while, so I stormed off…"

"And now you're regretting it?"

"Every damn word," Copper sighed again. "But that's not all: I had a run-in with Ash Goff not long ago, just after dinner; Tawny Brown caught the end of it, but she backed off the way she'd come – not wanting to be a witness, I guess."

"Witness to what?" Linen demanded. "What happened? I *did* see Ash Goff leave the mess just after you did."

"He must have figured that Kit and I had rowed and so he thought he could muscle in. He actually grabbed at my arm. So I slapped his face and told him where to go."

"Oops! If he reports it, you could be up for a court-martial, Cop!" the redhead warned tensely. "Assaulting a fellow officer is a serious offence! No wonder Tawny beat a retreat. What if she tells Kit?"

"Too late now," Copper said miserably. "How did you track me here?"

"Asked Spook, mentally of course, and then had the urge to head straight here, so I did. But let's make for your quarters and get you a Chocó-crème: you look as if you need one."

"Don't want one."

"Yes you do; come on."

As the two made their way to the elevator and deck nine, a prudent Lieutenant Brown had reached the mess, collected her drink and bagged a seat alongside Kit Locksmith and Doctors Faerin and Embertz, with the request that they invoke privacy.

"You've got a problem, Chief," were her opening words.

"Tell me about it," he grated dryly.

"This one's a doozie. I witnessed an assault just along the way about fifteen minutes ago."

"You what? You called it in?"

"I thought I'd better not, Chief. And I retreated before the victim spotted me."

Locksmith's eyes were instantly alert. "Victim?" he repeated. "What victim?"

Tawny shrugged. "Don't know the cause of the upset, but Ash Goff was evidently annoying Lieutenant Milkstone and she took the flat of her hand across his face with such force that he bounced off the wall. She spied me just before she put her boot where sol don't shine and backed off at high speed. I turned tail in the opposite direction. No other witnesses that I could tell."

"And you didn't call it in?" Locksmith demanded.

Brown shrugged again. "Lieutenant Goff *did* have hold of her by the arm. I figured it was a fair fight, more or less."

"Thanks."

"Welcome. But if Goff reports it, she'll be in trouble."

"Depends what *he* was doing," Faerin put in. "But if she's still affected by what went down in the lab this afternoon, she can claim mitigating circumstances."

"She won't," Kit said briefly. "Too stubborn."

"You got my report then?" Tawny asked her boss.

"Yup – a tad late, unfortunately."

"So I figured. You and Lieutenant Milkstone had a witness to *your* little spat earlier: young Murkyles. I shut him up before he could tell the whole watch."

"Thanks," Locksmith snorted laconically. "Nice to know my personal life now seems to be the hot topic around here."

"Have another caff, you'll feel better," Faerin suggested.

The caff was declined and the chat spun out until Brown had almost done, when an insistent trill on Locksmith's wrist-comm caused him to give vent to a mild expletive as he tabbed the device and demanded to know what was going on.

"Sensors have detected drill drone activation in one area," was the reply. "Just started. We've got a team on the way."

"Location?" Kit barked, rising, the hairs on the back of his neck starting to prickle in strange apprehension.

"Deck nine, section thirty four, location twenty four, repeat zero-nine, three-four, two-four."

"Dammit! I'm heading down. Locksmith out."

He was out of the mess at a run, Brown on his heels. Faerin took one look at Amber Embertz and shot to his feet likewise. Before anyone else in the mess could draw breath, they were off, the chief MO calling for medical back-up to the scene.

Copper had launched her perimeter field as she normally did as soon as she stepped through her billet door and checked that it showed clear. She was still numb with a feeling that she could not shake that her world had been blown apart by her own hand and she flopped onto the sofa in despair. Linen, understanding completely, threw her jacket on a chair and made for the drinks dispenser to call up their order. As Copper waited, ruminating, she was disturbed by a muffled rasping from beneath her feet.

"You hear that?"

The noise was disturbingly familiar and Copper lost no time in extracting her PPF from the table drawer. She stood, drawing away from what seemed to be the focus of the sound. She was not a moment too soon, as with no more than a soft puff of air, a thin cylinder shot through the deck just at the foot of her sofa. Aiming and firing were almost instinctive, but the shot did no more than slow the thing as it performed a gentle sweeping arc and made for her.

Quick thinking Linen grabbed her own discarded jacket and flung it over the device; the weight was enough to bring it down to the deck and Copper jumped hard onto where she thought it had landed.

"Shit, it's tough!" the redhead panted as the nose of the piece began to protrude through the tough fabric.

"Keep back! It's loaded and sensing lifesigns!" Copper called, raising her gun again as the drone pulled clear.

She had just released another shot when her door whooshed open and a pair of armed security guards stormed in.

"Drill drone!" yelled Linen from her spot behind the chair.

The first of the duo lost no time in directing a salvo at the drone, halting as the thing seemed to melt and drop. "Got the bastard!" he announced, raising his rifle up and away. "Get that capture net activated and check for more," he ordered his mate, coming forward for a closer look.

Even as he spoke, noises at the entry announced the arrival of Locksmith and Brown, who shouldered their way in, the chief calling for an update. The leading guard had just begun to deliver his verbal report when simultaneous cries from Linen and Copper alerted them that the drone was not quite dead.

"Its load's still active!" Linen bawled as all eyes followed the small red projectile as it shot skyward from the mass on the deck, the thrown capture net missing it by a fraction.

The tiny thing paused as if seeking its target and Copper, her mind taking in its direction at lightning speed, threw herself at the pair in the doorway, yelling at them to get down. Brown hit the deck but Kit stood his ground, arms opening instinctively to catch Copper. As her back arched and her feet stopped in their tracks, her weight caused him to stagger. She fell forwards but he held on, supporting her. She looked startled, eyes wide.

"Oh shit!" she said quietly as her head drooped to his neck.

"Check every frigging inch of this space!" Locksmith yelled as he unfroze and began to lower her to the deck. "Doctor!" he bawled over the rush of feet.

Faerin and Embertz were at his side in seconds.

"Team's heading in," the senior MO gasped. "Let me see… bloody thing's penetrated her jacket and it's got through her med-support. Hold her steady… Get me that capture net: I'm going to extract it. I want it in medbay."

Tawny Brown had retrieved the net and Embertz grabbed it and held it in readiness as Faerin carefully pulled the penetrative dart free, cursing that its load had been delivered. Linen had found one of Copper's scanners and handed it to the doctor, who actuated it promptly. Even as he did so the trauma team raced up, unpacking and setting up their gurney in seconds.

"Keep her face down! Get the breather on! Hand me that stim-pack! Got the drone-dart? You stay here, Chief, I'll keep you informed; let the colonel know. Move it, people!"

Locksmith grabbed Tawny Brown by an arm as the gurney and its crew disappeared off down the deck, whispering urgently in her ear. "Get a team together on the QT, get hold of Lixin Wale and put him on ice in the brig!"

"Understood."

As she strode off to do his bidding, the chief tabbed his link to demand the presence of a search team at his current location before he called Colonel Moritz, whose response indicated that she was already on her way, and indeed they could hear the thud of approaching feet down the passageway. It was then that Kit became aware of Linen's hard gaze and set mouth.

"It was deliberate targeting, wasn't it?" she said. "We're in the middle of nowhere and *still* it's going on. And how the hell didn't her perimeter scan pick the damn thing up?"

"I want to know that even more than you do," he responded grimly. "Tell me exactly what happened, from the moment you met up with her... here's the colonel... Ma'am."

"Go on," the commanding officer indicated as she reached them, her quick scan taking in the blast marks and debris.

* * *

Linen was included in the briefing that Colonel Moritz called two hours later. The lieutenant had been shunted out of her friend's quarters to allow security to carry out a thorough search and clean-up of the place and had been found by Trisk prowling deck nine, numb with delayed shock. He had hauled her into his quarters, fed her caff and called for answers. The strong security presence and the obvious source of the trouble had not escaped his eyes or those of their shipmates whose billets were along the same stretch. Trisk had later escorted her to the colonel's office and left her in the hands of Kynedd Faerin, also there with Kit Locksmith, Tawny Brown and Captain Merris Helmis.

Kynedd Faerin's report on Copper was mainly positive. The potent anaesthetic released by the dart was the same as that used in the incident in bay four and as a remedial response had been developed in the aftermath of that, the consequences were less severe than they might have been. Copper's clothing and skin-mimicking therapeutic support had slowed the dart, which had lost the impetus its carrier drone would have provided, but its own volatile delivery system had caused some burn damage and she would be out for hours.

Locksmith had called in one of his explosives experts to carry out a preliminary analysis of the fused remains of the drill drone. The results led him to conclude it was the same as those found earlier near the iso-bay, the bridge and in engineering, but this one had been loaded and given its location, its target was Copper. The drone also had an inbuilt anti-detection system that could not be picked up by a local perimeter security field; it was only because security's sensors had been specifically configured to detect drill drone activation and subsequent vibration that his duty team had found it at all. The one suspect that Locksmith's people had come up with and whom he had left loose was now in custody: Tawny Brown had had no problem locating and detaining Leading Officer Wale, an engineering non-comm. She and her team had tracked him to an engineering research lab on deck ten, taken him into custody and locked him in the most secure cell in the brig. She had also secured the lab and posted it off-limits.

Linen jumped on one piece of information. "If you'd picked this Wale up when first he came to your attention, he wouldn't have had the chance to get to Cop," she accused Locksmith.

"Belay that, Lieutenant," Helmis ordered icily. "*I* authorised the chief to leave Wale loose. And we have no evidence yet that he planted or activated the latest device, though I *have* checked his records and he's quite capable of setting up and initiating drill drones and their like. He enlisted for a two-year spell in Ground Ops to work as a technical engineer; on his release he joined civilian Law Enforcement, after which he re-enlisted in Fleet, in response to that recruitment drive months back," the captain explained to the group. "His earlier record entitled him to LO status."

"Ground Ops?" Linen looked startled. "Law Enforcement?" she repeated. "I wonder when, and who his buddies were, and if they kept up their friendship afterwards," she went on, with a questioning glance at the colonel.

Colonel Moritz realised at once what had alerted the redhead. "Ground Ops and then LE, as was your old associate Jecks; and *he* was certainly no friend of Ms Milkstone – or you. Wale's not been interrogated yet?" she demanded of her security chief.

"No, ma'am; I haven't had time. My priorities were to secure the area and ensure that no more devices were planted anywhere else. But I *will* be questioning him before I go off duty."

"Deck ten's below deck nine and our quarters," persisted Linen. "And where the armoury is," she added.

"We know *that*, Lieutenant," Locksmith interposed, his ice-water gaze quelling her.

"That engineering research lab isn't directly below Lieutenant Milkstone's quarters, but it's not too far off," Brown informed them. "We *are* checking that angle."

"But *why* Copper? She was deliberately targeted and it's more than the Jecks trouble," snapped Linen. "Somebody sure as hell has figured something and she's on their hit list. They want her out of commission…"

"But not permanently," Faerin interjected. "That shot was meant to incapacitate, not to kill."

"Huh! *That* wasn't Jecks agenda! But why Cop? So she can't do any more work on the alien tech? But that means I should be on their list, and Trisk."

"Lieutenant Milkstone has drawn more than a little attention to herself by her actions of late," the colonel pointed out. "And it's possible that her unique skills with regard to alien technology have been noticed and reported."

"By whom and to whom? We're in the middle of nowhere, the back of beyond, heading to the edge, so who does it profit? There's nobody else…" Linen paused for a second. "Oh hell! We're not alone in this pocket of space are we? Non-Fleet ships are out there; that supposedly high-spec boat that Greensands Minerals has its oily hands in for one, and I'm sure Magenta Firewall mentioned at least one other technically advanced ship, so there may be more. There *must* be other ships looking for first dibs and not afraid to scupper our mission or the Fleet to get it. And who'd believe this far out that if anything happened to us it would be anything but an accident? So do we reckon that the *Drake's* on some sort of bigger hit list, if we get in the way? What about malign alien influences on Jupiter Station? Does that mean…"

As Tawny Brown's eyes opened wide and a question formed on her lips, the colonel intervened. "That's enough, Lieutenant. For the moment we take every precaution that I deem necessary for the safety of this ship and her crew and for the completion of our mission. At this moment in time, we have had a security breach and there was a serious assault on one of my crew and I want more answers. Clear?"

"Yes, ma'am."

"You and I will interview Wale, Chief, and I want the whole session recorded," Colonel Moritz told Locksmith. "Merris, you see if you can dredge up any more on LO Lixin Wale. And you, Lieutenant Lyrican, as of now are off duty."

"Copper…"

"Is in the capable hands of Dr Faerin's team and will remain there until *he* says otherwise. Dismissed."

Linen trailed disconsolately back to her quarters. Trisk was still lively and must have been listening out, for he buzzed at the entry almost as soon as she made it in. His professed errand was to ask after Copper, as he had tried medbay and had been told to get lost. She brought him up to date, as he knew most of the story anyway. In return, he apprised her of a few rumours flying around their neck of the woods. That the culprit of the attack on deck nine was in custody was known, as was the victim. It was being mooted that there were reasons why Copper seemed to be the one that kept falling foul of the trouble aboard, but the general view was that it was likely to be due to her actions in thwarting some of the guilty. Trisk had taken it upon himself to waylay Ash Goff, who was as curious as everyone else as to what had gone down, and had put the fear of death on him by subtly hinting that anyone who was seen pestering Lieutenant Milkstone was liable to be detained and questioned.

"How was his face?" Linen asked curiously.

"Nary a mark," Trisk grinned. "Though I think his pride may be bruised a tad. I doubt he'll be telling tales."

"Thank heck for that. It wasn't mentioned in the briefing, so Tawny either said nothing or it's being kept quiet. This has got to stop, Trisk, or something's going to give. The crew must be getting jumpier by the sol. And that makes for poor morale and won't help the mission," Linen frowned.

"Who made *you* ship's counsellor?" he said with a smile. "Get some sleep: it *will* sort itself out, you'll see."

"Can't see anything at the moment," she groaned tiredly. "I'll see you for breakfast?"

"I'll knock on the way up. Oh seven thirty?"

* * *

When Linen and Trisk strode into the mess the following sol, the low hum grew a little louder, causing the redhead to murmur that if they were accosted by anyone, she would chew their ears off. She was still upset by the previous night's action and her temper not been improved by the dismissal she had received from medbay when she had called to enquire after Copper. The two had not long to wait until someone decided to join them, but as it was Colonel Moritz, who was alone and had asked permission to sit, Linen held fire, but took the precaution of setting privacy.

Copper had had a good night, the colonel told them, and was hoping to be back on duty soon: her reaction to the outcome of the trial in the lab was frustrating her and she needed answers. Having gone over the visual record, the colonel agreed. As for the other matter, it transpired that there *was* a link between Lixin Wale and Flinn Jecks: they had served together in Ground Ops, and both later joined Law Enforcement, although in the latter they had been stationed in different domes. With regard to the attack on Copper, Colonel Moritz refused to reveal any more of what had come out of the interrogation of Wale, other than that he appeared to be working single-handedly aboard the *Drake*, but reporting to others elsewhere. He had picked up his supplies and his orders on Jupiter Station and Kit Locksmith was dealing with that aspect of the case. Security had recovered his stash of drones and other interesting pieces, including targeting darts and a range of narcotics, not all of them benign.

"So whoever set him up probably has a massive network of lackeys," Linen concluded. "And how many did they manage to get assigned to the *Drake*, do we know, ma'am?"

"He's the last, we're pretty sure," Colonel Moritz said.

"I still don't get it. What made him think he'd get away with it? It was the same with the multiple attacks we had when we had all that fun in the armoury. But there, the perps knew that they would be able to get off the ship at Jupiter and probably had a forward plan. Out here, that isn't an option, unless they're really sure the *Drake* doesn't have a chance against whatever else is out here."

"Perhaps they *have* a forward plan that we haven't figured," Trisk suggested. "But from what I've seen of your pal Jecks, if this guy's of the same mould, he's a nasty piece of work."

"He's my problem," the colonel told them. "You two look into that reassembled piece of hardware that Dr Milkstone and her scanner put together *very carefully* and link me any details. Check with Dr Faerin as to when and for how long you can see her: she should be kept up to date. If you'll excuse me, I have other people to see."

With that, Ms Moritz collected her mug and set off to collar her first officer, who was seated with a couple of others over by the wall.

"He's *my* problem," Linen echoed to the colonel's back view. "She should make him Kit Locksmith's problem: he wouldn't be anybody's problem for much longer after that."

"That's what Tawny reckons," Trisk said unthinkingly.

"And how do you know that, Dr Addystone?"

"I spoke to her this morning before I called for you," Trisk admitted with a betraying lift to his shoulders.

"Aha! I thought so. Since when?"

"We're just friends."

"Hah! That's what Cop said about Kit and I believed it too," Linen said, amused. "Science and security: two sides of the same coin."

"At least it's put a smile on your face; but keep your hush."

"I promise," Linen agreed. "But we'd best get to the lab and get something done. And then we see Copper, whether Kynedd Faerin says so or not."

* * *

The two gazed at the small blue block in the secure steri-field that Trisk had set up around it. He had removed it from its case and its many layers of static film using robotic manipulators, as it still gave him the heebie-jeebies, he confessed.

"Copper felt the same: she said she was quaking in her boots and didn't know why, after our last session," Linen confirmed. "That's why she was so upset and ran off. She wanted to be alone to work it out, but couldn't – which of course led to her other troubles with Kit and Ash Goff."

"Strange, I'm not sure if this *is* a part-complete real whatever, or a replica, but it's showing the condensed sub-atomic structure I recorded earlier and there's a definite lattice support of novel molecules. I'm going to add a small block of solid human tissue cell-replicate to check for a reaction. In light of what it did to Copper's hand, there should be something. If Copper was here, she'd be able to let us have Spook's reaction."

"I can tell you that: he's seriously freaked. At least I am, and he sometimes lets me in on what he senses," the redhead told him. "I bet Junior's still in his closet. But you're right as far as I can work out: that design *does* sit proud of the base, as if it's got some function, like a mechanism that works if it's touched, at least by someone like Copper or you. But what happens if the right person or thing touches it or somehow gives it an order? Does it move, change, let you activate or access something?"

"Who knows?" Trisk asked. "Until we know what it's a part of, we'll not be able to work it out. But let's add this cube of cell-rep and see what we get."

What they got was a transient sputtering as the surface of the pale-coloured cube spat and fizzed and then sat quiescent. Trisk quickly retrieved his sample and the two science officers looked at it, Trisk hauling out his MEDIC.

"Surface destruction – it doesn't seem to have penetrated far, but definite damage and it's covered one whole face. See the mottling? The cells are ruptured but no other toxic elements detected. So now we know that whatever Copper's scanner did to bring these pieces together, we now have a working piece of alien tech – so like much of their stuff, pieces of it seem to carry the blueprints for the whole, and with the right constituents, you can make one. But there must be more to it that just damaging whatever it comes into contact with," Trisk noted.

"Has the piece itself changed?" Linen asked. "What does it gain from attacking organic matter like us? Satisfaction?"

"You have a point; let's compare a new scan with the one we took earlier."

A few minutes later and the two stood looking at one another in perplexity. With one accord, they wrapped up their work, carefully replacing the layers of static film and embedding it snugly in its case.

"At least it doesn't seem to react with inorganic material," Linen said with a sigh as she locked the sample away. "We'd best pass this on to the colonel: she'll no doubt bring her senior officers up to date ASAP. And then we go and see Cop."

"Agreed."

Copper was looking much livelier than the two had expected and was sipping some hot beverage when they rolled in shortly afterwards. She was hoping to be released in an hour or so, she told them. Whatever the knockout dart contained, it had left her no more than listless. Her back now matched her front, she told them ruefully. She had seen a scan of the area and it was burnt, but the damage was much less severe than phase-burn.

Linen looked her friend in the eye and gave a knowing smile. "Kit's been in and you two are happy bunnies again. Your face gives you away every time, Cop."

"He told me about Wale and the link to Jecks," Copper said to deflect any more teasing. "He said he and the colonel had grilled him but he wouldn't tell me the result of that."

"Colonel didn't tell us either," Trisk said. "But on another matter…"

As the two filled her in on what they had found, Copper's eyes set hard. "I wonder if that's why Spook was so wary of that pattern. He or his people in organic form have maybe suffered from it: they touch it, it sucks energy directly out of their tissues and causes acute surface, but not deep, damage. I wonder why?"

"Leaves them alive so it can use them again as a source of energy?" hazarded Trisk.

"That's obscene!" Linen exploded. "And there's no basis for that at all."

"Only a suggestion," Trisk said hurriedly. "But now we know we don't touch, if ever we see that pattern. Or in fact any piece of blue tech: it's not nice stuff. But our piece of hull in bay four – how much more do we do on that?"

"We've sent Ossy Inkscree's bots through it and got results but the box has got much more," Copper noted. "But that piece of hull has one advantage over a hard-holo ship…"

"Oh no you don't," Linen warned. "You do *not* use that box to try to force that piece of hull into a whole – we don't have enough organo-tech to do it in any case, even if we emptied every sample cartridge we have."

"We do have our own equivalent and that's the hull plating of the *Drake*," Copper argued. "We also have something else in bay four that's super-spec and was not retrofitted like the *Drake* was," she went on serenely, eyeing her friend meaningfully.

The subtle telepathy that the two shared rippled across the air gap separating them and Linen realised immediately what her friend meant. She gasped audibly.

"You cannot be serious! The colonel would never allow it for one. She'd have you locked up for even suggesting it, Copper

Milkstone! Absolutely no way! *I'd* have you locked in the brig if it was my call, before you had even got your thoughts in order."

"It's not your call, Lieutenant Lyrican," a voice at the entry to the bay said levelly. "And what is it that Lieutenant Milkstone cannot be serious about?"

"Timing, as ever," Copper muttered as the colonel stepped in and eyed the trio.

"I hear you're remarkably well for someone who was shot yestersol with a paralysing dart," Ms Moritz went on. "Now tell me why Lieutenant Lyrican is in such a flap."

Copper was discharged from medbay just after mid-sol and was borne off to the mess by her two colleagues, who were curious as to what the colonel had said to her in private. Linen and Trisk had been abruptly dismissed after the commanding officer had been apprised of what Copper proposed as a use for the lump of tech in outer bay four.

"Well, she didn't lock you in the brig," Linen observed. "But I bet she didn't agree with you, either."

"Not as such," Copper concurred. "But what she *did* say I wouldn't dare repeat in the mess. I'm not even sure I *can* tell you, though she didn't exactly say I couldn't. But I'll have to be quick as I have to see Jinn Limlite about my training schedule in less than an hour."

"Training! But you're just out of medbay! The doc will never approve it," Linen argued.

"Colonel's overruled him."

"What's going on, Cop?"

"Can't tell you here. We'd best get our lunch."

The three spent some break-time in calling up their personal comms as none of their colleagues seemed to want to come near them. Trisk put this down to fear that association with them attracted nothing but trouble. Linen was wryly amused to find a congratulatory note from Wolff Waterbone amongst her links, allied to a request for a copy of her pre-publication thesis, with all unpublished data and a short summary of her latest research.

"Cheek!" the redhead said. "He'll be able to call up a copy from the MDMC Acquisitions Informatics Bank or from the University of Mars research info-bank — all the LowColl data streams feed into that. He's just hoping for the uncut version and any extras he or his string-pullers can sink their teeth into.

He's a tad late anyhow: we've been doctored for sevensols. We never did see our overdue financial support from MDMC in any case, so why should I send him anything, even as a courtesy?"

"You should respond, to find out what he's up to," Copper told her. "MDMC evidently hasn't stopped digging and is very much interested in what the *Drake* and her mission is. I'd tell the colonel as well, on the QT, since I've had a similar request from our old chum Thulia. And a note from Mik Mack that MDMC has been harassing Thars for samples direct from the Warren."

"So they're having bad times back on Mars as well," Trisk put in. "But the colonel will be on top of that through her links to her old department. And there's naught we can do out here in the big empty."

After Copper's short visit to the personnel office up on level four, she made for her lab, where Linen and Trisk were sorting out their itineraries. Their next duty was one that they had been charged with some time ago and which had been relegated to the end of their task list by other, more important items. It was to start the analysis of the partial tri-dee sim of their target site of Lux Noctis, the body with which the *Griffon* had collided, and that had been constructed from the data amassed by the *Lithium Star*. The colonel had pressed them and had Ossy Inkscree remotely upload the data to the central ops unit in the tri-dee sim test facilities down in engineering, where the three could access it. Dr Inkscree and Lieutenant Halsen had had no time to do much with the simulation at present, as they had their hands full with their army of surf-sci bots, but would make full use of what their colleagues could come up with.

The target body they knew to be a large, ice-covered lump of mostly rocky material. The partial sim encompassed the areas where three impacts were believed to have had occurred in close proximity, including that of the *Griffon*. The three scientists were essentially tasked with analysing the sim of the crash sites to pinpoint search areas for a batch of Inkscree's bots and to scout for any clues as to what had pulled the *Griffon* and the other victims down onto the surface. The *Griffon* had not been large but she had been powerful and the colonel had no intention that the *Drake* fall victim to the same danger, if it still existed. As the *Lithium Star* had been able to scrape up samples and return home, it might be assumed that whatever had been operative at the time of the *Griffon's* demise was no longer so, but Colonel Moritz was taking no chances.

As soon as her friend reappeared, Linen had no hesitation in demanding the response of their commanding officer in relation to Copper's views on the use of the alien shard: the latter had in fact realised that as a piece of partly-functioning hull from an alien ship, it might be stimulated to regenerate into a whole, if sufficient material was available and the box utilised to facilitate it. The material she had in mind was the brand-new high-spec combat shuttle that had been delivered to the *Drake* from the auto-ship sent out from Mars and picked up at Jupiter. Linen had been partially correct in that the colonel would in no way sanction the misuse of her pristine shuttle for such a project, but having now seen the results of Copper's activities in the tri-dee facility, she was now more inclined to sanction restoration of the mass of alien tech in bay four into an approximation of its original. Sourcing suitable material was the main problem with that plan, for Colonel Moritz would not authorise the use of the *Drake's* limited supplies of spare hull plating.

The redhead was also intensely curious as to the appointment with the training officer, and was told to look out for a similar summons before long. Every officer with a recognised aptitude for flying would be required to put in more hours on simulators, as their commanding officer wanted every qualified person up to speed before the *Drake* reached her first objective. Copper had, however, been informed privately that she was to spend some of her drill time in the hard-holo of the small ship in the engineering sim suite.

"About which Jinn Limlite and his acolytes know nothing, I take it?" Linen demanded.

"Exactly. But I think Colonel Moritz and Dr Faerin had a bit of a disagreement about it," Copper admitted. "The doc has me down for more GHQ sims as well, or at least a couple of the advanced sims he puts his own guys through, Lor' knows why."

"Flight sims *and* health qualifications? The colonel has you earmarked for an away mission," Trisk said. "If we get to this minor planet in one piece and Ossy Inkscree's bots do okay, I'll bet she wants people on the surface, or at least doing fly-bys."

"Surface work will be fun," Copper said. "Gravity won't let us do more than stick to it for a start."

"The *Griffon* stuck to it and couldn't get off," Trisk observed dryly. "Something didn't want to let her go once they'd got her."

"Thanks for that. But we'd best start by having a look at this lump of rock we're supposed to be checking out once we get there. I'll have to pull down my holo-ship. I haven't operated it since I first tried it, and I want it complete, or as near as the box and the sim facility combined can get to full spec, as the colonel does want me to practice on it."

"And who'll be assigned to check up that you're not doing too much?" Linen enquired dangerously.

"I've to have a medi-tag fitted before I try another solo flight sim," Copper groaned. "I've just got rid of my last one, but Doc Faerin insisted. I'm not keen, as it means that any authorised person will be able to pinpoint my position at any time using the gear in medbay."

"Hah! Kit can do that from security," Linen said.

"There are a lot more authorised *and* unauthorised people in medbay," Copper retorted. "But at least it's not an implant, so I *will* be able to remove it."

"How useful," her friend grinned impishly. "Especially when you're off duty."

"Button it," she was told. "Another thing: security will drop off that tile that the colonel got at the market on Jupiter Station. She's had it locked away but wants me to have a closer look at it and see if I can pick anything else up. But I'd be grateful if you two were here when I did it."

"We wouldn't miss it," Trisk assured her. "When's it due?"

"Soon: it's to be handed to us directly, so maybe we'd better wait for it before we head to engineering. We've to log our time there anyway: no more spontaneous sorties, the colonel said."

"Wise woman," was Linen's view. "And it's your own damn fault. So who's to be with you when you next fly the little ship? It won't be one of the regular training officers, for sure, not even keeping a weather eye on your boards."

"I'm trusted to do it on my own, but I bet some alarm will go off if I overcook it. But it wouldn't hurt you to have a go, once I've figured it all out. You're a decent pilot."

"So's Kit, more than decent. And *he* knows about the holo-ship," the redhead declared.

"No," Copper said decidedly. "And he may not fit: the flight seat expands to accommodate the pilot, but there's a limit. I find it tight and the co-pilot's chair – or what I think is the co-pilot's chair – at back of me is the same."

"You don't want him to try it because it still takes a lot out of you and you think he'll put a stop to it," Linen noted shrewdly.

"No," Copper contradicted, not quite truthfully. "Because I still need Spook's help and Kit wouldn't have that – but you've got some affinity with Spook, so once I've figured most of it, you could gain at least a working knowledge."

Trisk was listening to the exchange and watching his friend carefully. "In case something happens to you, you mean."

Copper shrugged. "You got me. Some people out there don't like me and are trying to stop me; that's more than obvious. The colonel and senior officers are aware but what can they do?"

"And you're not scared?" Linen demanded.

"Of course I am. But I've got Spook."

"Someone at the door," Trisk noted as the buzzer sounded. "Tawny," he observed, tabbing the viewer. "It must be the tile. Come on in," he welcomed.

"Special delivery for the astrobio lab," Ms Brown proclaimed smilingly. "Which one of you wants it?"

"I'll take it," Linen announced swiftly. "It's wrapped up like a newborn," she observed. "It must be rare and precious. Want a caff, Tawny? We have the requisite facilities in our office."

"Can't, on duty," she said. "Good luck with whatever that is. I'll see you all later."

With that the security officer was gone. Linen smirked at Trisk. "Live wire," was all she said.

Copper sighed deeply. "You may as well unwrap it," she told her friend. "I can feel it from here, which is strange, as I can't see it and the colonel said she'd had it checked out and it's no more than a ceramic tile. I'd like to know who in hell the artisan was that produced it, though."

"Maybe it'll have a helpful holo-sticker," Linen suggested. "Spook here?"

"Spook's always here. So's Junior: he's come out of his closet and I can feel him round my neck, like a warm scarf. Just don't bring that thing too close, he may jump down my shirt."

"Seems to me you're getting more physical with these aliens. Better watch out, Kit will get jealous," the redhead said.

"Get on with it," was the only response.

As Linen unwound the layers of wrap, Copper could feel an itchy sensation at the back of her head that rose over her scalp, but she compelled herself to watch closely. The small blue tile would look typical among a group of the same, the twined lines of deep blue within and around the bordered pink diamond looking no more than an artist's fancy. But she felt there was a hidden meaning, if only she could grasp it. She tried to recall the other tiles that hung up the pole of the booth in the marketplace on level six at Jupiter Station, but they were a mix of colours.

"But all the same size," she said aloud.

"You what?" Linen demanded.

"The other tiles on that pole in the market: they were all the same shape and size, as if they were a set," she explicated. "But they were different patterns and colours, as far as I remember. Maybe the colonel should have bought the complete set: they might be a blueprint for something."

"Like a set of graphic warning plates?" Trisk suggested.

"That was the only one that caught your eye, so I doubt it," said Linen practically. "More likely a hidden message to the local bad guys: we're here, you've come to the right place. It might be their version of a password: if you're one of us, touch the plate and you can come in. If you're not, you get fried."

"You might not be a million clicks from the truth," Copper told her friend. "But I still don't like it and neither does Spook. And Junior's trying to be brave but he's doing the equivalent of peeping over my shoulder. I still think it's some sort of access button, but if you meet it, don't go there. Let me touch it."

"You think that's wise?" the redhead demanded.

"Colonel wants answers. This'll give her one," Copper said, reaching out with a probing forefinger.

The tile felt icy, icy cold, and a tingle ripped up Copper's finger to her wrist. She maintained her contact with the thing and her finger began to numb, the tingling sensation spreading slowly up her arm. She kept up a running commentary for the benefit of her friends and the recorder that was operational in the lab. Eventually, she pulled away, rubbing her affected right hand with her left.

"Interesting: I don't know if it's emotional, or Spook's had a hand in it or what," she said, flexing her fingers. "But there was a definite physical reaction. The feeling's ebbing away now, and I don't think there's any permanent effect, but it looks as if the image of this – thing – is now enough to trigger a reaction."

"Not for me," Linen said, picking up the tile and rubbing it. "You, Trisk?"

"Nothing," he said as he did the same. "You should repeat it when you're wearing your medi-tag and see what registers."

"Good plan. Well, we'd best head down to engineering and make a start on the partial tri-dee of that Lux Noctis rock that the *Griffon* and whatever else collided with. And I want to check my holo-ship: if I could fully complete her first, I'd be grateful."

"We'll help, but no fancy sim stuff," Linen warned. "Can we sit in as it's completing? It'll be a novel experience. I've never sat *in* a hard-holo while it's developing – usually you're at ops."

"We'd be sitting on each other's knees," Copper objected. "But if you insist..."

"We insist," Trisk interjected. "We'd like to know what you did and how you did it. I bet we didn't get the whole story last time we were down there."

The tri-dee facility on deck twenty had been logged out to them for the duration: the colonel had seen to that. It was still secure-tagged and none but the three, security personnel and the ship's most senior officers should be able to access it. It was as Copper recalled from her last visit, with the alien box positioned atop its auxiliary projector plate by the main ops station. The three locked the entry and called for lights. The almost complete ship was smaller than the *Drake's* shuttles. It hung suspended, its iridescent red-green hull taking up most of the operational space of the sim suite. Even in its quiescent state it glowed eerily in the dim light, the etched patterns on the smooth shell standing out clearly. It was shaped like a droplet of molten metal, with a rounded body tapering to a finer nose and it seemed to hover slightly above the deck. Its flattened underside implied that it could rest on a solid surface and the ragged edges at its larger end suggested that it was unfinished.

Copper quickly took a chair at the main ops station, pivoting back and forth as her swiftly moving hands called up the data she had stored earlier from her own instruments and made the linkage between the box and its associated projector plate. The activated energy transfer manifested as a pad of light between the plate and the box and the steady brightening of the green studs around the edge of the alien device. The three watched as the suspended holo began to pulse and the low-key sounds, as of a beast awakening, resonated across the chamber. As almost every regulator of the main ops station showed operational, the patterns on the glowing metallic hull began to shift, rippling and flowing and changing colour in rhythmic harmony as the sounds from the ship rose and fell.

"You're right, Cop," Linen breathed. "It *is* beautiful. It looks almost complete, but how do you get into it?"

"That's how I figure you need a mental as well as a physical link. I think there must be an operative entry plate, but I haven't worked that out. I just thought about wanting to get inside and the opening appeared and the ramp descended."

"I'm amazed you just stepped up," Trisk informed her. "I'd have freaked and then run, I think."

"Spook was there and it was okay," was the reply. "And he and Junior are with us now. It's up to full power, so let's try it."

She walked up to the teardrop-shaped hull of the ship and touched it lightly. In seconds an irised opening appeared and began to expand, swirling lines shooting away from the aperture. The ramp slowly slid out, and Copper made her easy way up the incline and into the body of the craft, the other two following more circumspectly. The inside space *was* tight, they noticed, but it did not resemble the interior of any shuttle they had ever seen. The command seat was set-in towards the tapered nose of the vessel and seemed to be a pod into which the pilot slid sideways, to face a semi-circular control bank. There was a similar, wider seat behind: *that* had no apparent flight controls, but it did have monitors and auxiliary side consoles. The inside surface of the craft consisted of what resembled interlocking hexagonal plates; projecting bulges at intervals suggested storage or auxiliary ops.

Overhead, similar bulges protruded into the space. The deck underfoot was a seamless pale green. The aft section was wider and higher than the fore and mid sections and was sealed by a flat bulkhead. There were no apertures through which the externals of the ship could be seen.

As Copper slid into the front seat, it wrapped around her to enclose her and a panel materialised within what seemed to be a viewing grid set into what would have been the forward flight window in a usual shuttle or fighter. An openwork circlet, lights chasing each other through its tracery of filaments, slid out of an overhead compartment and hovered above her. As she pulled it down to hang just above her head, Linen looked at Trisk, raised her eyebrows in a searching glance and slid into the seat behind. Trisk squeezed in beside her and both examined the console in front them as a smooth panel slid across to shut them in.

"You'd have to be good friends," Linen observed. "Next time we wear flight fatigues, they take up less room. Not much overhead space either. You're right, Cop: Kit would find this a tight fit. But I expect it would stretch to fit him. I note that you have adequate overhead space and can move your arms quite freely. No windows though."

"Want a window?" was the response as Copper manipulated some control and the bulkhead to Linen's right cleared.

"Hey, I can see the sim suite!"

Trisk was tapping a view-grid and playing with a series of softly glowing buttons that had materialised on the console in front of him and was ordered peremptorily to quit.

"So how do you run a flight sim?" he asked as he complied.

"This is the tricky bit," Copper admitted. "This is a hard-holo and I think I set it up as a ship in sim mode; it does *feel* as if you're in a sim and going nowhere, but it's more reactive than any sim I've tried before: if you do something stupid, you really feel it. It does respond to the controls but as I don't have the trick of them all yet, I have problems. But it also responds to mentally projected commands I think, maybe via this overhead net thing, unless it's Spook taking over when I go that route. I'm not sure, really. But make sure you're tied in, you'll need to be."

The two behind her soon found that she was not joking for a juddering as of take-off at speed had them thrust back into their seats and gasping. The next half hour was a dizzying excursion through what seemed to be a well-populated planetary system with numerous satellites that concealed more than a few nasty surprises, including some form of tractor beam that pulled them in until the ship's seams creaked, hostile vessels spewing fire and barrages of high-spec weaponry aimed in their direction. The ship wove and ducked, or seemed to, and the external details were relayed as tri-dee holos on the view-grids in front of and to the side of the ship's occupants.

As the sim slowed to a halt, Linen eased upwards with a deep sigh. "That was one of the roughest rides I've had in a while. Were you really in control of all that dodging and diving?"

"Most of it, though I think I had some help from the auto controls. But it was better than last time: I actually blacked out in one manoeuvre I tried," Copper confessed as she shut down. "But at least I found out that if *that* happens, the ship responds by initiating auto-mode and finishes the sim, so *it* must monitor the pilot and realise when he or she is unresponsive."

"Will the real version of this ship do that in actual flight and get the pilot out of trouble?" asked Trisk.

"I guess so," Copper said slowly. "If the colonel would only let me try to rebuild what we have in bay four..."

"Don't even go there," Linen warned. "You're supposed to have your medi-tag on while you're in here, aren't you?"

"That's my next stop: there's a reminder from Dr Faerin on my wrist-comm. But how do you like my ship?"

"*Your* ship? Since when?" demanded her redheaded friend.

"Since I went to the trouble of making the hard-holo. Once I do get a fully functional version set up, that'll be my ship too."

"Hah! That depends where you get the materials: if they're official then it's Mars Fleet's ship. Besides which, how in blazes will you be able to duplicate all the strange organo-controls and gizmos that allow mental manipulation, or whatever you call it, to operate such a ship? There's no way any of our technology would be able to reproduce that."

"I've been thinking of that," Copper said as she unstrapped herself from her pod seat and began to slide out. "Remember the asteroid Helixus, the one the *Fearless* was sent to investigate? Twelve percent of it was blasted out and filled with alien tech in which MDMC had a deep interest. And there was Elara with its base station or whatever full of dangerous weaponry – which of course suggests novel tech. They're now under military authority and the asteroid's being investigated by a Fleet science ship, as I expect Elara is. We got some data from them, but we didn't get the chance to probe deeply and carry out full analyses. But the existence of those bases implies similar out here somewhere."

"If you think we're going to find another, the chances are pretty slim," Trisk pointed out as he worked himself free of his seat. "Space is a big place after all. Not only that, even if we did – and believe me, I'm keeping a good lookout and so, I found out, is Doc Inkscree – do you *really* think the colonel would give you free rein just to hop down and scavenge what you wanted?"

"Maybe if I asked nicely," Copper said, grinning. "I wonder if the colonel ever got the results of what *was* found out about Helixus or the stuff on Elara."

"You can ask next time she joins us for dinner," Linen told her, following the other two out of the opening. "Meanwhile, I want to see what bruises your antics have landed me with. And we're here to have a look at our target rock and pick out a nice landing spot, aren't we?"

"We're here to analyse the *Lithium Star's* partial sim of it so that we can pull out the best areas for Ossy and Lyssa to drop their bots," Trisk reproved as the three hopped off the ramp. "The sim covers those crash site areas where the *Lithstar* picked up their samples, including the bits we got. We also have to search for clues as to what pulled the *Griffon* and the others in, if that *is* what happened."

"Which means pick out a landing spot," Linen argued. "You really think we'd come all this way, take a peek with a bunch of Ossy Inkscree's bots and then beat a retreat?"

"Depends what happens when we *do* take a peek with those damnable bots," Copper said. "I remember the fun we had with them down the Warren – they set off on their own little sorties and did their own thing and we had one helluva time trying to persuade them otherwise."

"First things first," Trisk interrupted firmly. "Copper, you take down your holo-ship, whether or not it's complete. Linen, you're with me. We'll start setting up the *Lithstar's* sim: it should be in the system."

* * *

Half an hour's hard graft resulted in a marked change to their surroundings. As the size of the facility was limited, only a part of the sim could be examined at any one time. The three gazed in some awe at their first sight of part of the minor planet that was their destination. Lux Noctis glinted in the dim light they had set up to view it, an icy coat over what the *Lithium Star* had reported as a rocky body. The surface was scored and pitted with craters and strewn with lumps and chunks of scree.

"Maybe the first victim originally tried to drop in to pick up fresh water," Copper grated. "If that *is* water ice, then there's a lot of it. Spook's people in organic form would need water, as would other aliens, I guess, or alien life as we imagine it."

"It's possible there may be liquid water down there," Trisk put in. "Internal heating by radioactive decay: it exists on some of the outer moons of the larger planets, but I guess you'd need to drill down. We must check the *Lithstar's* data to see what they recorded as they should have been able to pick it up."

"Doesn't explain why the ships were pulled in. Someone got there first, realised it was a handy place to have this far out for one reason or another, and set a booby-trap to keep their hold," was Linen's contribution. "But as the *Lithstar* got close enough that their science officers could drop a pod with the gear aboard to core, scrape, sort and store and they weren't harmed, what caused the earlier trouble must have left or been damaged or destroyed way before they got there."

"Or something that made it down but couldn't get back up deactivated the trap in the hopes of rescue?" Copper posited.

"Oh hell! Junior's people, maybe?" Linen asked

"Who knows? Worked in a way if that's what happened. We got Junior out of it. Though he's not happy about *that*." Copper indicated the part-sim of the cold, hard landscape that gleamed in the half-light. "But the debris found near some rocky bodies out at the edge by the *Wayfinder* on her mapping mission," she went on. "The colonel, or Major Moritz as she was then, figured it contained alien tech that was more recent than the stuff that had been dug up on Mars, and thus could mean big trouble. The *Lithium Star* was sent into the area and they found similar on this rock but stuck to bits of the *Griffon*, as were pieces of the blue tech that we think may once have belonged to aliens that are not as nice. But how long before the *Griffon* did the first alien ship or ships crash: years, decades, centuries? Or did one of the two deliberately or accidentally take out the *Griffon* and meet the same fate? I remember the unpleasant Colonel Karben telling us once that an alien ship did not take out the *Griffon*, but was she sure, or just annoyed at us because we guessed at some of MI's secrets?" she demanded of Linen.

"You got me. She was vexed at us, that was for sure."

"And if there *are* two alien ships, which I admit was my idea, and Spook's I think," Copper went on, "Is it remotely possible that whatever was the source of the blue replicative tech still has some life in it – like Spook?"

"Frock, you really think that could be the case?" the redhead whistled. "But look at that mess: it's a crash site all right. How clear can we get the holo? It looks like a quick job with little detail to me."

"I agree," Trisk said. "Though we have the scans the *Lithium Star's* science pod got as she went in. They should be part of the mix that Dr Inkscree linked through. I'll see if I can refine this section of the holo."

The details were a little clearer but the three realised that they would have a painstaking task going over the multiple crash site to find the optimum spot for the first sortie of Inkscree's army of surf-sci bots. It was as they were scanning outwards towards an area that had a reddish tint that they realised that the colour was the result of a large deposit of the red-green alien tech with which they were by now familiar. It was near the edge of the sim and at a distance from the site that the *Lithium Star* had sampled.

"Chunk of hull blown off one of the crashed ships and got stuck under that overhang?" Trisk posited, rotating the sector of holo. "It was maybe protected a bit and stayed in one piece."

Slowly Copper shook her head. "No. Spook's ship down in the Warren was put there intentionally and deliberately buried in the substrate – *I* think it was later seismic activity that released it enough that it was found."

"Are you saying that this could be similar?" Linen demanded. "They couldn't get off the rock, so they dug in?"

"I can't get a clearer image," Trisk grumbled. "But that does *not* look intact to me. And it's too small to be a ship."

"Unless it's a fighter or a shuttle," Copper remarked.

"It's small, whatever it is," Linen put in. "What's Spook got to say about it?"

Her friend's brow contracted in concentration as she stared closely at the hard-holo image. "Or an escape craft," she said finally. "Room for three, only two didn't make it?"

"No, it can't be," the redhead argued. "That's definitely red and reads like alien tech, but why is it so clear? And how would it have lasted this long frozen in space? There must have been random impacts even since the time the *Griffon* crashed."

"Out there, where there's nary a thing in local space? And that's a small target," Copper contended. "But that might be a logical starting point for Doc Inkscree's bots: that overhang may lead down into a fissure or similar, though it's not clear. Do we have more data on the sim that might equate to blue alien tech?" she asked Trisk. "We have comparatives in our data but I doubt the *Lithstar* would have had. It would make sense to send the bots into a relatively safe area first – if there *is* blue tech and any of it's been activated since the *Lithstar* went in, we don't want it compromising the bots."

"How?" demanded Linen.

"No idea, but if *we* can produce our own examples of alien tools based on fragments and some know how…"

"*And* a lot of friendly alien assistance," Trisk butted in.

"Granted, but we don't want to expose our bots to pointless risk if something else that's way in advance of us can do the same. Spook *can* interact physically with tech: if anything similar to him but spiteful is down there…"

"Which it wouldn't be now," Linen said practically. "Spook turned off that tractor that was pulling the *Lithstar* into Elara; it makes sense, doesn't it, that Junior's people could do the same? They must have arrived after the *Griffon*, got caught, deactivated the traps but couldn't save themselves as their ship had been too badly damaged."

"How far can Spook's people travel in non-organic form?" Trisk demanded. "And can they travel in space?"

Copper shook her head and shrugged. "Don't know. Spook

could travel back to his ship out at the Warren from Lowell, I'm sure, and he left the *Drake* to protect us and help the *Lithstar*, but he must have a way of replenishing his energy and could he do that in open space? But if Junior's people got to the edge after the *Griffon*, then they're way more advanced than Spook, even if they are the same people…"

"Might have been in space a long time," Linen disagreed. "It *was* the differences in tech from the original stuff on Mars that first gave MI and others the clue that it *was* the original Martians come back, but those differences didn't signpost technological developments that millennia would be expected to produce."

"Lots of good points," Copper conceded. "Let's get what we can out of this and wrap up, I need to get to medbay. Who tells Ossy Inkscree that we suggest he starts his bots off here because we think there's the chance that an alien escape pod's half-buried in the rockery?"

"That's your idea and you can't substantiate it," Trisk told her. "You tell the colonel and she tells Dr Inkscree what she feels he should know."

"If I was Doc Inkscree and I only got half a story, I'd be pissed," she responded dryly.

* * *

Copper's next stop was medbay and the acquisition of the medi-tag to monitor her health. Faerin set it up and menaced her with dire penalties if she removed it whilst on duty. Once free, she made for the lab, having agreed with her friends that they would examine the blue tile again before the evening meal.

Linen had the thing unwrapped. Copper knew as soon as she stepped through the door by the prickling of her scalp, but she continued her progress and halted by the bench, looking down at it. She paused before extending a tentative hand, curling her fingers back, reluctant to touch the icy cold surface.

"Hell, I really don't want to touch it," she said, tight-lipped. "But here goes…"

The freezing tingle that shot up her single finger to her wrist and up her arm caused her to curse volubly, cringing. She forced herself nonetheless to continue contact, ignoring the numbness that was now almost at her shoulder. It was a buzz at the comm station that caused the three to turn and Copper to release her contact with the tile.

"Five minutes out of my sight and she's at it again!" Faerin's furious tones rang out. "What's she been at this time?"

"What has the tag registered?" Trisk demanded practically.

He was left unanswered as the doctor demanded details, but Faerin was puzzled as to the cause of the reactions, which had presented as increased heartrate and sweating, an adrenalin rush and muscle contractions.

"Spook: it has to be," Linen said calmly. "You're displaying what *his* reaction would have been in solid form to a real piece of the blue stuff. You need to cut that link to him Cop, or he'll take over your entire life."

"It's not Spook," Copper said wearily. "It's Junior. He's now trying to protect me from what he thinks is trouble, which leads me to suspect he's been in contact with a genuine article before and knows what it does."

"Which means we should *not* take the samples of blue tech we have into the tri-dee suite and try to build them up into what might be a coherent piece of kit," Trisk advised.

"We've enough to do down there anyway," Linen agreed. "We need to report our assessments of our target site and *you've* been ordered to use the tri-dee for flight sims," she reminded Copper. "But now it's dinnertime. See you in the mess, Doc?"

"In a while: some of us have work to do," was the reply as Faerin linked off.

* * *

The next twelve sols were spent by the three science officers in refining their readings of the rocky body that was the *Drake's* ever-closing endpoint and in setting up potential sorties for Dr Inkscree's army of bots. They found their time intruded upon by training sessions and Copper at least suspected that the additional stints of bridge duty in her schedule had been ordered by the colonel to keep her from spending too much time in solo flight sims. The more she handled the now-complete hard-holo of the small alien craft, the more she became convinced that it was a fighter rather than a scout. On one lone foray along deck twenty, she had just reached the entry to the tri-dee suite when a familiar voice at her back bid her halt.

"You wouldn't be thinking of a solo in that mysterious ship of yours would you?"

"I thought you had fighter drill," she responded. "And how do you figure *I'm* headed for a flight sim?"

"You're wearing a flight-suit, you're logged in, but you're not in the deck thirteen suite," Kit told her, his blue eyes twinkling.

"You got me. The colonel wants me to get in more hours on my ship, so I'm here – and I have that damned medi-tag that Kynedd Faerin insisted I wear, so no sweat."

"*Your* ship?" he teased. "But you're pulling more hours than you have to. I know you were on the dark o'clock bridge watch last night, but I haven't seen you since breakfast and that was in the company of fifty other people. Care to show me what your little boat can do?"

"And then what?" Copper demanded.

"Oh, we'll think of something," he grinned down at her.

"What about your sim?"

"It can wait. Let's go."

Kit was impressed with the complete holo and surprised at the detail that Copper had been able to replicate within it. He found the secondary piloting space restricted, but not as much as he had expected from her description. He put this down to her reluctance to allow him aboard lest he realised that she was doing more than approved. He asked her bluntly if such was the case as he settled securely into the space that eased to fit him, examining the console that had emerged in front of him.

"You've been talking to Linen," was her only response as she deftly pulled down the filamentous circlet above her and set her boards, her hands moving smoothly over controls that seemed to mould to her fingers as the holo in her grid spun to show a starlit backdrop. "Tie yourself in," she added.

Copper ran a sim with which she was familiar and was one of the less taxing runs. As an experienced pilot and having flown various fighter designs, Kit was well aware that she was holding back, despite the abrupt take-off and sharp manoeuvring that had him slewing sideways in his seat. The details relayed on the view-grids around him were striking as the ship seemed to skim over a rugged frozen landscape, skirting steep-walled gullies and avoiding sheer cliffs at hair-raising speeds, but these were classic strategies that any instructor would set. The only dangers that seemed to have been coded were random explosions of geysers from the surface, for which the ship could compensate. As the pressure eased and the programme ended with a soft landing, Copper turned to gauge her companion's reaction.

Kit was nettled. "What was that supposed to be, a tourist trip to some ice resort? You could do that sort of flight in your sleep and so could I."

"So what do you want to see?" she retorted sharply.

"Run the last solo you did in this crate," he challenged her.

Her slight shake of the head gave her away and Kit persisted. "Run it. I'm not moving until you do."

Realising she would not be allowed off lightly, Copper turned back to her boards and called up a battle simulation that she had set using data from the *Drake's* encounters at Helixus and Elara. She had also sought input from Spook and the result was the capture of the ship in a tractor beam that pulled her off course and targeting by pulsed energy salvos that buffeted the hull in a series of jolts and caused the occupants to be assaulted by ear-piercing soundwaves and tossed about like ragdolls. Their first mission was to destroy the attack sources whilst retaining hull integrity. This involved such complex manoeuvring and turns of speed that Copper had lost consciousness for a few seconds on her last solo sim; she had received a sharp reprimand from Dr Faerin, who had been alerted by her medi-tag. This time she set Kit to auxiliary weapons support in the hopes that his assistance would make a difference, but the tactics she was forced to use to outfight her attackers were such that she again passed out. The final offensive by a trio of hostile fighters she tackled using knowledge she had gained from that first run and she brought the sim to an end by crash-landing safely on a small moon.

Once she had closed her view-grids and locked her controls down she twisted round to view her co-pilot. "Happy now?" she demanded.

"Out, now," was the grim response as Kit jerked his thumb towards the exit.

The two unsealed their seating units and slid out, Copper leading the way in silence. She could feel Kit's heavy breathing behind her and realised that he was as exhausted and drained as she was. She reached the bottom of the ramp first and turned to face the admonition she was expecting. He stood, arms folded, looking down at her, but his lips were twitching and the stern expression gave way to a wry smile.

"You are one helluva pilot," he acknowledged. "Come and give me a hug. And if you put me through that again, I'll have you hauled up on report for assaulting a fellow officer."

"Promises, promises," she murmured as she complied.

The two had secured the tri-dee facility and were heading out of engineering when a high-pitched siren began to sound and a flashing line of red light shot along the bulkheads. Seconds later a voice called out that it was no drill. With a startled glance at one another, Copper and Kit raced for the nearest elevator, the pounding feet of fellow crewmen heading for their own duty stations sounding in their ears. Kit had just called for deck five when Copper's wrist-comm buzzed and an urgent voice ordered her to the bridge. She acknowledged directly: she had recognised Colonel Moritz.

"Hell, I'm still in flight fatigues!"

"No-one will notice, believe me," Kit told her. "Be careful," he admonished as he gave her a quick kiss before jumping out at his own destination of deck three.

The bridge was humming when Copper arrived and reported in, excusing her appearance. She was ordered to the secondary science station alongside the chief SO, who was already there.

"What gives?" she asked as she locked in her ident and began to bring her console to life, assuming control of every science sensor array under her authority.

"Distress call," Inkscree replied shortly. "We've confirmed we're on our way. Get your station up to speed and set every external sensor to long-range scan."

"Aye, sir."

Comms had put the call on speaker and the crackling voice calling for aid rang out again. "*MSS Sapphire Sunset* to all ships in the area, we are under attack, repeat we are under attack."

29: SAPPHIRE SUNSET

In the split second it took her to comprehend the nature of the crisis and its victim, Copper realised why she had been called to the bridge. As she quickly brought her long-range sensors into line and began to scan ahead, she recalled an exchange with the colonel on the subject of the *Sapphire Sunset*. It had been on her first spell of bridge duty, after her report on the alien repair of a sample tube from the *Lithium Star* and her niggling feeling that an alien had somehow survived whatever had brought its ship down. Copper had posited then that the *Sunset*, with her faster than light drive, was heading out to the edge to search for alien artefacts over a large area. Colonel Moritz had not disputed it, or the idea that the *Sunset* was tasked with the drop-off of scores of surf-sci bots for short-range exploration. And now the ship was in trouble and she was carrying a large crew complement.

With her systems on line, Copper began a systematic search for the distressed ship's ion trail. She soon had it pinpointed and called it out as various reports from other bridge stations were being relayed. The crackle of comms as the *Sapphire Sunset* linked over her sensory data added to the tension that sparked the *Drake's* crew. A shockwave that seemed to stem from the large mass she was orbiting had slammed into the ship and knocked her off course; before she could recover she had grazed a tiny satellite of the body and had spun off at a tangent. She had hardly had time to stabilise when high-energy pulses from some sort of phase-beam weapon had been directed at her from the planetoid, which she had still been probing at the time.

"No tractor, but the tactics are familiar," the colonel noted as she perused her board for the input from her science stations. "Science and tactical, maintain scans and get me comparison readouts: I want to know if those beams are similar to those that hit the *Fearless* and the *Lithium Star*. Weapons stations, prepare long-range torpedoes for deployment; all defensive systems on line; helm, increase speed. And Number One, ready fighters: I don't want to use them but have the pilots stand by."

"Affirmative, ma'am," Helmis answered.

"*Sapphire Sunset's* holding her own," the tactical officer stated. "Pulses from surface are erratic and she's trying to get some distance from the source, but her main engines are crippled."

"Which means they were targeted," Copper frowned, mind whirring as she tried to take in the implications.

Ossy Inkscree to her right gave her more food for thought. "I'm picking up more than a trace of organo-tech in the local area," he announced. "Correlating: it's similar to the stuff we've met before, but that's not what's causing the trouble – it's too thinly spread."

"Let's see the data from the *Sunset's* science stations," Copper responded, something tugging at her brain. "*They* were detecting signals beneath the surface that equate to replicative and very durable organo-tech similar to the stuff on Helixus and Elara. The comp of the planetoid itself matches those bodies, but the *Sunset* didn't probe for internal structures. Let's check pulse-fire signatures… they match as well. Vespoltz, did the *Sunset* return fire?" she demanded of the tactical officer on her left.

"They tried," the lieutenant responded. "No effect."

"*No* effect?" Copper repeated. "Now that's strange."

"Why?" Inkscree wanted to know as the colonel strode over to examine the readouts and quiz her science officers.

"The *Fearless* returned fire; that triggered a heavier salvo from that structure on the asteroid they were trying to scavenge. Both she and the *Lithstar* were caught by restraining beams and shot at. But the *Sunset* wasn't pulled off course by a tractor. But if this *is* a station like the one on Elara, and it reads like one, it *should* have been updated…" she went on, puzzled.

"Here we are again," Colonel Moritz noted at her elbow. "Are you assuming that this body is part of that ancient alien defence system alerted because of increased sentient activity?"

"The data point to it, ma'am. If the *Sunset* had scanned for schematics it would have helped, though I see there's a note that she deployed surface gear. But the reaction to the *Sunset's* arrival is weak and *erratic*, as if something is interfering with its activity."

"You figured last time that when one of these bases was probed it scanned the intruder to work out how to disable it, launched an attack and then alerted its linked systems so they'd all recognise similar threats and know how to deal with them," Inkscree said to Copper. "Looks like their comms network's not working, if this *is* part of that network and not a rival one."

"That's not what's worrying me," she replied, looking at the colonel. "The *Lithstar* was finally scanned to obtain a standard ship's spec to avoid attack was my interpretation. The *Sapphire Sunset's* been hit but not taken down and the assault's irregular and weak – as if there's more than one force at work here."

The colonel's brow contracted as she scanned both the data and her science officer. "What are you saying?"

"Ancient tech, once shielded but since then breached and now under the influence of opposing factors?" guessed Copper. "Let's see: have we got definitive on the type of organo-tech the *Sunset* picked up? They must have all we know about the tech to date so they should have… let's split this out."

"What in hell are you doing, Milkstone?" demanded Inkscree as an updated report from the *Sapphire Sunset* rang out that the high-energy pulses were slowing.

A small hiss escaped Copper's pursed lips as she invited the chief SO to examine the data she had pulled up. "There's more than one type of organo-tech here, as we've found in the past. But *these* readings equate to more than a trace of the blue tech we've seen before and that means trouble. I'll get confirmation: we've got some in the lab. But remember what happened to the *Griffon*, or what you thought happened to her, ma'am: you told me and Linen that she was trying to get samples from an object that had crashed and the consensus was that either her systems failed and she went down or she was pulled in by a protective or destructive mechanism that was active. And some of the blue tech was found among the wreckage at *that* site and picked up by the *Lithstar*, which is why we have it now."

"Are you suggesting that this *is* one of these ancient bases and it's being undermined by some destructive elements?" the colonel asked.

"That's one interpretation, ma'am. The *Sunset* has picked up traces of hostile tech here, which we didn't read at either Elara or Helixus. If some sort of enemy, possibly a ship, arrived at the site in the past and tried to take out or subvert the base, it would have met resistance. This might be the result: deadlock until something happens, such as a data update. Or a ship shows and that provokes action. In fact, the same may have happened at our target: *that* may have once been a base that was attacked..."

"Conjecture," the colonel said, shaking her head. "Get what you can as we advance. If the attack on the *Sunset* is falling off, there's something active going on down there."

"Aye, ma'am."

Copper had just turned back to her console when Lieutenant Marco Vespoltz at tactical called out that another vessel had just popped up on his grid, and indeed comms confirmed a message incoming. The colonel was immediately on the alert.

"There's no other Mars Fleet ship in this area," she said to Captain Helmis. "Who are they?"

"This is the *EFS Dexterity* to *MSS Drake II*. We picked up the distress call from the *Sapphire Sunset*. Do you require assistance at this time?"

"An Earth Fleet ship? What's *she* doing out here?" muttered Helmis, tabbing his board to draw up pertinent information.

"The same as we are, but there's only one way to find out," the colonel told him as she resumed her seat. "This is *MSS Drake II*, Colonel Elle Moritz in command. What brings you into this neck of the system, *Dexterity*?"

The *EFS Dexterity*, part of the Earth explorer fleet and under the authority of a Captain Jed Ketter, was on a resources search mission, apparently. She was an older design of ship and far less advanced than the *Drake* but had some system akin to an FTL drive. Helmis had pulled up the data that she had recently been refitted and assigned on a classified mission, but as most Earth Fleet operations were listed thus it was no surprise. Ketter had heard of the *Drake*, and being an old hand was sufficiently savvy to know that a ship of her size and class was on more than a shakedown cruise. He was also honest enough to remark that the upsurge in unknown comms activity causing head-scratching amongst upper Fleet echelons was probably one of the reasons for increases to both Earth and Mars Fleet missions far from home. There were other Earth ships out this far, he told the colonel, but none close enough to render aid.

Colonel Moritz was cautious and knew that the situation into which she had committed her ship might spawn a few surprises; she thus accepted the offer of support on the proviso that the *Dexterity* stay in reserve until the *Drake* had evaluated current conditions. She also directed tactical to transmit the *Sunset's* data on the attack to their opposite numbers aboard the Earth ship.

The stricken Mars ship had in the interim reported a definite easing of the assault and had now been able to draw back from the source to a position where she could hold a high orbit. She had dropped off gear that she needed to retrieve, however, and intended to hold station.

"Surf-sci bots on exploratory, I bet," Copper muttered in an aside to Inkscree. "Hope she didn't send recon in after them."

Some swift manipulation and reconfiguration of her console confirmed her suspicions. "There must be at least five hundred of them in that nest! The ops system down there must have let bot-drop occur before targeting the *Sunset*. That was smart: see what they're doing, let them release their tech and then attack. That indicates intelligence. Hope it's not highly sentient: it might capture the nest of bots, reprogramme them maliciously and let them be rescued."

"You have one lurid imagination, Dr Milkstone! Just get on with your scans and let me know the second something shows that you don't like the look of," her chief retorted irritably.

The colonel was scanning her bridge stations' readouts and had caught part of the exchange. Once in possession of the gist of Copper's opinions, she looked askance at her officer.

"Once we're in full range, check it out *thoroughly*," she told her meaningfully. "Have Dr Addystone monitor the output of his lifeform probe from his lab station and if anything shows I want it called up here immediately. It's linked to every external scanning relay we have so he'll have his hands full. Dr Lyrican can assist."

"Aye, ma'am."

"Meanwhile, keep your long-distance scanners on that area of space; you too, tactical. I want to know what in hell's going on. I can't imagine the hostiles are running out of ammunition and have slowed their assault on that basis."

As the distance to the *Sapphire Sunset's* position decreased, the *Drake* was able to garner more data on the area of space into which they were headed. There had been no reports prior to the *Sunset* of any detailed survey, at least by Mars Fleet ships, but the evidence had been sufficient that the explorer ship had been refitted to a high spec and given her mission. She had been on the trail of increasing traces of suspected alien tech when she reached the planetoid that had launched the shockwave. As Inkscree had noted, the local area was thinly populated with signals of the types of organo-tech that had been encountered on Mars and out near the edge.

"Why send us and the *Sunset* out?" Copper asked the chief SO. "I realise her mission is broader and she doesn't have the means to put up a fight if she runs into serious trouble, but..."

"She's surveying a very large area and mapping what she finds in high detail, hence the payload of surf-sci bots, though hers are standardised. She's bringing samples aboard to analyse en route and transmit the data back home. She can send out manned or unmanned recon craft if she hits a high density region with a lot to investigate. And much of her storage space is taken up by gear that's to be dropped off for future missions, if suitable locations are found. She has a large crew yes, but her payload is enormous."

"Establishing a foothold in deep space to show whatever's out there that we have first dibs?" Copper asked shrewdly. "Fleet's seriously worried by the prospect of alien infiltration then, and so's Earth Fleet, given the presence of the *Dexterity*."

"Just keep your eyes on your boards," she was ordered.

* * *

Captain Leroy Fantodd of the *MSS Sapphire Sunset* was more than relieved by the advent of two ships off his bows. With damage to his main engines he needed assistance to get back on an even keel before he could head for the nearest outpost where his ship could be fully overhauled. He had ordered his teams to monitor the conditions on the rocky body, designated Blink 159, around which they orbited and the source of the shockwave had been pinpointed to an underground locus. The captain had the records transferred to the assisting ships and Copper aboard the

Drake was quick to analyse the data streaming into her station and add it to the readings her own arrays were picking up.

"Okay, hotshot," Ossy Inkscree demanded. "What do you make of it?"

"Surprise, surprise," she responded ironically. "Silico-carbon substrate, other typical minerals and water ice; I sense a pattern emerging yet again. And look what in-depth scanning shows: the definite presence of organics fused to the bedrock below surface in a regular pattern. A partly-shielded installation and synthetics are confirmed as the types of organo-tech we're familiar with – and some we're not," she added. "It's another of those outposts, I'm sure."

"What have you found, Lieutenant?" the colonel demanded as she stepped over.

"Red-green tech, replicative and non-replicative, that we have experience of; some other inclusions reading as organo-tech that I've not come across before; and definite and fairly significant amounts of the blue tech, samples of which we have in the lab."

"Define fairly significant," Inkscree instructed.

"Approximately point three percent of the whole, and that's a lot – certainly enough to undermine the other tech there, as there are higher levels at the source of the shockwave and close to the sources of hostile fire, as far as I can make out."

"Confirmed," the chief SO acknowledged.

"I see," Colonel Moritz mused. "I want verification that it *is* hostile tech down there and I'd like to know its extent and its capabilities. As I've no intention of provoking a hostile response by trying to take anything out, I also want your suggestions on what we do about it."

"Aye, ma'am," Copper agreed, although she was thinking that what *she* wanted was to sleep for a sevensol. "I'll try to locate the control centres – we can maybe send down an armed probe to disable?"

"Which would potentially leave friendly elements defenceless – no, that's not an option. I'm sure you'll think of something."

"Aye, ma'am." Copper knew that the colonel meant that Spook should be sent in to investigate.

As the commanding officer returned to her post to deal with the exchanges of information coming in from both the *Sapphire*

Sunset and the *Dexterity*, both science officers applied themselves to their tasks, homing in on the concentrations of structures that they could now clearly pick up using their own arrays.

"These regular nodes are probably control centres," Copper said as she pointed to the holo. "Just as we figured for Helixus and Elara: local high-energy hot spots linked to channels that are lined with deep depressions, all semi-organic and forming a maze of interconnected systems within the structures we see in this area here. And the lot occupies a fair chunk of planetoid. The whole set-up is bigger than the versions on Helixus and Elara, so maybe this is a bigger and more important base?"

She in fact knew that the nodes were centres for controlling the systems, as Spook had implied as much in the images he was invoking in her mind. She also knew that Spook was reluctant to make a sortie into a place where high levels of matter dangerous to his own people and to some humans was located. In thought, she recalled the sensations of being burned by her close contact to the tech, but her perceptions were heightened and she was seeing the effects of prolonged contact with the stuff. It was not pretty: she had a split-second image of her blackened and burnt skin after the fight on Jupiter Station that expanded to take in much of her whole body. It was enough to make her give a small gasp as the answer to a puzzle that had long eluded her was suddenly clear.

"What?" Inkscree demanded.

"Nothing," she rejoined, but could not stop her face creasing in impulsive sorrow and sympathy, realising at last why Spook had never let her see his organic form: he had been so badly burned by contact with the blue alien tech before he had merged with the life support unit aboard his ship that he feared she would be repulsed by his appearance.

"As if," she grieved internally as she automatically scanned her boards and tried to bring her mind back to the task with which she had been entrusted, knowing that her alien friend was trying to tell her something else that she was missing.

The alien early-warning cum defence complex *was* similar to those on Helixus and Elara and one of the series of connected posts she reckoned had been used by Spook's people as they moved into the Sol system millennia before. It seemed that they were all now waking up but something else had got to this one and was undermining its operation. The questions were who and when. She knew that Spook considered the culprits to be the entities that had driven his people off Mars in the distant past, or newer variants of the same. The original sub-surface organo-structures were composed of the earlier version of tech familiar to Copper, but other, more recent inclusions, similar to pieces that had been recovered by both the *Wayfinder* and the *Lithium Star*, were also present, which suggested more recent incursions by some species akin to Spook's original people.

Copper voiced her notion to Inkscree that the later tech was some sort of upgrade to the station that had been deployed remotely or installed by a ship that had made it off-planet: there was no sign of disturbance such as a crashed vessel that the *Sapphire Sunset* had picked up on her orbits of the body. It was logical to assume that those responsible for the hostile tech had thus arrived after the upgrading of the station. They had not stayed to check the results, Copper posited, suggesting that the station was quiescent at that time. When the station became operational, something had stirred and tried to destabilise the original systems. But the length of time that the blue tech had been down there was a serious issue: if those responsible were still around, it boded serious trouble for the local sentients. And as the reason for the *Drake's*, and other ships' presence out on the edge was the present substantial increase in what were deemed to be alien comms signals, the possibility was there that the intrusions were also recent.

"So what do we do about it?" Inkscree demanded. "We need to find a way to shut it down, or at least render it harmless."

"Without affecting the original constructs or their purpose," Copper added. "I wonder if we could use the *original* defensive parts of the base to neutralise the interference? The hostile tech seemed to have the upper hand at first, but the *Sunset* managed to break free when the initial power of the attack reduced."

"Could be they were low on weapons," Inkscree hazarded.

"Don't think so: the number and extent of structures down there are greater than those we found on Helixus and Elara and *they* had plenty of punch. I think the original tech is reasserting itself and is dealing with the situation; it may even be warning its linked stations. Dyxin, are you picking up any comms coming *off* that rock the *Sapphire Sunset* is orbiting?" she called over to the officer at the comms station in the well of the bridge.

"You what?" he responded, with a look over his shoulder at the command unit behind him.

"Just check it!" Copper returned. "Let's scan using *our* long-range arrays... There *is* a signal!" she crowed.

"Lieutenant Dyxin?" the colonel demanded.

"Confirmed," the young lieutenant returned, a little abashed. "How did you know?" he enquired of the science officer.

"Hunch," Copper replied, busily probing the body's surface.

"What have you got there, Lieutenant Milkstone?" Colonel Moritz demanded.

"The beam-weapon pulses have slowed to almost nothing, in fact they've stopped, *and* the planetoid's energy emissions have dwindled to background. So, apart from the directional comms signal, all we're reading points to station-keeping."

"Station-keeping?" the colonel repeated as Vespoltz at the tactical station confirmed the cessation of weapons fire.

"Matches the last readings we had from Elara base, ma'am, after the scan of the *Lithium Star*. But the comms signal is tight beam and it's heading out there, into unmapped space." Copper pointed, puzzled, to the holo she had pulled up. "Calling in back-up? There's still blue tech down there. I suspect it's being contained, but that doesn't mean it's safe to go down. I'd be very wary of deploying anything down there unless it's left behind: who knows what might be attached if it's brought back up? But I would be very interested in a thorough sub-surface exploration of that series of linked structures."

"Are you suggesting that if we send down a probe it will not be recognised as intrusive and deactivated or destroyed by the defence system?"

"No idea ma'am, but it might be worth a gamble. Unless the *Sunset* did and they haven't mentioned it – I note their bots are still nested, so they didn't have time to release them."

"Stand by."

Captain Fantodd denied the despatch of any physical probe: his ship had been targeted after close surface scans and the drop of a batch of stealth surface science bots to comb the body for the source of tech signs his long distance arrays had detected.

"Any probe might have trouble unless it can breach the surface," Inkscree pointed out to his junior officer. "But that's odd: I'm picking up increasing levels of remanent magnetisation in a small area that we can scan from here, just on the edge of the planetary limb that we have in view. Did the *Sunset's* readings show high RM in other areas now off our screens?"

"We had a lot of high remanent mag at our site on Isidis," Copper recalled as she checked the data. "It shifted constantly and we had endless trouble to get clear readings. Some of it *was* caused by… shit! …Just a fizzing second…"

She covered her involuntary slip by setting up the holo of an area of planetoid that was expressing fluctuating remanence, but even as she did so, an image from Spook was so strong that another insight sharply intruded. The RM intensity at one spot was so particularly high that she linked quickly through to Linen in their lab and bid her call up the relevant data from their Glory Hole and run a comparative on its similarity to the readings that the *Sunset* had recorded over the area below them.

"What now?" Colonel Moritz demanded as she stepped over, having caught some of the dialogue.

"Some of the high remanent magnetisation at our site out on Isidis and in other areas on Mars was deliberately induced to prevent detection of the alien ships buried there," Copper told her in a low, urgent voice. "We *know* it was activated to hide their tech. I don't know how…"

"Really?" the colonel said grimly, as Linen verified the match of RM intensity readings and demanded an explanation, while Inkscree expressed his surprise in a quiet expletive. "I don't recall *that* information in any verbal report that you or Ms Lyrican made to me."

Copper swallowed nervously. "Speculative on my part at first ma'am: I doubt you'd have believed us," she said softly. "But we recorded an instance of it while we were collecting our final samples out at the Warren – when we realised that our site had been breached from the military side, the remanent mag jumped appreciably. And that was just before we ran into Jecks and his unpleasant friend and were nearly fried."

"An *active* increase on Mars a few months back?" the voice of

Inkscree cut in incredulously.

"Belay, Doctor," the colonel snapped. "Are you implying that the magnetic anomaly down there was deliberately induced to hide something and it's now changing?"

"Not at all, ma'am: remanent mag fluxes are fairly common on Mars and elsewhere, though not at the scale we registered. But I have a feeling that there's more to *this* base station than meets the eye."

"I take it Dr Addystone has not reported anything of note from his lifeform scans?"

"None, ma'am. But if there *is* substantial interference down there, he may have a little difficulty."

"Begin scanning that area with *everything* we have in any case."

"Aye ma'am."

Copper frowned as she turned back to her station; she knew that Spook was still reluctant to head down, but he understood the dilemma that faced the *Drake*. She brought both Trisk and Linen up to date as far as possible and had them begin scans.

Meanwhile the *Sapphire Sunset* had pulled further away from Blink 159 to a higher position. Both the *Drake* and the *Dexterity* were holding high orbits and the colonel had reported the gist of her science officers' findings to her fellow commanders. All three ships were monitoring the small world and the local area, although the *Drake* had the advantage in that respect, as Spook was now on the surface probing the extent of the main base complex. It had come as a surprise to the alien entity that the hostile devices with which he was familiar were now limited by the newer additions made to the system by his successors and Copper could sense his relief that he was not in danger from the insidious relays that had been planted to subvert the original systems. She also sensed his disquiet that the agents of sabotage might in some way be aware of the reversion. Her primary concern was the time factor extant in the interference at the station: was it recent or had it occurred in the past? If it was recent, it could be assumed that there was a clear and present danger to the local sentients that called the Sol system home.

Copper passed on her concern to her chief and to Trisk and Linen in the lab as Spook ventured out towards the area of high RM that Dr Inkscree had noted. A drop in output allowed the

Drake's forward science arrays to home in on an area of bedrock that was pierced with cracks and hollows, some of which looked too regular to be natural. Trisk was peeved that his scans had yielded no evidence that could be construed as alien sentience in addition to Spook, but the area *was* a source of the reddish-green alien technology which was by now more than familiar to the science officers. The new structure bore little resemblance to the complex networks that formed the nearby base station relays however, and it was at first difficult to ascertain its purpose.

"Habitations?" Linen hazarded from her bolthole in the lab.

"No. It's an underground dock and repair facility," Copper said almost firmly. "Small, so for scouts, fighters and the like: it was probably used as a shielded base for resupply to a fleet."

"Yo, that's a doozie of a theory, Cop! How in hell do you verify that?"

"Yes, how in hell *do* you verify that, Lieutenant Milkstone?" the colonel enquired, coming over to check the data. "It's hardly the outcome of what your scanners are telling you."

In response, Copper requested that the overhead holo-grid be called into action. Colonel Moritz, with a quick look across to her first officer, nodded accord. Copper swiftly linked to it and soon had the visual of what seemed to be a maze of tunnels and caverns in the scanned area. As the scan beams zoomed through the spaces, a few mouths dropped open. Dipping RM readings had allowed fine-scale density analyses that showed distinct part-structures in some of the caverns opening off the larger tunnels. In one such space Copper halted the holo to refine the image.

"Recognise that?" she asked her audience as she tweaked the readings her arrays were gathering and a discernible form began to emerge within the hazy field.

Colonel Moritz certainly did. "Well I'll be... it's remarkably similar to that holo-ship you have in the tri-dee suite down on deck twenty..."

"Yes ma'am, I believe that's precisely what it is: at least it's what my instruments tell me. But it's not a holo. It's the real McCoy." She smiled meaningfully up at her commander.

"No, before you ask," she was told shortly. "I'm sending nothing down there, certainly not one of my crew and definitely not *you*, Lieutenant."

"Ma'am, may I respectfully…"

"No you may not."

"Damn right!" Linen's voice came clearly over the comm. "You've caused us enough trouble already!"

Copper closed the audio link to the lab with an oath as a few members of the bridge crew exchanged glances, wondering what in hell was going on. The colonel resumed her seat thoughtfully, having ordered a continuous scan of Blink 159, and after several exchanges with her opposite numbers aboard the two vessels alongside, the consensus was that the *Drake* would assist the *Sapphire Sunset* with her repairs and all three ships would remain in the area to monitor the current situation. The *Dexterity* had reported the incident back to her home base and the Martian commanders had agreed to submit a joint report to Mars Fleet.

With the red alert reduced to yellow, those officers due off duty were released. Copper was one of the bridge crew told to stand down, but as soon as her replacement had taken her place, she was ordered to attend Colonel Moritz to the bridge office.

"At ease," the colonel said mildly. "You need sleep," she continued, regarding her junior officer shrewdly.

"So do you," thought Copper, but left the words unsaid.

"I know," Ms Moritz went on with half a smile. "So that is where you are going next. We'll be staying in this area for a time, at least until the *Sunset* is fit to carry on and until I know what the situation is as far as that Earth ship is concerned."

"You mean we have first dibs on that rock out there and everything under it," Copper could not help herself interjecting.

"We do," the colonel agreed. "I will not require you on the bridge for the next few sols – you will spend some of your time in the engineering tri-dee facility getting to grips with that holo-ship that you seem to have been able to regenerate to the extent that you can fly sims in it. You'll spend more of your time in fighter simulations in our suites aboard and in actual space flight with an instructor, until I'm sure you can handle a fighter well enough to fly solo."

As Copper's eyes widened, the colonel continued briskly. "The rest of your duty time will be spent in the lab interpreting what's in that base station, to determine how we deactivate the hostile tech there. And I want at least one other pilot trained in handling that alien ship of yours. Whom do you recommend?"

Copper considered. "Linen would be the logical choice: she knows about it and Spook knows *her*; she's a fair pilot, though not on fighters; and I've already threatened her with learning the ropes. On the other hand, a very experienced pilot might be a better bet in the short term. Though there's only one that really fits the bill and I don't want to …" she bit her lip and halted.

"Commander Locksmith. I agree: I don't want to risk my chief of security either, but then I don't want to risk you or any of my crew. But it goes with the territory: we all signed up for Mars Fleet and we were certainly all made aware of the risks before we signed on. I'll have them both assigned; and if time permits, I'd like to try out this ship that you seem to consider your personal property. I'll get Jinn Limlite to organise rotas."

Copper had been ruminating and the colonel picked up on it, as she did most things. "Something else, Lieutenant?"

"Yes, ma'am – that shiny new combat shuttle we have in outer bay four…"

"What about it?"

"I'd like to try sims in that, if there are some available – there must be, otherwise why do we have it aboard?"

"With what view in mind?"

"To take it down to the surface when authorised – I *will* have to be on the team that goes down," she went on hurriedly as the colonel began to speak. "To gain entry to that facility if nothing else. But if that place is as I suspect, a dock and repair facility, it may be possible to upgrade our shuttle with alien tech, if …"

"*My* shuttle," Colonel Moritz corrected tartly. "And if you think I'll permit such an upgrade you are sadly mistaken. But you suspect or you know it's a repair dock?"

"I'm pretty sure, ma'am," Copper admitted. "It's shielded, so there must be a darn good reason it was hidden."

"If it's shielded, how did your instruments not only pick it up but produce the high-quality holos that you got?"

"Shielding was withdrawn to let me in. The other ships won't be able to scan the system so well," she said resignedly.

"Your Spook. I only hope its young sidekick isn't haunting the bridge – hell knows what it would get up to. I want to know exactly what you think we have on that planetoid, why you think so and how you got every scrap of data you have."

"Yes ma'am."

Forty minutes later, with the dialogue coming to an end and Copper dropping with exhaustion, a discreet buzz at the entry on the corridor side of the office caused the colonel to check the outer viewscreen. It was Kynedd Faerin.

"Probably coming to relieve you of duty on medical grounds, ma'am," she told the colonel.

"I'll overlook that insubordination in view of your severe fatigue, Lieutenant. Get out of here and get some sleep."

The doctor had come to order the same: Copper's medi-tag had been giving him some cause for concern. Satisfied that she was heading to her quarters, he stayed to talk to the colonel.

The lieutenant trudged off and was soon in her own billet. She did not have much time alone, however, for both Linen and Trisk were on the doorstep demanding answers. Wearily, she quickly showered and all three sat spinning the remainder of the night out in talk.

* * *

In compliance with orders, Copper spent hours over the next few sols in the sim suite on deck thirteen where Jinn Limlite had arranged a taxing run of fighter test programmes under the most qualified instructor aboard. She was also assigned training sims of the new combat shuttle, and found that she could handle it quite well. As the alert status had been reduced to blue, her lab work carried on with little respite, the body around which the *Drake* still orbited holding many mysteries yet to be probed. Off duty time she spent in the tri-dee facility with her precious holo-ship. She found that the colonel had informed both Linen and Kit that they would be required to gain experience in the alien craft. Kit was more than happy as it was one of the very few ways that he and Copper could snatch some time together: his own duties had not lessened despite the lull that had followed the attack on the *Sapphire Sunset*.

Her first actual space flight in a dual-control fighter with her instructor behind her was an achievement she would not forget, Copper realised, as she confidently swung her small craft in a tight loop around the *Drake* and brought it into the outer bay assigned her. She also realised that she would need a deal more practice before she would be able to pilot a fighter solo.

Meanwhile, business aboard the *Drake* carried on as several divisions carried out their own analyses of the local area. Ossy Inkscree maintained a persistent presence within range and the three astrobiologists were swiftly reaching the conclusion that it was about time that the chief SO was brought into the secret of their two alien shipmates. Trisk took it upon himself to mention their concerns to Colonel Moritz. She had been giving some thought to the issue the nearer they came to their primary target and warned the three that she intended to bring all her senior officers up to date on everything related to her science officers and their concerns, personal and otherwise.

"At least the colonel's the one that'll field any flak," Linen consoled her friend, who was more than aware that her name would be at the forefront of the briefing. "They all consider you as something out of the ordinary anyway: this will just confirm that they were right."

"Thanks for that. As long as the news doesn't slide too far down the ranks: there may be one or two thwarted spies aboard that security haven't got yet and this would be rumour to link home about despite the risks."

"Kit thinks we still have moles aboard?" enquired Trisk.

"Not necessarily but he has a suspicious mind and so have I; and that guy Wale's still in the brig. But let's finish this holo of that base station: Ossy wants it done before we go off duty."

"Or in our case, off to engineering," Linen sniffed. "I hope I'm never called on to fly a real version of your frigging boat: I find it hard work at the best of times. How does Kit handle it?"

"Very well but he likes it too much and takes risks. I know it's a sim, but I don't want a pattern of risk-taking setting in."

"Hark at who's talking! But let's finalise this holo. Ossy still wants to send a platoon of *his* bots down and get them back in one piece if the *Sunset's* are showing no sign of having been tampered with. Are the readings still showing no activity as far as the hostile tech is concerned, Trisk?"

"Confirmed, and we're on continuous monitoring. The chief SO of the *Sunset's* bringing her gear up slowly and keeping the bots off-ship until they can be checked out. I think Ossy would like to go over them himself."

The three finished their task within the allotted time. Trisk was left to tidy up and pass the completed base station holo to the *Drake's* chief SO whilst Copper and Linen hauled on down to deck twenty and a simulated duo flight in the alien holo-craft set up there.

An hour later and groaning in unison, the two waddled down the ramp of the ship. To Linen's surprise, the colonel was sitting at the main ops station; she was examining the link between the alien box and the auxiliary projector plate.

"Ma'am," Copper greeted her, realising that the subliminal images she had received from Spook had been to prepare her for the visit. "You'd like a ride?"

"If you're not too tired."

"Not for *this* ship," Copper replied.

"I'll sit it out here," Linen said hurriedly.

"You won't: I want to see how *you* handle the sim."

"Aye ma'am."

The colonel had very good reasons for her actions, as she relayed to the pair when she had seen each go through short but demanding exercises. Her senior officers were now up to speed on the presence of two alien crewmates, their links to Copper in the past and currently and the positive benefits to the *Drake* and her mission. The potential advantages of salvaging an intact alien fighter from the base below had also been discussed. The presence of the ship did not imply that it was spaceworthy, but the consensus had been that it would be wise to have more than one pilot capable of flying the thing. And if one ship was down there, it was possible that a thorough exploratory and analysis of the site might bring up another example. Copper doubted it, but held her tongue. One thought did occur.

"Dr Inkscree wants to send his bots on a recce to the base station; it may be useful to send them through the repair facility, as it may not have been penetrated by hostile technology. That will give us a much clearer picture than external scanning, as its shielding is still operative to a great extent."

The colonel pondered. "I'll discuss it with Inkscree. You two had better tie things up here and head off duty but morrow-sol you have a good look at that so-called repair facility."

"Aye, ma'am," the duo responded eagerly.

* * *

The mess was alive with the buzz of conversation as the two made their way in. Trisk was sat with Tawny Brown and waved them over. They were pointedly ignored by Ash Goff, who was in the company of Tany Melucca at the neighbouring table.

"Enjoy your flight sims?" Trisk enquired. "You're quite late."

"We had company," Linen explained. "The colonel decided she would like a look-see and she joined us *and* put us through our paces. She's nothing if not thorough," the redhead added.

"So when do you head down to the surface?" Trisk asked of Copper with a hint of mischief in his eyes.

"When the colonel says so."

"Huh! *If* she says so," Ash Goff muttered audibly.

"If you're going to listen in on our private conversation, you would be much better sitting with us," Linen told him bluntly. "You can even share my chippers."

It was obvious that Linen was in a playful mood and intent on teasing Goff. "So when's your next fighter flight, Cop?" she asked archly. "You could buzz the obs deck and we could stand there and wave. You'd be up for that, wouldn't you, Ash?"

"In around twelve hours and after that it's a sim of the new combat shuttle," Copper responded as Lieutenant Goff turned an annoyed face to them. "*And* we have all that stuff still to do in the lab. Too busy to be amusing you lot, so can it."

"We ought to send links to the folks back at Lowell," Linen continued, ignoring her friend's rebuke. "Not to mention Beagle and Viking One. Wonder if there's been any more mischief out at our site, with spies, security breaches and weapons fire?"

She continued in the same vein until Goff had had enough and stalked off elsewhere, Lieutenant Melucca at his side.

"Why do you always wind up his prop?" Copper complained.

"I enjoy it; and we may as well keep spreading the rumours that we're not to be tangled with. He drinks in every word even when he's pretending not to and I bet he talks about us behind our backs, at least to Tany, and she'll certainly spread the tales."

"You live on the edge," Tawny Brown told the redhead. "Mr Goff can pull rank, he *is* your senior."

"Not Cop's though," Linen replied brightly.

"Exactly," Copper replied. "Which makes me *your* senior and

I'm ordering you to button it."

"Grouchy. Is it because Kit's on a late shift?"

"Dangerous territory," Tawny grinned. "Let's get out of here, Trisk, before there's a fight."

The two left them to the table and Copper looked across at her friend, who was grinning ruefully. "Okay, what gives?"

The grin widened. "Not sure – I just feel light, airy, as if I've had a bump on the head and am a bit out of it. You know."

Copper looked fixedly at her, frowning, but a moment later, realisation dawned. "Hell!" she said. "I know!"

"What?"

Copper eyes searched her friend's face and then took in the space beyond her. "As if there are two of you dancing about in your head," she clarified.

"That's about it," Linen agreed, nodding. "So what is it? *Are* there two... oh hell!"

"The little sprite's bored and wants action; he figures you'll give him more free rein that I will," Copper said in a low voice. "You'd better disabuse him of that notion *right* now. And we'd best get back to mine. I'll need Spook's input on this one. How in blazes he managed to link to you..."

"Well, I'd always been jealous that you had a disembodied alien friend and I didn't," Linen replied perkily. "But now I see why I was so scared when the colonel ordered me to fly that sim in your holo-ship. Maybe I'll sleep in my closet tonight."

"Keep your voice down! Let's go!"

In the event, finding that Dr Faerin was still on duty, Copper hauled her friend off to medbay for a quick once over. She was relieved in some measure that she no longer felt like the minder of a young and increasingly adventurous alien, but her friend as a guardian gave her some cause for anxiety. Linen however, read as perfectly normal.

* * *

The following sol, Copper was not in a mood for the banter that her redheaded friend thought it witty to deliver after two gruelling flight drills. Linen's new buddy had also caused Trisk amusement and had given rise to a visit from the colonel, who had had the news from the chief MO. The steely green eyes of their commander effectively scared Linen into quiet submission but the drawback was that she would not settle to the work that had been planned once the colonel had gone. As Trisk was due to work on his and Faerin's alien probe system, Copper was left to analyse all the information they had garnered thus far on the repair centre of the base beneath them. In some annoyance, she took herself off to the tri-dee suite down in engineering, her purpose being to run the data through that to gain insight into the state of the facility and the use to which they could put it.

She was preparing to take down her holo-ship when some intuition made her stop. She sensed the nearness of Spook and sat, trying to fathom the message. "I wonder…" she muttered to herself, automatically powering up the cycle that would project the craft and allow her to operate a sim.

Quickly, she began to run the data stream from her sources through the main ops station and into the auxiliary projector site that linked to the alien box that generated the hard-holo of her ship. The bed of light above which the box hovered intensified its output and the green studs around its circumference glowed in eye-searing brightness.

"I wonder, I wonder…" she muttered again.

* * *

Three hours later, a buzzing in her ears brought Copper back to the awareness of her surroundings. She called up a visual of the exterior of her holo-ship to see what was going on. Colonel Moritz, Dr Faerin and Trisk were there. The latter was operating the main console and trying to shut down the holo.

"Shit!" Copper swore quietly as she quickly powered down her systems and closed off the run in which she had been so immersed that she had failed to notice the warning signal. "You should have kicked me up the butt," she mentally admonished Spook.

"I take it you have an explanation of why we had a power outage in this section of the deck?" the colonel demanded icily as Copper stumbled down the ramp.

"Lor', was it that bad?"

"You're ten seconds away from a disciplinary, Lieutenant."

Faerin, after a quick scan, pressed a hypo to her upper arm and then steered her deftly towards the ops console and a chair. "Sit," he commanded. "Exhaustion," he reported. "Mental and physical. What *were* you up to in there?"

Copper smiled wearily. "Exploring the labyrinth," she said. "Down there." She pointed to the floor. "The repair station: it's a maze of tunnels and repair bays. There are at least half a dozen small fighters down there. Mostly in bits and inoperable," she said. "They can be salvaged but we don't have enough gear to repair them. If back-up gets in, maybe they can lend a hand… There's one we can maybe jury-rig into a flyable crate."

"*What* are you saying, Dr Milkstone?" demanded the colonel. "What do you mean you were exploring the repair station?"

"Easy, Elle," Faerin warned.

"You were running a sim of the structure through your holo-ship," Trisk surmised as he ran experienced fingers over the ops console and took readings from various stations. "How on Mars did you manage to link our readings in and then persuade the sim generator of a holo-ship to run it as a sim? And how did you figure it could?"

"I suspect that the box, whatever it picked up from the piece of hull in bay four, identified it," Copper told him, leaning back with a sigh. "I knew it was drawing a lot of power to run the sim, I could feel it. But I didn't know it had caused an outage."

"How did you work out that you *could* call up a sim?" Trisk persisted.

"Had a feeling it might be possible."

"Are you seriously claiming that you have a simulation of that repair dock or whatever it is on that planet below and that you have explored it?" Colonel Moritz barked.

"Yes, ma'am. I can show you."

"You'll stay right where you are, Lieutenant," the doctor ordered, pushing her back down into the chair as she half-rose.

"You mentioned back-up getting in to lend a hand: what was it you meant by that?" the colonel continued frostily.

"The signal that's being sent out into unmapped space: the station's calling for help from its own. But we've no way to tell how long the call's been going, who or what's out there or when it was last heard from. They could be there now or they could have left this space a thousand years ago. Who's to say?"

"As we have had *recent* increases in comms and other activity out this way and back home, and we've reason to suspect said alien activity is *more* recent than not, I'd say the possibility exists that they're still there, or at least within calling distance," Trisk cut in, his eyes alight in anticipation. "With our own recent tech improvements, we can now get out this far fairly quickly. It's been picked up somehow and they're coming back."

"Who are *they*?" Copper asked.

"The sentients whose traces we've found on Mars and out here – and maybe the others you suspect drove them off. *We're* now ripe for exploitation: we've improved Mars, just as the first sentients did when they started to build their bases more than a few millennia ago. Or maybe they want to stop us expanding, in case we intrude on what they consider is their space – which of course may have been the case last time around."

"Same old, same old: a civilisation gets too big for its boots and either blows itself apart, or some bully comes in and blows it apart to steal its boots," Copper intoned bitterly.

"The station's calling for help from its own," repeated the colonel. "That's a mighty big supposition and not one I can call in without proof. I want that signal tracked and a probe sent out to detect anything that heads in, with *your* gear operational," she informed Faerin and Trisk. "As for you, Lieutenant, you will log every visit to this facility that you make *when* you make it and will only go in when authorised by a senior officer. And I want a look at your sim. If there *is* a fighter down there that can be salvaged safely, a team will be sent in. But it's a shielded space."

"Yes ma'am, but I'm sure I can get shields dropped to allow us entry," Copper said.

"I'll bet. Dr Addystone, you get back to your lab and start on that tracking probe; Kynedd, you'll sit in on this sim. Let's go, Lieutenant, and see what this holo-ship of yours can do."

If the colonel was impressed by the clarity and detail of the simulated ride through the channels and docking lacunae of the alien repair base, she failed to show it. Her main concerns lay in the means of making planetfall and breaching the system, and the safe retrieval of anything useful. She was less sanguine than her junior officer that the mission was feasible and relatively risk-free and listed several problems for Copper to sort out.

Once released from the sim suite, Copper's own priority was to find Linen and see what her friend had been up to in her absence. She intended to inform her on how matters stood, as she would require her undivided assistance in the sols ahead. Dr Lyrican was in a side lab examining the latest data streaming in via the science stations of all three ships in close proximity to the small planetoid. That there had been no more overt hostility indicated that the adverse influences *in situ* had been subdued. Linen had gleaned thus much from Junior, whom she reported to be more manageable now that he had taken on board her instinctive respect for and obedience to the colonel.

The remanent magnetisation that had puzzled Dr Inkscree was still shifting and was high, Linen reported, but she had been usefully employed in trying to find a way down to the repair facility without having to drill down through the surface: the original entry would have had to be large enough to take a small shuttle at least, she argued, hence it must be there somewhere.

"Good call," Copper congratulated. "Where's Trisk? He was sent to the lab to work on a probe to track that comm signal."

"Main lab," Linen edified her. "At least he was when I last saw him. Had lunch?"

"No."

"Then let's go and show our faces. We'll pick up Trisk on the way if he's still around. Junior and Spook can work out the front door to that dock down there while we're gone."

Lunch was rapid as Copper had had a few ideas and wanted to get moving on them. One issue eluding her was the source of power for the alien fighter: that it was some sort of fission that released large amounts of kinetic energy in a controlled manner was probable but how it was contained within the craft and how they would obtain a source was uncertain. Linen was pragmatic.

"Let Spook sort it out," she counselled. "You say he was a pilot as well as a senior commander, so he'll know and he knows you so he'll find a way to fix it. There's probably a store down there; they'd need to get any fighters or scouts out and to where they were going without a mothership of some sort in orbit."

"Too many probabilities," Copper argued. "Colonel needs concrete, not a heap of maybes, and I need to spend more time in space and in my holo-ship running sorties through that repair dock."

"You watch yourself. The colonel will have your hide if you

overdo it against orders, and so will Kit."

* * *

Several sols later and with space beneath her, Copper's small fighter spun in dark starlight. Her tactical grid had registered a ship heading in their direction. It was big, she knew, and she felt a prickle of anxiety. Her solo training run was almost complete but instinct compelled her to execute a banking turn and head out from the protection of the *Drake* for a closer look.

"Party time," Captain Helmis announced from his station on the bridge. "We have another ship on approach. ID indicates that she's the *SS Morgana Atlantis*, listed as a commercial survey vessel under the command of a Captain Nella Hellebore."

"I wonder we got that much," the colonel replied. "Merchant Fleet ops must be getting antsy. What's tactical got on her?"

"She's big, not far off our size; FTL drive and then some and a hull we can hardly get through, even with our covert scanners. So she's got top notch shielding as well as a repairable skin, and her weapons are considerable."

"But no match for ours," Colonel Moritz noted wryly. "How did they come up with that skin, I wonder? It's not quite the same as ours but it comes close. She's maintaining silence, but she sure as hell knows we're here, and I guess she may have her own ideas of why. Neat lines: she has…"

She was interrupted by comms. "Lieutenant Milkstone from her fighter, ma'am: she says it's urgent."

"Put it through. What is it, Milkstone?"

"That ship heading our way, ma'am. There are factors I don't like in some of her hull plating," Copper's voice echoed across. "It reads to me like a variant on that blue alien tech."

"Science, confirm!" snapped the colonel, rising to her feet.

"On it," Trisk called from his station. "I've got traces, but only partial," he verified. "I read them as parts of her weapons emplacements and her forr'ad scanning arrays but I can't get clear readings: she's heading in bow first and she's shielded."

"I concur," Copper called out. "I can head further out and get more from closer in."

"Belay that, Lieutenant Milkstone," the colonel commanded. "How much power do you have left?"

"Already in the red zone, ma'am: half an hour tops."

"Return to your bay and prepare for another sortie. You'll take out the combat shuttle in bay four."

"Aye ma'am," Copper agreed as several pairs of eyes turned to the commanding officer.

"Are you sure that's wise, Elle?" Helmis muttered in a low voice. "She's not flown it more than a couple of times."

"She can handle it, Merris. Comms, raise the *Morgana Atlantis* and tell them I'd like a word."

30: MORGANA ATLANTIS

Captain Nella Hellebore was a woman who had fought her way up from merchant cadetship at the minor fleet training centre of Phoenix College to the command of the *SS Morgana Atlantis* via several tough berths aboard ships of a few of the more colourful mercantile lines. She was little inclined for a long dialogue with a colonel of Mars Fleet known to her by repute, she was reticent about both her mission and the reasons for her ship's presence in the local area and she was mightily put out by the launch of a combat shuttle registered to the *MSS Drake II* that appeared to be heading in her direction.

Colonel Moritz made no apologies but clarified her own and the *EFS Dexterity's* position in response to the distress call from the *MSS Sapphire Sunset*. The *Morgana Atlantis*, she was told, had not picked up the signal, leaving the colonel to assume that another factor had triggered the commercial vessel's approach. What such a survey ship was doing in a sector of space that harboured definite and possibly large sources of alien material as well as the trade resources for which she was ostensibly scouting was simpler to figure, given her background and sponsorship.

Trading icily polite questions with Hellebore elicited only the further intelligence that her team had recorded local ore sources that were of interest to trading concerns back on Mars. As her scans had also shown that three other craft were in the area, she had ordered her ship to head in. A surprised whistle from Trisk alerted the colonel to another matter and as the science officer sent over details of what he had received from Copper aboard the combat shuttle, her eyebrows shot up and she requested her opposite number to stand by as she took in the implications.

As Hellebore's face melted into the ether, Colonel Moritz turned to Helmis. "Strange: she turns up when the hostile tech that was trying to outflank the original stuff on Blink 159 has been shut down *and* when we're preparing to make a sortie into a repair dock we know is well-hidden and close by. It's stranger still that she has traces of that same hostile tech in her hide – in her forr'ad weapons emplacements and scanning arrays but not elsewhere, it seems. And she has a scattering of tiny but very clever jamming devices attached to her outer hull in spots that bear a striking similarity to the ones that undermined our own scanners at Jupiter Station. Chief Locksmith developed a way to look for and disable them after our problems and Dr Milkstone no doubt has that locked into her scanning arrays, but I'd better see what Hellebore knows. When's the *En Hedu'anna* due?"

"Couple of hours," the first officer reported. "We can get her in ahead of that: with Perkin in command, she'll shift. I can make the call."

"Do it," the colonel directed as she re-established contact with the *Morgana Atlantis.*

Hellebore was ready for her: she was more than irritated that a shuttle from the *Drake* was close enough to give her ship an in-depth once over and was scanning sections of the large ship's hull in great detail. A request to desist had been ignored and the *Morgana Atlantis* had targeted the small craft, to no avail. Colonel Moritz countered by stating succinctly that her own scans had shown that a known form of alien technology was fused with parts of the civilian ship's hull, and the *Morgana Atlantis* was also hosting micro-jammers that could compromise external sensor arrays and potentially internal ship's systems.

Hellebore flatly rejected the colonel's evidence until she had been sent the relevant data on the jammers and had carried out her own checks, but she refused to discuss the components of her ship's hull and insisted that the *Drake's* combat shuttle be called off. As Copper veered away and back towards her own ship, a quick exchange elicited the intelligence that the *Morgana's* last port of call had been Jupiter Station. Her captain would not reveal her orders in respect of her mission there but she civilly thanked Colonel Moritz for her data and quickly cut comms to take the actions she deemed appropriate.

"Alien tech hasn't come as a surprise, but those jammers did," Captain Helmis observed sardonically. "Looks like Jupiter

Station's bad guys are still in operation then."

"If those hull inclusions were part of her when she left space dock, then there's trouble at home as well. She won't tell us more, but I'll see what Dr Milkstone's figured out. And I'll send word to Fleet Command; they'd better get working on it."

"The *En Hedu'anna* will be here in under an hour," Helmis continued. "I didn't pass on the details but they know we have *that* ship and an Earth Fleet ship as company. We're still heading down to surface to explore that shielded construction I take it?"

"We are. Lieutenant Milkstone will have to be on that trip for obvious reasons, but Chief Locksmith will pilot the shuttle down: he's an expert pilot and he's used sims of a ship close to what we think's down there, including a few runs through a sim of the structure. But if we find something worth bringing back, I want the *Morgana* as far out of range as possible."

"Mars Fleet hasn't planted a flag on that lump of rock, so we may have trouble claiming first dibs and telling her to back off."

"Why do you think I want reinforcements?" the colonel replied as she rose.

* * *

Copper was sure that the traces of hostile alien tech she had recorded on the *Morgana Atlantis* was all that was present on her hull but the ship's advanced capabilities made her reluctant to send Spook aboard. The vessel's external arrays were complex and it was possible that she carried some type of alien lifeform detection device similar to that developed by Trisk and Kynedd Faerin. There were certainly some minor systems that had not been recognised by the scanners aboard the combat shuttle.

Towards the end of Copper's briefing of Colonel Moritz, the news came in that the *MSS En Hedu'anna*, under the command of Captain Perkin Helmis, had arrived. Her advent added to the flurry of activity aboard the *Drake*, for final preparations were underway for the launch of a small shuttle to surface.

Careful exterior imaging under Linen's guidance had revealed a course of elevated ridges and overhangs a little way from the buried network of tunnels and caverns, beneath which several fissures pierced the bedrock. A stealthy sortie by a team of Dr Inkscree's surf-sci bots to the site had indicated that one of the fissures led directly to the edge of the structural zone. The cleft itself was sufficiently large to deploy a small craft but it was shielded and data intake by the bots had been imprecise. With Trisk's help, an enhanced scout probe that would precede the shuttle in had been organised. Copper was positive that with Spook alongside, local defensive mechanisms would recognise them and allow entry.

With the third Mars Fleet ship in place and Captain Ketter of the *Dexterity* aware of many of the issues, the colonel left her junior officer to proceed with her own tasks and set off to the bridge. Copper made for the lab to make sure everything was in place: she wanted Trisk and Linen, with Junior as back-up, to monitor everything that went forward. Kit as pilot and the most senior officer had been given command of the mission and he had assigned bioengineer Lieutenant Lyssa Halsen to the team. The fourth member was one of his own security officers.

"Don't take any unnecessary risks," was Linen's final caution as her friend made off to suit up in protective gear.

"As if Kit would let me," Copper returned. "But I'll be flying my ship back up if we can get a working power source into her."

"*Your* ship?" Trisk demanded.

"My ship: I doubt any other pilot would be able to get her into space. And the colonel's clearing outer bay five for her..."

"Providing you guarantee safety. One small doubt and I *will* advise her to call it off," Trisk told her seriously.

"I know: see you on the flipside."

Kit and the other two were already in the shuttle bay when Copper arrived, suited and ready. The craft had been prepped and was carrying added armaments as well as scanners. Ensign Ennis D'Arragh was toting a phase rifle and back-up pack that caused Copper to raise an eyebrow, but she made no comment and obeyed quickly when ordered aboard. Once in, the shuttle was sealed and primed for departure. Kit had insisted that full defence gear be utilised from the start and the four had their protective helmets and air supplies ready for deployment.

Permission being given, the small shuttle departed the *Drake* and set course. It would take fifteen minutes to reach the target area, from where Kit would negotiate his course beneath the series of overhangs that led to the insertion point. It was hoped that the remanent magnetisation still apparent in the area would foil any unwanted scanning from above and allow the shuttle to reach her first objective covertly.

The entry pinpointed by the bots was reached and the scout probe despatched as guide. Kit proceeded slowly in the dim glow of the shuttle's forward light arrays, every external scanner set to check the area around them, while Copper kept up a continuous commentary for the benefit of the officers listening in from the bridge and the main lab. The conduit they were following was narrow and far from straight, and the small craft wove a sinuous path through relatively smooth bedrock. Several minor channels pierced the way at intervals and passing scans indicated that they contained low levels of organo-technology and other materials that suggested a defensive capacity. Halsen had been tasked with keeping a wary eye on externals but she reported no increase in any readings that might suggest that the shuttle was being tracked by other than their own ship.

As the craft followed its guiding probe downwards and drew closer to the main parts of the buried formation, Ossy Inkscree at the *Drake's* science station called out that he was losing its signal, the results both of increases in magnetic flux and *in situ* shielding. Copper concurred: some sort of local sensor had been triggered by their passage and the shuttle and its probe were now beyond an energy curtain that was clearly registering on their own instruments. That it was benign could be inferred from their unimpeded progress and a gradual increase in the ambient lighting of their surroundings, to the extent that the shuttle's lights were hardly required and they could see that the tunnel was walled in a reflective pinkish coating.

"So far so good, then," Kit said with a quick nod at Copper beside him.

"Aye, sir," she returned. "This main branch should split at a node shortly and we'll have a choice of passageways. The probe has been programmed with the path to the bay we want to inspect. We should see wider recesses that open off the main way that have more structure to them and contain what are pieces of ship, if my deep-scan holos were accurate."

Their route followed the prescribed pattern, with apertures off that contained what looked like equipment linked to chunks of metallic material that may have been the shells of small craft.

They passed several before their shepherd probe led them into what was a slightly larger bay. Sitting there in the centre of the space was a small iridescent red-green, smooth-hulled ship, its tapering bow rising up and back to a slightly ridged stern. It sat on the ground on slightly protuberant landing extensors, the swirled patterns etched into its flanks cold and dark. Copper let out a soft sigh as she glowed in contentment: this was her ship.

"Lights," she breathed.

Kit increased the exterior lighting to illuminate the craft as he settled their shuttle down, but he hardly had need: some sensory system had kicked in and the muted ambient lighting began to increase until the small chamber glowed.

"Let's go," Copper announced.

"You're going nowhere, *Lieutenant*, until I've run checks," Kit said flatly. "Halsen, what have you got?"

"Seems clear, sir," was the reply as a chastened Copper began to run analyses of her own.

Spook, in a state of controlled excitement, had already gone to investigate what he recognised as a familiar object and as an expert in its use, Copper knew that he would be able to explore and understand every part of it. She had found that the bay held more than just the fighter, the equipment, instruments and parts that were required to carry out repairs and the means to enclose the bay for testing. There were closed off sections that led to other spaces. As she compared her readings with Lyssa Halsen, they jointly concluded that the spaces were multi-functional and were storage bays, routes to other parts of the facility and possibly habitation units.

Kit had deemed the local area safe, but in the low gravity and without a breathable atmosphere, full protection would have to be worn. He had tried to communicate his findings to the *Drake* but found that the interference that had grown since entering the site had blocked comms. His hand slapping his console in annoyance brought Copper out of the reflective state into which she had dropped and she scanned their surroundings and the shuttle's control boards carefully.

"They've maybe got troubles of their own and contact with a landing team on the surface might add to it," she suggested. "I'm picking up increasing shielding capacity down here and I bet it's for our protection."

"Are you saying we have something out there keeping an eye on us? In other words, something that knows we're here and is aware that all's not well up there?"

"We've been monitored from the second we arrived," she argued. "That's why environmental readings are in constant flux. The systems down here must be encoded to protect the resident lifeforms, and at the moment that's us. And as we can't call home, the *Drake* may have problems. And deactivate that rifle, Mr D'Arragh: there's nothing to shoot in here except us."

"There may be something dangerous out there, ma'am," the young officer countered. "And if there's trouble aboard…"

"College-trained security: no non-comm would argue a point or question an order from an officer," Kit snorted in laughter. "Put the gun down Ensign, we're showing clear. And I expect you want a closer look at that alien ship, Lieutenant Milkstone."

"Aye, sir. I'd like to try to get aboard and see how active her systems are."

"On my mark and not before," she was told dryly. "Get your helmets on people and check your air. And take the rifle with you, D'Arragh: once we're out there you can take the catch off."

Their bouncing gait in the low gravity carried the four across the bay to the alien ship sitting inertly on what appeared to be a soft but resilient floor. A rising hum audible through their head gear alerted them to something triggered by their activity and Copper, in the lead, held out an arm to halt their progress. They watched as the red-green hull before them began to gleam, the high-relief spiral motifs on its surface knitting and unravelling in undulating waves, their colours changing in sync. Copper raised a hand, palm outward and the hum became a tempo to match the beating of her heart. She smiled: the ship had awoken, had read her and accepted her. Concentrating, she tried to evoke the mental link that she knew was needed as part of the full control system of such a ship.

"There she goes!" she breathed softly, her hand automatically dropping to lower the phase rifle that D'Arragh had raised at the sight of a flaring iris in the flank of the strange craft.

"That's new," Kit remarked into the ether. "Didn't you have to touch your holo version to get that response?"

"This isn't a holo," she explicated as the short ramp dropped down smoothly and touched base. "Let's get aboard. I *will* have to go first," she went on as Kit grasped her arm.

"I'll be at your back," he said pointedly, drawing his sidearm and flicking off the catch. "Halsen and D'Arragh, you two stay out here and keep your eyes peeled."

The ship was so like the holo aboard the *Drake* that even Copper was surprised. She slid into her accustomed place as if it was natural to her and Kit slotted in behind, as he had done on the several sims they had shared.

"Don't even think of powering up – if this thing *has* power," he warned.

Aware that the others could hear every word, Copper replied only with an affirmative but her gloved hand reached out behind to grasp his in a comforting clasp.

"Checking systems," she continued, her senses taking in all she could see and feel around her. "We have some power," she announced. "Not much, but she's in one piece and she's armed. But there's more here than in the holo, a lot more. And there's more space – this one's slightly larger, I think. I'll link into the control system directly and see what I can bring up."

The view-grid lit to show the exterior of the craft as Copper pulled the overhead control net downwards. Being used to the composite controls of the *Drake's* newest combat shuttle, she found the added complexity of the alien craft less trouble than she had at first expected.

"I'll run a solo sim from here," she told Kit. "It's similar to my holo-ship, so it'll give me an idea of the additional controls I have."

"You will not: I've been aboard your holo-ship and I know the sims *you* run. It must have a dual control mode. I'll take the secondary pilot position, but I want full control at the flick of a switch and I *will* cut it if you run anything but a standard flight."

"Agreed," she said shortly. "I'm powering her up. Look out, outside: I don't think you'll notice apart from increased energy output, but you'd better stand back, just in case," she warned Halsen and D'Arragh, and had the satisfaction of seeing the pair retreat towards their own shuttle.

As promised, Copper ran the minimal simulation in order to

get a feel for flight in the ship and passed control to Kit when she felt she had the basics under her belt. He repeated her run and agreed that the vessel handled remarkably well, at least as a sim. For an alien ship, it was significant how well human pilots took to her. Copper was sure the reason lay in the close physical similarity of humans to Spook's people in their organic form but prudently kept her views to herself. She had noted that Halsen at least was monitoring every nuance of change in the output of the ship.

"She's fully operational," was Copper's final evaluation. "She *will* fly in space, she's as tight as a drum and I can programme an internal atmosphere, although I wouldn't do that in combat unless necessary…"

"Combat?" Kit queried.

"She's a fully-equipped fighter," Copper elucidated. "She *can* double as a scout, but she packs a lot more punch. Our main problem now is how to fuel her. She'll need her own supply. We'll have to check around here for spare energy cells, but I want to know what she has in her hold. We were never able to breach that in the holo-ship: I don't think I had sufficient data."

"Hold?" asked Kit.

"Whatever's behind that aft panel," explained Copper. "It's not the engines, or their equivalent: they and their fuel cells are beneath us."

"You must have a schematic or similar you can call up," said Kit. "The pilot would have to know what's on board and where. There are more controls in this position than there were on the holo-ship for sure. But we have limited time down here and it's running out. And I want to know what's going on back aboard the *Drake*. Any more sorties will have to be done later."

"I agree. Just a sec… you're right, an auxiliary console can be accessed here. The graphics I get but I don't understand *these* marks: they may be text. Reading some sort of power casing with what looks like a lot of gear linked to it… it's a life-support pod! Some sort of preservation capsule! That's how it worked! It extrudes into the main body of the ship in use."

Kit insisted that Copper complete her evaluation of the ship and asses its readiness to fly in very short order. Halsen, on the outside, had been carrying out a recce on her own account and had tracked down a door behind which she could read a number of discrete high energy sources. She construed the space to be a supply store and indicated her findings as soon as the other two had disembarked from the alien craft. A plate to the side of the door bore an inscription and shrugging, Copper put her gloved hand to it. The panel slid into the wall to reveal a small room, the perforated walls of which hosted neatly arranged modules of unknown purpose. With little time to survey them fully, Copper called on Spook and soon pinpointed the fuel cells she wanted.

"We'll take five," she instructed. "They'll have to be stacked aboard the fighter, but there should be aft space we can access from the outside. I'll check."

Circumnavigating the small craft, she quickly found her goal: it was similar to stacking the old shuttle used for ferrying gear to and from the Warren, she mused as she directed the stowage of five fuel cells and safely sealed the external hold.

"All ready, Commander," she announced as she turned. "I suggest I pilot this ship behind our shuttle. Dr Addystone will have monitoring gear ready to deploy the second he picks us up and will have her probed for everything from fresh air to toenail clippings to see if she's safe to bring aboard."

"And if she's not?" Kit demanded.

"I leave her outside and we worry about evac if and when we have to. A rescue pod can be sent out that can dock alongside if need be. The colonel is aware of the risks."

Copper was seriously elated and Kit was more than mindful of it, but he also knew that Colonel Moritz was keen to have an intact and safe alien ship as part of her arsenal. With only a warning look at Copper, therefore, he gave the order to make ready to depart and saw her settled securely into the fighter before he took his own place aboard the shuttle.

Copper was tense as she powered up, set the fighter in hover mode and prepared to follow the shuttle out. Kit, she knew, was watching her every move and only set his own ship in motion when she called in over her headset that she was ready. They retraced the route to the point at which communication with the *Drake* had been lost. Copper was able to tell from her own readings that the protective shielding cut out when craft reached the periphery. That event was signalled by a dimming of external lighting, but she also discovered another aspect of her new ship that truly excited her: at the margin of the safe zone, the pilot was prompted to activate the ship's cloaking function. As Spook urged her to comply, she called her findings across to Kit and requested that he keep an eye on her ship to observe the result.

"She's disappeared from my screen!" Halsen called out. "But I *am* picking up a distortion that's registering as unknown, so I can still track her."

"And I can hear you," Copper responded. "So our comms work at close range – or something's facilitating them," she added dryly. "I'll maintain the cloak, though I see it's an energy drain, until we find out what's happening aboard the *Drake*."

"Good call," Kit agreed. "But do *not* move away from us."

"Will comply."

It took a little time to re-establish communications with their ship and that was a formal order to return to their bay with all haste. Colonel Moritz demanding the reason for three and not four lifeforms registering made a wary Kit request that outer bay five be readied for their arrival and that Dr Addystone monitor their approach as agreed and update them on altered docking procedures if necessary. He was given the order to proceed and once above the influence of Blink 159, he and his crew could see why: the *Morgana Atlantis* was still very much in evidence and had assumed an orbit that was higher than but matched the *Drake's*. The *En Hedu'anna* was out of the shuttle's sensor range but she and the other two ships were surely in close proximity.

Kit brought the shuttle into outer bay five and into the most distant station he could. The bay was lit like a festival, with every security system in operation. Only when Copper had docked her small fighter safely was the order given to close bay doors. The second the great outer hatches were sealed, she uncloaked. The newly arrived officers sat waiting in their own craft as external scanners showed a detail of Kit's trained security guards line up across the exits.

"Best get out and meet the welcoming party," Kit grunted, unsealing the exit panel of the shuttle.

Copper was already descending the ramp from the fighter when the other three made it to the bay floor and they waited for her. Trisk and the colonel were at the entry and made their way over to meet the new arrivals, who strode towards them.

"So *that's* your ship, Lieutenant Milkstone," the colonel greeted her.

"That's my ship, ma'am; like her?"

"Dr Addystone deems her safe. You must have some sort of cloak: we detected a warp shift in local space behind the shuttle but that was it – and we *were* looking for it."

"Nice one, Trisk," Copper congratulated. "You figured. And yes ma'am, she has a cloak I can bring up. Smart: even the *Drake* can't do that. But why's the *Morgana Atlantis* still in our orbit?"

A sharp look greeted the tone but the response was that the vessel had recorded signs of viable ores in the area and had transmitted appropriate Mars Gov abstraction licences. She had also logged the signals being emitted into unmapped space from the sub-surface source of alien technology – to which a return signal from the same direction had just been detected by the probe that Trisk had sent out to track it, although no lifesigns had been identified thus far.

Copper paused. "We don't have enough firepower to set up a blockade and tell the *Morgana* politely to pull back," she said slowly. "But the signal's being sent and something out there is maybe replying to it? Are they the good guys promising back-up or the bad guys or strangers trying their luck?"

"Now you're back aboard, Dr Milkstone, we may be able to find out. But let me have a look at your ship."

Despite her own inspection, Trisk's minute examination and Copper's assurances, the colonel deemed it wise to set a guard around the bay. As an intact piece of active alien technology it was a prize worth a great deal of risk, and with a ship like the *Morgana Atlantis* on the doorstep, it was a prize to be protected.

On the way back to her office for a briefing, the colonel also brought Copper and Kit up to date on various other happenings during the few hours they had been off ship. The *Sapphire Sunset* had retrieved her surface gear and its payload of bots, which had been judged safe, and the *Sunset* had been repaired sufficiently that Captain Fantodd had decided to continue his own mission. The *Dexterity* was staying in the vicinity as her captain had sent out a few probes of his own to nearby bodies. The *En Hedu'anna* would stand as back-up for the *Drake* in the meanwhile and the

MSS Mina Fleming had been diverted their way and was closing.

* * *

Some time later, Linen was glad to welcome her friend back to the office to catch up on ship's gossip. The stand-off with the *Morgana Atlantis* was the hot topic in the mess as her captain was known in some circles to be persistent in pursuit of profit and sufficiently astute to scent more than that on the body below. Personal links had been put on hold since both Mars and Earth Fleet ships had detected covert scanning by the civilian ship but supra-light service comms directed to both Fleet HQs to protest the situation and other matters had crossed the spaceways.

"A shot across her bows would be my answer," Copper said shortly. "All this is hampering our work: we *were* supposed to be heading off to the rock where the *Griffon* and those other ships crashed but now we're stuck here awaiting developments. And I want flight practice in my ship, but that'll be curtailed until I get the go-ahead. And I'll need more fuel cells, but until I can get down there to get them, I'll have to hang fire on that."

"This isn't just about you, Cop," Linen reminded her gently.

"Sorry, grumpy and tired," she replied ruefully. "The colonel wants me to help figure a signal coming in on the same bearing as the one the station's sending out: it may not be a reply, but if it is, we might be in for some fun – or not."

"What? I hadn't heard!"

"It's not been broadcast ship-wide, I expect. But Trisk has the details, wherever the blazes he is. Kit's been told to sort out a response to the *Morgana Atlantis* and her scanning antics, our fighter pilots have been ordered to fly regular sorties and the rest of us are at yellow alert for the duration. And Colonel Moritz has strongly hinted that Spook might be useful in setting up a tech block to prevent the *Morgana* from accessing anything down on the surface. I felt like asking her how much he's being paid for his services."

"You didn't, did you?"

"Lor' no, I *have* sense. But I think if the station's monitoring gear can capture the spec of the *Morgana*, it can block her entry and it can warn the other stations about her and similar ships. If they match her, that is: we don't know how many civilian ships are out there that are more than they say on their labels."

"Hell, we didn't sign up for this, I'm sure. Weren't we told we could finish our PhDs and do a bit of cutting-edge science as we toured our corner of the galaxy in chic uniforms that would dazzle the masses?" Linen demanded as a cheery Trisk sailed in.

"You should've read the small print of the holo; it was under the bit that said we agreed to be shot at, beaten up and work all hours," Copper told her. "But what are you so happy about, Dr Addystone? Been given a pay rise?"

"Alas no; but I *have* captured a heap more comms that are beaming this way – and if I'm not mistook, long range scans are saying a large moving mass is responsible."

"Are you saying we have a ship coming in from unmapped space?" Copper breathed.

"No I'm not," he stated categorically. "I can't identify what it is but the source seems to be large and closing: the time from an outward pulse from the rock below to receipt of a return carrier wave with the *same* initial signal is getting shorter. Our comms arrays confirm. I think the initial signal is an ID so I've called it in to the bridge. It's supra-light, so they're at some distance yet and they're moving slowly, I think."

"How long 'til they're here?" Copper demanded sharply.

"Depends if they continue at the same rate or stop. If I were them, I'd stop: they must know we're scanning. Problem is, if our comms can get this data, so can the *Morgana Atlantis*. Unless we can block their scans, Dr Milkstone…"

"I know a subtle hint when I hear one. The colonel's put you up to this, hasn't she? I'll be in the lab. Link me through the data and do not disturb until I say so. Clear?"

"Any more of this bossiness and you'll be drafted into MI's Outer Mars Ops," Linen warned her friend. "Though I doubt they'd promote you over Colonel Karben's head…"

"Button it, Lyrican and tell Junior I want him there as well."

"What for?"

"Two aliens are better than one when they're on our side."

* * *

It was an hour later that an exhausted Copper reeled in with a request for strong caff. Trisk had gone one better, for he had paid a visit to Dr Faerin, explained the situation and been given a small bottle of liquid refreshment from the doc's secret supply.

"Off duty," he told his friends. "Here's to us! Now give us the lowdown on what you've been doing."

Copper had been able to connect so strongly with both aliens that she could direct them to the repair base below and see what they saw. She was almost certain that using that facility as a base rather than the station, which had been subverted and was thus potentially still weak, Spook could safely query the remoter tech and direct it to inhibit intrusion from ill-disposed sources. She could report partial success: the civilian ship had been analysed by probe beams and her specification captured. Copper had also aimed to establish if the return signal from unmapped space was friendly or a counterfeit designed to deceive, given the presence of hostile additions to the base station. Spook was convinced of its authenticity, she was sure. It was also her intention that only craft from the *Drake* would be allowed access to the repair base and only with one of their alien shipmates aboard, hence her request for Junior.

Linen was wary of the last objective. "So if you and Spook are out of it we can still get planetside? What are you up to?"

"I have to obey orders: I might be sent out on a mission and there's a need to get down there. The colonel made it clear that we need cover. I sent her a quick update, so she may stop in. But if the *Morgana* has worked out that whatever's responding to the base's signal is incoming, she may have plans to intercept."

"Her captain would be a fool if she did," was Trisk's opinion.

It was some time before the trio had a visit from the colonel. They were about to adjourn to the mess when she arrived to hear the full story. In return, she brought them up to date on her latest dealings with the captain of the *Morgana Atlantis*, who was aware that the Mars and Earth Fleet vessels had much more data than she had and that her ship had been probed from the surface. Her inference that the military were cooperating to block her caused a protest that fell on deaf ears. The *Morgana's* instruments had also detected the shuttle's return to the *Drake* and that foray was raising her hackles.

It was as the four were heading out that they felt a strange vibration around them; seconds later the red alert siren began to wail. Before the colonel could tab her link to demand the cause, the voice of Faela Khilph calling for her presence on the bridge rang out. The *Morgana Atlantis* had raised her shields and fired a salvo at the base station on Blink 159; she had then come about and launched a second at the *Drake*.

"Milkstone, you're with me: you two, to your stations."

"Aye, ma'am."

By the time Copper and the colonel made the bridge, Khilph had ordered her shields up and every battery online to target the civilian ship. The *En Hedu'anna* had come about and was circling in. The objective of the shot to the *Drake* was not lost on the bridge crew: the *Morgana* had targeted outer bay five.

Copper's first concern was her precious ship but a soothing internal voice assured her that she was safe. Tactical confirmed that the *Drake's* protective armour had withstood the shock and the self-healing hull plates were already repairing the damage. There had been a couple of minor casualties among the security crew assigned to the bay, but nothing worse. That was enough for the colonel, who immediately linked across to the *Morgana* threatening retaliatory action, a position backed by the captains of the *En Hedu'anna* and the *Dexterity*.

The trio of military ships assumed offensive positions around the civilian vessel and waited, holding fire but ready to respond on command, every targeting eye ranging across her hull. They waited for several minutes, but no further signs of a repeat were detected. Tactical finally reported that the *Morgana's* weapons systems were powering down, just as a comms request came in. It was an unknown face that materialised within the holo-grid to acknowledge Colonel Moritz. The latter was blunt.

"What the hell are you playing at? I have several injured crew on deck as a result of your unprovoked attack."

The response from the vessel's first officer Commander Vix Wyld she did not expect: Hellebore's actions in attempting an attack on the *Drake*, despite orders to the *Morgana Atlantis* from the board overseeing her mission to ease off, had so seriously alarmed her senior officers that the captain had been declared medically unfit to command and removed to the brig. Wyld had taken over and was willing to make reparations but refused to retreat from the area. The colonel ordered him to stand by and cut the link to discuss the matter with her fellow commanders. It was obvious that the *Morgana* was aware of the signal being beamed to the station by the unknown source that was now on approach and wanted to wait it out to see what came through.

Copper was by now more than cautious of what was coming towards them. She hailed Trisk in the lab to request that he and Linen maintain a watch on the readings from the probe sent out to detect the inbound mass and link through updates to her as they arose. Her own gear she set to scan in the same direction, to a sharp look from Inkscree at the main science station.

"It's picking up speed," Trisk came back after ten minutes, as word came through that the *MSS Mina Fleming* was on approach vector. "Patching through."

"It's massive all right, but I'm reading more than one discrete entity," Copper announced. "Have we life signs?"

"I concur, but negative on life signs," Trisk stated. "But if it's shielded how would we know? That indicator signal is still part of the carrier wave, but who or what are they?"

Dr Inkscree leaned over to have a good look, called the data over to the colonel and set it up on the bridge holo-grid. The colonel took it in grimly.

"Looks like we're going to have company sometime soon," she said dryly as she called on comms to monitor transmissions. "We assume they're hostile until we know they're not," she decided, after a quick word with the commanding officers of the other Fleet vessels, all of whom could now track the signals. "Contact the *Sapphire Sunset* and request her return: the more we have with us the better. And I'd like to know where the *Morgana Atlantis* stands on this: she surely can read what we can."

The *Sapphire Sunset* was quick to alter course and head back. Captain Neema Batoka of the *Mina Fleming*, now apprised of the situation, called in her support. A few short exchanges later and Commander Wyld of the *Morgana*, whilst refusing to submit to the authority of Mars Fleet, agreed to hold his ship in readiness if the situation proved hostile to their common interests.

"Knows what side his cookie's creamed," Copper muttered to Inkscree. "But I read at least five separate objects now, all on a parallel heading, configuration unknown."

"Sure of that, Lieutenant?" Colonel Moritz asked at her side.

"At the moment ma'am, yes. We're not getting specifics but I guess they're shielded. Though I would assume that they'd have cloaking capability," she added quietly. "But that uses power, and in any large vessel, it would use a lot."

"Friendly, neutral, hostile?"

"Don't know, ma'am; not yet. But I would keep *our* targeting eyes wide open and our weapons systems running hot."

"You're telling me how to run my ship again, Dr Milkstone. But I agree. Let me know if anything changes."

* * *

The next four hours were more or less a waiting game, with data being gathered on a continuous basis from every direction. The *Sapphire Sunset* had returned and had assumed orbit around Blink 159. Exchanges with the *Morgana Atlantis* were limited to civil rebuffs over the situation on the surface of the planetoid, Wyld now having worked out that he could not read what was happening as the analysis systems of the probes he sent out were being systematically scrambled. He blamed the *Drake* and what they had done to the place. The commanders of the Fleet vessels had met over closed links to discuss tactics and reports had been sent supra-light and urgent to both home worlds.

Colonel Moritz had sent her bridge crew off in relays for two hour rest spells, realising that she would need them up to speed. She herself had been ordered off the bridge by her first officer for the same reason. Linen and Trisk, given the task of manning the bridge science stations, reported that little had changed in the interim apart from the approach of a small flotilla of what was now known to be five sizeable craft. The science arrays had verified that the shielded hull structures bore some resemblance to the reddish-green alien organo-tech with which both science officers were familiar.

"Catch some sack time," Copper advised her friends when she reported back for duty. "You're liable to need it."

"For why?" Linen demanded.

"Spook's agitated and he's got me a tad rattled. I think that although our expected party may be friendly, whatever's at back of them might not be. Trisk, extend our long-range arrays as far as possible beyond the approaching unknowns, wide spread."

A few minutes later and Trisk looked up, wide-eyed. "Uh oh! Captain, we may have a problem."

Helmis strode over and was quickly apprised of the situation.

"It might be wise to get our other ships to initiate long-range scanning, sir," Copper advised. "If we can sweep as wide as possible, we can make sure we have only *one* other incoming."

With a shrewd look at her, Helmis called the colonel to the bridge and then relayed the data to his opposite numbers aboard the other vessels. Colonel Moritz was immediately aware of the potential implications once she had been brought up to speed.

"You think we have trouble?" she demanded of Copper.

"Yes, ma'am. The closer convoy is in constant contact with the station, as far as I can tell: I can't find any signals being sent this way from what's showing up further out. It's ambiguous, but the anomaly there reads mightily like a large power source – the energy readings are extremely high."

"Your interpretation of that?"

"It or they don't seem to be cloaked, so they don't feel the need. I would guess they're heavily armed and they outnumber the objects that are going to get here first. I don't like the look or feel of it – and neither does Spook."

"We'd better hope what's first is friendly or neutral. You're here for the present, Dr Milkstone; Addystone and Lyrican, you two get some rest if you haven't had any and then get back to your stations. I may need you on the bridge later."

The three complied, but Linen's face was set as she and Trisk stepped through the elevator door. "The lab," she stated grimly. "She wants us on the bridge because she has other plans for Cop that might just involve that little boat in outer bay five."

"That's what I reckon," Trisk agreed. "I'll take first watch, you grab an hour or so of sleep; then we swop. I'll make sure we have a supply of Oxypep handy – hell knows when we'll get more sleep if the balloon does go up."

Linen did not argue: she was unnerved and conscious that a very frightened Junior had picked up something that was scaring the sol-lights out of him.

* * *

It was less than an hour later that the red alert siren sounded throughout the ship and the call to battlestations rang out.

31: FIRST CONTACT

The holo-grid that extended down into the *Drake's* main bridge space was in continuous flux as data from every linked station streamed in to update the whole. Copper's task was to refine the material her science arrays were gathering and add it in. Inkscree on her right was similarly employed and she was conscious that every other position was equally active. The blast of the red alert had been muted to spare their ears but warning lights flashed from every bulkhead.

The minutes ticked by as the approaching blips grew larger and their outlines could be determined. No-one on the bridge of the *Drake* or their Fleet sister ships had seen anything like them. Wyld of the *Morgana Atlantis* also claimed to be baffled and was sufficiently alarmed to accept the authority of Colonel Moritz as commander of whatever action would be taken once the small fleet came within visual range.

The consensus was that five ships made up the group but none of the instruments trained on them could detect the nature of their weaponry, and the shifting nature of the readings that could be gleaned denoted some sort of constantly changing hull protection. Signals from the surface of the planetoid below had accelerated, implying huge data exchange. Copper's reading was that the station was either advising the newcomers that the local humans were friendly or warning them to expect trouble. Spook had shot off somewhere and a quick link from Linen indicated that Junior had done the same.

"They're slowing, ma'am!"

That was Vespoltz at tactical. Trisk confirmed from his lab and Copper quickly verified, calling that her readings were now clearer. The power levels of the approaching ships had stabilised to a degree that allowed a more detailed analysis of their lines.

"Show me!" Colonel Moritz demanded, rising.

Copper pulled up a visual of the vessel leading the group and quickly sent it to the main holo. The streamlined keel of the craft was an iridescent fusion of soft, metallic shades of shifting red, green and silver, almost bullet-shaped as it tapered towards what was possibly the stern of the ship, but with an aft section of what looked like a circular tailfin enclosing the rear hull. Parts of her exterior plating looked almost transparent against the blackness of space, but Copper realised that this was an optical illusion and down to the ship's chameleon outer coating.

"Your analysis of it, Lieutenant Milkstone?"

"She's beautiful," Copper breathed. "She is not targeting, nor has she armed weapons but she *is* scanning. And she's friendly: which is just as well, as she's got more firepower than two *Drake II* Class Explorer ships combined and I bet her crew knows how to use it."

"Her crew?" the colonel questioned sharply.

"I'm reading life signs. You got those, Trisk?"

"Just come up; she must be allowing scans as I had nothing before. But I'm reading very few lifeforms for a ship of her size: she's about the equivalent of one of our smaller corvettes."

"What kind of lifeforms, Dr Addystone?"

"Carbon-based organic overtones, ma'am; but strongly allied to some of the readings we're familiar with..."

"Spook," Copper clarified.

"More like Junior," Trisk put in. "There *are* differences, but we have a manned ship. The other ships are still shielded, so we can't read them."

"Then we treat them as potentially hostile until we know any different," Ms Moritz stated. "Can you render these lifeforms inoperative if you have to, Dr Addystone?"

"That depends on the non-organic moieties, ma'am and their ability to separate from their organic mass: so far we haven't been able to slow either Spook or Junior down."

Copper was outraged. "You mean you and Faerin tried?"

"*Dr* Faerin, and naturally we did. We had our orders. And we didn't tell you because you'd take it badly. We *have* developed an energy-dispersion beam that we think might disrupt an energy-based lifeform: it's untested as obviously we wouldn't use that against our own."

Biting down on her anger, Copper scanned her boards again. "Lead ship is leaving the group and drawing closer ma'am," she informed Colonel Moritz. "But what the… what's the *Morgana* doing? She's moving too – Vespoltz, is she on intercept?"

"That's what I read."

The colonel speedily resumed her seat, demanding an instant link to Vix Wyld. She ordered him to stand down, and receiving a negative, she bid Captain Batoka of the *Mina Fleming* target the *Morgana* and disable her if she continued on her present course, repeating her order to Wyld. He complied as the Mars Fleet ship came about, but maintained his vessel's targeting of the stranger.

Copper was seriously alarmed and quietly called on Trisk and Linen to maintain watch on the civilian ship, including scans of the forr'ad areas of her outer hull where certain of her weapons emplacements and scanning arrays included integral amounts of destructive alien organo-technology. She knew now that the two resident aliens from the *Drake* were aboard the oncoming ship, and though sure that they could leave at the first sign of trouble, she had no intention of taking chances. She was beginning to suspect why Spook had decided to investigate, with Junior along for the ride.

All six human ships maintained their positions as the small starship closed in on the *Drake*. She was half a kilometre away when she hove to, maintaining a stable orbit that matched that of the Mars Fleet ships around Blink 159. The colonel, with a look at her first officer, ordered comms to hail the vessel. A buzz of unknown fizz that may have been static was the only response received. As the seconds lengthened into minutes, the visual of the vessel shimmered as its hull flickered in the dark, and the comms officer shook his head in exasperation: he could make nothing of what was being sent.

Copper was aware of a growing gnawing in her belly that she knew was apprehension: Spook and Junior had returned and the former was proposing a course of action that she was more than reluctant to take. But as Spook had risked much to help her and her ship, she felt she had little option but to return the favour.

"Ma'am, I have a suggestion," she said, her voice sounding strained as it crossed the bridge to the command chair.

"I thought you might," the colonel responded softly, rising to make her way to the science station. "Has your Spook been over there to see what's what?" she demanded quietly.

Copper nodded. "Yes ma'am, with Junior. They're friendly; I'm picking up that they're akin to Junior. They want to connect to us but they can't, directly... but through me, with Spook, we may be able to establish a link..."

"And?"

"I suggest I take the alien fighter out to take a closer look..."

"No. You do that and the other ships out there will be more than aware we have such a craft aboard."

"Not if I cloak her..."

"A closer look? Is that *all* you'll be doing?"

The sceptical tone of the question alerted Copper to the fact that the colonel knew precisely what was on her mind. But its emphasis suggested that she was amenable to persuasion.

"That would depend on what I find when I get close enough, ma'am. We know these people have smaller craft: that suggests a means of landing aboard that ship. I've been through the repair bay down there and that gives me some idea of what to expect."

"I doubt that very much..."

"Ma'am, you won't persuade one of them over here, they're too few. And there's a lot of fear aboard that ship about what's heading in after them, *that* much I know. Which means trouble for us: if *they're* scared, what *is* out there? We can be sure it's not friendly, so where does that leave us if a massive fleet bursts out on top of us?"

In reply, the colonel called for an update on the signals being picked up by the long-range scanners of all the Fleet vessels that indicated a second unidentified energy source heading their way. The evidence not only pointed to a colossal incoming mass of power, but that it was building and seemed to be dispersing over a larger area. Its speed and direction were unchanged. Trisk had called in that the probe they had sent out to track the initial signal was active still. Its data suggested the likely presence of alien lifeforms but he could not relate them to those with which he was familiar or to those he had read from the ship close by. He was also reading what he deemed to be organo-technology.

"Trisk *is* the expert in the field," Copper remarked as comms were cut. "I realise that this is essentially a first contact situation, ma'am, and I may not even be able to make contact. But…"

"This isn't entirely your idea, is it Lieutenant?"

"No ma'am. But *that* looks like big trouble and it's coming closer."

"At the present rate of progress, how long 'til it gets here?" the colonel demanded of her science officers.

"Twenty three hours, if our scans are accurate and if current speed and heading are maintained," Inkscree replied.

"Stand by."

* * *

Bay five was eerily silent, its security personnel at attention around the perimeter as Copper, suited up in the best protective gear that the *Drake* possessed and with the colonel alongside, entered the bay. The guards had clearly been primed and knew what was going on. The farewell committee was there, Copper noted, and was not surprised. The hugs from Linen and Trisk she reciprocated silently as Colonel Moritz looked on. She knew what was coming from Kit: his grim mouth gave his opinion of the situation and despite the presence of the colonel he gave vent to his frustration. Copper was ready for him and took his hand gently.

"We're in it for the survival of all of us, Kit. These aliens are friendly and were here long before we were sentient enough to notice. They *will* look out for me. But hell is riding in less than a sol behind them and if we want to make it out, it'll take us and them – and whatever back-up we or they can call on, because this is no picnic. I *will* see you on the flipside, I promise."

"Damn you," he returned softly. "Just you look after yourself and come safe home. If there's one scratch, I'll have the hide of that Spook of yours if it's the last thing I do."

"He knows, believe me." She grinned crookedly, her heart in her eyes, and turned to go.

"Go after her and give her a kiss, you great idiot," Linen advised in a whisper. "Sir," she added as the blue eyes flashed a warning. "Junior, you're with me. And you're for the lab, Trisk: we'll all be welded to our stations for the duration."

"Aye ma'am. Funny, I wasn't aware of your promotion over me," he added with a quirky look at Colonel Moritz as they all turned to go. "And when did Copper start sounding like a third rate space holo-epic? Hell's riding in less than a sol behind?"

"She's scared," Linen said. "And so am I. What in blazes did I sign up for? I must have been flippy."

"No comment."

"Just make sure your juvenile Spookling is beside you and you're both in constant contact with Dr Milkstone, Lieutenant Lyrican," the colonel ordered. "*We* are for the bridge."

"Aye, ma'am."

As Linen took her place at the secondary science station, she could see the colonel in close discussion with her first officer. Captain Helmis was another one sceptical of the whole thing, unable to see what good would come of sending a small craft to scout out an alien starship about which they knew nothing and feared everything. He advised bringing both the *En Hedu'anna* and the *Mina Fleming* into the operation: as *Drake II* Class ships, they were equipped to a similar spec to themselves and could lend support in tracking Dr Milkstone. Even cloaked, her ship's displacement shift would be traceable by their scanners.

The colonel agreed, and as Copper prepped for launch, there was a quick exchange of information between the *Drake* and her sister ships as to their deployment positions. This activity as the vessels moved out did not go unnoticed by the remaining human-crewed ships but it was the *Morgana Atlantis* that linked in to demand why the *Drake* had launched some cloaked device: her superior equipment had picked up a shift in local space that had clearly come from one of the *Drake's* outer landing bays.

"They know damn well it was bay five!" Helmis snapped. "They've had covert eyes on us since they got here."

"As we've had on them," the colonel reminded him. "Wyld can sweat. We owe him no explanation. Patch me through to Dr Milkstone," she added to the comms officer.

Copper was as close to quaking as she could be within the confines of her small fighter but she responded equably that all was on target for a close visual appraisal and scan of the primary alien ship. She was made aware of the status of the craft around her and promptly had Spook keep watch on the *Morgana Atlantis* and request that his contacts aboard the alien ship do the same.

The shimmering synthesis of ever-changing shades of silvery red and green flowing through one another was mesmerising as Copper called up the external visual on her fighter's holo-grid, her hands automatically transferring the data to the *Drake*. In her mind she could hear the musical sounds that complemented the fluid movements as the tapered nose of the ship slid past her eyes and she made for the aft section with its encircling fin that seemed to be a part of yet unconnected with the hull. Close to, the almost translucent hull plating was now a misty green-white that shifted as the ship hung in space.

In her small fighter, Copper navigated around the hull in various orbits, taking in everything that her instruments could to transfer to the *Drake*. The hull appeared seamless, but knowing her own small craft, she realised that there had to be openings at more than one point. Spook, aware of her tactics, directed her amidships, towards what was the underside of the vessel. A shift in the colour of her hide showed suddenly as a solid block of green. As she watched, a panel rose upward to disappear into the plating above. She recognised the structure of the smooth conduit into the ship's interior: it was surfaced in a lustrous pink coating and lit like the interior of the repair facility of the nearby planetary body. A series of diminishing wall lights led inward.

"That's an invitation if ever I saw one, ma'am," she declared as she called in her observations. "I don't sense danger. Request permission to enter."

"I'm surprised she's asking," Helmis muttered dryly.

Colonel Moritz glanced towards Linen, who was gazing back. The redhead slowly nodded: Junior was assuring her that all was well. Trisk, monitoring from the lab, detected no overt threat and the readings from both *En Hedu'anna* and *Mina Fleming* were stable. And all knew that Kit was observing the situation from security. The four alien ships that had hung back remained at their stations, readings unchanging.

Copper locked in her controls for an entry to the bay as she would have done for docking within the *Drake*. As she passed into the space, she felt rather than saw her surroundings change and cut her cloak. The lighting increased and her forward path continued straight until a looming wall told her she was nearing an end point. She powered down to come to rest on a clearly-defined landing pad, running every sensor she had on external scan. Unlike the repair facility on Blink 159, there was no cut in comms and she remained in contact with her own people.

"The outer hull's closing up, Cop!" Linen called out.

"So is an inner panel behind me," Copper's voice came over the comm. "I'm reading externals now… there's a change to the atmosphere beyond my ship, the bay's pressurising. It's small, hardly bigger than my ship. Are you getting that, *Drake*?"

"We are," the colonel confirmed. "Proceed with extreme caution, Lieutenant. Can we track her within that ship, tactical?"

"Aye ma'am, scans are now penetrating the hull," Vespoltz returned. "On grid."

"She's a long way from the centre of the thing," Helmis said in an undertone. "But where's the bridge on a ship like that? If they have one, that is."

"I'll no doubt find out," Copper returned, having caught the aside. "Debarking now; and I think my escort's just turned up," she added with a snort of laughter.

"Lieutenant?"

"There's what looks like a small mechanoid appeared, ma'am, through an entry. Adjusting my suit's scanner to view ahead, so you should see more or less what I can. Atmosphere's reading as an oxygen-nitrogen mix, but I won't remove my breather unit. Gravity's similar to Mars: I don't know if that's for my convenience or theirs. Mine, I suspect."

Both Colonel Moritz and Captain Helmis were gazing at the section of holo-grid that had captured the visuals from Copper's scanner and most other eyes were locked on the same. They could see her route through the interior of the alien ship, in the wake of a metre-high blue metallic shape that looked to Linen curiously like her friend's holo-dragon with its elongated snout, tiny twisting ears, scaly blue body and short forelimbs. The mobile head of the thing twisted now and again to make sure she was following along the narrow passageway. There were no openings apparent and very few symbols that might represent signage although various rectangular outlines suggested entries.

At one of these the small guide stopped, its glittering green eyes looking up. The panel slid upwards to reveal an enclosed space lit in a pale white light. Copper followed her escort into it and the panel closed.

"Transport tube of some sort?" she hazarded. "There's a wall panel with coloured infill that's changing. I detect movement..."

"So do we," the colonel informed her. "You're on a straight trajectory inwards. We still read you loud and clear; from that I infer that we're being permitted to follow your progress. You're now heading upwards. It looks like your destination is towards the upper decks."

"The panel here *is* registering changing levels, I think, ma'am; though I can't read its output."

As her journey advanced over the next few minutes, Copper was apprised of current Fleet activities. Mars, Earth and all their associated stations and outposts were on alert, urgent supra-light reports having been despatched on a regular basis to both Fleet Command HQs. Mars Fleet had diverted the *MSS Lithium Star* their way and the *EFS Stephen Hawking*, an Earth ship, was also heading in: both would arrive in around nine hours.

"Coming to a halt," she interrupted, her stomach tightening into a knot as a slight shudder heralded the end of the ride and a panel to her right slid up to reveal a lighted space beyond.

The blue mechanoid scuttled forward and stopped outside, its flexible head twisting round to look at her, lights sparking from its green eyes. "This way, Copper," it said, gesturing.

"Bloody hell!" Helmis exclaimed as Copper began to laugh softly to cover her own astonishment, not unmixed with fear.

"Talk about making me feel at home," she said aloud. "This ship must have been able to make a link to the tech we have aboard, ma'am, and extract what it thought was relevant to me. And now it speaks."

"Spook's having a laugh," Linen articulated clearly. "Ask him if it can fly the ship."

"Belay that, Lieutenant," Copper responded as she stepped though the opening. "What the... would you look at that!"

She found herself on a platform that looked down into and circled a lower deck that she took to be the control centre of the ship. There was a perimeter barrier separating the raised section from the well below and she could see a number of outlines in varying shades set in at intervals around her own level that may have been panels to other areas or transport tubes. The walls around her shimmered in metallic shades of soft green and pink and a glance above showed a domed upper section with another galleried level encircling the space. She voiced her observations to the watchers aboard the *Drake* as she stepped forward to take hold of the rail and look over to the depth below. As she did so, a large pod detached from a side wall and began to move in the direction of her position.

"What's that?" she asked her diminutive guide, who merely looked up at her and rotated its tiny ears, its eyes sparkling.

Reaching the edge, the hulled pod settled alongside; a panel retracted and a matching gap appeared in the barrier. There was something vaguely familiar about the object and Copper stepped closer to examine the interior.

"It's like the bucket seat of my fighter!" she exclaimed. "Am I supposed to hop aboard?"

"This way, Copper," warbled her short friend in its curiously tinny voice, moving closer to the edge.

"Be careful, Lieutenant," Colonel Moritz warned.

"Affirmative ma'am," she responded as she slid sideways into the seat, twisting to settle into the tight space in her restrictive protective clothing.

As her seat expanded slightly to give her more room, she was faced with a semi-circular control console. Her forward and side views were clear; she could see beyond the confines of the pod to the space outside and also realised that she could call up a view-grid if necessary. Automatically she reached for the woven headpiece that provided additional control: it was there and it was active, its twinkling lights shooting through its component strands. As she pulled the device down over her breather unit, she spied the dragon-like form still on the platform.

"You coming?" she asked. "There's room at back of me. But don't touch anything," she warned as it zipped forward to climb into the cramped compartment behind her.

"You'll have to give him a name," Linen's voice came over the comm.

"Can it, Dr Lyrican. I'm sealing the unit: there's a retractable shell that closes the cockpit," she advised the *Drake*. "It's a self-contained capsule," she elucidated. "The controls are similar to my fighter but there are fewer for flight, more for analysis as well as environmental and tactical data... I don't quite get it. I can call up a spec of the ship on the view-grid I think. Ah, here's this place: it must be the main control centre, the bridge. Where are my weapons? What the... the unit's locking onto my own suit's controls and my own hand-held and abstracting the data!"

"All we can see is the interior of that unit, Lieutenant; what's going on outside?" the colonel demanded.

"A moment, ma'am," answered Copper, distracted, trying to assimilate the information that Spook was pressing on her. "I'm going to get this in motion if I can. It was sent up here on auto, so I guess it can be returned to its base the same way, but as it's not moving, I must be expected to pilot it. But what... uh oh! Another on approach!"

A second pod had appeared off her bow. She looked over. There was a form inside it, changeful through the shifting motes of colour that cloaked the forward windows, but Copper had a fleeting impression of familiarity. She adjusted her suit's scanner to capture the data. The face looking back at her was not human but it *was* a face, ovoid but tapering back as if stretched to fluted extensions either side that might be ears; it had a white down at its crest and a greenish tinge to the skin, but that may have been distortion. Its features were indistinct areas of dark. A skinny neck melted into the collar of some sort of metallic suit but a raised arm, also clad in the suit, ended in five elongated digits. These moved in unison, bending down and then straightening.

"*Drake*, you got it?" Copper breathed, mirroring the gesture.

"We got it," the colonel verified. "Science stations, capture every iota of that data."

"Junior's just gone over the two moons," Linen called out.

The windows of the opposite pod cleared and Copper could now see what she took to be eyes, two, and further apart than most human eyes would be, but in a similar place. Their colour she could not differentiate but they were light, large and seemed to flicker in the small face.

"Two nostrils, I think, two eyes – twofold symmetry then," the voice of Ossy Inkscree could be heard, sounding shaken.

"That's about right," Copper agreed, recalling the images that she, Linen and Trisk had seen when Junior had used the hard-holo projector dug up from the Warren to recall memories of his parents: they would have looked similar to what was before her, had they been substantial.

"Congratulations, Dr Milkstone: first verified contact with another sentient species," Captain Helmis said quietly.

"That we know about," Copper returned dryly. "This pod's scanned my gear and incorporated the data into itself: I'm now getting recognisable readings on the view-grid and info-console, if that's what this is. I'm reading an internal pod atmosphere of twenty percent oxygen to seventy nine nitrogen and trace others including argon. I'm going to remove my helmet."

"Careful, Lieutenant!" Colonel Moritz cut in.

"Aye ma'am. But as I've seen its face, I think it only fair that it should see mine."

Very gingerly, Copper undid the neck catches of her breather unit and slid it over her head, setting it to one side. She took a deep breath of the air around her. It was sweet and fresh and smelt of trees and salt water. Smiling, she reached up to pull the suspended control circlet closer to her scalp, looking over at her opposite number in the other pod. She then repeated the hand gesture it had used. Its eyes widened slightly and sparkled at her.

"Can you still hear me, ma'am? Good. Now we get the show on the road," she announced. "I guess I'll follow her."

"Her?"

"I get the impression she's female, ma'am, I can't think why. And I'm beginning to suspect what this pod is," Copper said. "She moves like my fighter, though not at speed. Let's see what we have in this place."

The area around the two pods was considerable but not huge. In circumference it was slightly larger than the bridge of the *Drake* but at least three times the depth. As she swept her small transport unit in an all-encompassing circle, Copper could see other pods that seemed to be locked into stations at various heights on bulkheads that resembled the hexagonal structure of the inside of her fighter. Various protrusions suggested other operational areas. From the depth of the well rose a stalk that ended in a flat surface with a triple indentation that looked as if it would take three pods of the size she occupied.

"That must be the command position," Copper conjectured. "This *is* the bridge of an alien starship. Each of those pods must be a crewed position. And there's a line on my view-grid from my current position to that central station."

"This way, Copper," said a voice at her back.

"If that's all that frigging blue dragon can say, it's going to get pretty monotonous," Linen remarked loudly.

"Can it, Dr Lyrican," the blue dragon replied.

"I see they based it on you," the redhead retorted as her friend's transport began to move towards the central location.

"These three docks are empty: does that mean no-one's in command up here?" Copper asked, puzzled. "My companion is moving into the central one of the three. I'm docking alongside: the pod just slots in. There must be an automatic system that locks down, as I show secure. What the…my cockpit's opening! So's hers. The air is still okay. The pods are being augmented by the controls of this station… we *have* locked in place, as if we've become part of it. There's a holo-grid rising up beyond us that's expanding out. Have you got that *Drake*? It's a tactical holo I think, but more detailed than ours."

"It's less than clear here, no specifics," the colonel replied.

"The entity sat next to me is manipulating some controls in front of her and that's definitely a tactical holo. I can see the other alien ships, you and the other Fleet ships and the shapes are distinct. Uh oh! I note the *Morgana Atlantis* is surrounded by what looks like a targeting field grid. From that I figure that she's considered unfriendly, or at least potentially so."

"We're still not getting that from your suit-scan," Helmis reported. "And our sister ships are getting a tad restless, ma'am, as are the *Dexterity* and the *Sapphire Sunset*: they want to know what's going on. The *En Hedu'anna* and the *Mina Fleming* tracked Lieutenant Milkstone's fighter as far as the ship but they lost her signal when she docked."

"Tell the commanding officers of *all* Fleet ships to stand by and prepare for a tight-beam secured transmission to be taken privately. I'll send it from my office. And if the *Morgana* as much as blinks, warn her we'll take action."

"Aye, ma'am; Wyld is still bending our ears demanding to know what we're playing at."

"Choke him off. And you, Lieutenant Milkstone, get as much information as you can on that ship and the current situation as far as its commander is concerned – if that's who's with you."

"Copy that, ma'am," Copper responded automatically.

As her eyes and other senses took in what was happening in response, she assumed, to the manoeuvres of her companion, a movement close by made her look up. She was just in time to see one of the suspended pods around her leave one site and flit to another in the wall of the large well that was the bridge of the ship, slotting into its site and rotating towards the centre of the space. The being beside her raised a hand and gestured towards the relocated pod and then to the view-grid that was part of the main console of her own pod, now a part of the station to which she was attached.

"I'm not sure but I think she's ordered one of her crew to move to that station," Copper called out. "And it's her tactical officer: it looks like there's something in the offing, Captain…"

Responding to a hint from Spook, Copper pulled the sensory circlet above her head closer, focussing on the actions about her and the data that was flowing across the linked consoles at the central command station. Suddenly she understood: probes that the ship had dropped on the way in were returning data that related to a fleet that was tailing them. That fleet was drawing closer, its progress plotted on the main holo-grid.

"My ship will need that," Copper said firmly, pointing, as she looked at her fellow and then indicated the *Drake* on the grid.

The message was received, for Captain Helmis announced that he was now receiving data on what closely resembled an incoming fleet as a direct link from the alien ship. As soon as Colonel Moritz resumed her chair, she was made aware of the situation. She ordered the circulation of the data to the other Fleet ships, and on a quick discussion with their commanders, she linked to the *Morgana* to update Wyld also.

It was quickly obvious that the next few hours would be a long haul. The capabilities and intentions of the advancing fleet were unclear and although hostility was now the expected outcome, its form was open to speculation. Responses from the home worlds were as expected: no retreat and gather as much data as possible to provide a heads-up if the incursion spread, though both Mars and Earth Fleets were preparing for action. Wyld would not divulge the orders to the *Morgana Atlantis* from home but it was noted by the Fleet ships that the civilian vessel had begun a systematic strengthening of her hull defences.

Colonel Moritz had ordered a reduced alert status to enable her crew to take time out on a rotational basis in view of the impending emergency. Copper was meanwhile trying to evaluate the alien ship and the mission that had called her and her sister ships to the small planetoid. She had seen links to what she took to be the commanders of the other four ships and knew that she had been introduced to each, as her small escort had advised her to return the raised hand that seemed to be the alien form of salute with the words, "Say hello, Copper." Various members of the small bridge crew had flown over in their pods to view the stranger and she had exchanged signals with each, listening to the soft chirruping that may have been their spoken language.

After over two hours of solid attention to absorb as much as she could of the bridge of the strange vessel, and stiff within the confines of her pod, Copper communed with Spook. She was sorely in need of bodily refreshment, and calling up the mental images of her quarters aboard the *Drake* and the officers' mess and its purpose, she hoped he could communicate the same to her hosts. She had voiced her wants aloud at the request of her blue friend, who seemed to recognise that there was a problem. The result was startling: her seat began to vibrate slowly, easing her cramped muscles; moments later, a pod hove alongside.

"Your aide, Copper," the blue dragon informed her.

"My what?"

"Your aide. To escort you to your personal space."

"My what?" Copper repeated, mystified. "Personal space? You mean quarters?"

"Personal space. As Captain Spook recommends," said a soft and melodious voice.

The words were hesitant but clear and they came from the entity alongside, who nodded slowly at her: the alien officer had evidently begun to identify human speech patterns and gestures, react to them, and imitate them.

"You're quicker than I am, ma'am," she smiled over with a responding nod of affirmation.

"It speaks?" the voice of Helmis sounded from her suit's communicator. "You're talking to it?"

"Her," Copper corrected. "The commanding officer seems to understand that I need a break. I've been assigned personal space and an aide, so I'm heading off to see what it's all about."

"You've got a billet aboard an alien starship?" Helmis said disbelievingly. "What next?"

"Dinner, I hope," Copper replied as she acknowledged the entity in the newly-arrived pod. "I'm starved."

"The sol you're not hungry is the sol the galaxy ends," Linen called over the comm. "Save some for me, I haven't had mine."

"Speech: so they communicate vocally and produce sound in organic form," Trisk deduced from the primary science station.

"Well, she seems to have ears," was Linen's contribution. "Let's see the visual of your quarters, I'm curious."

"Nosey, you mean," Copper replied as she detached her pod, realising that her escort's vehicle would not accommodate her.

She followed her appointed aide to the platform above and hove alongside the barrier, where an opening appeared to allow her to debark. She collected her breather unit, despite her blue friend's remark that it was unnecessary. The small entity hopped off behind her, evidently intent on following. Her aide was by that stage on the platform and gestured to the transport tube in which she had arrived. The alien was clad like the commander in a deep red glossy suit, but was visibly physically different, more thickset, with a skin deeper in colour and darker eyes. He walked upright on two legs, seemed sprightly and at full stretch was shorter than Copper.

"He asks that you follow him, Copper," the blue dragon said.

Copper had heard nothing. "So now you're telepathic," she remarked sardonically, looking down at the creature.

"Translator," it corrected.

"You'll have to give that dragon a name," Linen called out. "How about Scalenyx Junior?"

"Too long," her friend retorted as she stepped into the tube. "Nyx," she added. "You'll respond to Nyx," she told it, flicking its whirling left ear. "And what's my aide called?"

The response was a jumbled mass of soft syllables. "But he'll respond to Pyx," the dragon told her.

"Very funny. Let's move it – oops, we are! Now as you seem to have picked up dual language skills, ask Pyx what his captain's name is, and what this ship's called."

The lengthy reply earned Nyx another flicked ear but during the short ride outwards from the bridge, she gathered that the captain's name could be shortened to Flor. The ship's name was equally long and translated as *Interstellar Wanderer*, but as Copper had picked up only the first couple of syllables, she decided that *Sally* was as close as she was likely to get to its pronunciation.

Her personal space was marked by a gold-edged panel and a central symbol of a six-pointed star, eliciting a rude remark from Linen aboard the *Drake*. Entry was gained by a hand print, as a mime-show by her aide explained. As they entered, the space lit up in welcome and Copper looked around.

"I've seen bigger closets," was her opinion, but she dutifully listened to the details of its trappings translated by Nyx. "And now I'm signing off for a couple of hours," she informed her colleagues. "Some things you don't need to see or hear."

"Make sure your medi-tag's operational," a familiar voice cut in. "We *will* be monitoring it. And we'll alert you if we have to."

Copper laughed as she confirmed: Kit was evidently manning the security station on the bridge. She dismissed Pyx, who gave the familiar hand salute and left, but Nyx refused to budge. In the end she gave up and made her first attempt to extract a snack and a drink from the catering niche.

* * *

A buzzing above her head woke Copper and she dazedly sat up, demanding the time. Nyx informed her that she had napped for two hours precisely, as requested. As she slid off the narrow shelf that did duty as a couch and hit the switch that folded it up into a table and chair, she realised that the room had changed. The panel to the hygiene cubicle was open, a gentle steam was issuing from it and hung from a hook outside it was a one-piece uniform in shiny deep red that looked to be in her size.

"What am I supposed to do in there?" she asked Nyx.

"Scrub up. Undress and stand inside for two minutes. Your uniform is ready."

"This'll be the shortest shower I ever took. And you'll turn to face the wall and stay there until I say otherwise. I'm not having you record my ablutions for the record."

She continued to grumble until she stepped into the small space, when she found out just what scrub up meant: the whole cubicle became a swirling mass of soft wet brush and she was swept from head to foot. A warm gush of air through the brush dried most of her and she stepped out to find her discarded garments had been folded and placed on the table. They were clean and warm. And Nyx was still facing the wall.

"What the… this place will be the end of me," she protested as she dressed, carefully transferring her own devices to the new uniform, which was surprisingly lightweight, warm and much like the enviro-suit she had been used to as a researcher.

"This must be a breather unit," she said to herself, checking her appearance in a wall mirror. "Where are my weapons?"

"You won't need them, Copper."

"I'll be the judge of that. And you can turn around. Who moved my stuff?" she added, tweaking her wrist-comm.

"Automatic systems."

"I believe you. Milkstone to *Drake*: are you reading me?"

"Loud and clear, Lieutenant. Can you get a visual?"

"Good question, ma'am. Nyx, can I get a visual to my ship?"

"Yes. From the comm console on the wall. Linking now."

"I wish I knew how he did that," Copper complained as she took in the bridge of the *Drake* and was thankful to see several well-known faces at their stations.

"You've had some rest, Lieutenant?" the colonel said with a lift to her eyebrow at Copper's appearance.

"Yes, ma'am. I suspect I was hit with some sleepy stuff, as I don't remember a thing. When I awoke, I found this suit and it's a perfect fit: I judge that I'm a tad larger than most of my hosts. I'm not sure if it's a mark of respect or it has systems necessary aboard this ship."

"Both," Nyx told her.

"Nobody asked you. I'll head on up to the bridge and see what's happening there, ma'am. I take it there's been no change in circumstances otherwise?"

The approaching convoy was still advancing at the same rate, Copper was told. It was now clear that there were at least twelve distinct forms within the group. Data was being transferred as it was received by the alien probes to the *Drake* via the lead alien ship and all the vessels in the area were holding position. Other than that, there had been no further communications with the aliens: all attempts at contact had been ignored. The *Drake* had intercepted attempted links from the *Morgana Atlantis* to the *Sally*, but these had not been returned, as far as they were aware.

Copper found Pyx outside her quarters and requested escort to the bridge. He swiftly complied, turning smartly to indicate the nearest transport tube.

The control centre looked almost exactly as it had when she left it, she noted, the main alteration being the central holo; that was much more complex and contained clearer representations of the approaching fleet, as well as additional data. At a hint from Spook, she resumed the station she had occupied earlier, saluting Captain Flor, who was still there. She reckoned that they had about ten to twelve hours before the showdown began and meant to make the most of them by getting to grips with some of the technology within which she sat.

It was as she was informing Colonel Moritz that the targeting grid around the *Morgana Atlantis* had increased in intensity that she was alerted by Captain Flor of an incoming signal from the base station on the planetoid the humans called Blink 159. From the captain's halting speech and Nyx's rendition of the rest, she realised that the station had picked up signals via its relay of sister stations within and beyond the Sol system. With Spook's guidance, she called up the data on her own auxiliary holo-grid.

"There's going to be quite a party," she announced. "I have the specs of several ships that look to be homing in on this area of space. Two are Fleet; one is similar to the *Dexterity* and reads as an Earth Fleet heavy cruiser, so that'll be the *Stephen Hawking*. The other's the *Lithium Star*. But we have a large civilian whose outline looks uncannily similar to the *Morgana*. Do we have any evidence that she had a sister ship? Was Magenta Firewall right in her opinion that at least one other deep-space explorer ship was in the offing?"

"Three ships are not several, Lieutenant," the colonel noted.

"No ma'am. We also have three that read as alien heading in from beyond our exploratory range at speed: they're not in the same line as the hostiles approaching and this system has them tagged as friendly, or at least neutral – no targeting grids. But we have another on approach, also reading as alien and it's heading in from Lux Noctis, our mission target – the body where the *Griffon* crashed."

"Are you sure, Dr Milkstone?"

"Aye ma'am, it's quite clear here. It's labelled non-hostile at least and it should be here sooner than the *Hawking*; in about an hour from what I can figure from these readings. What I can't work out is if it *is* from where the *Griffon* and those other ships met their ends, who or what is piloting it? Unless another ship dropped off a pilot…"

"Or it's automatic," Trisk, now back in his lab and listening in, interjected.

"Something would still have had to set it off…"

"Remember the partial sim we set up of Lux Noctis for Doc Inkscree's bots," Linen put in. "We spotted a large lump of red-green tech near the limit of the crash site that seemed to be stuck below a ledge; you thought it was a small shuttle or escape pod that had been mostly concealed."

"I didn't believe it then," Inkscree grated from alongside her. "And from what I can see of what your friends have sent over, Dr Milkstone, I don't believe it now. Whatever *that* is, it's too big to be a shuttle."

"It's a good bit smaller than that ship you're in now," Linen noted. "But I agree with Dr Inkscree: it's large for a shuttle or an escape craft or similar, at least as far as *we* know."

Her friend's eyes opened wider as Captain Flor, who clearly had been following the exchange, indicated some readings and a holo she had called up on her own grid. It seemed to be the expanding spec of a space vessel of some kind.

"Well I'll be! A fusion, a bringing together of parts?" she asked of the alien captain.

"I confirm," was the response.

"The captain agrees," Nyx translated.

"Got it," said Copper shortly. "That, people, is a hybrid: it's a fusion of more than one ship, including scraps of the *Griffon* and bits of tech left by the *Lithium Star*. But *how*, Captain?" she asked Flor directly.

The answer was a soft flurry of musical speech that Copper had no means of understanding but for Spook and Nyx, who between them clarified what the story seemed to be. In fits and starts, with questions and answers that those aboard the *Drake* had difficulty following, she at last believed she had got the gist. She leant back, shaking her head in something akin to shock.

"So that place was an ops and repair base as well as this," she said at last. "It seems that a scout hostile got to the base a long time ago and tried to sabotage it; it was taken down but it wasn't destroyed completely. Enough life was left in it that they dug in and set up the trap that pulled the *Griffon* down when she went in to check out the remains of their ship, having registered it as alien tech. But the *Griffon* was tracked by another alien ship, one heading into the Sol system after eons in space and making for their ancient base; Spook's successors, in fact. They tried to help the *Griffon* but they got pulled in after the *Griffon* was destroyed. It seems that they dealt with the hostiles as far as they and the base's systems were able but their own ship was written off in the process. They tried an escape pod but it didn't make it..."

"Junior's folks!" Linen exploded. "Does that mean…"

"No," said Copper sadly. "They didn't survive; few of the crew did. The ones that did kept going long enough to protect Junior as best they could and to start salvage ops to build some sort of craft that *could* escape the place. But none of the crew survived long enough as organic entities to finish it. Junior bided his time until the *Lithstar* got there and hitched a ride. The *Sally* and her sister vessels found the structure and the information left by their people and began to complete the job, because *that* ship has a few surprises up its sleeve. And then the distress from this station came in, so they answered. A small team from the *Sally* and her sister ships were dropped off to fulfil the mission and what we have coming over the horizon is the result."

"I'll believe it when I see it," Inkscree reiterated as Colonel Moritz enquired as to the condition of the incoming ship and to what Copper meant by organic entities.

"She'll need additional upgrading, but she's another ship," Copper said mildly. "As for what's left of the original crew, I get the impression that there may be a couple of them in their non-organic forms still extant, but that's all."

"So in addition to the vessel from Lux Noctis, we have two military and one civilian incoming from this side, three possibly friendly unknowns from unmapped space and twelve of what we can now assume are definitely hostile less than half a sol behind them," the colonel summarised.

"Aye, ma'am, that's how we read it here. In fact, Captain Flor is updating me now... yes, ma'am?" Copper paused to take in what the alien commander was trying to communicate. "I see: our three unknown ships match our five friends here but they're larger, they're less well-armed, and – oh damn and hell!"

"What is it, Lieutenant?"

"They're not military, ma'am, they're alien civilian transports and they're racing in for safety: repeat they are non-combatant and they have a large number of civilians aboard, some of them young. Refugee ships, in other words. I'd say the stakes have just got higher, ma'am."

32: ANOTHER TASTE OF COMMAND

The three incoming blips formed a spearhead as they crossed the light lines of the projected holo of star-sprinkled space, their outlines coalescing into the elongated teardrop shapes that were recognisably alien. They had dropped their cloaking to use every available atom of power for speed, Flor informed Copper, who had cut her link to the *Drake* and was using her own station to analyse the incoming data. Colonel Moritz, she knew, was in closed session with her fellow Fleet commanders and an urgent supra-light communiqué had been sent to Fleet HQ. The small hybrid ship from Lux Noctis had increased speed and was on approach, and Wyld of the *Morgana Atlantis* was still at intervals bending the ears of Captain Merris Helmis.

As the flowing lines of the red-green skinned craft gleamed lustrously in her grid, Copper felt a thrill of tension sheeting her. The hybrid was a third the size of the *Sally*, similar but flatter in shape, her fluid-like metallic hull shot with golden streamers that flickered like flame from her stem to the complex tailfin that girdled her stern. Several stable dark patches evident against the mutable patterns on her plating Copper knew were docking bays and the many protrusions discernible as she closed were sensor arrays and weapons emplacements. The ship was sorely in need of energy cells and the wherewithal to complete her armoury and internal stations and Captain Flor had called up her own ship's inventory to inspect the *Sally's* supplies.

Copper had her own ideas, and after a quick mental exchange with Spook, she interrupted the captain. The ever-helpful Nyx provided rapid translation: the base station off which they hung included a repair facility probably furnished with much of what they would need to equip the hybrid ship. Their main problem was lack of time: with a hostile fleet now about ten hours away, any fitting would have to be carried out at lightning speed. And as far as she was aware, there were no auto repair systems or rigs down there that could be called in.

The alien captain listened carefully, understood instantly and before Copper could draw breath, was issuing orders and calling up various specs on her boards. Nyx was little help as he could relay only what he could link into of what was happening, but it seemed that there would be sorties from the *Sally* and her sister ships to the base for supplies. This was sufficient for Copper to call Captain Helmis and apprise him of the situation – the Fleet ships would need to know that action was impending and the *Morgana Atlantis* would also have to be contacted. Helmis sent the message through to the colonel and notified the first officers of the Mars and Earth Fleet vessels.

It was no surprise to find the colonel on the comm a short time after her meeting had finished. It had been agreed that the *Morgana* be informed of what was going down and Commander Wyld was furious when finally he was brought in. That the alien ships now in the area would be making flights to the planetoid, that the *Drake* was in contact with the lead ship and that one of her officers was aboard that ship, incensed him. That the aliens were in point of fact of the people that had built the base in the first place and the structures thus essentially belonged to them cut no ice: Wyld realised that the Fleet ships must have withheld a great deal of information from him that his people, with the superior facilities of the *Morgana*, could have analysed.

"And attempted to profit from," Colonel Moritz had added.

Commander Wyld had been infuriated by the observation and the colonel warned Copper that he might try to contact or approach the *Sally* on some pretext. Copper was sure that they could handle him: from what she had learned of her crewmates and their ship, they were more than capable of outsmarting and outshooting the *Morgana*.

The colonel had other news: the large civilian ship with an outline resembling that of the *Morgana Atlantis* was indeed her sister ship, the *SS Regan Arcadia*. Her ETA was in just over one hour and the Fleet ships had been primed to scan every speck of her to assess any hull anomalies such as alien tech or jammers. The *Lithium Star* would arrive shortly before. The colonel then came to the main point of her link: as a liaison aboard the *Sally*, Copper would be very useful to the joint Fleet if she remained aboard. It was not presented as a command, but Copper felt in her bones that it was the preferred option. Her eyes flickered over to Kit and to Linen, both still at their bridge posts.

"Captain Flor is of the same view, at least for now, and I see the point. I will of course comply, ma'am. I've more than plenty to do here just understanding the systems and as we're about to deploy a team to the base, as are *Sally Two* through *Sally Five*, I'd like to keep an eye on them – I *have* been through the place down there, so I have knowledge of it. And I think the captain has something in mind for me."

"Understood; Moritz out."

* * *

The next two hours were a frenzy of activity as far as the alien ships were concerned. Copper was amazed at the ingenuity and energy of her companions: they could fix the most complex of problems, they seemed to suffer no fatigue, for she saw none ease off, and the speed at which they worked was remarkable to her. She realised that inbuilt cyber systems in the uniforms they wore had much to do with it and the pods used for mobility around the open areas of the ship preserved their strength. She was given the opportunity to test these aids, for she was hauled in on a very short sim of the deployment of the *Sally* in a battle situation and found herself spinning from station to station in three dimensions in the well space that constituted the bridge. The alien captain, who had supervised the session, had her own reasons for the use of the time. Flor was able to communicate quite freely with Spook and it was he, with Nyx as support, who intimated to Copper the reasoning behind the drill. She pushed it to the back of her mind: she had other looming concerns.

The call signs of the *Lithium Star* and the *Regan Arcadia* were linked across by the *Drake*. Copper acknowledged briefly, most of her attention being focussed on the imminent approach of the three refugee ships and the disposition of their payloads. Captain Flor had noted that the repair facility spaces were well-protected and realised that with careful resource planning they could provide a safe haven for the civilians for the duration. The crews of the poorly-equipped refugee vessels had volunteered to maintain their ships as a last line of defence against the hostiles.

Civilian transfer would be a protracted affair, Copper mused, as the carrier ships were acutely under-crewed. After some rapid reckoning, she realised that the process could be hastened if she could call on her own people to assist. A quick dialogue with the colonel resulted a short time later in the requisitioning of several of the large recon vessels held by the *MSS Sapphire Sunset* as civilian transports. Captain Fantodd was less than enthusiastic, but agreed to the use of his craft, with his own people as pilots.

The arrival of the *EFS Stephen Hawking* ahead of schedule meant that all human aid that could be relied upon was in place. Her captain, Jane Stallban, had been briefed on the way in and was primed to take up position as close to the *Morgana Atlantis* as possible. Colonel Moritz still had reservations about that ship and was far from satisfied that her commander would obey orders if the present tense situation turned actively hostile. The newly arrived *Regan Arcadia* had proved clear of jammers but did read as having small amounts of alien tech fused to parts of her forward hull and close to two main weapons emplacements. Her captain, Erkon Elks, was as reticent as Hellebore had been when it came to discussing his ship's spec, leading the colonel to suspect that he was well aware of her novel aspects, but at least he heeded her warnings that the tech might prove dangerous to his own people.

With final relocation of the alien refugees to the repair base underway, Copper could at length cast her eyes over the internal upgrade of the hybrid ship and try to impress the spec into her brain. She took time away from the bridge of the *Sally* to return to her own billet for a discussion with her own commander. She had requested that the talk be private, citing acute urgency and its direct link to the current situation, as she wanted the *Drake's* bridge crew unaware of her intentions. The hostiles were now less than eight hours away and were being tracked by everything the local forces could muster.

Copper's explanation was short and to the point and as she watched the expressions that crossed the colonel's face, the now familiar gnawing fear in her belly grew. Colonel Moritz digested the information and expressed her dislike of the whole plan.

"It scares the hell out of me, ma'am," Copper admitted. "I see the logic behind it and given more time, I maybe could see a different way, but time we don't have. But there's one advantage the hybrid ship has that the rest of the Fleet don't, as yet."

As she detailed her knowledge, Copper knew intuitively that Colonel Moritz would agree with what Captain Flor and Spook between them had hatched, but the commander of the *Drake* would then have the problem of putting the plan to her fellow Fleet officers and finding volunteers. This would be a firing line like no other and a first for both Fleets. The hybrid ship created out at Lux Noctis was both alien and human and as such should be crewed by both. The *Sally* and her sister ships were unable to provide command support, being too poorly crewed themselves, but as Copper had long guessed, Spook had commanded ships in his organic form. With his strong mental and physical links to Copper, he was well able to operate with her and through her.

With the colonel's agreement buzzing in her head, along with a list of specifics she would need to generate, Copper took a last look around her small domain. Smiling grimly to herself, she detached her *Drake* insignia from the Fleet uniform that hung on the wall and pinned it to her protective alien-made suit. Her route to the bridge she had set into her wrist-comm and she made her way back, Nyx in tow, to brief Flor, suspecting that Spook had pre-empted her. How Colonel Moritz would handle the matter with her fellow officers she could not imagine, but she had other priorities: this was no recreational sim at Beagle Leisure Dome and the hybrid was no simulation starship.

Captain Flor's mouth was slightly stretched in what Copper took to be a smile and her light eyes glittered with a golden haze that was poignantly reminiscent of Linen. After settling her pod into its dock, Copper quickly related her conversation with Colonel Moritz, whilst Flor tilted her head in an attitude so close to listening that she had the strongest feeling that the captain was picking up more and more on human gestures. The briefing at an end, a prickling feeling alerted Copper to a shift in the air around her. She looked to the side to see two pods approaching; a further two were coming in on her other side. They all four came about to hover expectantly in her line of sight.

"Who are they?" she asked curiously.

"Your bridge crew, some of," Nyx put in.

Flor's face creased again in the elongated smile. "Most other ship's stations already are crewed but awaiting personnel from your ships as support," she explained in her soft voice.

Copper saluted the four around her and then turned to the captain. "I'll need a list of the positions we have to fill, ma'am. I suspect that some of our people won't be keen to be auxiliary."

"Too bad," Nyx said at her back. "Life is tough and then you croak."

"I'd like to know who programmed you, you sarky little sprite; you'll be more respectful when you translate for me. But enough already: Spook and I will need to get across to that ship as soon as possible, Captain."

"Data here on personnel transmitting now," Flor indicated her station. "Your fighter is ready. This is a translator device for attachment," she went on, handing over a thin circlet. "Orders will be relayed directly to the crew."

Copper took the band and looked at it inquisitively and then at Flor, who pointed to a similar device around her own scrawny neck that Copper did not remember having seen before.

"My science officers busy have been," Flor told her.

"They've just developed this?"

"We have had the technology always but your language is complex. Crew members will wear to assist communication but translator required still. New crew will also wear our uniforms: they will preserve biological stability and assist physical actions. My people were modified genetically to cope with environments we might find ourselves in: uniforms were developed to provide additional support," she explained.

"This is one amazing place, Captain. And I bet that's one amazing ship."

* * *

It was almost an hour later that Copper at last viewed the sleek outlines of her ship with her own eyes. The burnished red-green hull with its streaks of golden flame flickering in the dark of space grew larger as she homed in on the dock assigned to her small craft. She felt Spook close to her, relishing at last the awareness of command. Nyx behind her was maintaining an uncharacteristic silence. The shuttle in her wake carried the four officers assigned as part of the bridge crew; she knew they were a helmsman, a security officer with specialist knowledge of their adversaries, an engineer and her assigned first officer. Her aide Pyx, ranked the parallel of lieutenant, was also aboard, as were a few others. Pyx had been appointed as senior weapons officer. Unable to pronounce the protracted names of her alien crew, she had resorted to abbreviated forms and their designations as a means of communicating with them.

The spec of the vessel had been burned into her brain but as she docked her small fighter and waited until her boards read clear, she knew that she would still require Spook's guidance in navigating her way around. Her first duty would be to assume her place on the bridge but as she stepped down from her craft she did not expect to be greeted by two uniformed individuals that saluted her smartly in alien fashion. She returned the salute and waited.

"Captain Copper Milkstone," the first hailed her, his voice sounding strangely in his translator. "Lieutenant Hoof Engineer; this is Ensign Jeshin Security. We are your escort. We go this way Captain Copper, Captain Spook, Nyx Translator."

Amused at the greeting to Spook, but stifling her grin and the urge to correct his salutation, Copper stepped through the exit of the bay, marvelling again at the alien facility to pick up on the nuances of language, adapt the forms of speech used and update the translation devices. Once outside she stopped to look. As a hybrid that had been created from the shattered shells of both human and alien ships, the deck was narrow but exhibited the seamless structure and soft colour she had seen aboard the *Sally*. The bulkheads were smooth but inscribed hexagonal plates were interleaved at various junctions; panels let in along the way led off to other passageways and transport tubes.

They entered one such tube and Copper turned to her senior escort. "Lieutenant Hoof Engineer," she addressed him. "How many of the crew are now aboard and how many are human?"

"Twenty seven, of human only you," he replied. "We have sixteen more from our ships and await final tally from *Drake*."

As he waited for further questions she noted his similarity to Captain Flor, small and thin with pale greenish skin, though his cranial fuzz was soft fawn and his eyes a deeper golden-brown.

The security officer Jeshin seemed younger, less scrawny and with darker skin and a tuft of down on his scalp that was as red as Linen's curls. His eyes were green and were taking in his new human commander with open curiosity, as far as Copper could read his expression. He turned away quickly in what might have been mortification and Copper felt a tremor of amusement that most definitely came from Spook. It was then that she realised that the alien officers could sense Spook as surely as she did and react to his instructions.

In response to her questions, Hoof informed Copper of the nature of her crew and she was relieved that almost all essential ship's services were covered. There was no emergency bridge to call upon but with two non-organic crew members aboard in addition to Spook and the humans she could expect from the Fleet ships, she would be adequately if sparingly manned.

Although having seen the spec of the bridge of the ship, Copper had not quite taken in the arrangement. The deep well that was characteristic of the *Sally* was not part of the design, the hybrid being smaller and flatter, but the command module was set on a central podium and reached by a walkway that extended from the platform at which her transport tube had arrived. The platform continued to right and left around the perimeter of the bridge, supporting ship's stations behind a low rail, and ended in two further walkways that led back to the command position. A lower deck of control banks was set under the main level and reached by short flights of steps either side of the entryway. On the far side a large view-grid provided the medium for display of incoming data and ship's status and spanned both bridge levels. Copper looked round as every officer on deck stood to welcome her. The shimmering metallic green and pink walls cast a warm light on all the strange faces that looked up and across and Copper acknowledged the reception by the standard salute and the command to stand easy, aware that the four officers from the inbound shuttle destined for the bridge had beaten her there and three were already in position.

Realising that some sort of command acceptance speech was required, she expressed her pleasure at meeting the crew, her admiration of the work done to render the ship spaceworthy and her respect of the sacrifices made during the current crisis, trusting that the outcome would be worthy of their efforts, and knowing that all would do their duty. With Spook's reassuring presence beside her, she strode across to the command module and into the pod-like space that was reminiscent of the *Sally*. She locked herself in and skimmed her boards as the crew returned to their positions, aware of the very short time left to complete her ship's complement.

Copper's assigned first officer was Commander Othra, an engineering specialist. He requested permission to join her and she gestured to the adjunct position, adding a verbal affirmative. He was small, a grizzled veteran, she reckoned. His pale brown eyes flicked over his own station and then at her. He had spied the three glinting chevrons either side of her raised collar that Captain Flor had presented her with when she left the *Sally*: the insignia of command. Her cuffs also sported triple bands, well in view as she raised her arms to pull down the net-like circlet above her head that amplified the mental processes required to operate her station. She set her boards deftly, her hands moving with practiced skill over her controls. If he was impressed he gave no hint, but she thought she could detect a wry smile.

Copper now had the layout of the bridge and the disposition of the stations and could see which were manned and at what level. She knew that the human Fleet ships had been informed of the current situation and a quick link had been passed to her that volunteers were being organised. She suspected that there would not be a rush to join up, but had a shrewd suspicion of one or two that she might expect from the *Drake*. A hint from Spook caused her to order a full systems check; as she scanned the results, she was happy to note that as the engines powered up and the shields flicked on and off, everything seemed to be running at close to optimal. She then ordered a series of scanner and targeting tests, directing her newly-appointed comms officer to notify the surrounding ships of her intent. She was less than surprised to be told in response that Commander Vix Wyld of the *Morgana Atlantis* required an urgent word with the captain of the alien craft, having figured that they could understand him.

"Put me through to the *Drake*, I need information and I have news that I must pass on," Copper responded. "The *Morgana* can wait."

Colonel Moritz, aware that Copper had assumed command, was awaiting the first link with anticipation. The same could be said of her bridge crew, many of whom were openly staring as the link was made. Widened eyes took in their crewmate in her glossy red uniform, the glistening coronet suspended above her and the strangeness of her first officer, whom she introduced.

"Captain Milkstone," the colonel returned equably.

Copper felt a thrill akin to panic as she acknowledged with a slight nod and made for the bones of her communication: she wanted to know when the shuttles with her new crew would be arriving. Each one would be assigned an alien fellow officer to introduce them to their stations and their local facilities for the duration of their duty aboard the unified ship.

"Unified ship? Does your ship have a name, Captain?" asked the colonel with a quirky smile on her face.

"It does: this is the Unified Starship *Crucible*," Copper replied with a reciprocal smile: she had agreed the name with Captain Flor before she came aboard.

"*Crucible?*"

"Well, she *is* a melting pot," she explained. "It was either that or the *Hybrid*, and that's no name for a ship."

"So noted," Colonel Moritz said and proceeded with details as she linked across the list of personnel and their specialities.

Shuttles with volunteers who had agreed to serve aboard the part-alien ship were standing by on the *Drake*, the *En Hedu'anna* and the *Lithium Star*. The *Mina Fleming* had despatched one of her transports to pick up crew from the *Sapphire Sunset* and the *Dexterity*. As the *Stephen Hawking* had been detailed to keep her beady eyes on both civilian craft, it had been decided not to call on her for crew.

After thanking the colonel for her very speedy arrangements, acknowledging receipt of the crew list and ordering reception of the shuttles, Copper continued.

"On another note, ma'am: Captain Flor informs me that two of her sister ships will be breaking orbit to take up a defensive line beyond the immediate area. That should give us notice of what's coming in and their presence might delay the hostiles and buy us a little more time. And as I have Commander Wyld on the comm, I expect I'd better see what he wants."

"A piece of the action, I suspect," the colonel said.

"The piece he gets won't be what he's expecting," Copper replied. "My targeting eyes are on his ship and there they stay."

"Trouble?"

"My people reckon so," Copper confirmed, earning her a dry look from Colonel Moritz at her tone. "I'll link across further information as it becomes available. Anything else at your end, ma'am?"

"Not at present. I'll leave you to your duties, Captain. Moritz out."

Copper caught the unspoken goodwill, laced with regard, and smiled in response as the link was cut and she prepared to face the commander of the *Morgana Atlantis*. Wyld had trouble hiding his surprise at his first sight of an alien as he took in Othra and the bridge of the *Crucible*, but it was Copper who transfixed his eye: he had evidently not expected to see a human on the bridge of the latest-arrived and clearly alien starship. Copper for her part had difficulty controlling her face as he stated his name and rank and requested to speak to the captain, his eyes sliding back to Othra, assuming that he was in command and she was some sort of liaison.

"I'm Captain Copper Milkstone of the *US Crucible*," she told him evenly, her voice sounding odd in her ears: it was the first time she had announced her title to anyone. "You wished to speak to me, Commander?"

"You're human but your crew are alien?" he blurted out.

"I and my crew are my concern, *Commander.*"

With Spook as back-up, Copper felt sure of herself and she was far from happy at the readings on her command board that indicated that the *Morgana* was futilely scanning her ship and had released micro-probes in her direction, no doubt in an attempt to come sufficiently close to bypass her shielding. She tapped the board to alert Othra and sent the mental command through Spook to Pyx to take them out.

Wyld's major concern, delivered civilly enough, was that the *Crucible* was targeting his vessel and he wanted her to cease and desist. He also wanted to open friendly relations with the alien vessel, as his overtures to the other five had been unsuccessful.

"You were advised of the testing in advance, Commander. And I find it strange that you rebuke me for scanning your ship openly, whilst you attempt to scan mine covertly, and send out micro-probes to breach my defences. By the way, I *have* ordered their destruction, as I consider their deployment a hostile act."

Her eyes narrowed as she scrutinised him closely and awaited his reaction. That he was annoyed was certain, but he was also persistent. He justified his actions by asserting that he was defending his own against what he deemed to be aggression on her part and continued to express friendly overtures, requesting an account of her ship, her part aboard and her presence at the edge of human space.

"You can hardly lay claim to space this far from your home world, Commander, and around a base that does not belong to you or your people," she told him. "But give me your business here and perhaps I'll give you mine."

After a pause in which he realised that Copper had made good her threat of destroying his micro-probes, he confirmed that the *Morgana Atlantis* was a commercial survey ship on a resource-hunting mission but declined to provide specifics. As the nearby planetoid held masses of novel alien technology, he was naturally interested: contact with sentient alien life was part of his brief and the advent of several alien ships obviously fitted that category. The presence of what appeared to be a human aboard one of the ships was a puzzle that he would like clarified.

Copper was not about to oblige; she knew that he was well aware that the *Morgana's* hull included components of alien tech, and thus it was not as novel as he was implying. And as his ship had already opened fire on both the alien base station and on the *Drake*, she could hardly consider him friendly. As she taxed him with these points, he considered her shrewdly, evidently summing up the events over the past couple of sols.

"You're from the *Drake*, aren't you?" he challenged. "Were you the one sent aboard that lead alien ship? How long has Mars Fleet been in contact with these aliens?"

She grinned in reply. "I suggest you turn your targeting eyes and your scanners elsewhere," she advised. "Milkstone out."

She cut the link herself: her status update had shown that the first shuttle containing part of her human crew had just docked and she planned to greet them personally. They were from the *Drake* and she knew two of them very well.

Leaving Othra in command, Copper made her way down and across to the outer parts of the *Crucible*. She had ordered the shuttle into one of the larger bays and once pressurisation was complete, she led the welcoming committee forward. The pilot was first out, and observing that the strangers were not wearing breather units, he removed his own as he walked towards them.

"Permission to come aboard, Captain," he asked formally.

"Permission granted, Commander," she replied, her eyes and her smile giving him all the welcome he needed as she gave the salute. "You are all welcome aboard the *US Crucible*. These are your translators: you'll need to wear them at all times. Perhaps you'd introduce your squad, Commander Locksmith? Tactical and second helm," she added for the benefit of the attentive alien officers.

Kit's eyes widened a fraction at his own designation but with little time for niceties, he presented his crew to the alien group using a similar format. Copper greeted each as he named them, nodding in recognition. Linen, her smile wide, was first in line; Amber Embertz had volunteered as a medic, Oaky Grimsson as a flight engineer. She was touched that her old adversary Ash Goff had stepped up, as had comms officer Flax Dyxin and last but not least, young Ensign Flyte of security.

"And that would be Fetch?" she said wryly as she spotted a small brown and white dog at his feet.

"I can deactivate him if you wish, ma'am."

"He's fine as he is. You'll find our second comms officer is equally non-standard," she told him. "These officers will escort you to your quarters as you'll have to change into the protective gear necessary aboard the *Crucible*. You'll then be taken to your stations to be shown their operations. You've all been assigned billets on the same level, but given the lack of time, I'll see some of you on the bridge very shortly," she added to the whole team.

"I can come straight up to the bridge," Linen offered.

"You'll do as you're bid, Lieutenant Lyrican *and* Junior," was the dry reply. "But as you *are* assigned to the bridge, I'll see you both there."

"Aye, ma'am."

Copper saw two of them very soon after her own return to the bridge. Kit and Linen appeared with their deputies and were tied into their duty stations in fifteen minutes. Linen was quickly in full flow, as Copper had stepped over to the science position to check that the redhead could handle the controls and that Junior was on a tight rein.

"Why did you call her the *Crucible*?" Linen asked. "To remind you of the Carnelian Crucible back at Beagle?"

The sharp look on Copper's face made her change her tone hurriedly. "I had a few sims on your virtual ship, so I'm used to the controls, ma'am," she went on. "Junior wouldn't be left behind. Trisk wanted to come too, but the colonel would only let one of us loose and it had to be me. There were quite a few put their hands up once they knew you were in command," she continued impudently. "Lyssa Halsen, Axim Biggs and Faela Khilph all wanted to come, but the colonel vetoed it as she had to think of the *Drake*: the bad eggs we lost during our struggles earlier left us short and we only picked up a couple of security at Jupiter. She didn't want Commander Locksmith to come, but if she'd refused, she'd have had a mutiny on her hands," Linen crinkled up at her, winking over at Kit at his station. "Dyxin will be chuffed at his sidekick, if that's comms," she added, laughing.

"That's comms; you're settling in Commander?" Copper said as she moved over to the two officers at the tactical position.

Kit was running his fingers over his boards. "Yes, ma'am; as you know, I've had some experience with this technology."

"I know," said Copper, her hand on his shoulder tightening as she looked down. "Ensign Lomusan was one of *Sally's* tactical officers. She helped design this system and knows it inside out."

"Good."

Kit glanced up, his blue eyes piercing, his chin grazing the hand on his shoulder. Copper moved her little finger marginally to caress his cheek as she informed him that he should check in with Timri Helm: as second helm, he was liable be called in to take over at short notice. He acknowledged as she stepped away.

Linen winked knowingly at her friend as she passed and was rewarded by a slap on the head, to the wonder of her second, who had already been sufficiently amazed at the advent of a very young non-organic member of her own species on the bridge.

"The *Drake* is some ship," the redhead, a consummate reader of expressions, even alien ones it seemed, told her.

Copper had other concerns as she checked her updates and realised that shuttles from the *En Hedu'anna* and the *Lithium Star* were making their way in. She was looking forward to the arrival of two officers from the latter, both of whom would occupy bridge stations. Her engineer would be Lieutenant Erik Halsen; the weapons officer, who would shadow Pyx, was Lieutenant Gadget Blazells. She decided to let both craft dock before she headed out. She intended to meet them in a small repair bay: that way her latest crewmen would all get a view of their captain at the same time. Her welcome this time would be pared to the bare minimum: zero hour was approaching and she knew she would need all her strength on the bridge.

"Captain on deck!"

The call by one of her alien officers gave her wry pleasure as she called them to stand easy, stifling her amusement at the look on Gadget Blazells' face as his jaw dropped. The squad from the *Lithium Star* had evidently been told that their new captain was an officer from the *Drake* but had not been given a name. Her welcome was brief and delivered succinctly. Her relative youth caused a few quirky looks but she was becoming inured to the stares and wished them all well as she turned on her heel to leave. She could hear the rising rumble of talk as the panel at her back swished across: she was proving to be more of a sensation than her alien crewmembers.

Copper was met on her return to the bridge by Dr Zonota'a, a medic that Spook advised be assigned to the medical station. The doctor was scanning all the bridge officers in order that she had current baseline readings and would link to Amber Embertz in the event of problems with the human crew, she informed the captain. The stimulants often used by alien crew when risky situations required prolonged duty spells would be modified for human use and dispensed if needed. Copper took this to mean something like Oxypep, a stimulant originally used to counteract fatigue in those on long shifts, such as long-distance pilots, but these sols more often found in liquor cabinets to offset the effects of excessive consumption of the contents. She submitted to the doctor's scans and resumed her command chair to check in with Othra on current status, before her next trip to welcome the last of her crew in on the *Mina Fleming's* shuttle. The officers from the *Dexterity* would find the gravity different to their own as the *Crucible* was rigged for Martian conditions, which seemed to suit the alien crew, but other than that she hoped all would be well. Flax Dyxin had appeared and as Linen had surmised, his small colleague at comms was causing him some amusement, Copper realised when she stepped across to have a word.

The latest fleet news was that the captains of *Sally Two* and *Sally Four* had reported that they were preparing to leave orbit and head out to where the first wave of incoming hostiles was expected to materialise. The unknown fleet had continued on course and at the same rate of progress, which meant that they would be within shooting distance in a little over three standard hours Martian time. If the two alien advance ships could block their progress at least for a little time, it would give the rest of the Fleet some breathing space. All the refugees that had come in on the three large transports were now safely planetside and were digging in. The majority of the other stations in the ancient defensive network left by Spook's people that stretched across the Sol system had been activated; they would be brought on line lest the hostiles could not be stopped at system edge. Mars and Earth had mobilised more Fleet ships and merchant and other craft had been called in.

"I just hope this isn't going to be one massive anticlimax and all this is for nothing," Copper grumbled to her first officer.

"These beings are trouble," Othra stated, gesturing to the tactical display and the blips that were now more than obvious. "My people have resisted them for ages past: they claimed that we were violating their spaces and resources and that we should leave. We could not, of course, as our colonies had been there for generations, so they turned to hostility to force us. That is one reason that Captain Spook's people – my ancestors – tried to make a home on what is now your world," he explained.

"They were trying to make Mars habitable?"

"Indeed, Captain Copper: our people were dying out because of the depredations of *their* kind." Othra gestured again to the display. "On our original home, our early peoples were once a little like yours and our later technology assisted our survival in primitive conditions. My people had evolved over time to unlike their original forms but we knew that return to an earlier state was possible and would ensure that our kind would survive in some form. So we sent out groups of our people to colonise other worlds. As the third planet provided much of what we needed, we started there; but it was inhabited at the time by proto-sentients and so we could not make it a permanent base."

Copper stared at him. "Now that makes sense," she said. "I and a few of my people have what our chief medic aboard the *Drake* thinks is a predisposition to link to yours. We found what we thought was a tissue sample from one of your people. Our doctor detected a section of genetic coding material within it that resembled a tiny unit of redundant coding that's present in some humans, including me and Lieutenant Lyrican over there. *His* reading was that in ages past, some alien genetic material found its way into the human genome, though how we didn't know. And then you headed to my homeworld, Mars, to try to make it suitable for your people?"

"Indeed. And we were successful, at first. But then they came again, despite our series of early warning beacons and our ships. So we had to leave; but we left little for them to take."

"Scorched Mars policy: I figured," Copper told him. "Lucky for our civilisation they didn't hit Earth and lucky for me you did leave some of your technology behind, including Spook. I don't know what my life would have been without him. I would not be here, that's for sure," she smiled. "How did he end up being left behind, I wonder?"

"Ah. That we must investigate later. But here are more of your human bridge crew."

The two humans were Blazells and Halsen, escorted by their alien colleagues. Copper saluted them and stepped up to have a quick word. Halsen was soon settled with Hoof at engineering but Blazells, eyes darting every which way, seemed stunned and wondering what he had let himself in for. As his companion Pyx pointed to the weapons stations and the others alongside, the lieutenant suddenly spotted Linen, her blaze of red hair catching the light above her glossy uniform.

"Lyrican!" he exclaimed.

"Well met, Gadget! And how are you this fine sol?"

He was about to reply when something else caught his eye. "What is *that?*"

"That is the comms station and that is our resident translator and second comms officer," Copper informed him.

"Are you telling me you have a mechanoid as translator and comms officer?" Blazells demanded in utter disbelief as Nyx twinkled his green eyes at him. "It's a dragon!"

"We have a virtual dog as part of our security team," Linen called up. "And a few of our crew are non-physical. This is a ship like no other."

"You can say that again. And how did you wangle command of her, Milkstone?"

There was a sudden stillness and Blazells realised his gaffe as Copper turned steely eyes on him. "I'll overlook that this time in view of the novelty of the situation, *Lieutenant*. Assume your station and familiarise yourself with its operation; Lieutenant Pyx will induct you into the intricacies. Dismissed."

"Aye, ma'am," was the chastened reply, as Linen chuckled in the background and Dyxin announced that the *Mina Fleming's* shuttle with the last of the new crew had just docked.

The only highlight of the final trip out to the regions of the *Crucible* that housed her docking bays was a vaguely familiar face that Copper recognised among the mix of officers. The ensign wore the insignia of the *Sapphire Sunset* and he was looking at her in puzzlement and a slowly dawning recollection. Copper gave a searching glance as she ended her welcome aboard and made her way towards the young man.

"We've met before, haven't we? It's Jiff, isn't it?" she greeted him, amused to see him swallow nervously and confirm.

They had: he and three friends, fresh out of boot and newly assigned to the *Sapphire Sunset* had met Copper and Linen in Jinx in Beagle Central and had tried to dazzle them with life aboard a ship of the Fleet. Copper and her friend had pretended interest whilst trying to quiz them about the *Sunset* and her mission. Jiff and his buddy Keely had later met up with the two at the BC Hotel but the tryst had terminated swiftly when Jiff spotted the stat bars that Colonel Moritz had given the pair to acknowledge their status as linked to the Service and had figured that he was out of his depth. He now knew that he most certainly had been.

A summons requiring the captain's urgent presence on the bridge interrupted any further exchanges. Copper saluted swiftly and made off, speculating on what was about to happen. Spook had not warned her of any impending trouble but she had the odd feeling that something had occurred.

"Status?" she barked at Othra as soon as she had assumed her command chair.

"The ship *Morgana Atlantis* is on the move. An alert has been sent from the *Stephen Hawking* to all ships that she has raised her shields and is powering her weapons."

"That's crazy; she can't take on the whole fleet. Any move from the *Regan Arcadia*?"

"None, Captain. We are scanning the *Morgana Atlantis* as we know she has hostile attachments on her outer hull."

"And possibly inside as well," Copper said. "I know Spook certainly was very chary of going over there. Sound alert to stand by to assume duty stations: that's yellow alert. Comms, request what the *Morgana's* intentions are."

"This ship follows human alert system," confirmed Othra. "I recommend amber, Captain: *Morgana* has not heeded requests to stand down from our allied ships."

"I concur. Sound amber alert: all duty stations manned. I'm sorry for the crew that have just come aboard. They'll wonder what they've jumped into."

As the noise and activity around her intensified, Copper called for the expansion of the bridge holo-grid to track the *Morgana*. She sat alert, interacting with Spook as she watched the circuitous line that the civilian ship was taking.

"She's on a trajectory that will get her ahead of *Sally Two* and *Sally Four*! Dyxin, get me Commander Wyld of the *Morgana* on the comm!"

"On it," was the brief response.

Captain Flor had come to the same conclusion and was on the link. As the *Morgana* had rejected all hails, Copper had her full spec set up in the holo, calling for pinpoint data of the areas of hull that were affected by alien tech. The *Crucible* was armed with formidable scanning gear and it was with a shiver of horror that Copper realised what the data from her tactical and science stations were showing: the merged tech sported a recognisable pattern of raised whorls and curves, a pattern that had haunted her dreams over the past several months.

"They're autonomous!" she breathed. "I'd bet a month's pay that they're control centres for something and can be operated remotely when they get into range of hostile influences – and those hostile influences are less than three hours away!"

Othra had instantly grasped what she meant, knowing only too well what the blue tech might signify. "It is possible that the attachments are affecting the interior of the ship also: there are such devices. Perhaps *those* can affect some of the human crew?"

"I don't know but I've long suspected *that* particular pattern was part of a device designed to prevent a breach of whatever its parent structure protected: parts of the hull of the *Morgana Atlantis* in other words. Have you got that, Captain Flor? Sound red alert! All crew to battlestations! The *Crucible* has gear that no other ship of this Fleet has and it's time we used it. Pyx, prepare to deploy our phased organic disruptors set on the finest beam you can. Tactical, I want precision targeting of those areas of blue tech. Liaise with weapons: I want those inclusions out, with minimal damage to the *Morgana's* hull. Science, monitor the effects and keep me updated. Dyxin, get me Colonel Moritz!"

Copper was brief: she intended to intercept the *Morgana* and use her ship's superior artillery to disable the hostile inclusions on the great vessel's hull. The colonel was well aware that in the construction of the *Crucible*, in addition to the hulks of the ships that had been stranded and the extant structural technology on Lux Noctis, the aliens had incorporated deactivated hostile tech to produce a countermeasure that they believed would neutralise aggressive hostile structures, including those bonded to neutral matter; that gear was now part of the *Crucible's* weapons systems.

The colonel was equally brief. "It's one hell of a way to test a novel piece of kit," she said. "And your ship's not a match in any other way for the *Morgana*. The *Drake* will fly as your back-up. Have your navigation officer liaise with mine. Red alert! All hands to battlestations! Comms, patch me through to the rest of the Fleet but not the *Regan Arcadia*. *Crucible*, stand by."

"That's our Cop," Linen called to Kit at tactical as Copper directed her navigator, Lino'arr, to link to his equivalent aboard the *Drake*. "Feet first and all guns blazing. We'll have to hang on to the *Fleming's* shuttle; they won't have time to get her home."

"Attend to your duty, Lieutenant," was the sharp retort. "I'll need you to follow developments and notify me *and* the captain of the results of our actions exactly as they occur."

"Aye, sir!"

Captain Flor cut back in to advise Copper of her intention of shadowing the *Crucible*. She acknowledged, again trying to raise Wyld of the *Morgana*. There was something about the path of the ship that was baffling: she had powered up her weapons and raised her shields and her path would not intersect those of *Sally Two* or *Sally Four* but it would set her on a distinct bearing.

"She'll come out ahead of them and on a path that puts her straight on the track of what's coming in!" Copper exclaimed to Othra, realisation dawning as she directed her light beam at the tactical display depicting the civilian ship's projected course. "Is she aiming to intercept and take them down or to join them?"

"In either case, she *is* a danger," was Othra's opinion.

"Agreed: helm, prepare to come about on my mark. Lino'arr, plot us a course to intercept the *Morgana Atlantis*. Engineering, ready us for high-speed manoeuvring, hold shields at maximum; Pyx and Blazells, power up all weapons and keep them hot. All stations at the ready and tie yourselves in, people, this could be a rough ride. Anything from the *Morgana*, Dyxin?"

"Not a peep, ma'am."

"Then we go after them. Helm, on my mark... mark!"

33: SHOWDOWN

The *Crucible* shot through the dark of local space like an arrow, the *Drake* only moments behind on her port side and the *Sally* coming about to take up position on starboard. Copper had tied herself down securely, scanning the stations around her and on the lower bridge level. Her boards showed her crew at full alert and everyone in post, even those newly arrived via the *Mina Fleming*. Word had come in that the other Fleet ships had spread out to form a defensive shield around Blink 159 to protect the base and the civilians that had been left down there to fend for themselves.

"Comms, try to raise the *Morgana* again," Copper instructed. "Wyld must know we're on his tail."

"He's possibly waiting until we get into range, as his weapons systems are on line," Othra guessed. "Then he may target us."

"If I was him I'd already have us targeted," she replied. "He's got the range to launch his torpedoes, believe me. Why isn't he targeting?"

"Unknown, Captain."

Copper grinned: her first officer had not grasped the concept of the rhetorical question. "Linen, get every scanning beam you have on the *Morgana*: anything changes and I want to know. I'd like to get through her hull if I could, without harming the crew – or letting her know we've done it."

"Covert micro-breaching pods," Othra stated succinctly.

"We have that technology aboard?"

"We have. Tehoaar Science is familiar with the system," he explained, naming Linen's sidekick.

"Any other sneak technology that I should know about?"

Sarcasm was also a concept that Othra had not grasped as he listed a few other useful aids. The breaching pods, however, could be deployed once in close range of the target, had inbuilt cloaks to foil scanning and could be coded for several functions, including delivery of substances or drones. They were operated from the bridge science station. The main challenge in their use was precise targeting, Othra explained.

"Could onboard drones be programmed to search out and disable hostile technology?" Copper questioned.

"Yes, Captain, but it would take time, would work for only the types of technology recognised and would soon be identified by the technology itself as detrimental. We have dealt with our aggressors over many centuries and we know their strengths."

"That may be true, but that ship's human and the tech can't be widespread aboard. No time now, we're almost up on them. Comms, try to get me a direct link to the *Morgana*: this is their final warning."

The response to the *Crucible's* hail was met by static, although Nyx reported that he had detected a transitory tight-beam signal from the *Morgana* directed at the advancing fleet: he was trying to analyse its content. Suspicious both of that and the lack of targeting eyes, Copper called for a sensor sweep of the area around the hull of her ship. She also requested that Spook and her two other senior non-organic crew make an external sortie.

"In case they're doing to us what we might do to them, if we had time," she explained to her first officer. "If *we* have micro-breaching pods that are undetectable to normal scanning, you can bet your two front teeth that they do too."

"They *are* a human ship," Othra pointed out.

"They…"

She was interrupted by an abrupt call from Kit at tactical, echoed by Tehoaar at the science station. Their sweep had come up positive.

"We have incoming! A spread of hull-breaching stealth darts! On course for our main science arrays!"

"Take them down! I want them gone! Engineering, increase shielding to affected areas! Science, send out jamming signals to protect our arrays! Comms, warn *Drake* and *Sally* we're being targeted covertly. Science and tactical, get all you can on those damn darts and link on a tight beam to the *Drake*, the *Sally* and the rest of the Fleet! Helm, evasive! They're a tight spread!"

The tiny pin-pricks of light that were the lethal darts had been specifically programmed for the *Crucible*, for as the hybrid ship shot up at a tangent to avoid the cluster, it switched direction to follow. The crew were thrust down into their seats by the force of acceleration as the gravity compensators strove to cope. A few of the darts had penetrated the shields of the *Crucible* and crews on deck in the relevant areas were using hand weapons to cut them down as engineering techs worked flat out to repair the breaches. The complex organo-tech of the hull itself would recognise and learn from the attack and compensate but the damage had already been done.

"Pyx, deploy phased organic disruptors to target remaining darts! They're sure as hell not human tech. And then we go in. They don't target my ship and think they can get away with it!"

"Captain Spook and his team have dispersed but not disabled the final darts, Captain," Othra reported. "The *Drake* and the *Sally* were not targeted."

"So *we* were the mark. They know we're not a typical starship and they're taking our measure. Pyx, get those last few blips! Blazells, power up our other systems: I'll use them if I have to. Status on hull breach repairs?" she demanded of engineering.

The micro-breaches had been safely patched, she was told. A few minutes later and the final darts were reported destroyed; Copper thus recalled her three non-organic crew members. The *Morgana* had increased speed in her set direction but as far as they could tell she had not released additional missiles.

"Lino'arr, set us on a direct intercept of the *Morgana Atlantis*; Timri, give me full speed," she ordered her helmsman. "Tactical, get the spec of the *Morgana* up and direct the targeting of that blue tech on her hull. Pyx, you'll deploy our phased disruptors as soon as we're in range. Blazells, you get ready to loose with anything you have to if we're targeted. They turn their guns on us and you take them out. I want their weapons emplacements, their shields and their comms arrays targeted. Is that clear?"

"Aye, ma'am," the startled lieutenant replied.

"Are the *Drake* and the *Sally* still with us?" Copper called out.

"Aye, ma'am. They're coming about to follow us," Lomusan, Kit's second at tactical, reported.

The minutes ticked by as the *Crucible* slowly gained on her objective. Comms had been ordered to continue the attempted contact but had been unsuccessful. The vast shell of the *Morgana* began to fill the holo-grid as she came within the range of the phased organic disruptors. With a last look at her stations and a final check of her boards, Copper relayed her intentions to her sister vessels and ordered the all-out assault on the civilian ship.

The *Crucible* swept up in an arc, pulsed streams of micro-beams lancing from her discrete weapons arrays to shoot across the gap between the two craft. The hybrid ship wove an intricate path across the hull of the much larger *Morgana* to avoid lock-on by her targeting systems. Kit at tactical called out a warning that the areas of fused tech were expanding out across the *Morgana's* weapons emplacements and scanning arrays as their disruptors bit. Linen confirmed that the patterning was shifting but the organic mass of tech was stable.

"Show me!" barked Copper, face set, a feeling nagging at her that she had missed something.

Her concentration was broken by Lomusan alerting her that the *Morgana* was targeting them and preparing to fire her phase cannons. She bit her lip as she fought to pin down her thoughts, staring at the grid as the liquefying masses of blue came into focus. Fingers of the now molten substance had begun to flow across the spaces between the isolated sections.

"The merged areas are trying to link up! Blazells, target those subverted weapons and sensor arrays and take them out! Focus your beams on the centres, Pyx, and ignore the extrusions. Kit, you take auxiliary weapons and hit anything that comes at us. Get me the *Drake* and the *Sally*!"

As her crew moved to obey, Dyxin bawled out that an alert had been received: the *Regan Arcadia* was on the move, refusing to respond to hails, and had opened fire on the *Stephen Hawking*.

"Then we make this short! All weapons, take your targets out now! Helm, keep us out of range of those targeting eyes and once we've finished with the forward batteries, we neutralise the rest of her weapons. *Drake* and *Sally*, keep yourselves safe but take out any stray missiles and keep your eyes peeled for fighter launch: I bet she has a few and they may be unmanned. Othra, I want you at engineering to lend a hand with our shielding and prepare tractors. If she lets loose with escape craft, I want them where I can see them."

"Aye, Captain," the first officer responded, freeing himself from the confines of his station.

The main holo-grid wavered and flickered as the *Crucible*, small and highly manoeuvrable compared to her sister ships, scoured the hide of the *Morgana* to disable anything that might prove a danger or call for reinforcements. Flashes of fire from the *Drake* and the *Sally* lit her path as she wove up and across and her hull shuddered to the thwack of incoming fire that had made it past her defences. The *Morgana* was not military but she was powerfully armed and was well able to maintain an attack against three Fleet ships.

"Got them!" Linen crowed at last. "Patches of organo-tech on *Morgana's* hull now reading dead, Captain. Spread of hostile sections halted, mass reducing. It's worked!"

That may have worked but the civilian ship had another trick to play. A shuttle that read as having six lifeforms aboard was launched unexpectedly from a small side bay, its heading on a direct line for the *Crucible*. Othra requested permission to deploy tractors, but Copper had a strange feeling that may have been down to Spook.

"Belay!" she called. "Is that thing shielded?"

"Negative, Captain," Lomusan confirmed. "I read no shields or weapons but there is a large shielded area aboard the craft."

"Science, you scan that shuttle with everything you have. Dr Zonota'a, you do the same and get me the medical make-up of those six lifeforms. Helm, keep us out of range. I'd swear she was on a ramming course."

It was an alert from the *Drake* that advised something amiss: Trisk had also scented trouble and had linked his analyses to Dr Faerin. The six lifeforms were identical and read as perfect humans. Zonota'a verified the readings.

"Helm, keep our distance! Blazells, send a torpedo down their throats!"

"Torpedo away!"

The shuttle blew in an explosion several times greater than the power of the torpedo that had hit it.

"*Morgana* confirms she is standing down!" Dyxin announced from comms. "I have Commander Wyld on the link."

"About time," Copper muttered. "Put him through – and link it to the *Drake* and the *Sally*," she added, as Othra resumed his place at her side.

Vix Wyld was visibly dazed and had been injured. His story that he had not authorised the raising of his ship's shields or her weapons activation and that the systems had cut in automatically without warning and could not be shut down caused Copper to shake her head: his attempts to open an accord through her with Flor's people had hardly been subtle and the hull-breaching darts had been explicitly coded to target the *Crucible*. Apart from that, she knew the alien influence aboard the *Morgana* had been greatly reduced but not removed: Spook was sure and Captain Flor had sent a short note to the same effect. Wyld's course to intercept the hostile convoy that they now knew was about an hour away he explained by his conviction that he had to get his ship out of range of the Fleet vessels. He was aware that he had novel technology aboard, its ulterior function unknown to him, and he was by now also certain that some of his crew were not all that they seemed.

His immediate aim was damage limitation: the *Morgana* could barely defend herself and most of her comms and sensor arrays were out of action. Wyld planned to withdraw back towards the home system and take stock. He had no justification for the launch of a shuttle with fake lifesigns aboard and put it down to the subversive influences still aboard his vessel. Copper was not satisfied, but there was little she could do: the *Regan Arcadia* was almost within range and as the only Fleet ship with the capacity to neutralise the alien tech on her hull, the *Crucible* would yet again be in the firing line. She cut the link to take an advisory from Colonel Moritz, as the commanding officer of the human taskforce. Spook notwithstanding, she felt in need of a guiding hand.

The colonel was well aware that the experience of command in what was essentially a war situation was taking its toll on her young officer. She spoke calmly and informed Copper that the *Drake* would assume the lead against the *Regan*, with the *Crucible* as back-up. The *Sally* could shadow them and she had deputed the *En Hedu'anna* to track the *Morgana's* progress out of the local area. As the second civilian appeared to have much less hostile tech *in situ* and a captain that was more amenable than either Hellebore or Wyld to reason, it was realistic to suppose that she would be simpler to manage.

Flor concurred when brought into the strategy and added that she had ordered *Sally Two* and *Sally Four* to continue their course. She was still on line when a link to her from *Sally Two* indicated that the hostile fleet had stalled: the events around the downfall of the *Morgana* were possibly the cause and their speed had decreased to a crawl. Copper had only a moment to digest that news when the *Drake* was ordered to come about to face the rapidly approaching *Regan Arcadia*. She immediately directed her own helmsman to take up a wing position alongside the Mars Fleet vessel and prepare for the next engagement.

Other eyes and ears had been taking in the situation and the result was a soft voice in Copper's ear. She turned to find Dr Zonota'a with the equivalent of a hypo in hand. "Stimulant," the alien medic told her. "I have authorised it for everyone aboard."

There was something in the alien doctor's eyes that bespoke more than concern and Copper smiled at her, nodding assent. She hardly felt the jolt at her neck but immediately drew a deep breath and settled back into her command chair. The sol was far from over.

The *Regan Arcadia* was coming in on a flight path very similar to that of the *Morgana* and the three defending ships were alert to a similar strategy of the use of covert hostile assault weapons. As the *Drake* had reported that the *Regan* had refused to respond to hails, Copper called up her spec to locate the areas of her hull fused with alien tech, expecting to see the familiar etched spiral pattern that she was convinced signified a remotely operated self-directed mechanism.

"Fewer," Othra noted. "But the pattern matches that on the hull patches of the ship *Morgana*. We could deploy our covert micro-breaching pods with mobile drones in unaffected areas and try to reach those patches from the interior of the ship? We have no time to encode the drones for specific search and destroy tactics but we should be able to direct them to the areas affected and see how far into the ship their influence extends.

Once aboard, they would of course be detected by internal ship's security systems, but we may have a short time window. Lieutenant Tehoaar Science could be given the task. Lieutenant Linen Science is very adept and can work solo – although she has Junior Science as her attached initiate."

Copper could hardly hide a grin but agreed. "Do it."

She had only just uttered the phrase when an alert from Kit, now back at the tactical station, notified her that the *Regan* had altered course in a direct line for the *Crucible* and had deployed a spread of mines to halt the *Drake*. Kit had replicated the sensor sweep that had detected the hull-breaching darts of the *Morgana* but had come up negative.

"So they want us and they want us bad!" Copper spat. "Pyx, target your phased organic disruptors fine beam and destroy the mines heading for the *Drake*! Helm, hold our course until the *Drake's* clear and then bring us in on an intercept right on top of the *Regan* and as close to her hull as we can get. We'll have to risk close-range missiles but precision-target the areas of fused hostile tech and cut a track around each one: I don't want them attempting linkage. Dyxin, get me the *Drake* and the *Sally*."

Copper wasted no words, advising the Mars ship to pull back to give the *Crucible* manoeuvring room. She had realised that the *Regan*, although less heavily subverted than the *Morgana*, would have learnt from the previous encounter and would have new tricks in her arsenal. She advocated that they take her down quickly and thoroughly: the last thing the Fleet needed was trouble at its back when it was coming in at the front door. Flor concurred and proposed the positioning of *Sally Two* and *Sally Four* to cover any fighter deployment or attempted escape.

"Agreed," Copper said shortly. "Good luck! *Crucible* out."

Othra, checking his ops board, notified her that Tehoaar was organising the micro-breaching pods for use when ordered.

"Then we go in now – no warning. Weapons, stand by for a targeted strike as soon as you've got the range. Helm, take us in full throttle and close enough to the *Regan's* hull that we can see our faces in it. Spook, direct helm – you've been here before."

"Although the *Crucible* learns from previous attacks and alters hull configuration to compensate, *Regan Arcadia's* auto systems will target us and launch an offensive," Othra warned.

"I know, that's why I've asked Spook to intervene. If we can baffle their trackers, we have a chance of staying in one piece."

The webbing locking the crew in place tightened as a rising hum warned them of fast manoeuvring that was likely to cause destabilisation of the gravity system. Copper was suddenly very grateful for the sims she had used aboard her small alien fighter: she could cope with the rising wave of nausea. The hybrid ship screamed as she scoured the hull of the *Regan* that was closing in at a dizzying rate. The bridge holo spun in its grid as it displayed their path across the massive civilian ship, whose weapons were spewing lethal fire.

"Suggest use of deflecting shards to draw their fire!" Othra bellowed at her side.

"Do it!"

Copper had no idea what he meant but had no time to ask as her head was spinning as fast as the chasing lights in the sensory circlet above her head. *That* source provided the answer in a few seconds: deflecting shards were small reflective patches made of hull plating and with inbuilt tech that sent out signals to draw fire away from sensitive areas. It was notably effective against automated weapons.

Spook must have been a formidable helmsman in his time as the *Crucible* ducked and wove but held sufficiently long that Pyx could get a lock-on with his phased beams, which speared out again and again in light-streaks that cut the dark like fiery whips. Blazells had not been idle, as his targeting eyes had picked out the great ship's larger weapons loci and he was systematically taking them apart. As the pace slackened off, Linen's voice cut across the bridge.

"*Regan Arcadia's* hull now reading clear of operating organo-tech, Captain: no spread of hostile substances detected and the mass is dispersing. Good going, Pyx and Blazells, that was fast work," she added to the two officers at the weapons station. "Even the *Drake's* firepower was no match."

"Seven of our micro-breaching pods have pierced the *Regan's* hull, Captain," Othra reported, scanning his ops board closely. "Onboard drones are homing in on the areas infected by hostile technology. There *is* minor discharge to inner levels from the hull elements," he noted. "Capturing the data. But spread from there has essentially ceased. We are reading other hostile sources from within but we have too few drones to identify the full extent. Drones are gathering data to assist in refining our phased disruptors; we are transferring it to weapons station."

"Stand down weapons, but keep your targeting eyes on her," ordered Copper, checking her own board. "Nyx, keep a lookout for any transmission from the *Regan Arcadia* in any direction. She's ceased fire for the moment," she added to the first officer.

"Colonel Moritz for you, Captain," Dyxin called. "Captain Flor is also on line."

The colonel had linked in to inform Copper and Flor that she had received a capitulation message from Erkon Elks of the *Regan Arcadia*, citing circumstances beyond his control for the attacks on the *Hawking* and on the *Crucible*. His crew was at that moment disabling the automatic systems that had kicked in to take over his main bridge stations. He was also aware that his ship's hull had been infiltrated by drones from the hybrid ship and wanted an explanation and their immediate removal.

"I'll recall them *once* I have all the details they can pick up on the alien tech riddling that ship, as it's not just on her outer hull surface," Copper told the two. "My science team will send over the data once it's as complete as we can make it. Now what do we do about the *Regan*, ma'am?" she asked of the colonel.

"Your opinion, Captain Milkstone?"

"I'd want her out of local space," Copper said decidedly. "And possibly on a track back to her home base, though I'd be wary of that lest she pick up more bad habits or similar en route: she'll no doubt rendezvous with the *Morgana* and I expect they'll detour via Jupiter Station and that's a hive of felony if ever there was one, some of which is both hostile and alien. We can't leave her defenceless but I'd like to be assured that any hostile alien tech remaining aboard her is non-operational."

"I doubt you'll get that assurance, but I agree. Captain Flor, what is your view of the situation?"

Flor agreed on the *Regan's* removal from the neighbourhood and being familiar with the enemy tech, she concurred with the colonel that its complete removal or deactivation was unlikely. She was more interested in Copper's next move concerning her drones aboard the *Regan*.

"Their people are trying to find and disable our drones, but my team's keeping ahead of them. However, I'd like to speak to Captain Elks before I recall them," said Copper "That may give us a clue as to whether he was in close contact with the *Morgana* and was aware of the *Crucible's* ability to deal with the novel technology on his ship's hull – and of me: Commander Wyld was more than surprised to find me in command. I'd like you both to stay online when I do."

The two agreed and Dyxin put the link through. There was a pause: Elks had evidently been caught by surprise by contact from what was to him an alien ship. As his face appeared in the holo-grid and he caught sight of the bridge and the crew, his jaw dropped. Whatever he had been told, a ship crewed by both humans and aliens had thrown him. He confirmed his identity and asked to speak to the commanding officer with creditable calm however, and only a tightening of his lips gave any clue as to his discomfiture as his eyes flickered around the two who were obviously in the command position.

Copper let him size up the parts of her bridge he could see before she spoke. "Captain Elks: I'm Captain Copper Milkstone and this is the *US Crucible*. Why did you go out of your way to target my ship?"

"Out of my way?"

"The *MSS Drake II* was the lead ship: you deliberately spread mines in her path to stop her progress and you altered course to take on *my* ship. Why?"

He paused, still taking her in, not quite grasping her position or her authority, but eventually gave the reasons he had stated to Colonel Moritz earlier: his ship had switched to auto control without authorisation and his crew could not lock it down. His people were still in process of deactivating the relevant systems and he now had most of his ops back on line. He tendered his regrets and requested an opening of dialogue. He also warned that he would confiscate the drones sent out by the *Crucible* and wanted destruction of the data they had collected.

Copper raised an eyebrow and shook her head. She was not buying it: he was still hiding something.

"You fired on the *EFS Stephen Hawking* and broke out to follow a course which replicated that of the *Morgana Atlantis*, in the direction of incoming hostiles, once you knew the *Morgana* had been disabled. What was your motivation for that, Captain? Then you targeted my ship on the excuse that you couldn't help yourself. A ship like yours, with all that human – and alien – technology can do to make it the match of *any* human ship."

"You have my explanation and I can tell you nothing more. As a human in command of an alien ship, *you* are more than you seem and I would like very much to understand that."

"You don't stack up Captain, not by a long way; and until I get answers, I consider you hostile. Under whose orders do you operate? What is your mission? Why did you target my ship?"

"I have said all that I will say on that. You have a suspicious mind, Captain," Elks noted sourly.

"Damn straight I have. Subversion comes in many forms and I've seen enough of it and suffered enough from it to know that I will not risk any concessions I make backfiring: there will be time enough for dialogue when we have this neck of the system on an even keel. Take it up with your masters back on Mars or elsewhere if you have a problem with that. Milkstone out."

"Lor', aren't you glad she's on our side?" Linen remarked to Kit, irrepressible as usual, as the link was cut.

"Recall our drones," Copper ordered Othra. "We'll get no more from that ship and they'll get them sooner or later."

"Aye, Captain."

Copper was sure that there were still dark influences aboard the *Regan* and said as much to Colonel Moritz and Captain Flor, both of whom were equally wary. The data from the drones had confirmed that there was intact hostile tech aboard, although it was currently quiescent. Spook was certain that at least one or two of the crew were under hostile guidance, but there was little they could do. As with the *Morgana*, they had no option but to order her out of the immediate area. On Othra's advice a tracker probe was released to follow her progress, as no ship could be spared as escort: *Sally Two* had linked in to say that the hostile fleet had changed formation and had also picked up speed. At the current rate, they would reach the defending fleet's position in fifty five minutes Mars time.

* * *

None of the humans and few of the aliens aboard the *Crucible* had seen a hostile ship of the form incoming. Copper had called for the most detailed spec her tactical station could produce and she sat eyeing the malevolent shape that spun in her holo-grid. It was huge and bristling with weaponry, its dark hide seeming to shimmer beneath some form of energy barrier that coated it. As she took in the semi-cylindrical shape, its hull distended by myriad spiky protrusions, she could not shake the feeling that she was in some complex battle simulation, that this was unreal and that she would wake up soon. A touch on her arm made her turn: Zonota'a, a hypo in hand, was at her elbow.

"You've been monitoring my status," she deduced. "What's that, a sedative?"

"Negative. But it will help."

"Spook: I might have known. Go ahead, Doctor. With hell on the doorstep, I'll take all the help I can get."

Zonota'a had no sooner returned to her station than Othra, who had been busy with Pyx and Blazells at weapons, called her over. Grateful to stretch her legs, Copper made her way across to the small team that included engineers Oaky Grimsson and Hoof. She had noticed the huddle and various interactions with the officers at tactical and science but had been sufficiently wise to leave the crew to their own devices: the *Crucible* was at red alert but this was the calm before the storm and instinctively she knew that her people would perform to their utmost with no interference from her.

"Commander Othra?" she enquired formally, aware that the officers at every station nearby were listening in.

"You recall, Captain, that my people trapped on the world Lux Noctis used our technology and yours to begin to build this ship? We later assimilated inactivate hostile technology to create the phased disruptor beams that are now part of our weapons systems? We now know testing was successful against renegade human ships and we have upgraded our own systems with data acquired from our interactions with those vessels."

Copper nodded, wondering where this was going.

"Officers Pyx and Blazells have created schematics that may be used to produced attachments for retrofit of our ships with same technology; we have confirmed that materials are available on our repair station here, with hostile technology, to produce such weapons for our fleet, though not for human ships yet."

Othra gestured to a slowly spinning complex holo above the weapons station. "I recommend immediate despatch of plans to surface. Many of our people are now down there and they could begin the processing. It will take time of course and will not be in place when enemy fleet arrives, but it will aid home defence in the future. The plans can be relayed to all our stations in this system and to our remaining ships out there."

Copper digested the information, studying the faces watching hers. Whatever she had guessed might be going on, this was not it. As she examined schematics and asked questions, she could feel the tension in the air from both the humans and the aliens around her. She smiled at last and assented.

"We seem to have one helluva crew," she remarked aloud to Spook as she set off back to her own station.

"I think we have one helluva commanding officer," Blazells said quietly to Pyx.

Linen grinned over at Kit and winked: they concurred.

The tension on the bridge of the *Crucible* was rising palpably: Copper could sense it as she scanned her boards yet again. The two human civilian ships had left local space, both being tracked by the *En Hedu'anna* and the *Mina Fleming*. The science station of the *Crucible* was monitoring the probe she had sent in the wake of the *Regan*. The hostiles had slowed their approach again but were still moving, possibly more wary now that any help they had counted on from within the zone had been neutralised. *Sally Two* and *Sally Four* had reported attempted close surface scans of their hulls, which had been foiled by their shielding.

Colonel Moritz had taken command of the overall taskforce and of the human fleet but had agreed that Captain Flor would direct her own people. These did not include the crew of the *Crucible*: Copper was firmly told that she would obey the mission commander in matters of strategy. Comms and tactical stations were in process of making the various links across the fleet that would facilitate rapid data and communications exchange.

"All set," she announced grimly to Othra as the news came through that the lead ship of the approaching flotilla had called for a dialogue with the commander of the blocking force.

Although the defending fleet had more vessels, the massive size and armaments of the interlopers would, Copper guessed, more than match them. She questioned her first officer on his knowledge of the manoeuvrability, defensive mechanisms and weapons of the ships. As well as powerful torpedoes and pulsed energy bolts, the hostiles had disrupter beams that could deploy at close range, breaching pods and both manned and unmanned fighters. Their hulls were protected by self-healing energy fields that could be destabilised, Othra believed, by the phased organic disruptors that were now part of the *Crucible's* armaments, but that had yet to be tested on an enemy vessel.

Her bridge officers had meanwhile not been idle. Linen and Tehoaar had formed a close rapport and had been scanning the spec of the lead ship with every sensor they possessed. They had also been listening in to their seniors and the redhead had come to the conclusion that undermining the enemy by sending out fake signals to non-existent allies was one way of baffling them; she had hauled in Dyxin and Nyx to work on the details. Junior, with the alien equivalent of raising his hand in class, suggested that they needed something like a hard-holo projector that could throw a full-size holo-battleship into local space. He had once had such a device; he had used it to project small models of the real thing, weapons and all, he told Tehoaar, who was translating the young alien's telepathic links for Linen. If every ship had one, the fleet would look twice the size.

"You want something impossible done, get a child to do it," Linen remarked. "We'd need a duplicate of the box we used to project the hard-holo of Copper's fighter in our tri-dee sim suite back aboard the *Drake*," she mused, trying to call up a mental image of the device, which had been stored in Junior's favourite closet in the lab and which the young alien had used to call up holos of his parents. "But how we'd get convincing holos out into space in the time we've got left I don't know…"

Tehoaar was familiar with such devices and had picked up on Junior's notion quickly. The two science officers on the bridge had no time to investigate the practicalities or otherwise of such a project but with a quick link to their captain to apprise her of the situation, gave Junior the slack to hunt out other crewmen in science and engineering who could help.

Copper meanwhile was on her feet watching and listening, as was every other allied commander, to the talk between Colonel Moritz and the being who claimed to be in control of the hostile fleet that was now standing a few thousand kilometres off Blink 159. She and Othra were highly distrustful of the motives of the strange entity whose face was hidden by a helmet that masked every feature, suspecting that the reason for the discourse was a distraction to gain time for mischief. Every question of Colonel Moritz was parried by repeated requests for an account of the presence of the human and alien fleets in free space, where the new arrivals had come to claim their own.

It soon was obvious that several of the hostile vessels had deployed scanning beams, all of which were aimed at the human ships. Flor had ordered her own vessels into intercept positions to prevent them reaching the rest of the fleet, lest the Mars and Earth ships were insufficiently protected by their own shielding. That had caused an irate outburst from the hostile commander which had no effect on the colonel. The *Crucible's* shields could hold against the incursion, Othra told Copper, but he proposed that they return the compliment by scanning the leading enemy vessel. He also suggested that they send out a phalanx of micro-breaching pods, updated with the data gained from intercepting the *Regan Arcadia*, to a holding position, where they could target the lead ship. They *would* be detected, but if utilised, a few might make it through to deliver covert payloads of drones encoded to disable any independent ops clusters within the ship: the latter could potentially be despatched on search and destroy missions if the ship itself was taken down – Othra's people had met with such technology before.

"How aware are they of human covert technology?" queried Copper as she assented. "If they've arrived here in answer to the signals we know were sent out and haven't been in this sector, they may not have had experience of humans, even if they've had data transmitted to them from all the hostile influences in the Sol system. The *Drake* may have sensing or infiltration gear they've not met with before. Any changes in our readings of the hostile forces apart from those scanning beams?" she called out to her tactical and science stations. "The holo hasn't changed, but that doesn't mean they can't circumvent *our* scans. Liaise with the *Drake* on using her long-range science arrays linked to our systems, Lieutenant Lyrican: she may pick up something we don't. Commander Locksmith, you do the same with the *Drake's* tactical and security systems."

Othra was examining his ops board closely and communing with Spook, whom Copper could sense very near her. "Those hostile vessels are of older design," was his analysis. "They must have been in space for a very long time. Tehoaar, continuous scan of hull material of lead hostile vessel for changes related to data abstraction," he instructed. "The hulls of our vessels can gather and store data: it is absorbed at nodes and stored in hull fabric," he explained to Copper. "It allows our ships to react to hostile environments, to learn and update defences if necessary. Such systems can also be subverted to abstract data from others for offensive purposes. Changes showing use of the technology can be detected if you know what to search for: often the signals resemble hull-shielding shifts rather than scan beams."

"And the subject doesn't realise data's being recorded that might be used to undermine them. Very clever," Copper said. "And that's why the patterns on the hull of the *Crucible* shift: the ship continuously reacts to its environment to protect itself?"

"Exactly."

"What kind of range would such a system have if used to scan us?"

"Unknown. Ah! We have confirmation that such a system is operational! Captain Spook was correct."

"Notify the rest of the fleet that those hostiles are covertly probing for gaps in our defences and link them Tehoaar's data," Copper ordered her comms station. "Can we block the scans?"

"*We* can, now that we know. *Drake* and sister ships should be able to protect themselves; other vessels unknown," Othra said.

The warning to their fellow fleet vessels produced a manifest change in the deadlock. As soon as Colonel Moritz challenged the hostile commander with covert data abstraction, the linkage from the enemy ship was cut and the entire hostile fleet began to move as one, spreading out in an ever-widening formation, the lead vessel as the spear-point of a deadly battalion.

"Dammit!" Copper exploded. "They were getting ready for a full-scale assault and all this talk was a blind! Tie yourselves in, people, this could get rough! Spook, I want you at the helm with Timri. Comms and tactical, make sure our links to the fleet are tight; weapons, warm them up and keep them hot. Engineering, we'll need all you've got and then some. Science, keep your eyes peeled and liaise with tactical – I want to know what the hostiles are doing before they've done it. All hands, battlestations!"

As she spoke, Copper was webbing herself into her station, hauling her boards across and her sensory circlet closer. A jab on her arm distracted her as Zonota'a injected some stimulant or other into her bloodstream. She thus missed Linen call across to Kit that their captain was beginning to sound like a third-rate holo-flic script. His reply was terse, to the point and very uncomplimentary to the science officer.

Colonel Moritz had called battlestations for the whole fleet and ordered them to take position in a tight formation, with the *Drake* and her sister ships in the van. The *Crucible* was instructed to line up on the *Drake's* port side, with the *En Hedu'anna* and the *Mina Fleming* at starboard. The *Sapphire Sunset*, the *Lithium Star* and the two Earth ships made the second line of defence. *Sally Two* and *Sally Four* had been withdrawn and had joined the ships under Flor to take up flanking positions. The three alien transports with their limited crews were in place to protect Blink 159 and its refugee population.

Copper felt her head ring under the barrage of directions that was racing back and forth but gritted her teeth and scanned all her stations as she ordered her helmsman to tie into the *Drake's* navigation systems and maintain distance. With hard eyes she took in what the holo-grid was showing of the hostile advance. They were fast. Othra was watching her closely and nodded in grim accord as she ordered the release of their micro-breaching pods and their destructive drone payloads on a direct line to the lead vessel. Some inbuilt stimulus caused her to order a series of pulsed scanning beams on the same trajectory to confuse the sensory data that was no doubt being pulled in by the enemy.

"Tactical, can we crack their shielding and get more on their weaponry?"

"We could try linking our probe beams to the phased organic disruptors but they may interpret that as incoming fire," Kit responded.

"Hold for now…"

She was interrupted by the order from the *Drake* to expand their formation to match similar tactics by the enemy. The first salvo was not long in coming and the *Crucible's* hull rang to the buffet of incoming fire, deflected by her ever-changing organic-based shielding. Colonel Moritz had decided that attack was the best form of defence and had ordered her ships to advance, requesting Flor to hold back. It was soon clear that the *Crucible* was more manoeuvrable than her companion vessels and as the *Dexterity* cut in with the word that she had lost one of her main engines to a long-range torpedo that had cut through the first line of defence and would have to haul back a little, the colonel called her main line ships to break and attack. Flor had directed her fleet to extend their range as the hostiles began a widening pincer movement.

Now that the gloves were off, Copper lost no time in calling on tactical to expand the main grid holo with every piece of data they could get on the lead hostile vessel. Weapons were ordered to get a line on it and target it with the phased disruptors. The helm she left to Spook and Timri, with Othra keeping his eyes on engineering, hull integrity and the advance of their band of breaching pods: she was well aware that, sims notwithstanding, this was no ordinary combat situation.

"She's targeting us, Captain!" Kit called the warning.

"Evasive!" Copper bellowed. "Timri, keep them guessing! We're going in close!"

"*Sally Two* has been ordered in to cover our backs, Captain Copper!" the tinny voice of Nyx screeched over from comms.

"Just make sure we don't miss with a single shot," Copper responded as she was squashed back in her chair by the force of acceleration in response to an explosive banking turn as the *Crucible* rose up to avoid a stream of incoming phased fire.

For some compelling but indefinable reason, Copper wanted the lead ship down. The part of her that was now permanently linked to Spook was subliminally aware that he was responsible and given his experience with what was facing them, she nodded grimly to herself and ground her teeth as she read the rapidly updating holo-grid before her.

"We're hardly denting her!" she hissed. "And she's holding back, trying to figure just what we are: we should take advantage of that before she figures and warns her fleet."

"What do you recommend, Captain?" said Othra beside her.

"Her hull's crawling with enough armaments to take us and *Sally Two* down in one fell swoop. Launch a stream of deflecting shards towards her surface comms and sensor arrays and follow up with focussed bursts of phased organic disruptors. Get me *Sally Two*... Captain, request you target her aft weapons arrays. Helm, get us close enough to see our faces in her hull!"

"Aye, Captain," Timri called up as he cut through the cloud of deflecting shards that had been blasted from one of the *Crucible's* forr'ad torpedo tubes.

"Weapons, hit them with everything you have. Kit, you man the auxiliary weapons station and target those incoming missiles! I want them down!" Copper bawled as her quick eyes spotted a salvo that the enemy ship had let loose.

"Aye, ma'am!" he called, fighting to release his seat restraints.

"She's launched a breaching pod!" yelled Blazells. "Got it! Here's another!"

The huge ship had also changed course at speed to match the weaving and ducking smaller vessel that was stinging her hide and the crew on the bridge of the *Crucible* were flung this way and that as Timri at the helm, with Spook as back up, strove to compensate whilst coming ever closer to the enemy's hull. Nyx at comms was keeping pace with the situation of the rest of the defending fleet and had called out that the *Lithium Star* was out of action and limping out of range towards Blink 159.

There was a sustained juddering as an incoming missile that Kit had hit exploded close to the upper hull. The ship shook as she took one direct burst of phased fire amidships and a second struck her obliquely. As Lomusan at tactical called over that they had lost shield integrity in two sections, Copper glanced at her boards, tabbing her updates: a medbay alert was in progress.

"Hull damage repair ongoing," Halsen at engineering cut in. "Plating is holding but another strike in the same place and we'll lose it."

"Two of our micro-breaching pods have made it through the enemy's hull and have deployed their drones, Captain," Othra reported calmly. "I cannot track their progress but they should provide a diversion if nothing else."

Dyxin interrupted with the news that the *Sapphire Sunset* had launched two crewless recon craft as sacrificial pawns to slow the advance of the assault fleet, which had halted its structured attack. Each enemy vessel seemed now to be under orders to take out the opposing forces by any means necessary.

"I want this done!" Copper roared as another glancing blow struck the *Crucible* and she slewed up to avoid a second burst from the same source.

"Permission to launch fighters, Captain!" Linen yelled at the top of her lungs.

"What! We don't have fighters, apart from mine!" Copper yelled back.

"Junior does: virtual fighters. Permission to launch, ma'am?"

Copper's eyes blazed. "Hell's teeth! Granted. Just keep them out of my line of fire!"

"Enemy is matching our speed and attempting to foil our course changes, Captain," Timri reported. "She thinks she has our measure."

"Not yet she doesn't," Copper hissed as she mentally ordered Spook to pull out all the stops and take her ship in even closer.

"*Sally Two* reports that she has disabled approximately thirty percent of the enemy's aft weapons emplacements, but has lost some hull plating and one auxiliary engine!" announced Nyx.

"Tell her to haul back! Pyx, target those areas reading highest in organo-tech and take them out!"

"She's sending firepower after Junior's fighters!" crowed Linen gleefully.

"Then we end this now! Empty our arsenal in their faces! And send a shower of deflecting shards in with them, if we've any left: that should confuse their targeting."

"That's the last of our torpedoes, Captain but our phased disruptors still at fifteen percent capacity!" Blazells called.

"It looks as if we will not need them," Othra intoned softly.

The hostile ship veered away from them in a waltz of fire, a great split in her hull spewing flame. She broke apart, great splinters spinning off into space.

"Get us out of her path, helm!" Copper bellowed.

"Affirmative," responded Timri as he swung the *Crucible* up and away.

Copper had only time to draw breath when Dyxin's voice cut across the bridge. "The *Drake* has two on her! Requesting aid!"

"Bring us about, helm! Lino'arr, plot us an intercept to bring us up on the *Drake* with all speed. Kit, return to your station! Status on the rest of the fleet?"

"The *Hawking* is down; *Sally Three* is protecting her rear to let her escape. *En Hedu'anna* and *Mina Fleming* are holding their own but the *Sapphire Sunset* has lost engine power. Captain Flor has turned aside to assist but reports that the rest of her ships are being forced back towards the planet. Civilian ships have been ordered not to engage until under fire," the calm voice of Kit's second at tactical stated.

"Dammit! Expand that holo, I want to see the *Drake's* situation!"

The pride of Mars Fleet was beset: one advancing hostile was directing fire at her forward section and a second was aiming to come up under her. Copper took in the holo: she knew that the bridge and the primary centres were the main targets of the first ship and that the *Drake* did not have sufficient forr'ad firepower to breach the enemy's hull defences. If she turned to protect her most sensitive areas, she would leave her flanks vulnerable to attack – and that meant her fighter bays.

"Timri, can you get us between that hostile and the *Drake?*" she demanded, the lance point of her hand-held light beam encircling her chosen objective as the *Crucible's* path lit up on the holo like an arrow seeking its target. "Linen, you get Junior to deploy virtual fighters against the other: it might provide enough distraction to let us cut in. Pyx, choose your disruptor targets and make every burst count."

"Captain, I have sparse data collected by our drones that infiltrated the lead hostile before she was destroyed," Othra told her. "I can use it to plot a path for focussed disruptor fire: if we can disable the central memory core of the hostile vessel we can slow her attack."

"Do it – and get that information out to the fleet if you can."

"Two enemy ships have made it past our outer defences: they're homing in on Blink 159!" Kit called from tactical.

"There's nothing we can do for our people there. Continue on course," Copper instructed harshly.

The *Crucible* was highly responsive but had lost considerable engine power and with so little firepower left, Copper knew that her assault would have to be fast. The small hybrid ship shot up between the *Drake* and her main adversary, a tactic the hostile had not expected, as she had continued to rain fire on the Mars ship. A bolt hit the *Crucible*, and expecting a collision, the hostile veered away, but swept back in a banking turn that took her straight towards the great front mid-section that housed the *Drake's* main engines. Pyx and Blazells, choosing their targets carefully, hit every mark and the ship swerved away a second time. There was a cataclysmic eruption of flame that seemed like the universe exploding and the *Crucible* lost her helm control, spinning off into space in a sickening spiral that left her bridge crew gasping for breath, many of them flung like ragdolls around their stations.

"What the hell was that?" Copper screamed into the air as a searing pain cut across her midriff as she was thrown about, her chair webbing almost unable to cope with the stresses.

The bridge lighting flickered and then steadied as emergency backup cut in, ship's systems stabilised and Timri regained helm control. The red lights of the alert system had gone haywire and the eerily pulsing illumination turned the crew's faces to blood. Copper strove to focus, demanding updates from every station, pulling her boards back into place and hauling her sensory circlet downwards.

After a few garbled cries and bursts of static as the comms system came back on line, it was Othra who called out the news. One hostile had been taken out in a collision with the *Sally Two*: she had returned to assist her fellow vessel and with little power and weaponry had rammed the enemy craft. Both vessels were now one expanding bloom of flak. The second adversary had swiftly backed off and was en route to Blink 159. The *Drake* was damaged but still in fighting trim. One other hostile vessel had been destroyed but nine were left that were still operational.

"Damn and double damn!" was all that Copper could say, aware that her fight was over: the *Crucible* had nothing left but the wherewithal to maintain her integrity and limp to some sort of safety and her casualty list was alarmingly long.

She had little time to count the cost of her last battle: a curse from Dyxin at comms preceded his call that an assault on Blink 159 had begun: five hostiles not involved with the allied fleet were now headed straight for the planetoid. And an alert from *Sally One* had just been received: one of Flor's remote probes had detected a small body of unidentified blips heading at speed into the Sol system. Whoever they were, they were fast, they were shielded and they would be there in less than two hours.

The *Crucible* hung like a broken toy against the backdrop of star-spangled night. The *Drake* had come alongside to ascertain her status, but Copper was adamant: the mighty Mars ship would be more use out in the field with the remains of the allied fleet. The small hybrid vessel had power enough to maintain her position and her self-healing technology was already restoring what could be salvaged of her fabric and systems.

"See you on the flipside, Colonel," Copper smiled resolutely into the face looking searchingly at her.

"Roger that, Captain," Elle Moritz responded. "Good luck. *Drake* out."

"Othra, you take the conn," Copper directed her second-in-command, who was mercifully still in one piece. "We're going nowhere for the present and as I have what we humans term an advanced General Health Qualification, I can help Dr Zonota'a with the injuries to the human bridge crew."

"You seem to have many talents, Captain," the alien officer noted with a wry smile as he nodded confirmation.

Copper, ignoring the belt of pain that encircled her, unlocked her restraints and headed over to the medical station to pick up essential kit. She called Embertz to inform her of her intention, advising the doctor that she would call her for advisories as necessary. Dr Zonota'a was already on the deck by Lieutenant Hoof, who had taken a tumble and was out cold.

Linen was helping a bleeding Tehoaar back into her seat. The redhead herself was dishevelled and limping but a quick tally of her human crew told Copper that Kit was the only unconscious crewman and thus the one most in need of urgent aid. She was sick with apprehension as she knelt by him and ran her medi-scanner over his recumbent form: his seat restraints had come loose and he had been thrown against a bulkhead. She quickly cut him out of a tangle of webbing that had come away with him and eased him over onto his back. There were no bones broken, her scanner confirmed, but torn ligaments would have to be treated, as would a number of grazes and bumps caused by collisions with parts of the bridge. She strapped his left knee tightly and then patched what she could of the visible damage. A swelling lump over one eye was beginning to discolour as she methodically wiped the sweat and blood from his face.

"How's he doing?" said a voice at her elbow.

"He'll live," Copper replied. "What've you done to your leg?"

"Search me," Linen smiled in response. "But Blazells is griping away over there. If you give me a bundle of medi-wipes I can go see."

"You'll stay where you are, Lieutenant. I'm going to give Kit a shot of anti-inflammatory and some pain relief. You sit still and let me see that leg. Junior, you go stay with Tehoaar until Dr Zonota'a has time to deal with her."

"You can talk to him?" Linen asked in surprise.

"I'm now able to sense and communicate with all our non-organic crew," Copper said wearily. "I don't know how or when it kicked in, but it did. Everything's going to be all right, Junior," she added to the young alien, whose distress was apparent to her. "You go to Tehoaar, she needs you. And as for you, Dr Lyrican... pass me that med-patch, the small one."

As she quickly released the patch from its pack and applied it gently over the bump above Kit's eye, he groaned. Moments later, his eyes opened and Copper was relieved to note that both were bright enough.

"How many fingers am I holding up?" she asked him as he focussed on her face.

"One," he replied with an attempted grin, trying to reach up. "Time and place?" he added weakly.

"Behave. You're not my only patient, *Commander*. You lie still while I attend to Lieutenant Lyrican here."

"And who's going to be attending to you, Captain?" enquired Linen astutely, noticing how her friend winced as she turned.

"Belay that," Copper muttered, undoing a pack containing a small knee brace. "It's just a wrench," she told her. "I'll strap it up for support in the meantime and give you a shot. Keep off it if you can, but I want you back at station – I'll need you to get everything you can on what's approaching us from out yonder. As for you Commander Locksmith, you stay where you are until I or Dr Zonota'a say otherwise. Ensign Lomusan is well able to handle the tactical station."

"Aye, ma'am," Kit smiled.

Copper smiled gently in return as she rose to her feet. Her next stop was the weapons station, where Lieutenant Gadget Blazells was nursing one arm against his chest and rocking back and forth in his seat. He was still keeping wary eyes on his console, however, and exchanging words with Pyx at his side.

"We're upgrading our phased organic disruptor discharge system, Captain," he informed Copper, still awkward with her title. "We think we can cut the beams to make them finer and operate in longer bursts."

"Good. Leave that to Lieutenant Pyx for the moment, and let me have a look at that arm," she told him.

His eyes widened as he took in the medi-kit she was toting and the scanner that she had quickly run over the injured limb. He said nothing, however, as she adjusted a control and again checked her readings.

"I'm giving you a shot of pain control first," she apprised him, extracting a hypo and applying it to his upper arm. "I'll need you to relax that arm. It's a small fracture and should heal cleanly, but you've got a lot of swelling around it. I'll strap it for now: bone-sealing will have to be done by a registered medic, once we get back to something like normal."

"Will we get back to something like normal?" he asked, troubled. "Are we going to make it?"

She looked probingly into his face. "Trust me, we'll make it," she said calmly, hoping he would believe her: she herself was far from sure.

Copper's next port of call was Erik Halsen, who was sporting a bruised cheek and a cut to his head but insisted that he was fine otherwise. Her other human crew seemed to be intact and as she hobbled painfully back to the med-station with her gear, she was overtaken by Zonota'a.

"Sit there, Captain," the alien doctor instructed, indicating a chair. "I have authority to relieve you of command on medical grounds," she added quietly, a smile lighting her pale eyes.

"And you would, I suspect."

"Exactly. I have sent your readings to Dr Embertz. You have one cracked rib and muscle injury, we conclude. I have relevant treatment options here. Open protective suit, please: it is better if dressing applied closer to skin. Medication will penetrate."

"It's hardly private," Copper muttered as she obeyed, feeling a jab to her arm as the doctor's pain-relief hypo hit home.

"I also suggest you order respite for crew: food and rest."

"They'll have to stay at station, most of them," Copper told her. "Can you supply some nourishing brew that they can take to keep their strength up? I will not authorise off duty until we have enough cover."

"Agreed," Zonota'a said in a low tone, expertly feeding some strapping around Copper's middle and tightening it up.

"Damn shit, that hurts!"

"Good. Now you know how your patients feel."

"Once I *can* authorise off duty you'll be at the top of my list, Doctor. But what's our casualty list like?"

It seemed Zonota'a could read her extremely well. "We have nine severely injured crew, both human and my people; several more have non-life-threatening but serious injuries," she said calmly. "But we have no fatalities."

Copper leant back and closed her eyes with a sigh of intense relief. "Praise be," she breathed. "How are our medics coping?"

"Adequately, but they are overstretched."

"Keep me updated. I need to get back to my station. I'd like you to take a look at Commander Locksmith Tactical, when you get a moment," she added. "He's the most seriously injured of my human bridge crew and I don't want to pull a medic away from medbay if I can help it."

"Affirmative."

"Thank you, Doctor."

Copper felt the eyes of the alien physician follow her as she eased her way across to her station. She was utterly exhausted but in a strange way calm, as if nothing else now had the power to affect her. She was also aware of the eyes of many of her bridge crew as she settled into her chair gingerly and hauled her main ops board across. Something made her look up and she found Linen at her elbow.

"I thought I told you to keep to your station, Lieutenant," she said harshly.

Linen leaned in close. "You forgot to do your uniform up," she whispered. "You're showing the crew your underwear."

Copper looked down and found that the redhead was right. Cursing, she quickly sealed her suit and looked back into Linen's face. Something in the twinkling gold-brown eyes made her start to laugh softly.

"What would I do without you?" she asked her. "Get back to your station, and this time *stay* there."

"Have you remembered Kit? He's still on the deck."

"I have and Dr Zonota'a will look him over. Tell him."

"Aye, ma'am."

It was with something akin to relief that Copper noted that the *Crucible* was being left severely alone. Those combatants still in action appeared to be positioned between her and Blink 159. The field of flak that was all that was left of the *Sally Two* and the hostile she had taken out was still spreading but none of it was close enough to cause them serious trouble. Their view-grid holo had been updated with the latest data linked over from Flor, Othra told Copper as he slid in beside her. He had been lending a hand at engineering, where his extensive experience was being put to good use in directing repair of the ship's hull. The material of which the skin was composed needed substrate to self-heal the sections where they had lost a lot of plating and outer bulkheads were being utilised for the purpose. They could render the ship operational and with sufficient engine power to manoeuvre, the first officer noted, but with little left by way of weapons they would be of limited use in a battle situation.

"How much weaponry *is* little?" Copper demanded, scanning her ever-updating holos as they shifted.

"Phased organic disruptor capacity at three percent, standard energy pulse cannons at less than one percent; no torpedoes or short-range disruptor bolts left," he replied.

"But we have deflecting shards and our scanning arrays and sensors are operational – though our shielding has dropped by almost forty percent," she noted.

"Hostiles have reached optimum firing points for an attack on the station! Our civilian transport ships have been ordered to assume defensive positions and open fire!" Othra pointed to the holo as he spoke.

"They won't take that station out – it's too useful and too strategic," Copper said forcefully. "So the ships will be the main targets. And those four bastards there are holding our ships in check, they can't get through to protect. What in blazes is that coming in from the far side?"

"Captain, I'm reading her as the *Regan Arcadia*!" Lomusan called out.

"The *Drake* confirms that *Regan Arcadia* has returned to this sector," Dyxin added loudly from comms.

"Our side or theirs?"

"She appears to be firing on one of the hostiles attacking the station, Captain," Othra said evenly.

"*Drake* has called the *Regan* in as friendly and reports that two more hostiles are disengaging and making for Blink 159," Dyxin reported.

"Hell! They really want that station… can we power up sufficiently to head in?"

"Captain, we do not have the capacity to engage," Othra reminded her.

"We don't, but we do have Junior's hard-holo projector. If it could be modified to show that we do, or at least provide us with a virtual protective fighter wing, it may be enough to give us an edge. We'll need something: those unidentified blips that are heading in here have increased speed."

As she barked out orders and the activity intensified around her, Copper called up the data from her science station, where Linen had linked in the data stream from Flor's probes and was maintaining a close watch on the small group advancing towards them. They were still shielded and Copper could tell from her tactical update that they were now less than an hour away. She closed her eyes, the better to think things out. The fleet needed information and *her* ship had an advantage the rest did not: a very old entity that was more than knowledgeable about what was out there. A sudden collective intake of breath from several of her crew brought her back to full awareness. The blossoming of what seemed to be a ship blowing apart had appeared on the main holo-grid and it was directly above Blink 159.

"What in hell! Tactical, report!"

"As far as I can tell, there are several narrow-beam phased organic disruptor streams originating from our planetary station. They are targeting attacking ships," Lomusan responded.

"Show me!"

As the bridge holo expanded its detail and data poured across her boards, Copper understood. "The schematics we sent down there, the ones Pyx and Blazells worked out! They've managed to produce a working weapons system and are using it for planetary defence! Your people are the fastest, smartest bunch of techs I have ever come across," she breathed.

Othra accepted the compliment tranquilly. "So it seems. And Captain Spook has gone to investigate the fleet approaching?" he added shrewdly.

"You knew I'd asked him?"

"I knew. There is a danger if they are similar to the enemy forces we are facing here."

"I know, and so does he. Engineering, do we have enough power for manoeuvring thrusters?"

"Yes, ma'am," Halsen replied.

"Good. Helm, start moving us closer in to Blink 159 but keep us as far as possible out of range of our fleet and the three hostiles still engaged with them. Lino'arr, plot us a course that brings us up on the flanks of that outermost ship, but keep us in range of Captain Flor's probes: I don't want to lose their signals. And keep our remaining shielding at maximum. What's the status of planetary defence?"

"The civilian ships are holding their own, thanks to back-up from the surface," a well-known voice from tactical called out. "There's been no let-up in ground fire – they must have a good supply of gear down there."

Copper smiled over at Kit, who was back at station. As she did so, a sound at her elbow caused her to turn.

"Doctor?"

"Drink," Zonota'a directed, proffering a sealed cup. "Liquid nourishment; I have ordered the same for all human crew on duty. And equivalent for non-human crew."

As Copper quickly swallowed the drink, a call from Dyxin alerted her that two more enemy ships were down and that the *Regan Arcadia* had disabled another. She checked her boards and found there had been a cost: *Sally Five* was out of action and the *Drake* had lost two of the fighters that she had sent out to take out opposing fighters launched by one of the hostile ships. The *Sapphire Sunset* had managed to jury-rig her damaged engine and had returned to defend *Sally Five* from a pursuing vessel intent on destroying her.

"Those incoming blips have changed course and are on a line that will bring them up at our back!" Kit yelled over. "They're going all out, their speed is incredible!"

"Let me see!"

He was right: the blips had adopted a tight formation and there were at least eight of them. They were still shielded and their true shape and size could not be gauged by the *Crucible's* scanners. Copper could hear the curses from the science station as Linen strove to pierce the cloaking, but a strange elation had begun to seize her.

"Do we arm our remaining weapons and target, Captain?" Blazells asked a tad too loudly from his station.

"Negative, Lieutenant: we hold course and speed until they catch us up," she replied equally loudly. "Then we *all* head in."

A stunned silence, at least from the human crew, greeted the response. It was broken by Linen. "They're on our side."

Othra's face expanded in his strange alien grin. "Captain Spook made good time."

"Captain Spook's telepathic range is way greater than most of his own people, I imagine," Copper replied. "As my people say, the cavalry has come over the hill."

"Do we need a drum roll?" Linen demanded impishly.

"Just keep your eyes on your sensors, Lieutenant Lyrican. I want to know the moment they uncloak: reactions will be swift once our opponents realise they're outnumbered and outclassed. Dyxin, call the new arrivals in as friendly to our fleet."

The *Crucible* held her course but it was soon obvious that the advancing flotilla had been detected and deemed aggressive by the hostiles. As the battered remains of the allied fleet attempted to defend the most-damaged of their own ships and reel in their deployed fighters, the disruptor batteries of the planetary arrays intensified to shield them. The enemy forces were attempting to regroup to form a fighting wing and an urgent warning from the *Drake* alerted the defenders that at least two had dropped target-seeking mines in their wakes that were almost wholly composed of the blue organic tech – her science stations had confirmed.

"Hell! We need to take them out!" Copper snarled as she ordered Trisk's data to be displayed. "They're autonomous, so they'll work independently if they get through. *And* they can probably remain viable for millennia. Nyx, try to reach the base station and get them to target those mines: tell them to use fine-beam phased disruption. This is where we get our feet wet again! Lino'arr, plot us an intercept to get as many of those mines as we can; Timri, get us in as fast as you can. Pyx and Blazells, our phased discharge system: you reconfigured the beams to make them finer and extend their ops time. Get them up and running, effective immediately! We don't have much left, but transfer all weapons energy to those beams. Dyxin, inform Colonel Moritz and Captain Flor that we're heading in to deal with the mines. Othra, you and Spook liaise with our support forces and let them know."

"They're uncloaking!" That was Linen and as the holo within the confines of the grid spun and changed to accommodate the latest data, Copper paused for a second.

The newcomers were big, larger in scale than the *Sally* ships, and they shimmered against the star-dropped background as if shrouded in a diaphanous mist. Whatever messages had passed, seven of the group swept past the *Crucible* in an ever-widening formation, their object the melee that was local space around Blink 159. The eighth held position off her starboard as a shield.

"To allow us to deploy our weapons against the mines more effectively," Othra explained loudly as Copper was pushed back into her seat by the increasing acceleration. "Here we go!"

The *Crucible* banked and turned, her tactical and science ops working flat out to identify and target the small mines that were spreading like a field of scattered flowers. As one after another went down, the muted cheers of her officers levelled off. It seemed that an hour at least had passed before the weary voice of Gadget Blazells announced that all was over – the *Crucible* had not a drop of energy left in any weapons array that could be squeezed out.

"So now we count the cost," Copper intoned. "I only hope we got most of them."

"The future will tell us," her first officer said as he noted that the conflict was all but over: there were no hostiles to be seen, apart from the shards that were the remains of the four enemy vessels that had been destroyed in the final action.

The decision had been made not to pursue the fleeing ships. It was unlikely that they would regroup and return and there was too much to be done in the local zone to waste time and energy in a chase that was likely to be futile. Copper groaned as she called up reports from every section of her own ship. They had not lost any crew but medbay was in chaos and the walking wounded were more numerous that those who had escaped unscathed. They were lucky in that the *Crucible* could call on medical aid from the newcomers for her alien crewmembers and for technical assistance with ship's systems.

The latest arrivals were Othra's people, from an enclave that had successfully managed to avoid detection for centuries. They had initially been mobilised to assist the refugees that had found their way to Blink 159 in the three civilian ships that had come racing in. Those three large ships contained all that was left of the population of an outpost that had been attacked and destroyed, Othra informed Copper.

* * *

Counting the cost was a protracted business. Supra-light links had been made to both Mars and Earth and from thence to all the linked human outposts of the Sol system. Emergency aid would be some time coming, Colonel Moritz informed her fleet captains. The only ship that was almost completely intact was the recently-returned *Regan Arcadia*, and being one of the most advanced vessels in existence, her features were state-of-the-art. His crew had dealt with the residual rogue technology which had permeated his ship, Captain Elks informed the colonel, thanks to the initial work of the drones that Captain Milkstone had dealt him, and he promised all the support he could supply. Copper was still wary, realising that he must have found a way to circumvent the tracker probe that had been sent to track the *Regan Arcadia* and the *Morgana Atlantis* out of local space. But help was help and she assigned two non-organic crew members to the *Regan* to monitor the situation. She was adamant that she would accept no aid from the commercial ship and advised that any sent elsewhere be scanned before use, including personnel.

Despite a visit by Dr Embertz to ascertain her status, Copper refused to have her own injuries treated until she had personally checked in with all her crew. The leadership training drills she had taken part in at Beagle Basecamp seemed years in the past now, but somewhere at the back of her mind the ground rules lingered. She also resolutely refused to look at the lengthening list of casualties from the remaining allied vessels. The *Hawking* she knew had had to make planetfall on the far side of Blink 159 as she was no longer spaceworthy: the *Dexterity* was taking on her remaining crew. They had lost two of the *Sally* fleet, the rest of those were badly damaged and of the Mars ships, only the *En Hedu'anna* had escaped with limited damage and no fatalities. On a brighter note, the *MSS Ulugh Beg*, a *Drake* Class ship, had been diverted their way and would be with them in about ten sols. Another of the group, the *Annie J Cannon*, was being mobilised from Jupiter Station. The linked stations around the Sol system preserved by their alien allies had been updated; another series further out was being brought on line remotely. The main allied fleet had regrouped near Blink 159 and shuttles bearing essential personnel and supplies were criss-crossing the space lanes between ships as needed.

When at last Copper could relax on a medbay couch and allow Embertz to examine her, she was surprised to see nurse tech Axim Biggs in attendance. He had come over on a small transport from the *Drake* with additional medical supplies, he told her, having been released from duty by Dr Faerin. The *Drake* was coping remarkably well, Copper was pleased to hear: her only fatalities had been the two fighter pilots lost and a flight engineer on duty in one of the bays that had been hit.

"Three too many," Copper sighed as she settled back to allow whatever drugs Embertz had pumped into her to take effect. "Hell, I could sleep for a sevensol."

"I can arrange that, ma'am," Biggs informed her.

"You dare and I'll have you thrown in my brig and then court-martialled," she threatened.

That was the last she remembered until her eyes flicked open and she found herself in a small screened bay. She was still aboard the *Crucible* and could thus deduce that the happenings of the last few sols had not been some awful nightmare. She was no longer in her protective uniform but in a set of sleep-scrubs. Swearing profusely, she levered herself upright and attempted to stand. She had been cleaned up and her cracked rib had been strapped and, she hoped, mended, but she was aware of what felt like a hundred hurts on every part of her cramped anatomy.

"Who said you could get out of bed?" a voice demanded.

"I did," she replied shortly. "I'm in command here and don't you forget it, Nurse Biggs."

"Not in medbay you're not, Captain: Dr Zonota'a holds the reins here and her word's law. But you *can* sit up."

"Like hell, I have people to see to. How long have I been out and where's my uniform?"

He held her gaze for a long moment but could tell that he was not about to win any arguments. Ten hours, he told her as he indicated the door to a closet. With the nurse's assistance she was soon decently clad, and having downed some concoction that Briggs had insisted upon, she made her way out and into the main medbay.

The place was more orderly than it had been but every bed was filled and there were intensive care incubators ranged along one side that she knew contained the most severely injured of her crew. Every bay she checked was occupied and she lost no time in pulling up the medical records of those *in situ*. Not able to read the strange notation, she relied on the graphics, but from what she could see, most were improving. Her own people she could relate to without trouble and only hoped the light tones she directed at her alien crew were not being misread.

A small hiss and chirrup at her back made her turn and there was Nyx, his whirring green eyes looking up at her.

"Someone wishes to see you, Captain," the small mechanoid informed her. "He is in life-support system engineering suite for fitting but will be here shortly. Dr Zonota'a thinks it best that you should meet in private at first. This way."

Puzzled, Copper was led over to a small room that was an office of sorts, judging by the equipment contained there. She spent her time calling up ship's spec at a nearby info-point and updating on what had been going on while she had been out – on doctor's orders, apparently. Othra had been left in command and had authorised repair and upgrading. There was an alien ship berthed alongside the *Crucible* and she had been assisting with a number of logistical issues, including the setting up of the life-support system engineering suite. That was a medical cum technical facility to provide the links essential in the transition of fully organic lifeforms to cyber-enhanced or non-organic states, Nyx told her. That shook her as she realised the implications, but she put it to the back of her mind to check crew rotas, noting that ship's complement had been increased by a few recruits from the latest-arrived ships and refugees with special skills from Blink 159. They had been detailed to relieve the officers that had been at their stations for the duration.

Copper turned, a strange frisson of anxiety zipping up her spine, a fraction before the door slid soundlessly open. The tall figure standing beside Zonota'a was encased head to foot in a satiny, reddish-green uniform. It was not a design she had seen before but she knew instinctively what it was and who it was. Her hand strayed to her mouth, her face twisting up in an agony of pity, hope and love. She closed her eyes to squeeze away her tears and opened them again slowly. He was still there and was advancing towards her with a light, almost bouncing gait. The face-plate of the helmet was softly-featured and bore the gentle imprint of two wide-apart eye sockets, a nose and a wide gash of mouth: a benign face, an ageless face. Copper held her arms out wide as she advanced to meet him. He reciprocated the gesture, halting just short of her. She raised her arms to encircle his neck and rested her head on the metallic shoulder.

"Spook," she whispered. "Oh Spook…"

"Copper," he said in a voice that was reminiscent of Flor but deeper and more melodic as he gently put one arm round her.

Realising she had company, Copper straightened and stood back to take in the tall shape. "But why?" she sniffed, regaining some degree of composure. "You don't need a body."

"Not for interaction with my own people, no; but for contact with yours, it is necessary. This was not a technology open to me in my own time and now it is. I requested."

"You sound like yourself," she said, "As I heard you inside my head. Maybe that was why I took to Flor so quickly."

She gave a long, shuddering sigh. "And this is your ship. You're already Captain Spook to the crew. What *is* your real name anyway? You never told me."

"Now it is Spook," he said. "What it was is of no matter. My own are long gone. Perhaps some of them out there will come back and find me. But this is our ship, Captain Copper."

She shook her head. "No. I'm not ready to captain a ship long-term. I have a long haul in front of me before that. And my people here will want to go home, or at least back to their own ships. And the *Crucible*..."

"Will remain as the link between our peoples – that is, if your people will accept us within this system. We have many bases here that we can recolonise, we have several ships buried on your home world that may still be intact and we have knowledge and technology that your people may find useful."

"Such as the means to keep whatever those hostiles are away and to find what's left of their influence and help deal with it. We're a long way from seeing the last of it, I suspect. I bet the *Regan Arcadia* isn't as squeaky clean as her captain is claiming for a start."

If a non-organic being encased in a cyber suit could laugh, the sound that Spook expressed was probably a small chuckle, Copper guessed as she took a deep breath and prepared to head out. Zonota'a stepped back, tabbing her medi-scanner off.

"I take it I'm fine, Doctor?"

"You are as well as can be expected, Captain."

"Then I'm headed to the bridge. I want to see what my bridge crew and the rest of the fleet have been up to while I've been napping."

The bridge had been overhauled and looked much like it had when first Copper had viewed it. Several pairs of eyes swivelled in their direction and most of their owners snapped to attention as the two stepped forward, Nyx bringing up the rear. Linen, bright-eyed and energetic, was in post and waved. Othra sat in the command chair. He rose to let her take his place, bowing courteously and giving the alien salute to both her and Spook. He had obviously recognised the being within the suit.

"As you were, Commander," Copper said lightly, looking around her.

Lomusan held tactical, Halsen was at the engineering station alongside Oaky Grimsson and Hoof, and Timri was at the helm. There was no sign of Kit or Dyxin but Blazells, strapped up as he was, nodded over from the weapons station. The remaining bridge officers were new to her but she saluted them cordially, noting that they all wore translator rings around their necks. Those would become standard issue soon, she conjectured, if this human-alien alliance was sanctioned by Mars Gov and its Earth equivalent. She left Spook with Othra and made a tour of the bridge stations, stopping to have a word with each officer.

"You're getting to be quite sociable these sols, Captain, ma'am," her red-headed friend greeted her. "Kit's off duty and probably in his quarters, in case you wanted to stop in and see him," she added impudently. "I'm sure he'd be delighted."

"Can it, Lieutenant. Where's Junior?"

"With Tehoaar. He's taken to her – I think she reminds him of his mother. They're off duty as well. To be honest, she can deal with him a lot better than I can. She and her partner don't have offspring – her partner's Lino'arr, by the way. That's why they're both aboard."

"How in blazes do you know that?"

"I asked. You've been out for a while you know. I had to pass the time somehow."

"Being nosy… I take it you've had a break?"

"Certainly have – went just after you, in fact. Commander Othra ordered me off. That's Spook in the suit, isn't it?"

"Yes. How did you figure?"

"I can tell by the look on your face when you look at him. I've seen that look before. How did they do it?"

As Copper passed on as much as she knew, she suddenly felt light and airy, almost buoyant. "I need to talk to Colonel Moritz:

I take it she's still in command of our forces," she said. "We've a lot to discuss and a lot to pass on to the powers that be back home. But that's more her area of expertise than mine."

"Bet she calls you in to ride shotgun when she does," Linen predicted. "She and Captain Flor have been in touch with Othra over things but he'll brief you first, I guess. And then we'll be going home to the *Drake* will we, Captain, ma'am?"

"We'll be going home. But I'd better go see Othra."

Linen had been right and Othra took some time to brief both Copper and Spook over what had been arranged for the ships of both parts of the fleet. Flor's people would be staying put for the duration but supplies were to be sent out via Jupiter Station that would assist them. The Mars and Earth vessels would, with help on the way from both homeworlds and their colonies, be rendered as shipshape as possible. And the pair of non-organic crew from the *Crucible* that had been sent to check out the *Regan Arcadia* had reported that although contained, there were still some hostile influences aboard the commercial ship.

* * *

A few sols later and with most of her human crew more or less back on track, Copper headed over to the *Drake* alone for a pre-talk briefing with Colonel Moritz, who had set up a supralight meeting with Mars Fleet's upper echelons and invited Flor to be part of her team. It would be the first sight of an alien in Mars Fleet circles when the link went through. Captain Helmis would also be there, as well as Captain Ketter of the *Dexterity*.

The line-up of brass on the holo surprised even the colonel as the link was established to the conference room aboard the *Drake*. There were at least twenty high rankers arranged around the massive space, which was bristling with recording apparatus. Guards were stationed at each exit and several officials from Mars Gov were also in attendance. Copper was amused to note that her old adversary Ms Toxi Karben of Outer Mars Ops, now a full colonel, made one of the company.

It was a long meeting. Fleet Command had of necessity been kept informed of what had been going on and of the outcome of hostilities but the whole had to be gone over again for the benefit of those not in the inner circle. A recess was called after three hours and the main thing that Copper had taken from the proceedings to that point was that she had no inclination to be an admiral with a desk at Fleet HQ. She had not been called upon to give testimony, for which she was grateful, but had a hunch that it was only a pleasure deferred. She was not wrong.

It was Admiral Stannum who called her to the stand an hour after the council resumed. Copper had not met the admiral in person before but recognised the face of the woman who had launched the *MSS Drake II* all those months ago. It appeared that Stannum had been keeping a close eye on the flagship and her mission and had also been very aware of the *Crucible* and her conduct in the conflict. If Copper had been expecting praise she would have been very disappointed: her actions were dissected minutely and critically and she was called upon to explain her rationale at length. She did not mention Spook; as far as she was concerned it was none of the business of the council before her. She had schooled herself to remain calm despite the probing nature of the questions and had managed to sustain an outward appearance of composure until Stannum asked her bluntly, and with a searching glance at Flor, if she trusted their new alien allies. Her eyes blazed.

"You're damn straight I do! Without them, we would not be having this conversation. Without them, you'd have a frigging war fleet on your doorstep!"

"Belay that, Lieutenant," Stannum snapped.

"That's Captain – until I'm relieved of my command."

A certain amount of disorder ensued as several voices cut in, but the chairman of the assembly restored order and Stannum eventually stood down. There was little else directed at Copper and her anger kept her afloat until she could resume her seat. She was content to sit in the background while the next steps to be taken were talked out, although she was keenly aware that she was the subject of several pairs of long-distance eyes well after her part was over.

Flor was treated with as much curiosity as respect. Many were obviously startled that she could talk quite freely with the humans and was quite forthright in refusing to answer some questions. It was also obvious that a lot of talking out would have to be done before anything was resolved. The meeting was wound up with the threat of more to come and as the link was cut, Colonel Moritz turned to her young officer.

"You seem to have raised a few hackles, *Captain* Milkstone."

"I feel like taking a whip to their behinds, some of them," she responded, raising a chuckle from Captain Helmis. "I also feel like a glass of Dr Faerin's best scotch."

"I'll see what I can arrange," the colonel promised. "But we have a long road before us until we're shipshape again."

* * *

Five sols later the news filtered down that the *MSS Ulugh Beg* had made it into their neck of space. She was a welcome sight to many, not only as a symbol of a home that was still there, but as a welcome source of news, provisions and a touch of normality. Copper had bid farewell to most of her human crew. Linen had refused to budge and was not unduly pushed but Kit had no option but recall to the *Drake*. He had returned for a visit along with Colonel Moritz, who had come over for a tour of the ship and a long talk with both her present and her future captains. There had been a certain amount of pressure exerted on the colonel by Mars Fleet to engineer the appointment of human officers to the hybrid ship on a semi-permanent basis but she had resisted, knowing Copper's mindset. Colonel Moritz also had a few plans of her own that she intended to see carried out and was aware that Captain Milkstone, before resigning her temporary post, had one or two applications that *she* wished to see honoured.

Despite her disinclination for more interaction with the high and mighty of Mars Fleet, Copper had little option but to face another couple of long meetings with a newly-fledged dedicated council that had been swiftly assembled. The sessions included introductions to legislators from Mars Gov: draft policies were being pushed to bolster some sort of official alliance with Flor's people and her input was considered crucial. She was short and to the point: hostile alien technology was still extant around the Sol system, which led to the inescapable conclusion that the hostiles must have several toeholds and possibly adherents in human space. These could be on the homeworlds, on colonies or on stations. With Flor's people as support, trouble arising from such sources would be easier to handle. Such an alliance could have other advantages: the possibility of journeys beyond their own system and a share in technology that could advance human civilisation a few hundred years at least. Flor's people would also benefit if they were guaranteed possession of some of the many empty worlds within the Sol system for the several enclaves of her people that were still out beyond system edge. After all, Copper reminded the council, Mars had been home to their alien allies long before it was home to humankind.

Her own concerns took up most of her time, however, and it was some time later that a visit from a couple of her alien crew members gave Copper more pleasant food for thought. As she reported to the colonel, her first reaction was how to authorise the request with all speed. Tehoaar and Lino'arr wished formally to adopt Junior. Their captain's delight at their application was more than apparent to the couple, their only concern being that Linen would be upset. Junior himself was overjoyed to find himself with parents at last.

"If only everything could be fixed so simply," Copper said to her relieved red-headed friend over a caff after formalities had been completed. "I'm still wrangling with Captain LeFlynn over a promotion for Gadget Blazells – he doesn't consider that I have the seniority to authorise it, being a temporary captain."

"Get the colonel on board, she'll sort it," was Linen's advice.

"Good idea, as I have to see her about some other business anyway: she's coming over and Trisk wants a look see at the *Crucible*, so he'll be with her."

The other business that Copper and the colonel had in hand was the listing of all her human officers for commendations for their actions during the conflict. With Captain Flor's approval appended, they believed that they could hasten the obligatory administration: both Mars and Earth Fleet Commands were still sufficiently shaken by what might have been had the hostile fleet been successful, that they looked upon every request emanating from system edge with approbation.

* * *

Gadget Blazells was not the only officer to find himself a step up in rank. Copper had advocated honours for every one of her officers and to Linen's surprise, she found herself accepting the accolade of a commendation and a promotion at a ceremony aboard the *Drake* two months after the cessation of hostilities. The party had been quickly set up, as the *Crucible*, with Spook in the command chair, was to leave in a couple of sevensols to begin the long process of creating a series of footholds closer in to the human homeworlds. Blink 159 was now a permanent base for the refugees that had landed there and the new home port for the remnants of the *Sally* fleet.

Both Spook and Flor were present at the human ceremony aboard the Mars Fleet flagship, honoured guests of the colonel. She had brought them over for more than one reason, for as the call came up for Copper to receive her citation, an honour she had been advised was forthcoming, she was bid to stay and Captain Flor was called up. Copper assumed from that that the alien captain was to receive some sort of decoration for her part in the conflict, but Flor and Colonel Moritz had evidently been hatching something else between themselves. It was Captain Flor who was handed the small commemorative box, and she who announced in her soft tones that Lieutenant Milkstone was hereby promoted to Lieutenant Commander as she passed the box over with due ceremony.

Copper was incoherent and could only nod to her assembled friends and colleagues. Such a rapid promotion was virtually unique: the only person she knew who *had* been on the receiving end of such speedy advancement was in fact Colonel Moritz, not long before she had been given command of the *Drake*.

"Way to go, Cop! Just wait 'til we tell the folks back home!" Linen exploded as soon as her friend had returned to her seat and the congratulations of those most dear to her. "And Doc Faerin had best get that bottle of very old scotch out again, as he promised, remember, when you were made first lieutenant?"

"If ever you get your own ship, count me in as your chief SO," Trisk told her. "Life will be a blast!"

"You'll have to get used to answering to *Commander*," Kit murmured as he took her hand and leaned over to kiss her ear.

"I'll be relieved to: I'm not ready to be called Captain again for a very, very long time," Copper answered, squeezing his hand in return.

She turned to the upright form of Spook, who sat with them, and smiled up at the mask-like features of his headpiece, which she was already beginning to regard as the face he would have had in organic form.

"Congratulations, Copper," he said in his odd melodious voice. "I will miss you when I leave."

"I'll miss you more than I can say," she sighed, misty-eyed, stretching out to place her free hand on his red, metallic arm. "You've been more than my friend and mentor..."

"Yes, you saved our butts more than a couple of times, Captain Spook, sir," Linen informed him, grinning from ear to ear. "And I'll miss Junior – I got used to having *him* around, but he's much better off with Tehoaar and Lino'arr. But Copper's still got me to annoy her to bits: I don't intend to go away any time soon. And neither does Kit," she went on, winking at the pair. "You're stuck with *him* for the duration, Commander Copper, ma'am. But no canoodling on duty: the colonel will have both your hides."

"You're heading for a poke in the eye, *First* Lieutenant Lyrican..."

* * *

There was a crowd on the observation deck along the rail that edged the massive viewing portal. The panorama of stars spread to infinity, glowing in myriad colours as they enhanced the lustrously fluid lines of the small red-green hulled ship that slowly curved round to face the mighty *MSS Drake II*. The seemingly molten keel flickered as streamers of colour shot along her body from her rounded stem to the intricate tailfin encompassing her stern. The delicately shifting patterns on her hide seemed to grow and reduce as she made her final turn and halted, suspended in space like a beautiful, shimmering firebird.

"It's not the end of a beautiful friendship; and it's definitely the beginning of a glorious alliance," Copper told her friend as the *Crucible* slowly began to move, its radiance growing, to light up the space around itself like a nimbus as she headed inwards to her first port of call, the moon Elara.

"In more than one sense," Linen laughed lightly, looking over at the tall form of Commander Kit Locksmith, whose arm was tight around Copper's waist as he gazed at her friend with more than respect in his eyes. "I think you'd better watch out where they promote you to next, Cop. But at least if they do give you your own command, you can choose your own chief of security."

Copper let her have the last word.

FINIS

SUB MARTIS: STARSHIP - LEXIS

A

Arcadia Station A military station on Arcadia Planitia that is responsible for the administration of supplies to the Fleet.

Ares-Class Mark IV Shuttle A four-man military shuttle often used in training.

B

Batoka, Captain Neema Commanding Officer of the *MSS Mina Fleming*.

Beagle One Basecamp A new training base for recruits joining Mars Fleet that is located between Pillinger and Darwin Domes of Beagle Dome Complex.

Biggs, Axim A nurse tech aboard the *MSS Drake II*.

Biohazard Labs Military laboratories located between Fleet HQ and Korolev Station in Vastitas Borealis.

Birks, Mirrin A member of the Warren site station's security team who is also a site mechanic.

Biskott, Sergeant The main drill instructor at Beagle One Basecamp.

Blazells, Lieutenant Gadget A fellow-trainee of Copper and Linen at Beagle One Basecamp; posted to the *MSS Lithium Star*.

Blink 159 A planetoid at the edge of the main Sol System that hosts alien base and repair stations and that was breached by hostile forces.

Brown, Lieutenant Tawinna (Tawny) A security officer aboard the *MSS Drake II*.

C

Café Crème A small café in Precinct One of Jupiter Station.

Chenzen, Tilli A nurse assist aboard the *MSS Drake II*.

Chi, Sergeant A senior fitness instructor at Beagle One Basecamp.

Chinn, Lieutenant Zennik An officer aboard the *MSS Drake II*; a member of the Drake Singers.

D

D'Arragh, Ensign Ennis A security officer aboard the *MSS Drake II*.

Deck, Captain Bardin A Ground Operations medical doctor from the military basecamp close to the Warren site.

Dingle, Ensign Foxin (Foxy) A fellow-trainee of Copper and Linen at Beagle One Basecamp.

Disposable Cup, The A café on Jupiter Station.

Dyxin, Lieutenant Flax A comms officer aboard the *MSS Drake II*.

E

EFS Dexterity An Earth Fleet Explorer ship under the command of Captain Jed Ketter.

EFS Stephen Hawking An Earth Fleet Explorer ship under the command of Captain Jane Stallban.

Elara An outer satellite of Jupiter, part of which is composed of alien organo-tech that forms an ancient alien defensive post.

Elks, Captain Erkon Commanding Officer of the *SS Regan Arcadia*.

Embertz, Dr Amber A medical officer aboard the *MSS Drake II*.

F

Faerin, Dr Kynedd Chief Medical Officer of the *MSS Drake II*; ranked commander.

Fantodd, Captain Leroy Commanding Officer of the *MSS Sapphire Sunset*.

Fells, Joe A security guard at Beagle One Basecamp who has a brother with Fleet Security.

Ferret, Ensign Bass A fellow-trainee of Copper and Linen at Beagle One Basecamp.

Flor, Captain Commanding Officer of the alien starship

Interstellar Wanderer (known as the *Sally*).

Flyte, Ensign Lennik A junior security officer aboard the *MSS Drake II* who has a virtual dog called Fetch.

G

Gannet, Commander Helma First Officer of the *MSS Lithium Star*.

Grimsson, Lieutenant Oakwood (Oaky) An engineer aboard the *MSS Drake II*.

Goff, Lieutenant Ash A science officer, a geologist, aboard the *MSS Drake II*.

H

Halsen, Lieutenant Elyssal (Lyssa) A bioengineer aboard the *MSS Drake II*; sister of Lieutenant Erik Halsen

Halsen, Lieutenant Erik A flight engineer aboard the *MSS Lithium Star*; brother of Lieutenant Lyssa Halsen.

Helixus An asteroid in the main belt between Mars and Jupiter, part of which is composed of alien organo-tech that forms an ancient alien defensive post.

Hellebore, Captain Nella Commanding Officer of the *SS Morgana Atlantis*.

Helmis, Captain Merris First Officer (executive officer) of the *MSS Drake II*; brother of Captain Perkin Helmis.

Helmis, Captain Perkin Commanding Officer of the *MSS En Hedu'anna*; brother of Captain Merris Helmis.

Hoof, Lieutenant An engineer aboard the *US Crucible*.

I

Inkle, Ensign Dex A fellow-trainee of Copper and Linen at Beagle One Basecamp.

Inkscree, Dr Ossian (Ossy) Chief Science Officer of the *MSS Drake II*; ranked lieutenant commander, he is a nano-engineer.

Interstellar Wanderer The lead alien starship of a fleet of five and under the command of Captain Flor; known as the *Sally*.

Ivyleaf Designs An art business in Artisan Square, Pillinger Dome, Beagle Dome Complex; it caters for personal artistic adornment, particularly tattoos.

J

Jecks, Finn A subversive with military and law enforcement experience posing as a technician to gain access to the Warren site station; later an infiltrator aboard the *MSS Drake II*.

Jeshin, Ensign A security officer aboard the *US Crucible*.

K

Ketter, Captain Jed Commanding Officer of the Earth Fleet Explorer ship *EFS Dexterity*.

Kevloki, Sergeant A weapons instructor at Beagle One Basecamp.

Khilph, Lieutenant Commander Faela A senior navigation officer aboard the *MSS Drake II*.

Kivian, Lieutenant Bell A helmswoman aboard the *MSS Drake II*.

Korolev Station A military base in the northern polar region for the further training of Fleet and Ground Operations branches of the Service.

Kuillinor, Lieutenant Bloom A science officer and botanist aboard the *MSS Drake II*.

L

LeFlynn, Captain Mortin Commanding Officer of the *MSS Lithium Star*.

Limlite, Lieutenant Jinn The training liaison officer aboard the *MSS Drake II*.

Lino'arr The senior navigator aboard the *US Crucible*.

Locksmith, Lieutenant Kit Chief of Security aboard the *MSS Drake II*.

Lomusan, Ensign A tactical officer aboard the *US Crucible* and previously a tactical officer aboard the *Sally*.

Lux Noctis The name given to a minor planet out at the edge where the *MSS Griffon* and two alien ships crashed; discovered and named by the crew of the *MSS Lithium Star*.

M

MSS Annie J Cannon A *Drake II* Class Mars Fleet Explorer ship.

MSS En Hedu'anna A *Drake II* Class Mars Fleet Explorer ship

on a deep-space mission to the edge, under the command of
Captain Perkin Helmis.

MSS Mina Fleming A *Drake II* Class Mars Fleet Explorer ship
on a deep-space mission to the edge, under the command of
Captain Neema Batoka.

MSS Sapphire Sunset A Mars Fleet Explorer Corps personnel
and cargo carrier under the command of Captain Leroy
Fantodd.

MSS Swordfish A mid-range Mars Fleet Explorer Corps cruiser
tasked with mapping and space safety missions.

MSS Ulugh Beg A *Drake II* Class Mars Fleet Explorer ship on
a deep-space mission.

MV2 Flyer A two-man, low-atmosphere dual-control patrol
craft with military capability; often used in the first stages of
fighter pilot training.

Meldyn, Instructor Captain Max A Senior Flight Instructor at
Beagle One Basecamp; known as Max Meltdown.

Melucca, Lieutenant Tany A liaison officer aboard the *MSS
Drake II*.

Moritz, Colonel Elle Chryse Commanding Officer of the *MSS
Drake II*.

Murkyles, Ensign Kester A security officer aboard the *MSS
Drake II*.

N

Nightfall A seedy clothes emporium on Dowson Street,
Pillinger Dome, Beagle Dome Complex.

Nightfall, Nix The mysterious proprietrix of Nightfall.

Nyx Copper's escort and translator aboard the alien starship
Sally; later, comms officer and translator aboard the *US Crucible*;
he's a mechanoid blue dragon.

O

Okenite, Commandant Walt Commandant of Beagle One
Basecamp Fleet Training Centre.

Olympus Mons Support Squadron A Mars-based support
unit of Mars Fleet for transport, logistics and signals provision.

P

PPF Acronym for Personal Protection Firearm; a small hand weapon powered by charge caps that emits a disruptor energy burst sufficient to cause serious injury; requires a licence to own.

Pellin, Officer Dirk A law enforcement officer based at Beagle Dome Complex.

Pioneer II A dome complex at 119°E, 5°S, at the foot of Pavonis Mons. It is the location of a Fleet recruitment office.

Pyx, Lieutenant Copper's alien aide aboard the alien starship *Sally*; later her weapons officer aboard the *US Crucible*.

R

Rainbow Rookies A term used for Fleet Service trainees during their first spaceflight.

RedStar Bistro An eatery in Precinct One of Jupiter Station.

Rookie Road A local name for Private Road in Pillinger Dome, Beagle Dome Complex; so called as it linked the site of quarters for trainee law enforcement officers to Law Enforcement HQ.

Ruddin, Dr Texel Chief Science Officer of the *MSS Lithium Star*.

S

SS Fearless A high-spec exploratory starship belonging to and operated by the Mars Deep Mining Consortium; under the command of Captain Si Vendor.

SS Morgana Atlantis A high-tech commercial survey ship built by several groups; her mission was purportedly to search for rare mineral resources; initially commanded by Captain Nella Hellebore; later under the command of Commander Vix Wyld.

SS Regan Arcadia A high-tech commercial survey ship; sistership of the *Morgana Atlantis* and built by similar interested parties; her mission was recorded as the search for rare mineral resources; under the command of Captain Erkon Elks.

Sage, Lieutenant Commander Themis Chief Engineer of the *MSS Drake II*.

Sage, Lieutenant Merinna A junior engineer aboard a Fleet supply ship running between Mars and the bases beyond Jupiter; daughter of Commander Themis Sage.

Sally The abbreviated name Copper gives the alien ship she first boards, as she has trouble pronouncing the whole name (which translates as *Interstellar Wanderer*). Known later as *Sally One* to distinguish her from *Sally Two* through *Sally Five*.

Savich A small dome complex at the north-eastern edge of Hellas Planitia.

Skate, Ensign Bonny (Bon-Bon) A fellow-trainee of Copper and Linen at Beagle One Basecamp.

Skyller, Lieutenant Leo An officer aboard the *MSS Lithium Star*.

Sleet, Officer Jay A law enforcement officer based at Beagle Dome Complex.

Smoky Pearl Lounge A lounge in the BC Hotel in Pillinger Dome, Beagle Dome Complex.

Soapy Jim's A downmarket bar on level five, Jupiter Station.

Spokes, Fergalla A corrupt security guard aboard the *Drake II* who was involved in a plot to blow up the armoury.

Stallban, Captain Jane Commanding Officer of the Earth Fleet Explorer ship *EFS Stephen Hawking*.

Stannum, Admiral Vexilla An Admiral of Mars Fleet: she launched the *MSS Drake II*.

Station Ember A military station surrounded by a no-fly zone located at 2° N, 316° W in the Ismenius Lacus quadrangle.

Sunspot Surprise A cocktail speciality of the BC Hotel in Pillinger Dome, Beagle Dome Complex: caff liqueur syrup is added to a goblet, topped slowly by orange juice; tiny iced caff spheres are dropped in and a green cherry on a stick is added as garnish.

T

Tehoaar A science officer aboard the *US Crucible*.

Timri A helmsman aboard the *US Crucible*.

Tuffet, Major Tiff Quartermaster of the *MSS Drake II*.

Twilight Gallery A pricy art gallery on Zarnecki Avenue in Pillinger Dome, Beagle Dome Complex; located between Grady Way and Canillo Street.

U

US Crucible A hybrid starship built from remains of alien and human vessels that had crashed on the planetoid Lux Noctis.

V

Vendor, Captain Si Commanding Officer of the *SS Fearless*.
Vespoltz, Lieutenant Marco A tactical officer aboard the *MSS Drake II*.

W

Wale, Leading Officer Lixin A rogue engineering officer aboard the *MSS Drake II*.
Wingwarp, Ensign Charity A junior ops officer aboard the *MSS Drake II*.
Wyld, Commander Vix First Officer of the *SS Morgana Atlantis*.

Z

Zills, Ensign Zakarina (Zak) A fellow-trainee of Copper and Linen at Beagle One Basecamp.
Zonota'a, Dr A senior medical officer assigned to the bridge of the *US Crucible*.

ABOUT THE AUTHOR

SANDI CAYLESS is the author of *Sub Martis: Dome Lowell*, *Sub Martis: Dome Beagle*, *The Pirates' Web: Arianrhod*, and *The Ghost of Glow-Worm Alpha*. Her poem, *Ghost Walkers*, features in: *Futuredaze: An Anthology of YA Science Fiction*. For more, including images and maps, see: www.submartis.com.